# JEEVES AND WOOSTER

P. G. Wodehouse was born in Guildford, Surrey, in 1881 and educated at Dulwich College. After working for the Hong Kong and Shanghai Bank for two years, he left to earn his living as a journalist and storywriter.

During his lifetime he wrote over ninety books, and his work has won worldwide acclaim. He was hailed by *The Times* as 'A comic genius recognized in his lifetime as a classic and an old master of farce.' P. G. Wodehouse said: 'I believe there are two ways of writing novels. One is mine, making a sort of musical comedy without music and ignoring real life altogether; the other is going right deep down into life and not caring a damn.'

In 1975 he was created a Knight of the British Empire and he died on St Valentine's Day in the same year at the age of ninety-three.

ALSO IN ARROW BY P. G. WODEHOUSE

The Clicking of Cuthbert
Jeeves and the Feudal Spirit
Jeeves in the Offing
Joy in the Morning
The Mating Season
Nothing Serious
Uncle Dynamite
Right Ho, Jeeves

P. G. Wodehouse

# JEEVES AND WOOSTER

ARROW BOOKS

Arrow Books Limited
20 Vauxhall Bridge Road, London SW1V 2SA

An imprint of Random Century Group

London Melbourne Sydney Auckland
Johannesburg and agencies throughout
the world

Phototypeset by Input Typesetting Ltd, London
Printed and bound in Great Britain by
Cox & Wyman Ltd, Reading, Berkshire

ISBN 0 09 9916800 1

# CONTENTS

# =1=

I REACHED out a hand from under the blankets, and rang the bell for Jeeves.

'Good evening, Jeeves.'

'Good morning, sir.'

This surprised me.

'Is it morning?'

'Yes, sir.'

'Are you sure? It seems very dark outside.'

'There is a fog, sir. If you will recollect, we are now in Autumn – season of mists and mellow fruitfulness.'

'Season of what?'

'Mists, sir, and mellow fruitfulness.'

'Oh? Yes. Yes, I see. Well, be that as it may, get me one of those bracers of yours, will you?'

'I have one in readiness, sir, in the ice-box.'

He shimmered out, and I sat up in bed with that rather unpleasant feeling you get sometimes that you're going to die in about five minutes. On the previous night, I had given a little dinner at the Drones to Gussie Fink-Nottle as a friendly send-off before his approaching nuptials with Madeline, only daughter of Sir Watkyn Bassett, CBE, and these things take their toll. Indeed, just before Jeeves came in, I had been dreaming that some bounder was driving spikes through my head – not just ordinary spikes, as used by Jael the wife of Heber, but red-hot ones.

He returned with the tissue-restorer. I loosed it down the hatch, and after undergoing the passing discomfort, unavoidable when you drink Jeeves's patent morning revivers, of having the top of the skull fly up to the ceiling and the eyes shoot out of their sockets and rebound from the opposite wall like racquet balls, felt better. It would have been overstating it to say that even now Bertram was back again in mid-season form, but I had at least slid into the convalescent class and was equal to a spot of conversation.

'Ha!' I said, retrieving the eyeballs and replacing them in

position. 'Well, Jeeves, what goes on in the great world? Is that the paper you have there?'

'No, sir. It is some literature from the Travel Bureau. I thought that you might care to glance at it.'

'Oh?' I said. 'You did, did you?'

And there was a brief and – if that's the word I want – pregnant silence.

I suppose that when two men of iron will live in close association with one another, there are bound to be occasional clashes, and one of these had recently popped up in the Wooster home. Jeeves was trying to get me to go on a Round-The-World cruise, and I would have none of it. But in spite of my firm statements to this effect, scarcely a day passed without him bringing me a sheaf or nosegay of those illustrated folders which the Ho-for-the-open-spaces birds send out in the hope of drumming up custom. His whole attitude recalled irresistibly to the mind that of some assiduous hound who will persist in laying a dead rat on the drawing-room carpet, though repeatedly apprised by word and gesture that the market for same is sluggish or even non-existent.

'Jeeves,' I said, 'this nuisance must now cease.'

'Travel is highly educational, sir.'

'I can't do with any more education. I was full up years ago. No, Jeeves, I know what's the matter with you. That old Viking strain of yours has come out again. You yearn for the tang of the salt breezes. You see yourself walking the deck in a yachting cap. Possibly someone has been telling you about the Dancing Girls of Bali. I understand, and I sympathize. But not for me. I refuse to be decanted into any blasted ocean-going liner and lugged off round the world.'

'Very good, sir.'

He spoke with a certain what-is-it in his voice, and I could see that, if not actually disgruntled, he was far from being gruntled, so I tactfully changed the subject.

'Well, Jeeves, it was quite a satisfactory binge last night.'

'Indeed, sir?'

'Oh, most. An excellent time was had by all. Gussie sent his regards.'

'I appreciate the kind thought, sir. I trust Mr Fink-Nottle was in good spirits?'

'Extraordinarily good, considering that the sands are running out and that he will shortly have Sir Watkyn Bassett for a father-in-law. Sooner him than me, Jeeves, sooner him than me.'

I spoke with strong feeling, and I'll tell you why. A few months before, while celebrating Boat Race night, I had fallen into the clutches of the Law for trying to separate a policeman from his helmet, and after sleeping fitfully on a plank bed had been hauled up at Bosher Street next morning and fined five of the best. The magistrate who had inflicted this monstrous sentence – to the accompaniment, I may add, of some very offensive remarks from the bench – was none other than old Pop Bassett, father of Gussie's bride-to-be.

As it turned out, I was one of his last customers, for a couple of weeks later he inherited a pot of money from a distant relative and retired to the country. That, at least, was the story that had been put about. My own voice was that he had got the stuff by sticking like glue to the fines. Five quid here, five quid there – you can see how it would mount up over a period of years.

'You have not forgotten that man of wrath, Jeeves? A hard case, eh?'

'Possibly Sir Watkyn is less formidable in private life, sir.'

'I doubt it. Slice him where you like, a hellhound is always a hellhound. But enough of this Bassett. Any letters today?'

'No, sir.'

'Telephone communications?'

'One, sir. From Mrs Travers.'

'Aunt Dahlia? She's back in town, then?'

'Yes, sir. She expressed a desire that you would ring her up at your earliest convenience.'

'I will do even better,' I said cordially. 'I will call in person.'

And half an hour later I was toddling up the steps of her residence and being admitted by old Seppings, her butler. Little knowing, as I crossed that threshold, that in about two shakes of a duck's tail I was to become involved in an imbroglio that would test the Wooster soul as it had seldom been tested before. I allude to the sinister affair of Gussie Fink-Nottle, Madeline Bassett, old Pop Bassett, Stiffy Byng, the Rev. H. P. ('Stinker') Pinker, the eighteenth-century cow-creamer and the small, brown, leather-covered notebook.

No premonition of an impending doom, however, cast a cloud on my serenity as I buzzed in. I was looking forward with bright anticipation to the coming reunion with this Dahlia – she, as I may have mentioned before, being my good and deserving aunt, not to be confused with Aunt Agatha, who eats broken bottles and wears barbed wire next to the skin. Apart from the mere intellectual pleasure of chewing the fat with her, there was the glittering prospect that I might be able to cadge an invitation to lunch. And owing to the outstanding virtuosity of Anatole, her French cook, the browsing at her trough is always of a nature to lure the gourmet.

The door of the morning room was open as I went through the hall, and I caught a glimpse of Uncle Tom messing about with his collection of old silver. For a moment I toyed with the idea of pausing to pip-pip and enquire after his indigestion, a malady to which he is extremely subject, but wiser counsels prevailed. This uncle is a bird who, sighting a nephew, is apt to buttonhole him and become a bit informative on the subject of sconces and foliation, not to mention scrolls, ribbon wreaths in high relief and gadroon borders, and it seemed to me that silence was best. I whizzed by, accordingly, with sealed lips, and headed for the library, where I had been informed that Aunt Dahlia was at the moment roosting.

I found the old flesh-and-blood up to her Marcelwave in proof sheets. As all the world knows, she is the courteous and popular proprietress of a weekly sheet for the delicately nurtured entitled *Milady's Boudoir*. I once contributed an article to it on 'What The Well-Dressed Man is Wearing'.

My entry caused her to come to the surface, and she greeted me with one of those cheery view-halloos which, in the days when she went in for hunting, used to make her so noticeable a figure of the Quorn, the Pytchley and other organizations for doing the British fox a bit of no good.

'Hullo, ugly,' she said. 'What brings you here?'

'I understood, aged relative, that you wished to confer with me.'

'I didn't want you to come barging in, interrupting my work. A few words on the telephone would have met the case. But I suppose some instinct told you that this was my busy day.'

'If you were wondering if I could come to lunch, have no

anxiety. I shall be delighted, as always. What will Anatole be giving us?'

'He won't be giving you anything, my gay young tapeworm. I am entertaining Pomona Grindle, the novelist, to the midday meal.'

'I should be charmed to meet her.'

'Well, you're not going to. It is to be a strictly *tête-à-tête* affair. I'm trying to get a serial out of her for the *Boudoir*. No, all I wanted was to tell you to go to an antique shop in the Brompton Road – it's just past the Oratory – you can't miss it – and sneer at a cow-creamer.'

I did not get her drift. The impression I received was that of an aunt talking through the back of her neck.

'Do what to a what?'

'They've got an eighteenth-century cow-creamer there that Tom's going to buy this afternoon.'

The scales fell from my eyes.

'Oh, it's a silver whatnot, is it?'

'Yes. A sort of cream jug. Go there and ask them to show it to you, and when they do, register scorn.'

'The idea being what?'

'To sap their confidence, of course, chump. To sow doubts and misgivings in their mind and make them clip the price a bit. The cheaper he gets the thing, the better he will be pleased. And I want him to be in cheery mood, because if I succeed in signing the Grindle up for this serial, I shall be compelled to get into his ribs for a biggish sum of money. It's sinful what these best-selling women novelists want for their stuff. So pop off there without delay and shake your head at the thing.'

I am always anxious to oblige the right sort of aunt, but I was compelled to put in what Jeeves would have called a *nolle prosequi*. Those morning mixtures of his are practically magical in their effect, but even after partaking of them one does not oscillate the bean.

'I can't shake my head. Not today.'

She gazed at me with a censorious waggle of the right eyebrow.

'Oh, so that's how it is? Well, if your loathsome excesses have left you incapable of headshaking, you can at least curl your lip.'

'Oh, rather.'

'Then carry on. And draw your breath in sharply. Also try clicking the tongue. Oh, yes, and tell them you think it's modern Dutch.'

'Why?'

'I don't know. Apparently it's something a cow-creamer ought not to be.'

She paused, and allowed her eye to roam thoughtfully over my perhaps somewhat corpse-like face.

'So you were out on the tiles last night, were you, my little chickadee? It's an extraordinary thing – every time I see you, you appear to be recovering from some debauch. Don't you ever stop drinking? How about when you asleep?'

I rebutted the slur.

'You wrong me, relative. Except at times of special revelry, I am exceedingly moderate in my potations. A brace of cocktails, a glass of wine at dinner and possibly a liqueur with the coffee – that is Bertram Wooster. But last night I gave a small bachelor binge for Gussie Fink-Nottle.'

'You did, did you?' She laughed – a bit louder than I could have wished in my frail state of health, but then she is always a woman who tends to bring plaster falling from the ceiling when amused. 'Spink-Bottle, eh? Bless his heart! How was the old newt-fancier?'

'Pretty roguish.'

'Did he make a speech at this orgy of yours?'

'Yes. I was astounded. I was all prepared for a blushing refusal. But no. We drank his health, and he rose to his feet as cool as some cucumbers, as Anatole would say, and held us spellbound.'

'Tight as an owl, I suppose?'

'On the contrary. Offensively sober.'

'Well, that's a nice change.'

We fell into a thoughtful silence. We were musing on the summer afternoon down at her place in Worcestershire when Gussie, circumstances having so ordered themselves as to render him full to the back teeth with the right stuff, had addressed the young scholars of Market Snodsbury Grammar School on the occasion of their annual prize giving.

A thing I never know, when I'm starting out to tell a story

about a chap I've told a story about before, is how much explanation to bung in at the outset. It's a problem you've got to look at from every angle. I mean to say, in the present case, if I take it for granted that my public knows all about Gussie Fink-Nottle and just breeze ahead, those publicans who weren't hanging on my lips the first time are apt to be fogged. Whereas, if before kicking off I give about eight volumes of the man's life and history, other bimbos, who were so hanging will stifle yawns and murmur 'Old stuff. Get on with it.'

I suppose the only thing to do is to put the salient facts as briefly as possible in the possession of the first gang, waving an apologetic hand at the second gang the while, to indicate that they had better let their attention wander for a minute or two and that I will be with them shortly.

This Gussie, then, was a fish-faced pal of mine who, on reaching man's estate, had buried himself in the country and devoted himself entirely to the study of newts, keeping the little chaps in a glass tank and observing their habits with a sedulous eye. A confirmed recluse you would have called him, if you had happened to know the word, and you would have been right. By all the rulings of the form book, a less promising prospect for the whispering of tender words into shell-like ears and the subsequent purchase of platinum ring and licence for wedding it would have seemed impossible to discover in a month of Sundays.

But Love will find a way. Meeting Madeline Bassett one day and falling for her like a ton of bricks, he had emerged from his retirement and started to woo, and after numerous vicissitudes had clicked and was slated at no distant date to don the spongebag trousers and gardenia for buttonhole and walk up the aisle with the ghastly girl.

I call her a ghastly girl because she was a ghastly girl. The Woosters are chivalrous, but they can speak their minds. A droopy, soupy, sentimental exhibit, with melting eyes and a cooing voice and the most extraordinary views on such things as stars and rabbits. I remember her telling me once that rabbits were gnomes in attendance on the Fairy Queen and that the stars were God's daisy chain. Perfect rot, of course. They're nothing of the sort.

Aunt Dahlia emitted a low, rumbling chuckle, for that speech

13

of Gussie's down at Market Snodsbury has always been one of her happiest memories.

'Good old Spink-Bottle! Where is he now?'

'Staying at the Bassett's father's place – Totleigh Towers, Totleigh-in-the-Wold, Glos. He went back there this morning. They're having the wedding at the local church.'

'Are you going to it?'

'Definitely no.'

'No, I suppose it would be too painful for you. You being in love with the girl.'

I stared.

'In love? With a female who thinks that every time a fairy blows its wee nose a baby is born?'

'Well, you were certainly engaged to her once.'

'For about five minutes, yes, and through no fault of my own. My dear old relative,' I said, nettled, 'you are perfectly well aware of the inside facts of that frightful affair.'

I winced. It was an incident in my career on which I did not care to dwell. Briefly, what had occurred was this. His nerve sapped by long association with newts, Gussie had shrunk from pleading his cause with Madeline Bassett, and had asked me to plead it for him. And when I did so, the fat-headed girl thought I was pleading mine. With the result that when, after that exhibition of his at the prize giving, she handed Gussie the temporary mitten, she had attached herself to me, and I had had no option but to take the rap. I mean to say, if a girl has got it into her nut that a fellow loves her, and comes and tells him that she is returning her *fiancé* to store and is now prepared to sign up with him, what can a chap do?

Mercifully, things had been straightened out at the eleventh hour by a reconciliation between the two pills, but the thought of my peril was one at which I still shuddered. I wasn't going to feel really easy in my mind till the parson had said: 'Wilt thou, Augustus?' and Gussie had whispered a shy 'Yes.'

'Well, if it is of any interest to you,' said Aunt Dahlia, 'I am not proposing to attend that wedding myself. I disapprove of Sir Watkyn Bassett, and don't think he ought to be encouraged. There's one of the boys, if you want one!'

'You know the old crumb, then?' I said, rather surprised,

though of course it bore out what I often say – viz. that it's a small world.

'Yes, I know him. He's a friend of Tom's. They both collect old silver and snarl at one another like wolves about it all the time. We had him staying at Brinkley last month. And would you care to hear how he repaid me for all the loving care I lavished on him while he was my guest? Sneaked round behind my back and tried to steal Anatole!'

'No!'

'That's what he did. Fortunately, Anatole proved staunch – after I had doubled his wages.'

'Double them again,' I said earnestly. 'Keep on doubling them. Pour out money like water rather than lose that superb master of the roasts and hashes.'

I was visibly affected. The thought of Anatole, that peerless disher-up, coming within an ace of ceasing to operate at Brinkley Court, where I could always enjoy his output by inviting myself for a visit, and going off to serve under old Bassett, the last person in the world likely to set out a knife and fork for Bertram, had stirred me profoundly.

'Yes,' said Aunt Dahlia, her eye smouldering as she brooded on the frightful thing, 'that's the sort of hornswoggling high-binder Sir Watkyn Bassett is. You had better warn Spink-Bottle to watch out on the wedding day. The slightest relaxation of vigilance, and the old thug will probably get away with his tie-pin in the vestry. And now,' she said, reaching out for what had the appearance of being a thoughtful essay on the care of the baby in sickness and in health, 'push off. I've got about six tons of proofs to correct. Oh, and give this to Jeeves, when you see him. It's the "Husbands' Corner" article. It's full of deep stuff about braid on the side of men's dress trousers, and I'd like him to vet it. For all I know, it may be Red propaganda. And I can rely on you not to bungle that job? Tell me in your own words what it is you're supposed to do.'

'Go to antique shop – '

'– in the Brompton Road – '

'– in, as you say, the Brompton Road. Ask to see cow-creamer – '

'– and sneer. Right. Buzz along. The door is behind you.'

It was with a light heart that I went out into the street and hailed a passing barouche. Many men, no doubt, might have been a bit sick at having their morning cut into in this fashion, but I was conscious only of pleasure at the thought that I had it in my power to perform this little act of kindness. Scratch Bertram Wooster, I often say, and you find a Boy Scout.

The antique shop in the Brompton Road proved, as fore-shadowed, to be an antique shop in the Brompton Road and, like all antique shops except the swanky ones in the Bond Street neighbourhood, dingy outside and dark and smelly within. I don't know why it is, but the proprietors of these establishments always seem to be cooking some sort of stew in the back room.

'I say,' I began, entering; then paused as I perceived that the bloke in charge was attending to two other customers.

'Oh, sorry,' I was about to add, to convey the idea that I had horned in inadvertently, when the words froze on my lips.

Quite a slab of misty fruitfulness had drifted into the emporium, obscuring the view, but in spite of the poor light I was able to note that the smaller and elder of these two cus-tomers was no stranger to me.

It was old Pop Bassett in person. Himself. Not a picture.


There is a tough, bulldog strain in the Woosters which has often caused comment. It came out in me now. A weaker man, no doubt, would have tiptoed from the scene and headed for the horizon, but I stood firm. After all, I felt, the dead past was the dead past. By forking out that fiver, I had paid my debt to Society and had nothing to fear from this shrimp-faced son of a whatnot. So I remained where I was, giving him the surreptitious once-over.

My entry had caused him to turn and shoot a quick look at me, and at intervals since then he had been peering at me sideways. It was only a question of time, I felt, before the hidden chord in his memory would be touched and he would realize that the slight distinguished-looking figure leaning on its umbrella in the background was an old acquaintance. And now it was plain that he was hep. The bird in charge of the shop had pottered off into an inner room, and he came across to where I stood, giving me the up-and-down through his wind-shields.

'Hallo, hallo,' he said. 'I know you, young man. I never forget a face. You came up before me once.'

I bowed slightly.

'But not twice. Good! Learned your lesson, eh? Going straight now? Capital. Now, let me see, what was it? Don't tell me. It's coming back. Of course, yes. Bag-snatching.'

'No, no. It was –'

'Bag-snatching,' he repeated firmly. 'I remember it distinctly. Still, it's all past and done with now, eh? We have turned over a new leaf, have we not? Splendid. Roderick, come over here. This is most interesting.'

His buddy, who had been examining a salver, put it down and joined the party.

He was, as I had already been able to perceive, a breath-taking cove. About seven feet in height, and swathed in a plaid ulster which made him look about six feet across, he caught the eye and arrested it. It was as if Nature had intended to make a gorilla, and had changed its mind at the last moment.

But it wasn't merely the sheer expanse of the bird that impressed. Close to, what you noticed more was his face, which was square and powerful and slightly moustached towards the centre. His gaze was keen and piercing. I don't know if you have even seen those pictures in the papers of Dictators with tilted chins and blazing eyes, inflaming the populace with fiery words on the occasion of the opening of a new skittle alley, but that was what he reminded me of.

'Roderick,' said old Bassett, 'I want you to meet this fellow. Here is a case which illustrates exactly what I have so often maintained – that prison life does not degrade, that it does not warp the character and prevent a man rising on stepping-stones of his dead self to higher things.'

I recognized the gag – one of Jeeves's – and wondered where he could have heard it.

'Look at this chap. I gave him three months not long ago for snatching bags at railway stations, and it is quite evident that his term in jail has had the most excellent effect on him. He has reformed.'

'Oh, yes?' said the Dictator.

Granted that it wasn't quite 'Oh, yeah?' I still didn't like the way he spoke. He was looking at me with a nasty sort of supercilious expression. I remember thinking that he would have been the ideal man to sneer at a cow-creamer.

'What makes you think he has reformed?'

'Of course he has reformed. Look at him. Well groomed, well-dressed, a decent member of Society. What his present walk in life is, I do not know, but it is perfectly obvious that he is no longer stealing bags. What are you doing now, young man?'

'Stealing umbrellas, apparently,' said the Dictator. 'I notice he's got yours.'

And I was on the point of denying the accusation hotly – I had, indeed, already opened my lips to do so – when there suddenly struck me like a blow on the upper maxillary from a sock stuffed with wet sand the realization that there was a lot in it.

I mean to say, I remembered now that I had come out without my umbrella, and yet here I was, beyond any question of doubt, umbrellaed to the gills. What had caused me to take up the one that had been leaning against a seventeenth-century chair, I cannot say, unless it was the primeval instinct which makes a man without an umbrella reach out for the nearest one in sight, like a flower groping toward the sun.

A manly apology seemed in order. I made it as the blunt instrument changed hands.

'I say, I'm most frightfully sorry.'

Old Bassett said he was, too – sorry and disappointed. He said it was this sort of thing that made a man sick at heart.

The Dictator had to shove his oar in. He asked if he should call a policeman, and old Bassett's eyes gleamed for a moment. Being a magistrate makes you love the idea of calling policemen. It's like a tiger tasting blood. But he shook his head.

'No, Roderick. I couldn't. Not today – the happiest day of my life.'

The Dictator pursed his lips, as if feeling that the better the day, the better the deed.

'But listen,' I bleated, 'it was a mistake.'

'Ha!' said the Dictator.

'I thought that umbrella was mine.'

'That,' said old Bassett, 'is the fundamental trouble with you, my man. You are totally unable to distinguish between *meum* and *tuum*. Well, I am not going to have you arrested this time, but I advise you to be very careful. Come, Roderick.'

They biffed out, the Dictator pausing at the door to give me another look and say 'Ha!' again.

A most unnerving experience all this had been for a man of sensibility, as you may imagine, and my immediate reaction was a disposition to give Aunt Dahlia's commission the miss-in-balk and return to the flat and get outside another of Jeeves's pick-me-ups. You know how harts pant for cooling streams when heated in the chase. Very much that sort of thing. I realized now what madness it had been to go into the streets of London with only one of them under my belt, and I was on the point of melting away and going back to the fountain head, when the proprietor of the shop emerged from the inner room, accompanied by a rich smell of stew and a sandy cat, and enquired what he could do for me. And so, the subject having come up, I said that I understood that he had an eighteenth-century cow-creamer for sale.

He shook his head. He was a rather mildewed bird of gloomy aspect, almost entirely concealed behind a cascade of white whiskers.

'You're too late. It's promised to a customer.'

'Name of Travers?'

'Ah.'

'Then that's all right. Learn, O thou of unshuffled features and agreeable disposition,' I said, for one likes to be civil, 'that the above Travers is my uncle. He sent me here to have a look at the thing. So dig it out, will you? I expect it's rotten.'

'It's a beautiful cow-creamer.'

'Ha!' I said, borrowing a bit of the Dictator's stuff. 'That's what you think. We shall see.'

'I don't mind confessing that I'm not much of a lad for old silver, and though I have never pained him by actually telling him so, I have always felt that Uncle Tom's fondness for it is evidence of a goofiness which he would do well to watch and check before it spreads. So I wasn't expecting the heart to leap up to any great extent at the sight of this exhibit. But when the whiskered ancient pottered off into the shadows and came back with the thing. I scarcely knew whether to laugh or weep. The thought of an uncle paying hard cash for such an object got right in amongst me.

It was a silver cow. But when I say 'cow', don't go running away with the idea of some decent, self-respecting cudster such as you may observe loading grass into itself in the nearest meadow. This was a sinister, leering, Underworld sort of animal, the kind that would spit out of the side of its mouth for twopence. It was about four inches high and six long. Its back opened on a hinge. Its tail was arched, so that the tip touched the spine – thus, I suppose, affording a handle for the cream-lover to grasp. The sight of it seemed to take me into a different and dreadful world.

It was, consequently, an easy task for me to carry out the programme indicated by Aunt Dahlia. I curled the lip and clicked the tongue, all in one movement. I also drew in the breath sharply. The whole effect was that of a man absolutely out of sympathy with this cow-creamer, and I saw the mildewed cove start, as if he had been wounded in a tender spot.

'Oh, tut, tut, tut!' I said, 'Oh, dear, dear, dear! Oh, no, no, no, no, no! I don't think much of this,' I said, curling and clicking freely. 'All wrong.'

'All wrong?'

'All wrong. Modern Dutch.'

'Modern Dutch?' He may have frothed at the mouth, or he may not. I couldn't be sure. But the agony of spirit was obviously intense. 'What do you mean, Modern Dutch? It's eighteenth-century English. Look at the hallmark.'

'I can't see any hallmark.'

'Are you blind? Here, take it outside in the street. It's lighter there.'

'Right ho,' I said, and started for the door, sauntering at first in a languid sort of way, like a connoisseur a bit bored at having his time wasted.

I say 'at first', because I had only taken a couple of steps when I tripped over the cat, and you can't combine tripping over cats with languid sauntering. Shifting abruptly into high, I shot out of the door like someone wanted by the police making for the car after a smash-and-grab raid. The cow-creamer flew from my hands, and it was a lucky thing that I happened to barge into a fellow citizen outside, or I should have taken a toss in the gutter.

Well, not absolutely lucky, as a matter of fact, for it turned out to be Sir Watkyn Bassett. He stood there goggling at me with horror and indignation behind the pince-nez, and you could almost see him totting up the score on his fingers. First, bag-snatching, I mean to say; then umbrella-pinching; and now this. His whole demeanour was that of a man confronted with the last straw.

'Call a policeman, Roderick!' he cried, skipping like the high hills.

The Dictator sprang to the task.

'Police!' he bawled.

'Police!' yipped old Bassett, up in the tenor clef.

'Police!' roared the Dictator, taking the bass.

And a moment later something large loomed up in the fog and said: 'What's all this?'

Well, I dare say I could have explained everything, if I had stuck around and gone into it, but I didn't want to stick around and go into it. Side-stepping nimbly, I picked up the feet and was gone like the wind. A voice shouted 'Stop!' but of course I didn't. Stop, I mean to say! Of all the damn silly ideas. I legged it down byways and along side streets, and eventually fetched up somewhere in the neighbourhood of Sloane Square. There I got aboard a cab and started back to civilization.

My original intention was to drive to the Drones and get a bite of lunch there, but I hadn't gone far when I realized that I wasn't equal to it. I yield to no man in my appreciation of the Drones Club . . . its sparkling conversation, its camaraderie, its atmosphere redolent of all that is best and brightest in the metropolis . . . but there would, I knew, be a goodish bit of bread thrown hither and thither at its luncheon table, and I was in no vein to cope with flying bread. Changing my strategy in a flash, I told the man to take me to the nearest Turkish bath.

It is always my practice to linger over a Turkish b., and it was consequently getting late by the time I returned to the flat. I had managed to put in two or three hours' sleep in my cubicle, and that, taken in conjunction with the healing flow of persp. in the hot room and the plunge into the icy tank, had brought the roses back to my cheeks to no little extent. It was, indeed, practically with a merry tra-la-la on my lips that I latchkeyed my way in and made for the sitting room.

And the next moment my fizziness was turned off at the main by the sight of a pile of telegrams on the table.

# =2=

I DON'T know if you were among the gang that followed the narrative of my earlier adventures with Gussie Fink-Nottle – you may have been one of those who didn't happen to get around to it – but if you were you will recall that the dirty work on that occasion started with a tidal wave of telegrams, and you will not be surprised to learn that I found myself eyeing this mound of envelopes askance. Ever since then, telegrams in any quantity have always seemed to me to spell trouble.

I had had the idea at first glance that there were about twenty of the beastly things, but a closer scrutiny revealed only three. They had all been despatched from Totleigh-in-the-Wold, and they all bore the same signature.

They ran as follows:

The first:

> Wooster,
>   Berkeley Mansions,
>     Berkeley Square,
>       London.
> Come immediately. Serious rift Madeline and self. Reply.
>                                                 GUSSIE.

The second:

> Surprised receive no answer my telegram saying Come immediately serious rift Madeline and self. Reply.
>                                                 GUSSIE.

And the third:

> I say, Bertie, why don't you answer my telegrams? Sent you two today saying Come immediately serious rift Madeline and self. Unless you come earliest possible moment prepared lend

23

*every effort effect reconciliation, wedding will be broken off. Reply.*

GUSSIE.

I have said that that sojourn of mine in the T. bath had done much to re-establish the *mens sana in corpore* whatnot. Perusal of these frightful communications brought about an instant relapse. My misgivings, I saw, had been well founded. Something had whispered to me on seeing those bally envelopes that here we were again, and here we were.

The sound of the familiar footsteps had brought Jeeves floating out from the back premises. A glance was enough to tell him that all was not well with ye employer.

'Are you ill, sir?' he enquired solicitously.

I sank into a c. and passed an agitated h. over the b.

'Not ill, Jeeves, but all of a twitter. Read these.'

He ran his eye over the dossier, then transferred it to mine, and I could read in it the respectful anxiety he was feeling for the well-being of the young seigneur.

'Most disturbing, sir.'

His voice was grave. I could see that he hadn't missed the gist. The sinister import of those telegrams was as clear to him as it was to me.

We do not, of course, discuss the matter, for to do so would rather come under the head of speaking lightly of a woman's name, but Jeeves is in full possession of the facts relating to the Bassett-Wooster mix-up and thoroughly cognizant of the peril which threatens me from that quarter. There was no need to explain to him why I now lighted a feverish cigarette and hitched the lower jaw up with a visible effort.

'What do you suppose has happened, Jeeves?'

'It is difficult to hazard a conjecture, sir.'

'The wedding may be scratched, he says. Why? That is what I ask myself.'

'Yes, sir.'

'And I have no doubt that that is what you ask yourself?'

'Yes, sir.'

'Deep waters, Jeeves.'

'Extremely deep, sir.'

'The only thing we can say with any certainty is that in some way – how, we shall presumably learn later – Gussie has made an ass of himself again.'

I mused on Augustus Fink-Nottle for a moment, recalling how he had always stood by himself in the chump class. The best judges had been saying it for years. Why, at our private school, where I had first met him, he had been known as 'Fat-head', and that was in competition with fellows like Bingo Little, Freddie Widgeon and myself.

'What shall I do, Jeeves?'

'I think it would be best to proceed to Totleigh Towers, sir.'

'But how can I? Old Bassett would sling me out the moment I arrived.'

'Possibly if you were to telegraph to Mr Fink-Nottle, sir, explaining your difficulty, he might have some solution to suggest.'

This seemed sound. I hastened out to the post office, and wired as follows:

Fink-Nottle,
   Totleigh Towers,
      Totleigh-in-the-Wold.
   Yes, that's all very well. You say come here immediately, but how dickens can I? You don't understand relations between Pop Bassett and self. These not such as to make him welcome visit Bertram. Would inevitably hurl out on ear and set dogs on. Useless suggest putting on false whiskers and pretending be fellow come inspect drains, as old blighter familiar with features and would instantly detect imposture. What is to be done? What has happened? Why serious rift? What serious rift? How do you mean wedding broken off? Why dickens? What have you been doing to the girl? Reply.
                                                    BERTIE.

The answer to this came during dinner:

Wooster,
   Berkeley Mansions,
      Berkeley Square,
         London.
   See difficulty, but think can work it. In spite strained

*relations, still speaking terms Madeline. Am telling her have received urgent letter from you pleading be allowed come here. Expect invitation shortly.*

GUSSIE.

And on the morrow, after a tossing-on-pillow night, I received a bag of three.
The first ran:

*Have worked it. Invitation dispatched. When you come, will you bring book entitled* My Friends The Newts *by Loretta Peabody published Popgood and Grooly get any bookshop.*

GUSSIE.

The second:

*Bertie, you old ass, I hear you are coming here. Delighted, as something very important want you do for me.*

STIFFY.

The third:

*Please come here if you wish, but, oh Bertie, is this wise? Will not it cause you needless pain seeing me? Surely merely twisting knife wound.*

MADELINE.

Jeeves was bringing me the morning cup of tea when I read these missives, and I handed them to him in silence. He read them in same. I was able to imbibe about a fluid ounce of the hot and strengthening before he spoke.

'I think that we should start at once, sir.'

'I suppose so.'

'I will pack immediately. Would you wish me to call Mrs Travers on the telephone?'

'Why?'

'She has rung up several times this morning.'

'Oh? Then perhaps you had better give her a buzz.'

'I think it will not be necessary, sir. I fancy that this would be the lady now.'

26

A long and sustained peal had sounded from the front door, as if an aunt had put her thumb on the button and kept it there. Jeeves left the presence, and a moment later it was plain that his intuition had not deceived him. A booming voice rolled through the flat, the voice which once, when announcing the advent of a fox in their vicinity, had been wont to cause members of the Quorn and Pytchley to clutch their hats and bound in their saddles.

'Isn't that young hound awake yet, Jeeves? . . . Oh, there you are.'

Aunt Dahlia charged across the threshold.

At all times and on all occasions, owing to years of fox-chivvying in every kind of weather, this relative has a fairly purple face, but one noted now an even deeper mauve than usual. The breath came jerkily, and the eyes gleamed with a goofy light. A man with far less penetration than Bertram Wooster would have been able to divine that there before him stood an aunt who had got the pip about something.

It was evident that information which she yearned to uncork was bubbling within her, but she postponed letting it go for a moment in order to reproach me for being in bed at such an hour. Sunk, as she termed it in her forthright way, in hoggish slumber.

'Not sunk in hoggish slumber,' I corrected. 'I've been awake some little time. As a matter of fact, I was just about to partake of the morning meal. You will join me, I hope? Bacon and eggs may be taken as read, but say the word and we can do you a couple of kippers.'

She snorted with a sudden violence which twenty-four hours earlier would have unmanned me completely. Even in my present tolerably robust condition, it affected me rather like one of those gas explosions which slay six.

'Eggs! Kippers! What I want is a brandy and soda. Tell Jeeves to mix me one. And if he forgets to put in the soda, it will be all right with me. Bertie, a frightful thing has happened.'

'Push along into the dining saloon, my fluttering old aspen,' I said. 'We shall not be interrupted there. Jeeves will want to come in here to pack.'

'Are you off somewhere?'

'Totleigh Towers. I have had a most disturbing – '

'Totleigh Towers? Well, I'm dashed! That's just where I came to tell you you had jolly well got to go immediately.'

'Eh?'

'Matter of life and death.'

'How do you mean?'

'You'll soon see, when I've explained.'

'Then come along to the dining room and explain at your earliest convenience.'

'Now then, my dear old mysterious hinter,' I said, when Jeeves had brought the foodstuffs and withdrawn, 'tell me all.'

For an instant, there was silence, broken only by the musical sound of an aunt drinking brandy and soda and self lowering a cup of coffee. Then she put down her beaker, and drew a deep breath.

'Bertie,' she said, 'I wish to begin by saying a few words about Sir Watkyn Bassett, CBE. May greenfly attack his roses. May his cook get tight on the night of the big dinner party. May all his hens get the staggers.'

'Does he keep hens?' I said, putting a point.

'May his cistern start leaking, and may white ants, if there are any in England, gnaw away the foundations of Totleigh Towers. And when he walks up the aisle with his daughter Madeline, to give her away to that ass Spink-Bottle, may he get a sneezing fit and find that he has come out without a pocket handkerchief.'

She paused, and it seemed to me that all this, while spirited stuff, was not germane to the issue.

'Quite,' I said. 'I agree with you *in toto*. But what has he done?'

'I will tell you. You remember that cow-creamer?'

I dug into a fried egg, quivering a little.

'Remember it? I shall never forget it. You will scarcely believe this, Aunt Dahlia, but when I got to the shop, who should be there by the most amazing coincidence but this same Bassett – '

'It wasn't a coincidence. He had gone there to have a look at the thing, to see if it was all Tom had said it was. For – can you imagine such lunacy, Bertie? – that chump of an uncle of yours had told the man about it. He might have known that the fiend would hatch some devilish plot for his undoing. And

28

he did. Tom lunched with Sir Watkyn Bassett at the latter's club yesterday. On the bill of fare was a cold lobster, and this Machiavelli sicked him onto it.'

I looked at her incredulously.

'You aren't going to tell me,' I said, astounded, for I was familiar with the intensity delicate and finely poised mechanism of his tummy, 'that Uncle Tom ate lobster? After what happened last Christmas?'

'At this man's instigation, he appears to have eaten not only pounds of lobster, but forests of sliced cucumber as well. According to his story, which he was able to tell me this morning – he could only groan when he came home yesterday – he resisted at first. He was strong and resolute. But then circumstances were too much for him. Bassett's club, apparently, is one of those clubs where they have the cold dishes on a table in the middle of the room, so placed that wherever you sit you can't help seeing them.'

I nodded.

'They do at the Drones, too. Catsmeat Potter-Pirbright once hit the game pie from the far window six times with six consecutive rolls.'

'That was what caused poor old Tom's downfall. Bassett's lobster sales-talk he might have been strong enough to ignore, but the sight of the thing was too much for him. He yielded, tucked in like a starving Esquimau, and at six o'clock I got a call from the hall porter, asking me if I would send the car round to fetch away the remains, which had been discovered by the page boy writhing in a corner of the library. He arrived half an hour later, calling weakly for bicarbonate of soda. Bicarbonate of soda, my foot!' said Aunt Dahlia, with a bitter, mirthless laugh. 'He had to have two doctors and a stomach-pump.'

'And in the meantime -?' I said, for I could see whither the tale was tending.

'And in the meantime, of course, the fiend Bassett had nipped down and bought the cow-creamer. The man had promised to hold it for Tom till three o'clock, but naturally when three o'clock came and he didn't turn up and there was another customer clamouring for the thing, he let it go. So there you are. Bassett has the cow-creamer, and took it down to Totleigh last night.'

It was a sad story, of course, and one that bore out what I had so often felt about Pop Bassett – to wit, that a magistrate who could nick a fellow for five pounds, when a mere reprimand would more than have met the case, was capable of anything, but I couldn't see what she thought there was to be done about it. The whole situation seemed to me essentially one of those where you just clench the hands and roll the eyes mutely up to heaven and then start a new life and try to forget. I said as much, while marmalading a slice of toast.

She gazed at me in silence for a moment.

'Oh? So that's how you feel, is it?'

'I do, yes.'

'You admit, I hope, that by every moral law that cow-creamer belongs to Tom?'

'Oh, emphatically.'

'But you would take this foul outrage lying down? You would allow this stick-up man to get away with the swag? Confronted with the spectacle of as raw a bit of underhanded skulduggery as has ever been perpetrated in a civilized country, you would just sit tight and say "Well, well!" and do nothing?'

I weighed this.

'Possibly not "Well, well!" I concede that the situation is one that calls for the strongest comment. But I wouldn't do anything.'

'Well, I'm going to do something. I'm going to pinch the damn thing.'

I stared at her, astounded. I uttered no verbal rebuke, but there was a distinct 'Tut, tut!' in my gaze. Even though the provocation was, I admitted, severe, I could not approve of these strong-arm methods. And I was about to awaken her dormant conscience by asking her gently what the Quorn would think of these goings-on – or, for the matter of that, the Pytchley – when she added:

'Or, rather, you are!'

I had just lighted a cigarette as she spoke these words, and so, according to what they say in the advertisements, ought to have been nonchalant. But it must have been the wrong sort of cigarette, for I shot out of my chair as if somebody had shoved a bradawl through the seat.

'Who, me?'

'That's right. See how it all fits in. You're going to stay at Totleigh. You will have a hundred excellent opportunities of getting your hooks on the thing – '

'But, dash it!'

'- and I must have it, because otherwise I shall never be able to dig a cheque out of Tom for that Pomona Grindle serial. He simply won't be in the mood. And I signed the old girl up yesterday at a fabulous price, half the sum agreed upon to be paid in advance a week from current date. So snap into it, my lad. I can't see what you're making all this heavy weather about. It doesn't seem to me much to do for a loved aunt.'

'It seems to me a dashed lot to do for a loved aunt, and I'm jolly well not going to dream – '

'Oh, yes you are, because you know what will happen, if you don't.' She paused significantly. 'You follow me, Watson?'

I was silent. She had no need to tell me what she meant. This was not the first time she had displayed the velvet hand beneath the iron glove – or, rather, the other way about – in this manner.

For this ruthless relative has one all-powerful weapon which she holds constantly over my head like the sword of – who was the chap? – Jeeves would know – and by means of which she can always bend me to her will – viz. the threat that if I don't kick in she will bar me from her board and wipe Anatole's cooking from my lips. I shall not lightly forget the time when she placed sanctions on me for a whole month – right in the middle of the pheasant season, when this superman is at his incomparable best.

I made one last attempt to reason with her.

'But why does Uncle Tom want this frightful cow-creamer? It's a ghastly object. He would be far better without it.'

'He doesn't think so. Well, there it is. Perform this simple, easy task for me, or guests at my dinner table will soon be saying: "Why is it that we never seem to see Bertie Wooster here any more?" Bless my soul, what an amazing lunch that was that Anatole gave us yesterday! "Superb" is the only word. I don't wonder you're fond of his cooking. As you sometimes say, it melts in the mouth.'

I eyed her sternly.

'Aunt Dahlia, this is blackmail!'

'Yes, isn't it?' she said, and beetled off.

I resumed my seat, and ate a moody slice of cold bacon.
Jeeves entered.

'The bags are packed, sir.'

'Very good, Jeeves,' I said. 'Then let us be starting.'

'Man and boy, Jeeves,' I said, breaking a thoughtful silence
which had lasted for about eighty-seven miles, 'I have been in
some tough spots in my time, but this one wins the mottled
oyster.'

We were bowling along in the two-seater on our way to
Totleigh Towers, self at the wheel, Jeeves at my side, the personal effects in the dickey. We had got off round about eleven-
thirty, and the genial afternoon was now at its juiciest. It was
one of those crisp, sunny, bracing days with a pleasant tang in
the air, and had circumstances been different from what they
were, I should no doubt have been feeling at the peak of my
form, chatting gaily, waving to passing rustics, possibly even
singing some light snatch.

Unfortunately, however, if there was one thing circumstances
weren't, it was different from what they were, and there was
no suspicion of a song on the lips. The more I thought of what
lay before me at these bally Towers, the bowed-downer did the
heart become.

'The mottled oyster,' I repeated.

'Sir?'

I frowned. The man was being discreet, and this was no time
for discretion.

'Don't pretend you don't know all about it, Jeeves,' I said
coldly. 'You were in the next room throughout my interview
with Aunt Dahlia, and her remarks must have been audible in
Piccadilly.'

He dropped the mask.

'Well, yes, sir, I must confess that I did gather the substance
of the conversation.'

'Very well, then. You agree with me that the situation is a
lulu?'

'Certainly a somewhat sharp crisis in your affairs would
appear to have been precipitated, sir.'

I drove on, brooding.

'If I had my life to live again, Jeeves, I would start it as an orphan without any aunts. Don't they put aunts in Turkey in sacks and drop them in the Bosphorus?'

'Odalisques, sir, I understand. Not aunts.'

'Well, why not aunts? Look at the trouble they cause in the world. I tell you, Jeeves, and you may quote me as saying this – behind every poor, innocent, harmless blighter who is going down for the first time in the soup, you will find, if you look carefully enough, the aunt who shoved him into it.'

'There is much in what you say, sir.'

'It is no use telling me that there are bad aunts and good aunts. At the core, they are all alike. Sooner or later, out pops the cloven hoof. Consider this Dahlia, Jeeves. As sound an egg as ever cursed a foxhound for chasing a rabbit, I have always considered her. And she goes and hands me an assignment like this. Wooster, the pincher of policemen's helmets, we know. We are familiar with Wooster, the supposed bag-snatcher. But it was left for this aunt to present to the world a Wooster who goes to the houses of retired magistrates and, while eating their bread and salt, swipes their cow-creamers. Faugh!' I said, for I was a good deal overwrought.

'Most disturbing, sir.'

'I wonder how old Bassett will receive me, Jeeves.'

'It will be interesting to observe his reactions, sir.'

'He can't very well throw me out, I suppose, Miss Bassett having invited me?'

'No, sir.'

'On the other hand, he can – and I think he will – look at me over the top of his pince-nez and make rummy sniffing noises. The prospect is not an agreeable one.'

'No, sir.'

'I mean to say, even if this cow-creamer thing had not come up, conditions would be sticky.'

'Yes, sir. Might I venture to enquire if it is your intention to endeavour to carry out Mrs Travers's wishes?'

You can't fling the hands up in a passionate gesture when you are driving a car at fifty miles an hour. Otherwise, I should have done so.

'That is the problem which is torturing me, Jeeves. I can't make up my mind. You remember that fellow you've mentioned

to me once or twice, who let something wait upon something?
You know who I mean – the cat chap.'

'Macbeth, sir, a character in a play of that name by the late
William Shakespeare. He was described as letting "I dare not"
wait upon "I would", like the poor cat i' th' adage.'

'Well, that's how it is with me. I wobble, and I vacillate – if
that's the word?'

'Perfectly correct, sir.'

'I think of being barred from those menus of Anatole's, and
I say to myself that I will take a pop. Then I reflect that my
name at Totleigh Towers is already mud and that old Bassett is
firmly convinced that I am a combination of Raffles and a pea-
and-thimble man and steal everything I come upon that isn't
nailed down – '

'Sir?'

'Didn't I tell you about that? I had another encounter with
him yesterday, the worst to date. He now looks upon me as the
dregs of the criminal world – if not Public Enemy Number One,
certainly Number Two or Three.'

I informed him briefly of what had occurred, and conceive my
emotion when I saw that he appeared to be finding something
humorous in the recital. Jeeves does not often smile, but now a
distinct simper had begun to wreathe his lips.

'A laughable misunderstanding, sir.'

'Laughable, Jeeves?'

He saw that his mirth had been ill-timed. He reassembled the
features, ironing out the smile.

'I beg your pardon, sir. I should have said "disturbing".'

'Quite.'

'It must have been exceedingly trying, meeting Sir Watkyn in
such circumstances.'

'Yes, and it's going to be a dashed sight more trying if he
catches me pinching his cow-creamer. I keep seeing a vision of
him doing it.'

'I quite understand, sir. And thus the native hue of resolution
is sicklied o'er with the pale cast of thought, and enterprises of
great pitch and moment in this regard their currents turns awry
and lose the name of action.'

'Exactly. You take the words out of my mouth.'

I drove on, brooding more than ever.

'And here's another point that presents itself, Jeeves. Even if I want to steal cow-creamers, how am I going to find the time? It isn't a thing you can just take in your stride. You have to plan and plot and lay schemes. And I shall need every ounce of concentration for this business of Gussie's.'

'Exactly, sir. One appreciates the difficulty.'

'And, as if that wasn't enough to have on my mind, there is that telegram of Stiffy's. You remember the third telegram that came this morning. It was from Miss Stephanie Byng, Miss Bassett's cousin, who resides at Totleigh Towers. You've met her. She came to lunch at the flat a week or two ago. Smallish girl of about the tonnage of Jessie Matthews.'

'Oh, yes, sir. I remember Miss Byng. A charming young lady.'

'Quite. But what does she want me to do for her? That's the question. Probably something completely unfit for human consumption. So I've got that to worry about, too. What a life!'

'Yes, sir.'

'Still, stiff upper lip, I suppose, Jeeves, what?'

'Precisely, sir.'

During these exchanges, we had been breezing along at a fairish pace, and I had not failed to note that on a signpost which we had passed some little while back there had been inscribed the words 'Totleigh-in-the-Wold, 8 miles'. There now appeared before us through the trees a stately home of E.

I braked the car.

'Journey's End, Jeeves?'

'So I should be disposed to imagine, sir.'

And so it proved. Having turned in at the gateway and fetched up at the front door, we were informed by the butler that this was indeed the lair of Sir Watkyn Bassett.

'Childe Roland to the dark tower came, sir,' said Jeeves, as we alighted, though what he meant I hadn't an earthly. Responding with a brief 'Oh, ah,' I gave my attention to the butler, who was endeavouring to communicate something to me.

What he was saying, I now gathered, was that if desirous of mixing immediately with the inmates I had chosen a bad moment for hitting the place. Sir Watkyn, he explained, had popped out for a breather.

'I fancy he is somewhere in the grounds with Mr Roderick Spode.'

I started. After that affair at the antique shop, the name Roderick was, as you may imagine, rather deeply graven on my heart.

'Roderick Spode? Big chap with a small moustache and the sort of eye that can open an oyster at sixty paces?'

'Yes, sir. He arrived yesterday with Sir Watkyn from London. They went out shortly after lunch. Miss Madeline, I believe, is at home, but it may take some little time to locate her.'

'How about Mr Fink-Nottle?'

'I think he has gone for a walk, sir.'

'Oh? Well, right ho. Then I'll just potter about a bit.'

I was glad of the chance of being alone for a while, for I wished to brood. I strolled off along the terrace, doing so.

The news that Roderick Spode was on the premises had shaken me a good deal. I had supposed him to be some mere club acquaintance of old Bassett's, who confined his activities exclusively to the metropolis, and his presence at the Towers rendered the prospect of trying to unnerve the stoutest, twice as intimidating as it had been before, when I had supposed that I should be under the personal eye of Sir Watkyn alone.

Well, you can see that for yourself, I mean to say. I mean, imagine how some unfortunate Master Criminal would feel, on coming down to do a murder at the old Grange, if he found that not only was Sherlock Holmes putting in the weekend there, but Hercule Poirot, as well.

The more I faced up to the idea of pinching that cow-creamer, the less I liked it. It seemed to me that there ought to be a middle course, and that what I had to do was explore avenues in the hope of finding some formula. To this end, I paced the terrace with bent bean, pondering.

Old Bassett, I noted, had laid out his money to excellent advantage. I am a bit of a connoisseur of country houses, and I found this one well up to sample. Nice façade, spreading grounds, smoothly shaven lawns, and a general atmosphere of what is known as old-world peace. Cows were mooing in the distance, sheep and birds respectively bleating and tootling, and from somewhere near at hand there came the report of a gun, indicating that someone was having a whirl at the local rabbits.

Totleigh Towers might be a place where Man was vile, but undoubtedly every prospect pleased.

And I was strolling up and down, trying to calculate how long it would have taken the old bounder, fining, say, twenty people a day five quid apiece, to collect enough to pay for all this, when my attention was arrested by the interior of a room on the ground floor, visible through an open French window.

It was a sort of minor drawing room, if you know what I mean, and it gave the impression of being overfurnished. This was due to the fact that it was stuffed to bursting point with glass cases, these in their turn stuffed to bursting point with silver. It was evident that I was looking at the Bassett collection.

I paused. Something seemed to draw me through the French window. And the next moment, there I was, *vis-à-vis*, as the expression is, with my old pal the silver cow. It was standing in a smallish case over by the door, and I peered in at it, breathing heavily on the glass.

It was with considerable emotion that I perceived that the case was not locked.

I turned the handle. I dipped in, and fished it out.

Now, whether it was my intention merely to inspect and examine, or whether I was proposing to shoot the works, I do not know. The nearest I can remember is that I had no really settled plans. My frame of mind was more or less that of a cat in an adage.

However, I was not accorded leisure to review my emotions in what Jeeves would call the final analysis, for at this point a voice behind me said 'Hands up!' and, turning, I observed Roderick Spode in the window. He had a shotgun in his hand, and this he was pointing in a negligent sort of way at my third waistcoat button. I gathered from his manner that he was one of those fellows who like firing from the hip.

# =3=

I HAD described Roderick Spode to the butler as a man with an eye that could open an oyster at sixty paces, and it was an eye of this nature that he was directing at me now. He looked like a Dictator on the point of starting a purge, and I saw that I had been mistaken in supposing him to be seven feet in height. Eight, at least. Also the slowly working jaw muscles.

I hoped he was not going to say 'Ha!' but he did. And as I had not yet mastered the vocal cords sufficiently to be able to reply, that concluded the dialogue sequence for the moment. Then, still keeping his eyes glued on me, he shouted:

'Sir Watkyn!'

There was a distant sound of Eh-yes-here-I-am-what-is-it-ing.

'Come here, please. I have something to show you.'

Old Bassett appeared in the window, adjusting his pince-nez.

I had seen this man before only in the decent habiliments suitable to the metropolis, and I confess that even in the predicament in which I found myself I was able to shudder at the spectacle he presented in the country. It is, of course, an axiom, as I have heard Jeeves call it, that the smaller the man, the louder the check suit, and old Bassett's apparel was in keeping with his lack of inches. Prismatic is the only word for those frightful tweeds and, oddly enough, the spectacle of them had the effect of steadying my nerves. They gave me the feeling that nothing mattered.

'Look!' said Spode. 'Would you have thought such a thing possible?'

Old Bassett was goggling at me with a sort of stunned amazement.

'Good God! It's the bag-snatcher!'

'Yes. Isn't it incredible?'

'It's unbelievable. Why, damn it, it's persecution. Fellow follows me everywhere, like Mary's lamb. Never a free moment. How did you catch him?'

'I happened to be coming along the drive, and I saw a furtive figure slink in at the window. I hurried up, and covered him with my gun. Just in time. He had already begun to loot the place.'

'Well, I'm most obliged to you, Roderick. But what I can't get over is the chap's pertinacity. You would have thought that when we foiled that attempt of his in the Brompton Road, he would have given up the thing as a bad job. But no. Down he comes here next day. Well, he will be sorry he did.'

'I suppose this is too serious a case for you to deal with summarily?'

'I can issue a warrant for his arrest. Bring him along to the library, and I'll do it now. The case will have to go to the Assizes or the Sessions.'

'What will he get, do you think?'

'Not easy to say. But certainly not less than – '

'Hoy!' I said.

I had intended to speak in a quiet, reasonable voice – going on, after I had secured their attention, to explain that I was on these premises as an invited guest, but for some reason the word came out like something Aunt Dahlia might have said to a fellow member of the Pytchley half a mile away across a ploughed field, and old Bassett shot back as if he had been jabbed in the eye with a burned stick.

Spode commented on my methods of voice production.

'Don't shout like that!'

'Nearly broke my ear-drum,' grumbled old Bassett.

'But listen!' I yelled. 'Will you listen!'

A certain amount of confused argument then ensued, self trying to put the case for the defence and the opposition rather harping a bit on the row I was making. And in the middle of it all, just as I was showing myself in particularly good voice, the door opened and somebody said 'Goodness gracious!'

I looked round. Those parted lips . . . those saucerlike eyes . . . that slender figure, drooping slightly at the hinges . . .

Madeline Bassett was in our midst.

'Goodness gracious!' she repeated.

I can well imagine that a casual observer, if I had confided to him my qualms at the idea of being married to this girl, would have raised his eyebrows and been at a loss to understand. 'Bertie,' he would probably have said, 'you don't know what's good for you,' adding, possibly, that he wished he had half my complaint. For Madeline Bassett was undeniably of attractive exterior – slim, *svelte*, if that's the word, and bountifully equipped with golden hair and all the fixings.

But where the casual observer would have been making his bloomer was in overlooking that squashy soupiness of hers, that subtle air she had of being on the point of talking baby-talk. It was that that froze the blood. She was definitely the sort of girl who puts her hands over a husband's eyes, as he is crawling in to breakfast with a morning head, and says: 'Guess who!'

I once stayed at the residence of a newly married pal of mine, and his bride had had carved in large letters over the fireplace in the drawing room, where it was impossible to miss it, the legend: 'Two Lovers Built This Nest,' and I can still recall the look of dumb anguish in the other half of the sketch's eyes every time he came in and saw it. Whether Madeline Bassett, on entering the marital state, would go to such an awful extreme, I could not say, but it seemed most probable.

She was looking at us with a sort of pretty, wide-eyed wonder. 'Whatever is all the noise about?' she said. 'Why, Bertie! When did you get here?'

'Oh, hallo. I've just arrived.'

'Did you have a nice journey down?'

'Oh, rather, thanks. I came in the two-seater.'

'You must be quite exhausted.'

'Oh, no, thanks, rather not.'

'Well, tea will be ready soon. I see you've met Daddy.'

'And Mr Spode.'

'And Mr Spode.'

'I don't know where Augustus is, but he's sure to be in to tea.'

'I'll count the moments.'

Old Bassett has been listening to these courtesies with a dazed expression on the map – gulping a bit from time to time, like a fish that has been hauled out of a pond on a bent pin and isn't at all sure it is equal to the pressure of events. One followed the mental processes, of course. To him, Bertram was a creature of the underworld who stole bags and umbrellas and, what made it worse, didn't even steal them well. No father likes to see his ewe lamb on chummy terms with such a one.

'You don't mean you know this man?' he said.

Madeline Bassett laughed the tinkling, silvery laugh which was one of the things that had got her so disliked by the better element.

'Why, Daddy, you're too absurd. Of course I know him. Bertie Wooster is an old, old, a very dear old friend of mine. I told you he was coming here today.'

Old Bassett seemed not abreast. Spode didn't seem any too abreast, either.

'This isn't your friend Mr Wooster?'

'Of course.'

'But he snatches bags.'

'Umbrellas,' prompted Spode, as if he had been the King's Remembrancer or something.

'And umbrellas,' assented old Bassett. 'And makes daylight raids on antique shops.'

Madeline was not abreast – making three in all.

'Daddy!'

Old Bassett stuck to it stoutly.

'He does, I tell you. I've caught him at it.'

'*I've* caught him at it,' said Spode.

'We've both caught him at it,' said old Bassett. 'All over London. Wherever you go in London, there you will find this fellow stealing bags and umbrellas. And now in the heart of Gloucestershire.'

'Nonsense!' said Madeline.

I saw that it was time to put an end to all this rot. I was about fed up with that bag-snatching stuff. Naturally, one does not expect a magistrate to have all the details about the customers at his fingers' ends – pretty good, of course, remembering his *clientèle* at all – but one can't just keep passing a thing like that off tactfully.

'Of course it's nonsense,' I thundered. 'The whole thing is one of those laughable misunderstandings.'

I must say I was expecting that my explanation would have gone better than it did. What I had anticipated was that after a few words from myself, outlining the situation, there would have been roars of jolly mirth, followed by apologies and backslappings. But old Bassett, like so many of these police court magistrates, was a difficult man to convince. Magistrates' natures soon get warped. He kept interrupting and asking questions, and cocking an eye at me as he asked them. You know what I mean – questions beginning with 'Just one moment –' and 'You say –' and 'Then you are asking us to believe –' Offensive, very.

However, after a good deal of tedious spadework, I managed to get him straight on the umbrella, and he conceded that he might have judged me unjustly about that.

'But how about the bags?'

'There weren't any bags.'

'I certainly sentenced you for something at Bosher Street. I remember it vividly.'

'I pinched a policeman's helmet.'

'That's just as bad as snatching bags.'

Roderick Spode intervened unexpectedly. Throughout this – well, dash it, this absolute Trial of Mary Dugan – he had been standing by, thoughtfully sucking the muzzle of his gun and listening to my statements as if he thought it all pretty thin; but now a flicker of human feeling came into his granite face.

'No,' he said, 'I don't think you can go so far as that. When I was at Oxford, I once stole a policeman's helmet myself.'

I was astounded. Nothing in my relations with this man had given me the idea that he, too, had, so to speak, once lived in Arcady. It just showed, as I often say, that there is good in the worst of us.

Old Bassett was plainly taken aback. Then he perked up.

'Well, how about that affair at the antique shop? Hey? Didn't we catch him in the act of running off with my cow-creamer? What has he got to say to that?'

Spode seemed to see the force of this. He removed the gun, which he had replaced between his lips, and nodded.

'The bloke at the shop had given it to me to look at,' I said shortly. 'He advised me to take it outside, where the light was better.'

'You were rushing out.'

'Staggering out. I trod on the cat.'

'What cat?'

'It appeared to be an animal attached to the personnel of the emporium.'

'H'm! I saw no cat. Did you see a cat, Roderick?'

'No, no cat.'

'Ha! Well, we will pass over the cat – '

'But I didn't,' I said, with one of my lightning flashes.

'We will pass over the cat,' repeated old Bassett, ignoring the gag and leaving it lying there, 'and come to another point. What were you doing with that cow-creamer? You say you were looking at it. You are asking us to believe that you were merely subjecting it to a perfectly innocent scrutiny. Why? What was your motive? What possible interest could it have for a man like you?'

'Exactly,' said Spode. 'The very question I was going to ask myself.'

This bit of backing-up from a pal had the worst effect on old Bassett. It encouraged him to so great an extent that he now yielded completely to the illusion that he was back in his bally police court.

'You say the proprietor of the shop handed it to you. I put it to you that you snatched it up and were making off with it. And now Mr Spode catches you here, with the thing in your hands. How do you explain that? What's your answer to that? Hey?'

'Why, Daddy!' said Madeline.

I dare say you have been wondering at this pancake's silence during all the cut-and-thrust stuff which had been going on. It is readily explained. What had occurred was that shortly after saying 'Nonsense!' in the earlier portion of the proceedings, she had happened to inhale some form of insect life, and since then had been choking quietly in the background. And as the situation was far too tense for us to pay any attention to choking girls, she had been left to carry on under her own steam while the men threshed out the subject on the agenda paper.

She now came forward, her eyes still watering a bit.

'Why, Daddy,' she said, 'naturally your silver would be the first thing Bertie would want to look at. Of course, he is interested in it. Bertie is Mr Travers's nephew.'

'What!'

'Didn't you know that? Your uncle has a wonderful collection hasn't he, Bertie? I suppose he has often spoken to you of Daddy's.'

There was a pause. Old Bassett was breathing heavily. I didn't like the look of him at all. He glanced from me to the cow-creamer, and from the cow-creamer to me, then back from me to the cow-creamer again, and it would have taken a far less astute observer than Bertram to fail to read what was passing in his mind. If ever I saw a bimbo engaged in putting two and two together, that bimbo was Sir Watkyn Bassett.

'Oh!' he said.

Just that. Nothing more. But it was enough.

'I say,' I said, 'could I send a telegram?'

'You can telephone it from the library,' said Madeline. 'I'll take you there.'

She conducted me to the instrument and left me, saying that she would be waiting in the hall when I had finished. I leaped at it, established connection with the post office, and after a brief conversation with what appeared to be the village idiot, telephoned as follows:

Mrs Travers,
   47, Charles Street,
     Berkeley Square,
       London.

I paused for a moment, assembling the ideas, then proceeded thus:

*Deeply regret quite impossible carry out assignment re you know what. Atmosphere one of keenest suspicion and any sort of action instantly fatal. You ought to have seen old Bassett's eye just now on learning of blood relationship of self and Uncle Tom. Like ambassador finding veiled woman snooping round safe containing secret treaty. Sorry and all that, but nothing doing. Love.*

BERTIE

I then went down to the hall to join Madeline Bassett.

She was standing by the barometer, which, if it had had an ounce of sense in its head, would have been pointing to 'Stormy' instead of 'Set Fair': and as I hove alongside she turned and gazed at me with a tender goggle which sent a thrill of dread creeping down the Wooster spine. The thought that there stood one who was on distant terms with Gussie and might 'ere long return the ring and presents afflicted me with a nameless horror.

I resolved that if a few quiet words from a man of the world could heal the breach, they should be spoken.

'Oh, Bertie,' she said, in a low voice like beer trickling out of a jug, 'you ought not to be here!'

My recent interview with old Bassett and Roderick Spode had rather set me thinking along those lines myself. But I hadn't time to explain that this was no idle social visit, and that if Gussie hadn't been sending out SOSs I wouldn't have dreamed of coming within a hundred miles of the frightful place. She went on, looking at me as if I were a rabbit which she was expecting shortly to turn into a gnome.

'Why did you come? Oh, I know what you are going to say. You felt that, cost what it might, you had to see me again, just once. You could not resist the urge to take away with you one last memory, which you could cherish down the lonely years. Oh, Bertie, you remind me of Rudel.'

The name was new to me.'

'Rudel?'

'The Seigneur Geoffrey Rudel, Prince of Blay-en-Saintonge.'

I shook my head.

'Never met him, I'm afraid. Pal of yours?'

'He lived in the Middle Ages. He was a great poet. And he fell in love with the wife of the Lord of Tripoli.'

I stirred uneasily. I hoped she was going to keep it clean.

'For years he loved her, and at last he could resist no longer. He took ship to Tripoli, and his servants carried him ashore.'

'Not feeling so good?' I said, groping. 'Rough crossing?'

'He was dying. Of love.'

'Oh, ah.'

'They bore him into the Lady Melisande's presence on a litter, and he had just strength enough to reach out and touch her hand. Then he died.'

She paused, and heaved a sigh that seemed to come straight up from the cami-knickers. A silence ensued.

'Terrific,' I said, feeling I had to say something, though personally I didn't think the story a patch on the one about the travelling salesman and the farmer's daughter. Different, of course, if one had known the chap.

She sighed again.

'You see now why I said you reminded me of Rudel. Like him, you came to take one last glimpse of the woman you loved. It was dear of you, Bertie, and I shall never forget it. It will always remain with me as a fragrant memory, like a flower pressed between the leaves of an old album. But was it wise? should you not have been strong? Would it not have been better to have ended it all cleanly, that day when we said goodbye at Brinkley Court, and not to have reopened the wound? We had met, and you have loved me, and I had had to tell you that my heart was another's. That should have been our farewell.'

'Absolutely,' I said. I mean to say, all that was perfectly sound, as far as it went. If her heart really was another's, fine. Nobody more pleased than Bertram. The whole nub of the thing was – was it? 'But I had a communication from Gussie, more or less indicating that you and he were *p'fft*.'

She looked at me like someone who has just solved the cross-word puzzle with a shrewd 'Emu' in the top right-hand corner.

'So that was why you came! You thought that there might still be hope? Oh, Bertie, I'm sorry . . . sorry . . . so sorry.' Her eyes were misty with the unshed, and about the size of soup plates. 'No, Bertie, really there is no hope, none. You must not build dream castles. It can only cause you pain. I love Augustus. He is my man.'

'And you haven't parted brass rags?'

'Of course not.'

'Then what did he mean by saying "Serious rift Madeline and self"?'

'Oh, that?' She laughed another tinkling, silvery one. 'That was nothing. It was all too perfectly silly and ridiculous. Just the teeniest, weeniest little misunderstanding. I thought I had found him flirting with my cousin Stephanie, and I was silly and jealous. But he explained everything this morning. He was only taking a fly out of her eye.'

I suppose I might legitimately have been a bit shirty on learning that I had been hauled all the way down here for nothing, but I wasn't. I was amazingly braced. As I have indicated, that telegram of Gussie's had shaken me to my foundations, causing me to fear the worst. And now the All Clear had been blown, and I had received absolute inside information straight from the horse's mouth that all was hotsy-totsy between this blister and himself.

'So everything's all right, is it?'

'Everything. I have never loved Augustus more than I do now.'

'Haven't you, by Jove?'

'Each moment I am with him, his wonderful nature seems to open before me like some lovely flower.'

'Does it, egad?'

'Every day I find myself discovering some new facet of his extraordinary character. For instance . . . you have seen him quite lately, have you not?'

'Oh, rather. I gave him a dinner at the Drones only the night before last.'

'I wonder if you noticed any difference in him?'

I threw my mind back to the binge in question. As far as I could recollect, Gussie had been the same fish-faced freak I had always known.

'Difference? No, I don't think so. Of course, at that dinner I hadn't the chance to observe him very closely – subject his character to the final analysis, if you know what I mean. He sat next to me, and we talked of this and that, but you know how it is when you're a host – you have all sorts of things to divert your attention . . . keeping an eye on the waiters, trying to make the conversation general, heading Catsmeat Potter-Pirbright off from giving his imitation of Beatrice Lillie . . . a hundred little duties. But he seemed to me much the same. What sort of difference?'

'An improvement, if such a thing were possible. Have you not sometimes felt in the past, Bertie, that, if Augustus had a fault, it was a tendency to be a little timid?'

I saw what she meant.

'Oh, ah, yes, of course, definitely.' I remembered something Jeeves had once called Gussie. 'A sensitive plant, what?'

'Exactly. You know your Shelley, Bertie.'

'Oh, am I?'

'That is what I have always thought him – a sensitive plant, hardly fit for the rough and tumble of life. But recently – in this last week, in fact – he has shown, together with that wonderful dreamy sweetness of his, a force of character which I had not suspected that he possessed. He seems completely to have lost his diffidence.'

'By Jove, yes,' I said, remembering. 'That's right. Do you know, he actually made a speech at that dinner of mine, and a most admirable one. And, what is more – '

I paused. I had been on the point of saying that, what was more, he had made it from start to finish on orange juice, and not – as had been the case at the Market Snodsbury prize giving – with about three quarts of mixed alcoholic stimulants lapping about inside him: and I saw that the statement might be injudicious. That Market Snodsbury exhibition on the part of the adored object was, no doubt, something which she was trying to forget.

'Why, only this morning,' she said, 'he spoke to Roderick Spode quite sharply.'

'He did?'

'Yes. They were arguing about something, and Augustus told him to go and boil his head.'

'Well, well!' I said.

Naturally, I didn't believe it for a moment. Well, I mean to say! Roderick Spode, I mean – a chap who even in repose would have made an all-in wrestler pause and pick his words. The thing wasn't possible.

I saw what had happened, of course. She was trying to give the boyfriend a build-up and, like all girls, was overdoing it. I've noticed the same thing in young wives, when they're trying to kid you that Herbert or George or whatever the name may be has hidden depths which the vapid and irreflective observer might overlook. Women never know when to stop on these occasions.

I remember Mrs Bingo Little once telling me, shortly after their marriage, that Bingo said poetic things to her about sunsets – his best friends being perfectly well aware, of course, that the old egg never noticed a sunset in his life and that, if he did by a fluke ever happen to do so, the only thing he would say about it would be that it reminded him of a slice of roast beef, cooked just right.

However, you can't call a girl a liar; so, as I say, I said: 'Well, well!'

'It was the one thing that was needed to make him perfect. Sometimes, Bertie, I ask myself if I am worthy of so rare a soul.'

'Oh, I wouldn't ask yourself rot like that,' I said heartily. 'Of course you are.'

'It's sweet of you to say so.'

'Not a bit. You two fit like pork and beans. Anyone could see that it was a what-d'you-call-it . . . ideal union. I've known Gussie since we were kids together, and I wish I had a bob for every time I've thought to myself that the girl for him was somebody just like you.'

'Really?'

'Absolutely. And when I met you, I said: "That's the bird! There she spouts!" When is the wedding to be?'

'On the twenty-third.'

'I'd make it earlier.'

'You think so?'

'Definitely. Get it over and done with, and then you'll have it off your mind. You can't be married too soon to a chap like Gussie. Great chap. Splendid chap. Never met a chap I respected more. They don't often make them like Gussie. One of the fruitiest.'

She reached out and grabbed my hand and pressed it. Unpleasant, of course, but one had to take the rough with the smooth.

'Ah, Bertie! Always the soul of generosity!'

'No, no, rather not. Just saying what I think.'

'It makes me so happy to feel that . . . all this . . . has not interfered with your affection for Augustus.'

'I should say not.'

'So many men in your position might have become embittered.'

'Silly asses.'

'But you are too fine for that. You can still say these wonderful things about him.'

'Oh, rather.'

'Dear Bertie!'

And on this cheery note we parted, she to go messing about on some domestic errand, I to head for the drawing room and get a spot of tea. She, it appeared, did not take tea, being on a diet.

And I had reached the drawing room, and was about to shove open the door, which was ajar, when from the other side there came a voice. And what it was saying was:

'So kindly do not talk rot, Spode!'

There was no possibility of mistake as to whose voice it was. From his earliest years, there has always been something distinctive and individual about Gussie's *timbre*, reminding the hearer partly of an escape of gas from a gas pipe and partly of a sheep calling to its young in the lambing season.

Nor was there any possibility of mistake about what he had said. The words were precisely as I have stated, and to say that I was surprised would be to put it too weakly. I saw now that it was perfectly possible that there might be something, after all, in that wild story of Madeline Bassett's. I mean to say, an Augustus Fink-Nottle who told Roderick Spode not to talk rot was an Augustus Fink-Nottle who might quite well have told him to go and boil his head.

I entered the room, marvelling.

Except for some sort of dim female abaft the teapot, who looked as if she might be a cousin by marriage or something of that order, only Sir Watkyn Bassett, Roderick Spode and Gussie were present. Gussie was straddling the hearth rug with his legs apart, warming himself at the blaze which should, one would have said, been reserved for the trouser seat of the master of the house, and I saw immediately what Madeline Bassett had meant when she said that he had lost his diffidence. Even across the room one could see that, when it came to self-confidence, Mussolini could have taken his correspondence course.

He sighted me as I entered, and waved what seemed to me a dashed patronizing hand. Quite the ruddy Squire graciously receiving the deputation of tenantry.

'Ah, Bertie. So here you are.'

'Yes.'

'Come in, come in and have a crumpet.'

'Thanks.'

'Did you bring that book I asked you to?'

'Awfully sorry. I forgot.'

'Well, of all the muddle-headed asses that ever stepped, you certainly are the worst. Others abide our question, thou art free.'

And dismissing me with a weary gesture, he called for another potted-meat sandwich.

I have never been able to look back on my first meal at Totleigh Towers as among my happiest memories. The cup of tea on arrival at a country house is a thing which, as a rule, I particularly enjoy. I like the crackling logs, the shaded lights, the scent of buttered toast, the general atmosphere of leisured cosiness. There is something that seems to speak to the deeps in me in the beaming smile of my hostess and the furtive whisper of my host, as he plucks at my elbow and says 'Let's get out of here and go and have a whisky and soda in the gun room.' It is on such occasions as this, it has often been said, that you catch Bertram Wooster at his best.

But now all sense of *bien-être* was destroyed by Gussie's peculiar manner – that odd suggestion he conveyed of having bought the place. It was a relief when the gang had finally drifted away, leaving us alone. There were mysteries here which I wanted to probe.

I thought it best, however, to begin by taking a second opinion on the position of affairs between himself and Madeline. She had told me that everything was now hunky-dory once more, but it was one of those points on which you cannot have too much assurance.

'I saw Madeline just now,' I said. 'She tells me that you are sweethearts still. Correct?'

'Quite correct. There was a little temporary coolness about my taking a fly out of Stephanie Byng's eye, and I got a bit panicked and wired you to come down. I thought you might possibly plead. However, no need for that now. I took a strong line, and everything is all right. Still, stay a day or two, of course, as you're here.'

'Thanks.'

'No doubt you will be glad to see your aunt. She arrives tonight, I understand.'

I could make nothing of this. My Aunt Agatha, I knew, was in a nursing home with jaundice. I had taken her flowers only a couple of days before. And naturally it couldn't be Aunt

Dahlia, for she had mentioned nothing to me about any plans for infesting Totleigh Towers.

'Some mistake,' I said.

'No mistake at all. Madeline showed me the telegram that came from her this morning, asking if she could be put up for a day or two. It was dispatched from London, I noticed, so I suppose she has left Brinkley.'

I stared.

'You aren't talking about my Aunt Dahlia?'

'Of course I'm talking about your Aunt Dahlia.'

'You mean Aunt Dahlia is coming here tonight?'

'Exactly.'

This was nasty news, and I found myself chewing the lower lip a bit in undisguised concern. This sudden decision to follow me to Totleigh Towers could mean only one thing, that Aunt Dahlia, thinking things over, had become mistrustful of my will to win, and had felt it best to come and stand over me and see that I did not shirk the appointed task. And as I was fully resolved to shirk it, I could envisage some dirty weather ahead. Her attitude toward a recalcitrant nephew would, I feared, closely resemble that which in the old tally-ho days she had been wont to adopt towards a hound which refused to go to cover.

'Tell me,' continued Gussie, 'what sort of voice is she in these days? I ask, because if she is going to make those hunting noises of hers at me during her visit, I shall be compelled to tick her off pretty sharply. I had enough of that sort of thing when I was staying at Brinkley.'

I would have liked to go on musing on the unpleasant situation which had arisen, but it seemed to me that I had been given the cue to begin my probe.

'What's happened to you, Gussie?' I asked.

'Eh?'

'Since when have you been like this?'

'I don't understand you.'

'Well, to take an instance, saying you're going to tick Aunt Dahlia off. At Brinkley, you cowered before her like a wet sock. And, to take another instance, telling Spode not to talk rot. By the way, what was he talking rot about?'

'I forgot. He talks so much rot.'

'I wouldn't have the nerve to tell Spode not to talk rot,' I said frankly. My candour met with an immediate response.

'Well, to tell you the truth, Bertie,' said Gussie, coming clean, 'neither would I, a week ago.'

'What happened a week ago?'

'I had a spiritual rebirth. Thanks to Jeeves. There's a chap, Bertie!'

'Ah!'

'We are as little children, frightened of the dark, and Jeeves is the wise nurse who takes us by the hand and – '

'Switches the light on?'

'Precisely. Would you care to hear about it?'

I assured him that I was all agog. I settled myself in my chair and, putting match to gasper, awaited the inside story.


Gussie stood silent for a moment. I could see that he was marshalling his facts. He took off his spectacles and polished them.

'A week ago, Bertie,' he began, 'my affairs had reached a crisis. I was faced by an ordeal, the mere prospect of which blackened the horizon. I discovered that I would have to make a speech at the wedding breakfast.'

'Well, naturally.'

'I know, but for some reason I had not foreseen it, and the news came as a stunning blow. And shall I tell you why I was so overcome by stark horror at the idea of making a speech at the wedding breakfast? It was because Roderick Spode and Sir Watkyn Basset would be in the audience. Do you know Sir Watkyn intimately?'

'Not very. He once fined me five quid at his police court.'

'Well, you can take it from me that he is a hard nut, and he strongly objects to having me as a son-in-law. For one thing, he would have liked Madeline to marry Spode – who, I may mention, has loved her since she was so high.'

'Oh, yes?' I said, courteously concealing my astonishment that anyone except a certified boob like himself could deliberately love this girl.

'Yes. But apart from the fact that she wanted to marry me, he didn't want to marry her. He looks upon himself as a Man of Destiny, you see, and feels that marriage would interfere with his mission. He takes a line through Napoleon.'

I felt that before proceeding further I must get the low-down on this Spode. I didn't follow all this Man of Destiny stuff.

'How do you mean, his mission? Is he someone special?'

'Don't you ever read the papers? Roderick Spode is the founder and head of the Saviours of Britain, a Fascist organization better known as the Black Shorts. His general idea, if he doesn't get knocked on the head with a bottle in one of the frequent brawls in which he and his followers indulge, is to make himself a Dictator.'

'Well, I'm blowed!'

I was astounded at my keenness of perception. The moment I had set eyes on Spode, if you remember, I had said to myself 'What ho! A Dictator!' and a Dictator he had proved to be. I couldn't have made a better shot, if I had been one of those detectives who see a chap walking along the street and deduce that he is a retired manufacturer of poppet valves named Robinson with rheumatism in one arm, living at Clapham.

'Well, I'm dashed! I thought he was something of that sort. That chin . . . Those eyes . . . And, for the matter of that, that moustache. By the way, when you say "shorts", you mean "shirts", of course.'

'No. By the time Spode formed his association, there were no shirts left. He and his adherents wear black shorts.'

'Footer bags, you mean?'

'Yes.'

'How perfectly foul.'

'Yes.'

'Bare knees?'

'Bare knees.'

'Golly!'

'Yes.'

A thought struck me, so revolting that I nearly dropped my gasper.

'Does old Bassett wear black shorts?'

'No. He isn't a member of the Saviours of Britain.'

'Then how does he come to be mixed up with Spode? I met them going around London like a couple of sailors on shore leave.'

'Sir Watkyn is engaged to be married to his aunt – a Mrs Wintergreen, widow of the late Colonel H. H. Wintergreen, of Pont Street.'

I mused for a moment, reviewing in my mind the scene in the antique-bin.

When you are standing in the dock, with a magistrate looking at you over his pince-nez and talking about you as 'the prisoner Wooster', you have ample opportunity for drinking him in, and what had struck me principally about Sir Watkyn Bassett that day at Bosher Street had been his peevishness. In that shop, on the other hand, he had given the impression of a man who has found the blue bird. He had hopped about like a carefree cat on hot bricks, exhibiting the merchandise to Spode with little chirps of 'I think your aunt would like this?' and 'How about this?' and so forth. And now a clue to that fizziness had been provided.

'Do you know, Gussie,' I said, 'I've an idea he must have clicked yesterday.'

'Quite possibly. However, never mind about that. That is not the point.'

'No, I know. But it's interesting.'

'No, it isn't.'

'Perhaps you're right.'

'Don't let us go wandering off into side issues,' said Gussie, calling the meeting to order. 'Where was I?'

'I don't know.'

'I do. I was telling you that Sir Watkyn disliked the idea of having me for a son-in-law. Spode also was opposed to the match. Nor did he make any attempt to conceal the fact. He used to come popping out at me from round corners and muttering threats.'

'You couldn't have liked that.'

'I didn't.'

'Why did he mutter threats?'

'Because though he would not marry Madeline, even if she would have him, he looks on himself as a sort of knight, watching over her. He keeps telling me that the happiness of that little girl is very dear to him, and that if ever I let her down, he will break my neck. That is the gist of the threats he mutters, and that was one of the reasons why I was a bit agitated when

Madeline became distant in her manner, on catching me with Stephanie Byng.'

'Tell me, Gussie, what were you and Stiffy actually doing?'

'I was taking a fly out of her eye.'

I nodded. If that was his story, no doubt he was wise to stick to it.

'So much for Spode. We now come to Sir Watkyn Bassett. At our very first meeting I could see that I was not his dream man.'

'Me, too.'

'I became engaged to Madeline, as you know, at Brinkley Court. The news of the betrothal was, therefore, conveyed to him by letter, and I imagine that the dear girl must have hauled up her slacks about me in a way that led him to suppose that what he was getting was a sort of cross between Robert Taylor and Einstein. At any rate, when I was introduced to him as the man who was to marry his daughter, he just stared for a moment and said "What?" Incredulously, you know, as if he were hoping that this was some jolly practical joke and that the real chap would shortly jump out from behind a chair and say "Boo!" When he at last got onto it that there was no deception, he went off into a corner and sat there for some time, holding his head in his hands. After that I used to catch him looking at me over the top of his pince-nez. It unsettled me.'

I wasn't surprised. I have already alluded to the effect that over-the-top-of-the-pince-nez look of old Bassett's had had on me, and I could see that, if directed at Gussie, it might quite conceivably have stirred the old egg up a good deal.

'He also sniffed. And when he learned from Madeline that I was keeping newts in my bedroom, he said something very derogatory – under his breath, but I heard him.'

'You've got the troupe with you, then?'

'Of course. I am in the middle of a very delicate experiment. An American professor has discovered that the full moon influences the love life of several undersea creatures, including one species of fish, two starfish groups, eight kinds of worms and a ribbon-like seaweed called Dictyota. The moon will be full in two or three days, and I want to find out if it affects the love life of newts, too.'

'But what *is* the love life of newts, if you boil it right down?

Didn't you tell me once that they just waggled their tails at one another in the mating season?'

'Quite correct.'

I shrugged my shoulders.

'Well, all right, if they like it. But it's not my idea of molten passion. So old Bassett didn't approve of the dumb chums?'

'No. He didn't approve of anything about me. It made things most difficult and disagreeable. Add Spode, and you will understand why I was beginning to get thoroughly rattled. And then, out of a blue sky, they sprang it on me that I would have to make a speech at the wedding breakfast – to an audience, as I said before, of which Roderick Spode and Sir Watkyn Bassett would form a part.'

He paused, and swallowed convulsively, like a Pekingese taking a pill.

'I am a shy man, Bertie. Diffidence is the price I pay for having a hyper-sensitive nature. And you know how I feel about making speeches under any conditions. The mere idea appals me. When you lugged me into that prize-giving affair at Market Snodsbury, the thought of standing on a platform, faced by a mob of pimply boys, filled me with a panic terror. It haunted my dreams. You can imagine, then, what it was like for me to have to contemplate that wedding breakfast. To the task of haranguing a flock of aunts and cousins I might have steeled myself. I don't say it would have been easy, but I might have managed it. But to get up with Spode on one side of me and Sir Watkyn Bassett on the other . . . I didn't see how I was going to face it. And then out of the night that covered me, black as the pit from pole to pole, there shone a tiny gleam of hope. I thought of Jeeves.'

His hand moved upwards, and I think this idea was to bare his head reverently. The project was, however, rendered null and void by the fact that he hadn't a hat on.

'I thought of Jeeves,' he repeated, 'and I took the train to London and placed my problem before him. I was fortunate to catch him in time.'

'How do you mean, in time?'

'Before he left England.'

'He isn't leaving England.'

'He told me that you and he were starting off almost immediately on one of those Round-The-World cruises.'

'Oh, no, that's all off. I didn't like the scheme.'

'Does Jeeves say it's all off?'

'No, but I do.'

'Oh?'

He looked at me rather oddly, and I thought he was going to say something more on the subject. But he only gave a rummy sort of short laugh, and resumed his narrative.

'Well, as I say, I went to Jeeves, and put the facts before him. I begged him to try to find some way of getting me out of this frightful situation in which I was enmeshed – assuring him that I would not blame him if he failed to do so, because it seemed to me, after some days of reviewing the matter, that I was beyond human aid. And you will scarcely credit this, Bertie, I hadn't got more than halfway through the glass of orange juice with which he had supplied me, when he solved the whole thing. I wouldn't have believed it possible. I wonder what that brain of his weighs?'

'A good bit, I fancy. He eats a lot of fish. So it was a winner, was it, this idea?'

'It was terrific. He approached the matter from the psychological angle. In the final analysis, he said, disinclination to speak in public is due to fear of one's audience.'

'Well, I could have told you that.'

'Yes, but he indicated how this might be cured. We do not, he said, fear those whom we despise. The thing to do, therefore, is to cultivate a lofty contempt for those who will be listening to one.'

'How?'

'Quite simple. You fill your mind with scornful thoughts about them. You keep saying to yourself: "Think of that pimple on Smith's nose" . . . "Consider Jones's flapping ears" . . . "Remember the time Robinson got hauled up before the beak for travelling first-class with a third-class ticket" . . . "Don't forget you once saw the child Brown being sick at a children's party" . . . and so on. So that when you are called upon to address Smith, Jones, Robinson and Brown, they have lost their sting. You dominate them.'

I pondered on this.

'I see. Well, yes, it sounds good, Gussie. But would it work in practice?'

'My dear chap, it works like a charm. I've tested it. You recall my speech at that dinner of yours?'

I started.

'You weren't despising us?'

'Certainly I was. Thoroughly.'

'What, me?'

'You, and Freddie Widgeon, and Bingo Little, and Catsmeat Potter-Pirbright, and Barmy Fotheringay-Phipps, and all the rest of those present. "Worms!" I said to myself. "What a crew!" I said to myself. "There's old Bertie," I said to myself. "Golly!" I said to myself, "what I know about *him*!" With the result that I played on you as on a lot of stringed instruments, and achieved an outstanding triumph.'

I must say I was conscious of a certain chagrin. A bit thick, I mean, being scorned by a goof like Gussie – and that at a moment when he had been bursting with one's meat and orange juice.

But soon more generous emotions prevailed. After all, I told myself, the great thing – the fundamental thing to which all other considerations must yield – was to get this Fink-Nottle safely under the wire and off on his honeymoon. And but for this advice of Jeeves's, the muttered threats of Roderick Spode and the combined sniffing and looking over the top of the pince-nez of Sir Watkyn Bassett might well have been sufficient to destroy his morale entirely and cause him to cancel the wedding arrangements and go off hunting newts in Africa.

'Well, yes,' I said, 'I see what you mean. But dash it, Gussie, conceding the fact that you might scorn Barmy Fotheringay-Phipps and Catsmeat Potter-Pirbright and – stretching the possibilities a bit – me, you couldn't despise Spode.'

'Couldn't I?' He laughed a light laugh. 'I did it on my head. And Sir Watkyn Bassett, too. I tell you, Bertie, I approach this wedding breakfast without a tremor. I am gay, confident, debonair. There will be none of that blushing and stammering and twiddling the fingers and plucking at the tablecloth which you see in most bridegrooms on these occasions. I shall look these men in the eye, and make them wilt. As for the aunts and cousins, I shall have them rolling in the aisles. The moment Jeeves spoke those words, I settled down to think of all the things about Roderick Spode and Sir Watkyn Bassett which expose them to the just contempt of their fellow men. I could tell you fifty things about Sir Watkyn alone which would make you wonder how such a moral and physical blot on the English scene could have been tolerated all these years. I wrote them down in a notebook.'

'You wrote them down in a notebook?'

'A small, leather-covered notebook. I bought it in the village.'

I confess that I was a bit agitated. Even though he presumably kept it under lock and key, the mere existence of such a book made one uneasy. One did not care to think what the upshot and outcome would be were it to fall into the wrong hands. A brochure like that would be dynamite.

'Where do you keep it?'

'In my breast pocket. Here it is. Oh, no, it isn't. That's funny,' said Gussie. 'I must have dropped it somewhere.'

## 4

I DON'T know if you have had the same experience, but a thing I have found in life is that from time to time, as you jog along, there occur moments which you are able to recognize immediately with the naked eye as high spots. Something tells you that they are going to remain etched, if etched is the word I want, for ever on the memory and will come back to you at intervals down the years, as you are dropping off to sleep, banishing that drowsy feeling and causing you to leap on the pillow like a gaffed salmon.

One of these well-remembered moments in my own case was the time at my first private school when I sneaked down to the headmaster's study at dead of night, my spies having informed me that he kept a tin of biscuits in the cupboard under the bookshelf; to discover, after I was well inside and a modest and unobtrusive withdrawal impossible, that the old bounder was seated at his desk and – by what I have always thought a rather odd coincidence – actually engaged in the composition of my end-of-term report, which subsequently turned out a stinker.

It was a situation in which it would be paltering with the truth to say that Bertram retained unimpaired his customary *sang-froid*. But I'm dashed if I can remember staring at the Rev. Aubrey Upjohn on that occasion with half the pallid horror which had shot into the map at these words of Gussie's.

'Dropped it?' I quavered.

'Yes, but it's all right.'

'All right?'

'I mean, I can remember every word of it.'

'Oh, I see. That's fine.'

'Yes.'

'Was there much of it?'

'Oh, lots.'

'Good stuff?'

'Of the best.'

'Well, that's splendid.'

I looked at him with growing wonder. You would have thought that by this time even this pre-eminent sub-normal would have spotted the frightful peril that lurked. But no. His tortoiseshell-rimmed spectacles shone with a jovial light. He was full of *élan* and *espièglerie*, without a care in the world. All right up to the neck, but from there on pure concrete – that was Augustus Fink-Nottle.

'Oh, yes,' he said, 'I've got it all carefully memorized, and I'm extremely pleased with it. During this past week I have been subjecting the characters of Roderick Spode and Sir Watkyn Bassett to a pitiless examination. I have probed these two gumboils to the very core of their being. It's amazing the amount of material you can assemble, once you begin really analysing people. Have you ever heard Sir Watkyn Bassett dealing with a bowl of soup? It's not unlike the Scottish express going through a tunnel. Have you ever seen Spode eat asparagus?'

'No.'

'Revolting. It alters one's whole conception of Man as Nature's last word.'

'Those were two of the things you wrote in the book?'

'I gave them about half a page. They were just trivial, surface faults. The bulk of my researches went much deeper.'

'I see. You spread yourself?'

'Very much so.'

'And it was all bright, snappy stuff?'

'Every word of it.'

'That's great. I mean to say, no chance of old Bassett being bored when he reads it.'

'Reads it?'

'Well, he's just as likely to find the book as anyone, isn't he?'

I remember Jeeves saying to me once, apropos of how you can never tell what the weather's going to do, that full many a glorious morning had he seen flatter the mountain tops with sovereign eye and then turn into a rather nasty afternoon. It was the same with Gussie now. He had been beaming like a searchlight until I mentioned this aspect of the matter, and the radiance suddenly disappeared as if it had been switched off at the main.

He stood gaping at me very much as I had gaped at the Rev. A. Upjohn on the occasion to which I have alluded above. His expression was almost identical with that which I had once surprised on the face of a fish, whose name I cannot recall, in the royal aquarium at Monaco.

'I never thought of that!'

'Start now.'

'Oh, my gosh!'

'Yes.'

'Oh, my golly!'

'Quite.'

'Oh, my sainted aunt!'

'Absolutely.'

He moved to the tea table like a man in a dream, and started to eat a cold crumpet. His eyes, as they sought mine, were bulging.

'Suppose old Bassett does find that book, what do you think will ensue?'

I could answer that one.

'He would immediately put the bee on the wedding.'

'You don't really think that?'

'I do.'

He choked over his crumpet.

'Of course he would,' I said. 'You say he has never been any too sold on you as a son-in-law. Reading that book isn't going to cause a sudden change for the better. One glimpse of it, and he will be countermanding the cake and telling Madeline that she shall marry you over his dead body. And she isn't the sort of girl to defy a parent.'

'Oh, my gosh!'

'Still, I wouldn't worry about that, old man,' I said, pointing out the bright side, 'because long before it happened, Spode would have broken your neck.'

He plucked feebly at another crumpet.

'This is frightful, Bertie.'

'Not too good, no.'

'I'm in the soup.'

'Up to the thorax.'

'What's to be done?'

'I don't know.'

'Can't you think of anything?'

'Nothing. We must just put our trust in a higher power.'

'Consult Jeeves, you mean?'

I shook the lemon.

'Even Jeeves cannot help us here. It is a straight issue of finding and recovering that notebook before it can get to old Bassett. Why on earth didn't you keep it locked up somewhere?'

'I couldn't. I was always writing fresh stuff in it. I never knew when the inspiration would come, and I had to have it handy.'

'You're sure it was in your breast pocket?'

'Quite sure.'

'It couldn't be in your bedroom, by any chance?'

'No. I always kept it on me – so as to have it safe.'

'Safe. I see.'

'And also, as I said before, because I had constant need of it. I'm trying to think where I saw it last. Wait a minute. It's beginning to come back. Yes, I remember. By the pump.'

'What pump?'

'The one in the stable yard, where they fill the buckets for the horses. Yes, that is where I saw it last, before lunch yesterday. I took it out to jot down a note about the way Sir Watkyn slopped his porridge about at breakfast, and I had just completed my critique when I met Stephanie Byng and took the fly out of her eye. Bertie!' he cried, breaking off. A strange light had come into his spectacles. He brought his fist down with a bang on the table. Silly ass. Might have known he would upset the milk. 'Bertie, I've just remembered something. It is as if a curtain had been rolled up and all was revealed. The whole scene is rising before my eyes. I took the book out, and entered the porridge item. I then put it back in my breast pocket. Where I keep my handkerchief.'

'Well?'

'Where I keep my handkerchief,' he repeated. 'Don't you understand? Use your intelligence, man. What is the first thing you do, when you find a girl with a fly in her eye?'

I uttered an exclamash.

'Reach for your handkerchief!'

'Exactly. And draw it out and extract the fly with the corner of it. And if there is a small, brown leather-covered notebook alongside the handkerchief – '

'It shoots out – '

'And falls to earth – '

'- you know not where.'

'But I do know where. That's just the point. I could lead you to the exact spot.'

For an instant I felt braced. Then moodiness returned.

'Yesterday before lunch, you say? Then someone must have found it by this time.'

'That's just what I'm coming to. I've remembered something else. Immediately after I had coped with the fly, I recollect hearing Stephanie saying "Hallo, what's that?" and seeing her stop and pick something up. I didn't pay much attention to the episode at the time, for it was just at that moment that I caught sight of Madeline. She was standing in the entrance of the stable yard, with a distant look on her face. I may mention that in order to extract the fly I had been compelled to place a hand under Stephanie's chin, in order to steady the head.'

'Quite.'

'Essential on these occasions.

'Definitely.'

'Unless the head is kept rigid, you cannot operate. I tried to point this out to Madeline, but she wouldn't listen. She swept away, and I swept after her. It was only this morning that I was able to place the facts before her and make her accept my explanation. Meanwhile, I had completely forgotten the Stephanie-stooping-picking-up incident. I think it is obvious that the book is now in the possession of this Byng.'

'It must be.'

'Then everything's all right. We just seek her out and ask her to hand it back, and she does so. I expect she will have got a good laugh out of it.'

'Where is she?'

'I seem to remember her saying something about walking down to the village. I think she goes and hobnobs with the curate. If you're not doing anything, you might stroll and meet her.'

'I will.'

'Well, keep an eye open for that Scottie of hers. It probably accompanied her.'

'Oh, yes. Thanks.'

I remembered that he had spoken to me of this animal at my dinner. Indeed, at the moment when the *sole meunière* was being served, he had shown me the sore place on his leg, causing me to skip that course.

'It biteth like a serpent.'

'Right ho. I'll be looking out. And I might as well start at once.'

It did not take me long to get to the end of the drive. At the gates, I paused. It seemed to me that my best plan would be to linger here until Stiffy returned. I lighted a cigarette, and gave myself up to meditation.

Although slightly easier in the mind than I had been, I was still much shaken. Until that book was back in safe storage, there could be no real peace for the Wooster soul. Too much depended on its recovery. As I had said to Gussie, if old Bassett started doing the heavy father and forbidding banns, there wasn't a chance of Madeline sticking out her chin and riposting with a modern 'Is zat so?' A glance at her was enough to tell one that she belonged to that small group of girls who still think a parent should have something to say about things: and I was willing to give a hundred to eight that, in the circumstances which I had outlined, she would sigh and drop a silent tear, but that when all the smoke had cleared away Gussie would be at liberty.

I was still musing in sombre and apprehensive vein, when my meditations were interrupted. A human drama was developing in the road in front of me.

The shades of evening were beginning to fall pretty freely by now, but the visibility was still good enough to enble me to observe that up the road there was approaching a large, stout, moon-faced policeman on a bicycle. And he was, one could see, at peace with all the world. His daily round of tasks may or may not have been completed, but he was obviously off duty for the moment, and his whole attitude was that of a policeman with nothing on his mind but his helmet.

Well, when I tell you that he was riding without his hands, you will gather to what lengths the careless gaiety of this serene slop had spread.

And where the drama came in was that it was patent that his attention had not yet been drawn to the fact that he was being chivvied – in the strong, silent, earnest manner characteristic of this breed of animal – by a fine Aberdeen terrier. There he was, riding comfortably along, sniffing the fragrant evening breeze; and there was the Scottie, all whiskers and eyebrows, haring after him hell-for-leather. As Jeeves said later, when I described the scene to him, the whole situation resembled some great moment in a Greek tragedy, where somebody is stepping high, wide and handsome, quite unconscious that all the while Nemesis is at his heels, and he may be right.

The constable, I say, was riding without his hands: and but for this the disaster, when it occurred, might not have been so complete. I was a bit of a cyclist myself in my youth – I think I have mentioned that I once won a choir boys' handicap at some village sports – and I can testify that when you are riding without your hands, privacy and a complete freedom from interruption are of the essence. The merest suggestion of an unexpected Scottie connecting with the ankle bone at such a time, and you swoop into a sudden swerve. And, as everybody knows, if the hands are not firmly on the handlebars, a sudden swerve spells a smeller.

And so it happened now. A smeller – and among the finest I have ever been privileged to witness – was what this officer of the law came. One moment he was with us, all merry and bright; the next he was in the ditch, a sort of *macédoine* of arms and legs and wheels, with the terrier standing on the edge, looking down at him with that rather offensive expression of virtuous smugness which I have often noticed on the faces of Aberdeen terriers in their clashes with humanity.

And as he threshed about in the ditch, endeavouring to unscramble himself, a girl came round the corner, an attractive young prune upholstered in heather-mixture tweeds, and I recognized the familiar features of S. Byng.

After what Gussie had said, I ought to have been expecting Stiffy, of course. Seeing an Aberdeen terrier, I should have gathered that it belonged to her. I might have said to myself: If Scotties come, can Stiffy be far behind?

Stiffy was plainly vexed with the policeman. You could see it in her manner. She hooked the crook of her stick over the Scottie's collar and drew him back; then addressed herself to the man, who had now begun to emerge from the ditch like Venus rising from the foam.

'What on earth,' she demanded, 'did you do that for?'

It was no business of mine, of course, but I couldn't help feeling that she might have made a more tactful approach to what threatened to be a difficult and delicate conference. And I could see that the policeman felt the same. There was a good deal of mud on his face, but not enough to hide the wounded expression.

'You might have scared him out of his wits, hurling yourself about like that. Poor old Bartholomew, did the ugly man nearly squash him flat?'

Again I missed the tactful note. In describing this public servant as ugly, she was undoubtedly technically correct. Only if the competition had consisted of Sir Watkyn Bassett, Oofy Prosser of the Drones, and a few more fellows like that, could he have hoped to win to success in a beauty contest. But one doesn't want to rub these things in. Suavity is what you need on these occasions. You can't beat suavity.

The policeman had now lifted himself and bicycle out of the abyss, and was putting the latter through a series of tests, to ascertain the extent of the damage. Satisfied that it was slight, he turned and eyed Stiffy rather as old Bassett had eyed me on the occasion when I had occupied the Bosher Street dock.

'I was proceeding along the public highway,' he began, in a slow, measured tone, as if he were giving evidence in court, 'and the dorg leaped at me in a verlent manner. I was zurled from my bersicle – '

Stiffy seized upon the point like a practised debater.

'Well, you shouldn't ride a bicycle. Bartholomew hates bicycles.'

'I ride a bersicle, miss, because if I didn't I should have to cover my beat on foot.'

'Do you good. Get some of the fat off you.'

'That,' said the policeman, no mean debater himself, producing a notebook from the recesses of his costume and blowing a water-beetle off it, 'is not the point at tissue. The point at tissue is that this makes twice that the animal has committed an aggravated assault on my person, and I shall have to summons you once more, miss, for being in possession of a savage dorg not under proper control.'

The thrust was a keen one, but Stiffy came back strongly.

'Don't be an ass, Oates. You can't expect a dog to pass up a policeman on a bicycle. It isn't human nature. And I'll bet you started it, anyway. You must have teased him, or something, and I may as well tell you that I intend to fight this case to the House of Lords. I shall call this gentleman as a material witness.' She turned to me, and for the first time became aware that I was no gentleman, but an old friend. 'Oh, hallo, Bertie.'

'Hallo, Stiffy.'

'When did you get here?'

'Oh, recently.'

'Did you see what happened?'

'Oh, rather. Ringside seat throughout.'

'Well, stand by to be subpoenaed.'

'Right ho.'

The policeman had been taking a sort of inventory and writing it down in the book. He was now in a position to call the score.

'Piecer skin scraped off right knee. Bruise or contusion on left elbow. Scratch on nose. Uniform covered with mud and'll have to go and be cleaned. Also shock – severe. You will receive the summons in due course, miss.'

He mounted his bicycle and rode off, causing the dog Bartholomew to make a passionate bound that nearly unshipped him from the restraining stick. Stiffy stood for a moment looking after him a bit yearningly, like a girl who wished that she had half a brick handy. Then she turned away, and I came straight down to brass tacks.

'Stiffy,' I said, 'passing lightly over all the guff about being charmed to see you again and how well you're looking and all that, have you got a small, brown, leather-covered notebook that Gussie Fink-Nottle dropped in the stable yard yesterday?'

She did not reply, seeming to be musing – no doubt on the recent Oates. I repeated the question, and she came out of the trance.

'Notebook?'

'Small, brown, leather-covered one.'

'Full of a lot of breezy personal remarks?'

'That's the one.'

'Yes, I've got it.'

I flung the hands heavenwards and uttered a joyful yowl. The dog Bartholomew gave me an unpleasant look and said something under his breath in Gaelic, but I ignored him. A kennel of Aberdeen terriers could have rolled their eyes and bared the wisdom tooth without impairing this ecstatic moment.

'Gosh, what a relief!'

'Does it belong to Gussie Fink-Nottle?'

'Yes.'

'You mean to say that it was Gussie who wrote those really excellent character studies of Roderick Spode and Uncle Watkyn? I wouldn't have thought he had it in him.'

'Nobody would. It's a most interesting story. It appears – '

'Though why anyone should waste time on Spode and Uncle Watkyn when there was Oates simply crying out to be written about, I can't imagine. I don't think I have ever met a man, Bertie, who gets in the hair so consistently as this Eustace Oates. He makes me tired. He goes swanking about on that bicycle of his, simply asking for it, and then complains when he gets it. And why should he discriminate against poor Bartholomew in this sickening way? Every red-blooded dog in the village has had a go at his trousers, and he knows it.'

'Where's that book, Stiffy?' I said, returning to the *res*.

'Never mind about books. Let's stick to Eustace Oates. Do you think he means to summons me?'

I said that, reading between the lines, that was rather the impression I had gathered, and she made what I believe is known as a *moue* . . . Is it *moue*? . . . Shoving out the lips, I mean, and drawing them quickly back again.

'I'm afraid so, too. There is only one word for Eustace Oates, and that is "malignant". He just goes about seeking whom he may devour. Oh, well, more work for Uncle Watkyn.'

'How do you mean?'

'I shall come up before him.'

'Then he does still operate, even though retired?' I said, remembering with some uneasiness the conversation between this ex-beak and Roderick Spode in the collection room.

'He only retired from Bosher Street. You can't choke a man off magistrating, once it's in his blood. He's a Justice of the Peace now. He holds a sort of Star Chamber court in the library. That's where I always come up. I'll be flitting about, doing the flowers, or sitting in my room with a good book, and the butler comes and says I'm wanted in the library. And there's Uncle

Watkyn at the desk, looking like Judge Jeffreys, with Oates waiting to give evidence.'

I could picture the scene. Unpleasant, of course. The sort of thing that casts a gloom over a girl's home life.

'And it always ends the same way, with him putting on the black cap and soaking me. He never listens to a word I say. I don't believe the man understands the ABC of justice.'

'That's how he struck me, when I attended his tribunal.'

'And the worst of it is, he knows just what my allowance is, so can figure out exactly how much the purse will stand. Twice this year he's skinned me to the bone, each time at the instigation of this man Oates – once for exceeding the speed limit in a built-up area, and once because Bartholomew gave him the teeniest little nip on the ankle.'

I tut-tutted sympathetically, but I was wishing that I could edge the conversation back to that notebook. One so frequently finds in girls a disinclination to stick to the important subject.

'The way Oates went on about it, you would have thought Bartholomew had taken his pound of flesh. And I suppose it's all going to happen again now. I'm fed up with this police persecution. One might as well be in Russia. Don't you loathe policemen, Bertie?'

I was not prepared to go quite so far as this in my attitude towards an, on the whole, excellent body of men.

'Well, not *en masse*, if you understand the expression. I suppose they vary, like other sections of the community, some being full of quiet charm, others not so full. I've met some very decent policemen. With the one on duty outside the Drones I am distinctly chummy. *In re* this Oates of yours, I haven't seem enough of him, of course, to form an opinion.'

'Well, you can take it from me that he's one of the worst. And a bitter retribution awaits him. Do you remember the time you gave me lunch at your flat? You were telling me about how you tried to pinch that policeman's helmet in Leicester Square.'

'That was when I first met your uncle. It was that that brought us together.'

'Well, I didn't think much of it at the time, but the other day it suddenly came back to me, and I said to myself: "Out of the mouths of babes and sucklings!" For months I had been trying to think of a way of getting back at this man Oates, and you had showed it to me.'

I started. It seemed to me that her words could bear but one interpretation.

'You aren't going to pinch his helmet?'

'Of course not.'

'I think you're wise.'

'It's man's work. I can see that. So I've told Harold to do it. He has often said he would do anything in the world for me, bless him.'

Stiffy's map, as a rule, tends to be rather grave and dreamy, giving the impression that she is thinking deep, beautiful thoughts. Quite misleading, of course. I don't suppose she would recognize a deep, beautiful thought, if you handed it to her on a skewer with tartare sauce. Like Jeeves, she doesn't often smile, but now her lips had parted – ecstatically, I think – I should have to check up with Jeeves – and her eyes were sparkling.

'What a man!' she said. 'We're engaged, you know.'

'Oh, are you?'

'Yes, but don't tell a soul. It's frightfully secret. Uncle Watkyn mustn't know about it till he has been well sweetened.'

'And who is this Harold?'

'The curate down in the village.' She turned to the dog Bartholomew. 'Is lovely kind curate going to pinch bad, ugly policeman's helmet for his muzzer, zen, and make her very, very happy?' she said.

Or words to that general trend. I can't do the dialect of course.

I stared at the young pill, appalled at her moral code, if you could call it that. You know, the more I see of women, the more I think that there ought to be a law. Something has got to be done about this sex, or the whole fabric of Society will collapse, and then what silly asses we shall all look.

'Curate?' I said. 'But, Stiffy, you can't ask a curate to go about pinching policemen's helmets.'

'Why not?'

'Well, it's most unusual. You'll get the poor bird unfrocked.'

'Unfrocked?'

'It's something they do to parsons when they catch them

bending. And this will inevitably be the outcome of the frightful task you have apportioned to the sainted Harold.'

'I don't see that it's a frightful task.'

'You aren't telling me that it's the sort of thing that comes naturally to curates?'

'Yes, I am. It ought to be right up Harold's street. When he was at Magdalen, before he saw the light, he was the dickens of a chap. Always doing things like that.'

Her mention of Magdalen interested me. It had been my own college.

'Magdalen man, is he? What year? Perhaps I know him.'

'Of course you do. He often speaks to you, and was delighted when I told him you were coming here. Harold Pinker.'

I was astounded.

'Harold Pinker? Old Stinker Pinker? Great Scott! One of my dearest pals. I've often wondered where he had got to. And all the while he had sneaked off and become a curate. It just shows you how true it is that one-half of the world doesn't know how the other three-quarters lives. Stinker Pinker, by Jove! You really mean that old Stinker cures souls?'

'Certainly. And jolly well, too. The nibs think very highly of him. Any moment now, he may get a vicarage, and then watch his smoke. He'll be a Bishop some day.'

The excitement of discovering a long-lost buddy waned. I found myself returning to the practical issues. I became grave.

And I'll tell you why I became grave. It was all very well for Stiffy to say that this thing would be right up old Stinker's street. She didn't know him as I did. I had watched Harold Pinker through the formative years of his life, and I knew him for what he was – a large, lumbering, Newfoundland puppy of a chap – full of zeal, yes: always doing his best, true; but never quite able to make the grade; a man, in short, who if there was a chance of bungling an enterprise and landing himself in the soup, would snatch at it. At the idea of him being turned on to perform the extraordinarily delicate task of swiping Constable Oates's helmet, the blood froze. He hadn't a chance of getting away with it.

I thought of Stinker, the youth. Built rather on the lines of Roderick Spode, he had played Rugby football not only for his University but also for England, and at the art of hurling an opponent into a mud puddle and jumping on his neck with cleated boots had had few, in any, superiors. If I had wanted someone to help me out with a mad bull, he would have been my first choice. If by some mischance I had found myself trapped in the underground den of the Secret Nine, there was nobody I would rather have seen coming down the chimney than the Rev. Harold Pinker.

But mere thews and sinews do not qualify a man to pinch policemen's helmets. You need finesse.

'He will, will he?' I said. 'A fat lot of bishing he's going to do, if he's caught sneaking helmets from members of his flock.'

'He won't be caught.'

'Of course he'll be caught. At the old Alma Mater he was always caught. He seemed to have no .notion whatsoever of going about a thing in a subtle, tactful way. Chuck it, Stiffy. Abandon the whole project.'

'No.'

'Stiffy!'

'No. The show must go on.'

I gave it up. I could see plainly that it would be mere waste of time to try to argue her out of her girlish daydreams. She had the same type of mind, I perceived, as Roberta Wickham, who once persuaded me to go by night to the bedroom of a fellow guest at a country house and puncture his hot-water bottle with a darning needle on the end of a stick.

'Well, if it must be, it must be, I suppose,' I said resignedly. 'But at least impress upon him that it is essential, when pinching policemen's helmets, to give a forward shove before applying the upwards lift. Otherwise, the subject's chin catches in the strap. It was to overlooking this vital point that my own downfall in Leicester Square was due. The strap caught, the cop was enabled to turn and clutch, and before I knew what had happened I was in the dock, saying "Yes, your Honour" and "No, your Honour" to your Uncle Watkyn.'

I fell into a thoughtful silence, as I brooded on the dark future lying in wait for an old friend. I am not a weak man, but I was beginning to wonder if I had been right in squelching so curtly Jeeves's efforts to get me off on a Round-The-World cruise. Whatever you may say against these excursions – the cramped conditions of shipboard, the possibility of getting mixed up with a crowd of bores, the nuisance of having to go and look at the Taj Mahal – at least there is this to be said in their favour, that you escape the mental agony of watching innocent curates dishing their careers and forfeiting all chance of rising to great heights in the Church by getting caught bonneting their parishioners.

I heaved a sigh, and resumed the conversation.

'So you and Stinker are engaged, are you? Why didn't you tell me when you lunched at the flat?'

'It hadn't happened then. Oh, Bertie, I'm so happy I could bite a grape. At least, I shall be, if we can get Uncle Watkyn thinking along "Bless you, my children" lines.'

'Oh, yes, you were saying, weren't you? About him being sweetened. How do you mean, sweetened?'

'That's what I want to have a talk with you about. You remember what I said in my telegram, about there being something I wanted you to do for me?'

I started. A well-defined uneasiness crept over me. I had forgotten all about that telegram of hers.

'It's something quite simple.'

I doubted it. I mean to say, if her idea of a suitable job for curates was the pinching of policemen's helmets, what sort of an assignment, I could not but ask myself, was she likely to hand to me? It seemed that the moment had come for a bit of in-the-bud-nipping.

'Oh, yes?' I said. 'Well, let me tell you here and now that I'm jolly well not going to do it.'

'Yellow, eh?'

'Bright yellow. Like my Aunt Agatha.'

'What's the matter with her?'

'She's got jaundice.'

'Enough to give her jaundice, having a nephew like you. Why, you don't even know what it is.'

'I would prefer not to know.'

'Well, I'm going to tell you.'

'I do not wish to listen.'

'You would rather I unleashed Bartholomew? I notice he has been looking at you in that odd way of his. I don't believe he likes you. He does take sudden dislikes to people.'

The Woosters are brave, but not rash. I allowed her to lead

me to the stone wall that bordered the terrace, and we sat down. The evening, I remember, was one of perfect tranquillity, featuring a sort of serene peace. Which just shows you.

'I won't keep you long,' she said. 'It's all quite simple and straightforward. I shall have to begin, though, by telling you why we have had to be so dark and secret about the engagement. That's Gussie's fault.'

'What has he done?'

'Just been Gussie, that's all. Just gone about with no chin, goggling through his spectacles and keeping newts in his bedroom. You can understand Uncle Watkyn's feelings. His daughter tells him she is going to get married. "Oh, yes?" he says. 'Well, let's have a dekko at the chap." And along rolls Gussie. A nasty jar for a father.'

'Quite.'

'Well, you can't tell me that a time when he is reeling under the blow of having Gussie for a son-in-law is the moment for breaking it to him that I want to marry the curate.'

I saw her point. I recollected Freddie Threepwood telling me that there had been trouble at Blandings about a cousin of his wanting to marry a curate. In that case, I gathered, the strain had been eased by the discovery that the fellow was the heir of a Liverpool shipping millionaire; but, as a broad, general rule, parents do not like their daughters marrying curates, and I take it that the same thing applies to uncles with their nieces.

'You've got to face it. Curates are not so hot. So before anything can be done in the way of removing the veil of secrecy, we have got to sell Harold to Uncle Watkyn. If we play our cards properly, I am hoping that he will give him a vicarage which he has in his gift. Then we shall begin to get somewhere.'

I didn't like her use of the word 'we', but I saw what she was driving at, and I was sorry to have to insert a spanner in her hopes and dreams.

'You wish me to put in a word for Stinker? You would like me to draw your uncle aside and tell him what a splendid fellow Stinker is? There is nothing I would enjoy more, my dear Stiffy, but unfortunately we are not on those terms.'

'No, no, nothing like that.'

'Well, I don't see what more I can do.'

'You will,' she said, and again I was conscious of that subtle feeling of uneasiness. I told myself that I must be firm. But I could not but remember Roberta Wickham and the hot-water bottle. A man thinks he is being chilled steel – or adamant, if you prefer the expression – and suddenly the mists clear away and he finds that he has allowed a girl to talk him into something frightful. Samson had the same experience with Delilah.

'Oh?' I said, guardedly.

She paused in order to tickle the dog Bartholomew under the left ear. Then she resumed.

'Just praising Harold to Uncle Watkyn isn't any use. You need something much cleverer than that. You want to engineer some terrifically brainy scheme that will put him over with a bang. I thought I had got it a few days ago. Do you ever read *Milady's Boudoir*?'

'I once contributed an article to it on "What The Well-Dressed Man Is Wearing", but I am not a regular reader. Why?'

'There was a story in it last week about a Duke who wouldn't let his daughter marry the young secretary, so the secretary got a friend of his to take the Duke out on the lake and upset the boat, and then he dived in and saved the Duke, and the Duke said "Right ho".'

I resolved that no time should be lost in quashing this idea.

'Any notion you may have entertained that I am going to take Sir W. Bassett out in a boat and upset him can be dismissed instanter. To start with, he wouldn't come out on a lake with me.'

'No. And we haven't a lake. And Harold said that if I was thinking of the pond in the village, I could forget it, as it was much too cold to dive into ponds at this time of year. Harold is funny in some ways.'

'I applaud his sturdy common sense.'

'Then I got an idea from another story. It was about a young lover who gets a friend of his to dress up as a tramp and attack the girl's father, and then he dashes in and rescues him.'

I patted her hand gently.

'The flaw in all these ideas of yours,' I pointed out, 'is that the hero always seems to have a half-witted friend who is eager to place himself in the foulest positions on his behalf. In Stinker's case, this is not so. I am fond of Stinker – you could even go so far as to say that I love him like a brother – but there are sharply defined limits to what I am prepared to do to further his interests.'

'Well, it doesn't matter, because he put the presidential veto on that one, too. Something about what the vicar would say if it all came out. But he loves my new one.'

'Oh, you've got a new one?'

'Yes, and it's terrific. The beauty of it is that Harold's part in it is above reproach. A thousand vicars couldn't get the goods on him. The only snag was that he has to have someone working with him, and until I heard you were coming down here I couldn't think who we were to get. But now you have arrived, all is well.'

'It is, is it? I informed you before, young Byng, and I now inform you again that nothing will induce me to mix myself up with your loathesome schemes.'

'Oh, but, Bertie, you must! We're relying on you. And all you have to do is practically nothing. Just steal Uncle Watkyn's cow-creamer.'

I don't know what you would have done, if a girl in heather-mixture tweeds had sprung this on you, scarcely eight hours after a mauve-faced aunt had sprung the same. It is possible that you would have reeled. Most chaps would, I imagine. Personally, I was more amused than aghast. Indeed, if memory serves me aright, I laughed. If so, it was just as well, for it was about the last chance I had.

'Oh, yes?' I said. 'Tell me more,' I said, feeling that it would be entertaining to allow the little blighter to run on. 'Steal his cow-creamer, eh?'

'Yes. It's a thing brought back from London yesterday for his collection. A sort of silver cow with a kind of blotto look on its face. He thinks the world of it. He had it on the table in front of him at dinner last night, and was gassing away about it. And it was then that I got the idea. I thought that if Harold could pinch it, and then bring it back, Uncle Watkyn would be so grateful that he would start spouting vicarages like a geyser. And then I spotted the catch.'

'Oh, there was a catch?'

'Of course. Don't you see? How would Harold be supposed to have got the thing? If a silver cow is in somebody's collection, and it disappears, and next day a curate rolls round with it, that curate has got to do some good, quick explaining. Obviously, it must be made to look like an outside job.'

'I see. You want me to put on a black mask and break in through the window and snitch this *objet d'art* and hand it over to Stinker? I see. I see.'

I spoke with satirical bitterness, and I should have thought that anyone could have seen that satirical bitterness was what I was speaking with, but she merely looked at me with admiration and approval.

'You are clever, Bertie. That's exactly it. Of course, you needn't wear a mask.'

'You don't think it would help me throw myself into the part?' I said with s. b., as before.

'Well, it might. That's up to you. But the great thing is to get through the window. Wear gloves, of course, because of the fingerprints.'

'Of course.'

'Then Harold will be waiting outside, and he will take the thing from you.'

'And after that I go off and do my stretch at Dartmoor?'

'Oh, no. You escape in the struggle, of course.'

'What struggle?'

'And Harold rushes into the house, all over blood – '

'Whose blood?'

'Well, I said yours, and Harold thought his. There have got to be signs of a struggle to make it more interesting, and my idea was that he should hit you on the nose. But he said the thing would carry greater weight if he was all covered with gore. So how we've left it is that you both hit each other on the nose. And then Harold rouses the house and comes in and shows Uncle Watkyn the cow-creamer and explains what happened, and everything's fine. Because, I mean, Uncle Watkyn couldn't just say "Oh, thanks" and leave it at that, could he? He would be compelled, if he had a spark of decency in him, to cough up that vicarage. Don't you think it's a wonderful scheme, Bertie?'

I rose. My face was cold and hard.

'Most. But I'm sorry – '

'You don't mean you won't do it, now that you see that it

will cause you practically no inconvenience at all? It would only take about ten minutes of your time.'

'I do mean I won't do it.'

'Well, I think you're a pig.'

'A pig, maybe, but a shrewd, level-headed pig. I wouldn't touch the project with a bargepole. I tell you I know Stinker. Exactly how he would muck the thing up and get us all landed in the jug, I cannot say, but he would find a way. And now I'll take that book, if you don't mind.'

'What book? Oh, that one of Gussie's.'

'Yes.'

'What do you want it for?'

'I want it,' I said gravely, 'because Gussie is not fit to be in charge of it. He might lose it again, in which event it might fall into the hands of your uncle, in which event he would certainly kick the stuffing out of the Gussie-Madeline wedding arrangements, in which event I would be up against it as few men have ever been up against it before.'

'You?'

'None other.'

'How do you come into it?'

'I will tell you.'

And in a few terse words I outlined for her the events which had taken place at Brinkley Court, the situation which had arisen from those events and the hideous peril which threatened me if Gussie's entry were to be scratched.

'You will understand,' I said, 'that I am implying nothing derogatory to your cousin Madeline, when I say that the idea of being united to her in the bonds of holy wedlock is one that freezes the gizzard. The fact is in no way to her discredit. I should feel just the same about marrying many of the world's noblest women. There are certain females whom one respects, admires, reveres, but only from a distance. If they show any signs of attempting to come closer, one is prepared to fight them off with a blackjack. It is to this group that your cousin Madeline belongs. A charming girl, and the ideal mate for Augustus Fink-Nottle, but ants in the pants to Bertram.'

She drank this in.

'I see. Yes, I suppose Madeline is a bit of a Gawd-help-us.'

'The expression "Gawd-help-us" is one which I would not

have gone so far as to use myself, for I think a chivalrous man ought to stop somewhere. But since you have brought it up, I admit that it covers the facts.'

'I never realized that that was how things were. No wonder you want that book.'

'Exactly.'

'Well, all this has opened up a new line of thought.'

That grave, dreamy look had come into her face. She massaged the dog Bartholomew's spine with a pensive foot.

'Come on,' I said, chafing at the delay. 'Slip it across.'

'Just a moment. I'm trying to straighten it all out in my mind. You know, Bertie, I really ought to take that book to Uncle Watkyn.'

'What!'

'That's what my conscience tells me to do. After all, I owe a lot to him. For years he has been a second father to me. And he ought to know how Gussie feels about him, oughtn't he? I mean to say, a bit tough on the old buster, cherishing what he thinks is a harmless newt-fancier in his bosom, when all the time it's a snake that goes about criticizing the way he drinks soup. However, as you're being so sweet and are going to help Harold and me by stealing that cow-creamer, I suppose I shall have to stretch a point.'

We Woosters are pretty quick. I don't suppose it was more than a couple of minutes before I figured out what she meant. I read her purpose, and shuddered.

She was naming the Price of the Papers. In other words, after being blackmailed by an aunt at breakfast, I was now being blackmailed by a female crony before dinner. Pretty good going, even for this lax post-war world.

'Stiffy!' I cried.

'It's no good saying "Stiffy!" Either you sit and do your bit, or Uncle Watkyn gets some racy light reading over his morning egg and coffee. Think it over, Bertie.'

She hoisted the dog Bartholomew to his feet, and trickled off towards the house. The last I saw of her was a meaning look, directed at me over her shoulder, and it went through me like a knife.

I had slumped back onto the wall, and I sat there, stunned. Just how long, I don't know, but it was a goodish time. Winged creatures of the night barged into me, but I gave them little attention. It was not till a voice suddenly spoke a couple of feet or so above my bowed head that I came out of the coma.

'Good evening, Wooster,' said the voice.

I looked up. The cliff-like mass looming over me was Roderick Spode.

I suppose even Dictators have their chummy moments, when they put their feet up and relax with the boys, but it was plain from the outset that if Roderick Spode had a sunnier side, he had not come with any idea of exhibiting it now. His manner was curt. One sensed the absence of the bonhomous note.

'I should like a word with you, Wooster.'

'Oh, yes?'

'I have been talking to Sir Watkyn Bassett, and he has told me the whole story of the cow-creamer.'

'Oh, yes?'

'And we know why you are here.'

'Oh, yes?'

'Stop saying "Oh, yes?" you miserable worm, and listen to me.'

Many chaps might have resented his tone. I did myself, as a matter of fact. But you know how it is. There are some fellows you are right on your toes to tick off when they call you a miserable worm, others not quite so much.

'Oh, yes,' he said, saying it himself, dash it, 'it is perfectly plain to us why you are here. You have been sent by your uncle to steal this cow-creamer for him. You needn't trouble to deny it. I found you with the thing in your hands this afternoon. And now, we learn, your aunt is arriving. The muster of the vultures, ha!'

He paused a moment, then repeated 'The muster of the vultures,' as if he thought pretty highly of it as a gag. I couldn't see that it was so very hot myself.

'Well, what I came to tell you, Wooster, was that you are being watched – watched closely. And if you are caught stealing that cow-creamer, I can assure you that you will go to prison. You need entertain no hope that Sir Watkyn will shrink from creating a scandal. He will do his duty as a citizen and a Justice of the Peace.'

Here he laid a hand upon my shoulder, and I can't remember when I have experienced anything more unpleasant. Apart from what Jeeves would have called the symbolism of the action, he had a grip like the bite of a horse.

'Did you say "Oh, yes?"' he asked.

'Oh, no,' I assured him.

'Good. Now, what you are saying to yourself, no doubt, is that you will not be caught. You imagine that you and this precious aunt of yours will be clever enough between you to steal the cow-creamer without being detected. It will do you no good, Wooster. If the thing disappears, however cunningly you and your female accomplice may have covered your traces, I shall know where it has gone, and I shall immediately beat you to a jelly. To a jelly,' he repeated, rolling the words round his tongue as if they were vintage port. 'Have you got that clear?'

'Oh, quite.'

'You are sure you understand?'

'Oh, definitely.'

'Splendid.'

A dim figure was approaching across the terrace, and he changed his tone to one of a rather sickening geniality.

'What a lovely evening, is it not? Extraordinarily mild for the time of year. Well, I mustn't keep you any longer. You will be wanting to go and dress for dinner. Just a black tie. We are quite informal here. Yes?'

The word was addressed to the dim figure. A familiar cough revealed its identity.

'I wished to speak to Mr Wooster, sir. I have a message for him from Mrs Travers. Mrs Travers presents her compliments, sir, and desires me to say that she is in the Blue Room and would be glad if you could make it convenient to call upon her there as soon as possible. She has a matter of importance which she wishes to discuss.'

I heard Spode snort in the darkness.

'So Mrs Travers has arrived?'

'Yes, sir.'

'And has a matter of importance to discuss with Mr Wooster?'

'Yes, sir.'

'Ha!' said Spode, and biffed off with a short, sharp laugh.

I rose from my seat.

'Jeeves,' I said, 'stand by to counsel and advise. The plot has thickened.'

## 5

I SLID into the shirt, and donned the knee-length under-wear.
'Well, Jeeves,' I said, 'how about it?'

During the walk to the house I had placed him in possession
of the latest developments, and had left him to turn them over
in his mind with a view to finding a formula, while I went along
the passage and took a hasty bath. I now gazed at him hopefully,
like a seal awaiting a bit of fish.

'Thought of anything, Jeeves?'

'Not yet, sir, I regret to say.'

'What, no results whatever?'

'None, sir, I fear.'

I groaned a hollow one, and shoved on the trousers. I had
become so accustomed to having this gifted man weigh in with
the ripest ideas at the drop of the hat that the possibility of his
failing to deliver on this occasion had not occurred to me. The
blow was a severe one, and it was with a quivering hand that
I now socked the feet. A strange frozen sensation had come over
me, rendering the physical and mental processes below par. It
was as though both limbs and bean had been placed in a refriger-
ator and overlooked for several days.

'It may be, Jeeves,' I said, a thought occurring, 'that you
haven't got the whole scenario clear in your mind. I was able
to give you only the merest outline before going off to scour
the torso. I think it would help if we did what they do in the
thrillers. Do you ever read thrillers?'

'Not very frequently, sir.'

'Well, there's always a bit where the detective, in order to
clarify his thoughts, writes down a list of suspects, motives,
times when, alibis, clues and what not. Let us try this plan.
Take pencil and paper, Jeeves, and we will assemble the facts.
Entitle the thing "Wooster, B. – position of." Ready?'

'Yes, sir.'

'Right. Now, then. Item One – Aunt Dahlia says that if I

84

don't pinch that cow-creamer and hand it over to her, she will bar me from her table, and no more of Anatole's cooking.'

'Yes, sir.'

'We now come to Item Two – viz., if I do pinch the cow-creamer and hand it over to her, Spode will beat me to a jelly.'

'Yes, sir.'

'Furthermore – Item Three – if I pinch it and hand it over to her and don't pinch it and hand it over to Harold Pinker, not only shall I undergo the jellying process alluded to above, but Stiffy will take that notebook of Gussie's and hand it over to Sir Watkyn Bassett. And you know and I know what the result of that would be. Well, there you are. That's the set-up. You've got it?'

'Yes, sir. It is certainly a somewhat unfortunate state of affairs.'

I gave him one of my looks.

'Jeeves,' I said, 'don't try me too high. Not at a moment like this. Somewhat unfortunate, forsooth! Who was it you were telling me about the other day, on whose head all the sorrows of the world had come?'

'The Mona Lisa, sir.'

'Well, if I met the Mona Lisa at this moment, I would shake her by the hand and assure her that I knew just how she felt. You see before you, Jeeves, a toad beneath the harrow.'

'Yes, sir. The trousers perhaps a quarter of an inch higher, sir. One aims at the carelessly graceful break over the instep. It is a matter of the nicest adjustment.'

'Like that?'

'Admirable, sir.'

I sighed.

'There are moments, Jeeves, when one asks oneself "Do trousers matter?" '

'The mood will pass, sir.'

'I don't see why it should. If you can't think of a way out of this mess, it seems to me that it is the end. Of course,' I proceeded on a somewhat brighter note, 'you haven't really had time to get your teeth into the problem yet. While I am at dinner, examine it once more from every angle. It is just possible that an inspiration might pop up. Inspirations do, don't they? All in a flash, as it were?'

'Yes, sir. The mathematician Archimedes is related to have discovered the principle of displacement quite suddenly one morning, while in his bath.'

'Well, there you are. And I don't suppose he was such a devil of a chap. Compared with you, I mean.'

'A gifted man, I believe, sir. It has been a matter of general regret that he was subsequently killed by a common soldier.'

'Too bad. Still, all flesh is as grass, what?'

'Very true, sir.'

I lighted a thoughtful cigarette and, dismissing Archimedes for the nonce, allowed my mind to dwell once more on the ghastly jam into which I had been thrust by young Stiffy's ill-advised behaviour.

'You know, Jeeves,' I said, 'when you really start to look into it, it's perfectly amazing how the opposite sex seems to go out of its way to snooter me. You recall Miss Wickham and the hot-water bottle?'

'Yes, sir.'

'And Gwladys what-was-her-name, who put her boyfriend with the broken leg to bed in my flat?'

'Yes, sir.'

'And Pauline Stoker, who invaded my rural cottage at dead of night in a bathing suit?'

'Yes, sir.'

'What a sex! What a sex, Jeeves! But none of that sex, however deadlier than the male, can be ranked in the same class with this Stiffy. Who was the chap lo whose name led all the rest – the bird with the angel?'

'Abou ben Adhem sir.'

'That's Stiffy. She's the top. Yes, Jeeves?'

'I was merely about to enquire, sir, if Miss Byng, when she uttered her threat of handing over Mr Fink-Nottle's notebook to Sir Watkyn, by any chance spoke with a twinkle in her eye?'

'A roguish one, you mean, indicating that she was merely pulling my leg? Not a suspicion of it. No, Jeeves, I have seen untwinkling eyes before, many of them, but never a pair so totally free from twinkle as hers. She wasn't kidding. She meant business. She was fully aware that she was doing something which even by female standards was raw, but she didn't care. The whole fact of the matter is that all this modern emancipation of women has resulted in them getting it up their noses and not giving a damn what they do. It was not like this in Queen Victoria's day. The Prince Consort would have had a word to say about a girl like Stiffy, what?'

'I can conceive that His Royal Highness might quite possibly not have approved of Miss Byng.'

'He would have had her over his knee, laying into her with a slipper, before she knew where she was. And I wouldn't put it past him to have treated Aunt Dahlia in a similar fashion. Talking of which, I suppose I ought to be going and seeing the aged relative.'

'She appeared very desirous of conferring with you, sir.'

'Far from mutual, Jeeves, that desire. I will confess frankly that I am not looking forward to the *séance*.'

'No, sir?'

'No. You see, I sent her a telegram just before tea, saying that I wasn't going to pinch that cow-creamer, and she must have left London long before it arrived. In other words, she has come expecting to find a nephew straining at the leash to do her bidding, and the news will have to be broken to her that the deal is off. She will not like this, Jeeves, and I don't mind telling you that the more I contemplate the coming chat, the colder the feet become.'

'If I might suggest, sir – it is, of course, merely a palliative – but it has often been found in times of despondency that the assumption of formal evening dress has a stimulating effect on the morale.'

'You think I ought to put on a white tie? Spode told me black.'

'I consider that the emergency justifies the departure, sir.'

'Perhaps you're right.'

And, of course, he was. In these delicate matters of psychology he never errs. I got into the full soup and fish, and was immediately conscious of a marked improvement. The feet became warmer, a sparkle returned to the lack-lustre eyes, and the soul seemed to expand as if someone had got to work on it with a bicycle pump. And I was surveying the effect in the mirror, kneading the tie with gentle fingers and running over in my mind a few things which I proposed to say to Aunt Dahlia if she started getting tough, when the door opened and Gussie came in.

At the sight of this bespectacled bird, a pang of compassion shot through me, for a glance was enough to tell me that he was not abreast of stop-press events. There was visible in his demeanour not one of the earmarks of a man to whom Stiffy had been confiding her plans. His bearing was buoyant, and I exchanged a swift, meaning glance with Jeeves. Mine said 'He little knows!' and so did his.

'What ho!' said Gussie. 'What ho! Hallo, Jeeves.'

'Good evening, sir.'

'Well, Bertie, what's the news? Have you seen her?'

The pang of compash became more acute. I heaved a silent sigh. It was to be my mournful task to administer to this old friend a very substantial sock on the jaw, and I shrank from it.

Still, these things have to be faced. The surgeon's knife, I mean to say.

'Yes,' I said. 'Yes, I've seen her. Jeeves, have we any brandy?'

'No, sir.'

'Could you get a spot?'

'Certainly, sir.'

'Better bring the bottle.'

'Very good, sir.'

He melted away, and Gussie stared at me in honest amazement.

'What's all this? You can't start swigging brandy just before dinner.'

'I do not propose to. It is for you, my suffering old martyr at the stake, that I require the stuff.'

'I don't drink brandy.'

'I'll bet you drink this brandy – yes, and call for more. Sit down, Gussie, and let us chat awhile.'

And deposing him in the armchair, I engaged him in desultory conversation about the weather and the crops. I didn't want to spring the thing on him till the restorative was handy. I prattled on, endeavouring to infuse into my deportment a sort of bedside manner which would prepare him for the worst, and it was not long before I noted that he was looking at me oddly.

'Bertie, I believe you're pie-eyed.'

'Not at all.'

'Then what are you babbling like this for?'

'Just filling in till Jeeves gets back with the fluid. Ah, thank you, Jeeves.'

I took the brimming beaker from his hand, and gently placed Gussie's fingers round the stem.

'You had better go and inform Aunt Dahlia that I shall not be able to keep our tryst, Jeeves. This is going to take some time.'

'Very good, sir.'

I turned to Gussie, who was now looking like a bewildered halibut.

'Gussie,' I said, 'drink that down, and listen. I'm afraid I have bad news for you. About that notebook.'

'About the notebook?'

'Yes.'

'You don't mean she hasn't got it?'

'That is precisely the nub or crux. She has, and she is going to give it to Pop Bassett.'

I had expected him to take it fairly substantially, and he did. His eyes, like stars, started from their spheres and he leaped from the chair, spilling the contents of the glass and causing the room to niff like the saloon bar of a pub on a Saturday night.

'What!'

'That is the posish, I fear.'

'But, my gosh!'

'Yes.'

'You don't really mean that?'

'I do.'

'But why?'

'She has her reasons.'

'But she can't realize what will happen.'

'Yes, she does.'

'It will mean ruin!'

'Definitely.'

'Oh, my gosh!'

It has often been said that disaster brings out the best in the Woosters. A strange calm descended on me. I patted his shoulder.

'Courage, Gussie! Think of Archimedes.'

'Why?'

'He was killed by a common soldier.'

'What of it?'

'Well, it can't have been pleasant for him, but I have no doubt he passed out smiling.'

My intrepid attitude had a good effect. He became more composed. I don't say that even now we were exactly like a couple of French aristocrats waiting for the tumbril, but there was a certain resemblance.

'When did she tell you this?'

'On the terrace not long ago.'

'And she really meant it?'

'Yes.'

'There wasn't – '

'A twinkle in her eyes? No. No twinkle.'

'Well, isn't there any way of stopping her?'

I had been expecting him to bring this up, but I was sorry he had done so. I foresaw a period of fruitless argument.

'Yes,' I said. 'There is. She says she will forgo her dreadful purpose if I steal old Bassett's cow-creamer.'

'You mean that silver cow thing he was showing us at dinner last night?'

'That's the one.'

'But why?'

I explained the position of affairs. He listened intelligently, his face brightening.

'Now I see! Now I understand! I couldn't imagine what her idea was. Her behaviour seemed so absolutely motiveless. Well, that's fine. That solves everything.'

I hated to put a crimp in his happy exuberance, but it had to be done.

'Not quite, because I'm jolly well not going to do it.'

'What! Why not?'

'Because, if I do, Roderick Spode says he will beat me to a jelly.'

'What's Roderick Spode got to do with it?'

'He appears to have espoused that cow-creamer's cause. No doubt from esteem for old Bassett.'

'H'm! Well, you aren't afraid of Roderick Spode.'

'Yes, I am.'

'Nonsense! I know you better than that.'

'No, you don't.'

He took a turn up and down the room.

'But, Bertie, there's nothing to be afraid of in a man like Spoke, a mere mass of beef and brawn. He's bound to be slow on his feet. He would never catch you.'

'I don't intend to try him out as a sprinter.'

'Besides, it isn't as if you had to stay on here. You can be off the moment you've put the thing through. Send a note down to this curate after dinner, telling him to be on the spot at midnight, and then go to it. Here is the schedule, as I see it. Steal cow-creamer – say, twelve-fifteen to twelve-thirty, or call it twelve-forty, to allow for accidents. Twelve-forty-five, be at stables, starting up your car. Twelve-fifty, out on the open road, having accomplished a nice, smooth job. I can't think what you're worrying about. The whole thing seems childishly simple to me.'

'Nevertheless – '

'You won't do it?'

'No.'

He moved to the mantelpiece, and began fiddling with a statuette of a shepherdess of sorts.

'Is this Bertie Wooster speaking?' he asked.

'It is.'

'Bertie Wooster whom I admired so at school – the boy we used to call "Daredevil Bertie"?'

'That's right.'

'In that case, I suppose there is nothing more to be said.'

'No.'

'Our only course is to recover the book from the Byng.'

'How do you propose to do that?'

He pondered, frowning. Then the little grey cells seemed to stir.

'I know. Listen. That book means a lot to her, doesn't it?'

'It does.'

'This being so, she would carry it on her person, as I did.'

'I suppose so.'

'In her stocking, probably. Very well, then.'

'How do you mean, very well, then?'

'Don't you see what I'm driving at?'

'No.'

'Well, listen. You could easily engage her in a sort of friendly romp, if you know what I mean, in the course of which it would be simple to . . . well, something in the nature of a jocular embrace . . .'

I checked him sharply. There are limits, and we Woosters recognize them.

'Gussie, are you suggesting that I prod Stiffy's legs?'

'Yes.'

'Well, I'm not going to.'

'Why not?'

'We need not delve into my reasons,' I said, stiffly. 'Suffice it that the shot is not on the board.'

He gave me a look, a kind of wide-eyed, reproachful look, such as a dying newt might have given him, if he had forgotten to change its water regularly. He drew in his breath sharply.

'You certainly have altered completely from the boy I knew at school,' he said. 'You seem to have gone all to pieces. No pluck. No dash. No enterprise. Alcohol, I suppose.'

He sighed and broke the shepherdess, and we moved to the door. As I opened it, he gave me another look.

'You aren't coming down to dinner like that, are you? What are you wearing a white tie for?'

'Jeeves recommended it, to keep up the spirits.'

'Well, you're going to feel a perfect ass. Old Bassett dines in a velvet smoking-jacket with soup stains across the front. Better change.'

There was a good deal in what he said. One does not like to look conspicuous. At the risk of lowering the morale, I turned to doff the tails. And as I did so there came to us from the drawing room below the sound of a fresh young voice chanting, to the accompaniment of a piano, what exhibited all the symptoms of being an old English folk song. The ear detected a good deal of 'Hey nonny nonny', and all that sort of thing.

This uproar had the effect of causing Gussie's eyes to smoulder behind the spectacles. It was as if he were feeling that this was just that little bit extra which is more than man can endure.

'Stephanie Byng!' he said bitterly. 'Singing at a time like this!'

He snorted, and left the room. And I was just finishing tying the black tie, when Jeeves entered.

'Mrs Travers,' he announced formally.

An 'Oh, golly!' broke from my lips. I had known, of course, hearing that formal announcement, that she was coming, but so does a poor blighter taking a stroll and looking up and seeing a chap in an aeroplane dropping a bomb on his head know that that's coming, but it doesn't make it any better when it arrives.

I could see that she was a good deal stirred up – all of a doodah would perhaps express it better – and I hastened to bung her civilly into the armchair and make my apologies.

'Frightfully sorry I couldn't come and see you, old ancestor,' I said. 'I was closeted with Gussie Fink-Nottle upon a matter deeply affecting our mutual interests. Since we last met, there have been new developments, and my affairs have become somewhat entangled, I regret to say. You might put it that Hell's foundations are quivering. That is not overstating it, Jeeves?'

'No, sir.'

She dismissed my protestations with a wave of the hand.

'So you're having your troubles, too, are you? Well, I don't know what new developments there have been at your end, but there has been a new development at mine, and it's a stinker. That's why I've come down here in such a hurry. The most rapid action has got to be taken, or the home will be in the melting-pot.'

I began to wonder if even the Mona Lisa could have found the going so sticky as I was finding it. One thing after another, I mean to say.

'What is it?' I asked. 'What's happened?'

She choked for a moment, then contrived to utter a single word.

'Anatole!'

'Anatole?' I took her hand and pressed it soothingly. 'Tell me, old fever patient,' I said, 'what, if anything, are you talking about? How do you mean, Anatole?'

'If we don't look slippy, I shall lose him.'

A cold hand seemed to clutch at my heart.

'Lose him?'

'Yes.'

'Even after doubling his wages?'

'Even after doubling his wages. Listen, Bertie. Just before I left home this afternoon, a letter arrived for Tom from Sir Watkyn Bassett. When I say "just before I left home", that was what made me leave home. Because do you know what was in it?'

'What?'

'It contained an offer to swap the cow-creamer for Anatole, and Tom is seriously considering it!'

I stared at her.

'What? Incredulous!'

'Incredible, sir.'

'Thank you, Jeeves. Incredible! I don't believe it. Uncle Tom would never contemplate such a thing for an instant.'

'Wouldn't he? That's all you know. Do you remember Pomeroy, the butler we had before Seppings?'

'I should say so. A noble fellow.'

'A treasure.'

'A gem. I never could think why you let him go.'

'Tom traded him to the Bessington-Copes for an oviform chocolate pot on three scroll feet.'

I struggled with a growing despair.

'But surely the delirious old ass — or, rather Uncle Tom — wouldn't fritter Anatole away like that?'

'He certainly would.'

She rose, and moved restlessly to the mantelpiece. I could see that she was looking for something to break as a relief to her surging emotions — what Jeeves would have called a palliative — and courteously drew her attention to a terra cotta figure of the Infant Samuel At Prayer. She thanked me briefly, and hurled it against the opposite wall.

'I tell you, Bertie, there are no lengths to which a really loony collector will not go to secure a coveted specimen. Tom's actual words, as he handed me the letter to read, were that it would give him genuine pleasure to skin old Bassett alive and personally drop him into a vat of boiling oil, but that he saw no alternative but to meet his demands. The only thing that stopped him wiring him there and then that it was a deal was my telling him that you had gone to Totleigh Towers expressly to pinch the cow-creamer, and that he would have it in his hands almost immediately. How are you coming along in that direction,

Bertie? Formed your schemes? All your plans cut and dried? We can't afford to waste time. Every moment is precious.'

I felt a trifle boneless. The news, I saw, would now have to be broken, and I hoped that that was all there would be. This aunt is a formidable old creature, when stirred, and I could not but recall what had happened to the Infant Samuel.

'I was going to talk to you about that,' I said. 'Jeeves, have you that document we prepared?'

'Here it is, sir.'

'Thank you, Jeeves. And I think it might be a good thing if you were to go and bring a spot more brandy.'

'Very good, sir.'

He withdrew, and I slipped her the paper, bidding her read it attentively. She gave it the eye.

'What's all this?'

'You will soon see. Note how it is headed. "Wooster, B. – position of." Those words tell the story. They explain,' I said, backing a step and getting ready to duck, 'why it is that I must resolutely decline to pinch that cow-creamer.'

'What!'

'I sent you a telegram to that effect this afternoon, but, of course, it missed you.'

She was looking at me pleadingly, like a fond mother at an idiot child who has just pulled something exceptionally goofy.

'But, Bertie, dear, haven't you been listening? About Anatole? Don't you realize the position?'

'Oh, quite.'

'Then have you gone cuckoo? When I say "gone", of course – '

I held up a checking hand.

'Let me explain, aged r. You will recall that I mentioned to you that there had been some recent developments. One of these is that Sir Watkyn Bassett knows all about this cow-creamer-pinching scheme and is watching my every movement. Another is that he has confided his suspicions to a pal of his named Spode. Perhaps on your arrival here you met Spode?'

'That big fellow?'

'Big is right, though perhaps "supercolossal" would be more the *mot juste*. Well, Sir Watkyn, as I say, has confided his suspicions to Spode, and I have it from the latter personally that if that cow-creamer disappears, he will beat me to a jelly. That is why nothing constructive can be accomplished.'

A silence of some duration followed these remarks. I could see that she was chewing on the thing and reluctantly coming to the conclusion that it was no idle whim of Bertram's that was causing him to fail her in her hour of need. She appreciated the cleft stick in which he found himself and, unless I am vastly mistaken, shuddered at it.

This relative is a woman who, in the days of my boyhood and adolescence, was accustomed frequently to clump me over the side of the head when she considered that my behaviour warranted this gesture, and I have often felt in these days that she was on the point of doing it again. But beneath this earhole-sloshing exterior there beats a tender heart, and her love for Bertram is, I know, deep-rooted. She would be the last person to wish to see him get his eyes bunged up and have that well-shaped nose punched out of position.

'I see,' she said, at length. 'Yes. That makes things difficult, of course.'

'Extraordinarily difficult. If you care to describe the situation as an *impasse*, it will be all right with me.'

'Said he would beat you to a jelly, did he?'

'That was the expression he used. He repeated it, so that there should be no mistake.'

'Well, I wouldn't for the world have you manhandled by that big stiff. You wouldn't have a chance against a gorilla like that. He would tear the stuffing out of you before you could say "Pip-pip". He would rend you limb from limb and scatter the fragments to the four winds.'

I winced a little.

'No need to make a song about it, old flesh and blood.'

'You're sure he meant what he said?'

'Quite.'

'His bark may be worse than his bite.'

I smiled sadly.

'I see where you're heading, Aunt Dahlia,' I said. 'In another minute you will be asking if there wasn't a twinkle in his eye as he spoke. There wasn't. The policy which Roderick Spode outlined to me at our recent interview is the policy which he will pursue and fulfil.'

'Then we seem to be stymied. Unless Jeeves can think of something.' She addressed the man, who had just entered with the brandy – not before it was time. I couldn't think why he had taken so long over it. 'We are talking of Mr Spode, Jeeves.'

'Yes, madam?'

'Jeeves and I have already discussed the Spode menace,' I said moodily, 'and he confesses himself baffled. For once, that substantial brain has failed to click. He has brooded, but no formula.'

Aunt Dahlia had been swigging the brandy gratefully, and there now came into her face a thoughtful look.

'You know what has just occurred to me?' she said.

'Say on, old thicker than water,' I replied, still with that dark moodiness. 'I'll bet it's rotten.'

'It's not rotten at all. It may solve everything. I've been wondering if this man Spode hasn't some shady secret. Do you know anything about him, Jeeves?'

'No, madam.'

'How do you mean, a secret?'

'What I was turning over in my mind was the thought that, if he had some chink in his armour, one might hold him up by means of it, thus drawing his fangs. I remember, when I was a girl, seeing your Uncle George kiss my governess, and it was amazing how it eased the strain later on, when there was any question of her keeping me in after school to write out the principal imports and exports of the United Kingdom. You see what I mean? Suppose we knew that Spode had shot a fox, or something? You don't think much of it?' she said, seeing that I was pursing my lips dubiously.

'I can see it as an idea. But there seems to me to be one fatal snag – viz. that we don't know.'

'Yes, that's true.' She rose. 'Oh, well, it was just a random thought, I merely threw it out. And now I think I will be returning to my room and spraying my temples with *eau-de-Cologne*. My head feels as if it were about to burst like shrapnel.'

The door closed. I sank into the chair which she had vacated, and mopped the b.

'Well, that's over,' I said thankfully. 'She took the blow better than I had hoped, Jeeves. The Quorn trains its daughters well. But, stiff though her upper lip was, you could see that she felt it deeply, and that brandy came in handy. By the way, you were the dickens of a while bringing it. A St Bernard dog would have been there and back in half the time.'

'Yes, sir. I am sorry. I was detained in conversation by Mr Fink-Nottle.'

I sat pondering.

'You know, Jeeves,' I said, 'that wasn't at all a bad idea of Aunt Dahlia's about getting the goods on Spode. Fundamentally, it was sound. If Spode had buried the body and we knew where, it would unquestionably render him a negligible force. But you say you know nothing about him.'

'No, sir.'

'And I doubt if there is anything to know, anyway. There are some chaps, one look at whom is enough to tell you that they are pukka sahibs who play the game and do not do the things that aren't done, and prominent among these, I fear, is Roderick Spode. I shouldn't imagine that the most rigorous investigation would uncover anything about him worse than that moustache of his, and to the world's scrutiny of that he obviously has no objection, or he wouldn't wear the damned thing.'

'Very true, sir. Still, it might be worth while to institute enquiries.'

'Yes, but where?'

'I was thinking of the Junior Ganymede, sir. It is a club for gentlemen's personal gentlemen in Curzon Street, to which I have belonged for some years. The personal attendant of a gentleman of Mr Spode's prominence would be sure to be a member, and he would, of course, have confided to the secretary a good deal of material concerning him, for insertion in the club book.'

'Eh?'

'Under Rule Eleven, every new member is required to supply the club with full information regarding his employer. This not only provides entertaining reading, but serves as a warning to members who may be contemplating taking service with gentlemen who fall short of the ideal.'

A thought struck me, and I started. Indeed, I started rather violently.

'What happened when you joined?'

'Sir?'

'Did you tell them all about me?'

'Oh, yes, sir.'

'What, everything? The time when old Stoker was after me and I had to black up with boot polish in order to assume a rudimentary disguise?'

'Yes, sir.'

'And the occasion on which I came home after Pongo Twistleton's birthday party and mistook the standard lamp for a burglar?'

'Yes, sir. The members like to have these things to read on wet afternoons.'

'They do, do they? And suppose some wet afternoon Aunt Agatha reads them? Did that occur to you?'

'The contingency of Mrs Spenser Gregson obtaining access to the club book is a remote one.'

'I dare say. But recent events under this very roof will have shown you how women do obtain access to books.'

I relapsed into silence, pondering on this startling glimpse he had accorded of what went on in institutions like the Junior Ganymede, of the existence of which I had previously been unaware. I had known, of course, that at nights, after serving the frugal meal, Jeeves would put on the old bowler hat and slip round the corner, but I had always supposed his destination to have been the saloon bar of some neighbouring pub. Of clubs in Curzon Street I had had no inkling.

Still less had I had an inkling that some of the fruitiest of Bertram Wooster's possibly ill-judged actions were being inscribed in a book. The whole thing to my mind smacked rather unpleasantly of Abou ben Adhem and Recording Angels, and I found myself frowning somewhat.

Still, there didn't seem much to be done about it, so I returned to what Constable Oates would have called the point at tissue.

'Then what's your idea? To apply to the Secretary for information about Spode?'

'Yes, sir.'

'You think he'll give it to you?'

'Oh, yes, sir.'

'You mean he scatters these data — these extraordinarily dangerous data — these data that might spell ruin if they fell into the wrong hands — broadcast to whoever asks for them?'

'Only to members, sir.'

'How soon could you get in touch with him?'

'I could ring him up on the telephone immediately, sir.'

'Then do so, Jeeves, and if possible chalk the call up to Sir Watkyn Bassett. And don't lose your nerve when you hear the girl say "Three minutes". Carry on regardless. Cost what it may, ye Sec. must be made to understand – and understand thoroughly – that now is the time for all good men to come to the aid of the party.'

'I think I can convince him that an emergency exists, sir.'

'If you can't, refer him to me.'

'Very good, sir.'

He started off on his errand of mercy.

'Oh, by the way, Jeeves,' I said, as he was passing through the door, 'did you say you had been talking to Gussie?'

'Yes, sir.'

'Had he anything new to report?'

'Yes, sir. It appears that his relations with Miss Bassett have been severed. The engagement is broken off.'

He floated out, and I leaped three feet. A dashed difficult thing to do, when you're sitting in an armchair, but I managed it.

'Jeeves!' I yelled.

But he had gone, leaving not a wrack behind.

From downstairs there came the sudden booming of the dinner gong.

# =6=

IT has always given me a bit of a pang to look back at that dinner and think that agony of mind prevented me sailing into it in the right carefree mood, for it was one which in happier circumstances I would have got my nose down to with a will. Whatever Sir Watkyn Bassett's moral shortcomings, he did his guests extraordinarily well at the festive board, and even in my preoccupied condition it was plain to me in the first five minutes that his cook was a woman who had the divine fire in her. From a Grade A soup we proceeded to a toothsome fish, and from the toothsome fish to a salmi of game which even Anatole might have been proud to sponsor. Add asparagus, a jam omelette and some spirited sardines on toast, and you will see what I mean.

All wasted on me, of course. As the fellow said, better a dinner of herbs when you're all buddies together than a regular blow-out when you're not, and the sight of Gussie and Madeline Bassett sitting side by side at the other end of the table turned the food to ashes in my m. I viewed them with concern.

You know what engaged couples are like in mixed company, as a rule. They put their heads together and converse in whispers. They slap and giggle. They pat and prod. I have even known the female member of the duo to feed her companion with a fork. There was none of this sort of thing about Madeline Bassett and Gussie. He looked pale and corpse-like, she cold and proud and aloof. They put in the time for the most part making bread pills and, as far as I was able to ascertain, didn't exchange a word from start to finish. Oh, yes, once – when he asked her to pass the salt, and she passed the pepper, and he said 'I meant the salt,' and she said 'Oh, really?' and passed the mustard.

There could be no question whatever that Jeeves was right. Brass rags had been parted by the young couple, and what was weighing upon me, apart from the tragic aspect, was the mystery of it all. I could think of no solution, and I looked forward to the conclusion of the meal, when the women should have legged it and I would be able to get together with Gussie over the port and learn the inside dope.

To my surprise, however, the last female had no sooner passed through the door than Gussie, who had been holding it open, shot through after her like a diving duck and did not return, leaving me alone with my host and Roderick Spode. And as they sat snuggled up together at the far end of the table, talking to one another in low voices, and staring at me from time to time as if I had been a ticket-of-leave man who had got in by crashing the gate and might be expected, unless carefully watched, to pocket a spoon or two, it was not long before I, too, left. Murmuring something about fetching my cigarette case, I sidled out and went up to my room. It seemed to me that either Gussie or Jeeves would be bound to look in there sooner or later.

A cheerful fire was burning in the grate, and to while away the time I pulled the armchair up and got out the mystery story I had brought with me from London. As my researches in it had already shown me, it was a particularly good one, full of crisp clues and meaty murders, and I was soon absorbed. Scarcely, however, had I really had time to get going on it, when there was a rattle at the door handle, and who should amble in but Roderick Spode.

I looked at him with not a little astonishment. I mean to say, the last chap I was expecting to invade my bedchamber. And it wasn't as if he had come to apologize for his offensive attitude on the terrace, when in addition to muttering menaces he had called me a miserable worm, or for those stares at the dinner table. One glance at his face told me that. The first thing a chap who has come to apologize does is to weigh in with an ingratiating simper, and of this there was no sign.

As a matter of fact, he seemed to me to be looking slightly more sinister than ever, and I found his aspect so forbidding that I dug up an ingratiating simper myself. I didn't suppose it would do much towards conciliating the blighter, but every little helps.

'Oh, hallo, Spode,' I said affably. 'Come on in. Is there something I can do for you?'

Without replying, he walked to the cupboard, threw it open

with a brusque twiddle and glared into it. This done, he turned and eyed me, still in that unchummy manner.

'I thought Fink-Nottle might be here.'

'He isn't.'

'So I see.'

'Did you expect to find him in the cupboard?'

'Yes.'

'Oh?'

There was a pause.

'Any message I can give him if he turns up?'

'Yes. You can tell him that I am going to break his neck.'

'Break his neck?'

'Yes. Are you deaf? Break his neck.'

I nodded pacifically.

'I see. Break his neck. Right. And if he asks why?'

'He knows why. Because he is a butterfly who toys with women's hearts and throws them away like soiled gloves.'

'Right ho.' I hadn't had a notion that that was what butterflies did. Most interesting. 'Well, I'll let him know if I run across him.'

'Thank you.'

He withdrew, slamming the door, and I sat musing on the odd way in which history repeats itself. I mean to say, the situation was almost identical with the one which had arisen some few months earlier at Brinkley, when young Tuppy Glossop had come in to my room with a similar end in view. True, Tuppy, if I remembered rightly, had wanted to pull Gussie inside out and make him swallow himself, while Spode had spoken of breaking his neck, but the principle was the same.

I saw what had happened, of course. It was a development which I had rather been anticipating. I had not forgotten what Gussie had told me earlier in the day about Spode informing him of his intention of leaving no stone unturned to dislocate his cervical vertebrae should he ever do Madeline Bassett wrong. He had doubtless learned the facts from her over the coffee, and was now setting out to put his policy into operation.

As to what these facts were, I still had not the remotest. But it was evident from Spode's manner that they reflected little credit on Gussie. He must, I realized, have been making an ass of himself in a big way.

A fearful situation, beyond a doubt, and if there had been anything I could have done about it, I would have done same without hesitation. But it seemed to me that I was helpless, and that Nature must take its course. With a slight sigh, I resumed my gooseflesher, and was making fair progress with it, when a hollow voice said: 'I say, Bertie!' and I sat up quivering in every limb. It was as if a family spectre had edged up and breathed down the back of my neck.

Turning, I observed Augustus Fink-Nottle appearing from under the bed.

Owing to the fact that the shock had caused my tongue to get tangled up with my tonsils, inducing an unpleasant choking sensation, I found myself momentarily incapable of speech. All I was able to do was goggle at Gussie, and it was immediately evident to me, as I did so, that he had been following the recent conversation closely. His whole demeanour was that of a man vividly conscious of being just about half a jump ahead of Roderick Spode. The hair was ruffled, the eyes wild, the nose twitching. A rabbit pursued by a weasel would have looked just the same – allowing, of course, for the fact that it would not have been wearing tortoiseshell-rimmed spectacles.

'That was a close call, Bertie,' he said, in a low, quivering voice. He crossed the room, giving a little at the knees. His face was a rather pretty greenish colour. 'I think I'll lock the door, if you don't mind. He might come back. Why he didn't look under the bed, I can't imagine. I always thought these Dictators were so thorough.'

I managed to get the tongue unhitched.

'Never mind about beds and Dictators. What's all this about you and Madeline Bassett?'

He winced.

'Do you mind not talking about that?'

'Yes, I do mind not talking about it. It's the only thing I want to talk about. What on earth has she broken off the engagement for? What did you do to her?'

He winced again. I could see that I was probing an exposed nerve.

'It wasn't so much what I did to her – it was what I did to Stephanie Byng.'

'To Stiffy?'

'Yes.'

'What did you do to Stiffy?'

He betrayed some embarrassment.

'I – er . . . Well, as a matter of fact, I . . . Mind you, I can see now that it was a mistake, but it seemed a good idea at the time . . . You see, the fact is . . .'

'Get on with it.'

He pulled himself together with a visible effort.

'Well, I wonder if you remember, Bertie, what we were saying up here before dinner . . . about the possibility of her carrying that notebook on her person . . . I put forward the theory, if you recall, that it might be in her stocking . . . and I suggested if you recollect, that one might ascertain . . .'

I reeled. I had got the gist. 'You didn't – '

'Yes.'

'When?'

Again that look of pain passed over his face.

'Just before dinner. You remember we heard her singing folk songs in the drawing room. I went down there, and there she was at the piano, all alone . . . At least, I thought she was all alone . . . And it suddenly struck me that this would be an excellent opportunity to . . . What I didn't know, you see, was that Madeline, though invisible for the moment, was also present. She had gone behind the screen in the corner to get a further supply of folk songs from the chest in which they are kept . . . and . . . well, the long and short of it is that, just as I was . . . well, to cut a long story short, just as I was . . . How shall I put it? . . . Just as I was, so to speak, getting on with it, out she came . . . and . . . Well, you see what I mean . . . I mean, coming so soon after that taking-the-fly-out-of-the-girl's-eye-in-the-stable-yard business, it was not easy to pass it off. As a matter of fact, I didn't pass it off. That's the whole story. How are you on knotting sheets, Bertie?'

I could not follow what is known as the transition of thought.

'Knotting sheets?'

'I was thinking it over under the bed, while you and Spode were chatting, and I came to the conclusion that the only thing to be done is for us to take the sheets off your bed and tie knots in them, and then you can lower me down from the window.

They do it in books, and I have an idea I've seen it in the movies. Once outside, I can take your car and drive up to London. After that, my plans are uncertain. I may go to California.'

'California?'

'It's seven thousand miles away. Spode would hardly come to California.'

I stared at him aghast.

'You aren't going to do a bolt?'

'Of course I'm going to do a bolt. Immediately. You heard what Spode said?'

'You aren't afraid of Spode?'

'Yes, I am.'

'But you were saying yourself that he's a mere mass of beef and brawn, obviously slow on his feet.'

'I know. I remember. But that was when I thought he was after you. One's views change.'

'But, Gussie, pull yourself together. You can't just run away.'

'What else can I do?'

'Why, stick around and try to effect a reconciliation. You haven't had a shot at pleading with the girl yet.'

'Yes, I have. I did it at dinner. During the fish course. No good. She just gave me a cold look, and made bread pills.'

I racked the bean. I was sure there must be an avenue somewhere, waiting to be explored, and in about half a minute I spotted it.

'What you've got to do,' I said, 'is to get the notebook. If you secured that book and showed it to Madeline, its contents would convince her that your motives in acting as you did towards Stiffy were not what she supposed, but pure to the last drop. She would realize that your behaviour was the outcome of . . . it's on the tip of my tongue . . . of a counsel of desperation. She would understand and forgive.'

For a moment, a faint flicker of hope seemed to illumine his twisted features.

'It's a thought,' he agreed. 'I believe you've got something there, Bertie. That's not a bad idea.'

'It can't fail. *Tout comprendre, c'est tout pardonner* about sums it up.'

The flicker faded.

'But how can I get the book? Where is it?'

'It wasn't on her person?'

'I don't think so. Though my investigations were, in the circumstances, necessarily cursory.'

'Then it's probably in her room.'

'Well, there you are. I can't go searching a girl's room.'

'Why not? You see that book I was reading when you popped up. By an odd coincidence – I call it a coincidence, but probably these things are sent to us for a purpose – I had just come to a bit where a gang had been doing that very thing. Do it now, Gussie. She's probably fixed in the drawing room for the next hour or so.'

'As a matter of fact, she's gone to the village. The curate is giving an address on the Holy Land with coloured slides to the Village Mothers at the Working Men's Institute, and she is playing the piano accompaniment. But even so . . . No, Bertie, I can't do it. It may be the right thing to do . . . in fact, I can see that it is the right thing to do . . . but I haven't the nerve. Suppose Spode came in and caught me.'

'Spode would hardly wander into a young girl's room.'

'I don't know so much. You can't form plans on any light-hearted assumption like that. I see him as a chap who wanders everywhere. No. My heart is broken, my future a blank, and there is nothing to be done but accept the fact and start knotting sheets. Let's get at it.'

'You don't knot any of my sheets.'

'But, dash it, my life is at stake.'

'I don't care. I decline to be a party to this craven scooting.'

'Is this Bertie Wooster speaking?'

'You said that before.'

'And I say it again. For the last time, Bertie, will you lend me a couple of sheets and help knot them?'

'No.'

'Then I shall just have to go off and hide somewhere till dawn, when the milk train leaves. Goodbye, Bertie. You have disappointed me.'

'You have disappointed *me*. I thought you had guts.'

'I have, and I don't want Roderick Spode fooling about with them.'

He gave me another of those dying-newt looks, and opened the door cautiously. A glance up and down the passage having apparently satisfied him that it was, for the moment, Spodeless, he slipped out and was gone. And I returned to my book. It was the only thing I could think of that would keep me from sitting torturing myself with agonizing broodings.

Presently I was aware that Jeeves was with me. I hadn't heard him come in, but you often don't with Jeeves. He just streams silently from spot A to spot B, like some gas.

I WOULDN'T say that Jeeves was actually smirking, but there was a definite look of quiet satisfaction on his face, and I suddenly remembered what this sickening scene with Gussie had caused me to forget – viz. that the last time I had seen him he had been on his way to the telephone to ring up the Secretary of the Junior Ganymede Club. I sprang to my feet eagerly. Unless I had misread that look, he had something to report.

'Did you connect with the Sec., Jeeves?'

'Yes, sir. I have just finished speaking to him.'

'And did he dish the dirt?'

'He was most informative, sir.'

'Has Spode a secret?'

'Yes, sir.'

I smote the trouser leg emotionally.

'I should have known better than to doubt Aunt Dahlia. Aunts always know. It's a sort of intuition. Tell me all.'

'I fear I cannot do that, sir. The rules of the club regarding the dissemination of material recorded in the book are very rigid.'

'You mean your lips are sealed?'

'Yes, sir.'

'Then what was the use of telephoning?'

'It is only the details of the matter which I am precluded from mentioning, sir. I am at perfect liberty to tell you that it would greatly lessen Mr Spode's potentiality for evil, if you were to inform him that you know all about Eulalie, sir.'

'Eulalie?'

'Eulalie, sir.'

'That would really put the stopper on him?'

'Yes, sir.'

I pondered. It didn't sound much to go on.

'You're sure you can't go a bit deeper into the subject?'

'Quite sure, sir. Were I to do so, it is probable that my resignation would be called for.'

'Well, I wouldn't want that to happen, of course.' I hated to think of a squad of butlers forming a hollow square while the Committee snipped his buttons off. 'Still, you really are sure that if I look Spode in the eye and spring this gag, he will be baffled? Let's get this quite clear. Suppose you're Spode, and I walk up to you and say "Spode, I know all about Eulalie," that would make you wilt?'

'Yes, sir. The subject of Eulalie, sir, is one which the gentleman, occupying the position he does in the public eye, would, I am convinced, be most reluctant to have ventilated.'

I practised it for a bit. I walked up to the chest of drawers with my hands in my pockets, and said, 'Spode, I know all about Eulalie.' I tried again, waggling my finger this time. I then had a go with folded arms, and I must say it still didn't sound too convincing.

However, I told myself that Jeeves always knew.

'Well, if you say so, Jeeves. Then the first thing I had better do is find Gussie and give him this life-saving information.'

'Sir?'

'Oh, of course, you don't know anything about that, do you? I must tell you, Jeeves, that, since we last met, the plot has thickened again. Were you aware that Spode has long loved Miss Bassett?'

'No, sir.'

'Well, such is the case. The happiness of Miss Bassett is very dear to Spode, and now that her engagement has gone phut for reasons highly discreditable to the male contracting party, he wants to break Gussie's neck.'

'Indeed, sir?'

'I assure you. He was in here just now, speaking of it, and Gussie, who happened to be under the bed at the time, heard him. With the result that he now talks of getting out of the window and going to California. Which, of course, would be fatal. It is imperative that he stays on and tries to effect a reconciliation.'

'Yes, sir.'

'He can't effect a reconciliation, if he is in California.'

'No, sir.'

'So I must go and try to find him. Though, mark you, I doubt if he will be easily found at this point in his career. He is probably on the roof, wondering how he can pull it up after him.'

My misgivings were proved abundantly justified. I searched the house assiduously, but there were no signs of him. Somewhere, no doubt, Totleigh Towers hid Augustus Fink-Nottle, but it kept its secret well. Eventually, I gave it up, and returned to my room, and stap my vitals if the first thing I beheld on entering wasn't the man in person. He was standing by the bed, knotting sheets.

The fact that he had his back to the door and that the carpet was soft kept him from being aware of my entry till I spoke. My 'Hey!' – a pretty sharp one, for I was aghast at seeing my bed thus messed about – brought him spinning round, ashen to the lips.

'Woof!' he exclaimed. 'I thought you were Spode!'

Indignation succeeded panic. He gave me a hard stare. The eyes behind the spectacles were cold. He looked like an annoyed turbot.

'What do you mean, you blasted Wooster,' he demanded, 'by sneaking up on a fellow and saying "Hey!" like that? You might have given me heart failure.'

'And what do you mean, you blighted Fink-Nottle,' I demanded in my turn, 'by mucking up my bed linen after I specifically forbade it? You have sheets of your own. Go and knot those.'

'How can I? Spode is sitting on my bed.'

'He is?'

'Certainly he is. Waiting for me. I went there after I left you, and there he was. If he hadn't happened to clear his throat, I'd have walked right in.'

I saw that it was high time to set this disturbed spirit at rest.

'You needn't be afraid of Spode, Gussie.'

'What do you mean, I needn't be afraid of Spode? Talk sense.'

'I mean just that. Spode, *qua* menace, if *qua* is the word I want, is a thing of the past. Owing to the extraordinary perfection of Jeeves's secret system, I have learned something about him which he wouldn't care to have generally known.'

'What?'

'Ah, there you have me. When I said I had learned it, I should have said that Jeeves had learned it, and unfortunately Jeeves's lips are sealed. However, I am in a position to slip it across the man in no uncertain fashion. If he attempts any rough stuff, I will give him the works.' I broke off, listening. Footsteps were coming along the passage. 'Ah!' I said. 'Someone approaches. This may quite possibly be the blighter himself.'

An animal cry escaped Gussie.

'Lock that door!'

I waved a fairly airy hand.

'It will not be necessary,' I said. 'Let him come. I positively welcome this visit. Watch me deal with him, Gussie. It will amuse you.'

I had guessed correctly. It was Spode, all right. No doubt he had grown weary of sitting on Gussie's bed, and had felt that another chat with Bertram might serve to vary the monotony. He came in, as before, without knocking, and as he perceived Gussie, uttered a wordless exclamation of triumph and satisfaction. He then stood for a moment, breathing heavily through the nostrils.

He seemed to have grown a bit since our last meeting, being now about eight foot six, and had my advices *in re* getting the bulge on him proceeded from a less authoritative source, his aspect might have intimidated me quite a good deal. But so sedulously had I been trained through the years to rely on Jeeves's lightest word that I regarded him without a tremor.

Gussie, I was sorry to observe, did not share my sunny confidence. Possibly I had not given him a full enough explanation of the facts in the case, or it may have been that, confronted with Spode in the flesh, his nerve had failed him. At any rate, he now retreated to the wall and seemed, as far as I could gather, to be trying to get through it. Foiled in this endeavour, he stood looking as if he had been stuffed by some good taxidermist, while I turned to the intruder and gave him a long, level stare, in which surprise and hauteur were nicely blended.

'Well, Spode,' I said, 'what is it now?'

I had put a considerable amount of top spin on the final word, to indicate displeasure, but it was wasted on the man. Giving the question a miss like the deaf adder of Scripture, he began to advance slowly, his gaze concentrated on Gussie. The jaw muscles, I noted, were working as they had done on the occasion when he had come upon me toying with Sir Watkyn Bassett's collection of old silver: and something in his manner suggested that he might at any moment start beating his chest with a hollow drumming sound, as gorillas do in moments of emotion.

'Ha!' he said.

Well, of course, I was not going to stand any rot like that. This habit of his of going about the place saying 'Ha!' was one that had got to be checked, and checked promptly.

'Spode!' I said sharply, and I have an idea that I rapped the table.

He seemed for the first time to become aware of my presence. He paused for an instant, and gave me an unpleasant look.

'Well, what do *you* want?'

I raised an eyebrow or two.

'What do I want? I like that. That's good. Since you ask, Spode, I want to know what the devil you mean by keeping coming into my private apartment, taking up space which I require for other purposes and interrupting me when I am chatting with my personal friends. Really, one gets about as much privacy in this house as a strip-tease dancer. I assume that you have a room of your own. Get back to it, you fat slob, and stay there.'

I could not resist shooting a swift glance at Gussie, to see how he was taking all this, and was pleased to note on his face the burgeoning of a look of worshipping admiration, such as a distressed damsel of the Middle Ages might have directed at a knight on observing him getting down to brass tacks with the dragon. I could see that I had once more become to him the old Daredevil Wooster of our boyhood days, and I had no doubt that he was burning with shame and remorse as he recalled those sneers and jeers of his.

Spode, also, seemed a good deal impressed, though not so favourably. He was staring incredulously, like one bitten by a rabbit. He seemed to be asking himself if this could really be the shrinking violet with whom he had conferred on the terrace.

He asked me if I had called him a slob, and I said I had.

'A fat slob?'

'A fat slob. It is about time,' I proceeded, 'that some public-spirited person came along and told you where you got off. The trouble with you, Spode, is that just because you have succeeded in inducing a handful of half-wits to disfigure the London scene by going about in black shorts, you think you're someone. You hear them shouting, "Heil, Spode!" and you imagine it is the Voice of the People. That is where you make your bloomer. What the Voice of the People is saying is: "Look at that frightful ass Spode swanking about in footer bags! Did you ever in your puff see such a perfect perisher?" '

He did what is known as struggling for utterance.

'Oh?' he said. 'Ha! Well, I will attend to you later.'

'And I,' I retorted, quick as a flash, 'will attend to you now.' I lit a cigarette. 'Spode,' I said, unmasking my batteries, 'I know your secret!'

'Eh?'

'I know all about – '

'All about what?'

It was to ask myself precisely that question that I had paused. For, believe me or believe me not, in this tense moment, when I so sorely needed it, the name which Jeeves had mentioned to me as the magic formula for coping with this blister had completely passed from my mind. I couldn't even remember what letter it began with.

It's an extraordinary thing about names. You've probably noticed it yourself. You think you've got them, I mean to say, and they simply slither away. I've often wished I had a quid for every time some bird with a perfectly familiar map has come up to me and Hallo-Woostered, and had me gasping for air because I couldn't put a label to him. This always makes one feel at a loss, but on no previous occasion had I felt so much at a loss as I did now.

'All about what?' said Spode.

'Well, as a matter of fact,' I had to confess, 'I've forgotten.'

A sort of gasping gulp from up-stage directed my attention to Gussie again, and I could see that the significance of my words had not been lost on him. Once more he tried to back: and as he realized that he had already gone as far as he could go, a glare of despair came into his eyes. And then, abruptly, as Spode began to advance upon him, it changed to one of determination and stern resolve.

I like to think of Augustus Fink-Nottle at the moment. He showed up well. Hitherto, I am bound to say, I had never regarded him highly as a man of action. Essentially the dreamer type, I should have said. But now he couldn't have smacked into it with a prompter gusto if he had been a rough-and-tumble fighter on the San Francisco waterfront from early childhood.

Above him, as he stood glued to the wall, there hung a fairish-sized oil-painting of a chap in knee-breeches and a three-cornered hat gazing at a female who appeared to be chirruping to a bird of sorts – a dove, unless I am mistaken, or a pigeon. I had noticed it once or twice since I had been in the room, and had, indeed, thought of giving it to Aunt Dahlia to break instead of the Infant Samuel at Prayer. Fortunately, I had not done so, or Gussie would not now have been in a position to tear it from its moorings and bring it down with a nice wristy action on Spode's head.

I say 'fortunately', because if ever there was a fellow who needed hitting with oil paintings, that fellow was Roderick Spode. From the moment of our first meeting, his every word and action had proved abundantly that this was the stuff to give him. But there is always a catch in these good things, and it took me only an instant to see that this effort of Gussie's, though well meant, had achieved little of constructive importance. What he should have done, of course, was to hold the picture sideways, so as to get the best out of the stout frame. Instead of which, he had used the flat of the weapon, and Spode came through the canvas like a circus rider going through a paper hoop. In other words, what had promised to be a decisive blow had turned out to be merely what Jeeves would call a gesture.

It did, however, divert Spode from his purpose for a few seconds. He stood there blinking, with the thing round his neck like a ruff, and the pause was sufficient to enable me to get into action.

Give us a lead, make it quite clear to us that the party has warmed up and that from now on anything goes, and we Woosters do not hang back. There was a sheet lying on the bed where Gussie had dropped it when disturbed at his knotting, and to snatch this up and envelop Spode in it was with me the work of a moment. It is a long time since I studied the subject, and before committing myself definitely I should have to consult Jeeves, but I have an idea that ancient Roman gladiators used to do much the same sort of thing in the arena, and were rather well thought of in consequence.

I suppose a man who has been hit over the head with a picture of a girl chirruping to a pigeon and almost immediately afterwards enmeshed in a sheet can never really retain the cool, intelligent outlook. Any friend of Spode's, with his interests at heart, would have advised him at this juncture to keep quite still and not stir till he had come out of the cocoon. Only thus, in a terrain so liberally studded with chairs and things, could a purler have been avoided.

He did not do this. Hearing the rushing sound caused by Gussie exiting, he made a leap in its general direction and took the inevitable toss. At the moment when Gussie, moving well, passed through the door, he was on the ground, more inextricably entangled than ever.

My own friends, advising me, would undoubtedly have recommended an immediate departure at this point, and looking back, I can see that where I went wrong was in pausing to hit the bulge which, from the remarks that were coming through at that spot, I took to be Spode's head, with a china vase that stood on the mantelpiece not far from where the Infant Samuel had been. It was a strategical error. I got home all right and the vase broke into a dozen pieces, which was all to the good – for the more of the property of a man like Sir Watkyn Bassett that was destroyed, the better – but the action of dealing this buffet caused me to overbalance. The next moment, a hand coming out from under the sheet had grabbed my coat.

It was a serious disaster, of course, and one which might well have caused a lesser man to feel that it was no use going on struggling. But the whole point about the Woosters, as I have had occasion to remark before, is that they are not lesser men. They keep their heads. They think quickly, and they act quickly. Napoleon was the same. I have mentioned that at the moment when I was preparing to inform Spode that I knew his secret, I had lighted a cigarette. This cigarette, in its holder, was still between my lips. Hastily removing it, I pressed the glowing end on the ham-like hand which was impeding my getaway.

The results were thoroughly gratifying. You would have thought that the trend of recent events would have put Roderick Spode in a frame of mind to expect anything and be ready for it, but this simple manœuvre found him unprepared. With a sharp cry of anguish, he released the coat, and I delayed no longer. Bertram Wooster is a man who knows when and when not to be among those present. When Bertram Wooster sees a lion in his path, he ducks down a side street. I was off at an impressive speed, and would no doubt have crossed the threshold with a burst which would have clipped a second or two off Gussie's time, had I not experienced a head-on collision with a solid body which happened to be entering at the moment. I remember thinking, as we twined our arms about each other, that at Totleigh Towers, if it wasn't one thing, it was bound to be something else.

I fancy that it was the scent of *eau-de-Cologne* that still clung to her temples that enabled me to identify this solid body as that of Aunt Dahlia, though even without it the rich, hunting-field expletive which burst from her lips would have put me on the right track. We came down in a tangled heap, and must have rolled inwards to some extent, for the next thing I knew, we were colliding with the sheeted figure of Roderick Spode, who when last seen had been at the other end of the room. No doubt the explanation is that we had rolled nor'-nor'-east and he had been rolling sou'-sou'-west, with the result that we had come together somewhere in the middle.

Spode, I noticed, as Reason began to return to her throne, was holding Aunt Dahlia by the left leg, and she didn't seem to be liking it much. A good deal of breath had been knocked out of her by the impact of a nephew on her midriff, but enough remained to enable her to expostulate, and this she was doing with all the old fire.

'What is this joint?' she was demanding heatedly. 'A loony bin? Has everybody gone crazy? First I meet Spink-Bottle racing along the corridor like a mustang. Then you try to walk through me as if I were thistledown. And now the gentleman in the burnous has started tickling my ankle – a thing that hasn't happened to me since the York and Ainsty Hunt Ball of the year nineteen-twenty-one.'

These protests must have filtered through to Spode, and presumably stirred his better nature, for he let go, and she got up, dusting her dress.

'Now, then,' she said, somewhat calmer. 'An explanation, if you please, and a categorical one. What's the idea? What's it all about? Who the devil's that inside the winding-sheet?'

I made the introductions.

'You've met Spode, haven't you? Mr Roderick Spode, Mrs Travers.'

Spode had now removed the sheet, but the picture was still in position, and Aunt Dahlia eyed it wonderingly.

'What on earth have you got that thing round your neck for?' she asked. Then, in more tolerant vein: 'Wear it if you like, of course, but it doesn't suit you.'

Spode did not reply. He was breathing heavily. I didn't blame him, mind you – in his place, I'd have done the same – but the sound was not agreeable, and I wished he wouldn't. He was also gazing at me intently, and I wished he wouldn't do that, either. His face was flushed, his eyes were bulging, and one had the odd illusion that his hair was standing on end – like quills upon the fretful porpentine, as Jeeves once put it when describing to me the reactions of Barmy Fotheringay-Phipps on seeing a dead snip, on which he had invested largely, come in sixth in the procession at the Newmarket Spring Meeting.

I remember once, during a temporary rift with Jeeves, engaging a man from the registry office to serve me in his stead, and he hadn't been with me a week when he got blotto one night and set fire to the house and tried to slice me up with a carving knife. Said he wanted to see the colour of my insides, of all bizarre ideas. And until this moment I had always looked on that episode as the most trying in my experience. I now saw that it must be ranked second.

This bird of whom I speak was a simple, untutored soul and Spode a man of good education and upbringing, but it was plain that there was one point at which their souls touched. I don't suppose they would have seen eye to eye on any other subject you could have brought up, but in the matter of wanting to see the colour of my insides their minds ran on parallel lines. The only difference seemed to be that whereas my employee had planned to use a carving knife for his excavations, Spode appeared to be satisfied that the job could be done all right with the bare hands.

'I must ask you to leave us, madam,' he said.

'But I've only just come,' said Aunt Dahlia.

'I am going to thrash this man within an inch of his life.'

It was quite the wrong tone to take with the aged relative.

She has a very clannish spirit and, as I have said, is fond of Bertram. Her brow darkened.

'You don't touch a nephew of mine.'

'I am going to break every bone in his body.'

'You aren't going to do anything of the sort. The idea! . . . Here, you!'

She raised her voice sharply as she spoke the concluding words, and what had caused her to do so was the fact that Spode at this moment made a sudden move in my direction.

Considering the manner in which his eyes were gleaming and his moustache bristling, not to mention the gritting teeth and the sinister twiddling of the fingers, it was a move which might have been expected to send me flitting away like an adagio dancer. And had it occurred somewhat earlier, it would undoubtedly have done so. But I did not flit. I stood where I was, calm and collected. Whether I folded my arms or not, I cannot recall, but I remember that there was a faint, amused smile upon my lips.

For that brief monosyllable 'you' had accomplished what a quarter of an hour's research had been unable to do – viz. the unsealing of the fount of memory. Jeeve's words came back to me with a rush. One moment, the mind a blank: the next, the fount of memory spouting like nobody's business. It often happens this way.

'One minute, Spode,' I said quietly. 'Just one minute. Before you start getting above yourself, it may interest you to learn that I know all about Eulalie.'

It was stupendous. I felt like one of those chaps who press buttons and explode mines. If it hadn't been that my implicit faith in Jeeves had led me to expect solid results, I should have been astounded at the effect of this pronouncement on the man. You could see that it had got right in amongst him and churned him up like an egg whisk. He recoiled as if he had run into something hot, and a look of horror and alarm spread slowly over his face.

The whole situation recalled irresistibly to my mind something that had happened to me once up at Oxford, when the heart was young. It was during Eights Week, and I was sauntering on the river-bank with a girl named something that has slipped my mind, when there was a sound of barking and a large, hefty dog came galloping up, full of beans and buck and obviously intent on mayhem. And I was just commending my soul to God, and feeling that this was where the old flannel trousers got about thirty bob's worth of value bitten out of them, when the girl, waiting till she saw the whites of its eyes, with extraordinary presence of mind suddenly opened a coloured Japanese umbrella in the animal's face. Upon which, it did three back somersaults and retired into private life.

Except that he didn't do any back somersaults, Roderick Spode's reactions were almost identical with those of this nonplussed hound. For a moment, he just stood gaping. Then he said 'Oh?' Then his lips twisted into what I took to be his idea of a conciliatory smile. After that, he swallowed six – or it may have been seven – times, as if he had taken aboard a fish bone. Finally, he spoke. And when he did so, it was the nearest thing to a cooing dove that I have ever heard – and an exceptionally mild-mannered dove, at that.

'Oh, do you?' he said.

'I do,' I replied.

If he had asked me what I knew about her, he would have had me stymied, but he didn't.

'Er – how did you find out?'

'I have my methods.'

'Oh?' he said.

'Ah,' I replied, and there was silence again for a moment.

I wouldn't have believed it possible for so tough an egg to sidle obsequiously, but that was how he now sidled up to me. There was a pleading look in his eyes.

'I hope you will keep this to yourself, Wooster? You will keep it to yourself, won't you, Wooster?'

'I will –'

'Thank you, Wooster.'

'– provided,' I continued, 'that we have no more of these extraordinary exhibitions on your part of – what's the word?'

He sidled a bit closer.

'Of course, of course. I'm afraid I have been acting rather hastily.' He reached out a hand and smoothed my sleeve. 'Did I rumple your coat, Wooster? I'm sorry. I forgot myself. It shall not happen again.'

'It had better not. Good Lord! Grabbing fellows' coats and

saying you're going to break chaps' bones. I never heard of such a thing.'

'I know, I know. I was wrong.'

'You bet you were wrong. I shall be very sharp on that sort of thing in the future, Spode.'

'Yes, yes, I understand.'

'I have not been at all satisfied with your behaviour since I came to this house. The way you were looking at me at dinner. You may think people don't notice these things, but they do.'

'Of course, of course.'

'And calling me a miserable worm.'

'I'm sorry I called you a miserable worm, Wooster. I spoke without thinking.'

'Always think, Spode. Well, that is all. You may withdraw.'

'Good night, Wooster.'

'Good night, Spode.'

He hurried out with bowed head, and I turned to Aunt Dahlia, who was making noises like a motor-bicycle in the background. She gazed at me with the air of one who has been seeing visions. And I suppose the whole affair must have been extraordinarily impressive to the casual bystander.

'Well, I'll be – '

Here she paused – fortunately, perhaps, for she is a woman who, when strongly moved, sometimes has a tendency to forget that she is no longer in the hunting-field, and the verb, had she given it utterance, might have proved a bit too fruity for mixed company.

'Bertie! What was all that about?'

I waved a nonchalant hand.

'Oh, I just put it across the fellow. Merely asserting myself. One has to take a firm line with chaps like Spode.'

'Who is this Eulalie?'

'Ah, there you've got me. For information on that point you will have to apply to Jeeves. And it won't be any good, because the club rules are rigid and members are permitted to go only just so far. Jeeves,' I went on, giving credit where credit was due, as is my custom, 'came to me some little while back and told me that I had only to inform Spode that I knew all about Eulalie to cause him to curl up like a burnt feather. And a burnt feather, as you have seen, was precisely what he did curl up like. As to who the above may be, I haven't the foggiest. All that I can say is that she is a chunk of Spode's past – and, one fears, a highly discreditable one.'

I sighed, for I was not unmoved.

'One can fill in the picture for oneself, I think, Aunt Dahlia? The trusting girl who learned too late that men betray . . . the little bundle . . . the last mournful walk to the riverbank . . . the splash . . . the bubbling cry . . . I fancy so, don't you? No wonder the man pales beneath the tan a bit at the idea of the world knowing of that.'

Aunt Dahlia drew a deep breath. A sort of Soul's Awakening look had come into her face.

'Good old blackmail! You can't beat it. I've always said so and I always shall. It works like magic in an emergency. Bertie,' she cried, 'do you realize what this means?'

'Means, old relative?'

'Now that you have got the goods on Spode, the only obstacle to your sneaking that cow-creamer has been removed. You can stroll down and collect it tonight.'

I shook my head regretfully. I had been afraid she was going to take that view of the matter. It compelled me to dash the cup of joy from her lips, always an unpleasant thing to have to do to an aunt who dandled one on her knee as a child.

'No,' I said. 'There you're wrong. There, if you will excuse me saying so, you are talking like a fathead. Spode may have ceased to be a danger to traffic, but that doesn't alter the fact that Stiffy still has the notebook. Before taking any steps in the direction of the cow-creamer, I have got to get it.'

'But why? Oh, but I suppose you haven't heard. Madeline Bassett has broken off her engagement with Spink-Bottle. She told me so in the strictest confidence just now. Well, then. The snag before was that young Stephanie might cause the engagement to be broken by showing old Bassett the book. But if it's broken already – '

I shook the bean again.

'My dear old faulty reasoner,' I said, 'you miss the gist by a mile. As long as Stiffy retains that book, it cannot be shown to Madeline Bassett. And only by showing it to Madeline Bassett can Gussie prove to her that his motive in pinching Stiffy's legs was not what she supposed. And only by proving to her that

his motive was not what she supposed can he square himself
and effect a reconciliation. And only if he squares himself and
effects a reconciliation can I avoid the distasteful necessity of
having to marry this bally Bassett myself. No, I repeat. Before
doing anything else, I have got to have that book.'

My pitiless analysis of the situation had its effect. It was plain
from her manner that she had got the strength. For a space, she
sat chewing the lower lip in silence, frowning like an aunt who
has drained the bitter cup.

'Well, how are you going to get it?'

'I propose to search her room.'

'What's the good of that?'

'My dear old relative, Gussie's investigations have already
revealed that the thing is not on her person. Reasoning closely,
we reach the conclusion that it must be in her room.'

'Yes, but, you poor ass, whereabouts in her room? It may be
anywhere, And wherever it is, you can be jolly sure it's carefully
hidden. I suppose you hadn't thought of that.'

As a matter of fact, I hadn't, and I imagine that my sharp
'Oh ah!' must have revealed this, for she snorted like a bison
at the water trough.

'No doubt you thought it would be lying out on the dressing
table. All right, search her room, if you like. There's no actual
harm in it, I suppose. It will give you something to do and keep
you out of the public houses. I, meanwhile, will be going off
and starting to think of something sensible. It's time one of us
did.'

Pausing at the mantelpiece to remove a china horse which
stood there and hurl it to the floor and jump on it, she passed
along. And I, somewhat discomposed, for I had thought I had
got everything neatly planned out and it was a bit of a jar to
find that I hadn't, sat down and began to bend the brain.

The longer I bent it the more I was forced to admit that the
flesh and blood had been right. Looking round this room of my
own, I could see at a glance a dozen places where, if I had had
a small object to hide like a leather-covered notebook full of
criticisms of old Bassett's method of drinking soup, I could have
done so with ease. Presumably, the same conditions prevailed
in Stiffy's lair. In going thither, therefore, I should be embarking
on a quest well calculated to baffle the brightest bloodhound,

let alone a chap who from childhood up had always been rotten at hunt-the-slipper.

To give the brain a rest before having another go at the problem, I took up my goose-flesher again. And, by Jove, I hadn't read more than half a page when I uttered a cry. I had come upon a significant passage.

'Jeeves,' I said, addressing him as he entered a moment later, 'I have come upon a significant passage.'

'Sir?'

I saw that I had been too abrupt, and that footnotes would be required.

'In this thriller I'm reading,' I explained. 'But wait. Before showing it to you, I would like to pay you a stately tribute on the accuracy of your information *re* Spode. A hearty vote of thanks, Jeeves. You said the name Eulalie would make him wilt, and it did. Spode, *qua* menace . . . is it *qua?*'

'Yes, sir. Quite correct.'

'I thought so. Well, Spode, *qua* menace, is a spent egg. He has dropped out and ceased to function.'

'That is very gratifying, sir.'

'Most. But we are still faced by this Becher's Brook, that young Stiffy continues in possession of the notebook. That notebook, Jeeves, must be located and re-snitched before we are free to move in any other direction. Aunt Dahlia has just left in despondent mood, because, while she concedes that the damned thing is almost certainly concealed in the little pimple's sleeping quarters, she sees no hope of fingers being able to be laid upon it. She says it may be anywhere and is undoubtedly carefully hidden.'

'That is the difficulty, sir.'

'Quite. But that is where this significant passage comes in. It points the way and sets the feet upon the right path. I'll read it to you. The detective is speaking to his pal, and the "they" refers to some bounders at present unidentified, who have been ransacking a girl's room, hoping to find the missing jewels. Listen attentively, Jeeves. "They seem to have looked everywhere, my dear Postlethwaite, except in the one place where they might have expected to find something. Amateurs, Postlethwaite, rank amateurs. They never thought of the top of the cupboard, the thing any experienced crook thinks of at once, because" – note carefully what follows – "because he knows it is every woman's favourite hiding-place." '

I eyed him keenly.

'You see the profound significance of that, Jeeves?'

'If I interpret your meaning aright, sir, you are suggesting the Mr Fink-Nottle's notebook may be concealed at the top of the cupboard in Miss Byng's apartment?'

'Not "may", Jeeves, "must". I don't see how it can be conce-aled anywhere else but. That detective is no fool. If he says a thing is so, it is so. I have the utmost confidence in the fellow, and am prepared to follow his lead without question.'

'But surely, sir, you are not proposing – '

'Yes, I am. I'm going to do it immediately. Stiffy has gone to the Working Men's Institute, and won't be back for ages. It's absurd to suppose that a gaggle of Village Mothers are going to be sated with coloured slides of the Holy Land, plus piano accompaniment, in anything under two hours. So now is the time to operate while the coast is clear. Gird up your loins, Jeeves, and accompany me.'

'Well, really, sir – '

'And don't say "Well, really, sir". I have had occasion to rebuke you before for this habit of yours of saying "Well, really, sir" in a soupy sort of voice, when I indicate some strategic line of action. What I want from you is less of the "Well, really, sir" and more of the buckling-to spirit. Think feudally, Jeeves. Do you know Stiffy's room?'

'Yes, sir.'

'Then Ho for it!'

I cannot say, despite the courageous dash which I had exhi-bited in the above slab of dialogue, that it was in any too bobbish a frame of mind that I made my way to our destination. In fact, the nearer I got, the less bobbish I felt. It had been just the same the time I allowed myself to be argued by Roberta Wickham into going and puncturing that hot-water bottle. I hate these surreptitious prowlings. Bertram Wooster is a man who likes to go through the world with his chin up and both feet on the ground, not to sneak about on tiptoe with his spine tying itself into reefer knots.

It was precisely because I had anticipated some such reactions that I had been so anxious that Jeeves should accompany me and lend moral support, and I found myself wishing that he would buck up and lend a bit more than he was doing. Willing service and selfless co-operation were what I had hoped for, and he was not giving me them. His manner from the very start betrayed an aloof disapproval. He seemed to be dissociating himself entirely from the proceedings, and I resented it.

Owing to this aloofness on his part and this resentment on mine, we made the journey in silence, and it was in silence that we entered the room and switched on the light.

The first impression I received on giving the apartment the once-over was that for a young shrimp of her shaky moral outlook Stiffy had been done pretty well in the matter of sleeping accommodation. Totleigh Towers was one of those country houses which had been built at a time when people planning a little nest had the idea that a bedroom was not a bedroom unless you could give an informal dance for about fifty couples in it, and this sanctum could have accommodated a dozen Stiffys. In the rays of the small electric light up in the ceiling, the bally thing seemed to stretch for miles in every direction, and the thought that if that detective had not called his shots correctly, Gussie's notebook might be concealed anywhere in these great spaces, was a chilling one.

I was standing there, hoping for the best, when my meditations were broken in upon by an odd, gargling sort of noise, something like static and something like distant thunder, and to cut a long story short this proved to proceed from the larynx of the dog Bartholomew.

He was standing on the bed, stropping his front paws on the coverlet, and so easy was it to read the message in his eyes that we acted like two minds with but a single thought. At the exact moment when I soared like an eagle onto the chest of drawers, Jeeves was skimming like a swallow onto the top of the cupboard. The animal hopped from the bed and, advancing into the middle of the room, took a seat, breathing through the nose with a curious whistling sound, and looking at us from under his eyebrows like a Scottish elder rebuking sin from the pulpit.

And there for a while the matter rested.

# =8=

JEEVES was the first to break a rather strained silence.

'The book does not appear to be here, sir.'

'Eh?'

'I have searched the top of the cupboard, sir, but I have not found the book.'

It may be that my reply erred a trifle on the side of acerbity. My narrow escape from those slavering jaws had left me a bit edgy.

'Blast the book, Jeeves! What about this dog?'

'Yes, sir.'

'What do you mean – "Yes, sir"?'

'I was endeavouring to convey that I appreciate the point which you have raised, sir. The animal's unexpected appearance unquestionably presents a problem. While he continues to maintain his existing attitude, it will not be easy for us to prosecute the search for Mr Fink-Nottle's notebook. Our freedom of action will necessarily be circumscribed.'

'Then what's to be done?'

'It is difficult to say, sir.'

'You have no ideas?'

'No, sir.'

I could have said something pretty bitter and stinging at this – I don't know what, but something – but I refrained. I realized that it was rather tough on the man, outstanding though his gifts were, to expect him to ring the bell every time, without fail. No doubt that brilliant inspiration of his which had led to my signal victory over the forces of darkness as represented by R. Spode had taken it out of him a good deal, rendering the brain for the nonce a bit flaccid. One could but wait and hope that the machinery would soon get going again, enabling him to seek new high levels of achievement.

And, I felt as I continued to turn the position of affairs over in my mind, the sooner, the better, for it was plain that nothing was going to budge this canine excrescence except an offensive on a major scale, dashingly conceived and skilfully carried out. I don't think I have ever seen a dog who conveyed more vividly the impression of being rooted to the spot and prepared to stay there till the cows – or, in this case, his proprietress – came home. And what I was going to say to Stiffy if she returned and found me roosting on her chest of drawers was something I had not yet thought out in any exactness of detail.

Watching the animal sitting there like a bump on a log, I soon found myself chafing a good deal. I remember Freddie Widgeon, who was once chased onto the top of a wardrobe by an Alsatian during a country house visit, telling me that what he had disliked most about the thing was the indignity of it all – the blow to the proud spirit, if you know what I mean – the feeling, in fine, that he, the Heir of the Ages, as you might say, was camping out on a wardrobe at the whim of a bally dog.

It was the same with me. One doesn't want to make a song and dance about one's ancient lineage, of course, but after all the Woosters did come over with the Conqueror and were extremely pally with him: and a fat lot of good it is coming over with Conquerors, if you're simply going to wind up by being given the elbow by Aberdeen terriers.

These reflections had the effect of making me rather peevish, and I looked down somewhat sourly at the animal.

'I call it monstrous, Jeeves,' I said, voicing my train of thought, 'that this dog should be lounging about in a bedroom. Most unhygienic.'

'Yes, sir.'

'Scotties are smelly, even the best of them. You will recall how my Aunt Agatha's McIntosh niffed to heaven while enjoying my hospitality. I frequently mentioned it to you.'

'Yes, sir.'

'And this one is even riper. He should obviously have been bedded out in the stables. Upon my Sam, what with Scotties in Stiffy's room and newts in Gussie's, Totleigh Towers is not far short of being a lazar house.'

'No, sir.'

'And consider the matter from another angle,' I said, warming to my theme. 'I refer to the danger of keeping a dog of this nature and disposition in a bedroom, where it can spring out ravening on anyone who enters. You and I happen to be able to take care of ourselves in an emergency such as has arisen, but suppose we had been some highly strung house-maid.'

'Yes, sir.'

'I can see her coming into the room to turn down the bed. I picture her as a rather fragile girl with big eyes and a timid expression. She crosses the threshold. She approaches the bed. And out leaps this man-eating dog. One does not like to dwell upon the sequel.'

'No, sir.'

I frowned.

'I wish,' I said, 'that instead of sitting there saying "Yes, sir" and "No, sir", Jeeves, you would do something.'

'But what can I do, sir?'

'You can get action, Jeeves. That is what is required here – sharp, decisive action. I wonder if you recall a visit we once paid to the residence of my Aunt Agatha at Woollam Chersey in the county of Herts. To refresh your memory, it was the occasion on which, in company with the Right Honourable A. B. Filmer, the Cabinet Minister, I was chivvied onto the roof of a shack on the island in the lake by an angry swan.'

'I recall the incident vividly, sir.'

'So do I. And the picture most deeply imprinted on my mental retina – is that the correct expression?'

'Yes, sir.'

'– is of you facing that swan in the most intrepid "You-can't-do-that-there-here" manner and bunging a raincoat over its head, thereby completely dishing its aims and plans and compelling it to revise its whole strategy from the bottom up. It was a beautiful bit of work. I don't know when I have seen a finer.'

'Thank you, sir. I am glad if I gave satisfaction.'

'You certainly, did, Jeeves, in heaping measure. And what crossed my mind was that a similar operation would make this dog feel pretty silly.'

'No doubt, sir. But I have no raincoat.'

'Then I would advise seeing what you can do with a sheet. And in case you are wondering if a sheet would work as well, I may tell you that just before you came to my room I had had admirable results with one in the case of Mr Spode. He just couldn't seem to get out of the thing.'

'Indeed, sir?'

'I assure you, Jeeves. You could wish no better weapon than a sheet. There are some on the bed.'

'Yes, sir. On the bed.'

There was a pause. I was loath to wrong the man, but if this wasn't a *nolle prosequi*, I didn't know one when I saw one. The distant and unenthusiastic look on his face told me that I was right, and I endeavoured to sting his pride, rather as Gussie in our *pourparlers* in the matter of Spode had endeavoured to sting mine.

'Are you afraid of a tiny little dog, Jeeves?'

He corrected me respectfully, giving it as his opinion that the undersigned was not a tiny little dog, but well above the average in muscular development. In particular, he drew my attention to the animal's teeth.

I reassured him.

'I think you would find that if you were to make a sudden spring, his teeth would not enter into the matter. You could leap onto the bed, snatch up a sheet, roll him up in it before he knew what was happening, and there we would be.'

'Yes, sir.'

'Well, are you going to make a sudden spring?'

'No, sir.'

A rather stiff silence ensued, during which the dog Bartholomew continued to gaze at me unwinkingly, and once more I found myself noticing – and resenting – the superior, sanctimonious expression on his face. Nothing can ever render the experience of being treed on top of a chest of drawers by an Aberdeen terrier pleasant, but it seemed to me that the least you can expect on such an occasion is that the animal will meet you halfway and not drop salt into the wound by looking at you as if he were asking if you were saved.

It was in the hope of wiping this look off his face that I now made a gesture. There was a stump of candle standing in the parent candlestick beside me, and I threw this at the little blighter. He ate it with every appearance of relish, took time out briefly in order to be sick, and resumed his silent stare. And at this moment the door opened and in came Stiffy – hours before I had expected her.

The first thing that impressed itself upon one on seeing her was that she was not in her customary buoyant spirits. Stiffy, as a rule, is a girl who moves jauntily from spot to spot – youthful elasticity is, I believe, the expression – but she entered now with a slow and dragging step like a Volga boatman. She cast a dull eye at us, and after a brief 'Hallo, Bertie. Hallo, Jeeves,' seemed to dismiss us from her thoughts. She made for the dressing-table and having removed her hat, sat looking at herself in the mirror with sombre eyes. It was plain that for some reason the soul had got a flat tyre, and seeing that unless I opened the conversation there was going to be one of those awkward pauses, I did so.

'What ho, Stiffy.'

'Hallo.'

'Nice evening. Your dog's just been sick on the carpet.'

All this, of course, was merely by way of leading into the main theme, which I now proceeded to broach.

'Well, Stiffy, I suppose you're surprised to see us here?'

'No, I'm not. Have you been looking for that book?'

'Why, yes. That's right. We have. Though, as a matter of fact, we hadn't got really started. We were somewhat impeded by the bow-wow.' (Keeping it light, you notice. Always the best way on these occasions.) 'He took our entrance in the wrong spirit.'

'Oh?'

'Yes. Would it be asking too much of you to attach a stout lead to his collar, thus making the world safe for democracy?'

'Yes, it would.'

'Surely you wish to save the lives of two fellow creatures?'

'No, I don't. Not if they're men. I loathe all men. I hope Bartholomew bites you to the bone.'

I saw that little was to be gained by approaching the matter from this angle. I switched to another *point d'appui*.

'I wasn't expecting you,' I said. 'I thought you had gone to the Working Men's Institute, to tickle the ivories in accompaniment to old Stinker's coloured lecture on the Holy Land.'

'I did.'

'Back early, aren't you?'

'Yes. The lecture was off. Harold broke the slides.'

'Oh?' I said, feeling that he was just the sort of chap who would break slides. 'How did that happen?'

131

She passed a listless hand over the brow of the dog Bartholomew, who had stepped up to fraternize.

'He dropped them.'

'What made him do that?'

'He had a shock, when I broke off our engagement.'

'What!'

'Yes.' A gleam came into her eyes, as if she were reliving unpleasant scenes, and her voice took on the sort of metallic sharpness which I have so often noticed in that of my Aunt Agatha during our get-togethers. Her listlessness disappeared, and for the first time she spoke with a girlish vehemence. 'I got to Harold's cottage, and I went in, and after we'd talked of this and that for a while, I said "When are you going to pinch Eustace Oates's helmet, darling?" And would you believe it, he looked at me in a horrible, sheepish, hang-dog way and said that he had been wrestling with his conscience in the hope of getting its OK, but that it simply wouldn't hear of him pinching Eustace Oates's helmet, so it was all off. "Oh?" I said, drawing myself up. "All off, is it? Well, so is our engagement," and he dropped a double handful of coloured slides of the Holy Land, and I came away.'

'You don't mean that?'

'Yes, I do. And I consider that I have had a very lucky escape. If he is the sort of man who is going to refuse me every little thing I ask, I'm glad I found it out in time. I'm delighted about the whole thing.'

Here, with a sniff like the tearing of a piece of calico, she buried the bean in her hands, and broke into what are called uncontrollable sobs.

Well, dashed painful, of course, and you wouldn't be far wrong in saying that I ached in sympathy with her distress. I don't suppose there is a man in the W1 postal district of London more readily moved by a woman's grief than myself. For two pins, if I'd been a bit nearer, I would have patted her head. But though there is this kindly streak in the Woosters, there is also a practical one, and it didn't take me long to spot the bright side to all this.

'Well, that's too bad,' I said. 'The heart bleeds. Eh, Jeeves?'

'Distinctly, sir.'

'Yes, by Jove, it bleeds profusely, and I suppose all that one can say is that one hopes that Time, the great healer, will eventually stitch up the wound. However, as in these circs you will, of course, no longer have any use for that notebook of Gussie's, how about handing it over?'

'What?'

'I said that if your projected union with Stinker is off, you will, of course, no longer wish to keep that notebook of Gussie's among your effects – '

'Oh, don't bother me about notebooks now.'

'No, no, quite. Not for the world. All I'm saying is that if – at your leisure – choose the time to suit yourself – you wouldn't mind slipping it across – '

'Oh, all right. I can't give it you now, though. It isn't here.'

'Not here?'

'No. I put it . . . Hallo, what's that?'

What had caused her to suspend her remarks just at the point when they were becoming fraught with interest was a sudden tapping sound. A sort of tap-tap-tap. It came from the direction of the window.

This room of Stiffy's, I should have mentioned, in addition to being equipped with four-poster beds, valuable pictures, richly upholstered chairs and all sorts of things far too good for a young squirt who went about biting the hand that had fed her at luncheon at its flat by causing it the utmost alarm and despondency, had a balcony outside its window. It was from this balcony that the tapping sound proceeded, leading one to infer that someone stood without.

That the dog Bartholomew had reached this conclusion was shown immediately by the lissom agility with which he leaped at the window and started trying to bite his way through. Up till this moment he had shown himself a dog of strong reserves, content merely to sit and stare, but now he was full of strange oaths. And I confess that as I watched his champing and listened to his observations I congratulated myself on the promptitude with which I had breezed onto that chest of drawers. A bone-crusher, if ever one drew breath, this Bartholomew Byng. Reluctant as one always is to criticize the acts of an all-wise Providence, I was dashed if I could see why a dog of his size should have been fitted out with the jaws and teeth of a crocodile. Still, too late of course to do anything about it now.

Stiffy, after that moment of surprised inaction which was to be expected in a girl who hears tapping sounds at her window, had risen and gone to investigate. I couldn't see a thing from where I was sitting, but she was evidently more fortunately placed. As she drew back the curtain, I saw her clap a hand to her throat, like someone in a play, and a sharp cry escaped her, audible even above the ghastly row which was proceeding from the lips of the frothing terrier.

'Harold!' she yipped, and putting two and two together I gathered that the bird on the balcony must be old Stinker Pinker, my favourite curate.

It was with a sort of joyful yelp, like that of a woman getting together with her demon lover, that the little geezer had spoken his name, but it was evident that reflection now told her that after what had occurred between this man of God and herself this was not quite the tone. Her next words were uttered with a cold, hostile intonation. I was able to hear them, because she had stooped and picked up the bounder Bartholomew, clamping a hand over his mouth to still his cries – a thing I wouldn't have done for a goodish bit of money.

'What do you want?'

Owing to the lull in Bartholomew, the stuff was coming through well now. Stinker's voice was a bit muffled by the intervening sheet of glass, but I got it nicely.

'Stiffy!'

'Well?'

'Can I come in?'

'No, you can't.'

'But I've brought you something.'

A sudden yowl of ecstasy broke from the young pimple.

'Harold! You angel lamb! You haven't got it, after all?'

'Yes.'

'Oh, Harold, my dream of joy!'

She opened the window with eager fingers, and a cold draught came in and played about my ankles. It was not followed, as I had supposed it would be, by old Stinker. He continued to hang about on the outskirts, and a moment later his motive in doing so was made clear.

'I say, Stiffy, old girl, is that hound of yours under control?'

'Yes, rather. Wait a minute.'

She carried the animal to the cupboard and bunged him in, closing the door behind him. And from the fact that no further bulletins were received from him, I imagine he curled up and went to sleep. These Scotties are philosophers, well able to adapt themselves to changing conditions. They càn take it as well as dish it out.

'All clear, angel,' she said, and returned to the window, arriving there just in time to be folded in the embrace of the Incoming Stinker.

It was not easy for some moments to sort out the male from the female ingredients in the ensuing tangle, but eventually he disengaged himself and I was able to see him steadily and see him whole. And when I did so, I noticed that there was rather more of him than there had been when I had seen him last. Country butter and the easy life these curates lead had added a pound or two to an always impressive figure. To find the lean, finely trained Stinker of my nonage, I felt that one would have to catch him in Lent.

But the change in him, I soon perceived, was purely superficial. The manner in which he now tripped over a rug and cannoned into an occasional table, upsetting it with all the old thoroughness, showed me that at heart he still remained the same galumphing man with two left feet, who had always been constitutionally incapable of walking through the great Gobi desert without knocking something over.

Stinker's was a face which in the old College days had glowed with health and heartiness. The health was still there – he looked like a clerical beetroot – but of heartiness at this moment one noted rather a shortage. His features were drawn, as if Conscience were gnawing at his vitals. And no doubt it was, for in one hand he was carrying the helmet which I had last observed perched on the dome of Constable Eustace Oates. With a quick, impulsive movement, like that of a man trying to rid himself of a dead fish, he thrust it at Stiffy, who received it with a soft, tender squeal of ecstasy.

'I brought it,' he said dully.

'Oh, Harold!'

'I brought your gloves, too. You left them behind. At least, I've brought one of them. I couldn't find the other.'

135

'Thank you, darling. But never mind about gloves, my wonder man. Tell me everything that happened.'

He was about to do so, when he paused, and I saw that he was staring at me with a rather feverish look in his eyes. Then he turned and stared at Jeeves. One could read what was passing in his mind. He was debating within himself whether we were real, or whether the nervous strain to which he had been subjected was causing him to see things.

'Stiffy,' he said, lowering his voice, 'don't look now, but is there something on top of that chest of drawers?'

'Eh? Oh, yes, that's Bertie Wooster.'

'Oh, it is?' said Stinker, brightening visibly. 'I wasn't quite sure. Is that somebody on the cupboard, too?'

'That's Bertie's man Jeeves.'

'How do you do?' said Stinker.

'How do you do, sir?' said Jeeves.

We climbed down, and I came forward with outstretched hand, anxious to get the reunion going.

'What ho, Stinker.'

'Hallo, Bertie.'

'Long time since we met.'

'It is a bit, isn't it?'

'I hear you're a curate now.'

'Yes, that's right.'

'How are the souls?'

'Oh, fine, thanks.'

There was a pause, and I suppose I would have gone on to ask him if he had seen anything of old So-and-so lately or knew what had become of old What's-his-name, as one does when the conversation shows a tendency to drag on these occasions of ancient College chums meeting again after long separation, but before I could do so, Stiffy, who had been crooning over the helmet like a mother over the cot of her sleeping child, stuck it on her head with a merry chuckle, and the spectacle appeared to bring back to Stinker like a slosh in the waistcoat the realization of what he had done. You've probably heard the expression 'The wretched man seemed fully conscious of his position.' That was Harold Pinker at this juncture. He shied like a startled horse, knocked over another table, tottered to a chair, knocked that over, picked it up and sat down, burying his face in his hands.

'If the Infants' Bible Class should hear of this!' he said, shuddering strongly.

I saw what he meant. A man in his position has to watch his step. What people expect from a curate is a zealous performance of his parochial duties. They like to think of him as a chap who preaches about Hivites, Jebusites and what not, speaks the word in season to the backslider, conveys soup and blankets to the deserving bed-ridden and all that sort of thing. When they find him de-helmeting policemen, they look at one another with the raised eyebrow of censure, and ask themselves if he is quite the right man for the job. That was what was bothering Stinker and preventing him being the old effervescent curate whose jolly laugh had made the last School Treat go with such a bang.

Stiffy endeavoured to hearten him.

'I'm sorry, darling. If it upsets you, I'll put it away.' She crossed to the chest of drawers, and did so. 'But why it should,' she said, returning, 'I can't imagine. I should have thought it would have made you so proud and happy. And now tell me everything that happened.'

'Yes,' I said. 'One would like the first-hand story.'

'Did you creep up behind him like a leopard?' asked Stiffy.

'Of course he did,' I said, admonishing the silly young shrimp. 'You don't suppose he pranced up in full view of the fellow? No doubt you trailed him with unremitting snakiness, eh, Stinker, and did the deed when he was relaxing on a stile or somewhere over a quiet pipe?'

Stinker sat staring straight before him, that drawn look still on his face.

'He wasn't on the stile. He was leaning against it. After you left me, Stiffy, I went for a walk to think things over, and I had just crossed Plunkett's meadow and was going to climb the stile into the next one, when I saw something dark in front of me, and there he was.'

I nodded. I could visualize the scene.

'I hope,' I said, 'that you remembered to give the forward shove before the upwards lift?'

'It wasn't necessary. The helmet was not on his head. He had taken it off and put it on the ground. And I just crept up and grabbed it.'

I started, pursing the lips a bit.

'Not quite playing the game, Stinker.'

'Yes, it was,' said Stiffy, with a good deal of warmth. 'I call it very clever of him.'

I could not recede from my position. At the Drones, we hold strong views on these things.

'There is a right way and a wrong way of pinching policemen's helmets,' I said firmly.

'You're talking absolute nonsense,' said Stiffy. 'I think you were wonderful, darling.'

I shrugged my shoulders.

'How do you feel about it, Jeeves?'

'I scarcely think that it would be fitting for me to offer an opinion, sir.'

'No,' said Stiffy. 'And it jolly well isn't fitting for you to offer an opinion, young pie-faced Bertie Wooster. Who do you think you are,' she demanded, with renewed warmth, 'coming strolling into a girl's bedroom, sticking on dog about the right way and wrong way of pinching helmets? It isn't as if you were such a wonder at it yourself, considering that you got collared and hauled up next morning at Bosher Street, where you had to grovel to Uncle Watkyn in the hope of getting off with a fine.'

I took this up promptly.

'I did not grovel to the old disease. My manner throughout was calm and dignified, like that of a Red Indian at the stake. And when you speak of me hoping to get off with a fine – '

Here Stiffy interrupted, to beg me to put a sock in it.

'Well, all I was about to say was that the sentence stunned me. I felt so strongly that it was a case for a mere reprimand. However, this is beside the point – which is that Stinker in the recent encounter did not play to the rules of the game. I consider his behaviour morally tantamount to shooting a sitting bird. I cannot alter my opinion.'

'And I can't alter my opinion that you have no business in my bedroom. What are you doing here?'

'Yes, I was wondering that,' said Stinker, touching on the point for the first time. And I could see, of course, how he might quite well be surprised at finding this mob scene in what he had supposed the exclusive sleeping apartment of the loved one.

I eyed her sternly.

'You know what I am doing here. I told you. I came – '

'Oh, yes. Bertie came to borrow a book, darling. But' – here her eyes lingered on mine in a cold and sinister manner – 'I'm afraid I can't let him have it just yet. I have not finished with it myself. By the way,' she continued, still holding me with that compelling stare, 'Bertie says he will be delighted to help us with that cow-creamer scheme.'

'Will you, old man?' said Stinker eagerly.

'Of course he will,' said Stiffy. 'He was saying only just now what a pleasure it would be.'

'You won't mind me hitting you on the nose?'

'Of course he won't.'

'You see, we must have blood. Blood is of the essence.'

'Of course, of course, of course,' said Stiffy. Her manner was impatient. She seemed in a hurry to terminate the scene. 'He quite understands that.'

'When would you feel like doing it, Bertie?'

'He feels like doing it tonight,' said Stiffy. 'No sense in putting things off. Be waiting outside at midnight, darling. Everybody will have gone to bed by then. Midnight will suit you, Bertie? Yes, Bertie says it will suit him splendidly. So that's all settled. And now you really must be going, precious. If somebody came in and found you here, they might think it odd. Good night, darling.'

'Good night, darling.'

'Good night, darling.'

'Good night, darling.'

'Wait!' I said, cutting in on these revolting exchanges, for I wished to make a last appeal to Stinker's finer feelings.

'He can't wait. He's got to go. Remember, angel. On the spot, ready to the last button, at twelve pip emma. Good night, darling.'

'Good night, darling.'

'Good night, darling.'

'Good night, darling.'

They passed onto the balcony, the nauseous endearments

receding in the distance, and I turned to Jeeves, my face stern and hard.

'Faugh, Jeeves!'

'Sir?'

'I said "Faugh!" I am a pretty broadminded man, but this has shocked me – I may say to the core. It is not so much the behaviour of Stiffy that I find so revolting. She is a female, and the tendency of females to be unable to distinguish between right and wrong is notorious. But that Harold Pinker, a clerk in Holy Orders, a chap who buttons his collar at the back, should countenance this thing appals me. He knows she has got that book. He knows that she is holding me up with it. But does he insist on her returning it? No! He lends himself to the raw work with open enthusiasm. A nice look-out for the Totleigh-in-the-Wold flock, trying to keep on the straight and narrow path with a shepherd like that! A pretty example he sets to this Infants' Bible Class of which he speaks! A few years of sitting at the feet of Harold Pinker and imbibing his extraordinary views on morality and ethics, and every bally child on the list will be serving a long stretch at Wormwood Scrubs for blackmail.'

I paused, much moved. A bit out of breath, too.

'I think you do the gentleman an injustice, sir.'

'Eh?'

'I am sure that he is under the impression that your acquiescence in the scheme is due entirely to goodness of heart and a desire to assist an old friend.'

'You think she hasn't told him about the notebook?'

'I am convinced of it, sir. I could gather that from the lady's manner.'

'I didn't notice anything about her manner.'

'When you were about to mention the notebook, it betrayed embarrassment, sir. She feared lest Mr Pinker might enquire into the matter and, learning the facts, compel her to make restitution.'

'By Jove, Jeeves, I believe you're right.'

I reviewed the recent scene. Yes, he was perfectly correct. Stiffy, though one of those girls who enjoy in equal quantities the gall of an army mule and the calm *insouciance* of a fish on a slab of ice, had unquestionably gone up in the air a bit when

I had seemed about to explain to Stinker my motives for being in the room. I recalled the feverish way in which she had hustled him out, like a small bouncer at a pub ejecting a large customer.

'Egad, Jeeves!' I said, impressed.

There was a muffled crashing sound from the direction of the balcony. A few moments later, Stiffy returned.

'Harold fell off the ladder,' she explained, laughing heartily. 'Well, Bertie, you've got the programme all clear? Tonight's the night!'

I drew out a gasper and lit it.

'Wait!' I said. 'Not so fast. Just one moment, young Stiffy.'

The ring of quiet authority in my tone seemed to take her aback. She blinked twice, and looked at me questioningly, while I, drawing in a cargo of smoke, expelled it nonchalantly through the nostrils.

'Just one moment,' I repeated.

In the narrative of my earlier adventures with Augustus Fink-Nottle at Brinkley Court, with which you may or may not be familiar, I mentioned that I had once read a historical novel about a Buck or Beau or some such cove who, when it became necessary for him to put people where they belonged, was in the habit of laughing down from lazy eyelids and flicking a speck of dust from the irreproachable Mechlin lace at his wrists. And I think I stated that I had had excellent results from modelling myself on this bird.

I did so now.

'Stiffy,' I said, laughing down from lazy eyelids and flicking a speck of cigarette ash from my irreproachable cuff, 'I will trouble you to disgorge that book.'

The questioning look became intensified. I could see that all this was perplexing her. She had supposed that she had Bertram nicely ground beneath the iron heel, and here he was, popping up like a two-year-old, full of the fighting spirit.

'What do you mean?'

I laughed down a bit more.

'I should have supposed,' I said, flicking, 'that my meaning was quite clear. I want that notebook of Gussie's, and I want it immediately, without any more back chat.'

Her lips tightened.

'You will get it tomorrow – if Harold turns in a satisfactory report.'

'I shall get it now.'

'Ha jolly ha!'

' "Ha jolly ha!" to you, young Stiffy, with knobs on,' I retorted with quiet dignity. 'I repeat, I shall get it now. If I don't, I shall go to old Stinker and tell him all about it.'

'All about what?'

'All about everything. At present, he is under the impression that my acquiescence in your scheme is due entirely to goodness of heart and a desire to assist an old friend. You haven't told him about the notebook. I am convinced of it. I could gather that from your manner. When I was about to mention the notebook, it betrayed embarrassment. You feared lest Stinker might enquire into the matter and, learning the facts, compel you to make restitution.'

Her eyes flickered. I saw that Jeeves had been correct in his diagnosis.

'You're talking absolute rot,' she said, but it was with a quaver on the v.

'All right. Well, toodle-oo. I'm off to find Stinker.'

I turned on my heel and, as I expected, she stopped me with a pleading yowl.

'No, Bertie, don't! You mustn't!'

I came back.

'So! You admit it? Stinker knows nothing of your . . .' The powerful phrase which Aunt Dahlia had employed when speaking of Sir Watkyn Bassett occurred to me – ' of your underhanded skulduggery.'

'I don't see why you call it underhanded skulduggery.'

'I call it underhanded skulduggery because that is what I consider it. And that is what Stinker, dripping as he is with high principles, will consider it when the facts are placed before him.' I turned on the h. again. 'Well, toodle-oo once more.'

'Bertie, wait!'

'Well?'

'Bertie, darling – '

I checked her with a cold wave of the cigarette-holder.

'Less of the "Bertie, darling". "Bertie, darling", forsooth! Nice time to start the "Bertie, darling"-ing.'

'But, Bertie darling, I want to explain. Of course I didn't dare tell Harold about the book. He would have had a fit. He would have said it was a rotten trick, and of course I knew it was. But there was nothing else to do. There didn't seem any other way of getting you to help us.'

'There wasn't.'

But you are going to help us, aren't you?'

'I am not.'

'Well, I do think you might.'

'I dare say you do, but I won't.'

Somewhere about the first or second line of this chunk of dialogue, I had observed her eyes begin to moisten and her lips to tremble, and a pearly one had started to steal down the cheek. The bursting of the dam, of which that pearly one had been the first preliminary trickle, now set in with great severity. With a brief word to the effect that she wished she were dead and that I would look pretty silly when I gazed down at her coffin, knowing that my inhumanity had put her there, she flung herself on the bed and started going *oomp*.

It was the old uncontrollable sob-stuff which she had pulled earlier in the proceedings, and once more I found myself a bit unmanned. I stood there irresolute, plucking nervously at the cravat. I have already alluded to the effect of a woman's grief on the Woosters.

'Oomp,' she went.

'Oomp . . . Oomp . . .'

'But, Stiffy, old girl, be reasonable. Use the bean. You can't seriously expect me to pinch that cow-creamer.'

'It oomps everything to us.'

'Very possibly. But listen. You haven't envisaged the latent snags. Your blasted uncle is watching my every move, just waiting for me to start something. And even if he wasn't, the fact that I would be co-operating with Stinker renders the thing impossible. I have already given you my views on Stinker as a partner in crime. Somehow, in some manner, he would muck everything up. Why, look at what happened just now. He couldn't even climb down a ladder without falling off.'

'Oomp.'

'And, anyway, just examine this scheme of yours in pitiless analysis. You tell me the wheeze is for Stinker to stroll in all over blood and say he hit the marauder on the nose. Let us suppose he does so. What ensues? "Ha!" says your uncle, who doubtless knows a clue as well as the next man. "Hit him on the nose, did you? Keep your eyes skinned, everybody, for a bird with a swollen nose." And the first thing he sees is me with a beezer twice the proper size. Don't tell me he wouldn't draw conclusions.'

I rested my case. It seemed to me that I had made out a pretty good one, and I anticipated the resigned. 'Right ho. Yes, I see what you mean. I suppose you're right.' But she merely oomped the more, and I turned to Jeeves, who hitherto had not spoken.

'You follow my reasoning, Jeeves?'

'Entirely, sir.'

'You agree with me, that the scheme, as planned, would merely end in disaster?'

'Yes, sir. It undoubtedly presents certain grave difficulties. I wonder if I might be permitted to suggest an alternative one.'

I stared at the man.

'You mean you have found a formula.'

'I think so, sir.'

His words had de-oomped Stiffy. I don't think anything else in the world would have done it. She sat up, looking at him with a wild surmise.

'Jeeves! Have you really?'

'Yes, miss.'

'Well, you certainly are the most wonderfully woolly baa-lamb that ever stepped.'

'Thank you, miss.'

'Well, let us have it, Jeeves,' I said, lighting another cigarette and lowering self into a chair. 'One hopes, of course, that you are right, but I should have thought personally that there were no avenues.'

'I think we can find one, sir, if we approach the matter from the psychological angle.'

'Oh, psychological?'

'Yes, sir.'

'The psychology of the individual?'

'Precisely, sir.'

'I see. Jeeves,' I explained to Stiffy, who, of course, knew the man only slightly, scarcely more, indeed, than as a silent figure

144

that had done some smooth potato-handing when she had lunched at my flat, 'is and always has been a whale on the psychology of the individual. He eats it alive. What individual, Jeeves?'

'Sir Watkyn Bassett, sir.'

I frowned doubtfully.

'You propose to try to soften that old public enemy? I don't think it can be done, except with a knuckleduster.'

'No, sir. It would not be easy to soften Sir Watkyn, who, as you imply, is a man of strong character, not easily moulded. The idea I have in mind is to endeavour to take advantage of his attitude towards yourself. Sir Watkyn does not like you, sir.'

'I don't like him.'

'No, sir. But the important thing is that he has conceived a strong distaste for you, and would consequently sustain a severe shock, were you to inform him that you and Miss Byng were betrothed and were anxious to be united in matrimony.'

'What! You want me to tell him that Stiffy and I are that way?'

'Precisely, sir.'

I shook the head.

'I see no percentage in it, Jeeves. All right for a laugh, no doubt – watching the old bounder's reactions I mean – but of little practical value.'

Stiffy, too, seemed disappointed. It was plain that she had been hoping for better things.

'It sounds goofy to me,' she said. 'Where would that get us Jeeves?'

'If I might explain miss. Sir Watkyn's reactions would, as Mr Wooster suggests, be of a strongly defined character.'

'He would hit the ceiling.'

'Exactly, miss. A very colourful piece of imagery. And if you were then to assure him that there was no truth in Mr Wooster's statement, adding that you were, in actual fact, betrothed to Mr Pinker, I think the overwhelming relief which he would feel at the news would lead him to look with a kindly eye on your union with that gentlemen.'

Personally, I had never heard anything so potty in my life, and my manner indicated as much. Stiffy, on the other hand, was all over it. She did the first few steps of a Spring dance.

'Why, Jeeves, that's marvellous!'

'I think it would prove effective, miss.'

'Of course, it would. It couldn't fail. Just imagine, Bertie, darling, how he would feel if you told him I wanted to marry you. Why, if after that I said "Oh, no, it's all right, Uncle Watkyn. The chap I really want to marry is the boy who cleans the boots," he would fold me in his arms and promise to come and dance at the wedding. And when he finds that the real fellow is a splendid, wonderful, terrific man like Harold, the thing will be a walk-over. Jeeves, you really are a specific dream-rabbit.'

'Thank you, miss. I am glad to have given satisfaction.'

I rose. It was my intention to say goodbye to all this. I don't mind people talking rot in my presence, but it must not be utter rot. I turned to Stiffy, who was now in the later stages of her Spring dance, and addressed her with curt severity.

'I will now take the book, Stiffy.'

She was over by the cupboard, strewing roses. She paused for a moment.

'Oh, the book. You want it?'

'I do. Immediately.'

'I'll give it you after you've seen Uncle Watkyn.'

'Oh?'

'Yes. It isn't that I don't trust you, Bertie, darling, but I should feel much happier if I knew that you knew I had still got it, and I'm sure you want me to feel happy. You toddle off and beard him, and then we'll talk.'

I frowned.

'I will toddle off,' I said coldly, 'but beard him, no. I don't seem to see myself bearding him!'

She stared.

'But Bertie, this sounds as if you weren't going to sit in.'

'It was how I meant it to sound.'

'You wouldn't fail me, would you?'

'I would. I would fail you like billy-o.'

'Don't you like the scheme?'

'I do not. Jeeves spoke a moment ago of his gladness at having given satisfaction. He has given me no satisfaction whatsoever. I consider that the idea he has advanced marks the absolute zero in human goofiness, and I am surprised that he should have entertained it. The book, Stiffy, if you please – and slippily.'

She was silent for a space.

'I was rather asking myself,' she said, 'if you might not take this attitude.'

'And now you know the answer,' I riposted. 'I have. The book, if you please.'

'I'm not going to give you the book.'

'Very well. Then I go to Stinker and tell him all.'

'All right. Do. And before you can get within a mile of him, I shall be up in the library, telling Uncle Watkyn all.'

She waggled her chin, like a girl who considers that she has put over a swift one: and, examining what she had said, I was compelled to realize that this was precisely what she had put over. I had overlooked this contingency completely. Her words gave me pause. The best I could do in the way of a come-back was to utter a somewhat baffled 'H'm!' There is no use attempting to disguise the fact – Bertram was nonplussed.

'So there you are. Now, how about it?'

It is never pleasant for a chap who has been doing the dominant male to have to change his stance and sink to ignoble pleadings, but I could see no other course. My voice, which had been firm and resonant, took on a melting tremolo.

'But, Stiffy, dash it! You wouldn't do that?'

'Yes, I would, if you don't go and sweeten Uncle Watkyn.'

'But how can I go and sweeten him? Stiffy, you can't subject me to this fearful ordeal.'

'Yes, I can. And what's so fearful about it? He can't eat you.'

I conceded this.

'True. But that's about the best you can say.'

'It won't be any worse than a visit to the dentist.'

'It'll be worse than six visits to six dentists.'

'Well, think how glad you will be when it's over.'

I drew little consolation from this. I looked at her closely, hoping to detect some signs of softening. Not one. She had been as tough as a restaurant steak, and she continued as tough as a restaurant steak. Kipling was right. D. than them. No getting round it.

I made one last appeal.

'You won't recede from your position?'

'Not a step.'

'In spite of the fact – excuse me mentioning it – that I gave you a dashed good lunch at my flat, no expense spared?'

'No.'

I shrugged my shoulders, as some Roman gladiator – one of those chaps who threw knotted sheets over people, for instance – might have done on hearing the call-boy shouting his number in the wings.

'Very well, then,' I said.

She beamed at me maternally.

'That's the spirit. That's my brave little man.'

At a less preoccupied moment, I might have resented her calling me her brave little man, but in this grim hour it scarcely seemed to matter.

'Where is this frightful uncle of yours?'

'He's bound to be in the library now.'

'Very good. Then I will go to him.'

I don't know if you were ever told as a kid that story about the fellow whose dog chewed up the priceless manuscript of the book he was writing. The blow-out, if you remember, was that he gave the animal a pained look and said: 'Oh, Diamond, Diamond, you – or it may have been thou – little know – or possibly knowest – what you – or thou – has – or hast – done.' I heard it in the nursery, and it has always lingered in my mind. And why I bring it up now is that this was how I looked at Jeeves as I passed from the room. I didn't actually speak the gag, but I fancy he knew what I was thinking.

I could have wished that Stiffy had not said 'Yoicks! Tally-ho!' as I crossed the threshold. It seemed to me in the circumstances flippant and in dubious taste.

# =9=

IT has been well said of Bertram Wooster by those who know him best that there is a certain resilience in his nature that enables him as a general rule to rise on stepping-stones of his dead self in the most unfavourable circumstances. It isn't often that I fail to keep the chin up and the eye sparkling. But as I made my way to the library in pursuance of my dreadful task, I freely admit that Life had pretty well got me down. It was with leaden feet, as the expression is, that I tooled along.

Stiffy had compared the binge under advisement to a visit to the dentist, but as I reached journey's end I was feeling more as I had felt in the old days of school when going to keep a tryst with the head master in his study. You will recall me telling you of the time I sneaked down by night to the Rev. Aubrey Upjohn's lair in quest of biscuits and found myself unexpectedly cheek by jowl with the old bird, I in striped non-shrinkable pyjamas, he in tweeds and a dirty look. On that occasion, before parting, we had made a date for half-past four next day at the same spot, and my emotions were almost exactly similar to those which I had experienced on that far-off afternoon, as I tapped on the door and heard a scarcely human voice invite me to enter.

The only difference was that while the Rev. Aubrey had been alone, Sir Watkyn Bassett appeared to be entertaining company. As my knuckles hovered over the panel, I seemed to hear the rumble of voices, and when I went in I found that my ears had not deceived me. Pop Bassett was seated at the desk, and by his side stood Constable Eustace Oates. It was a spectacle that rather put the lid on the shrinking feeling from which I was suffering. I don't know if you have ever been jerked before a tribunal of justice, but if you have you will bear me out when I say that the memory of such an experience lingers, with the result that when later you are suddenly confronted by a sitting magistrate and a standing policeman, the association of ideas gives you a bit of a shock and tends to unman.

A swift keen glance from old B. did nothing to still the fluttering pulse.

'Yes, Mr Wooster?'

'Oh – ah – could I speak to you for a moment?'

"Speak to me?' I could see that a strong distaste for having his sanctum cluttered up with Woosters was contending in Sir Watkyn Bassett's bosom with a sense of the obligations of a host. After what seemed a nip-and-tuck struggle, the latter got its nose ahead. 'Why, yes . . . That is . . . If you really . . . Oh, certainly . . . Pray take a seat.'

I did so, and felt a good deal better. In the dock, you have to stand. Old Bassett, after a quick look in my direction to see that I wasn't stealing the carpet, turned to the constable again.

'Well, I think that is all, Oates.'

'Very good, Sir Watkyn.'

'You understand what I wish you to do?'

'Yes, sir.'

'And with regard to that other matter, I will look into it very closely, bearing in mind what you have told me of your suspicions. A most rigorous investigation shall be made.'

The zealous officer clumped out. Old Bassett fiddled for a moment with the papers on his desk. Then he cocked an eye at me.

'That was Constable Oates, Mr Wooster.'

'Yes.'

'You know him?'

'I've seen him.'

'When?'

'This afternoon.'

'Not since then?'

'No.'

'Are you quite sure?'

'Oh, quite.'

'H'm.'

He fiddled with the papers again, then touched on another topic.

'We were all disappointed that you were not with us in the drawing-room after dinner, Mr Wooster.'

This, of course, was a bit embarrassing. The man of sensibility

150

does not like to reveal to this host that he has been dodging him like a leper.

'You were much missed.'

'Oh, was I? I'm sorry. I had a bit of a headache, and went and ensconsed myself in my room.'

'I see. And you remained there?'

'Yes.'

'You did not by any chance go for a walk in the fresh air, to relieve your headache?'

'Oh, no. Ensconsed all the time.'

'I see. Odd. My daughter Madeline tells me that she went twice to your room after the conclusion of dinner, but found it unoccupied.'

'Oh, really? Wasn't I there?'

'You were not.'

'I suppose I must have been somewhere else.'

'The same thought had occurred to me.'

'I remember now. I did saunter out on two occasions.'

'I see.'

He took up a pen and leaned forward, tapping it against his left forefinger.

'Somebody stole Constable Oates's helmet tonight,' he said, changing the subject.

'Oh, yes.'

'Yes. Unfortunately he was not able to see the miscreant.'

'No?'

'No. At the moment when the outrage took place, his back was turned.'

'Dashed difficult, of course, to see miscreants, if your back's turned.'

'Yes.'

'Yes.'

There was a pause. And as, in spite of the fact that we seemed to be agreeing on every point, I continued to sense a strain in the atmosphere, I tried to lighten things with a gag which I remembered from the old *in statu pupillari* days.

'Sort of makes you say to yourself *Quis custodiet ipsos custodes*, what?'

'I beg your pardon?'

'Latin joke,' I exclaimed. '*Quis* – who – *custodiet* – shall guard – *ipsos custodes* – the guardians themselves? Rather funny, I mean to say,' I proceeded, making it clear to the meanest intelligence, 'a chap who's supposed to stop chaps pinching things from chaps having a chap come along and pinch something from him.'

'Ah, I see your point. Yes, I can conceive that a certain type of mind might detect a humorous side to the affair. But I can assure you, Mr Wooster, that that is not the side which presents itself to me as a Justice of the Peace. I take the very gravest view of the matter, and this, when once he is apprehended and placed in custody, I shall do my utmost to persuade the culprit to share.'

I didn't like the sound of this at all. A sudden alarm for old Stinker's well-being swept over me.

'I say, what do you think he would get?'

'I appreciate your zeal for knowledge, Mr Wooster, but at the moment I am not prepared to confide in you. In the words of the late Lord Asquith, I can only say "Wait and see". I think it is possible that your curiosity may be gratified before long.'

I didn't want to rake up old sores, always being a bit of a lad for letting the dead past bury its dead, but I thought it might be as well to give him a pointer.

'You fined me five quid,' I reminded him.

'So you informed me this afternoon,' he said, pince-nezing me coldly. 'But if I understood correctly what you were saying, the outrage for which you were brought before me at Bosher Street was perpetrated on the night of the annual boat race between the Universities of Oxford and Cambridge, when a certain licence is traditionally granted by the authorities. In the present case, there are no such extenuating circumstances. I should certainly not punish the wanton stealing of Government property from the person of Constable Oates with a mere fine.'

'You don't mean it would be chokey?'

'I said that I was not prepared to confide in you, but having gone so far I will. The answer to your question, Mr Wooster, is in the affirmative.'

There was a silence. He sat tapping his finger with the pen. I, if memory serves me correctly, straightening my tie. I was deeply concerned. The thought of poor old Stinker being bunged into the Bastille was enough to disturb anyone with a kindly interest in his career and prospects. Nothing retards a curate's advancement in his chosen profession more surely than a spell in the jug.

He lowered the pen.

'Well, Mr Wooster, I think that you were about to tell me what brings you here?'

I started a bit. I hadn't actually forgotten my mission, of course, but all this sinister stuff had caused me to shove it away at the back of my mind, and the suddenness with which it now came popping out gave me a bit of a jar.

I saw that there would have to be a few preliminary *pourparlers* before I got down to the nub. When relations between a bloke and another bloke are of a strained nature, the second bloke can't charge straight into the topic of wanting to marry the first bloke's niece. Not, that is to say, if he has a nice sense of what is fitting, as the Woosters have.

'Oh, ah, yes. Thanks for reminding me.'

'Not at all.'

'I just thought I'd drop in and have a chat.'

'I see.'

What the thing wanted, of course, was edging into, and I found I had got the approach. I teed up with a certain access of confidence.

'Have you ever thought about love, Sir Watkyn?'

'I beg your pardon?'

'About love. Have you ever brooded on it to any extent?'

'You have not come here to discuss love?'

'Yes, I have. That's exactly it. I wonder if you have noticed a rather rummy thing about it – viz. that it is everywhere. You can't get away from it. Love, I mean. Wherever you go, there it is, buzzing along in every class of life. Quite remarkable. Take newts, for instance.'

'Are you quite well, Mr Wooster?'

'Oh, fine, thanks. Take newts, I was saying. You wouldn't think it, but Gussie Fink-Nottle tells me they get it right up their noses in the mating season. They stand in line by the hour, waggling their tails at the local belles. Starfish, too. Also under-sea worms.'

'Mr Wooster – '

'And, according to Gussie, even ribbonlike seaweed. That

surprises you, eh? It did me. But he assures me that it is so. Just where a bit of ribbonlike seaweed thinks it is going to get by pressing its suit is more than I can tell you, but at the time of the full moon it hears the voice of Love all right and is up and doing with the best of them. I suppose it builds on the hope that it will look good to other bits of ribbonlike seaweed, which, of course, would also be affected by the full moon. Well, be that as it may, what I'm working round to is that the moon is pretty full now, and if that's how it affects seaweed you can't very well blame a chap like me for feeling the impulse, can you?'

'I am afraid – '

'Well, can you?' I repeated, pressing him strongly. And I threw in an 'eh, what?' to clinch the thing.

But there was no answering spark of intelligence in his eye. He had been looking like a man who had missed the finer shades, and he still looked like a man who had missed the finer shades.

'I am afraid, Mr Wooster, that you will think me dense, but I have not the remotest notion what you are talking about.'

Now that the moment for letting him have it in the eyeball had arrived, I was pleased to find that the all-of-a-twitter feeling which had gripped me at the outset had ceased to function. I don't say that I had become exactly debonair and capable of flicking specks of dust from the irreproachable Mechlin lace at my wrists, but I felt perfectly calm.

What had soothed the system was the realization that in another half-jiffy I was about to slip a stick of dynamite under this old buster which would teach him that we are not put into the world for pleasure alone. When a magistrate has taken five quid off you for what, properly looked at, was a mere boyish peccadillo which would have been amply punished by a waggle of the forefinger and a brief 'Tut, tut!' it is always agreeable to make him jump like a pea on a hot shovel.

'I'm talking about me and Stiffy.'

'Stiffy?'

'Stephanie.'

'Stephanie? My niece?'

'That's right. Your niece. Sir Watkyn,' I said, remembering a good one, 'I have the honour to ask you for your niece's hand.'

'You – what?'

'I have the honour to ask you for your niece's hand.'

'I don't understand.'

'It's quite simple. I want to marry young Stiffy. She wants to marry me. Surely you've got it now? Take a line through that ribbonlike seaweed.'

There was no question as to its being value for money. On the cue 'niece's hand', he had come out of his chair like a rocketing pheasant. He now sank back, fanning himself with the pen. He seemed to have aged quite a lot.

'She wants to marry you?'

'That's the idea.'

'But I was not aware that you knew my niece.'

'Oh, rather. We two, if you care to put it that way, have plucked the gowans fine. Oh, yes, I know Stiffy, all right. Well, I mean to say, if I didn't, I shouldn't want to marry her, should I?'

He seemed to see the justice of this. He became silent, except for a soft, groaning noise. I remembered another good one.

'You will not be losing a niece. You will be gaining a nephew.'

'But I don't want a nephew, damn it!'

Well, there was that, of course.

He rose, and muttering something which sounded like 'Oh, dear! Oh, dear!' went to the fireplace and pressed the bell with a weak finger. Returning to his seat, he remained holding his head in his hands until the butler blew in.

'Butterfield,' he said in a low, hoarse voice, 'find Miss Stephanie and tell her that I wish to speak to her.'

A stage wait then occurred, but not such a long one as you might have expected. It was only about a minute before Stiffy appeared. I imagine she had been lurking in the offing, expectant of his summons. She tripped in, all merry and bright.

'You want to see me, Uncle Watkyn? Oh, hallo, Bertie.'

'Hallo.'

'I didn't know you were here. Have you and Uncle Watkyn been having a nice talk?'

Old Bassett, who had gone into a coma again, came out of it and uttered a sound like the death-rattle of a dying duck.

' "Nice",' he said, 'is not the adjective I would have selected.' He moistened his ashen lips. 'Mr Wooster has just informed me that he wishes to marry you.'

I must say that young Stiffy gave an extemely convincing performance. She stared at him. She stared at me. She clasped her hands. I rather think she blushed.

'Why Bertie!'

Old Bassett broke the pen. I had been wondering when he would.

'Oh, Bertie! You have made me very proud.'

'Proud?' I detected an incredulous note in old Bassett's voice. 'Did you say "proud"?'

'Well, it's the greatest compliment a man can pay a woman, you know. All the nibs are agreed on that. I'm tremendously flattered and grateful . . . and, well, all that sort of thing. But, Bertie dear, I'm terribly sorry. I'm afraid it's impossible.'

I hadn't supposed that there was anything in the world capable of jerking a man from the depths so effectively as one of those morning mixtures of Jeeves's, but these words acted on old Bassett with an even greater promptitude and zip. He had been sitting in his chair in a boneless, huddled sort of way, a broken man. He now started up, with gleaming eyes and twitching lips. You could see that hope had dawned.

'Impossible? Don't you want to marry him?'

'No.'

'He said you did.'

'He must have been thinking of a couple of other fellows. No, Bertie, darling, it cannot be. You see, I love somebody elše.'

Old Bassett started.

'Eh? Who?'

'The most wonderful man in the world.'

'He has a name, I presume?'

'Harold Pinker.'

'Harold Pinker? . . . Pinker . . . The only Pinker I know is – '

'The curate. That's right. He's the chap.'

'You love the curate?'

'Ah!' said Stiffy, rolling her eyes up and looking like Aunt Dahlia when she had spoken of the merits of blackmail. 'We've been secretly engaged for weeks.'

It was plain from old Bassett's manner that he was not prepared to classify this under the heading of tidings of great joy. His brows were knitted, like those of some diner in a restaurant who, sailing into his dozen oysters, finds that the first one to pass his lips is a wrong 'un. I saw that Stiffy had shown a shrewd knowledge of human nature, if you could call his that, when she had told me that this man would have to be heavily sweetened before the news could be broken. You could see that he shared the almost universal opinion of parents and uncles that curates were nothing to start strewing roses out of a hat about.

'You know that vicarage that you have in your gift, Uncle Watkyn? What Harold and I were thinking was that you might give him that, and then we could get married at once. You see, apart from the increased dough, it would start him off on the road to higher things. Up till now, Harold has been working under wraps. As a curate, he has had no scope. But slip him a vicarage, and watch him let himself out. There is literally no eminence to which that boy will not rise, once he spits on his hands and starts in.'

She wriggled from base to apex with girlish enthusiasm, but there was no girlish enthusiasm in old Bassett's demeanour. Well, there wouldn't be, of course, but what I mean is there wasn't.

'Ridiculous!'

'Why?'

'I could not dream – '

'Why not?'

'In the first place, you are far too young – '

'What nonsense. Three of the girls I was at school with were married last year. I'm senile compared with some of the infants you see toddling up the aisle nowadays.'

Old Bassett thumped the desk – coming down, I was glad to see, on an upturned paper fastener. The bodily anguish induced by this lent vehemence to his tone.

'The whole thing is quite absurd and utterly out of the question. I refuse to consider the idea for an instant.'

'But what have you got against Harold?'

'I have nothing, as you put it, against him. He seems zealous in his duties and popular in the parish – '

'He's a baa-lamb.'

'No doubt.'

'He played football for England.'

'Very possibly.'

157

'And he's marvellous at tennis.'

'I dare say he is. But that is not a reason why he should marry my niece. What means has he, if any, beyond his stipend?'

'About five hundred a year.'

'Tchah!'

'Well, I don't call that bad. Five hundred's pretty good sugar, if you ask me. Besides, money doesn't matter.'

'It matters a great deal.'

'You really feel that, do you?'

'Certainly. You must be practical.'

'Right ho, I will. If you'd rather I married for money, I'll marry for money. Bertie, it's on. Start getting measured for the wedding trousers.'

Her words created what is known as a genuine sensation. Old Bassett's 'What!' and my 'Here, I say, dash it!' popped out neck and neck and collided in mid air, my heart-cry having, perhaps, an even greater horse-power than his. I was frankly appalled. Experience has taught me that you never know with girls, and it might quite possibly happen, I felt, that she would go through with this frightful project as a gesture. Nobody could teach me anything about gestures. Brinkley Court in the preceding summer had crawled with them.

'Bertie is rolling in the stuff and, as you suggest, one might do worse than take a whack at the Wooster millions. Of course, Bertie dear, I am only marrying you to make you happy. I can never love you as I love Harold. But as Uncle Watkyn has taken this violent prejudice against him – '

Old Bassett hit the paper fastener again, but this time didn't seem to notice it.

'My dear child, don't talk such nonsense. You are quite mistaken. You must have completely misunderstood me. I have no prejudice against this young man Pinker. I like and respect him. If you really think your happiness lies in becoming his wife, I would be the last man to stand in your way. By all means, marry him. The alternative – '

He said no more, but gave me a long, shuddering look. Then, as if the sight of me were more than his frail strength could endure, he removed his gaze, only to bring it back again and give me a short quick one. He then closed his eyes and leaned back in his chair, breathed stertorously. And as there didn't seem anything to keep me, I sidled out. The last I saw of him, he was submitting without any great animation to a niece's embrace.

I suppose that when you have an uncle like Sir Watkyn Bassett on the receiving end, a niece's embrace is a thing you tend to make pretty snappy. It wasn't more than about a minute before Stiffy came out and immediately went into her dance.

'What a man! What a man! What a man! What a man! What a man!' she said, waving her arms and giving other indications of *bien-être*. 'Jeeves,' she explained, as if she supposed that I might imagine her to be alluding to the recent Bassett. 'Did he say it would work? He did. And was he right? He was. Bertie, could one kiss Jeeves?'

'Certainly not.'

'Shall I kiss you?'

'No, thank you. All I require from you, young Byng, is that notebook.'

'Well, I must kiss someone, and I'm dashed if I'm going to kiss Eustace Oates.'

She broke off. A graver look came into her dial.

'Eustace Oates!' she repeated meditatively. 'That reminds me. In the rush of recent events, I had forgotten him. I exchanged a few words with Eustace Oates just now, Bertie, while I was waiting on the stairs for the balloon to go up, and he was sinister to a degree.'

'Where's that notebook?'

'Never mind about the notebook. The subject under discussion is Eustace Oates and his sinisterness. He's on my trail about that helmet.'

'What!'

'Absolutely. I'm Suspect Number One. He told me that he reads a lot of detective stories, and he says that the first thing a detective makes a bee-line for is motive. After that, opportunity. And finally clues. Well, as he pointed out, with that high-handed behaviour of his about Bartholomew rankling in my bosom, I had a motive all right, and seeing that I was out and about at the time of the crime I had the opportunity, too. And as for clues, what do you think he had with him, when I saw him? One of my gloves! He had picked it up on the scene of the outrage – while measuring footprints or looking for cigar ash, I suppose. You remember when Harold brought me back my gloves, there was only one of them. The other he apparently dropped while scooping in the helmet.'

A sort of dull, bruised feeling weighed me down as I mused on this latest manifestation of Harold Pinker's goofiness, as if a strong hand had whanged me over the cupola with a blackjack. There was such a sort of hideous ingenuity in the way he thought up new methods of inviting ruin.

'He would!'

'What do you mean, he would?'

'Well, he did, didn't he?'

'That's not the same as saying he would – in a beastly sneering, supercilious tone, as if you were so frightfully hot yourself. I can't understand you, Bertie – the way you're always criticizing poor Harold. I thought you were so fond of him.'

'I love him like a b. But that doesn't alter my opinion that of all the pumpkin-headed foozlers who ever preached about Hivites and Jebusites, he is the foremost.'

'He isn't half as pumpkin-headed as you.'

'He is, at a conservative estimate, about twenty-seven times as pumpkin-headed as me. He begins where I leave off. It may be a strong thing to say, but he's more pumpkin-headed than Gussie.'

With a visible effort, she swallowed the rising choler.

'Well, never mind about that. The point is that Eustace Oates is on my trail, and I've got to look slippy and find a better safe-deposit vault for that helmet than my chest of drawers. Before I know where I am, the Ogpu will be searching my room. Where would be a good place, do you think?'

I dismissed the thing wearily.

'Oh dash it, use your own judgement. To return to the main issue, where is that notebook?'

'Oh, Bertie, you're a perfect bore about that notebook. Can't you talk of anything else?'

'No, I can't. Where is it?'

'You're going to laugh when I tell you.'

I gave her an austere look.

'It is possible that I may some day laugh again – when I have got well away from this house of terror, but there is a fat chance of my doing so at this early date. Where is that book?'

'Well, if you really must know, I hid it in the cow-creamer.'

Everyone, I imagine, has read stories in which things turned black and swam before people. As I heard these words, Stiffy turned black and swam before me. It was as if I had been looking at a flickering negress.

'You – what?'

'I hid it in the cow-creamer.'

'What on earth did you do that for?'

'Oh, I thought I would.'

'But how am I to get it?'

A slight smile curved the young pimple's mobile lips.

'Oh, dash it, use your own judgement,' she said. 'Well, see you soon, Bertie.'

She biffed off, and I leaned limply against the banisters, trying to rally from this frightful wallop. But the world still flickered, and a few moments later I became aware that I was being addressed by a flickering butler.

'Excuse me, sir. Miss Madeline desired me to say that she would be glad if you could spare her a moment.'

I gazed at the man dully, like someone in a prison cell when the jailer has stepped in at dawn to notify him that the firing squad is ready. I knew what this meant, of course. I had recognized this butler's voice for what it was – the voice of doom. There could be only one thing that Madeline Bassett would be glad if I could spare her moment about.

'Oh, did she?'

'Yes, sir.'

'Where is Miss Bassett?'

'In the drawing-room, sir.'

'Right ho.'

I braced myself with the old Wooster grit. Up came the chin, back went the shoulders.

'Lead on,' I said to the butler, and the butler led on.

# =10=

THE sound of soft and wistful music percolating through the drawing-room door as I approached did nothing to brighten the general outlook: and when I went in and saw Madeline Bassett seated at the piano, drooping on her stem a goodish deal, the sight nearly caused me to turn and leg it. However, I fought down the impulse and started things off with a tentative 'What ho.'

The observation elicited no immediate response. She had risen, and for perhaps half a minute stood staring at me in a sad sort of way, like the Mona Lisa on one of the mornings when the sorrows of the world had been coming over the plate a bit too fast for her. Finally, just as I was thinking I had better try to fill in with something about the weather, she spoke.

'Bertie – '

It was, however, only a flash in the pan. She blew a fuse, and silence supervened again.

'Bertie – '

No good. Another wash-out.

I was beginning to feel the strain a bit. We had had one of these deaf-mutes-getting-together sessions before, at Brinkley Court, in the summer, but on that occasion I had been able to ease things along by working in a spot of stage business during the awkward gaps in the conversation. Our previous chat as you may or possibly may not recall, had taken place in the Brinkley dining-room in the presence of a cold collation, and it had helped a lot being in a position to bound forward at intervals with a curried egg or a cheese straw. In the absence of these food stuffs, we were thrown back a good deal on straight staring, and this always tends to embarrass.

Her lips parted. I saw that something was coming to the surface. A couple of gulps, and she was off to a good start. 'Bertie, I wanted to see you . . . I asked you to come because I wanted to say . . . I wanted to tell you . . . Bertie, my engagement to Augustus is at an end.'

'Yes.'

'You knew?'

'Oh, rather. He told me.'

'Then you know why I asked you to come here. I wanted to say – '

'Yes.'

'That I am willing – '

'Yes.'

'To make you happy.'

She appeared to be held up for a moment by a slight return of the old tonsil trouble, but after another brace of gulps she got it out.

'I will be your wife, Bertie.'

I suppose that after this most chaps would have thought it scarcely worthwhile to struggle against the inev., but I had a dash at it. With such vital issues at stake, one would have felt a chump if one had left any stone unturned.

'Awfully decent of you,' I said civilly, 'Deeply sensible of the honour, and what not. But have you thought? Have you reflected? Don't you feel you're being a bit rough on poor old Gussie?'

'What! After what happened this evening?'

'Ah, I wanted to talk to you about that. I always think, don't you, that it is as well on these occasions, before doing anything drastic, to have a few words with a seasoned man of the world and get the real low-down. You wouldn't like later on to have to start wringing your hands and saying "Oh, if I had only known!" In my opinion, the whole thing should be re-examined with a view to threshing out. If you care to know what I think, you're wronging Gussie.'

'Wronging him? When I saw him with my own eyes – '

'Ah, but you haven't got the right angle. Let me explain.'

'There can be no explanation. We will not talk about it any more, Bertie. I have blotted Augustus from my life. Until tonight I saw him only through the golden mist of love, and thought him the perfect man. This evening he revealed himself as what he really is – a satyr.'

'But that's just what I'm driving at. That's just where you're making your bloomer. You see – '

'We will not talk about it any more.'

163

'But – '

'Please!'

'Oh, right ho.'

I tuned out. You can't make any headway with that *tout comprendre, c'est tout pardonner* stuff if the girl won't listen.

She turned the bean away, no doubt to hide a silent tear, and there ensued a brief interval during which she swabbed the eyes with a pocket handerkchief and I, averting my gaze, dipped the beak into a jar of *pot-pourri* which stood on the piano.

Presently, she took the air again.

'It is useless, Bertie. I know, of course, why you are speaking like this. It is that sweet, generous nature of yours. There are no lengths to which you will not go to help a friend, even though it may mean the wrecking of your own happiness. But there is nothing you can say that will change me. I have finished with Augustus. From tonight he will be to me merely a memory – a memory that will grow fainter and fainter through the years as you and I draw ever closer together. You will help me to forget. With you beside me, I shall be able in time to exorcize Augustus's spell ... And now I suppose I had better go and tell Daddy.'

I started. I could still see Pop Bassett's face when he had thought that he was going to draw me for a nephew. It would be a bit thick, I felt, while he was still quivering to the roots of the soul at the recollection of that hair's-breadth escape, to tell him that I was about to become his son-in-law. I was not fônd of Pop Bassett, but one has one's humane instincts.

'Oh, my aunt!' I said. 'Don't do that!'

'But I must. He will have to know that I am to be your wife. He is expecting me to marry Augustus three weeks from tomorrow.'

I chewed this over. I saw what she meant, of course. You've got to keep a father posted about these things. You can't just let it all slide and have the poor old egg rolling up to the church in a topper and a buttonhole, to find that the wedding is off and nobody bothered to mention it to him.

'Well, don't tell him tonight,' I urged. 'Let him simmer a bit. He's just had a pretty testing shock.'

'A shock?'

'Yes. He's not quite himself.'

A concerned look came into her eyes, causing them to bulge a trifle.

'So I was right. I thought he was not himself, when I met him coming out of the library just now. He was wiping his forehead and making odd little gasping noises. And when I asked him if anything was the matter, he said that we all had our cross to bear in this world, but that he supposed he ought not to complain, because things were not so bad as they might have been. I couldn't think what he meant. He then said he was going to have a warm bath and take three aspirins and go to bed. What was it? What had happened?'

I saw that to reveal the full story would be to complicate an already fairly well complicated situation. I touched, accordingly, on only one aspect of it.

'Stiffy had just told him she wanted to marry the curate.'

'Stephanie? The curate? Mr Pinker?'

'That's right. Old Stinker Pinker. And it churned him up a good deal. He appears to be a bit allergic to curates.'

She was breathing emotionally, like the dog Bartholomew just after he had finished eating the candle.

'But . . . But . . .'

'Yes?'

'But does Stephanie love Mr Pinker?'

'Oh, rather. No question about that.'

'But then – '

I saw what was in her mind, and nipped in promptly.

'Then there can't be anything between her and Gussie, you were going to say? Exactly. This proves it, doesn't it? That's the very point I've been trying to work the conversation round to from the start.'

'But he – '

'Yes, I know he did. But his motives in doing so were as pure as the driven snow. Purer, if anything. I'll tell you all about it, and I am prepared to give you a hundred to eight that when I have finished you will admit that he was more to be pitied then censured.'

Give Bertram Wooster a good, clear story to unfold, and he can narrate it well. Starting at the beginning with Gussie's aghastness at the prospect of having to make a speech at the wedding breakfast, I took her step by step through the subsequent developments, and I may say that I was as limpid as dammit. By the time I had reached the final chapter, I had her a bit squiggle-eyed but definitely wavering on the edge of conviction.

'And you say Stephanie has hidden this notebook in Daddy's cow-creamer?'

'Plumb spang in the cow-creamer.'

'But I never heard such an extraordinary story in my life.'

'Bizarre, yes, but quite capable of being swallowed, don't you think? What you have got to take into consideration is the psychology of the individual. You may say that you wouldn't have a psychology like Stiffy's if you were paid for it, but it's hers all right.'

'Are you sure you are not making all this up, Bertie?'

'Why on earth?'

'I know your altruistic nature so well.'

'Oh, I see what you mean. No, rather not. This is the straight official stuff. Don't you believe it?'

'I shall, if I find the notebook where you say Stephanie put it. I think I had better go and look.'

'I would.'

'I will.'

'Fine.'

She hurried out, and I sat down at the piano and began to play 'Happy Days Are Here Again' with one finger. It was the only method of self-expression that seemed to present itself. I would have preferred to get outside a curried egg or two, for the strain had left me weak, but, as I have said, there were no curried eggs present.

I was profoundly braced. I felt like some Marathon runner who, after sweating himself to the bone for hours, at length breasts the tape. The only thing that kept my bracedness from being absolutely unmixed was the lurking thought that in this ill-omened house there was always the chance of something unforeseen suddenly popping up to mar the happy ending. I somehow couldn't see Totleigh Towers throwing in the towel quite so readily as it appeared to be doing. It must, I felt, have something up its sleeve.

Nor was I wrong. When Madeline Bassett returned a few minutes later, there was no notebook in her hand. She reported total inability to discover so much as a trace of a notebook in the spot indicated. And, I gathered from her remarks, she had ceased entirely to be a believer in that notebook's existence.

I don't know if you have ever had a bucket of cold water right in the mazzard. I received one once in my boyhood through the agency of a groom with whom I had had some difference of opinion. That same feeling of being knocked endways came over me now.

I was at a loss and nonplussed. As Constable Oates had said, the first move the knowledgeable bloke makes when rummy goings-on are in progress is to try to spot the motive, and what Stiffy's motive could be for saying the notebook was in the cow-creamer, when it wasn't, I was unable to fathom. With a firm hand this girl had pulled my leg, but why – that was the point that baffled – why had she pulled my leg?

I did my best.

'Are you sure you really looked?'

'Perfectly sure.'

'I mean, carefully.'

'Very carefully.'

'Stiffy certainly swore it was there.'

'Indeed?'

'How do you mean, indeed?'

'If you want to know what I mean, I do not believe there ever was a notebook.'

'You don't credit my story?'

'No, I do not.'

Well, after that, of course, there didn't seem much to say. I may have said 'Oh?' or something along those lines – I'm not sure – but if I did, that let me out. I edged to the door, and pushed off in a sort of daze, pondering.

You know how it is when you ponder. You become absorbed, concentrated. Outside phenomena do not register on the what-is-it. I suppose I was fully halfway along the passage leading to my bedroom before the beastly row that was going on there penetrated to my consciousness, causing me to stop, look and listen.

This row to which I refer was a kind of banging row, as if somebody were banging on something. And I had scarcely said to myself 'What ho, a banger!' when I saw who this banger was. It was Roderick Spode, and what he was banging on was the door of Gussie's bedroom. As I came up, he was in the act of delivering another buffet on the woodwork.

The spectacle had an immediate tranquillizing effect on my jangled nervous system. I felt a new man. And I'll tell you why.

Everyone, I suppose, has experienced the sensation of comfort and relief which comes when you are being given the run-around by forces beyond your control and suddenly discover someone on whom you can work off the pent-up feelings. The merchant prince, when things are going wrong, takes it out of the junior clerk. The junior clerk goes and ticks off the office boy. The office boy kicks the cat. The cat steps down the street to find a smaller cat, which in its turn, the interview concluded, starts scouring the countryside for a mouse.

It was so with me now. Snootered to bursting point by Pop Bassetts and Madeline Bassetts and Stiffy Byngs and what not, and hounded like the dickens by a remorseless Fate, I found solace in the thought that I could still slip it across Roderick Spode.

'Spode!' I cried sharply.

He paused with lifted fist and turned an inflamed face in my direction. Then, as he saw who had spoken, the red light died out of his eyes. He wilted obsequiously.

'Well, Spode, what is all this?'

'Oh, hallo, Wooster. Nice evening.'

I proceeded to work off the pent-up f's.

'Never mind what sort of an evening it is,' I said. 'Upon my word, Spode, this is too much. This is just that little bit above the odds which compels a man to take drastic steps.'

'But, Wooster – '

'What do you mean by disturbing the house with this abominable uproar? Have you forgotten already what I told you about checking this disposition of yours to run amok like a raging hippopotamus? I should have thought that after what I said you would have spent the remainder of the evening curled up with a good book. But no. I find you renewing your efforts to assault and batter my friends. I must warn you, Spode, that my patience is not inexhaustible.'

'But, Wooster, you don't understand.'

'What don't I understand?'

'You don't know the provocation I have received from this pop-eyed Fink-Nottle.' A wistful look came into his face. 'I must break his neck.'

'You are not going to break his neck.'

'Well, shake him like a rat.'

'Nor shake him like a rat.'

'But he says I'm a pompous ass.'

'When did Gussie say that to you?'

'He didn't exactly say it. He wrote it. Look. Here it is.'

Before my bulging eyes he produced from his pocket a small, brown, leather-covered notebook.

Harking back to Archimedes just once more, Jeeves's description of him discovering the principle of displacement, though brief, had made a deep impression on me, bringing before my eyes a very vivid picture of what must have happened on that occasion. I had been able to see the man testing the bath water with his toe . . . stepping in . . . immersing the frame. I had accompanied him in spirit through all the subsequent formalities – the soaping of the loofah, the shampooing of the head, the burst of song . . .

And then, abruptly, as he climbs towards the high note, there is a silence. His voice has died away. Through the streaming suds you can see that his eyes are glowing with a strange light. The loofah falls from his grasp, disregarded. He utters a triumphant cry. 'Got it! What ho! The principle of displacement!' And out he leaps, feeling like a million dollars.

In precisely the same manner did the miraculous appearance of this notebook affect me. There was that identical moment of stunned silence, followed by the triumphant cry. And I have no doubt that, as I stretched out a compelling hand, my eyes were glowing with a strange light.

'Give me that book, Spode!'

'Yes, I would like you to look at it, Wooster. Then you will see what I mean. I came upon this,' he said, 'in rather a remarkable way. The thought crossed my mind that Sir Watkyn might feel happier if I were to take charge of that cow-creamer of his. There have been a lot of burglaries in the neighbourhood,' he added hastily, 'a lot of burglaries, and those French windows are never really safe. So I – er – went to the collection-room, and took it out of its case. I was surprised to hear something bumping about inside it. I opened it, and found this book. Look,' he said, pointing a banana-like finger over my shoulder. 'There is what he says about the way I eat asparagus.'

I think Roderick Spode's idea was that we were going to pore over the pages together. When he saw me slip the volume into my pocket, I sensed the feeling of bereavement.

'Are you going to keep the book, Wooster?'

'I am.'

'But I wanted to show it to Sir Watkyn. There's a lot about him in it, too.'

'We will not cause Sir Watkyn needless pain, Spode.'

'Perhaps you're right. Then I'll be getting on with breaking this door down?'

'Certainly not,' I said sternly. 'All you do is pop off.'

'Pop off?'

'Pop off. Leave me, Spode. I would be alone.'

I watched him disappear round the bend, then rapped vigorously on the door.

'Gussie.'

No reply.

'Gussie, come out.'

'I'm dashed if I do.'

'Come out, you ass. Wooster speaking.'

But even this did not produce immediate results. He explained later that he was under the impression that it was Spode giving a cunning imitation of my voice. But eventually I convinced him that this was indeed the boyhood friend and no other, and there came the sound of furniture being dragged away, and presently the door opened and his head emerged cautiously, like that of a snail taking a look round after a thunderstorm.

Into the emotional scene which followed I need not go in detail. You will have witnessed much the same sort of thing in the pictures, when the United States Marines arrive in the nick of time to relieve the beleaguered garrison. I may sum it up by saying that he fawned upon me. He seemed to be under the impression that I had worsted Roderick Spode in personal combat and it wasn't worthwhile to correct it. Pressing the notebook into his hand, I sent him off to show it to Madeline Bassett, and proceeded to my room.

Jeeves was there, messing about at some professional task.

It had been my intention, on seeing this man again, to put him through it in no uncertain fashion for having subjected me to the tense nervous strain of my recent interview with Pop Bassett. But now I greeted him with the cordial smile rather than the acid glare. After all, I told myself, his scheme had dragged home the gravy, and in any case this was no moment for recriminations. Wellington didn't go about ticking people off after the battle of Waterloo. He slapped their backs and stood them drinks.

'Aha, Jeeves! You're there, are you?'

'Yes, sir.'

'Well, Jeeves, you may start packing the effects.'

'Sir?'

'For the homeward trip. We leave tomorrow.'

'You are not proposing, then, sir, to extend your stay at Totleigh Towers?'

I laughed one of my gay, jolly ones.

'Don't ask foolish questions, Jeeves. Is Totleigh Towers a place where people extend their stays, if they haven't got to? And there is now no longer any necessity for me to linger on the premises. My work is done. We leave first thing tomorrow morning. Start packing, therefore, so that we shall be in a position to get off the mark without an instant's delay. It won't take you long?'

'No, sir. There are merely the two suitcases.'

He hauled them from beneath the bed, and opening the larger of the brace began to sling coats and things into it, while I, seating myself in the armchair, proceeded to put him abreast of recent events.

'Well, Jeeves, that plan of yours worked all right.'

'I am most gratified to hear it, sir.'

'I don't say that the scene won't haunt me in my dreams for some little time to come. I make no comment on your having let me in for such a thing. I merely state that it proved a winner. An uncle's blessing came popping out like a cork out of a champagne bottle, and Stiffy and Stinker are headed for the altar rails with no more fences ahead.'

'Extremely satisfactory, sir. Then Sir Watkyn's reactions were as we had anticipated?'

'If anything, more so. I don't know if you have ever seen a stout bark buffeted by the waves?'

'No, sir. My visits to the seaside have always been made in clement weather.'

'Well, that was what he resembled on being informed by me that I wanted to become his nephew by marriage. He looked and behaved like the Wreck of the *Hesperus*. You remember? It sailed the wintry sea, and the skipper had taken his little daughter to bear him company.'

'Yes, sir. Blue were her eyes as the fairy-flax, her cheeks like the dawn of day, and her bosom was white as the hawthorn buds that open in the month of May.'

'Quite. Well, as I was saying, he reeled beneath the blow and let water in at every seam. And when Stiffy appeared, and told him that it was all a mistake and that the *promesso sposo* was in reality old Stinker Pinker, his relief knew no bounds. He instantly gave his sanction to their union. Could hardly get the words out quick enough. But why am I wasting time telling you all this, Jeeves? A mere side issue. Here's the real front-page stuff. Here's the news that will shock the *chancelleries*. I've got that notebook.'

'Indeed, sir?'

'Yes, absolutely got it. I found Spode with it and took it away from him, and Gussie is even now showing it to Miss Bassett and clearing his name of the stigma that rested upon it. I shouldn't be surprised if at this very moment they were locked in a close embrace.'

'A consummation devoutly to be wished, sir.'

'You said it, Jeeves.'

'Then you have nothing to cause you further concern, sir.'

'Nothing. The relief is stupendous. I feel as if a great weight had been rolled from my shoulders. I could dance and sing. I think there can be no question that exhibiting that notebook will do the trick.'

'None, I should imagine, sir.'

'I say, Bertie,' said Gussie, trickling in at this juncture with the air of one who has been passed through a wringer, 'a most frightful thing has happened. The wedding's off.'

# =11=

I STARED at the man, clutching the brow and rocking on my base.

'Off?'

'Yes.'

'Your wedding?'

'Yes.'

'It's off?'

'Yes.'

'What – *off*?'

'Yes.'

I don't know what the Mona Lisa would have done in my place. Probably just what I did.

'Jeeves,' I said. 'Brandy!'

'Very good, sir.'

He rolled away on his errand of mercy, and I turned to Gussie, who was tacking about the room in a dazed manner, as if filling in the time before starting to pluck straws from his hair.

'I can't bear it!' I heard him mutter. 'Life without Madeline won't be worth living.'

It was an astounding attitude, of course, but you can't argue about fellows' tastes. One man's peach is another man's poison, and *vice versa*. Even my Aunt Agatha, I remembered, had roused the red-hot spark of pash in the late Spenser Gregson.

His wandering had taken him to the bed, and I saw that he was looking at the knotted sheet which lay there.

'I suppose,' he said, in an absent, soliloquizing voice, 'a chap could hang himself with that.'

I resolved to put a stopper on this trend of thought promptly. I had got more or less used by now to my bedroom being treated as a sort of meeting-place of the nations, but I was dashed if I was going to have it turned into the spot marked with an X. It was a point on which I felt strongly.

'You aren't going to hang yourself here.'

'I shall have to hang myself somewhere.'

173

'Well, you don't hang yourself in my bedroom.'

He raised his eyebrows.

'Have you any objection to my sitting in your armchair?'

'Go ahead.'

'Thanks.'

He seated himself, and stared before him with glazed eyes.

'Now, then, Gussie,' I said, 'I will take your statement. What is all this rot about the wedding being off?'

'It is off.'

'But didn't you show her the notebook?'

'Yes. I showed her the notebook.'

'Did she read its contents?'

'Yes.'

'Well, didn't she *tout comprendre*?'

'Yes.'

'And *tout pardonner*?'

'Yes.'

'Then you must have got your facts twisted. The wedding can't be off.'

'It is, I tell you. Do you think I don't know when a wedding's off and when it isn't? Sir Watkyn has forbidden it.'

This was an angle I had not foreseen.

'Why? Did you have a row or something?'

'Yes. About newts. He didn't like me putting them in the bath.'

'You put newts in the bath?'

'Yes.'

Like a keen cross-examining counsel, I swooped on the point.

'Why?'

His hand fluttered, as if about to reach for a straw.

'I broke the tank. The tank in my bedroom. The glass tank I keep my newts in. I broke the glass tank in my bedroom, and the bath was the only place to lodge the newts. The basin wasn't large enough. Newts need elbowroom. So I put them in the bath. Because I had broken the tank. The glass tank in my bedroom. The glass tank I keep my – '

I saw that if allowed to continue in this strain he might go on practically indefinitely, so I called him to order with a sharp rap of a china vase on the mantelpiece.

'I get the idea,' I said, brushing the fragments into the fire-place. 'Proceed. How does Pop Bassett come into the picture?'

'He went to take a bath. It never occurred to me that anyone would be taking a bath as late as this. And I was in the drawing-room, when he burst in shouting: "Madeline, that blasted Fink-Nottle has been filling my bathtub with tadpoles!" And I lost my head a little, I'm afraid. I yelled: "Oh, my gosh, you silly old ass, be careful what you're doing with those newts. Don't touch them. I'm in the middle of a most important experiment." '

'I see. And then – '

'I went on to tell him how I wished to ascertain whether the full moon affected the love life of newts. And a strange look came into his face, and he quivered a bit, and then he told me that he had pulled out the plug and all my newts had gone down the waste pipe.'

I think he would have preferred at this point to fling himself on the bed and turn his face to the wall, but I headed him off. I was resolved to stick to the *res*.

'Upon which you did what?'

'I ticked him off properly. I called him every name I could think of. In fact, I called him names that I hadn't a notion I knew. They just seemed to come bubbling up from my subconsciousness. I was hampered a bit at first by the fact that Madeline was there, but it wasn't long before he told her to go to bed, and then I was really able to express myself. And when I finally paused for breath, he forbade the banns and pushed off. And I rang the bell and asked Butterfield to bring me a glass of orange juice.'

I started.

'Orange juice?'

'I wanted picking up.'

'But orange juice? At such a time?'

'It was what I felt I needed.'

I shrugged my shoulders.

'Oh, well,' I said.

'Just another proof, of course, of what I often say – that it takes all sorts to make a world.

'As a matter of fact, I could do with a good long drink now.'

'The tooth-bottle is at your elbow.'

'Thanks . . . Ah! That's the stuff!'

'Have a go at the jug.'

'No, thanks. I know when to stop. Well, that's the position, Bertie. He won't let Madeline marry me, and I'm wondering if there is any possible way of bringing him round. I'm afraid there isn't. You see, it wasn't only that I called him names – '

'Such as?'

'Well, louse, I remember, was one of them. And skunk, I think. Yes, I'm pretty sure I called him a wall-eyed skunk. But he might forgive that. The real trouble is that I mocked at that cow-creamer of his.'

'Cow-creamer!'

I spoke sharply. He had started a train of thought. An idea had begun to burgeon. For some little time I had been calling on all the resources of the Wooster intellect to help me to solve this problem, and I don't often do that without something breaking loose. At this mention of the cow-creamer, the brain seemed suddenly to give itself a shake and start off across country with its nose to the ground.

'Yes. Knowing how much he loved and admired it, and searching for barbed words that would wound him, I told him it was modern Dutch. I had gathered from his remarks at the dinner table last night that that was the last thing it ought to be. "You and your eighteen-century cow-creamers!" I said. "Pah! Modern Dutch!" or words to that effect. The thrust got home. He turned purple, and broke off the wedding.'

'Listen, Gussie,' I said. 'I think I've got it.'

His face lit up. I could see that optimism had stirred and was shaking a leg. This Fink-Nottle has always been of an optimistic nature. Those who recall his address to the boys of Market Snodsbury Grammar School will remember that it was largely an appeal to the little blighters not to look on the dark side.

'Yes, I believe I see the way. What you have got to do, Gussie, is pinch that cow-creamer.'

His lips parted, and I thought an 'Eh, what?' was coming through, but it didn't. Just silence and a couple of bubbles.

'That is the first, essential step. Having secured the cow-creamer, you tell him it is in your possession and say: "Now, how about it?" I feel convinced that in order to recover that foul cow he would meet any terms you care to name. You know what collectors are like. Practically potty, every one of them. Why, my Uncle Tom wants the thing so badly that he is actually prepared to yield up his supreme cook, Anatole, in exchange for it.'

'Not the fellow who was functioning at Brinkley when I was there?'

'That's right.'

'The chap who dished up those *nonettes de poulet Agnes Sorel*?'

'That very artist.'

'You really mean that your uncle would consider Anatole well lost if he could secure this cow-creamer?'

'I have it from Aunt Dahlia's own lips.'

He drew a deep breath.

'Then you're right. This scheme of yours would certainly solve everything. Assuming, of course, that Sir Watkyn values the thing equally highly.'

'He does. Doesn't he, Jeeves?' I said, putting it up to him, as he trickled in with the brandy. 'Sir Watkyn Bassett has forbidden Gussie's wedding,' I explained, 'and I've been telling him that all he has to do in order to make him change his mind is to get hold of that cow-creamer and refuse to give it back until he coughs up a father's blessing. You concur?'

'Undoubtedly, sir. If Mr Fink-Nottle possesses himself of the *objet d'art* in question, he will be in a position to dictate. A very shrewd plan, sir.'

'Thank you, Jeeves. Yes, not bad, considering that I had to think on my feet and form my strategy at a moment's notice. If I were you, Gussie, I would put things in train immediately.'

'Excuse me, sir.'

'You spoke, Jeeves?'

'Yes, sir. I was about to say that before Mr Fink-Nottle can put the arrangements in operation there is an obstacle to be surmounted.'

'What's that?'

'In order to protect his interests, Sir Watkyn has posted Constable Oates on guard in the collection-room.'

'What!'

'Yes, sir.'

The sunshine died out of Gussie's face, and he uttered a stricken sound like a gramophone record running down.

'However, I think that with a little finesse it will be perfectly possible to eliminate this factor. I wonder if you recollect, sir, the occasion at Chufnell Hall, when Sir Roderick Glossop had become locked up in the potting-shed, and your efforts to release him appeared likely to be foiled by the fact that Police Constable Dobson had been stationed outside the door?'

'Vividly, Jeeves.'

'I ventured to suggest that it might be possible to induce him to leave his post by conveying word to him that the parlourmaid Mary, to whom he was betrothed, wished to confer with him in the raspberry bushes. The plan was put into effect and proved successful.'

'True, Jeeves. But,' I said dubiously, 'I don't see how anything like that could be worked here. Constable Dobson, you will recall, was young, ardent, romantic – just the sort of chap who would automatically go leaping into raspberry bushes if you told him there were girls there. Eustace Oates has none of the Dobson fire. He is well stricken in years and gives the impression of being a settled married man who would rather have a cup of tea.'

'Yes, sir, Constable Oates is, as you say, of a more sober temperament. But it is merely the principle of the thing which I would advocate applying to the present emergency. It would be necessary to provide a lure suited to the psychology of the individual. What I would suggest is that Mr Fink-Nottle should inform the officer that he has seen his helmet in your possession.'

'Egad, Jeeves!'

'Yes, sir.'

'I see the idea. Yes, very hot. Yes, that would do it.'

Gussie's glassy eye indicating that all this was failing to register, I explained.

'Earlier in the evening, Gussie, a hidden hand snitched this *gendarme's* lid, cutting him to the quick. What Jeeves is saying is that a word from you to the effect that you have seen it in my room will bring him bounding up here like a tigress after its lost cub, thus leaving you a clear field in which to operate. That is your idea in essence, is it not, Jeeves?'

'Precisely, sir.'

178

Gussie brightened visibly.

'I see. It's a ruse.'

'That's right. One of the ruses, and not the worst of them. Nice work, Jeeves.'

'Thank you, sir.'

'That will do the trick, Gussie. Tell him I've got his helmet, wait while he bounds out, nip to the glass case and trouser the cow. A simple programme. A child could carry it out. My only regret, Jeeves, is that this appears to remove any chance Aunt Dahlia might have had of getting the thing. A pity there has been such a wide popular demand for it.'

'Yes, sir. But possibly Mrs Travers, feeling that Mr Fink-Nottle's need is greater than hers, will accept the disappointment philosophically.'

'Possibly. On the other hand, possibly not. Still, there it is. On these occasions when individual interests clash, somebody has got to draw the short straw.'

'Very true, sir.'

'You can't be expected to dish out happy endings all round – one per person, I mean.'

'No, sir.'

'The great thing is to get Gussie fixed. So buzz off, Gussie, and Heaven speed your efforts.'

I lit a cigarette.

'A very sound idea, that, Jeeves. How did you happen to think of it?'

'It was the officer himself who put it into my head, sir, when I was chatting with him not long ago. I gathered from what he said that he actually does suspect you of being the individual who purloined his helmet.'

'Me? Why on earth? Dash it, I scarcely know the man. I thought he suspected Stiffy.'

'Originally, yes, sir. And it is still his view that Miss Byng was the motivating force behind the theft. But he now believes that the young lady must have had a male accomplice, who did the rough work. Sir Watkyn, I understand, supports him in this theory.'

I suddenly remembered the opening passages of my interview with Pop Bassett in the library, and at last got on to what he had been driving at. Those remarks of his which had seemed to me then mere idle gossip had had, I now perceived, a sinister under-current of meaning. I had supposed that we were just two of the boys chewing over the latest bit of hot news, and all the time the thing had been a probe or quiz.

'But what makes them think that I was the male accomplice?'

I gather that the officer was struck by the cordiality which he saw to exist between Miss Byng and yourself, when he encountered you in the road this afternoon, and his suspicions became strengthened when he found the young lady's glove on the scene of the outrage.'

'I don't get you, Jeeves.'

'He supposes you to be enamoured of Miss Byng, sir, and thinks that you were wearing her glove next your heart.'

'If it had been next my heart, how could I have dropped it?'

'His view is that you took it out to press to your lips, sir.'

'Come, come, Jeeves. Would I start pressing gloves to my lips at the moment when I was about to pinch a policeman's helmet?'

'Apparently Mr Pinker did, sir.'

I was on the point of explaining to him that what old Stinker would do in any given situation and what the ordinary, normal person with a couple of ounces more brain than a cuckoo clock would do were two vastly different things, when I was interrupted by the re-entrance of Gussie. I could see by the buoyancy of his demeanour that matters had been progressing well.

'Jeeves was right, Bertie,' he said. 'He read Eustace Oates like a book.'

'The information stirred him up?'

'I don't think I have ever seen a more thoroughly roused policeman. His first impulse was to drop everything and come dashing up here right away.'

'Why didn't he?'

'He couldn't quite bring himself to, in view of the fact that Sir Watkyn had told him to stay there.'

I followed the psychology. It was the same as that of the boy who stood on the burning deck, whence all but he had fled.

'Then the procedure, I take it, will be that he will send word to Pop Bassett, notifying him of the facts and asking permission to go ahead?'

'Yes. I expect you will have him with you in a few minutes.'

'Then you ought not to be here. You should be lurking in the hall.'

'I'm going there at once. I only came to report.'

'Be ready to slip in the moment he is gone.'

'I will. Trust me. There won't be a hitch. It was a wonderful idea of yours, Jeeves.'

'Thank you, sir.'

'You can imagine how relieved I'm feeling, knowing that in about five minutes everything will be all right. The only thing I'm a bit sorry for now,' said Gussie thoughtfully, 'is that I gave the old boy that notebook.'

He threw out this appalling statement so casually that it was a second or two before I got its import. When I did, a powerful shock permeated my system. It was as if I had been reclining in the electric chair and the authorities had turned on the juice.

'You gave him the notebook!'

'Yes. Just as he was leaving. I thought there might be some names in it which I had forgotten to call him.'

I supported myself with a trembling hand on the mantelpiece.

'Jeeves!'

'Sir?'

'More brandy!'

'Yes, sir.'

'And stop doling it out in those small glasses, as if it were radium. Bring the cask.'

Gussie was regarding me with a touch of surprise.

'Something the matter, Bertie?'

'Something the matter?' I let out a mirthless 'Ha! Well, this has torn it.'

'How do you mean? Why?'

'Can't you see what you've done, you poor chump? It's no use pinching that cow-creamer now. If old Bassett has read the contents of that notebook, nothing will bring him round.'

'Why not?'

'Well, you saw how they affected Spode. I don't suppose Pop Bassett is any fonder of reading home truths about himself than Spode is.'

'But he's had the home truths already. I told you how I ticked him off.'

'Yes, but you could have got away with that. Overlook it,

please . . . spoken in hot blood . . . strangely forgot myself . . . all that sort of stuff. Coldly reasoned opinions, carefully inscribed day by day in a notebook, are a very different thing.'

I saw that it had penetrated at last. The greenish tinge was back in his face. His mouth opened and shut like that of a goldfish which sees another goldfish nip in and get away with the ant's egg which it had been earmarking for itself.

'Oh, gosh!'

'Yes.'

'What can I do?'

'I don't know.'

'Think. Bertie, think!'

I did so, tensely, and was rewarded with an idea.

'Tell me,' I said, 'what exactly occurred at the conclusion of the vulgar brawl? You handed him the book. Did he dip into it on the spot?'

'No. He shoved it away in his pocket.'

'And did you gather that he still intended to take a bath?'

'Yes.'

'Then answer me this. What pocket? I mean the pocket of what garment? What was he wearing?'

'A dressing gown.'

'Over – think carefully, Fink-Nottle, for everything hangs on this – over shirt and trousers and things?'

'Yes, he had his trousers on. I remember noticing.'

'Then there is still hope. After leaving you, he would have gone to his room to shed the upholstery. He was pretty steamed up, you say?'

'Yes, very much.'

'Good. My knowledge of human nature, Gussie, tells me that a steamed-up man does not loiter about feeling in his pocket for notebooks and steeping himself in their contents. He flings off the garments, and legs it to the *salle de bain*. The book must still be in the pocket of his dressing gown – which, no doubt, he flung on the bed or over a chair – and all you have to do is nip into his room and get it.'

I had anticipated that this clear thinking would produce the joyous cry and the heartfelt burst of thanks. Instead of which, he merely shuffled his feet dubiously.

'Nip into his room?'

'Yes.'

'But dash it!'

'Now, what?'

'You're sure there isn't some other way?'

'Of course there isn't.'

'I see . . . You wouldn't care to do it for me, Bertie?'

'No, I would not.'

'Many fellows would, to help an old school friend.'

'Many fellows are mugs.'

'Have you forgotten those days at the dear old school?'

'Yes.'

'You don't remember the time I shared my last bar of milk chocolate with you?'

'No.'

'Well, I did, and you told me then that if ever you had an opportunity of doing anything for me . . . However, if these obligations – sacred, some people might consider them – have no weight with you, I suppose there is nothing more to be said.'

He pottered about for a while, doing the old cat-in-an-adage stuff: then, taking from his breast pocket a cabinet photograph of Madeline Bassett, he gazed at it intently. It seemed to be the bracer he required. He eyes lit up. His face lost its fishlike look. He strode out, to return immediately, slamming the door behind him.    'I say, Bertie, Spode's out there!'

'What of it?'

'He made a grab at me.'

'Made a grab at you?'

I frowned. I am a patient man, but I can be pushed too far. It seemed incredible, after what I had said to him, that Roderick Spode's hat was still in the ring. I went to the door, and threw it open. It was even as Gussie had said. The man was lurking.

He sagged a bit, as he saw me. I addressed him with cold severity.

'Anything I can do for you, Spode?'

'No. No, nothing, thanks.'

'Push along, Gussie,' I said, and stood watching him with a protective eye as he sidled round the human gorilla and disappeared along the passage. Then I turned to Spode.

'Spode,' I said in a level voice, 'did I or did I not tell you to leave Gussie alone?'

He looked at me pleadingly.

'Couldn't you possibly see your way to letting me do something to him, Wooster? If it was only to kick his spine up through his hat?'

'Certainly not.'

'Well, just as you say, of course.' He scratched his cheek discontentedly. 'Did you read that notebook, Wooster?'

'No.'

'He says my moustache is like the faint discoloured smear left by a squashed blackbeetle on the side of a kitchen sink.'

'He always was a poetic sort of chap.'

'And that the way I eat asparagus alters one's whole conception of Man as Nature's last word.'

'Yes, he told me that, I remember. He's about right, too. I was noticing at dinner. What you want to do, Spode, in future is lower the vegetable gently into the abyss. Take it easy. Don't snap at it. Try to remember that you are a human being and not a shark.'

'Ha, ha! "A human being and not a shark." Cleverly put, Wooster. Most amusing.'

He was still chuckling, though not frightfully heartily I thought, when Jeeves came along with a decanter on a tray.

'The brandy, sir.'

'And about time, Jeeves.'

'Yes, sir. I must once more apologize for my delay. I was detained by Constable Oates.'

'Oh? Chatting with him again?'

'Not so much chatting, sir, as staunching the flow of blood.'

'Blood?'

'Yes, sir. The officer had met with an accident.'

My momentary pique vanished, and in its place there came a stern joy. Life at Totleigh Towers had hardened me, blunting the gentler emotions, and I derived nothing but gratification from the news that Constable Oates had been meeting with accidents. Only one thing, indeed, could have pleased me more – if I had been informed that Sir Watkyn Bassett had trodden on the soap and come a purler in the bath tub.

'How did that happen?'

'He was assaulted while endeavouring to recover Sir Watkyn's cow-creamer from a midnight marauder, sir.'

Spode uttered a cry.

'The cow-creamer has not been stolen?'

'Yes sir.'

It was evident that Roderick Spode was deeply affected by the news. His attitude towards the cow-creamer had, if you remember, been fatherly from the first. Not lingering to hear more, he galloped off, and I accompanied Jeeves into the room, agog for details.

'What happened, Jeeves?'

'Well, sir, it was a little difficult to extract a coherent narrative from the officer, but I gather that he found himself restless and fidgety – '

'No doubt owing to his inability to get in touch with Pop Bassett, who, as we know, is in his bath, and receive permission to leave his post and come up here after his helmet.'

'No doubt, sir. And being restless, he experienced a strong desire to smoke a pipe. Reluctant, however, to run the risk of being found to have smoked while on duty – as might have been the case had he done so in an enclosed room, where the fumes would have lingered – he stepped out into the garden.'

'A quick thinker, this Oates.'

'He left the French window open behind him. And some little time later his attention was arrested by a sudden sound from within.'

'What sort of sound?'

'The sound of stealthy footsteps, sir.'

'Someone stepping stealthily, as it were?'

'Precisely, sir. Followed by the breaking of glass. He immediately hastened back to the room – which was, of course, in darkness.'

'Why?'

'Because he had turned the light out, sir.'

I nodded. I followed the idea.

'Sir Watkyn's instruction to him had been to keep his vigil in the dark, in order to convey to a marauder the impression that the room was unoccupied.'

I nodded again. It was a dirty trick, but one which would spring naturally to the mind of an ex-magistrate.

'He hurried to the case in which the cow-creamer had been deposited, and struck a match. This almost immediately went

185

out, but not before he had been able to ascertain that the *objet d'art* had disappeared. And he was still in the process of endeavouring to adjust himself to the discovery, when he heard a movement and, turning, perceived a dim figure stealing out through the French window. He pursued it into the garden, and was overtaking it and might shortly have succeeded in effecting an arrest, when there sprang from the darkness a dim figure –'

'The same dim figure?'

'No, sir. Another one.'

'A big night for dim figures.'

'Yes, sir.'

'Better call them Pat and Mike, or we shall be getting mixed.'

'A and B perhaps, sir?'

'If you prefer it, Jeeves. He was overtaking dim figure A, you say, when dim figure B sprang from the darkness –'

'– and struck him upon the nose.'

I uttered an exclamash. The thing was a mystery no longer.

'Old Stinker!'

'Yes, sir. No doubt Miss Byng inadvertently forgot to apprise him that there had been a change in the evening's arrangements.'

'And he was lurking there, waiting for me.'

'So one would be disposed to imagine, sir.'

I inhaled deeply, my thoughts playing about the constable's injured beezer. There, I was feeling, but for whatever it is, went Bertram Wooster, as the fellow said.

'This assault diverted the officer's attention, and the object of his pursuit was enabled to escape.'

'What became of Stinker?'

'On becoming aware of the officer's identity, he apologized, sir. He then withdrew.'

'I don't blame him. A pretty good idea, at that. Well, I don't know what to make of this, Jeeves. This dim figure. I am referring to dim figure A. Who could it have been? Had Oates any views on the subject?'

'Very definite views, sir. He is convinced that it was you.'

I stared.

'Me? Why the dickens has everything that happens in this ghastly house got to be me?'

'And it is his intention, as soon as he is able to secure Sir Watkyn's co-operation, to proceed here and search your room.'

'He was going to do that, anyway, for the helmet.'

'Yes, sir.'

'This is going to be rather funny, Jeeves. It will be entertaining to watch these two blighters ferret about, feeling sillier and sillier asses as each moment goes by and they find nothing.'

'Most diverting, sir.'

'And when the search is over and they are standing there baffled, stammering out weak apologies, I shall get a bit of my own back. I shall fold my arms and draw myself up to my full height – '

There came from without the hoof beats of a galloping relative, and Aunt Dahlia whizzed in.

'Here, shove this away somewhere, young Bertie,' she panted, seeming touched in the wind.

And so saying, she thrust the cow-creamer into my hands.

# =12=

I N my recent picture of Sir Watkyn Basset reeling beneath the
blow of hearing that I wanted to marry into his family, I
compared his garglings, if you remember, to the death rattle of
a dying duck. I might now have been this duck's twin brother,
equally stricken. For some moments I stood there, quacking
feebly: then with a powerful effort of the will I pulled myself
together and cheesed the bird imitation. I looked at Jeeves. He
looked at me. I did not speak, save with the language of the
eyes, but his trained senses enabled him to read my thoughts
unerringly.

'Thank you, Jeeves.'

I took the tumbler from him, and lowered perhaps half an
ounce of the raw spirit. Then, the dizzy spell overcome, I transferred my gaze to the aged relative, who was taking an easy in
the armchair.

It is pretty generally admitted, both in the Drones Club and
elsewhere, that Bertram Wooster in his dealings with the
opposite sex invariably shows himself a man of the nicest chivalry – what you sometimes hear described as a *parfait gentil*
knight. It is true that at the age of six, when the blood ran hot,
I once gave my nurse a juicy one over the top knot with a
porringer, but the lapse was merely a temporary one. Since then,
though few men have been more sorely tried by the sex, I have
never raised a hand against a woman. And I can give no better
indication of my emotions at this moment than by saying that,
*preux chevalier* though I am, I came within the veriest toucher
of hauling off and letting a revered aunt have it on the side of
the head with a *papier mâché* elephant – the only object on the
mantelpiece which the fierce rush of life at Totleigh Towers had
left still unbroken.

She, while this struggle was proceeding in my bosom, was at
her chirpiest. Her breath recovered, she had begun to prattle
with a carefree gaiety which cut me like a knife. It was obvious

from her demeanour that, stringing along with the late Diamond, she little knew what she had done.

'As nice a run,' she was saying, 'as I have had since the last time I was out with the Berks and Bucks. Not a check from start to finish. Good clean British sport at its best. It was a close thing though, Bertie. I could feel that cop's hot breath on the back of my neck. If a posse of curates hadn't popped up out of a trap and lent a willing hand at precisely the right moment, he would have got me. Well, God bless the clergy, say I. A fine body of men. But what on earth were policemen doing on the premises? Nobody ever mentioned policemen to me.'

'That was Constable Oates, the vigilant guardian of the peace of Totleigh-in-the-Wold,' I replied, keeping a tight hold on myself lest I should howl like a banshee and shoot up to the ceiling. 'Sir Watkyn had stationed him in the room to watch over his belongings. He was lying in the wait. I was the visitor he expected.'

'I'm glad you weren't the visitor he got. The situation would have been completely beyond you, my poor lamb. You would have lost your head and stood there like a stuffed wombat, to fall an easy prey. I don't mind telling you that when that man suddenly came in through the window, I myself was for a moment paralyzed. Still, all's well that ends well.'

I shook a sombre head.

'You err, my misguided old object. This is not an end, but a beginning. Pop Bassett is about to spread a drag-net.'

'Let him.'

'And when he and the constable come and search this room?'

'They wouldn't do that.'

'They would and will. In the first place, they think the Oates helmet is here. In the second place, it is the officer's view, relayed to me by Jeeves, who had it from him first hand as he was staunching the flow of blood, that it was I whom he pursued.'

Her chirpiness waned. I had expected it would. She had been beaming. She beamed no longer. Eyeing her steadily, I saw that the native hue of resolution had become sicklied o'er with the pale cast of thought.

'H'm! This is awkward.'

'Most.'

'If they find the cow-creamer here, it may be a little difficult to explain.'

She rose, and broke the elephant thoughtfully.

'The great thing,' she said, 'is not to lose our heads. We must say to ourselves: "What would Napoleon have done?" He was the boy in a crisis. He knew his onions. We must do something very clever, very shrewd, which will completely baffle these bounders. Well, come on, I'm waiting for suggestions.'

'Mine is that you pop off without delay, taking that beastly cow with you.'

'And run into the search party on the stairs! Not if I know it. Have you any ideas, Jeeves?'

'Not at the moment, madam.'

'You can't produce a guilty secret of Sir Watkyn's out of the hat, as you did with Spode?'

'No, madam.'

'No, I suppose that's too much to ask. Then we've got to hide the thing somewhere. But where? It's the old problem, of course – the one that makes life so tough for murderers – what to do with the body. I suppose the old Purloined Letter stunt wouldn't work?'

'Mrs Travers is alluding to the well-known story by the late Edgar Allan Poe, sir,' said Jeeves, seeing that I was not abreast. 'It deals with the theft of an important document, and the character who had secured it foiled the police by placing it in full view in a letter-rack, his theory being that what is obvious is often overlooked. No doubt Mrs Travers wishes to suggest that we deposit the object on the mantelpiece.'

I laughed a hollow one.

'Take a look at the mantelpiece! It is as bare as a wind-swept prairie. Anything placed there would stick out like a sore thumb.'

'Yes, that's true,' Aunt Dahlia was forced to admit.

'Put the bally thing in the suitcase, Jeeves.'

'That's no good. They're bound to look there.'

'Merely as a palliative,' I explained. 'I can't stand the sight of it any longer. In with it, Jeeves.'

'Very good, sir.'

A silence ensued, and it was just after Aunt Dahlia had broken it to say how about barricading the door and standing a siege that there came from the passage the sound of approaching footsteps.

'Here they are,' I said.

'They seem in a hurry,' said Aunt Dahlia.

She was correct. These were running footsteps. Jeeves went to the door and looked out.

'It is Mr Fink-Nottle, sir.'

And the next moment Gussie entered, going strongly.

A single glance at him was enough to reveal to the discerning eye that he had not been running just for the sake of the exercise. His spectacles were glittering in a hunted sort of way, and there was more than a touch of the fretful porpentine about his hair.

'Do you mind if I hide here till the milk train goes, Bertie?' he said. 'Under the bed will do. I shan't be in your way.'

'What's the matter?'

'Or, still better, the knotted sheet. That's the stuff.'

A snort like a minute-gun showed that Aunt Dahlia was in no welcoming mood.

'Get out of here, you foul Spink-Bottle,' she said curtly. 'We're in conference. Bertie, if an aunt's wishes have any weight with you, you will stamp on this man with both feet and throw him out on his ear.'

I raised a hand.

'Wait! I want to get the strength of this. Stop messing about with those sheets, Gussie, and explain. Is Spode after you again? Because if so –'

'Not Spode. Sir Watkyn.'

Aunt Dahlia snorted again, like one giving an encore in response to a popular demand.

'Bertie –'

I raised another hand.

'Half a second, old ancestor. How do you mean Sir Watkyn? Why Sir Watkyn? What on earth is he chivvying you for?'

'He's read the notebook.'

'What!'

'Yes.'

'Bertie, I am only a weak woman –'

I raised a third hand. This was no time for listening to aunts.

'Go on, Gussie,' I said dully.

He took off his spectacles and wiped them with a trembling

handkerchief. You could see that he was a man who had passed through the furnace.

'When I left you, I went to his room. The door was ajar, and I crept in. And when I had got in, I found that he hadn't gone to have a bath, after all. He was sitting on the bed in his underwear, reading the notebook. He looked up, and our eyes met. You've no notion what a frightful shock it gave me.'

'Yes, I have. I once had a very similar experience with the Rev. Aubrey Upjohn.'

'There was a long, dreadful pause. Then he uttered a sort of gurgling sound and rose, his face contorted. He made a leap in my direction. I pushed off. He followed. It was neck and neck down the stairs, but as we passed through the hall he stopped to get a hunting crop, and this enabled me to secure a good lead, which I – '

'Bertie,' said Aunt Dahlia, 'I am only a weak woman, but if you won't tread on this insect and throw the remains outside, I shall have to see what I can do. The most tremendous issues hanging in the balance . . . Our plan of action still to be decided on . . . Every second of priceless importance . . . and he comes in here, telling us the story of his life. Spink-Bottle, you ghastly goggle-eyed piece of gorgonzola, will you hop it or will you not?'

There is a compelling force about the old flesh and blood, when stirred, which generally gets her listened to. People have told me that in her hunting days she could make her wishes respected across two ploughed fields and a couple of spinneys. The word 'not' had left her lips like a high-powered shell, and Gussie, taking it between the eyes, rose some six inches into the air. When he returned to terra firms, his manner was apologetic and conciliatory.

'Yes, Mrs Travers. I'm just going, Mrs Travers. The moment we get the sheet working, Mrs Travers. If you and Jeeves will just hold this end, Bertie . . .'

'You want them to let you down from the window with a sheet?'

'Yes, Mrs Travers. Then I can borrow Bertie's car and drive to London.'

'It's a long drop.'

'Oh, not so very, Mrs Travers.'

'You may break your neck.'

'Oh, I don't think so, Mrs Travers.'

'But you may,' argued Aunt Dahlia. 'Come on, Bertie,' she said, speaking with real enthusiasm, 'hurry up. Let the man down with the sheet, can't you? What are you waiting for?'

I turned to Jeeves. 'Ready, Jeeves?'

'Yes, sir.' He coughed gently. 'And perhaps if Mr Fink-Nottle is driving your car to London, he might take your suitcase with him and leave it at the flat.'

I gasped. So did Aunt Dahlia. I stared at him. Aunt Dahlia the same. Our eyes met, and I saw in hers the same reverent awe which I have no doubt she viewed in mine.

I was overcome. A moment before, I had been dully conscious that nothing could save me from the soup. Already I had seemed to hear the beating of its wings. And now this!

Aunt Dahlia, speaking of Napoleon, had claimed that he was pretty hot in an emergency, but I was prepared to bet that not even Napoleon could have topped this superb effort. Once more, as so often in the past, the man had rung the bell and was entitled to the cigar or coconut.

'Yes, Jeeves,' I said, speaking with some difficulty, 'that is true. He might, mightn't he?'

'Yes, sir.'

'You won't mind taking my suitcase, Gussie? If you're borrowing the car, I shall have to go by train. I'm leaving in the morning myself. And it's a nuisance hauling about a lot of luggage.'

'Of course.'

'We'll just loose you down on the sheet and drop the suitcase after you. All set, Jeeves?'

'Yes, sir.'

'Then upsy-daisy!'

I don't think I have ever assisted at a ceremony which gave such universal pleasure to all concerned. The sheet didn't split, which pleased Gussie. Nobody came to interrupt us, which pleased me. And when I dropped the suitcase, it hit Gussie on the head, which delighted Aunt Dahlia. As for Jeeves, one could see that the faithful fellow was tickled pink at having been able to cluster round and save the young master in his hour of peril. His motto is 'Service'.

The stormy emotions through which I had been passing had not unnaturally left me weak, and I was glad when Aunt Dahlia, after a powerful speech in which she expressed her gratitude to our preserver in well-phrased terms, said that she would hop along and see what was going on in the enemy's camp. Her departure enabled me to sink into the armchair in which, had she remained, she would unquestionably have parked herself indefinitely. I flung myself on the cushioned seat and emitted a woof that came straight from the heart.

'So that's that, Jeeves!'

'Yes, sir.'

'Once again your swift thinking has averted disaster as it loomed.'

'It is very kind of you to say so, sir.'

'Not kind, Jeeves. I am merely saying what any thinking man would say. I didn't chip in while Aunt Dahlia was speaking, for I saw that she wished to have the floor, but you may take it that I was silently subscribing to every sentiment she uttered. You stand alone, Jeeves. What size hat do you take?'

'A number eight, sir.'

'I should have thought larger. Eleven or twelve.'

I helped myself to a spot of brandy, and sat rolling it round my tongue luxuriantly. It was delightful to relax after the strain and stress I had been through.

'Well, Jeeves, the going has been pretty tough, what?'

'Extremely, sir.'

'One begins to get some idea of how the skipper of the *Hesperus*'s little daughter must have felt. Still, I suppose these tests and trials are good for the character.'

'No doubt, sir.'

'Strengthening.'

'Yes, sir.'

'However, I can't say I'm sorry it's all over. Enough is always enough. And it is all over, one feels. Even this sinister house can surely have no further shocks to offer.'

'I imagine not, sir.'

'No, this is the finish. Totleigh Towers has shot its bolt, and at long last we are sitting pretty. Gratifying, Jeeves.'

'Most gratifying, sir.'

'You bet it is. Carry on with the packing. I want to get it done and go to bed.'

He opened the small suitcase, and I lit a cigarette and proceeded to stress the moral lesson to be learned from all this rannygazoo.

'Yes, Jeeves, "gratifying" is the word. A short while ago, the air was congested with V-shaped depressions, but now one looks north, south, east and west and describes not a single cloud on the horizon – except the fact that Gussie's wedding is still off, and that can't be helped. Well, this should certainly teach us, should it not, never to repine, never to despair, never to allow the upper lip to unstiffen, but always to remember that, no matter how dark the skies may be, the sun is shining somewhere and will eventually come smiling through.'

I paused. I perceived that I was not securing his attention. He was looking down with an intent, thoughtful expression on his face.

'Something the matter, Jeeves?'

'Sir?'

'You appear preoccupied.'

'Yes, sir. I have just discovered that there is a policeman's helmet in this suitcase.'

I HAD been right about the strengthening effect on the character of the vicissitudes to which I had been subjected since
clocking in at the country residence of Sir Watkyn Bassett. Little
by little, bit by bit, they had been moulding me, turning me
from a sensitive clubman and *boulevardier* to a man of chilled
steel. A novice to conditions in this pest house, abruptly handed
the news item which I had just been handed, would, I imagine,
have rolled up the eyeballs and swooned where he sat. But I,
toughened and fortified by the routine of one damn thing after
another which constituted life at Totleigh Towers, was enabled
to keep my head and face the issue.

I don't say I didn't leave my chair like a jack-rabbit that has
sat on a cactus, but having risen I wasted no time in fruitless
twitterings. I went to the door and locked it. Then, tight-lipped
and pale, I came back to Jeeves, who had now taken the helmet
from the suitcase and was oscillating it meditatively by its strap.

His first words showed me that he had got the wrong angle
on the situation.

'It would be wiser, sir,' he said with a faint reproach, 'to have
selected some more adequate hiding place.'

I shook my head. I may even have smiled – wanly, of course.
My swift intelligence had enabled me to probe to the bottom
of this thing.

'Not me, Jeeves. Stiffy.'

'Sir?'

'The hand that placed that helmet there was not mine, but
that of S. Byng. She had it in her room. She feared lest a search
might be instituted, and when I last saw her was trying to think
of a safer spot. This is her idea of one.'

I sighed.

'How do you imagine a girl gets a mind like Stiffy's, Jeeves?'

'Certainly the young lady is somewhat eccentric in her actions,
sir.'

'Eccentric? She could step straight into Colney Hatch, and no questions asked. They would lay down the red carpet for her. The more the thoughts dwell on that young shrimp, the more the soul sickens in horror. One peers into the future, and shudders at what one sees there. One has to face it, Jeeves – Stiffy, who is pure padded cell from the foundations up, is about to marry the Rev. H. P. Pinker, himself about as pronounced a goop as ever broke bread, and there is no reason to suppose – one has to face this, too – that their union will not be blessed. There will, that is to say, 'ere long be little feet pattering about the home. And what one asks oneself is – Just how safe will human life be in the vicinity of those feet, assuming – as one is forced to assume – that they will inherit the combined loopiness of two such parents? It is with a sort of tender pity, Jeeves, that I think of the nurses, the governesses, the private-school masters and the public-school masters who will lightly take on the responsibility of looking after a blend of Stephanie Byng and Harold Pinker, little knowing that they are coming up against something hotter than mustard. However,' I went on, abandoning these speculations, 'all this, though of absorbing interest, is not really germane to the issue. Contemplating that helmet and bearing in mind the fact that the Oates-Bassett comedy duo will be arriving at any moment to start their search, what would you recommend?'

'It is a little difficult to say, sir. A really effective hiding place for so bulky an object does not readily present itself.'

'No. The damn thing seems to fill the room, doesn't it?'

'It unquestionably takes the eye, sir.'

'Yes. The authorities wrought well when they shaped this helmet for Constable Oates. They aimed to finish him off impressively, not to give him something which would balance on top of his head like a peanut, and they succeeded. You couldn't hide a lid like this in an impenetrable jungle. Ah, well,' I said, 'we will just have to see what tact and suavity will do. I wonder when these birds are going to arrive. I suppose we may expect them very shortly. Ah! That would be the hand of doom now, if I mistake not, Jeeves.'

But in assuming that the knocker who had just knocked on the door was Sir Watkyn Bassett, I had erred. It was Stiffy's voice that spoke.

'Bertie, let me in'

There was nobody I was more anxious to see, but I did not immediately fling wide the gates. Prudence dictated a preliminary enquiry.

'Have you got that bally dog of yours with you?'

'No. He's being aired by the butler.'

'In that case, you may enter.'

When she did so, it was to find Bertram confronting her with folded arms and a hard look. She appeared, however, not to note my forbidding exterior.

'Bertie, darling – '

She broke off, checked by a fairly animal snarl from the Wooster lips.

'Not so much of the "Bertie, darling". I have just one thing to say to you, young Stiffy, and it is this: Was it you who put that helmet in my suitcase?'

'Of course it was. That's what I was coming to talk to you about. You remember I was trying to think of a good place. I racked the brain quite a bit, and then suddenly I got it.'

'And now I've got it.'

The acidity of my tone seemed to surprise her. She regarded me with girlish wonder – the wide-eyed kind.

'But you don't mind do you, Bertie, darling?'

'Ha!'

'But why? I thought you would be so glad to help me out.'

'Oh, yes?' I said, and I meant it to sting.

'I couldn't risk having Uncle Watkyn find it in my room.'

'You preferred to have him find it in mine?'

'But how can he? He can't come searching your room.'

'He can't, eh?'

'Of course not. You're his guest.'

'And you suppose that that will cause him to hold his hand?' I smiled one of those bitter, sardonic smiles. 'I think you are attributing to the old poison germ a niceness of feeling and a respect for the laws of hospitality which nothing in his record suggests that he possesses. You can take it from me that he definitely is going to search the room, and I imagine that the only reason he hasn't arrived already is that he is still scouring the house for Gussie.'

'Gussie?'

'He is at the moment chasing Gussie with a hunting crop. But a man cannot go on doing that indefinitely. Sooner or later he will give it up, and then we shall have him here, complete with magnifying glass and bloodhounds.'

The gravity of the situash had at last impressed itself upon her. She uttered a squeak of dismay, and her eyes became a bit soup-platey.

'Oh, Bertie! Then I'm afraid I've put you in rather a spot.'

'That covers the facts like a dust-sheet.'

'I'm sorry now I ever asked Harold to pinch the thing. I was a mistake. I admit it. Still, after all, even if Uncle Watkyn does come here and find it, it doesn't matter much, does it?'

'Did you hear that, Jeeves?'

'Yes, sir.'

'Thank you, Jeeves. What makes you suppose that I shall meekly assume the guilt and not blazon the truth forth to the world?'

I wouldn't have supposed that her eyes could have widened any more, but they did perceptibly. Another dismayed squeak escaped her. Indeed, such was its volume that it might perhaps be better to call it a squeal.

'But Bertie!'

'Well?'

'Bertie, listen!'

'I'm listening.'

'Surely you will take the rap? You can't let Harold get it in the neck. You were telling me this afternoon that he would be unfrocked. I won't have him unfrocked. Where is he going to get if they unfrock him? That sort of thing gives a curate a frightful black eye. Why can't you say you did it? All it would mean is that you would be kicked out of the house, and I don't suppose you're so anxious to stay on, are you?'

'Possibly you are not aware that your bally uncle is proposing to send the perpetrator of this outrage to chokey.'

'Oh, no. At the worst, just a fine.'

'Nothing of the kind. He specifically told me chokey.'

'He didn't mean it. I expect there was – '

'No, there was not a twinkle in his eye.'

'Then that settles it. I can't have any precious, angel Harold doing a stretch.'

'How about your precious, angel Bertram?'

'But Harold's sensitive.'

'So am I sensitive.'

'Not half so sensitive as Harold. Bertie, surely you aren't going to be difficult about this? You're much too good a sport. Didn't you tell me once that the Code of the Woosters was "Never let a pal down"?'

She had found the talking point. People who appeal to the Code of the Woosters rarely fail to touch a chord in Bertram. My iron front began to crumble.

'That's all very fine – '

'Bertie, darling!'

'Yes, I know, but, dash it all – '

'Bertie!'

'Oh, well!'

'You will take the rap?'

'I suppose so.'

She yodelled ecstatically, and I think that if I had not side-stepped she would have flung her arms about my neck. Certainly she came leaping forward with some such purpose apparently in view. Foiled by my agility, she began to tear off a few steps of that Spring dance to which she was so addicted.

'Thank you, Bertie, darling. I knew you would be sweet about it. I can't tell you how grateful I am, and how much I admire you. You remind me of Carter Paterson . . . no, that's not it . . . Nick Carter . . . no, not Nick Carter . . . Who does Mr Wooster remind me of, Jeeves?'

'Sidney Carton, miss.'

'That's right. Sidney Carton. But he was smalltime stuff compared with you, Bertie. And, anyway, I expect we are getting the wind up quite unnecessarily. Why are we taking it for granted that Uncle Watkyn will find the helmet, if he comes and searches the room? There are a hundred places where you can hide it.'

And before I could say 'Name three!' she had pirouetted to the door and pirouetted out. I could hear her dying away in the distance with a song on the lips.

My own, as I turned to Jeeves, were twisted in a bitter smile.

'Women, Jeeves!'

'Yes, sir.'

'Well, Jeeves,' I said, my hand stealing towards the decanter, 'this is the end!'

'No, sir.'

I started with a violence that nearly unshipped my front uppers.

'Not the end?'

'No, sir.'

'You don't mean you have an idea?'

'Yes, sir.'

'But you told me just now you hadn't.'

'Yes, sir. But since then I have been giving the matter some thought, and am now in a position to say "Eureka!" '

'Say what?'

'Eureka, sir. Like Archimedes.'

'Did he say Eureka? I thought it was Shakespeare.'

'No, sir. Archimedes. What I would recommend is that you drop the helmet out of the window. It is most improbable that it will occur to Sir Watkyn to search the exterior of the premises, and we shall be able to recover it at our leisure.' He paused, and stood listening. 'Should this suggestion meet with your approval, sir, I feel that a certain haste would be advisable. I fancy I can hear the sound of approaching footsteps.'

He was right. The air was vibrant with their clumping. Assuming that a herd of bison was not making its way along the second-floor passage of Totleigh Towers, the enemy were upon us. With the nippiness of a lamb in the fold on observing the approach of Assyrians, I snatched up the helmet, bounded to the window and loosed the thing into the night. And scarcely had I done so, when the door opened, and through it came – in the order named – Aunt Dahlia, wearing an amused and indulgent look, as if she were joining in some game to please the children: Pop Bassett, in a purple dressing gown, and Police Constable Oates, who was dabbing at his nose with a pocket-handkerchief.

'So sorry to disturb you, Bertie,' said the aged relative courteously.

'Not at all,' I replied with equal suavity. 'Is there something I can do for the multitude?'

'Sir Watkyn has got some extraordinary idea into his head about wanting to search your room.'

'Search my room?'

'I intend to search it from top to bottom,' said old Bassett, looking very Bosher Street-y.

I glanced at Aunt Dahlia, raising the eyebrows.

'I don't understand. What's all this about?'

She laughed indulgently.

'You will scarcely believe it, Bertie, but he thinks that cow-creamer is here.'

'Is it missing?'

'It's been stolen.'

'You don't say!'

'Yes.'

'Well, well, well!'

'He's very upset about it.'

'I don't wonder.'

'Most distressed.'

'Poor old bloke!'

I placed a kindly hand on Pop Basset's shoulder. Probably the wrong thing to do, I can see, looking back, for it did not soothe.

'I can do without your condolences, Mr Wooster, and I should be glad if you would not refer to me as a bloke. I have every reason to believe that not only is my cow-creamer in your possession, but Constable Oates's helmet, as well.'

A cheery guffaw seemed in order. I uttered it.

'Ha, ha!'

Aunt Dahlia came across with another.

'Ha, ha!'

'How dashed absurd!'

'Perfectly ridiculous.'

'What on earth would I be doing with cow-creamers?'

'Or policemen's helmets?'

'Quite.'

'Did you ever hear such a weird idea?'

'Never. My dear old host,' I said, 'let us keep perfectly calm and cool and get all this straightened out. In the kindliest spirit, I must point out that you are on the verge – if not slightly past the verge – of making an ass of yourself. This sort of thing won't do, you know. You can't dash about accusing people of nameless crimes without a shadow of evidence.'

'I have all the evidence I require, Mr Wooster.'

'That's what you think. And that, I maintain, is where you are making the floater of lifetime. When was this modern Dutch gadget of yours abstracted?'

He quivered beneath the thrust, pinkening at the tip of the nose.

'It is not modern Dutch!'

'Well, we can thresh that out later. The point is: when did it leave the premises?'

'It has not left the premises.'

'That, again, is what you think. Well, when was it stolen?'

'About twenty minutes ago.'

'Then there you are. Twenty minutes ago I was up here in my room.'

This rattled him. I had thought it would.

'You were in your room?'

'In my room.'

'Alone?'

'On the contrary. Jeeves was here.'

'Who is Jeeves?'

'Don't you know, Jeeves? This is Jeeves. Jeeves . . . Sir Watkyn Bassett.'

'And who may you be, my man?'

'That's exactly what he is – my man. May I say my right-hand man?'

'Thank you, sir.'

'Not at all, Jeeves. Well-earned tribute.'

Pop Bassett's face was disfigured, if you could disfigure a face like his, by an ugly sneer

'I regret, Mr Wooster, that I am not prepared to accept as conclusive evidence of your innocence the unsupported word of your manservant.'

'Unsupported, eh? Jeeves, go and page Mr Spode. Tell him I want him to come and put a bit of stuffing into my alibi.'

'Very good, sir.'

He shimmered away, and Pop Bassett seemed to swallow something hard and jagged.

'Was Roderick Spode with you?'

'Certainly he was. Perhaps you will believe him?'

'Yes, I would believe Roderick Spode.'

'Very well, then. He'll be here in a moment.'

He appeared to muse.

'I see. Well, apparently I was wrong, then, in supposing that you are concealing my cow-creamer. It must have been purloined by somebody else.'

'Outside job, if you ask me,' said Aunt Dahlia.

'Possibly the work of an international gang,' I hazarded.

'Very likely.'

'I expect it was all over the place that Sir Watkyn had bought the thing. You remember Uncle Tom had been counting on getting it, and no doubt he told all sorts of people where it had gone. It wouldn't take long for the news to filter through to the international gangs. They keep their ear to the ground.'

'Damn clever, those gangs,' assented the aged relative.

Pop Bassett had seemed to me to wince a trifle at the mention of Uncle Tom's name. Guilty conscience doing its stuff, no doubt – gnawing, as these guilty consciences do.

'Well, we need not discuss the matter further,' he said. 'As regards the cow-creamer, I admit that you have established your case. We will now turn to Constable Oate's helmet. That, Mr Wooster, I happen to know positively, is in your possession.'

'Oh, yes?'

'Yes. The constable received specific information on the point from an eyewitness. I will proceed, therefore, to search your room without delay.'

'You really feel you want to?'

'I do.'

I shrugged the shoulders.

'Very well,' I said, 'very well. If that is the spirit in which you interpret the duties of a host, carry on. We invite inspection. I can only say that you appear to have extraordinarily rummy views on making your guests comfortable over the weekend. Don't count on my coming here again.'

I had expressed the opinion to Jeeves that it would be entertaining to stand by and watch this blighter and his colleague ferret about, and so it proved. I don't know when I have extracted more solid amusement from anything. But all these good things have to come to an end at last. About ten minutes later, it was plain that the bloodhounds were planning to call it off and pack up.

To say that Pop Bassett was wry, as he desisted from his efforts and turned to me, would be to understate it.

'I appear to owe you an apology, Mr Wooster,' he said.

'Sir W. Bassett,' I rejoined, 'you never spoke a truer word.'

And folding my arms and drawing myself up to my full height, I let him have it.

The exact words of my harangue have, I am sorry to say, escaped my memory. It is a pity that there was nobody taking them down in shorthand, for I am not exaggerating when I say that I surpassed myself. Once or twice, when a bit lit at routs and revels, I have spoken with an eloquence which, rightly or wrongly, has won the plaudits of the Drones Club, but I don't think that I have ever quite reached the level to which I now soared. You could see the stuffing trickling out of old Bassett in great heaping handfuls.

But as I rounded into my perforation, I suddenly noticed that I was failing to grip. He had ceased to listen, and was staring past me at something out of my range of vision. And so worth looking at did this spectacle, judging from his expression, appear to be that I turned in order to take a dekko.

It was the butler who had so riveted Sir Watkyn Bassett's attention. He was standing in the doorway, holding in his right hand a silver salver. And on that salver was a policeman's helmet.

# =14=

I REMEMBER old Stinker Pinker, who towards the end of his career at Oxford used to go in for social service in London's tougher districts, describing to me once in some detail the sensations he had experienced one afternoon, while spreading the light in Bethnal Green, on being unexpectedly kicked in the stomach by a costermonger. It gave him, he told me, a strange, dreamy feeling, together with an odd illusion of having walked into a thick fog. And the reason I mention it is that my own emotions at this moment were extraordinarily similar.

When I had last seen this butler, if you recollect, on the occasion when he had come to tell me that Madeline Bassett would be glad if I could spare her a moment, I mentioned that he had flickered. It was not so much at a flickering butler that I was gazing now as at a sort of heaving mist with a vague suggestion of something butlerine vibrating inside it. Then the scales fell from my eyes, and I was enabled to note the reactions of the rest of the company.

They were all taking it extremely big. Pop Bassett, like the chap in the poem which I had to write out fifty times at school for introducing a white mouse into the English Literature hour, was plainly feeling like some watcher of the skies when a new planet swims into his ken, while Aunt Dahlia and Constable Oates resembled respectively stout Cortez staring at the Pacific and all his men looking at each other with a wild surmise, silent upon a peak in Darien.

It was a goodish while before anybody stirred. Then, with a choking cry like that of a mother spotting her long-lost child in the offing, Constable Oates swooped forward and grabbed the lid, clasping it to his bosom with visible ecstasy.

The movement seemed to break the spell. Old Bassett came to life as if someone had pressed a button.

'Where – where did you get that, Butterfield?'

'I found it in a flowerbed, Sir Watkyn.'

'In a flowerbed?'

'Odd,' I said. 'Very strange.'

'Yes, sir. I was airing Miss Byng's dog, and happening to be passing the side of the house I observed Mr Wooster drop something from his window. It fell into the flowerbed beneath, and upon inspection proved to be this helmet.'

Old Bassett drew a deep breath.

'Thank you, Butterfield.'

The butler breezed off, and old B., revolving on his axis, faced me with gleaming pince-nez.

'So!' he said.

There is never very much you can do in the way of a telling come-back when a fellow says 'So!' to you. I preserved a judicious silence.

'Some mistake,' said Aunt Dahlia, taking the floor with an intrepidity which became her well. 'Probably came from one of the other windows. Easy to get confused on a dark night.'

'Tchah!'

'Or it may be that the man was lying. Yes, that seems a plausible explanation. I think I see it all. This Butterfield of yours is the guilty man. He stole the helmet, and knowing that the hunt was up and detection imminent, decided to play a bold game and try to shove it off on Bertie. Eh, Bertie?'

'I shouldn't wonder, Aunt Dahlia. I shouldn't wonder at all.'

'Yes, that is what must have happened. It becomes clearer every moment. You can't trust these saintly looking butlers an inch.'

'Not an inch.'

'I remember thinking the fellow had a furtive eye.'

'Me, too.'

'You noticed it yourself, did you?'

'Right away.'

'He reminds me of Murgatroyd. Do you remember Murgatroyd at Brinkley, Bertie?'

'The fellow before Pomeroy? Stoutish cove?'

'That's right. With a face like a more than usually respectable archbishop. Took us all in, that face. We trusted him implicitly. And what was the result? Fellow pinched a fish slice, put it up the spout and squandered the proceeds at the dog races. This Butterfield is another Murgatroyd.'

'Some relation, perhaps.'

'I shouldn't be surprised. Well, now that's all satisfactorily settled and Bertie dismissed without a stain on his character, how about all going to bed? It's getting late, and if I don't have my eight hours, I'm a rag.'

She had injected into the proceedings such a pleasant atmosphere of all-pals-together and hearty let's-say-no-more-about-it that it came quite as a shock to find that old Bassett was failing to see eye to eye. He proceeded immediately to strike the jarring note.

'With your theory that somebody is lying, Mrs Travers, I am in complete agreement. But when you assert that it is my butler, I must join issue with you. Mr Wooster has been exceedingly clever – most ingenious – '

'Oh, thanks.'

'- but I am afraid that I find myself unable to dismiss him, as you suggest, without a stain on his character. In fact, to be frank with you, I do not propose to dismiss him at all.'

He gave me the pince-nez in a cold and menacing manner. I can't remember when I've seen a man I liked the look of less.

'You may possibly recall, Mr Wooster, that in the course of our conversation in the library I informed you that I took the very gravest view of this affair. Your suggestion that I might be content with inflicting a fine of five pounds, as was the case when you appeared before me at Bosher street convicted of a similar outrage, I declared myself unable to accept. I assured you that the perpetrator of this wanton assault on the person of Constable Oates would, when apprehended, serve a prison sentence. I see no reason to revise that decision.'

This statement had a mixed press. Eustace Oates obviously approved. He looked up from the helmet with a quick encouraging smile and but for the iron restraint of discipline would, I think, have said 'Hear, hear!' Aunt Dahlia and I, on the other hand, didn't like it.

'Here, come, I say now, Sir Watkyn, really, dash it,' she expostulated, always on her toes when the interests of the clan were threatened. 'You can't do that sort of thing.'

'Madam, I both can and will.' He twiddled a hand in the direction of Eustace Oates. 'Constable!'

He didn't add 'Arrest this man!' or 'Do you duty!' but the officer got the gist. He clumped forward zealously. I was rather expecting him to lay a hand on my shoulder or to produce the gyves and apply them to my wrists, but he didn't. He merely lined up beside me as if we were going to do a duet and stood there looking puff-faced.

Aunt Dahlia continued to plead and reason.

'But you can't invite a man to your house and the moment he steps inside the door calmly bung him into the coop. If that is Gloucestershire hospitality, then heaven help Gloucestershire.'

'Mr Wooster is not here on my invitation, but on my daughter's.'

'That makes no difference. You can't wriggle out of it like that. He is your guest. He has eaten your salt. And let me tell you, while we are on the subject, that there was a lot too much of it in the soup tonight.'

'Oh, would you say that?' I said. 'Just about right, it seemed to me.'

'No. Too salty.'

Pop Bassett intervened.

'I must apologize for the shortcomings of my cook. I may be making a change before long. Meanwhile, to return to the subject with which we were dealing, Mr Wooster is under arrest, and tomorrow I shall take the necessary steps to – '

'And what's going to happen to him tonight?'

'We maintain a small but serviceable police station in the village, presided over by Constable Oates. Oates will doubtless be able to find him accommodation.'

'You aren't proposing to lug the poor chap off to a police station at this time of night? You could at least let him doss in a decent bed.'

'Yes, I see no objection to that. One does not wish to be unduly harsh. You may remain in this room until tomorrow, Mr Wooster.'

'Oh, thanks.'

'I shall lock the door – '

'Oh, quite.'

'And take charge of the key – '

'Oh, rather.'

'And Constable Oates will patrol beneath the window for the remainder of the night.'

'Sir?'

'This will check Mr Wooster's known propensity for dropping things from windows. You had better take up your station at once, Oates.'

'Very good, sir.'

There was a note of quiet anguish in the officer's voice, and it was plain that the smug satisfaction with which he had been watching the progress of events had waned. His views on getting his eight hours were apparently the same as Aunt Dahlia's. Saluting sadly, he left the room in a depressed sort of way. He had his helmet again, but you could see that he was beginning to ask himself if helmets were everything.

'And now, Mrs Travers, I should like, if I may, to have a word with you in private.'

They oiled off, and I was alone.

'I don't mind confessing that my emotions, as the key turned in the lock, were a bit poignant. On the one hand, it was nice to feel that I had got my bedroom to myself for a few minutes, but against that you had to put the fact that I was in what is known as durance vile and not likely to get out of it.

Of course, this was not new stuff to me, for I had heard the bars clang outside my cell door that time at Bosher Street. But on that occasion I had been able to buoy myself up with the reflection that the worst the aftermath was likely to provide was a rebuke from the bench or, as subsequently proved to be the case, a punch in the pocket-book. I was not faced, as I was faced now, by the prospect of waking on the morrow to begin serving a sentence of thirty days' duration in a prison where it was most improbable that I would be able to get my morning cup of tea.

Nor did the consciousness that I was innocent seem to help much. I drew no consolation from the fact that Stiffy Byng thought me like Sidney Carton. I had never met the chap, but I gathered that he was somebody who had taken it on the chin to oblige a girl, and to my mind this was enough to stamp him as a priceless ass. Sidney Carton and Bertram Wooster, I felt – nothing to choose between them. Sidney, one of the mugs – Bertram, the same.

I went to the window and looked out. Recalling the moody distaste which Constable Oates had exhibited at the suggestion that he should stand guard during the night hours, I had a faint hope that, once the eye of authority was removed, he might have ducked the assignment and gone off to get his beauty sleep. But no. There he was, padding up and down on the lawn, the picture of vigilance. And I had just gone to the washhand-stand to get a cake of soap to bung at him, feeling that this might soothe the bruised spirit a little, when I heard the door handle rattle.

I stepped across and put my lips to the woodwork.

'Hallo.'

'It is I, sir. Jeeves.'

'Oh, hallo, Jeeves.'

'The door appears to be locked, sir.'

'And you can take it from me, Jeeves, that appearances do not deceive. Pop Bassett locked it, and has trousered the key.'

'Sir?'

'I've been pinched.'

'Indeed, sir?'

'What was that?'

'I said "Indeed, sir?" '

'Oh, did you? Yes. Yes, indeed. And I'll tell you why.'

I gave him a *précis* of what had happened. It was not easy to hear, with a door between us, but I think the narrative elicited a spot of respectful tut-tutting.

'Unfortunate, sir.'

'Most. Well, Jeeves, what is your news?'

'I endeavoured to locate Mr Spode, sir, but he had gone for a walk in the grounds. No doubt he will be returning shortly.'

'Well, we shan't require him now. The rapid march of events has taken us far past the point where Spode could have been of service. Anything else been happening at your end?'

'I have had a word with Miss Byng, sir.'

'I should like a word with her myself. What had she to say?'

'The young lady was in considerable distress of mind, sir, her union with the Reverend Mr Pinker having been forbidden by Sir Watkyn.'

'Good Lord, Jeeves! Why?'

'Sir Watkyn appears to have taken umbrage at the part played by Mr Pinker in allowing the purloiner of the cow-creamer to effect his escape.'

'Why do you say "his"?'

'From motives of prudence, sir. Walls have ears.'

'I see what you mean. That's rather neat, Jeeves.'

'Thank you, sir.'

I mused a while on this latest development. There were certainly aching hearts in Gloucestershire all right this p.m. I was conscious of a pang of pity. Despite the fact that it was entirely owing to Stiffy that I found myself in my present predic., I wished the young loony well and mourned for her in her hour of disaster.

'So he has bunged a spanner into Stiffy's romance as well as Gussie's, has he? That old bird has certainly been throwing his weight about tonight, Jeeves.'

'Yes, sir.'

'And not a thing to be done about it, as far as I can see. Can you see anything to be done about it?'

'No, sir.'

'And switching to another aspect of the affair, you haven't any immediate plans for getting me out of this, I suppose?'

'Not adequately formulated, sir. I am turning over an idea in my mind.'

'Turn well, Jeeves. Spare no effort.'

'But it is at present merely nebulous.'

'It involves finesse, I presume?'

'Yes, sir.'

I shook my head. Waste of time really, of course, because he couldn't see me. Still, I shook it.

'It's no good trying to be subtle and snaky now, Jeeves. What is required is rapid action. And a thought has occurred to me. We were speaking not long since of the time when Sir Roderick Glossop was immured in the potting-shed, with Constable Dobson guarding every exit. Do you remember what old Pop Stoker's idea was for coping with the situation?'

'If I recollect rightly, sir, Mr Stoker advocated a physical assault upon the officer. "Bat him over the head with a shovel!" was, as I recall, his expression.'

'Correct, Jeeves. Those were his exact words. And though we scouted the idea at the time, it seemed to me now that he displayed a considerable amount of rugged good sense. These practical, self-made men have a way of going straight to the point and avoiding side issues. Constable Oates is on sentry go beneath my window. I still have the knotted sheets and they can readily be attached to the leg of the bed or something. So if you would just borrow a shovel somewhere and step down – '

'I fear, sir – '

'Come on, Jeeves. This is no time for *nolle prosequis*. I know you like finesse, but you must see that it won't help us now. The moment has arrived when only shovels can serve. You could go and engage him in conversation, keeping the instrument concealed behind your back, and waiting for the psychological – '

'Excuse me, sir. I think I hear somebody coming.'

'Well, ponder over what I have said. Who is coming?'

'It is Sir Watkyn and Mrs Travers, sir. I fancy they are about to call upon you.'

'I thought I shouldn't get this room to myself for long. Still, let them come. We Woosters keep open house.'

When the door was unlocked a few moments later, however, only the relative entered. She made for the old familiar armchair, and dumped herself heavily in it. Her demeanour was sombre, encouraging no hope that she had come to announce that Pop Bassett, wiser counsels having prevailed, had decided to set me free. And yet I'm dashed if that wasn't precisely what she had come to announce.

'Well, Bertie,' she said, having brooded in silence for a space, 'you can get on with your packing.'

'Eh?'

'He's called it off.'

'Called it off?'

'Yes. He isn't going to press the charge.'

'You mean I'm not headed for chokey?'

'No.'

'I'm as free as the air, as the expression is?'

'Yes.'

I was so busy rejoicing in spirit that it was some moments before I had leisure to observe that the buck-and-wing dance which I was performing was not being abetted by the old flesh and blood. She was still carrying on with her sombre sitting, and I looked at her with a touch of reproach.

'You don't seem very pleased.'

'Oh, I'm delighted.'

'I fail to detect the symptoms,' I said, rather coldly. 'I should have thought that a nephew's reprieve at the foot of the scaffold, as you might say, would have produced a bit of leaping and springing about.'

A deep sigh escaped her.

'Well, the trouble is, Bertie, there is a catch in it. The old buzzard has made a condition.'

'What is that?'

'He wants Anatole.'

I stared at her.

'Wants Anatole?'

'Yes. That is the price of your freedom. He says he will agree not to press the charge if I let him have Anatole. The darned old blackmailer!'

A spasm of anguish twisted her features. It was not so very long since she had been speaking in high terms of blackmail and giving it her hearty approval, but if you want to derive real satisfaction from blackmail, you have to be at the right end of it. Catching it coming, as it were, instead of going, this woman was suffering.

I wasn't feeling any too good myself. From time to time in the course of this narrative I have had occasion to indicate my sentiments regarding Anatole, that peerless artist, and you will remember that the relative's account of how Sir Watkyn Bassett had basely tried to snitch him from her employment during his visit to Brinkley Court had shocked me to my foundations.

It is difficult, of course, to convey to those who have not tasted this wizard's products the extraordinary importance which his roasts and boileds assume in the scheme of things to those who have. I can only say that once having bitten into one of his dishes you are left with the feeling that life will be deprived of all its poetry and meaning unless you are in a position to go on digging in. The thought that Aunt Dahlia was prepared to sacrifice this wonder man merely to save a nephew from the cooler was one that struck home and stirred.

I don't know when I have been so profoundly moved. It was with a melting eye that I gazed at her. She reminded me of Sidney Carton.

'You were actually contemplating giving up Anatole for my sake?' I gasped.

'Of course.'

'Of course jolly well not! I wouldn't hear of such a thing.'

'But you can't go to prison.'

'I certainly can, if my going means that that supreme maestro will continue working at the old stand. Don't dream of meeting old Bassett's demands.'

'Bertie! Do you mean this?'

'I should say so. What's a mere thirty days in the second division? A bagatelle. I can do it on my head. Let Bassett do his worst. And,' I added in a softer voice, 'when my time is up and I come out into the world once more a free man, let Anatole do his best. A month of bread and water or skilly or whatever they feed you on in these establishments will give me a rare appetite. On the night when I emerge, I shall expect a dinner that will live in legend and song.'

'You shall have it.'

'We might be sketching out the details now.'

'No time like the present. Start with caviare? Or *cantaloup*?'

'And *cantaloup*. Followed by a strengthening soup.'

'Thick or clear?'

'Clear.'

'You aren't forgetting Anatole's *Velouté aux fleurs de courgette*?'

'Not for a moment. But how about his *Consommé aux Pommes d'Amour*?'

'Perhaps you're right.'

'I think I am. I feel I am.'

'I'd better leave the ordering to you.'

'It might be wisest.'

I took pencil and paper, and some ten minutes later I was in a position to announce the result.

'This, then,' I said, 'subject to such additions as I may think out in my cell, is the menu as I see it.'

And I read as follows:

*Le Diner*

*Caviar Frais*
*Cantaloup*
*Consommé aux Pommes d'Amour*

*Sylphides à la crème d'Écrevisses*
*Mignonette de poulet petit Duc*
*Points d'ásperges à la Mistinguette*
*Suprême de fois gras au champagne*
*Neige aux Perles des Alpes*
*Timbale de ris de veau Toulousaine*
*Salade d'endive et de céleri*
*Le Plum Pudding*
*L'Etoile au Berger*
*Bénédictins Blancs*
*Bombe Néro*
*Friandises*
*Diablotins*
*Fruits*

'That about covers it, Aunt Dahlia?'

'Yes, you don't seem to have missed out much.'

'Then let's have the man in and defy him. Bassett!' I cried.

'Bassett!' shouted Aunt Dahlia.

'Bassett!' I bawled, making the welkin ring.

It was still ringing when he popped in, looking annoyed.

'What the devil are you shouting at me like that for?'

'Oh, there you are, Bassett.' I wasted no time in getting down to the agenda. 'Bassett, we defy you.'

The man was plainly taken aback. He threw a questioning look at Aunt Dahlia. He seemed to be feeling that Bertram was speaking in riddles.

'He is alluding,' explained the relative, 'to that idiotic offer of yours to call the thing off if I let you have Anatole. Silliest idea I ever heard. We've been having a good laugh about it. Haven't we, Bertie?'

'Roaring our heads off,' I assented.

He seemed stunned.

'Do you mean that you refuse?'

'Of course we refuse. I might have known my nephew better than to suppose for an instant that he would consider bringing sorrow and bereavement to an aunt's home in order to save himself unpleasantness. The Woosters are not like that, are they, Bertie?'

'I should say not.'

'They don't put self first.'

'You bet they don't.'

'I ought never to have insulted him by mentioning the offer to him. I apologize, Bertie.'

'Quite all right, old flesh and blood.'

She wrung my hand.

'Good night, Bertie, and goodbye – or, rather *au revoir*. We shall meet again.'

'Absolutely. When the fields are white with daisies, if not sooner.'

'By the way, didn't you forget *Nomais de la Méditerranée au Fenouil*?'

'So I did. And *Selle d'Agneau aux laitues á la Grecque*. Shove them on the charge sheet, will you?'

Her departure, which was accompanied by a melting glance of admiration and esteem over her shoulder as she navigated across the threshold, was followed by a brief and, on my part, haughty silence. After a while, Pop Bassett spoke in a strained and nasty voice.

'Well, Mr Wooster, it seems that after all you will have to pay the penalty of your folly.'

'Quite.'

'I may say that I have changed my mind about allowing you to spend the night under my roof. You will go to the police station.'

'Vindictive, Bassett.'

'Not at all. I see no reason why Constable Oates should be deprived of his well-earned sleep merely to suit your convenience. I will send for him.' He opened the door. 'Here, you!'

It was a most improper way of addressing Jeeves, but the faithful fellow did not appear to resent it.

'Sir?'

'On the lawn outside the house you will find Constable Oates. Bring him here.'

'Very good, sir. I think Mr Spode wishes to speak to you, sir.'

'Eh?'

'Mr Spode, sir. He is coming along the passage now.'

Old Bassett came back into the room, seeming displeased.

'I wish Roderick would not interrupt me at a time like this,'

217

he said querulously. 'I cannot imagine what reason he can have for wanting to see me.'

I laughed lightly. The irony of the thing amused me.

'He is coming – a bit late – to tell you that he was with me when the cow-creamer was pinched, thus clearing me of the guilt.'

'I see. Yes, as you say, he is somewhat late. I shall have to explain to him . . . Ah, Roderick.'

The massive frame of R. Spode had appeared in the doorway.

'Come in, Roderick, come in. But you need not have troubled, my dear fellow. Mr Wooster has made it quite evident that he had nothing to do with the theft of my cow-creamer. It was that that you wished to see me about, was it not?'

'Well – er – no,' said Roderick Spode.

There was an odd, strained look on the man's face. His eyes were glassy and, as far as a thing of that size was capable of being fingered, he was fingering his moustache. He seemed to be bracing himself for some unpleasant task.

'Well – er – no,' he said. 'The fact is, I hear there's been some trouble about that helmet I stole from Constable Oates.'

There was a stunned silence. Old Bassett goggled. I goggled. Roderick Spode continued to finger his moustache.

'It was a silly thing to do,' he said. 'I see that now. I – er – yielded to a uncontrollable impulse. One does sometimes, doesn't one? You remember I told you I once stole a policeman's helmet at Oxford. I was hoping I could keep quiet about it, but Wooster's man tells me that you have got the idea that Wooster did it, so of course I had to come and tell you. That's all. I think I'll go to bed,' said Roderick Spode. 'Good night.'

He edged off, and the stunned silence started functioning again.

I suppose there have been men who looked bigger asses than Sir Watkyn Bassett at this moment, but I have never seen one myself. The tip of his nose had gone bright scarlet, and his pince-nez were hanging limply to the parent nose at an angle of forty-five. Consistently though he had snootered me from the very inception of our relations, I felt almost sorry for the poor old blighter.

'H'rrmph!' he said at length.

He struggled with the vocal cords for a space. They seemed to have gone twisted on him.

'It appears that I owe you an apology, Mr Wooster.'

'Say no more about it, Bassett.'

'I am sorry that all this has occurred.'

'Don't mention it. My innocence is established. That is all that matters. I presume that I am now at liberty to depart?'

'Oh, certainly, certainly. Good night, Mr Wooster.'

'Good night, Bassett. I need scarcely say, I think, that I hope this will be a lesson to you.'

I dismissed him with a distant nod, and stood there wrapped in thought. I could make nothing of what had occurred. Following the old and tried Oates method of searching for the motive, I had to confess myself baffled. I could only suppose that this was the Sidney Carton spirit bobbing up again.

And then a sudden blinding light seemed to flash upon me.

'Jeeves!'

'Sir?'

'Were you behind this thing?'

'Sir?'

'Don't keep saying "Sir?" You know what I'm talking about. Was it you who egged Spode on to take the rap?'

I wouldn't say he smiled – he practically never does – but a muscle abaft the mouth did seem to quiver slightly for an instant.

'I did venture to suggest to Mr Spode that it would be a graceful act on his part to assume the blame, sir. My line of argument was that he would be saving you a great deal of unpleasantness, while running no risk himself. I pointed out to him that Sir Watkyn, being engaged to marry his aunt, would hardly be likely to inflict upon him the sentence which he had contemplated inflicting upon you. One does not send gentlemen to prison if one is betrothed to their aunts.'

'Profoundly true, Jeeves. But I still don't get it. Do you mean he just right-hoed? Without a murmur?'

'Not precisely without a murmur, sir. At first, I must confess, he betrayed a certain reluctance. I think I may have influenced his decision by informing him that I knew all about – '

I uttered a cry.

'Eulalie?'

'Yes, sir.'

A passionate desire to get to the bottom of this Eulalie thing swept over me.

'Jeeves, tell me. What did Spode actually do to the girl? Murder her?'

'I fear I am not at liberty to say, sir.'

'Come on, Jeeves.'

'I fear not, sir.'

I gave it up.

'Oh, well!'

I started shedding the garments. I climbed into the pyjamas. I slid into bed. The sheets being inextricably knotted, it would be necessary, I saw, to nestle between the blankets, but I was prepared to rough it for one night.

The rapid surge of events had left me pensive. I sat with my arms round my knees, meditating on Fortune's swift changes.

'An odd thing, life, Jeeves.'

'Very odd, sir.'

'You never know where you are with it, do you? To take a simple instance, I little thought half an hour ago that I would be sitting here in carefree pyjamas, watching you pack for the getaway. A very different future seemed to confront me.'

'Yes, sir.'

'One would have said that a curse had come upon me.'

'One would, indeed, sir.'

'But now my troubles, as you might say, have vanished like the dew on the what-is-it. Thanks to you.'

'I am delighted to have been able to be of service, sir.'

'You have delivered the goods as seldom before. And yet, Jeeves, there is always a snag.'

'Sir?'

'I wish you wouldn't keep saying "Sir?" What I mean is, Jeeves, loving hearts have been sundered in this vicinity and are still sundered. I may be all right – I am – but Gussie isn't all right. Nor is Stiffy all right. That is the fly in the ointment.'

'Yes, sir.'

'Though, pursuant on that, I never could see why flies shouldn't be in ointment. What harm do they do?'

'I wonder, sir – '

'Yes, Jeeves?'

'I was merely about to enquire if it is your intention to bring an action against Sir Watkyn for wrongful arrest and defamation of character before witnesses.'

'I hadn't thought of that. You think an action would lie?'

'There can be no question about it, sir. Both Mrs Travers and I could offer overwhelming testimony. You are undoubtedly in a position to mulct Sir Watkyn in heavy damages.'

'Yes, I suppose you're right. No doubt that was why he went up in the air to such an extent when Spode did his act.'

'Yes, sir. His trained legal mind would have envisaged the peril.'

'I don't think I ever saw a man go so red in the nose. Did you?'

'No, sir.'

'Still, it seems a shame to harry him further. I don't know that I want actually to grind the old bird into the dust.'

'I was merely thinking, sir, that were you to threaten such an action, Sir Watkyn, in order to avoid unpleasantness, might see his way to ratifying the betrothals of Miss Bassett and Mr Fink-Nottle and Miss Byng and the Reverend Mr Pinker.'

'Golly, Jeeves! Put the bite on him, what?'

'Precisely, sir.'

'The thing shall be put in train immediately.'

I sprang from the bed and nipped to the door.

'Bassett!' I yelled.

There was no immediate response. The man had presumably gone to earth. But after I had persevered for some minutes, shouting 'Bassett!' at regular intervals with increasing volume, I heard the distant sound of pattering feet, and along he came, in a very different spirit from that which he had exhibited on the previous occasion. This time it was more like some eager waiter answering the bell.

'Yes, Mr Wooster?'

I led the way back into the room, and hopped into bed again.

'There is something you wish to say to me, Mr Wooster?'

'There are about a dozen things I wish to say to you, Bassett, but the one we will touch on at the moment is this. Are you aware that your headstrong conduct in sticking police officers on to pinch me and locking me in my room has laid you open to an action for – what was it, Jeeves?'

'Wrongful arrest and defamation of character before witnesses, sir.'

That's the baby. I could soak you for millions. What are you going to do about it?'

He writhed like an electric fan.

'I'll tell you what you are going to do about it,' I proceeded. 'You are going to issue your OK on the union of your daughter Madeline and Augustus Fink-Nottle and also on that of your niece Stephanie and the Rev. H. P. Pinker. And you will do it now.'

A short struggle seemed to take place in him. It might have lasted longer, if he hadn't caught my eye.

'Very well, Mr Wooster.'

'And touching that cow-creamer. It is highly probable that the international gang that got away with it will sell it to my Uncle Tom. Their system of underground information will have told them that he is in the market. Not a yip out of you, Bassett, if at some future date you see that cow-creamer in his collection.'

'Very well, Mr Wooster.'

'And one other thing. You owe me a fiver.'

'I beg your pardon?'

'In repayment of the one you took off me at Bosher Street. I shall want that before I leave.'

'I will write you a cheque in the morning.'

'I shall expect it on the breakfast tray. Good night, Bassett.'

'Good night, Mr Wooster. Is that brandy I see over there? I think I should like a glass, if I may.'

'Jeeves, a snootful for Sir Watkyn Bassett.'

'Very good, sir.'

He drained the beaker gratefully, and tottered out. Probably quite a nice chap, if you knew him.

Jeeves broke the silence.

'I have finished the packing, sir.'

'Good. Then I think I'll curl up. Open the windows, will you?'

'Very good, sir.'

'What sort of a night is it?'

'Unsettled, sir. It has begun to rain with some violence.'

The sound of a sneeze came to my ears.

'Hallo, who's that Jeeves? Somebody out there?'

'Constable Oates, sir.'

'You don't mean he hasn't gone off duty?'

'No, sir. I imagine that in his preoccupation with other matters it escaped Sir Watkyn's mind to send word to him that there was no longer any necessity to keep his vigil.'

I sighed contentedly. It needed but this to complete my day. The thought of Constable Oates prowling in the rain like the troops of Midian, when he could have been snug in bed toasting his pink toes on the hot-water bottle, gave me a curiously mellowing sense of happiness.

'This is the end of a perfect day, Jeeves. What's that thing of yours about larks?'

'Sir?'

'And, I rather think, snails.'

'Oh, yes, sir. "The year's at the Spring, the day's at the morn, morning's at seven, the hill side's dew-pearled – " '

'But the larks, Jeeves? The snails? I'm pretty sure larks and snails entered into it.'

'I am coming to the larks and snails, sir. "The lark's on the wing, the snail's on the thorn – " '

'Now you're talking. And the tab line?'

' "God's in His heaven, all's right with the world." '

'That's it in a nutshell. I couldn't have put it better myself. And yet, Jeeves, there is just one thing. I do wish you would give me the inside facts about Eulalie.'

'I fear, sir – '

'I would keep it dark. You know me – the silent tomb.'

'The rules of the Junior Ganymede are extremely strict, sir.'

'I know. But you might stretch a point.'

'I am sorry, sir – '

I made the great decision.

'Jeeves,' I said, 'give me the low-down, and I'll come on that World Cruise of yours.'

He wavered.

'Well, in the strictest confidence, sir – '

'Of course.'

'Mr Spode designs ladies' underclothing, sir. He has a considerable talent in that direction, and has indulged it secretly for some years. He is the founder and proprietor of the emporium in Bond Street known as Eulalie Sœurs.'

'You don't mean that?'

'Yes, sir.'

'Good Lord, Jeeves! No wonder he didn't want a thing like that to come out.'

'No, sir. It would unquestionably jeopardize his authority over his followers.'

'You can't be a successful Dictator and design women's underclothing.'

'No, sir.'

'One or the other. Not both.'

'Precisely, sir.'

I mused.

'Well, it was worth it, Jeeves. I couldn't have slept, wondering about it. Perhaps that cruise won't be so very foul, after all?'

'Most gentlemen find them enjoyable, sir.'

'Do they?'

'Yes, sir. Seeing new faces.'

'That's true. I hadn't thought of that. The faces will be new, won't they? Thousands and thousands of people, but no Stiffy.'

'Exactly, sir.'

'You had better get the tickets tomorrow.'

'I have already procured them, sir. Good night, sir.'

The door closed. I switched off the light. For some moments I lay there listening to the measured tramp of Constable Oates's feet and thinking of Gussie and Madeline Bassett and of Stiffy and old Stinker Pinker, and of the hotsy-totsiness which now prevailed in their love lives. I also thought of Uncle Tom being handed the cow-creamer and of Aunt Dahlia seizing the psychological moment and nicking him for a fat cheque for *Milady's Boudoir*. Jeeves was right, I felt. The snail was on the wing and the lark on the thorn – or, rather, the other way round – and God was in His heaven and all right with the world.

And presently the eyes closed, the muscles relaxed, the breathing became soft and regular, and sleep which does something which has slipped my mind to the something sleave of care poured over me in a healing wave.

P. G. Wodehouse

# THANK YOU, JEEVES

# PREFACE

This is the first of the full-length novels about Jeeves and Bertie Wooster, and it is the only book of mine which I tried to produce without sitting down at the typewriter and getting a crick in the back.

Not that I ever thought of dictating it to a stenographer. How anybody can compose a story by word of mouth, face to face with a bored looking secretary with a notebook is more than I can imagine. Yet many authors think nothing of saying 'Ready, Miss Spelvin? Take dictation. Quote No comma Lord Jasper Murgatroyd comma close quote said no better make it hissed Evangeline comma quote I would not marry you if you were the last man on earth close quote period Quote Well comma, I'm not the last man on earth comma so the point does not arise comma close quote replied Lord Jasper comma twirling his moustache cynically period And so the long day wore on.'

If I started to do that sort of thing I should be feeling all the time that the girl was saying to herself as she took it down, 'Well comma this beats me period How comma with homes for the feeble-minded touting for customers on every side comma has a fathead like this Wodehouse succeeded in remaining at large all these years mark of interrogation.'

But I did get one of those machines where you talk into a mouthpiece and have your observations recorded on wax, and I started *Thank You, Jeeves*, on it. And after the first few paragraphs I thought I would turn back and play the stuff over to hear how it sounded.

It sounded too awful for human consumption. Until that moment I had never realized that I had a voice like that of a very pompous school-master addressing the young scholars in his charge from the pulpit in the school chapel. There was a kind of foggy dreariness about it that chilled the spirits. It stunned me, I had been hoping, if all went well, to make *Thank You, Jeeves*, an amusing book – gay, if you see what I mean, rollicking if you still follow me and debonair, and it was plain to me that a man with a voice like that could never come within several miles of being debonair. With him at the controls the thing would develop into one of those dim tragedies of peasant life which we return to the library after a quick glance at Page One. I sold the machine next day and felt like the Ancient Mariner when he got rid of the albatross. So now I confine myself to the good old typewriter.

Writing my stories I enjoy. It is the thinking them out that is apt to blot the sunshine from my life. You can't think out plots like mine without getting a suspicion from time to time that something has gone seriously wrong with the brain's two hemispheres and the broad band of transversely running fibres known as the corpus collosum. It is my practice to make about 400 pages of notes before starting a novel, and during this process there always comes a moment when I say to myself 'Oh, what a noble mind is here o'erthrown'. The odd thing is that just as I am feeling that I must get a proposer and seconder and have myself put up for the loony bin, something always clicks and after that all is joy and jollity.

P. G. Wodehouse

# =1=
# JEEVES GIVES NOTICE

I WAS a shade perturbed. Nothing to signify, really, but still just a spot concerned. As I sat in the old flat, idly touching the strings of my banjolele, an instrument to which I had become greatly addicted of late, you couldn't have said that the brow was actually furrowed, and yet, on the other hand, you couldn't have stated absolutely that it wasn't. Perhaps the word 'pensive' about covers it. It seemed to me that a situation fraught with embarrassing potentialities had arisen.

'Jeeves,' I said, 'do you know what?'

'No, sir.'

'Do you know whom I saw last night?'

'No, sir.'

'J. Washburn Stoker and his daughter, Pauline.'

'Indeed, sir?'

'They must be over here.'

'It would seem so, sir.'

'Awkward, what?'

'I can conceive that after what occurred in New York it might be distressing for you to encounter Miss Stoker, sir. But I fancy the contingency need scarcely arise.'

I weighed this.

'When you start talking about contingencies arising, Jeeves, the brain seems to flicker and I rather miss the gist. Do you mean that I ought to be able to keep out of her way?'

'Yes, sir.'

'Avoid her?'

'Yes, sir.'

I played five bars of 'Old Man River' with something of abandon. His pronouncement had eased my mind. I followed his reasoning. After all, London's a large place. Quite simple not to run into people, if you don't want to.

'It gave me rather a shock, though.'

'I can readily imagine so, sir.'

'Accentuated by the fact that they were accompanied by Sir Roderick Glossop.'

'Indeed, sir?'

'Yes. It was at the Savoy Grill. They were putting on the nosebag together at a table by the window. And here's rather a rummy thing, Jeeves. The fourth member of the party was Lord Chuffnell's aunt, Myrtle. What would she be doing in that gang?'

'Possibly her ladyship is an acquaintance either of Mr Stoker, Miss Stoker, or Sir Roderick, sir.'

'Yes, that may be so. Yes, that might account for it. But it surprised me, I confess.'

'Did you enter into conversation with them, sir?'

'Who, me? No, Jeeves. I was out of the room like a streak. Apart from wishing to dodge the Stokers, can you see me wantonly and deliberately going and chatting with old Glossop?'

'Certainly he has never proved a very congenial companion in the past, sir.'

'If there is one man in the world I hope never to exchange speech with again, it is that old crumb.'

'I forgot to mention, sir, that Sir Roderick called to see you this morning.'

'What!'

'Yes, sir.'

'He called to see me?'

'Yes, sir.'

'After what has passed between us?'

'Yes, sir.'

'Well, I'm dashed!'

'Yes, sir. I informed him that you had not yet risen, and he said that he would return later.'

'He did, did he?' I laughed. One of those sardonic ones. 'Well, when he does, set the dog on him.'

'We have no dog, sir.'

'Then step down to the flat below and borrow Mrs Tinkler-Moulke's Pomeranian. Paying social calls after the way he behaved in New York! I never heard of such a thing. Did you ever hear of such a thing, Jeeves?'

'I confess that in the circumstances his advent occasioned me surprise, sir.'

'I should think it did. Good Lord! Good heavens! Good gosh! The man must have the crust of a rhinoceros.'

And when I have given you the inside story, I think you will agree with me that my heat was justified. Let me marshal my facts and go to it.

About three months before, noting a certain liveliness in my Aunt Agatha, I had deemed it prudent to pop across to New York for a space to give her time to blow over. And about half-way through my first week there, in the course of a beano of some description at the Sherry-Netherland, I made the acquaintance of Pauline Stoker.

She got right in amongst me. Her beauty maddened me like wine.

'Jeeves,' I recollect saying, on returning to the apartment, 'who was the fellow who on looking at something felt like somebody looking at something? I learned the passage at school, but it has escaped me.'

'I fancy the individual you have in mind, sir, is the poet Keats, who compared his emotions on first reading Chapman's Homer to those of stout Cortez when with eagle eyes he stared at the Pacific.'

'The Pacific, eh?'

'Yes, sir. And all his men looked at each other with a wild surmise, silent upon a peak in Darien.'

'Of course. It all comes back to me. Well, that's how I felt this afternoon on being introduced to Miss Pauline Stoker. Press the trousers with special care tonight, Jeeves. I am dining with her.'

In New York, I have always found, one gets off the mark quickly in matters of the heart. This, I believe, is due to something in the air. Two weeks later I proposed to Pauline. She accepted me. So far, so good. But mark the sequel. Scarcely forty-eight hours after that a monkey wrench was bunged into the machinery and the whole thing was off.

The hand that flung that monkey wrench was the hand of Sir Roderick Glossop.

In these memoirs of mine, as you may recall, I have had occasion to make somewhat frequent mention of this old pot of poison. A bald-domed, bushy-browed blighter, ostensibly a nerve specialist, but in reality, as everybody knows, nothing more nor less than a high-priced loony-doctor, he has been cropping up in my path for years, always with the most momentous results. And it so happened that he was in New York when the announcement of my engagement appeared in the papers.

What brought him there was one of his periodical visits to J. Washburn Stoker's second cousin, George. This George was a man who, after a lifetime of doing down the widow and orphan, had begun to feel the strain a bit. His conversation was odd, and he had a tendency to walk on his hands. He had been a patient of Sir Roderick's for some years, and it was the latter's practice to dash over to New York every once in a while to take a look at him. He arrived on the present occasion just in time to read over the morning coffee and egg the news that Bertram Wooster and Pauline Stoker were planning to do the Wedding Glide. And, as far as I can ascertain, he was at the telephone, ringing up the father of the bride-to-be, without so much as stopping to wipe his mouth.

Well, what he told J. Washburn about me I cannot, of course, say: but, as a venture, I imagine he informed him that I had once been engaged to his daughter, Honoria, and that he had broken off the match because he had decided that I was barmy to the core. He would have touched, no doubt, on the incident of the cats and the fish in my bedroom: possibly, also, on the episode of the stolen hat and my habit of climbing down water-spouts: winding up, it may be, with a description of the unfortunate affair of the punctured hot-water bottle at Lady Wickham's.

A close friend of J. Washburn's and a man on whose judgment J.W. relied, I take it that he had little difficulty in persuading the latter that I was not the ideal son-in-law. At any rate, as I say, within a mere forty-eight hours of the holy moment I was notified that it would be unnecessary for me to order the new sponge-bag trousers and gardenia, because my nomination had been cancelled.

And it was this man who was having the cool what's-the-word to come calling at the Wooster home. I mean, I ask you!

I resolved to be pretty terse with him.

I was still playing the banjolele when he arrived. Those who know Bertram Wooster best are aware that he is a man of sudden, strong enthusiasms and that, when in the grip of one of these, he becomes a remorseless machine – tense, absorbed, single-minded.

It was so in the matter of this banjolele-playing of mine. Since the night at the Alhambra when the supreme virtuosity of Ben Bloom and his Sixteen Baltimore Buddies had fired me to take up the study of the instrument, not a day had passed without its couple of hours' assiduous practice. And I was twanging the strings like one inspired when the door opened and Jeeves shovelled in the foul strait-waistcoat specialist to whom I have just been alluding.

In the interval which had elapsed since I had first been apprised of the man's desire to have speech with me, I had been thinking things over: and the only conclusion to which I could come was that he must have had a change of heart of some nature and decided that an apology was due me for the way he had behaved. It was, therefore, a somewhat softened Bertram Wooster who now rose to do the honours.

'Ah, Sir Roderick,' I said. 'Good morning.'

Nothing could have exceeded the courtesy with which I had spoken. Conceive of my astonishment, therefore, when his only reply was a grunt, and an indubitably unpleasant grunt, at that. I felt that my diagnosis of the situation had been wrong. Right off the bull's-eye I had been. Here was no square-shooting apologizer. He couldn't have been glaring at me with more obvious distaste if I had been the germ of *dementia praecox*.

Well, if that was the attitude he was proposing to adopt, well, I mean to say. My geniality waned. I drew myself up coldly, at the same time raising a stiff eyebrow. And I was just about to work off the old To-what-am-I-indebted-for-this-visit gag, when he chipped in ahead of me.

'You ought to be certified!'

'I beg your pardon?'

'You're a public menace. For weeks, it appears, you have been making life a hell for all your neighbours with some hideous musical instrument. I see you have it with you now. How dare you play that thing in a respectable block of flats? Infernal din!'

I remained cool and dignified.

'Did you say "infernal din"?'

'I did.'

'Oh? Well, let me tell you that the man that hath no music in himself . . .' I stepped to the door. 'Jeeves,' I called down the passage, 'what was it Shakespeare said the man who hadn't music in himself was fit for?'

'Treasons, stratagems, and spoils, sir.'

'Thank you, Jeeves. Is fit for treasons, stratagems, and spoils,' I said, returning.

He danced a step or two.

'Are you aware that the occupant of the flat below, Mrs Tinkler-Moulke, is one of my patients, a woman in a highly nervous condition. I have had to give her a sedative.'

I raised a hand.

'Spare me the gossip from the loony-bin,' I said distantly. 'Might I inquire, on my side, if you are aware that Mrs Tinkler-Moulke owns a Pomeranian?'

'Don't drivel.'

'I am not drivelling. This animal yaps all day and not infrequently far into the night. So Mrs Tinkler-Moulke has had the nerve to complain of my banjolele, has she? Ha! Let her first pluck out the Pom which is in her own eye,' I said, becoming a bit scriptural.

He chafed visibly.

'I am not here to talk about dogs. I wish for your assurance that you will immediately cease annoying this unfortunate woman.'

I shook the head.

'I am sorry she is a cold audience, but my art must come first.'

'That is your final word, is it?'

'It is.'

'Very good. You will hear more of this.'

'And Mrs Tinkler-Moulke will hear more of this,' I replied, brandishing the banjolele.

I touched the buzzer.

'Jeeves,' I said, 'show Sir R. Glossop out!'

I confess that I was well pleased with the manner in which I had comported myself during this clash of wills. There was a time, you must remember, when the sudden appearance of old Glossop in my sitting-room would have been enough to send me bolting for cover like a rabbit. But since then I had passed through the furnace, and the sight of him no longer filled me with a nameless dread. With a good deal of quiet self-satisfaction I proceeded to play 'The Wedding of the Painted Doll', 'Singin' In the Rain', 'Three Little Words', 'Goodnight, Sweetheart', 'My Love Parade', 'Spring Is Here', 'Whose Baby Are You?' and part of 'I Want an

Automobile With a Horn That Goes Toot-Toot', in the order named: and it was as I was approaching the end of this last number that the telephone rang.

I went to the instrument and stood listening. And, as I listened, my face grew hard and set.

'Very good, Mr Manglehoffer,' I said coldly. 'You may inform Mrs Tinkler-Moulke and her associates that I choose the latter alternative.'

I touched the bell.

'Jeeves,' I said, 'there has been a spot of trouble.'

'Indeed, sir?'

'Unpleasantness is rearing its ugly head in Berkeley Mansions, W.1. I note also a lack of give-and-take and an absence of the neighbourly spirit. I have just been talking to the manager of this building on the telephone, and he has delivered an ultimatum. He says I must either chuck playing the banjolele or clear out.'

'Indeed, sir?'

'Complaints, it would seem, have been lodged by the Honourable Mrs Tinkler-Moulke, of C.6; by Lieutenant-Colonel J. J. Bustard, D.S.O., of B.5; and Sir Everard and Lady Blennerhassett, of B.7. All right. So be it. I don't care. We shall be well rid of these Tinkler-Moulkes, these Bustards, and these Blennerhassetts. I leave them without a pang.'

'You are proposing to move, sir?'

I raised the eyebrows.

'Surely, Jeeves, you cannot imagine that I ever considered any other course?'

'But I fear you will encounter a similar hostility elsewhere, sir.'

'Not where I am going. It is my intention to retire to the depths of the country. In some old world, sequestered nook I shall find a cottage, and there resume my studies.'

'A cottage, sir?'

'A cottage, Jeeves. If possible, honeysuckle-covered.'

The next moment, you could have knocked me down with a toothpick. There was a brief pause, and then Jeeves, whom I have nurtured in my bosom, so to speak, for years and years and years, gave a sort of cough and there proceeded from his lips these incredible words:

'In that case, I fear I must give my notice.'

There was a tense silence. I stared at the man.

235

'Jeeves,' I said, and you wouldn't be far out in describing me as stunned, 'did I hear you correctly?'

'Yes, sir.'

'You actually contemplate leaving my entourage?'

'Only with the greatest reluctance, sir. But if it is your intention to play that instrument within the narrow confines of a country cottage . . .'

I drew myself up.

'You say "that instrument", Jeeves. And you say it in an unpleasant, soupy voice. Am I to understand that you dislike this banjolele?'

'Yes, sir.'

'You've stood it all right up to now.'

'With grave difficulty, sir.'

'And let me tell you that better men than you have stood worse than banjoleles. Are you aware that a certain Bulgarian, Elia Gospodinoff, once played the bagpipes for twenty-four hours without a stop? Ripley vouches for this in his "Believe It Or Not".'

'Indeed, sir?'

'Well, do you suppose Gospodinoff's personal attendant kicked? A laughable idea. They are made of better stuff than that in Bulgaria. I am convinced that he was behind the young master from start to finish of his attempt on the Central European record, and I have no doubt frequently rallied round with ice packs and other restoratives. Be Bulgarian, Jeeves.'

'No, sir. I fear I cannot recede from my position.'

'But, dash it, you say you *are* receding from your position.'

'I should have said, I cannot abandon the stand which I have taken.'

'Oh.'

I mused awhile.

'You mean this, Jeeves?'

'Yes, sir.'

'You have thought it all out carefully, weighing the pros and cons, balancing this against that?'

'Yes, sir.'

'And you are resolved?'

'Yes, sir. If it is really your intention to continue playing that instrument, I have no option but to leave.'

The Wooster blood boiled over. Circumstances of recent years have so shaped themselves as to place this blighter in a position which you might describe as that of a domestic Mussolini: but, forgetting this and sticking simply to cold fact, what *is* Jeeves, after all? A valet. A salaried attendant. And a fellow simply can't go on truckling – do I mean truckling? I know it begins with a 't' – to his valet for ever. There comes a moment when he must remember that his ancestors did dashed well at the Battle of Crecy and put the old foot down. This moment had now arrived.

'Then, leave, dash it!'

'Very good, sir.'

# =2=
# CHUFFY

I CONFESS that it was in sombre mood that I assembled the stick, the hat, and the lemon-coloured gloves some half-hour later and strode out into the streets of London. But though I did not care to think what existence would be like without Jeeves, I had no thought of weakening. As I turned the corner into Piccadilly, I was a thing of fire and chilled steel; and I think in about another half-jiffy I should have been snorting, if not actually shouting the ancient battle cry of the Woosters, had I not observed on the skyline a familiar form.

This familiar form was none other than that of my boyhood friend, the fifth Baron Chuffnell – the chap, if you remember, whose Aunt Myrtle I had seen the previous night hobnobbing with the hellhound, Glossop.

The sight of him reminded me that I was in the market for a country cottage and that here was the very chap to supply same.

I wonder if I have ever told you about Chuffy? Stop me if I have. He's a fellow I've known more or less all my life, he and self having been at private school, Eton and Oxford together. We don't see a frightful lot of one another nowadays, however, as he spends most of his time down at Chuffnell Regis on the coast of Somersetshire, where he owns an enormous great place with about a hundred and fifty rooms and miles of rolling parkland.

Don't run away, however, on the strength of this, with the impression that Chuffy is one of my wealthier cronies. He's dashed hard up, poor bloke, like most fellows who own land, and only lives at Chuffnell Hall because he's stuck with it and can't afford to live anywhere else. If somebody came to him and offered to buy the place, he would kiss him on both cheeks. But who wants to buy a house that size in these times? He can't even let it. So he sticks on there most of the year, with nobody to talk to except the local doctor and parson and his Aunt Myrtle and her twelve-year-old son, Seabury, who live at the Dower House in the park. A pretty mouldy existence for one who at the University gave bright promise of becoming one of the lads.

Chuffy also owns the village of Chuffnell Regis – not that that does him much good, either. I mean to say, the taxes on the estate and all the expenses of repairs and what not come to pretty nearly as much as he gets out of the rents, making the thing more or less of a washout. Still, he is the landlord, and, as such, would doubtless have dozens of cottages at his disposal and probably be only too glad of the chance of easing one of them off on to a reputable tenant like myself.

'You're the very chap I wanted to see, Chuffy,' I said accordingly, after our initial what-ho-ing. 'Come right along with me to the Drones for a bite of lunch. I can put a bit of business in your way.'

He shook his head, wistfully, I thought.

'I'd like it, Bertie, but I'm due at the Carlton in five minutes. I'm lunching with a man.'

'Give him a miss.'

'I couldn't.'

'Well, bring him along, then, and we'll make it a threesome.'

Chuffy smiled rather wanly.

'I don't think you'd enjoy it, Bertie. He's Sir Roderick Glossop.'

I goggled. It's always a bit of a shock, when you've just parted from Bloke A., to meet Bloke B. and have Bloke B. suddenly bring Bloke A. into the conversation.

'Sir Roderick Glossop?'

'Yes.'

'But I didn't know you knew him.'

'I don't, very well. Just met him a couple of times. He's a great friend of my Aunt Myrtle.'

'Ah! That explains it. I saw her dining with him last night.'

'Well, if you come to the Carlton, you'll see me lunching with him today.'

'But, Chuffy, old man, is this wise? Is this prudent? It's an awful ordeal breaking bread with this man. I know. I've done it.'

'I dare say, but I've got to go through with it. I had an urgent wire from him yesterday, telling me to come up and see him without fail, and what I'm hoping is that he wants to take the Hall for the summer or knows somebody who does. He would hardly wire like that unless there was something up. No, I shall have to stick it, Bertie. But I'll tell you what I will do. I'll dine with you tomorrow night.'

I would have been all for it, of course, had the circs been different, but I had to refuse. I had formed my plans and made my arrangements and they could not be altered.

'I'm sorry, Chuffy. I'm leaving London tomorrow.'

'You are?'

'Yes. The management of the building where I reside has offered me the choice between clearing out immediately or ceasing to play the banjolele. I elected to do the former. I am going to take a cottage in the country somewhere, and that's what I meant when I said I could put business in your way. Can you let me have a cottage?'

'I can give you your choice of half a dozen.'

'It must be quiet and secluded. I shall be playing the banjolele a good deal.'

'I've got the very shack for you. On the edge of the harbour and not a neighbour within a mile except Police-Sergeant Voules. And he plays the harmonium. You could do duets.'

'Fine!'

'And there's a troupe of nigger minstrels down there this year. You could study their technique.'

'Chuffy, it sounds like heaven. And we shall be able to see something of each other for a change.'

'You don't come playing your damned banjolele at the Hall.'

'No, old man. But I'll drop over to lunch with you most days.'

'Thanks.'

'Don't mention it.'

'By the way, what has Jeeves got to say about all this? I shouldn't have thought he would have cared about leaving London.'

I stiffened a little.

'Jeeves has nothing to say on that or any other subject. We have parted brass-rags.'

'What!'

I had anticipated that the news would stagger him.

'Yes,' I said, 'from now on, Jeeves will take the high road and I'll take the low road. He had the immortal rind to tell me that if I didn't give up my banjolele he would resign. I accepted his portfolio.'

'You've really let him go?'

'I have.'

'Well, well, well!'

I waved a hand nonchalantly.

'These things happen,' I said. 'I'm not pretending I'm pleased, of course, but I can bite the bullet. My self-respect would not permit me to accept the man's terms. You can push a Wooster just so far. "Very good, Jeeves," I said to him. "So be it. I shall watch your future career with considerable interest." And that was that.'

We walked on for a bit in silence.

'So you've parted with Jeeves, have you?' said Chuffy, in a thoughtful sort of voice. 'Well, well, well! Any objection to my looking in and saying good-bye to him?'

'None whatever.'

'It would be a graceful act.'

'Quite.'

'I've always admired his intellect.'

'Me too. No one more.'

'I'll go round to the flat after lunch.'

'Follow the green line,' I said, and my manner was airy and even careless. This parting of the ways with Jeeves had made me feel a bit as if I had just stepped on a bomb and was trying to piece myself together again in a bleak world, but we Woosters can keep the stiff upper lip.

I lunched at the Drones and spent the afternoon there. I had much to think of. Chuffy's news that there was a troupe of nigger minstrels performing on the Chuffnell Regis sands had definitely weighed the scale down on the side of the advantages of the place. The fact that I would be in a position to forgather with these experts and possibly pick up a hint or two from their banjoist on fingering and execution enabled me to bear with fortitude the prospect of being in a spot where I would probably have to meet the Dowager Lady Chuffnell and her son Seabury pretty frequently. I had often felt how tough it must be for poor old Chuffy having this pair of pustules popping in and out all the time. And in saying this I am looking straight at little Seabury, a child who should have been strangled at birth. I have no positive proof, but I have always been convinced that it was he who put the lizard in my bed the last time I stayed at the Hall.

But, as I say, I was prepared to put up with this couple in return for the privilege of being in close communication with a really hot banjoist, and most of these nigger minstrel chaps can pick the strings like nobody's business. It was not, therefore, the thought of them which, as I returned to the flat to dress for dinner, was filling me with a strange moodiness.

No. We Woosters can be honest with ourselves. What was giving me the pip was the reflection that Jeeves was about to go out of my life. There never had been anyone like Jeeves, I felt, as I climbed sombrely into the soup and fish, and there never would be. A wave of not unmanly sentiment poured over me. I was conscious of a pang. And when my toilet was completed and I stood before the mirror, surveying that perfectly pressed coat, those superbly creased trousers, I came to a swift decision.

Abruptly, I went into the sitting-room and leaned on the bell.

'Jeeves,' I said. 'A word.'

'Yes, sir?'

'Jeeves,' I said, 'touching on our conversation this morning.'

'Yes, sir?'

'Jeeves,' I said, 'I have been thinking things over. I have come to the conclusion that we have both been hasty. Let us forget the past. You may stay on.'

'It is very kind of you, sir, but . . . are you still proposing to continue the study of that instrument?'

I froze.

'Yes, Jeeves, I am.'

'Then I fear, sir . . .'

It was enough. I nodded haughtily.

'Very good, Jeeves. That is all. I will of course, give you an excellent recommendation.'

'Thank you, sir. It will not be necessary. This afternoon I entered the employment of Lord Chuffnell.'

I started.

'Did Chuffy sneak round here this afternoon and scoop you in?'

'Yes, sir. I go with him to Chuffnell Regis in about a week's time.'

'You do, do you? Well, it may interest you to know that I repair to Chuffnell Regis tomorrow.'

'Indeed, sir?'

'Yes. I have taken a cottage there. We shall meet at Philippi,
Jeeves.'

'Yes, sir.'

'Or am I thinking of some other spot?'

'No, sir, Philippi is correct.'

'Very good, Jeeves.'

'Very good, sir.'

Such, then, is the sequence of events which led up to Bertram
Wooster, on the morning of July the fifteenth, standing at the door
of Seaview Cottage, Chuffnell Regis, surveying the scene before
him through the aromatic smoke of a meditative cigarette.

# =3=
# RE-ENTER THE DEAD PAST

You know, the longer I live, the more I feel that the great wheeze in life is to be jolly well sure what you want and not let yourself be put off by pals who think they know better than you do. When I had announced at the Drones, on my last day in the metropolis, that I was retiring to this secluded spot for an indeterminate period, practically everybody had begged me, you might say with tears in their eyes, not to dream of doing such a cloth-headed thing. They said I should be bored stiff.

But I had carried on according to plan, and here I was, on the fifth morning of my visit, absolutely in the pink and with no regrets whatsoever. The sun was shining. The sky was blue. And London seemed miles away – which it was, of course. I wouldn't be exaggerating if I said that a great peace enveloped the soul.

A thing I never know when I'm telling a story is how much scenery to bung in. I've asked one or two scriveners of my acquaintance, and their views differ. A fellow I met at a cocktail party in Bloomsbury said that he was all for describing kitchen sinks and frowsty bedrooms and squalor generally, but the beauties of Nature no. Whereas, Freddie Oaker, of the Drones, who does tales of pure love for the weeklies under the pen-name of Alicia Seymour, once told me that he reckoned that flowery meadows in springtime alone were worth at least a hundred quid a year to him.

Personally, I've always rather barred long descriptions of the terrain, so I will be on the brief side. As I stood there that morning, what the eye rested on was the following. There was a nice little splash of garden, containing a bush, a tree, a couple of flower beds, a lily pond with a statue of a nude child with a bit of a tummy on him, and to the right a hedge. Across this hedge, Brinkley, my new man, was chatting with our neighbour, Police Sergeant Voules, who seemed to have looked in with a view to selling eggs.

There was another hedge straight ahead, with the garden gate in it, and over this one spied the placid waters of the harbour, which was much about the same as any other harbour, except that some time during the night a whacking great yacht had rolled up and cast anchor in it. And of all the objects under my immediate advisement I noted this yacht with the most pleasure and approval. White in colour, in size resembling a young liner, it lent a decided tone to the Chuffnell Regis foreshore.

Well, such was the spreading prospect. Add a cat sniffing at a snail on the path and me at the door smoking a gasper, and you have the complete picture.

No, I'm wrong. Not quite the complete picture, because I had left the old two-seater in the road, and I could just see the top part of it. And at this moment the summer stillness was broken by the tooting of its horn, and I buzzed to the gate with all possible speed for fear some fiend in human shape was scratching my paint. Arriving at destination, I found a small boy in the front seat, pensively squeezing the bulb, and was about to administer one on the side of the head when I recognized Chuffy's cousin, Seabury, and stayed the hand.

'Hallo,' he said.

'What ho,' I replied.

My manner was reserved. The memory of that lizard in my bed still lingered. I don't know if you have ever leaped between the sheets, all ready for a spot of sleep, and received an unforeseen lizard up the left pyjama leg? It is an experience that puts its stamp on a man. And while, as I say, I had no legal proof that this young blighter had been the author of the outrage, I entertained suspicions that were tantamount to certainty. So now I not only spoke with a marked coldness but also gave him the fairly frosty eye.

It didn't seem to jar him. He continued to regard me with that supercilious gaze which had got him so disliked among the right-minded. He was a smallish, freckled kid with aeroplane ears, and he had a way of looking at you as if you were something he had run into in the course of a slumming trip. In my Rogues' Gallery of repulsive small boys I suppose he would come about third – not quite so bad as my Aunt Agatha's son. Young Thos., or Mr Blumenfeld's Junior, but well ahead of little Sebastian Moon, my Aunt Dahlia's Bonzo, and the field.

After staring at me for a moment as if he were thinking that I had changed for the worse since he last saw me, he spoke.

'You're to come to lunch.'

'Is Chuffy back, then?'

'Yes.'

Well, of course, if Chuffy had returned, I was at his disposal. I shouted over the hedge to Brinkley that I would be absent from the midday meal and climbed into the car and we rolled off.

'When did he get back?'

'Last night.'

'Shall we be lunching alone?'

'No.'

'Who's going to be there?'

'Mother and me and some people.'

'A party? I'd better go back and put on another suit.'

'No.'

'You think this one looks all right?'

'No, I don't. I think it looks rotten. But there isn't time.'

This point settled, he passed into the silence for a while. A brooding kid. He came out of it to give me some local gossip.

'Mother and I are living at the Hall again.'

'What!'

'Yes. There's a smell at the Dower House.'

'Even though you've left it?' I said, in my keen way.

He was not amused.

'You needn't try to be funny. If you really want to know, I expect it's my mice.'

'Your what?'

'I've started breeding mice and puppies. And, of course, they nif a bit,' he added in a dispassionate sort of way. 'But mother thinks it's the drains. Can you give me five shillings?'

I simply couldn't follow his train of thought. The way his conversation flittered about gave me that feeling you get in dreams sometimes.

'Five shillings?'

'Five shillings.'

'What do you mean, five shillings?'

'I mean five shillings.'

'I dare say. But what I want to know is how have we suddenly got on to the subject? We were discussing mice, and you introduce this five shillings motif.'

'I want five shillings.'

'Admitting that you may possibly want that sum, why the dickens should I give it to you?'

'For protection.'

'What!'

'Protection.'

'What from?'

'Just protection.'

'You don't get any five shillings out of me.'

'Oh, all right.'

He sat silent for a space.

'Things happen to guys that don't kick in their protection money,' he said dreamily.

And on this note of mystery the conversation concluded, for we were moving up the drive of the Hall and on the steps I perceived Chuffy standing. I stopped the car and got out.

'Hallo, Bertie,' said Chuffy.

'Welcome to Chuffnell Hall,' I replied. I looked round. The kid had vanished. 'I say, Chuffy,' I said, 'young blighted Seabury. What about him?'

'What about him?'

'Well, if you ask me, I should say he has gone off his rocker. He's just been trying to touch me for five bob and babbling about protection.'

Chuffy laughed heartily, looking bronzed and fit.

'Oh, that. That's his latest idea.'

'How do you mean?'

'He's been seeing gangster films.'

The scales fell from my eyes.

'He's turned racketeer?'

'Yes. Rather amusing. He goes round collecting protection money from everybody according to their means. Makes a good thing out of it, too. Enterprising kid. I'd pay up if I were you. I have.'

I was shocked. Not so much at the information that the foul child had given this additional evidence of a diseased mind as that Chuffy should be exhibiting this attitude of amused tolerance. I eyed him keenly. Right from the start this morning I had thought his manner strange. Usually, when you meet him, he is brooding over his financial situation and is rather apt to greet you with the lack-lustre eye and the careworn frown. He had been like that five

247

days ago in London. What, then, had caused him to beam all over the place like this and even to go as far as to speak of little Seabury with what amounted to something perilously near to indulgent affection? I sensed a mystery and decided to apply the acid test.

'How is your Aunt Myrtle?'

'She's fine.'

'Living at the Hall now, I hear.'

'Yes.'

'Indefinitely?'

'Oh, yes.'

It was enough.

One of the things, I must mention, which has always made poor old Chuffy's lot so hard is his aunt's attitude toward him. She has never quite been able to get over that matter of the succession. Seabury, you see, was not the son of Chuffy's late uncle, the fourth Baron: he was simply something Lady Chuffnell had picked up *en route* in the course of a former marriage and, consequently, did not come under the head of what the Peerage calls 'issue'. And, in matters of succession, if you aren't issue, you haven't a hope. When the fourth Baron pegged out, accordingly, it was Chuffy who copped the title and estates. All perfectly square and aboveboard, of course, but you can't get women to see these things, and the relict's manner, Chuffy has often told me, was consistently unpleasant. She had a way of clasping Seabury in her arms and looking reproachfully at Chuffy as if he had slipped over a fast one on mother and child. Nothing actually said, you understand, but her whole attitude that of a woman who considers she has been the victim of sharp practice.

The result of this had been that the Dowager Lady Chuffnell was not one of Chuffy's best-loved buddies. Their relations had always been definitely strained, and what I'm driving at is that usually, when you mention her name, a look of pain comes into Chuffy's clean-cut face and he winces a little, as if you had probed an old wound.

Now he was actually smiling. Even that remark of mine about her living at the Hall had not jarred him. Obviously, there were mysteries here. Something was being kept from Bertram.

I tackled him squarely.

'Chuffy,' I said, 'what does this mean?'

'What does what mean?'

'This bally cheeriness. You can't deceive me. Not old Hawk-eye Wooster. Come clean, my lad, something is up. What is all the ruddy happiness about?'

He hesitated. For a moment he eyed me narrowly.

'Can you keep a secret?'

'No.'

'Well, it doesn't matter much, because it'll be in the *Morning Post* in a day or two. Bertie,' said Chuffy, in a hushed voice, 'do you know what's happened? I'm getting Aunt Myrtle off this season.'

'You mean somebody wants to marry her?'

'I do.'

'Who is this half-wit?'

'Your old friend, Sir Roderick Glossop.'

I was stupefied.

'What!'

'I was surprised, too.'

'But old Glossop can't be contemplating matrimony.'

'Why not? He's been a widower more than two years.'

'Oh, I dare say it's possible to make up some kind of a story for him. But what I mean is, he doesn't seem to go with orange blossoms and wedding cake.'

'Well, there it is.'

'Well, I'm dashed!'

'Yes.'

'Well, there's one thing, Chuffy, old man. This means that little Seabury will be getting a really testing stepfather and old Glossop just the stepson I could have wished him. Both have been asking for something on these lines for years. But fancy any woman being mad enough to link her lot with his. Our Humble Heroines!'

'I wouldn't say the heroism was all on one side. About fifty-fifty, I should call it. There is a lot of good in this Glossop, Bertie.'

I could not accept this. It seemed to me loose thinking.

'Aren't you going a bit far, old man? Admitted that he is taking your Aunt Myrtle off your hands . . .'

'And Seabury.'

'And Seabury, true. But, even so, would you really say there was good in the old pest? Remember all the stories I've told you about him from time to time. They show him in a very dubious light.'

'Well, he's doing me a bit of good, anyway. Do you know what it was he wanted to see me about so urgently that day in London?'

'What?'

'He's found an American he thinks he can sell the Hall to.'

'Not really?'

'Yes. If all goes well, I shall at last get rid of this blasted barracks and have a bit of money in my pocket. And all the credit will be due to Uncle Roderick, as I like to think of him. So you will kindly refrain, Bertie, from nasty cracks at his expense and, in particular, from mentioning him in the same breath with young Seabury. You must learn to love Uncle Roddie for my sake.'

I shook my head.

'No, Chuffy, I fear I cannot recede from my opposition.'

'Well, go to hell, then,' said Chuffy agreeably. 'Personally, I regard him as a life-saver.'

'But are you sure this thing is going to come off? What would this fellow want with a place the size of the Hall?'

'Oh, that part of it is simple enough. He's a great pal of old Glossop's and the idea is that he shall put up the cash and let Glossop run the house as a sort of country club for his nerve patients.'

'Why doesn't old Glossop simply rent it from you?'

'My dear ass, what sort of state do you suppose the place is in these days? You talk as if you could open it and step straight into it. Most of the rooms haven't been used for forty years. It wants at least fifteen thousand quid spent on it, to put it in repair. More. Besides new furniture, fittings and so on. If some millionaire like this chap doesn't take it on, I shall have it on my hands for the rest of my life.'

'Oh, he's a millionaire, is he?'

'Yes, that part of it is all right. All I'm worrying about is getting his signature on the dotted line. Well, he's coming to lunch today, and it's going to be a good one, too. He's apt to soften up a good bit after a fat lunch, isn't he?'

'Unless he's got dyspepsia. Many American millionaires have. This man of yours may be one of those fellows who can't get outside more than a glass of milk and a dog biscuit.'

Chuffy laughed jovially.

'Not much. Not old Stoker.' He suddenly began to leap about like a lamb in the spring-time. 'Hullo-ullo-ullo!'

250

A car had drawn up at the steps and was discharging passengers.

Passenger A. was J. Washburn Stoker. Passenger B. was his daughter, Pauline. Passenger C. was his young son, Dwight. And Passenger D. was Sir Roderick Glossop.

# =4=
# ANNOYING PREDICAMENT OF PAULINE STOKER

I MUST say I was pretty well a-twitter. It was about as juicy a biff as I had had for years. To have encountered this segment of the dead past in London would have been bad enough. Running into the gang down here like this, with the prospect of a lengthy luncheon party ahead, was a dashed sight worse. I removed the lid with as much courtly grace as I could muster up, but the face had coloured with embarrassment and I was more or less gasping for air.

Chuffy was being the genial host.

'Hullo-ullo-ullo! Here you all are. How are you Mr Stoker? How are you Sir Roderick? Hullo, Dwight. Er – good morning, Miss Stoker. May I introduce my friend, Bertie Wooster? Mr Stoker, my friend, Bertie Wooster. Dwight, my friend, Bertie Wooster. Miss Stoker, my friend, Bertie Wooster. Sir Roderick Glossop, my friend, Bertie ... Oh, but you know each other already, don't you?'

I was still under the ether. You will agree that all this was enough to rattle any chap. I surveyed the mob. Old Stoker was glaring at me. Old Glossop was glaring at me. Young Dwight was staring at me. Only Pauline appeared to find no awkwardness in the situation. She was as cool as an oyster on the half-shell and as chirpy as a spring breeze. We might have been meeting by appointment. Where Bertram could find only a tentative 'Pip-pip!' she bounded forward, full of speech, and grabbed the old hand warmly.

'Well, well, well! Old Colonel Wooster in person! Fancy finding you here, Bertie! I called you up in London, but they told me you had left.'

'Yes. I came down here.'

'I see you did, you little blob of sunshine. Well, sir, this has certainly made my day. You're looking fine, Bertie. Don't you think he's looking lovely, father?'

Old Stoker appeared reluctant to set himself up as a judge of male beauty. He made a noise like a pig swallowing half a cabbage, but refused to commit himself further. Dwight, a solemn child, was drinking me in in silence. Sir Roderick, who had turned purple, was now fading away to a lighter shade, but still looked as if his inner feelings had sustained a considerable wallop.

At this moment, however, the Dowager Lady Chuffnell came out. She was one of those powerful women who look like female Masters of Hounds, and she handled the mob scene with quiet efficiency. Before I knew where I was, the whole gang had gone indoors, and I was alone with Chuffy. He was staring at me in an odd manner and doing a bit of lower-lip biting.

'I didn't know you knew these people, Bertie.'

'I met them in New York.'

'You saw something of Miss Stoker there?'

'A little.'

'Only a little?'

'Quite a little.'

'I thought her manner seemed rather warm.'

'Oh, no. About normal.'

'I should have imagined you were great friends.'

'Oh, no. Just fairly pally. She goes on like that with everyone.'

'She does?'

'Oh, yes. Big-hearted you see.'

'She has got a delightful, impulsive, generous, spontaneous, genuine nature, hasn't she?'

'Absolutely.'

'Beautiful girl, Bertie.'

'Oh, very.'

'And charming.'

'Oh, most.'

'In fact, attractive.'

'Oh, quite.'

'I saw a good deal of her in London.'

'Yes?'

'We went to the Zoo and Madame Tussaud's together.'

'I see. And what does she seem to feel about this buying the house binge?'

'She seems all for it.'

'Tell me, laddie,' I said, anxious to get off the current subj., 'how do the prospects look?'

He knitted the Chuffnell brow.

'Sometimes good. Sometimes not.'

'I see.'

'Uncertain.'

'I understand.'

'This Stoker chap makes me nervous. He's friendly enough as a general rule, but I can't help feeling that at any moment he may fly off the handle and scratch the entire fixture. You can't tell me if there are any special subjects to avoid when talking to him, can you?'

'Special subjects?'

'Well, you know how it is with a stranger. You say it's a fine day, and he goes all white and tense, because you've reminded him that it was on a fine day that his wife eloped with the chauffeur.'

I considered.

'Well, if I were you,' I said, 'I wouldn't harp too much on the topic of B. Wooster. I mean, if you were thinking of singing my praises . . .'

'I wasn't.'

'Well, don't. He doesn't like me.'

'Why not?'

'Just one of those unreasonable antipathies. And I was thinking, old man, if it's all the same to you, it might be better if I didn't join the throng at the luncheon table. You can tell your aunt I've got a headache.'

'Well, if the sight of you is going to infuriate him . . . What makes him bar you so much?'

'I don't know.'

'Well, I'm glad you told me. You had better sneak off.'

'I will.'

'And I suppose I ought to be joining the others.'

He went indoors, and I started to take a turn or two up and down the gravel. I was glad to be alone. I wished to muse upon this matter of his attitude towards Pauline Stoker.

I wonder if you would mind just going back a bit and running the mental eye over that part of our conversation which had had to do with the girl.

Anything strike you about it?

No?

Oh, well, to get the full significance, of course, you ought to have been there and observed him. I am a man who can read faces, and Chuffy's had seemed to me highly suggestive. Not only had its expression, as he spoke of Pauline, been that of a stuffed frog with a touch of the Soul's Awakening about it, but it had also turned a fairly deepish crimson in colour. The tip of the nose had wiggled, and there had been embarrassment in the manner. The result being that I had become firmly convinced that the old schoolmate had copped it properly. Quick work, of course, seeing that he had only known the adored object a few days, but Chuffy is like that. A man of impulse and hot-blooded impetuosity. You find the girl, and he does the rest.

Well, if it was so, it was all right with me. Nothing of the dog in the manger about Bertram. As far as I was concerned, Pauline Stoker could hitch up with anyone she liked and she would draw a hearty 'Go to it!' from the discarded suitor. You know how it is on quiet reflection in these affairs. For a time the broken heart, and then suddenly the healing conviction that one is jolly well out of it. I could still see that Pauline was one of the most beautiful girls I had ever met, but of the ancient fire which had caused me to bung my heart at her feet that night at the Plaza there remained not a trace.

Analysing this, if analysing is the word I want, I came to the conclusion that this changed outlook was due to the fact that she was so dashed dynamic. Unquestionably an eyeful, Pauline Stoker had the grave defect of being one of those girls who want you to come and swim a mile before breakfast and rout you out when you are trying to snatch a wink of sleep after lunch for a merry five sets of tennis. And now that the scales had fallen from my eyes, I could see that what I required for the rôle of Mrs Bertram Wooster was something rather more on the lines of Janet Gaynor.

But in Chuffy's case these objections fell to the ground. He, you see, is very much on the dynamic side himself. He rides, swims, shoots, chivvies foxes with loud cries, and generally bustles about. He and this P. Stoker would make the perfect pair, and I felt that if there was anything I could do to push the thing along, it should be done unstintedly.

So when at this point I saw Pauline coming out of the house and bearing down on me, obviously with a view to exchanging notes and picking up the old threads and what not, I did not leg it but greeted her with a bright 'What ho!' and allowed her to steer me into the shelter of a path that led through the rhododendron shrubbery.

All of which goes to show what lengths a Wooster will proceed when it is a question of helping a pal, because the last thing I really wanted was to be closeted with this girl. The first shock of meeting her was over, but I was still feeling far from yeasty at the prospect of a heart-to-heart talk. As our relations had been severed by post and the last time we had forgathered we had been an engaged couple, I wasn't quite sure what was the correct note to strike.

However, the thought that I might be able to put in a word for old Chuffy nerved me to the ordeal, and we parked ourselves on a rustic bench and got down to the agenda.

'How perfectly extraordinary finding you here, Bertie,' she began. 'What are you doing in these parts?'

'I am temporarily in retirement,' I replied, pleased to find the conversational exchanges opening on what I might call an unemotional note. 'I needed a place where I could play the banjolele in solitude, and I took this cottage.'

'What cottage?'

'I've got a cottage down by the harbour.'

'You must have been surprised to see us.'

'I was.'

'More surprised than pleased, eh?'

'Well, of course, old thing, I'm always delighted to meet you, but when it comes to your father *and* old Glossop . . .'

'He's not one of your greatest admirers, is he? By the way, Bertie, *do* you keep cats in your bedroom?'

I stiffened a little.

'There have been cats in my bedroom, but the incident to which you allude is one that is susceptible of a ready . . .'

'All right. Never mind. Take it as read. But you ought to have seen father's face when he heard about it. Talking of father's face, I should get a big laugh if I saw it now.'

I could not allow this. Goodness knows, I'm as fond of a chuckle as the next man, but J. Washburn Stoker's face had never made me so much as smile. He was a cove who always reminded me of a pirate of the Spanish Main — a massive blighter and piercing-eyed, to boot. So far from laughing at the sight of him, I had never yet failed to feel absolutely spineless in his presence.

'If he suddenly came round the corner, I mean, and found us with our heads together like this. He's convinced that I'm still pining for you.'

'You don't mean that?'

'I do, honestly.'

'But, dash it . . .'

'It's true, I tell you. He looks on himself as the stern Victorian father who has parted the young lovers and has got to exercise ceaseless vigilance to keep them from getting together again. Little knowing that you never had a happier moment in your life than when you got my letter.'

'No, I say!'

'Bertie, be honest. You know you were delighted.'

'I wouldn't say that.'

'You don't have to. Mother knows.'

'No, dash it, really! I wish you wouldn't talk like that. I always esteemed you most highly.'

'You did what? Where do you pick up these expressions?'

'Well, I suppose from Jeeves, mostly. My late man. He had a fine vocabulary.'

'When you say "late", do you mean he's dead? Or just unpunctual?'

'He's left me. He didn't like me playing the banjolele. Words passed, and he is now with Chuffy.'

'Chuffy?'

'Lord Chuffnell.'

'Oh?'

There was a pause. She sat listening for a moment to a couple of birds who were having an argument in a near-by tree.

'Have you known Lord Chuffnell long?' she asked.

'Oh, rather.'

'You're great friends?'

'Bosom is the *mot juste*.'

'Good. I hoped you were. I wanted to talk to you about him. I can confide in you, can't I, Bertie?'

'Of course.'

'I knew I could. That's the comfort of having been engaged to a man. When you break it off, you feel such a sister.'

'I don't regard you as a blister at all,' I said warmly. 'You had a perfect right . . .'

'Not blister. Sister!'

'Oh, sister? You mean, you look on me as a brother.'

'Yes, as a brother. How quick you are. And I want you to be very brotherly now. Tell me about Marmaduke.'

'I don't think I know him.'

'Lord Chuffnell, idiot.'

'Is his name Marmaduke? Well, well! How true it is that one doesn't know how the other half of the world lives, what? Marmaduke!' I said, laughing heartily. 'I remember he was always evasive and secretive about it at school.'

She seemed annoyed.

'It's a beautiful name!'

I shot one of my swift, keen glances at her. This, I felt, must mean something. Nobody would say Marmaduke was a beautiful name wantonly and without good reason. And, sure enough, the eyes were gleaming and the epidermis a pretty pink.

'Hullo!' I said. 'Hullo, hullo, hullo! Hullo!'

Her demeanour was defiant.

'All right, all right!' she said. 'Less of the Sherlock stuff. I'm not trying to hide anything. I was just going to tell you.'

'You love this . . . ha, ha! Excuse me . . . this Marmaduke?'

'I'm crazy about him.'

'Good! Well, if what you say . . .'

'Don't you worship the way his hair fluffs up behind?'

'I have better things to do than go about staring at the back of Chuffy's head. But, as I was about to remark, if what you say is really so, be prepared for tidings of great joy. I'm a pretty close observer, and a certain bulbous look in the old boy's eyes when a recent conversation happened to turn in your direction has convinced me that he is deeply enamoured of you.'

She wiggled her shoulder impatiently, and in a rather peevish manner hoofed a passing earwig with a shapely foot.

'I know that, you chump. Do you think a girl can't tell?'

I was frankly nonplussed.

'Well, if he loves you and you love him, I fail to comprehend what you are beefing about?'

'Why, can't you understand? He's obviously dippy about me, but not a yip from him.'

'He will not speak?'

'Not a syllable.'

'Well, why would he? Surely you realize that there is a certain decency in these matters, a certain decorum? Naturally he wouldn't say anything yet. Dash it, give the man a chance. He's only known you five days.'

'I sometimes feel that he was a king in Babylon when I was a Christian slave.'

'What makes you think that?'

'I just do.'

'Well, you know best, of course. Very doubtful, I should have said myself. And, anyway, what do you want me to do about it?'

'Well, you're a friend of his. You could give him a hint. You could tell him there's no need for cold feet. . . .'

'It is not cold feet. It is delicacy. As I just explained, we men have our code in these matters. We may fall in love pretty nippily, but after that we consider it decorous to back-pedal a while. We are the parfait gentle knights, and we feel that it ill beseems us to make a beeline for a girl like a man charging into a railway restaurant for a bowl of soup. We . . .'

'What utter nonsense! You asked me to marry you after you had known me two weeks.'

'Ah, but there you were dealing with one of the Wild Woosters.'

'Well, I can't see . . .'

'Yes?' I said 'Proceed. You have our ear.'

But she was looking past me at something to the south-east; and, turning, I perceived that we were no longer alone.

There, standing in an attitude of respectful courtliness, with the sunshine playing upon his finely-chiselled features, was Jeeves.

# =5=
# BERTIE TAKES THINGS
# IN HAND

I NODDED affably. This man and I might have severed our
professional relations, but a Wooster is always debonair.

'Ah, Jeeves.'

'Good afternoon, sir.'

Pauline appeared interested.

'Is this Jeeves?'

'This is Jeeves.'

'So you don't like Mr Wooster's banjolele?'

'No, miss.'

I preferred that this delicate matter be not discussed, and it may
be, in consequence, that I spoke a little curtly.

'Well, Jeeves? What is it?'

'Mr Stoker, sir. He is inquiring after Miss Stoker's whereabouts.'

Well, of course, there's always that old one about them being at
the wash, but this seemed to me neither the time nor the place. I
turned to the girl with an air of courteous dismissal.

'You'd better push along.'

'I suppose so. You won't forget what I said?'

'The matter,' I assured her, 'shall have my prompt attention.'

She legged it, and Jeeves and I were alone together in the great
solitude. I lit a cigarette nonchalantly.

'Well, Jeeves.'

'Sir?'

'I mean to say, we meet again.'

'Yes, sir.'

'Philippi, what?'

'Yes, sir.'

'I hope you're getting on all right with Chuffy?'

'Everything is most pleasant, sir. I trust your new personal
attendant is giving satisfaction?'

'Oh, quite. A sterling fellow.'

'I am extremely gratified to hear it, sir.'

There was a pause.

'Er, Jeeves,' I said.

A rummy thing. It had been my intention, after exchanging these few civilities, to nod carelessly and leave the fellow. But it's so dashed difficult to break the habit of years. I mean to say, here was I and here was Jeeves, and a problem had been put up to me of just the type concerning which I had always been wont to seek his advice and counsel, and now something seemed to keep me rooted to the spot. And instead of being aloof and distant and passing on with the slight inclination of the head which, as I say, I had been planning, I found myself irresistibly impelled to consult him just as if there had been no rift at all.

'Er – Jeeves,' I said.

'Sir?'

'I should rather like, if you have a moment to spare, to split a word with you.'

'Certainly, sir.'

'I wish to canvass your views regarding old Chuffy.'

'Very good, sir.'

His face was wearing that expression of quiet intelligence combined with a feudal desire to oblige which I had so often seen upon it, and I hesitated no longer.

'You will agree with me that something's got to be done about the fifth Baron, I take it?'

'I beg your pardon, sir?'

I was impatient with this – what the dickens is the word I want?

'Come, come, Jeeves. You know what I mean as well as I do. A little less coyness and a bit more of the old rallying round spirit. You can't tell me you've been in his employment for nearly a week without observing and deducing and forming your conclusions.'

'Am I correct in supposing, sir, that you are alluding to his lordship's feelings towards Miss Stoker?'

'Exactly.'

'I am, of course, aware that his lordship is experiencing for the young lady a sentiment deeper and warmer than that of ordinary friendship, sir.'

'Would I be going too far if I said that he was potty about her?'

'No, sir. The expression would meet the facts of the case quite adequately.'

'Very well, then. Now, mark this. She, too, loves, Jeeves.'

'Indeed, sir?'

'She was telling me so specifically when you came along. She confessed herself dippy about the man. And she's very upset, poor fish. Extremely upset. Her feminine intuition has enabled her to read his secret. She detects the lovelight in his eyes. And she is all for it. And what is worrying her is that he does not tell his love, but lets concealment like . ! . like what, Jeeves?'

'A worm i' the bud, sir.'

'Feed on his something . . .'

'Damask cheek, sir.'

'Damask? You're sure?'

'Quite sure, sir.'

'Well, then, what on earth is it all about? He loves her. She loves him. So what's the snag? In conversing with her just now, I advanced the theory that what was holding him back was delicacy, but I didn't really believe it. I know Chuffy. A swift performer, if ever there was one. If he didn't propose to a girl by the end of the first week, he would think he was losing his grip. Yet now look at him. Missing on every cylinder. Why?'

'His lordship is a gentleman of scruples, sir.'

'How do you mean?'

'He feels that, being of straitened means himself, he has not the right to propose marriage to a young lady as wealthy as Miss Stoker.'

'But, dash it, Love laughs at . . . no, it doesn't . . . it's at locksmiths, isn't it?'

'At locksmiths, yes, sir.'

'Besides, she isn't as rich as all that. Just comfortably off, I should have said.'

'No, sir. Mr Stoker's fortune amounts to as much as fifty million dollars.'

'What! You're talking through your hat, Jeeves.'

'No, sir. I understand that that was the sum which he inherited recently under the will of the late Mr George Stoker.'

I was stunned.

'Good Lord, Jeeves! Has Second Cousin George kicked the bucket?'

'Yes, sir.'

'And left all his money to old Stoker?'

'Yes, sir.'

'Now I see. Now I understand— This explains everything. I was wondering how he managed to be going about buying vast estates. The yacht in the harbour is his, of course?'

'Yes, sir.'

'Well, well, well! But, dash it, George must have had nearer relations.'

'Yes, sir. I understand that he disliked them all.'

'You know about him, then?'

'Yes, sir. I saw a good deal of his personal attendant when we were in New York. A man named Benstead.'

'He was potty, wasn't he?'

'Certainly extremely eccentric, sir.'

'Any chance of one of those other relations contesting the will?'

'I do not imagine so, sir. But in such a case Mr Stoker would rely on Sir Roderick Glossop, of course, to testify that the late Mr Stoker, while possibly somewhat individual in his habits, was nevertheless perfectly sane. The testimony of so eminent a mental specialist as Sir Roderick would be unassailable.'

'You mean he'd say why shouldn't a fellow walk about on his hands, if he wants to? Saves shoe leather, and so forth?'

'Exactly, sir.'

'Then there's no chance of Miss Stoker ever being anything except the heiress of a bird with fifty million dollars shoved away behind the brick in the fire-place?'

'Virtually none, sir.'

I brooded on this.

'H'm. And unless old Stoker buys the Hall, Chuffy will continue to be Kid Lazarus, the man without a bean. One spots the drama of the situation. And yet, why, Jeeves? Why all this fuss about money? After all, plenty of bust blokes have married oofy girls before now.'

'Yes, sir. But his lordship is a gentleman of peculiar views on this particular matter.'

I mused. Yes, I reflected, it was quite true. Chuffy is a fellow who has always been odd on the subject of money. It's something to do with the Pride of the Chuffnells, I suppose. I know that for years and years I have been trying to lend him of my plenty, but he has always steadfastly refused to put the bite on me.

'It's difficult,' I said. 'One fails for the moment to see the way out. And yet you may be wrong, Jeeves. After all, you're only guessing.'

'No, sir. His lordship did me the honour to confide in me.'

'Really? How did the subject come up?'

'Mr Stoker had expressed a wish that I should enter his employment. He approached me in the matter. I informed his lordship. His lordship instructed me to hold out hopes.'

'You can't mean that he wants you to leave him and go to old Stoker?'

'No, sir. He specifically stated the reverse, with a good deal of vehemence. But he was anxious that I should not break off the negotiations with a definite refusal until the sale of Chuffnell Hall has gone through.'

'I see. I follow his strategy. He wanted you to jolly old Stoker along and keep him sweetened till he had signed the fatal papers?'

'Precisely, sir. It was this conversation that led up to his lordship revealing his personal position as concerns Miss Stoker. Until his financial status is sufficiently sound to justify him in doing so, his self-respect will not permit him to propose marriage to the young lady.'

'Silly ass!'

'I would not have ventured to employ precisely that term myself, sir, but I confess that I regard his lordship's attitude as somewhat hyper-quixotic.'

'We must talk him out of it.'

'Impossible, sir, I fear. I endeavoured to do so myself, but my arguments were of no avail. His lordship has a complex.'

'A what?'

'A complex, sir. It seems that he once witnessed a musical comedy, in which one of the dramatis personæ was a certain impecunious peer, Lord Wotwotleigh, who was endeavouring to marry an American heiress, and this individual appears to have made a lasting impression on his mind. He stated to me in the most unequivocal terms that he refused to place himself in a position where comparisons might be instituted.'

'But suppose the sale of the house does not go through?'

'In that case, I fear, sir . . .'

'The damask cheek will continue to do business at the old stand indefinitely?'

'Exactly, sir.'

'You really are sure it is "damask"?'

'Yes, sir.'

'But it doesn't seem to mean anything.'

'An archaic adjective, sir. I fancy it is intended to signify a healthy complexion.'

'Well, Chuffy's got that.'

'Yes, sir.'

'But what good's a healthy complexion if you don't get the girl?'

'Very true, sir.'

'What would you advise, Jeeves?'

'I fear I have nothing to suggest at the moment, sir.'

'Come, come, Jeeves.'

'No, sir. The difficulty being essentially a psychological one, I find myself somewhat baffled. As long as the image of Lord Wotwotleigh persists in his lordship's consciousness, I fear that there is nothing to be done.'

'Of course there is. Why this strange weakness, Jeeves? It is not like you. Obviously, the fellow must be shoved over the brink.'

'I do not quite follow you, sir.'

'Of course you do. The thing's perfectly clear. Here's old Chuffy, for the nonce just hanging dumbly round the girl. What he needs is a jolt. If he thought there was grave danger of some other bloke scooping her up, wouldn't that make him forget these dashed silly ideas of his and charge in, breathing fire through the nostrils?'

'Jealously is undoubtedly an extremely powerful motivating force, sir.'

'Do you know what I am going to do, Jeeves?'

'No, sir.'

'I am going to kiss Miss Stoker and take care that Chuffy sees me do it.'

'Really, sir, I should not advocate . . .'

'Peace, Jeeves. I have got the whole thing taped out. It came to me in a flash, as we were talking. After lunch, I shall draw Miss Stoker aside to this seat. You will arrange that Chuffy follows her. Waiting till I see the whites of his eyes, I shall fold her in a close embrace. If that doesn't work, nothing will.'

'I consider that you would be taking a decided risk, sir. His lordship is in a highly emotional condition.'

'Well, a Wooster can put up with a punch in the eye for the sake of a pal. No, Jeeves, I desire no further discussion. The thing is settled. All that remains is to fix the times. I suppose lunch would be over by about two-thirty. . . . Incidentally, I'm not going in to lunch myself.'

'No, sir?'

'No. I cannot face that gang. I shall remain out here. Bring me some sandwiches and a half-bot of the best.'

'Very good, sir.'

'And, by the way, the french windows of the dining-room will be open in weather like this. Sneak near them from time to time during lunch and bend an ear. Something of importance might be said.'

'Very good, sir.'

'Put plenty of mustard on the sandwiches.'

'Very good, sir.'

'And at two-thirty inform Miss Stoker that I would like a word with her. And at two-thirty-one inform Lord Chuffnell that she would like a word with him. The rest you can leave to me.'

'Very good, sir.'

# COMPLICATIONS SET IN

THERE was a fairly longish interval before Jeeves returned with the food-stuffs. I threw myself on them with some abandon.

'You've been the dickens of a time.'

'I followed your instructions, sir, and listened at the dining-room window.'

'Oh? With what result?'

'I was not able to hear anything that gave an indication of Mr Stoker's views regarding the purchase of the house, but he appeared in affable mood.'

'That's promising. Full of sparkle, eh?'

'Yes, sir. He was inviting all those present to a party on his yacht.'

'He's staying on here, then?'

'For some little time, I gathered, sir. Apparently something has gone wrong with the propeller of the vessel.'

'He probably gave it one of his looks. And this party?'

'It appears that it is Master Dwight Stoker's birthday tomorrow, sir. The party, I gathered, was to be in celebration of the event.'

'And was the suggestion well received?'

'Extremely, sir. Though Master Seabury appeared to experience a certain chagrin at Master Dwight's somewhat arrogant assertion that he betted this was the first time that Master Seabury had ever so much as smelled a yacht.'

'What did he say?'

'He retorted that he had been on millions of yachts. Indeed, if I am not mistaken, trillions was the word he employed.'

'And then?'

'From a peculiar noise which he made with his mouth, I received the impression that Master Dwight was sceptical concerning this claim. But at this moment Mr Stoker threw oil upon the troubled waters by announcing his intention of hiring the troupe of negro minstrels to perform at the party. It appears that his lordship had mentioned their presence in Chuffnell Regis.'

'And that went well?'

'Very well, indeed, sir. Except that Master Seabury said that he betted Master Dwight had never heard negro minstrels before. From a remark passed shortly afterwards by her ladyship, I gathered that Master Dwight had thrown a potato at Master Seabury; and for a while a certain unpleasantness seemed to threaten.'

I clicked my tongue.

'I wish somebody would muzzle those kids and chain them up. They'll queer the whole thing.'

'The imbroglio was fortunately short-lived, sir. I left the whole company on what appeared to be the most amicable terms. Master Dwight protested that his hand had slipped, and the apology was gracefully received.'

'Well, bustle back and see if you can hear some more.'

'Very good, sir.'

I finished my sandwiches and half-bot, and lit a cigarette, wishing that I had told Jeeves to bring me some coffee. But you don't have to tell Jeeves things like that. In due course, up he rolled with the steaming cupful.

'Luncheon has just concluded, sir.'

'Ah! Did you see Miss Stoker?'

'Yes, sir. I informed her that you desired a word with her, and she will be here shortly.'

'Why not now?'

'His lordship engaged her in conversation immediately after I had given her your message.'

'Had you told him to come here, too?'

'Yes, sir.'

'No good, Jeeves. I see a flaw. They will arrive together.'

'No, sir. On observing his lordship making in this direction, I can easily detain him for a moment on some matter.'

'Such as—?'

'I have long been desirous of canvassing his lordship's views as to the desirability of purchasing some new socks.'

'H'm! You know what you are when you get on to the subject of socks, Jeeves. Don't get carried away and keep him talking for an hour. I want to get this thing over.'

'I quite understand, sir.'

'When did you see Miss Stoker?'

'About a quarter of an hour ago, sir.'

'Funny, she doesn't turn up. I wonder what they're talking about?'

'I could not say, sir.'

'Ah!'

I had observed a gleam of white among the bushes. The next moment, the girl appeared. She was looking more beautiful than ever, her eyes, in particular, shining like twin stars. Nevertheless, I did not waver in my view that I was jolly glad it was Chuffy who, if all went well, was going to marry her, and not me. Odd, how a girl may be a perfect knock-out, and yet one can still feel that to be married to her would give one the absolute pip. That's life, I suppose.

'Hallo, Bertie,' said Pauline. 'What's all this about your having a headache? You seem to have been doing yourself pretty well, in spite of it.'

'I found I could peck a bit. You had better take these things back, Jeeves.'

'Very good, sir.'

'And you won't forget that, if his lordship should want me, I'm here.'

'No, sir.'

He gathered up the plate, cup and bottle and disappeared. And whether I was sorry to see him go or not, I couldn't have said. I was feeling a good deal worked up. Taut, if you know what I mean. On edge. Tense. The best idea I can give you of my emotions at this juncture is to say that they rather resembled those I had once felt when starting to sing 'Sonny Boy' at Beefy Bingham's Church Lads entertainment down in the East End.

Pauline had grabbed my arm, and was beginning to make some species of communication.

'Bertie,' she was saying . . .

But at this point I caught sight of Chuffy's head over a shrub, and I felt that the moment had come to act. It was one of those things that want doing quickly or not at all. I waited no longer. Folding the girl in my arms, I got home on her right eyebrow. It wasn't one of my best, I will admit, but it was a kiss within the meaning of the act, and I fancied that it ought to produce results.

And so, no doubt, it would have done, had the fellow who entered left at this critical point been Chuffy. But it wasn't. What with only being able to catch a fleeting glimpse of a Homburg hat through the foliage, I appeared to have made an unfortunate floater. The bloke who now stood before us was old Pop Stoker, and I confess I found myself a prey to a certain embarrassment.

It was, you must admit, not a little awkward. Here was an anxious father who combined with a strong distaste for Bertram Wooster the notion that his daughter was madly in love with him: and the first thing he saw when he took an after-lunch saunter was the two of us locked in a close embrace. It was enough to give any parent the jitters, and I was not surprised that his demeanour was that of stout Cortez staring at the Pacific. A fellow with fifty millions in his kick doesn't have to wear the mask. If he wants to give any selected bloke a nasty look, he gives him a nasty look. He was giving me one now. It was a look that had both alarm and anguish in it, and I realized that Pauline's statement regarding his views had been accurate.

Fortunately, the thing did not go beyond looks. Say what you like against civilization, it comes in dashed handy in a crisis like this. It may be a purely artificial code that keeps a father from hoofing his daughter's kisser when they are fellow guests at a house, but at this moment I felt that I could do with all the purely artificial codes that were going.

There was just one instant when his foot twitched and it seemed as if what you might call the primitive J. Washburn Stoker was about to find self-expression. Then civilization prevailed. With one more of those looks he collected Pauline, and the next moment I was alone and at liberty to think the thing over.

And it was as I was doing so with the help of a soothing cigarette that Chuffy bounded into my little sylvan glade. He too appeared to have something on his mind, for he was noticeably pop-eyed.

'Look here, Bertie,' he began without preamble, 'what's all this I hear?'

'What's all what you hear, old man?'

'Why didn't you tell me you had been engaged to Pauline Stoker?'

I raised an eyebrow. It seemed to me that a touch of the iron hand would not be out of place. If you see a fellow's going to be austere with you, there's nothing like jumping in and being austere with him first.

'I fail to understand you, Chuffnell,' I said stiffly. 'Did you expect me to send you a post card?'

'You could have told me this morning.'

'I saw no reason to do so. How did you hear about it, anyhow?'

'Sir Roderick Glossop happened to mention it.'

'Oh, he did, did he? Well, he's an authority on the subject. He was the bird who broke it off.'

'What do you mean?'

'He happened to be in New York at the time, and it was the work of a moment with him to tap old Stoker on the chest and urge him to give me the push. The whole thing didn't last more than forty-eight hours from kick-off to finish.'

Chuffy eyed me narrowly.

'You swear that?'

'Certainly.'

'Only forty-eight hours?'

'Less.'

'And there's nothing between you now?'

His demeanour was not matey, and I began to perceive that in arranging that Stoker and not he should be the witness of the recent embrace the guardian angel of the Woosters had acted dashed shrewdly.

'Nothing.'

'You're sure?'

'Nothing whatever. So charge in, Chuffy, old man,' I said, patting his shoulder in an elder-brotherly manner. 'Follow the dictates of the old heart and fear nothing. The girl is potty about you.'

'Who told you that?'

'She did.'

'Herself?'

'In person.'

'She does really love me?'

'Passionately, I gathered.'

A look of relief came into the old egg's care-worn face. He passed a hand over the forehead and generally relaxed.

'Well, that's all right, then. Sorry, if I appeared a bit rattled for a moment. When a fellow's just got engaged to a girl, it's rather a jar to find that she was engaged to somebody else about two months before.'

I was astounded.

'Are you engaged? Since when?'

'Since shortly after lunch.'

'But how about Wotwotleigh?'

'Who told you about Wotwotleigh?'

'Jeeves. He said the shadow of Wotwotleigh brooded over you like a cloud.'

'Jeeves talks too much. As a matter of fact, Wotwotleigh didn't enter into the matter at all. Immediately before I fixed things up with Pauline, old Stoker told me that he had decided to buy the house.'

'Really!'

'Absolutely. I think it was the port that did it. I lushed him up on the last of the '85.'

'You couldn't have done a wiser thing. Your own idea?'

'No. Jeeves's.'

I could not restrain a wistful sigh.

'Jeeves is a wonder.'

'A marvel.'

'What a brain!'

'Size nine-and-a-quarter, I should say.'

'He eats a lot of fish. What a pity he has no ear for music,' I said moodily. Then I stifled regret and tried not to think of my bereavement but of Chuffy's bit of luck. 'Well, this is fine,' I said heartily. 'I hope you will be very, very happy. I can honestly say that I always looked on Pauline as one of the nicest girls I was ever engaged to.'

'I wish you would stop harping on that engagement.'

'Quite.'

'I'm trying to forget that you were ever engaged to her.'

'Quite, quite.'

'When I think that you were once in a position to . . .'

'But I wasn't. Never lose sight of the fact that the betrothal only lasted two days, during both of which I was in bed with a nasty cold.'

'But when she accepted you, you must have . . .'

'No, I didn't. A waiter came into the room with a tray of beef sandwiches and the moment passed.'

'Then you never . . . ?'

'Absolutely never.'

'She must have had a great time, being engaged to you. One round of excitement. I wonder what on earth made her accept you?'

This had puzzled me too, more than a little. I can only suppose that there is something in me that strikes a chord in the bosoms of these forceful females. I've known it happen before, on the occasion when I got engaged to Honoria Glossop.

'I once consulted a knowledgeable pal,' I said, 'and his theory was that the sight of me hanging about like a loony sheep awoke the maternal instinct in Woman. There may be something in this.'

'Possibly,' agreed Chuffy. 'Well, I'll be getting along. I suppose Stoker will want to talk to me about the house. You coming?'

'No, thanks. The fact of the matter is, old man, I'm not so dashed keen on mingling with your little troupe. I could stand your Aunt Myrtle. I could even stand little Seabury. But add Stoker and Glossop, and the going becomes too sticky for Bertram. I shall take a stroll about the estate.'

This demesne or seat of Chuffy's was a topping place for a stroll, and I should have thought he would have had a certain regret at the thought that it was passing out of his hands, to become a private loony-bin. But I suppose when you've been cooped up in a house for years with an Aunt Myrtle and a cousin Seabury for next-door neighbours, you lose your taste for it. I spent an agreeable two hours messing about, and it was well along into the late afternoon when the imperative need for a cup of tea sent me sauntering round to the back premises, where I anticipated finding Jeeves.

A scullery-maid of sorts directed me to his quarters, and I sat down in the comfortable certainty that ere long the steaming pot and buttered toast would be to the fore. The happy ending of which Chuffy had recently apprised me had induced contentment, and a nice hot cup and slab of toast would, I felt, just top the thing off.

'In fact, Jeeves,' I said, 'even muffins would scarcely be out of place on an occasion like this. I find it very gratifying to reflect that Chuffy's storm-tossed soul has at last come safely into harbour. You heard about Stoker promising to buy the house?'

'Yes, sir.'

'And the engagement?'

'Yes, sir.'

'I suppose old Chuffy is feeling great.'

'Not altogether, sir.'

'Eh?'

'No, sir. I regret to say that there has been something in the nature of a hitch.'

'What! They can't have quarrelled already?'

'No, sir. His lordship's relations with Miss Stoker continue uniformly cordial. It is with Mr Stoker that he is on distant terms.'

'Oh, my God!'

'Yes, sir.'

'What happened?'

'The origin of the trouble was a physical contest between Master Dwight Stoker and Master Seabury, sir. You may recollect my mentioning that during luncheon there appeared to be a lack of perfect sympathy between the young gentlemen.'

'But you said—'

'Yes, sir. Matters were smoothed over at the time, but they came to a head again some forty minutes after the conclusion of the meal. The young gentlemen had gone off together to the small morning-room, and there, it appears, Master Seabury endeavoured to exact from Master Dwight the sum of one shilling and sixpence for what he termed protection.'

'Oh, golly!'

'Yes, sir. Master Dwight, I gathered, declined in a somewhat high-spirited manner to kick in, as I believe the expression is, and one word led to another, with the result that at about three-thirty sounds indicative of a brawl were heard proceeding from the morning-room, and the senior members of the party, repairing thither, discovered the young gentlemen on the floor surrounded by the debris of a china cabinet which they had overturned in their struggle. At the moment of their arrival, Master Dwight appeared to be having somewhat the better of the exchanges, for he was seated on Master Seabury's chest, bumping his head on the carpet.'

It will give you some idea of the grave concern which this narrative was occasioning me, when I say that my emotion on hearing this was not a sober ecstasy at the thought that after all these long years somebody had at last been treating little Seabury's head as it ought to be treated, but a sickening dismay. I could see whither all this was tending.

'Gosh, Jeeves!'

'Yes, sir.'

'And then?'

'The action then became, as it were, general, sir.'

'The old brigade lent a hand?'

'Yes, sir, the initiative being taken by Lady Chuffnell.'

I moaned.

'It would be, Jeeves. Chuffy has often told me that her attitude towards Seabury resembles that of a tigress towards its cub. In Seabury's interests she has always been inclined to stamp on the world's toes and give it the elbow. I have heard Chuffy's voice absolutely quiver when describing the way in which, in the days before he contrived to shoot them off to the Dower House and they were still living at the Hall, she always collared the best egg at breakfast and slipped it to the little one. But go on.'

'On witnessing the position of affairs, her ladyship uttered a sharp cry and struck Master Dwight with considerable force on the right ear.'

'Upon which, of course . . . ?'

'Precisely, sir. Mr Stoker, espousing the cause of his son, aimed a powerful kick at Master Seabury.'

'And got him, Jeeves? Tell me he got him.'

'Yes, sir. Master Seabury was rising at the moment, and his attitude was exceptionally well adapted for the receipt of such an attack. The next moment, a heated altercation had broken out between her ladyship and Mr Stoker. Her ladyship called to Sir Roderick for support, and he – somewhat reluctantly, it appeared to me – proceeded to take Mr Stoker to task for the assault. High words ensued, and the upshot of it was that Mr Stoker with a good deal of warmth informed Sir Roderick that if he supposed that he, Mr Stoker, intended to purchase Chuffnell Hall after what had occurred, he, Sir Roderick, was in grave error.'

I buried the head in the hands.

'Upon this . . .'

'Yes, get it over, Jeeves. I can see what's coming.'

'Yes, sir. I agree with you that the whole affair has something of the dark inevitability of Greek tragedy. Upon this, his lordship, who had been an agitated auditor, gave vent to a startled exclamation and urged Mr Stoker to disclaim these words. It was his lordship's view that Mr Stoker, having given his promise to purchase Chuffnell Hall, could not, as an honourable man, recede from his obligation. Upon Mr Stoker replying that he did not care what he had promised or what he had not promised and continuing to asseverate that not a penny of his money should be expended in the direction indicated, his lordship, I regret to say, became somewhat unguarded in his speech.'

I moaned another bar or two. I knew what old Chuffy was capable of when his generous nature was stirred. I had heard him coaching his college boat at Oxford.

'He ticked Stoker off?'

'With considerable vigour, sir. Stating in an extremely candid manner his opinion of the latter's character, commercial probity, and even appearance.'

'That must have put the lid on it.'

'It did appear to create a certain coldness, sir.'

'And then?'

'That terminated the distressing scene, sir. Mr Stoker returned to the yacht with Miss Stoker and Master Dwight. Sir Roderick has gone to secure accommodation for himself at the local inn. Lady Chuffnell is applying arnica to Master Seabury in his bedroom. His lordship, I believe, is taking the dog for a run in the west park.'

I mused.

'When all this happened, had Chuffy told Stoker he wanted to marry Miss Stoker?'

'No, sir.'

'Well, I don't see how he can very well do it now.'

'I fancy the announcement would not be cordially received, sir.'

'They will have to meet by stealth.'

'Even that will be a little difficult, sir. I should have mentioned that I chanced to be an auditor of a conversation between Mr and Miss Stoker, from the substance of which I gathered that it was the gentleman's intention to keep Miss Stoker virtually in durance while on board the yacht, not permitting her to go ashore during the remainder of their enforced stay in the harbour.'

'But you said he didn't know anything about the engagement.'

'Mr Stoker's motive in immuring Miss Stoker on the vessel is not to prevent her encountering his lordship, but to obviate any chance of her meeting you, sir. The fact that you embraced the young lady has convinced him that her affection for you has persisted since your parting in New York.'

'You're sure you really heard all this?'

'Yes, sir.'

'How did you come to do that?'

'I was conversing with his lordship at the moment on one side of a screen of bushes, when the conversation which I have described broke out on the other side. There was no alternative but to overhear Mr Stoker's remarks.'

I started visibly.

'You were talking with Chuffy, did you say?'

'Yes, sir.'

'And he heard all that, too?'

'Yes, sir.'

'About me kissing Miss Stoker?'

'Yes, sir.'

'Did it seem to stir him up?'

'Yes, sir.'

'What did he say?'

'He mentioned something about scooping out your insides, sir.'

I wiped the brow.

'Jeeves,' I said, 'this calls for careful thought.'

'Yes, sir.'

'Advise me, Jeeves.'

'Well, sir, I think it might be judicious if you were to attempt to persuade his lordship that the spirit in which you embraced Miss Stoker was a purely brotherly one.'

'Brotherly? You think I could get away with that?'

'I fancy so, sir. After all, you are an old friend of the young lady. It would be quite understandable that you should bestow a kindly and dispassionate kiss upon her on learning of her betrothal to so close an intimate as his lordship.'

I rose.

'It may work, Jeeves. It is, at least, worth trying. I shall now leave you, to prepare myself for the ordeal before me with silent meditation.'

'Your tea will be here in a moment, sir.'

'No, Jeeves. This is no time for tea. I must concentrate. I must have that story right before he arrives. I dare say I shall be getting a call from him shortly.'

'It would not surprise me if you were to find his lordship

277

awaiting you at your cottage now, sir.'

He was absolutely correct. No sooner had I crossed the threshold than something exploded out of the arm-chair and there was Chuffy, gazing bleakly upon me.

'Ah!' he said, speaking the word between clenched teeth and generally comporting himself in an unpleasant and disturbing manner. 'Here you are at last!'

I slipped him a sympathetic smile.

'Here I am, yes. And I have heard all. Jeeves told me. Too bad, too bad. I little thought, old man, when I bestowed a brotherly kiss on Pauline Stoker by way of congratulating her on your engagement, that all this trouble would be bobbing up so soon afterwards.'

He continued to give me the eye.

'Brotherly?'

'Essentially brotherly.'

'Old Stoker didn't seem to think so.'

'Well, we know what sort of a mind old Stoker has got, don't we?'

'Brotherly? H'm!'

I registered manly regret.

'I suppose I shouldn't have done it . . .'

'It was lucky for you I wasn't there when you did.'

'. . . But you know how it is when a fellow you've been at private school, Eton and Oxford with gets engaged to a girl on whom you look as a sister. One is carried away.'

It was plain that a struggle was going on in the old boy's bosom. He glowered a bit and paced the room a bit and, happening to trip over a footstool, he kicked it a bit. Then he became calmer. You could see Reason returning to her throne.

'Well, all right,' he said. 'But in future a little less of this fraternal stuff.'

'Quite.'

'Switch it off. Resist the impulse.'

'Certainly.'

'If you want sisters, seek them elsewhere.'

'Just so.'

'I don't want to feel, when I'm married, that at any moment I may come into the room and find a brother-and-sister act in progress.'

'I quite understand, old man. Then you still intend to marry this Pauline?'

'Intend to marry her? Of course I intend to marry her. I'd look a silly ass not marrying a girl like that, wouldn't I?'

'But how about the old Chuffnell scruples?'

'What are you talking about?'

'Well, if Stoker is not going to buy the Hall, aren't you rather by way of being back in the position you were in before, when you would not tell your love, but let the thought of Wotwotleigh like a worm i' the bud feed on your damask cheek?'

He gave a slight shudder.

'Bertie,' he said, 'don't remind me of a time when I must have been absolutely potty. I can't imagine how I ever felt like that. You can take it as official that my views have changed. I don't care now if I haven't a bean and she's got a packet. If I can dig up seven-and-six for the licence and the couple of quid or whatever it is for the man behind the Prayer Book, this wedding is going through.'

'Fine.'

'What does money matter?'

'Quite.'

'I mean, love's love.'

'You never spoke a truer word, laddie. If I were you, I'd write her a letter embodying those views. You see, she may think that, now your finances are rocky once more, you will want to edge out.'

'I will. And, by Jove!'

'What?'

'Jeeves shall take it to her. Thus removing any chance of old Stoker intercepting it.'

'Could he, do you think?'

'My dear chap! A born letter-intercepter. You can see it in his eye.'

'I mean, could Jeeves take it? I don't see how.'

'I should have told you that Stoker wanted Jeeves to leave me and enter his service. At the time I thought I had never heard such crust in my life, but now I am all for it. Jeeves shall go to him.'

I got on to the ruse or scheme.

'I see what you mean. Operating under the Stoker banner, he will be free to come and go.'

'Exactly.'

'He can take a letter from you to her and then one from her to you and then one from you to her and then one from her to you and then one from you to her and then one . .'

'Yes, yes. You've got the idea. And in the course of this correspondence we can fix up some scheme for meeting. Have you any idea how long it takes to clear the decks for a wedding?'

'I'm not sure. I believe, if you get a special licence, you can do it like a flash.'

'I'll get a special licence. Two. Three. Well, this has certainly put the butter on the spinach. I feel a new man. I'll go and tell Jeeves at once. He can be on that yacht this evening.'

At this point he suddenly stopped. The brow darkened once more and he shot another of those searching looks at me.

'I suppose she really does love me?'

'Dash it, old man, didn't she say so?'

'She said so, yes. Yes, she said so. But can you believe what a girl says?'

'My dear chap!'

'Well, they're great kidders. She may have been fooling me.'

'Morbid, laddie.'

He brooded a bit.

'It seemed so dashed odd that she should have let you kiss her.'

'I took her by surprise.'

'She could have sloshed you on the ear.'

'Why? She naturally divined that the embrace was purely brotherly.'

'Brotherly, eh?'

'Wholly brotherly.'

'Well, it may be so,' said Chuffy doubtfully. 'Have you any sisters, Bertie?'

'No.'

'But, if you had, you would kiss them?'

'Repeatedly.'

'Well . . . Oh, well . . . Well, perhaps it's all right.'

'You can believe a Wooster's word, can't you?'

'I don't know so much. I remember you once, the morning after the Boat Race our second year at Oxford, telling the magistrates your name was Eustace H. Plimsoll and that you lived at The Laburnams, Alleyn Road, West Dulwich.'

'That was a special case, calling for special measures.'

'Yes, of course ... Yes ... Well. ... Well, I suppose it's all right. You really do swear there's absolutely nothing between you and Pauline now?'

'Nothing. We have often laughed heartily at the thought of that moment's madness in New York.'

'I never heard you.'

'Well, we have done – frequently.'

'Oh? ... In that case ... Well, yes, I suppose ... Well, anyway, I'll go off and write that letter.'

For some time after he had left me, I remained with the feet up on the mantelpiece, relaxing. Taking it all in all, it had been a pretty strenuous day, and I was feeling the strain a bit. The recent exchange of thoughts with Chuffy alone had taken it out of the nervous system considerably. And when Brinkley came in and wanted to know when I would have dinner, the thought of sitting down to a solitary steak and fried in the cottage didn't appeal. I felt restless, on edge.

'I shall dine out, Brinkley,' I said.

This successor to Jeeves had been sent down by the agency in London, and I'm bound to say he wasn't the fellow I'd have selected if I had had time to go round to the place and make a choice in person. Not at all the man of my dreams. A melancholy blighter, with a long, thin, pimple-studded face and deep, brooding eyes, he had shown himself averse from the start to that agreeable chit-chat between employer and employed to which the society of Jeeves had accustomed me. I had been trying to establish cordial relations ever since he had arrived, but with no success. Outwardly he was all respectfulness, but inwardly you could see that he was a man who was musing on the coming Social Revolution and looked on Bertram as a tyrant and an oppressor.

'Yes, Brinkley, I shall dine out.'

He said nothing, merely looking at me as if he were measuring me for my lamp-post.

'I have had a fatiguing day, and I feel a need for the lights and the wine. Both of these, I should imagine, may be had in Bristol. And there ought to be a show of some kind playing there, don't you think? It's one of the Number One touring towns.'

He sighed slightly. All this talk of my going to shows was distressing him. What he really wanted was to see me sprinting down Park Lane with the mob after me with dripping knives.

'I shall take the car and drive over there. You can have the evening off.'

'Very good, sir,' he moaned.

I gave it up. The man annoyed me. I hadn't the slightest objection to his spending his time planning massacres for the bourgeoisie, but I was dashed if I could see why he couldn't do it with a bright and cheerful smile. Dismissing him with a gesture, I went round to the garage and got the car out.

It was only a matter of thirty miles or so to Bristol, and I got there in nice time for a comfortable bite before the theatre. The show was a musical comedy which I had seen on several occasions during its London run, but it stood up quite well on a further visit, and altogether I was feeling rested and refreshed when I started back home.

I suppose it would have been getting on for midnight when I fetched up at the rural retreat: and, being about ready for sleep by now, I lost no time in lighting a candle and toddling upstairs. As I opened the door of my room, I recollect I was thinking how particularly well a dollop of slumber would go: and I was just making for the bed with a song on my lips, so to speak, when something suddenly sat up in it.

The next moment I had dropped the candle and the room was plunged into darkness. But not before I had seen quite enough to be getting along with.

Reading from left to right, the contents of the bed consisted of Pauline Stoker in my heliotrope pyjamas with the old gold stripe.

# =7=
# A VISITOR FOR BERTIE

THE attitude of fellows towards finding girls in their bedroom shortly after midnight varies. Some like it. Some don't. I didn't. I suppose it's some old Puritan strain in the Wooster blood. I drew myself up censoriously and shot a sternish glance in her direction. Absolutely wasted, of course, because it was pitch dark.

'What . . . What . . What . . . ?'

'It's all right.'

'All right?'

'Quite all right.'

'Oh?' I said, and I don't pretend to disguise the fact that I spoke bitterly. I definitely meant it to sting.

I stooped to pick up the candle, and the next moment I had uttered a startled cry.

'Don't make such a noise!'

'But there's a corpse on the floor.'

'There isn't. I should have noticed it.'

'There is, I tell you. I was groping about for the candle, and my fingers touched something cold and still and clammy.'

'Oh, that's my swimming suit.'

'Your swimming suit?'

'Well, do you think I came ashore by aeroplane?'

'You swam here from the yacht?'

'Yes.'

'When?'

'About half an hour ago.'

In that level-headed, practical way of mine, I went straight to the root of the matter.

'Why?' I asked.

A match scratched and a candle by the bed flamed up and lent a bit of light to the scene. Once more I was able to observe those pyjamas, and I'm bound to admit they looked extraordinarily dressy. Pauline was darkish in her general colour scheme, and heliotrope suited her. I said as much, always being ready to give credit where credit is due.

'You look fine in that slumber-wear.'

'Thanks.'

She blew out the match, and gazed at me in a sort of wondering way.

'You know, Bertie, steps should be taken about you.'

'Eh?'

'You ought to be in some sort of a home.'

'I am,' I replied coldly and rather cleverly. 'My own. The point I wish to thresh out is, what are you doing in it?'

Womanlike, she evaded the issue.

'What on earth did you want to kiss me like that for in front of father? You needn't tell me you were carried away by my radiant beauty. No, it was just plain, straight goofiness, and I can quite understand now why Sir Roderick told father that you ought to be under restraint. Why are you still at large? You must have a pull of some kind.'

We Woosters are pretty sharp on this sort of thing. I spoke with a good deal of asperity.

'The incident to which you allude is readily explained. I thought he was Chuffy.'

'Thought who was Chuffy?'

'Your father.'

'If you're trying to make out that Marmaduke looks the least bit like father you must be cuckoo,' she replied with a warmth equal to my own. I gathered that she was not a great admirer of the parent's appearance, and I'm not saying she wasn't right. 'Besides, I don't see what you mean.'

I explained.

'The idea was to let Chuffy observe you in my embrace, so that the generous fire would be stirred within him and he would get keyed up to proposing to you, feeling that if he didn't get action right speedily he might lose you.'

Her manner softened.

'You didn't think that out by yourself?

'I did.' I was somewhat nettled. 'Why everybody should imagine that I can't get ideas without the assistance of Jeeves . . .'

'But that was very sweet of you.'

'We Woosters *are* sweet, exceedingly sweet, when a pal's happiness is in the balance.'

'I can see now why I accepted you that night in New York,' she said meditatively. 'There's a sort of woolly-headed duckiness about you. If I wasn't so crazy about Marmaduke, I could easily marry you, Bertie.'

'No, no,' I said, with some alarm. 'Don't dream of it. I mean to say . . .'

'Oh, it's all right. I'm not going to. I'm going to marry Marmaduke; that's why I'm here.'

'And now,' I said, 'we've come right back to it. Once more we have worked round to the very point concerning which I most desire enlightenment. What on earth is the idea behind all this? You say you swam ashore from the yacht? Why? You came and dumped yourself in my little home. Why?'

'Because I wanted somewhere to lie low till I could get clothes, of course. I can't go to the Hall in a swimming suit.'

I began to follow the train of thought.

'Oh, you swam ashore to get to Chuffy?'

'Of course. Father was keeping me a prisoner on board the yacht, and this evening your man Jeeves . . .'

I winced.

'My late man.'

'All right. Your late man. Your late man Jeeves arrived with an early letter from Marmaduke. Oh, boy!'

'How do you mean, oh, boy?'

'Was that a letter? I cried six pints when I read it.'

'Hot stuff?'

'It was beautiful. It throbbed with poetry.'

'It did?'

'Yes.'

'This letter?'

'Yes.'

'Chuffy's letter?'

'Yes. You seem surprised.'

I was a bit. One of the very best, old Chuffy, of course, but I wouldn't have said he could write letters like that. But then one has got to take into consideration the fact that when I've been with him he has generally been eating steak-and-kidney pudding or cursing horses for not running fast enough. On such occasions, the poetic side of a man is not uppermost.

'So this letter stirred you up, did it?'

'You bet it stirred me up. I felt I couldn't wait another day without seeing him. What was that poem about a woman wailing for her demon lover?'

'Ah, there you have me. Jeeves would know.'

'Well, that's what I felt like. And, talking of Jeeves, what a man! Sympathy? He drips with it.'

'Oh, you confided in Jeeves?'

'Yes. And told him what I was going to do.'

'And he didn't try to stop you?'

'Stop me? He was all for it.'

'He was, was he?'

'You should have seen him. Such a kind smile. He said you would be delighted to help me.'

'He did, eh?'

'He spoke most highly of you.'

'Really?'

'Oh, yes, he thinks a lot of you. I remember his very words. "Mr Wooster, miss," he said, "is, perhaps, mentally somewhat negligible, but he has a heart of gold." He said that as he was lowering me from the side of the boat by a rope, having first made sure that the coast was clear. I couldn't dive, you see, because of the splash.'

I was chewing the lip in some chagrin.

'What the devil did he mean, "mentally negligible"?'

'Oh, you know. Loopy.'

'Tchah!'

'Eh?'

'I said "Tchah!"'

'Why?'

'Why?' I was a good deal moved. 'Well wouldn't you say "Tchah!" if your late man was going about the place telling people you were mentally negligible. . . .'

'But with a heart of gold.'

'Never mind the heart of gold. The point is that my man, my late man, a fellow I have always looked on more as some sort of an uncle than a personal attendant, is shooting to and fro bellowing out at the top of his voice that I am mentally negligible and filling my bedroom with girls. . . .'

'Bertie! Are you annoyed?'

'Annoyed!'

'You sound annoyed. And I can't see why. I should have thought you would have been only too glad of the chance of helping me to get the man I love. Having this heart of gold I hear so much about.'

'The point is not whether I have a heart of gold. Heaps of people have hearts of gold and yet would be upset at finding girls in their bedrooms in the small hours. What you don't seem to realize, what you and this Jeeves of yours have omitted to take into your calculations, is that I have a reputation to keep up, an unspotted name to maintain in its pristine purity. This cannot be done by entertaining girls who come in, in the middle of the night, without so much as a by-your-leave and coolly pinch your heliotrope pyjamas . . .'.

'You didn't expect me to sleep in a wet swimming suit?'

'. . . and leap into your bed . . .'

She uttered an exclamation.

'I know what this reminds me of. I've been trying to think ever since you came in. The story of the Three Bears. You must have been told it as a kid. "There's somebody in my bed. . . ." Wasn't that what the Big Bear said?'

I frowned doubtfully.

'As I recollect it, it was something about porridge. "Who's been eating my porridge?" '

'I'm sure there was a bed in it.'

'Bed? Bed? I can't remember any bed. On the subject of the porridge, however, I am absolutely. . . . But we are wandering from the point once more. What I was saying was that a reputable bachelor like myself, who has never had his licence so much as endorsed, can scarcely be blamed for looking askance at girls in heliotrope pyjamas in his bed. . . .'

'You said they suited me.'

'They do suit you.'

'You said I looked fine in them.'

'You do look fine in them, but once more you are refusing to meet the issue squarely. The point is . . .'

'How many points is that? I seem to have counted about a dozen.'

'There is only one point, and I am endeavouring to make it

clear. In a nutshell, what will people say when they find you here?'

'But they won't find me here.'

'You think so? Ha! What about Brinkley?'

'Who's he?'

'My man.'

'Your late man?'

I clicked the tongue.

'My new man. At nine tomorrow morning he will bring me tea.'

'Well, you'll like that.'

'He will bring it to this room. He will approach the bed. He will place it on the table.'

'What on earth for?'

'To facilitate my getting at the cup and sipping.'

'Oh, you mean he will put the tea on the table. You said he would put the bed on the table.'

'I never said anything of the sort.'

'You did. Distinctly.'

I tried to reason with the girl.

'My dear child,' I said, 'I must really ask you to use your intelligence. Brinkley is not a juggler. He is a well-trained gentleman's gentleman, and would consider it a liberty to put beds on tables. And why should he put beds on tables? The idea would never occur to him. He . . .'

She interrupted my reasoning.

'But wait a minute. You keep babbling about Brinkley, but there isn't a Brinkley.'

'There is a Brinkley. One Brinkley. And one Brinkley coming into this room at nine o'clock tomorrow morning and finding you in that bed will be enough to start a scandal which will stagger humanity.'

'I mean, he can't be in the house.'

'Of course he's in the house.'

'Well, he must be deaf, then. I made enough noise getting in to wake six gentlemen's gentlemen. Apart from smashing a window at the back . . .'

'Did you smash a window at the back?'

'I had to, or I couldn't have got in. It was the window of some sort of bedroom on the ground floor.'

'Why, dash it, that's Brinkley's bedroom.'

'Well, he wasn't in it.'

'Why on earth not? I gave him the evening off, not the night.'

'I can see what has happened. He's away on a toot somewhere, and won't be back for days. Father had a man who did that once. He went out for his evening from our house on East Sixty-Seventh Street, New York, on April the fourth in a bowler hat, grey gloves and a check suit, and the next we heard of him was a telegram from Portland, Oregon, on April the tenth, saying he had overslept himself and would be back shortly. That's what your Brinkley must have done.'

I must say I drew a good deal of comfort from the idea.

'Let us hope so,' I said. 'If he is really trying to drown his sorrows, it ought to take him weeks.'

'So, you see, you've been making a fuss about nothing. I always say . . .'

But what it was she always said, I was not privileged to learn. For at that moment she broke off with a sharp squeak.

Somebody was knocking on the front door.

# =8=
# POLICE PERSECUTION

WE looked at each other with a wild surmise, silent upon a first-floor back in Chuffnell Regis. That frightful sound, coming unexpectedly like that in the middle of the peaceful summer night, had been enough to strike the chit-chat from anybody's lips. And what rendered it so particularly unpleasant to us, personally, was the fact that we had both jumped simultaneously to the same ghastly conclusion.

'It's father!' Pauline gargled, and with a swift flip of her finger she doused the candle.

'What did you do that for?' I said, a good deal pipped. The sudden darkness seemed to make things worse.

'So that he shouldn't see a light in the window, of course. If he thinks you're asleep he may go away.'

'What a hope!' I retorted, as the knocking, which had eased off for a moment, started again with more follow-through than ever.

'Well, I suppose you had better go down,' said the girl in a subdued sort of voice. 'Or' – she seemed to brighten – 'shall we pour water on him from the staircase window?'

I started violently. She had made the suggestion as if she considered it one of her best and brightest, and I suddenly realized what it meant to play the host to a girl of her temperament and personality. All that I had ever heard or read about the reckless younger generation seemed to come back to me.

'Don't dream of it!' I whispered urgently. 'Dismiss the project utterly and absolutely from your mind.'

I mean to say, a dry J. Washburn Stoker seeking an errant daughter was bad enough. A J. Washburn Stoker stimulated to additional acerbity by a jugful of $H_2O$ on his head, I declined to contemplate. Goodness knows, I wasn't keen on going down and passing the time of night with the man, but if the alternative was to allow his loved one to drench him to the skin and then wait while he tore the walls down with his bare hands I proposed to do so immediately.

'I'll have to see him,' I said.

'Well, be careful.'

'How do you mean, careful?'

'Oh, just careful. Still, of course, he may not have a gun.'

I swallowed a trifle.

'What exactly would you say the odds were, for and against?'

She mused awhile.

'I'm trying to remember if father is a Southerner or not.'

'A what?'

'I know he was born at a place called Carterville, but I can't recollect if it was Carterville, Kentucky, or Carterville, Massachusetts.'

'What the dickens difference does it make?'

'Well, if you smirch the honour of a Southerner's family, he's apt to shoot.'

'Would your father consider it smirched the family honour, your being here?'

'Bound to, I should think.'

I couldn't help agreeing with her. It did seem to me offhand that a purist might consider the smirching pretty good, but I hadn't time to weigh the point, because the knocker got going again with renewed vim.

'Well, dash it,' I said, 'wherever this ghastly parent of yours was born, I shall have to go down and talk to him. That door will be splitting asunder soon.'

'Don't get closer to him than you can help.'

'I won't.'

'He was a great wrestler when he was a young man.'

'You needn't tell me any more about your father.'

'I only meant, I wouldn't let him get hold of you, if you can help. Is there anywhere I can hide?'

'No.'

'Why not?'

'I don't know why not,' I replied, a little curtly. 'They don't build these country cottages with secret rooms and under-ground passages. When you hear me open the front door, stop breathing.'

'Do you want me to suffocate?'

Well, of course, a Wooster does not put such thoughts into words, but I'm bound to say this struck me as a jolly good idea. Forbearing the reply, I hurried down the stairs and flung open the front door. Well, when I say flung, I opened it a matter of six inches, not omitting to keep it on the chain.

'Hallo?' I said. 'Yes?'

I don't know when I've felt such a chunk of relief as surged over me the next moment.

'Oy!' said a voice. 'Taken your time, haven't you? What's the matter with you, young man? Deaf or something?'

It wasn't in its essentials a musical voice, being on the thick side and a shade roopy. If I'd been its owner, I'd have given more than a little thought to the subject of tonsils. But it had one supreme merit which out-weighed all its defects. It wasn't the voice of J. Washburn Stoker.

'Frightfully sorry,' I said. 'I was thinking of this and that. Sort of reverie, if you know what I mean.'

The voice spoke again, not without a pretty goodish modicum of suavity this time.

'Oh, I beg your pardon, sir. I thought you was the young man Brinkley.'

'Brinkley's out,' I said, feeling that if he ever returned I would have a word to say to him about the hours at which his pals paid social calls. 'Who are you?'

'Sergeant Voules, sir.'

I opened the door. It was pretty dark outside, but I could recognize the arm of the Law all right. This Voules was a bird built rather on the lines of the Albert Hall, round in the middle and not much above. He always looked to me as if Nature had really intended to make two police sergeants and had forgotten to split them up.

'Ah, Sergeant!' I said.

Careless, debonair. Not a thing on Bertram's mind, you would have supposed, but his hair.

'Anything I can do for you, Sergeant?'

My eyes were getting accustomed to the darkness by this time, and I was enabled to spot certain objects of interest by the wayside. The principal one was another policeman. Tall and lean and stringy, this one.

'This is my young nephew, sir. Constable Dobson.'

Well, I wasn't exactly in the mood for a social reunion, and I could have wished that the sergeant, if he wanted to make me one of the family and all pals together, so to speak, had selected some other time, but I inclined the bean gracefully in the constable's direction and uttered a kindly 'Ah, Dobson!' I rather think, if I remember, that I also said something about its being a fine night.

But apparently this wasn't just one of those chummy gatherings which recall the old-time *salon*.

'Are you aware, sir, that there's a window broke at the back of your residence? My young nephew here spotted it and thought best to wake me up and have me investigate. A ground-floor window, sir, with a whole pane of glass gone from it.'

I simpered slightly.

'Oh, that? Yes, Brinkley did that yesterday. Silly ass!'

'You know about it, then, sir?'

'Oh, yes. Oh, yes. Quite all right, Sergeant.'

'Well, you know best if it's quite all right, sir, but I should say there was a danger of marauders getting through.'

And at this juncture the chump of a constable, who had hitherto not spoken, shoved his oar in.

'I thought I did see a marauder getting through, Uncle Ted.'

'What! Then why didn't you tell me before, you young muttonhead? And don't call me Uncle Ted when we're on duty.'

'No, Uncle Ted.'

'You'd best let us make a search of the 'ouse, sir,' said Sergeant Voules.

Well, I put the presidential veto on this pretty quick.

'Certainly not, Sergeant,' I said. 'Quite out of the q.'

'It would be wiser, sir.'

'I'm sorry,' I said, 'but it can't be done.'

He seemed piqued and discontented.

'Well, please yourself, sir, but you're shackling the police, that's what you're doing. There's too much shackling of the police these days. There was a piece in the *Mail* about it yesterday. Perhaps you read it?'

'No.'

'On the middle page. Unshackle the police, it said because public alarm is growing in Great Britain owing to the continuous increase of crime in the lonely rural districts. I clipped it out to paste in my album. The number of indictable offences, it said, has rose from one three four five eight one in 1929 to one four seven nought three one in 1930, with a marked increase of seven per cent in crimes of violence, and is this disturbing state of things due to slackness on the part of the police, it said? No, it said, it's not. It's because the police are shackled.'

The man was obviously cut to the quick. Dashed awkward.

'Well, I'm sorry,' I said.

'Yes, sir, and you're going to be sorrier when you go upstairs to your bedroom and a marauder cuts your throat from ear to ear.'

'Fight against these gloomy views, my dear old police sergeant,' I said. 'I anticipate no such contingency. I've just come from upstairs, and I give you my word there were no marauders.'

'Probably lurking, sir.'

'Biding their time,' suggested Constable Dobson.

Sergeant Voules sighed heavily.

'I wouldn't like nothing to happen to you, sir, seein' you're a close friend of his lordship's. But as you prove obdurate . . .'

'Oh, nothing could happen to anyone in a place like Chuffnell Regis.'

'Don't you believe it, sir. Chuffnell Regis is going down. I would never have thought to have seen a troupe of nigger minstrels singing comic songs within a stone's-throw of my police station.'

'You view them with concern?'

'There's been fowls missing,' said Sergeant Voules darkly. 'Several fowls. And I have my suspicions. Well, come along, Constable. If we're to be shackled, there's nothing to keep us here. Good night, sir.'

'Good night.'

I shut the door and buzzed back to the bedroom. Pauline was sitting up in bed, more or less agog.

'Who was it?'

'The constabulary.'

'What did they want?'

'Apparently they saw you getting in.'

'What a lot of trouble I'm giving you, Bertie.'

'Oh, no. Only too pleased. Well, I suppose I might as well be pushing along.'

'Are you going?'

'In the circumstances,' I replied a little frigidly. 'I can hardly doss on the premises. I shall withdraw to the garage.'

'Isn't there a sofa downstairs?'

'There is. Noah's. He brought it ashore on Mount Ararat. I shall be better off in the car.'

'Oh, Bertie, I *am* giving you a lot of trouble.'

I softened slightly. After all, the poor girl was scarcely to be blamed for what had occurred. As Chuffy had remarked earlier in the evening, love's love.

'Don't you worry, old thing. We Woosters can rough it when it is a matter of giving two fond hearts a leg-up. You put your little head on the pillow and curl your little pink toes up and doze off. I shall be all right.'

And, so saying, I uncorked a kindly smile, popped off, trickled down the stairs, opened the front door, and out into the scented night; and I don't suppose I was a dozen yards from the house when a heavy hand fell on my shoulder, occasioning me both mental and physical distress, and a shadowy form said: 'Gotcher!'

'Ouch!' I replied.

The shadowy form now revealed itself as that of Constable Dobson of the Chuffnell Regis police force. He was in apologetic vein.

'I'm sure I beg your pardon, sir. I thought you was the marauder.'

I forced myself to be airy and affable. The young squire setting the lower orders at their ease.

'Quite all right, Constable. Quite all right. Just going for a stroll.'

'I understand, sir. Breath of air.'

'You have put it in a nutshell. A breath, as you astutely observe, of air. The house is quite close.'

'Yes, sir. Just over there.'

'I mean stuffy.'

'Oh, yes, sir. Well, good night, sir.'

'Tra-la, Constable.'

I proceeded on my way, a little shaken. I had left the garage door open, and I felt my way to the old two-seater, glad to be alone once more. In certain moods, no doubt, one would have found Constable Dobson a delightful and stimulating companion, but tonight I preferred his absence. I climbed into the car and, leaning back, endeavoured to compose myself for sleep.

Now, whether I should have been able to achieve the dreamless had the conditions remained right, I cannot say. The point is pretty moot. As two-seaters go, I had always found mine fairly comfortable, but then I had never before tried to get the eight hours in it, and you would be surprised at the number of knobs and protuberances which seem suddenly to sprout out of a car's upholstery when you seek to convert it into a bed.

But, as it happened, I was not given a square chance of making the test. I don't suppose I could have counted more than about a platoon and a half of sheep when a light suddenly flashed on the features and a voice instructed me to come on out of it.

I sat up.

'Ah, Sergeant!' I said.

Another awkward meeting. Embarrassment on both sides.

'Is that you, sir?'

'Yes.'

'Sorry to have disturbed you, sir.'

'Not at all.'

'Can't say it occurred to me that it might be you in here, sir.'

'I thought I'd try to get a bit of sleep in the old car, Sergeant.'

'Yes, sir.'

'Such a warm night.'

'Just so, sir.'

His voice was respectful, but I could not conquer a suspicion that he was beginning to look a bit askance. There was something in his manner that gave me the idea that he considered Bertram eccentric.

'Stuffy indoors.'

'Yes, sir?'

'I often park myself in the car in the summertime.'

'Yes, sir?'

'Good night, Sergeant.'

'Good night, sir.'

Well, you know how it is when someone butts in on you just as you are shaping for the beauty sleep. It breaks the spell, if you know what I mean. I curled up again, but I soon saw that all efforts in the direction of the restful night in my present environment would be fruitless. I counted about five more medium-sized flocks, but it was no good. Steps, I realized, would have to be taken through other channels.

I hadn't done a great deal of exploring in these grounds of mine, but it so happened that one morning a sharp shower had driven me to the shelter of a species of shed or outhouse down in the south-west corner of the estate where the gardener-by-the-day stacked his tools and flower-pots and what not. And, unless memory deceived me, there had been in that outhouse or shed a pile of sacking on the floor.

Well, you may say that sacking, considered in the light of a bed, isn't everybody's money, and in saying so you would be perfectly correct. But after half an hour in the seat of a Widgeon Seven, even sacking begins to look pretty good to you. It may be a little hardish on the frame, and it may smell a good deal of mice and the deep-delved earth, but there remains just one point to be put forward in its favour – viz. that it enables one to stretch the limbs. And stretching the limbs was the thing I felt now that I wanted to do most.

In addition to smelling of mice and mould, the particular segment of sacking on which some two minutes later I was reclining had a marked aroma of by-the-day gardener; and there was a moment when I had to ask myself if the mixture wasn't a shade too rich. But these things grow on one in time, and at the end of about a quarter of an hour I was rather enjoying the blend of scents than otherwise. I can recall inflating the lungs and more or less drinking it in. At the end of about half an hour a soothing drowsiness had begun to steal over me.

And at the end of about thirty-five minutes the door flew open and there was the old, familiar lantern shining in again.

'Ah!' said Sergeant Voules.

And Constable Dobson said the same.

I realized that the time had come to strike a forceful note with these two pests. I am all for not shackling the police, but what I maintain is that if the police come dodging about a householder's garden all night, routing him out every time he is on the point of snatching a little repose, they have jolly well got to be shackled.

'Yes?' I said, and there was a touch of the imperious old aristocrat in my manner. 'What is it now?'

Constable Dobson had been saying something in a pretty self-satisfied sort of way about having seen me creeping through the darkness and tracking me like a leopard, and Sergeant Voules, who was a man who believed in keeping nephews in their place, was remarking that he had seen me first and had tracked me just as much like a leopard as Constable Dobson: but at these crisp words a sudden silence fell upon them.

'Is that you *again*, sir?' inquired the sergeant in rather an awed voice.

'Yes, it is, dash it! What, may I ask, is the meaning of this incessant chivying? Sleep under these conditions becomes impossible.'

'Very sorry, sir. It never occurred to me that it could be you.'

'And why not?'

'Well, sleeping in a shed, sir . . .'

'You do not dispute the fact that it is my shed?'

'No, sir. But it sort of seems funny.'

'I see nothing funny in it whatsoever.'

'Uncle Ted means "odd", sir.'

'Not so much of what Uncle Ted means. And don't call me Uncle Ted. What it sort of seemed to us, sir, was peculiar.'

'I cannot subscribe to your opinion, Sergeant,' I said stiffly. 'I have a perfect right, have I not, to sleep where I please?'

'Yes, sir.'

'Exactly. It might be the coal cellar. It might be the front-door steps. It happens to be this shed. I will now thank you, Sergeant, to withdraw. At this rate, I shan't drop off till daybreak.'

'Are you intending to remain here the rest of the night, sir?'

'Certainly. Why not?'

I had got him. He was at a loss.

'Well, I suppose there's no reason why you shouldn't, if you want to, sir. But it seems . . .'

'Odd,' said Constable Dobson.

'Peculiar,' said Sergeant Voules. 'It seems peculiar, having a bed of your own, sir, if I might say so . . .'

I had had enough of this.

'I hate beds,' I said curtly. 'Can't stand them. Never could.'

'Very good, sir.' He paused a moment. 'Quite a warm day today, sir.'

'Quite.'

'My young nephew here pretty near got a touch of the sun. Didn't you, Constable?'

'Ah!' said Constable Dobson.

'Made him come over all funny.'

'Indeed?'

'Yes, sir. Sort of seemed to addle the brain.'

I endeavoured without undue brusqueness to convey to this man the idea that I did not consider one in the morning a suitable time for discussing his nephew's addled brain.

'You must give me all the family medical gossip another day,' I said. 'At the moment, I wish to be alone.'

'Yes, sir. Good night, sir.'

'Good night, Sergeant.'

'If I might ask the question, sir, do you feel a sort of burning feeling about the temples?'

'I beg your pardon?'

'Does your head throb, sir?'

'It's beginning to.'

'Ah! Well, good night, sir, again.'

'Good night, Sergeant.'

'Good night, sir.'

'Good night, Constable.'

'Good night, sir.'

The door closed softly. I could hear them whispering for a moment or two, like a couple of specialists holding a conference outside the sick-room. Then they appeared to ooze off, for all became quiet save for the lapping of the waves on the shore. And, by Jove, so sedulously did these waves lap that gradually a drowsiness crept over me and not ten minutes after I had made up my mind that I should never get to sleep again in this world I was off as comfortably as a babe or suckling.

It couldn't last, of course – not in a place like Chuffnell Regis, a hamlet containing more Nosey Parkers to the square foot than any other spot in England. The next thing I remember is someone joggling my arm.

I sat up. There was the good old lantern once more.

'Now, listen . . .' I was beginning, with a generous strength, when the words froze on my lips.

The fellow who was joggling my arm was Chuffy.

# =9=
# LOVERS' MEETINGS

IT has been well said of Bertram Wooster that he is a man who is at all times glad to see his friends and can be relied upon to greet them with a cheery smile and a gay quip. But though in the main this is correct, I make one proviso – viz. that the conditions be right. On the present occasion they were not. When an old schoolmate's fiancée is roosting in your bed in a suit of your personal pyjamas, it is hard to frisk round this old schoolmate with any abandon when he suddenly appears in the immediate vicinity.

I uttered, accordingly, no gay quip. I couldn't even manage the cheery smile. I just sat goggling at the man wondering how he had got there, how long he proposed to remain, and what the chances were of Pauline Stoker suddenly shoving her head out of window and shouting to me to come and grapple with a mouse or something.

Chuffy was bending over me with a sort of bedside manner. In the background I could see Sergeant Voules hovering with something of the air of a trained nurse. What had become of Constable Dobson, I did not know. It seemed too jolly to think that he was dead, so I took it that he had returned to his beat.

'It's all right, Bertie,' said Chuffy soothingly. 'It's me, old man.'

'I found his lordship by the side of the harbour,' explained the sergeant.

I must say I chafed a bit. I saw what had happened. When you tear a lover of Chuffy's calibre from the girl of his heart, he does not just mix himself a final spot and turn in – he goes and stands beneath her window. And if she's on a yacht, anchored out in the middle of a harbour, this can only be done, of course, by infesting the waterfront. All quite in order, no doubt, but in the present circs dashed inconvenient, to use the mildest term. And what was making me chafe was the thought that if only he had got to his parking place a bit earlier he would have been in a position to welcome the girl as she came ashore, thus obviating all the present awkwardness.

'The sergeant was worried about you, Bertie. He seemed to think your manner was strange. So he brought me along to have a look at you. Very sensible of you, Voules.'

'Thank you, m'lord.'

'A sound move.'

'Thank you, m'lord.'

'You couldn't have done a wiser thing.'

'Thank you, m'lord.'

It was sickening to hear them.

'So you've got a touch of the sun, Bertie?'

'I have not got a touch of any bally sun.'

'Voules thought so.'

'Voules is an ass.'

The sergeant bridled somewhat.

'Begging your pardon, sir, you informed me that your head throbbed, and I assumed that the brain was addled.'

'Exactly. You must have gone slightly off your rocker, old chap,' said Chuffy gently, 'musn't you? To be sleeping out here, I mean, what?'

'Why shouldn't I sleep out here?'

I saw Chuffy and the sergeant exchange glances.

'But you've got a bedroom, old fellow. You've got a nice bedroom, haven't you? I should have thought you would have found it so much snugger and jollier in your cosy little bedroom.'

The Woosters have all been pretty quick thinkers. I saw that I had got to make this move of mine seem plausible.

'There's a spider in my bedroom.'

'A spider, eh? Pink?'

'Pinkish.'

'With long legs?'

'Fairly long legs.'

'And hairy, I shouldn't wonder?'

'Very hairy.'

The rays of the lantern were falling on Chuffy's face, and at this point I observed a subtle change come into his expression. A moment before, he had been solicitous old Doctor Chuffnell, gravely concerned about the sorely sick patient whom he had been called in to treat. He now grinned in a most unpleasant manner and, rising, drew Sergeant Voules aside and addressed a remark to

301

him which told me that he had placed an entirely wrong construction on the matter.

'It's all right, Sergeant. Nothing to worry about. He's simply as tight as an owl.'

I think he imagined he was speaking in a tactful undertone, but his words came clearly to my ears, as did the sergeant's reply.

'Is that so, m'lord?' said Sergeant Voules. And his voice was the voice of a sergeant to whom all things have been made clear.

'That's all that's the trouble. Completely boiled. You notice the glassy look in the eyes?'

'Yes, m'lord.'

'I've seen him like this before. Once, after a bump-supper at Oxford, he insisted that he was a mermaid and wanted to dive into the college fountain and play the harp there.'

'Young gents will be young gents,' said Sergeant Voules in a tolerant and broad-minded manner.

'We must put him to bed.'

I jumped up. Horror-stricken. Trembling like a leaf.

'I don't want to go to bed!'

Chuffy stroked my arm soothingly.

'It's all right, Bertie. Quite all right. We understand. No wonder you were frightened. Beastly great spider. Enough to frighten any one. But it's all right now. Voules and I will come up to your room with you and kill it. You aren't scared of spiders, Voules?'

'No, m'lord.'

'You hear that, Bertie? Voules will stand by you. Voules can tackle any spider. How many spiders was it you were telling me you took on in India once, Voules?'

'Ninety-six, m'lord.'

'Big ones, if I remember rightly?'

'Whackers, m'lord.'

'There, Bertie. You see there's nothing to be afraid of. You take this arm, Sergeant. I'll take the other. Just relax, Bertie. We'll hold you up.'

Looking back, I am not certain whether I didn't do the wrong thing at this juncture. It may be that a few well-chosen words would have served me better. But you know how it is about well-chosen words. When you need them most, you can't find any. The sergeant had begun to freeze on to my left arm, and I couldn't think of a single remark. So, in lieu of conversation, I punched him in the tummy and made a dash for the open spaces.

Well, you can't go far at a high rate of speed in a dark shed littered with the belongings of a by-the-day gardener. I suppose there were quite half a dozen things I could have come a purler over. The one which actually caused me to take the toss was a watering-can. I fell with a dull, sickening thud, and when reason returned to her throne I found I was being carried through the summer night in the direction of the house. Chuffy had got me under the arms, and Sergeant Voules was attached to my feet. And, thus linked, we passed through the front door and up the stairs. It wasn't, perhaps, actually the frog's march, but it was quite near enough to it to wound my *amour propre*.

Not that I was thinking such a frightful lot about my *amour propre* at the moment. We had reached the bedroom door now, and what I was asking myself was, What would the harvest be when Chuffy opened it and noted contents?

'Chuffy,' I said, and I spoke earnestly, 'don't go into that room!'

But it's no good speaking earnestly if your head's hanging down and your tongue has got tangled up with your back teeth. All that actually emerged was a sort of gargle, and Chuffy completely misunderstood it.

'I know, I know,' he said. 'Never mind. Soon be in beddy-bye now.'

I considered his manner offensive, and would have said so, but at this moment speech was, so to speak, wiped from my lips, as it were, by amazement. With a quick heave, my bearers had suddenly dumped me on the bed, and all that the frame had encountered was a blanket and pillow. Of anything in the nature of a girl in heliotrope pyjamas there was absolutely no trace.

I lay there, wondering. Chuffy had found the candle and lighted it, and I was now in a position to look about me.

Pauline Stoker had absolutely disappeared. Leaving not a wrack behind, as I remember Jeeves saying once.

Dashed odd.

Chuffy was dismissing his assistant.

'Thanks, Sergeant. I can manage now.'

'You're sure, m'lord?'

'Yes, it's quite all right. He always drops off to sleep on these occasions.'

'Then I think I'll be going, m'lord. It's a bit late for me.'

'Yes, pop off. Good night.'

'Good night, m'lord.'

The sergeant clumped down the stairs, making enough row for two sergeants, and Chuffy, with something of the air of a mother brooding over a sleeping child, took off my boots.

'That's my little man,' he said. 'Now you lie quite quiet, Bertie, and take things easy.'

It is a thing I have often wondered, whether I would or would not have commented upon what I considered the insufferably patronizing note in his voice as he called me his little man. I wanted to, but I saw that it would be fruitless unless I could think of something more than a little biting: and it was while I was searching in my mind for the telling phrase that the door of the hanging cupboard outside the room opened and Pauline Stoker came strolling in as if she hadn't a care in the world. In fact, she seemed distinctly entertained.

'What a night, what a night!' she said amusedly. 'A close call that, Bertie. Who were those men I heard going out?'

And then she suddenly sighted Chuffy, gave a kind of gasping squeak, and the love light came into her eyes as if somebody had pressed a switch.

'Marmaduke!' she cried, and stood there, staring.

But, by Jove, it was the poor old schoolmate who was doing the real staring, in the truest and fullest sense of the word. I've seen starers in my time, many of them, but never one who came within a mile of putting up the performance which Chuffy did then. The eyebrows had shot up, the jaw had fallen, and the eyes were protruding from one to two inches from the parent sockets. He also appeared to be trying to say something, but in this he flopped badly. Nothing came through except a rather unpleasant whistling sound, not quite so loud as the row your radio makes when you twiddle the twiddler a bit too hard but in other respects closely resembling it.

Pauline, meanwhile, had begun to advance with the air of a woman getting together with her demon lover, and a sort of pity for the girl shot through the Wooster bosom. I mean to say, any observant outsider like myself could see so clearly that she had got quite the wrong angle on the situation. I could read Chuffy like a book, and I knew that she was totally mistaken in what she supposed to be his emotions at this juncture. That odd noise he was making I could diagnose, not as the love call which she appeared to think it, but as the stern and censorious gruffle of a man who, finding his loved one on alien premises in heliotrope pyjamas, is stricken to the core, cut to the quick, and as sore as a gumboil.

But she, poor simp, being so dashed glad to behold him, had not so much as begun to suspect that he, the circs being what they were, might possibly not be equally glad to behold her. With the result that when at this juncture he stepped back and folded his arms with a bitter sneer, it was as if he had jabbed her in the eye with a burnt stick. The light faded from her face, and in its stead there appeared the hurt, bewildered look of a barefoot dancer who, while half-way through The Vision of Salome, steps on a tin tack.

'Marmaduke!'

Chuffy unleashed another bitter sneer.

'So!' he said, finding speech — if you can call that speech.

'What do you mean? Why are you looking like that?'

I thought it about time that I put in a word. I had risen from the bed on Pauline's entry and for some moments had been teetering towards the door with a sort of sketchy idea of making for the great open spaces. But partly because I felt that it ill beseemed a Wooster to leg it at such a time and partly because I had no boots on, I had decided to remain. I now intervened, coming across with the word in season.

'What you want on an occasion like this, Chuffy, old man,' I said, 'is simple faith. The poet Tennyson tells us . . .'

'Shut up,' said Chuffy. 'I don't want to hear anything from you.'

'Right ho,' I said. 'But, all the same, simple faith *is* better than Norman blood, and you can't get away from it.'

Pauline was looking a bit fogged.

'Simple faith? What . . . Oh!' she said, abruptly signing off. And I noted that the features were suffused with a crimson blush.

'Oh!' she said.

The cheeks continued to glow. But now it was not the blush of modesty that hotted them up. That first '*Oh!*' I take it, had been caused by her catching sight of her pyjamaed limbs and suddenly getting on to the equivocal nature of her position. The second one was different. It was the heart cry of a woman who is madder than a hornet.

I mean, you know how it is. A sensitive and high-spirited girl goes through the deuce of an ordeal to win through to the bloke she loves, jumping off yachts, swimming through dashed cold water, climbing into cottages, and borrowing other people's speak, and is expecting the tender smile and the whispered endearments, gets instead the lowering frown, the curled lip, the suspicious eye, and – in a word – the raspberry. Naturally, she's a bit upset.

'Oh!' she said, for the third time, and her teeth gave a little click, most unpleasant. 'So that's what you think?'

Chuffy shook his head in an impatient sort of way.

'Of course I don't.'

'You do.'

'I don't.'

'Yes, you do.'

'I don't think anything of the kind,' said Chuffy. 'I know that Bertie has been . . .'

'. . . Scrupulously correct in his behaviour throughout,' I suggested.

'. . . sleeping in a potting shed,' continued Chuffy, and I must say it didn't sound half as good as my version. 'That's not the point. The fact remains that in spite of being engaged to me and pretending this afternoon that you were tickled pink to be engaged to me, you are still so much in love with Bertie that you can't keep away from him. You think I don't know all about your being engaged to him in New York, but I do. Oh, I'm not complaining,' said Chuffy, looking rather like Saint Sebastian on receipt of about the fifteenth arrow. 'You have a perfect right to love who you like . . .'

'Whom, old man,' I couldn't help saying. Jeeves has made me rather a purist in these matters.

'Will you keep quiet!'

'Of course, of course.'

'You keep shoving your oar in. . . .'

'Sorry, sorry. Shan't occur again.'

Chuffy, who had been gazing at me as if he would have liked to strike me with a blunt instrument, gazed once more at Pauline as if he would have liked to strike her with a blunt instrument.

'But . . .' He paused. 'Now you've made me forget what I was going to say,' he said in a rather peevish manner.

Pauline took the floor. She was still on the pink side, and her eyes were gleaming glitteringly. I've seen my Aunt Agatha's eyes gleam just like that when she prepared to tick me off for some fancied misdemeanour. Of the love light no traces remained.

'Well, then, perhaps you'll listen to what *I'm* going to say. I suppose you have no objection to my putting in a word?'

'None,' said Chuffy.

'None, none,' I said.

Pauline was beyond a question stirred to the core. I could see her toes wiggling.

'In the first place, you make me sick!'

'Indeed?'

'Yes, indeed. In the second place, I hope I shall never see you again in this world or the next.'

'Really?'

'Yes, really. I hate you. I wish I'd never met you. I think you're a worse pig than any you've got up at that beastly house of yours.'

This interested me.

'I didn't know you kept pigs, Chuffy.'

'Black Berkshires,' he said absently. 'Well, if that's how you . . .'

'There's money in pigs.'

'Well, all right,' said Chuffy. 'If that's how you feel, well, all right.'

'You bet it's all right.'

'That's what I said, it's all right.'

'My Uncle Henry . . .'

'Bertie,' said Chuffy.

'Hallo?'

'I don't want to hear about your Uncle Henry. I am not interested in your Uncle Henry. It will be all right with me if your damned Uncle Henry trips over his feet and breaks his blasted neck.'

'Too late, old man. He passed away three years ago. Pneumonia. I was only saying he kept pigs. Made a good thing out of them, too.'

'Will you stop . . .'

307

'Yes, and will you,' said Pauline. 'Are you going to spend the night here? I wish you would leave off talking and go.'

'I will,' said Chuffy.

'Do,' said Pauline.

'Good night,' said Chuffy.

He strode to the head of the stairs.

'But one last word . . .' he said with a wide, passionate gesture.

Well, I could have told the poor old chap that you can't do that sort of thing in these old-world country cottages. His knuckles hit a projecting beam, he danced in agony, over-balanced, and the next moment was on his way to the ground floor like a sack of coals.

Pauline Stoker ran to the banisters and looked over.

'Are you hurt?' she cried.

'Yes,' yelled Chuffy.

'Good,' cried Pauline.'

She came back into the room, and the front door slammed like the bursting of an over-wrought heart.

# =10=
# ANOTHER VISITOR

I DREW a deepish breath. With the departure of the male half of the sketch a certain strain seemed to have gone out of the atmosphere. Excellent companion though I had always found him in the past, Chuffy had not shown himself at his chummiest during the recent scene, with the result that for some little time I had been feeling rather like Daniel in the lions' den.

Pauline was panting somewhat. Not exactly snorting, but coming very near to what you might call the borderland of the snort. Her eyes were hard and bright. Deeply moved. She picked up her bathing suit.

'Push off, Bertie,' she said.

I had been hoping for a quiet chat, in the course of which we would review the situation, touching on this point and on that, and strive to ascertain what to do for the best.

'But listen. . . .'

'I want to change.'

'Change what?'

'Put on my swimming suit.'

I could not follow her.

'Why?'

'Because I am going to swim.'

'Swim?'

'Swim.'

I stared.

'You aren't going back to the yacht?'

'I am going back to the yacht.'

'But I wanted to talk about Chuffy.'

'I never wish to hear his name mentioned again.'

It seemed time to be the wise old mediator.

'Oh, come!'

'Well?'

'When I say "Oh, come!" ' I explained, 'I mean surely you don't

309

intend to give the poor blighter the permanent air on account of a trifling lovers' tiff?'

She looked at me in rather a peculiar manner.

'Would you mind repeating that?' Just the last three words.'

'Trifling lovers' tiff?'

She breathed heavily, and for a moment I experienced a return of that lions' den sensation.

'I wasn't sure I had caught them correctly,' she said.

'I mean to say you get (*a*) a girl and (*b*) a bloke and stir up their generous natures, and the result is that each says lots of things she or he doesn't mean.'

'Oh? Well, let me tell you I meant every word I said. I told him I never wanted to speak to him again. I don't. I told him I hated him. I do. I called him a pig. He is.'

'Now, that's rummy about Chuffy's pigs. I had no notion he kept them.'

'Why not? Birds of a feather.'

There seemed nothing much more to say about pigs.

'Aren't you a bit hard?'

'Am I?'

'And rather rough on Chuffy?'

'Am I?'

'You wouldn't say his attitude was excusable?'

'I would not.'

'Must have been a shock for the poor old chap, I mean, barging in and finding you here.'

'Bertie.'

'Hallo?'

'Ever been hit over the head with a chair?'

'No.'

'Well, you soon may be.'

I began to see she was in a difficult mood.

'Oh, well!'

'Does that mean the same as "Oh, come!"?'

'No. All I was driving at was that it seems a pity. Two loving hearts sundered for ever – *bingo*!'

'Yes?'

'Still, if that's the way you feel, well, that's the way you feel, what?'

'Yes.'

'We now come to this idea of swimming home. Potty, it strikes me as.'

'There's nothing to keep me here now, is there?'

'No. But the midnight swim. . . . You're going to find it pretty cold.'

'And wet. I don't care.'

'And how are you going to get aboard?'

'I'll get aboard. I can climb up by the thing they hang the anchor from. I've done it before. So will you remove yourself and let me change.'

I went out on to the landing. And presently she emerged in the bathing suit.

'You needn't see me out.'

'Of course I will, if you're really going.'

'I'm going, all right.'

'Well, if you must.'

Outside the front door the air seemed nippier than ever. The mere thought of plunging into the harbour gave me the shivers. But it had no effect on her. She slipped off into the darkness without a word, and I went upstairs to bed.

You might have thought that after garages and potting sheds the fact that I was in a bed would have resulted in instant slumber. But no. I couldn't get off. The more I tried, the more I found the mind turning to what you might call the tragedy in which I had so recently participated. I don't mind admitting that my heart ached for Chuffy. It also ached for Pauline. It ached for both of them.

I mean to say, consider the facts. Two thoroughly sound eggs, destined for each other, you might almost say, through all eternity, giving each other the bird like this for no reason whatever, really. Pitiful. Rotten. No good to man or beast. The more I thought of it, the sillier it seemed.

And yet there it was. Words had passed. Relations had been severed. The whole binge was irrevocably off.

There is only one thing for the sympathetic bystander to do on these occasions, and I realized now that it was madness not to have done it before going to bed and attempting sleep. I slid out from between the sheets and went downstairs.

The whisky bottle was in the cupboard. So was the siphon. So was the glass. I mixed myself a healing beaker and sat down. And, as I did so, I observed on the table a sheet of paper.

311

It was a note from Pauline Stoker.

DEAR BERTIE,

You were right about it being cold. I couldn't face the swim. But there's a boat down by the landing stage. I shall row to the yacht and set it adrift. I've come back to borrow your overcoat. I didn't want to disturb you, so I climbed in through the window. I'm afraid you will have to sacrifice the coat, as of course I shall have to throw it overboard when I get to the yacht. Sorry.

P.S.

You notice the style? Curt. Staccato. Evidence of the wounded heart and the heavy mind. I felt sorrier for her than ever, but glad she probably wasn't going to get a cold in the head. As for the coat, a careless shrug of the shoulders covered that. I did not grudge it her, though new and silk-lined. Only too pleased, about summed up my attitude in the matter.

I tore up the note and returned to my spot.

There is nothing like a strong w-and-s for calming the system. In about another quarter of an hour I was feeling so soothed that I could contemplate bed once more, this time confident that the betting was at least eight to three that a refreshing slumber would be my portion.

I rose accordingly, and was just about to ankle upstairs, when for the second time that night there was the dickens of a knocking on the front door.

I don't know that you would call me an irascible man. I rather think not. Ask them about me at the Drones, and they will probably tell you that Bertram Wooster, wind and weather permitting, is as a general rule suavity itself. But, as I had been compelled to show Jeeves in the matter of the banjolele, I can be pushed too far. It was with drawn brow and cold eye that I now undid the chain. I was just about ready to give Sergeant Voules — for I assumed that it was he — the ticking-off of a life-time.

'Voules,' I was preparing to say, 'enough is enough. This police persecution must stop. It is monstrous and uncalled-for. We are not in Russia, Voules. There are such things, I would have you remember, Voules, as strong letters to *The Times*.'

That, or something like it, is what I would have said to Sergeant Voules: and what caused me to refrain was not weakness or pity, but the fact that the man attached to the knocker wasn't Voules at all. It was J. Washburn Stoker, and he was regarding me with a sort of hard-boiled fury which, but for the fact that I had just finished a life-giving snort and knew that his daughter Pauline was safely off the premises, would undoubtedly have tickled me up not a little.

As it was, I remained tranquil.

'Yes?' I said.

I had packed so much cold surprise and hauteur into the word that a lesser man might well have keeled over backwards as if hit by a bullet. J. W. Stoker took it without blinking. He pushed past me into the house, then turned and grabbed me by the shoulder.

'Now, then!' he said.

I disengaged myself coldly. I had to wriggle out of my pyjama jacket to do so, but I managed it.

'I beg your pardon?'

'Where's my daughter?'

'Your daughter Pauline?'

'I have only one daughter.'

'And you ask me where this one daughter is?'

'I know where she is.'

'Then why did you ask?'

'She's here.'

'Then give me my pyjama jacket and tell her to come in,' I said.

I've never actually seen a man grind his teeth, so I wouldn't care to state definitely that this is what J. Washburn Stoker did at this juncture. He may have done. He may not have done. All I can say authoritatively is that the muscles stood out on his cheeks and his jaws began to work as if he were chewing gum. It was not a pleasant spectacle, but thanks to the fact that I had mixed that whisky and splash particularly strong so as to facilitate sleep I was enabled to endure it with fortitude and phlegm.

'She's in this house!' he said, continuing to grind, if he was grinding.

'What makes you think that?'

'I'll tell you what makes me think that. I went to her stateroom half an hour ago, and it was empty.'

'But why on earth should you suppose she's come here?'

'Because I know she's infatuated with you.'

'Not at all. She regards me as a sister.'

'I am going to search this house.'

313

'Charge right ahead.'

He dashed upstairs and I returned to my spot. Not the same spot. Another one. I felt that in the circumstances a repeat was justified. And presently my visitor, who had gone up like a lion, came down like a lamb. I suppose a parent who has barged into a comparative stranger's cottage in the small hours in search of a missing daughter, feels more or less of a silly ass. I know I should, and apparently this Stoker did, for he shuffled a bit and I could see that a lot of the steam or motive force had gone out of him.

'I owe you an apology, Mr Wooster.'

'Don't give it a thought.'

'I took it for granted when I found Pauline gone . . .'

'Dismiss the whole thing from your mind. Might have happened to anybody. Faults on both sides and so forth. You'll have a certain something before you go?'

It seemed to me that it would be a prudent move to detain him on the premises for as long as possible, so as to give Pauline plenty of time to get back to the old boat. But he wouldn't be tempted. His mind was evidently too occupied for spots.

'It beats me where she can have gone,' he said, and you would have been astounded at the mildness and even chummy pathos with which he spoke. It was as if Bertram had been some wise old friend to whom he was bringing his little troubles. The man seemed positively punctured. A child could have played with him.

I endeavoured to throw out a word of cheer.

'I expect she's gone for a swim.'

'At this time of night?'

'Girls do rummy things.'

'And she's a curious girl. This infatuation of hers for you, for instance.'

This seemed to me lacking in tact, and I would have frowned slightly, had I not remembered that I wished to disabuse him, if disabuse is what I'm driving at, of the idea that any such infatuation existed.

'Correct this notion that Miss Stoker is under my fatal spell.' I urged him. 'She laughs herself sick at the sight of me.'

'I did not get that impression this afternoon.'

'Oh, that? Just brother and sister stuff. It shan't occur again.'

'It had better not,' he said, returning for a moment to what I might call his earlier manner. 'Well, I won't keep you up, Mr Wooster. I apologize again for making a darned fool of myself.'

I did not quite slap him on the back, but I made a sort of backslapping gesture.

'Not at all,' I said. 'Not at all. I wish I had a quid for every time I've made a darned fool of *myself*.'

And on these cordial terms we parted. He went down the garden path, and I, having waited up about ten minutes on the chance that somebody else might come playing a social call, drained my glass and popped up to bed.

Something attempted, something done, had earned a night's repose, or as near as you can get to a night's repose in a place full of Stokers and Paulines and Vouleses and Chuffys and Dobsons. It was not long before the weary eyelids closed and I was off.

It seems almost incredible, considering what the night life of Chuffnell Regis was like, but the next thing that woke me was not a girl leaping out from under the bed, her father bounding in with blood in his eye, or a police sergeant playing ragtime on the knocker, but actually the birds outside my window heralding in a new day.

Well, when I say heralding, it was about ten-thirty of a fine summer morning, and the sunshine streaming in through the window seemed to be calling to me to get up and see what I could do to an egg, a rasher, and the good old pot of coff.

I had a hasty bath and shave and trotted down to the kitchen, full of *joie de vivre*.

# =11=
# SINISTER BEHAVIOUR OF A
# YACHT-OWNER

I T was not until I had finished breakfast and was playing the
banjolele in the front garden that something seemed to whisper
reproachfully in my ear that I had no right to be feeling as perky as
this on what was so essentially the morning after. Dirty work had
been perpetrated overnight. Tragedy had stalked through the
home. Scarcely ten hours earlier I had been a witness of a scene
which, if I were the man of fine fibre I liked to think myself, should
have removed all the sunshine from my life. Two loving hearts,
one of which I had been at school and Oxford with, had gone to
the mat together in my presence and having chewed holes in one
another had parted in anger, never — according to present
schedule — to meet again. And here I was, care-free and callous,
playing 'I Lift Up My Finger And I Say Tweet-Tweet' on the
banjolele.

All wrong. I switched to 'Body and Soul', and a sober sadness
came upon me.

Something, I felt, must be done. Steps must be taken and
avenues explored.

But I could not conceal from myself that the situation was
complex. Usually, in my experience, when one of my pals has
broken off diplomatic relations with a girl or vice versa they have
been staying in a country house together or at least living in
London, where it wasn't so dashed difficult to arrange a meeting
and join their hands with a benevolent smile. But in this matter of
Chuffy and Pauline Stoker, consider the facts. She was on the
yacht, virtually in irons. He was at the Hall, three miles inland.
And anybody who wanted to do any hand-joining had got to be a
much more mobile force than I was. True, my standing with old
Stoker had improved a bit overnight, but there had been no hint
on his part of any disposition to give me the run of his yacht. I
seemed to have about as much chance of getting in touch with

Pauline and endeavouring to reason with her as if she had never come from America at all.

Quite a prob., I mean to say, and I was still brooding on it when the garden gate clicked and I perceived Jeeves walking up the path.

'Ah, Jeeves,' I said.

My manner probably seemed to him a little distant, and I jolly well meant it to. What Pauline had told me about his loose and unconsidered remarks with reference to my mentality had piqued me considerably. It was not the first time he had said that sort of thing, and one has one's feelings.

But if he sensed the hauteur, he affected to ignore it. His bearing continued placid and unmoved.

'Good morning, sir.'

'Have you come from the yacht?'

'Yes, sir.'

'Was Miss Stoker there?'

'Yes, sir. She appeared at the breakfast table. I was somewhat surprised to see her. I had assumed that it was her intention to remain ashore and establish communication with his lordship.'

I laughed shortly.

'They established communication, all right?'

'Sir?'

I put down the banjolele and looked at him sternly.

'A nice thing you let all and sundry in for last night!' I said.

'Sir?'

'You can't get out of it by saying "Sir?" Why on earth didn't you stop Miss Stoker from swimming ashore yestreen?'

'I could scarcely take the liberty, sir, of thwarting the young lady in an enterprise on which her heart was so plainly set.'

'She says you urged her on with word and gesture.'

'No, sir. I merely expressed sympathy with her stated aims.'

'You said I would be delighted to put her up for the night.'

'She had already decided to seek refuge in your house, sir. I did nothing more than hazard the opinion that you would do all that lay in your power to assist her.'

'Well, do you know what the outcome was – the upshot, if I may use the term? I was pursued by the police.'

'Indeed, sir?'

'Yes. Naturally I couldn't sleep in the house, with every nook

317

and cranny bulging with blighted girls, so I withdrew to the garage. I had hardly been there ten minutes before Sergeant Voules arrived.'

'I have not met Sergeant Voules, sir.'

'With him Constable Dobson.'

'I am acquainted with Constable Dobson. A nice young fellow. He is keeping company with Mary, the parlourmaid at the Hall. A red-haired girl, sir.'

'Resist the urge to talk about the colour of parlourmaids' hair, Jeeves,' I said coldly. 'It is not germane to the issue. Stick to the point. Which is that I spent a sleepless night, chased to and fro by the gendarmerie.'

'I am sorry to hear that, sir.'

'Eventually Chuffy arrived. Forming a totally erroneous diagnosis of the case, he insisted on helping me to my room, removing my boots, and putting me to bed. He was thus occupied when Miss Stoker strolled in, wearing my heliotrope pyjamas.'

'Most disturbing, sir.'

'It was. They had the dickens of a row, Jeeves.'

'Indeed, sir?'

'Eyes flashed, voices were raised. Eventually Chuffy fell downstairs and went moodily out into the night. And the point is – the nub of the thing is – what is to be done about it?'

'It is a situation that will require careful thought, sir.'

'You mean you have not had any ideas yet?'

'I have only this moment heard what transpired, sir.'

'True. I was forgetting that. Have you had speech with Miss Stoker this morning?'

'No, sir.'

'Well, I can see no point in your going to the Hall and tackling Chuffy. I have given this matter a good deal of thought, Jeeves, and it is plain to me that Miss Stoker is the one who will require the persuasive word, the nicely reasoned argument – in short, the old oil. Last night Chuffy wounded her deepest feelings, and it's going to take a lot of spadework to bring her round. In comparison, the problem of Chuffy is simple. I shouldn't be surprised if even now he was kicking himself soundly for having behaved so like a perfect chump. One day of quiet meditation, at the outside, should be enough to convince him that he wronged the girl. To go and reason with Chuffy is simply a waste of time.

Leave him alone, and Nature will effect the cure. You had better go straight back to the yacht and see what you can do at the other end.'

'It was not with the intention of interviewing his lordship that I came ashore, sir. Once more I must reiterate that, until you informed me just now, I was not aware that anything in the nature of a rift had occurred. My motive in coming here was to hand you a note from Mr Stoker.'

I was puzzled.

'A note?'

'Here it is, sir.'

I opened it, still fogged, and read contents. I can't say I felt much clearer when I had done so.

'Rummy, Jeeves.'

'Sir?'

'This is a letter of invitation.'

'Indeed, sir?'

'Absolutely. Bidding me to the feast. "Dear Mr Wooster," writes Pop Stoker. "I shall be frightfully bucked if you will come and mangle a spot of garbage on the boat tonight. Don't dress." I give you the gist of the thing. Peculiar, Jeeves.'

'Certainly unforeseen, sir.'

'I forgot to tell you that among my visitors last night was this same Stoker. He bounded in, shouting that his daughter was on the premises, and searched the house.'

'Indeed, sir?'

'Well, of course, he didn't find any daughter, because she was already on her way back to the yacht, and he seemed conscious of having made rather an ass of himself. His manner on departing was chastened. He actually spoke to me civilly — a thing I'd have taken eleven to four on that he didn't know how to do. But does that explain this sudden gush of hospitality? I don't think so. Last night he seemed apologetic rather than matey. There was no indication whatever that he wished to start one of those great friendships.'

'I think it is possible that a conversation which I had this morning with the gentleman, sir . . .'

'Ah! It was you, was it, who caused this pro-Bertram sentiment?'

'Immediately after breakfast, sir, Mr Stoker sent for me and inquired if I had once been in your employment. He said that he fancied that he recalled having seen me at your apartment in New York. On my replying in the affirmative, he proceeded to question me with regard to certain incidents in the past.'

'The cats in the bedroom?'

'And the hot-water bottle episode.'

'The purloined hat?'

'And also the matter of your sliding down pipes, sir.'

'And you said—?'

'I explained that Sir Roderick Glossop had taken a biased view of these occurrences, sir and proceeded to relate their inner history.'

'And he—?'

'— seemed pleased, sir. He appeared to think that he had misjudged you. He said that he ought to have known better than to believe information proceeding from Sir Roderick – to whom he alluded as a bald-headed old son of a something which for the moment has escaped my memory. It was, I imagine, shortly after this that he must have written this letter inviting you to dinner sir.'

I was pleased with the man. When Bertram Wooster finds the old feudal spirit flourishing, he views it with approval and puts that approval into words.

'Thank you, Jeeves.'

'Not at all, sir.'

'You have done well. Regarding the matter from one aspect, of course, it is negligible whether Pop Stoker thinks I'm a loony or not. I mean to say, a fellow closely connected by ties of blood with a man who used to walk about on his hands is scarcely in a position, where the question of sanity is concerned, to put on dog and set himself up as an . . .'

'*Arbiter elegentiarum*, sir?'

'Quite. It matters little to me, therefore, from one point of view, what old Stoker thinks about my upper storey. One shrugs the shoulders. But, setting that aside, I admit that this change of heart is welcome. It has come at the right time. I shall accept his invitation. I regard it as . . .'

'The *amende honorable*, sir?'

'I was going to say olive branch.'

'Or olive branch. The two terms are virtually synonymous. The French phrase I would be inclined to consider perhaps slightly the more exact in the circumstances – carrying with it, as it does, the implication of remorse, of the desire to make restitution. But if you prefer the expression "olive branch", by all means employ it, sir.'

'Thank you, Jeeves.'

'Not at all, sir.'

'I suppose you know that you have made me completely forget what I was saying?'

'I beg your pardon, sir. I should not have interrupted. If I recollect, you were observing that it was your intention to accept Mr Stoker's invitation.'

'Ah, yes. Very well then. I shall accept his invitation – whether as an olive branch or an *amende honorable* is wholly immaterial and doesn't matter a single, solitary damn, Jeeves. . . .'

'No, sir.'

'And shall I tell you why I shall accept his invitation? Because it will enable me to get together with Miss Stoker and plead Chuffy's cause.'

'I understand, sir.'

'Not that it's going to be easy. I hardly know what line to take.'

'If I might make the suggestion, sir, I should imagine that the young lady would respond most satisfactorily to the statement that his lordship was in poor health.'

'She knows he's as fit as a fiddle.'

'Poor health induced since her parting from him by distress of mind.'

'Ah! I get you. Distraught?'

'Precisely, sir.'

'Contemplating self-destruction?'

'Exactly, sir.'

'Her gentle heart would be touched by that, you think?'

'Very conceivably, sir.'

'Then that is the vein I shall work. I see this invitation says dinner at seven. A bit on the early side, what?'

'I presume that the arrangements have been made with a view to the convenience of Master Dwight, sir. This would be the birthday-party of which I informed you yesterday.'

'Of course, yes. With negroe minstrel entertainment to follow. They are coming all right, I take it?'

'Yes, sir. The Negroes will be present.'

'I wonder if there would be any chance of a word with the one who plays the banjo. There are certain points in his execution I would like to consult him about.'

'No doubt it could be arranged, sir.'

He seemed to speak with a certain reserve, and I could see that he felt that the conversation had taken an embarrassing turn. Probing the old sore, I mean.

Well, the best thing to do on these occasions, I've always found, is to be open and direct.

'I'm making great progress with the banjolele, Jeeves.'

'Indeed, sir?'

'Would you like me to play you 'What Is This Thing Called Love?''

'No, sir.'

'Your views on the instrument are unchanged?'

'Yes, sir.'

'Still, it can't be helped. No hard feelings.'

'No, sir.'

'Unfortunate, though.'

'Most unfortunate, sir.'

'Well, tell old Stoker that I shall be there at seven prompt with my hair in a braid.'

'Yes, sir.'

'Or should I write a brief, civil note?'

'No, sir. I was instructed to bring back a verbal reply.'

'Right ho, then.'

'Very good, sir.'

At seven on the dot, accordingly, I stepped aboard the yacht and handed the hat and light overcoat to a passing salt. It was with mixed feelings that I did so, for conflicting emotions were warring in the bosom. On the one hand, the keen ozone of Chuffnell Regis had given me a good appetite, and I knew from recollections of his hosp. in New York that J. Washburn Stoker did his guests well. On the other, I had never been what you might call tranquil in his society, and I was not looking forward to it particularly now. You might put it like this if you cared to – the Fleshly or corporeal Wooster was anticipating the binge with pleasure, but his spiritual side rather recoiled a bit.

In my experience, there are two kinds of elderly American. One, the stout and horn-rimmed, is matiness itself. He greets you as if you were a favourite son, starts agitating the cocktail shaker before you know where you are, slips a couple into you with a merry laugh, claps you on the back, tells you a dialect story about two Irishmen named Pat and Mike, and, in a word, makes life one grand, sweet song.

The other, which runs a good deal to the cold, grey stare and the square jaw, seems to view the English cousin with concern. It is not Elfin. It broods. It says little. It sucks in its breath in a pained way. And every now and again you catch its eye, and it is like colliding with a raw oyster.

Of this latter class or species J. Washburn Stoker had always been the perpetual vice-president.

It was with considerable relief, therefore, that I found that tonight he had eased off a bit. While not precisely affable, he gave a distinct impression of being as nearly affable as he knew how.

'I hope you have no objection to a quiet family dinner, Mr Wooster?' he said, having shaken the hand.

'Rather not. Dashed good of you to ask me,' I replied, not to be outdone in the courtesies.

'Just you and Dwight and myself. My daughter is lying down. She has a headache.'

This was something of a jar. In fact, it seemed to me to take what you might describe as the whole meaning out of this expedition.

'Oh?' I said.

'I am afraid she found her exertions last night a little too much for her,' said Pop Stoker, with something of the old fish-like expression in the eye: and, reading between the lines, I rather gathered that Pauline had been sent to bed without her supper in disgrace. Old Stoker was not one of your broad-minded, modern parents. There was, as I had had occasion to notice before, a distinct touch of the stern and rockbound old Pilgrim Father about him. A man, in short, who, in his dealings with his family, believed in the firm hand.

Observing that eye, I found it a bit difficult to shape the kindly inquiries.

'Then you – er . . . she – er—?'

'Yes. You were quite right, Mr Wooster. She had gone for a swim.'

And once more, as he spoke, I caught a flash of the fishlike. I could see that Pauline's stock was far from high this p.m., and I would have liked to put in a word for the poor young blighter. But beyond an idea of saying that girls would be girls, which I abandoned, I could think of nothing.

At this moment, however, a steward of sorts announced dinner, and we pushed in.

I must say that there were moments during that dinner when I regretted that occurrences which could not be overlooked had resulted in the absence from the board of the Hall party. You will question this statement, no doubt, inclining to the view that all a dinner-party needs to make it a success is for Sir Roderick Glossop, the Dowager Lady Chuffnell, and the latter's son, Seabury, not to be there. Nevertheless, I stick to my opinion. There was a certain uncomfortable something about the atmosphere which more or less turned the food to ashes in my mouth. If it hadn't been that this man, this Stoker, had gone out of his way to invite me, I should have said that I was giving him a pain in the neck. Most of the time he just sat and champed in a sort of dark silence, like a man with something on his mind. And when he did speak it was with a marked what-d'you-call-it. I mean to say, not actually out of the corner of his mouth, but very near it.

I did my best to promote a flow of conversation. But it was not till young Dwight had left the table and we were lighting the cigars that I seemed to hit on a topic that interested, elevated, and amused.

'A fine boat, this, Mr Stoker,' I said.

For the first time, something approaching animation came into the face.

'Not many better.'

'I've never done much yachting. And, except at Cowes one year, I've never been on a boat this size.'

He puffed at his cigar. An eye came swivelling round in my direction, then pushed off again.

'There are advantages in having a yacht.'

'Oh, rather.'

'Plenty of room to put your friends up.'

'Heaps.'

'And, when you've got 'em, they can't get away so easy as they could ashore.'

It seemed a rummy way of looking at it, but I supposed a man like Stoker would naturally have a difficulty in keeping guests. I mean, I took it that he had had painful experiences in the past. And nothing, of course, makes a host look sillier to have somebody arrive at his country house for a long visit and then to find, round about lunch-time the second day, that he has made a quiet sneak for the railway station.

'Care to look over the boat?' he asked.

'Fine,' I said.

'I'd be glad to show it to you. This is the main saloon we're in.'

'Ah,' I said.

'I'll show you the state-rooms.'

He rose, and we went along passages and things. We came to a door. He opened it and switched on the light.'

'This is one of our larger guest-rooms.'

'Very nice, too.'

'Go in and take a look round.'

Well, there wasn't much to see that I couldn't focus from the threshold, but one has to do the civil thing on these occasions. I toddled over and gave the bed a prod.

And, as I did so, the door slammed. And when I nipped round, the old boy had disappeared.

Rather rummy, was my verdict. In fact, distinctly rummy. I went across and gave the handle a twist.

The bally door was locked.

'Hoy!' I called.

No answer.

'Hey!' I said. 'Mr Stoker.'

Only silence, and lots of it.

I went and sat down on the bed. This seemed to me to want thinking about.

# =12=
# START SMEARING, JEEVES!

I CAN'T say I liked the look of things. In addition to being at a loss
and completely unable to follow the scenario, I was also
distinctly on the uneasy side. I don't know if you ever read a book
called 'The Masked Seven'? It's one of those goosefleshers and
there's a chap in it, Drexdale Yeats, a private investigator, who
starts looking for clues in a cellar one night, and he's hardly
collected a couple when – *bingo* – there's a metallic clang and
there he is with the trapdoor shut and someone sniggering nastily
on the other side. For a moment his heart stood still, and so did
mine. Excluding the nasty snigger (which Stoker might quite well
have uttered without my hearing it), it seemed to me that my case
was more or less on all fours with his. Like jolly old Drexdale, I
sensed some lurking peril.

Of course, mark you, if something on these lines had occurred
at some country house where I was staying, and the hand that had
turned the key had been that of a pal of mine, a ready explanation
would have presented itself. I should have set it down as a spot of
hearty humour. My circle of friends is crammed with fellows who
would consider it dashed diverting to bung you into a room and
lock the door. But on the present occasion I could not see this
being the solution. There was nothing roguish about old Stoker.
Whatever view you might take of this fishy-eyed man, you would
never call him playful. If Pop Stoker put his guests in cold storage,
his motive in so doing was sinister.

Little wonder, then, that as he sat on the edge of the bed
pensively sucking at his cigar, Bertram was feeling uneasy. The
thought of Stoker's second cousin, George, forced itself upon the
mind. Dotty, beyond a question. And who knew but what that
dottiness might not run in the family? It didn't seem such a long
step, I mean to say, from a Stoker locking people in state-rooms to
a Stoker with slavering jaws and wild, animal eyes coming back
and doing them a bit of no good with the meat axe.

When, therefore, there was a click and the door opened,

revealing mine host on the threshold, I confess that I rather drew myself together somewhat and pretty well prepared myself for the worst.

His manner, however, was reassuring. Puff-faced, yes, but not fiend-in-human-shape-y. The eyes were steady and the mouth lacked foam. And he was still smoking his cigar, which I felt was promising. I mean, I've never met any homicidal loonies, but I should imagine that the first thing they would do before setting about a fellow would be to throw away their cigars.

'Well, Mr Wooster?'

I never have known quite what to answer when blokes say "Well?" to me, and I didn't now.

'I must apologize for leaving you so abruptly,' proceeded the Stoker, 'but I had to get the concert started.'

'I'm looking forward to the concert,' I said.

'A pity,' said Pop Stoker. 'Because you're going to miss it.'

He eyed me musingly.

'There was a time, when I was younger, when I would have broken your neck,' he said.

I didn't like the trend the conversation was taking. After all, a man is as young as he feels, and there was no knowing that he wouldn't suddenly get one of these – what do you call them? – illusions of youth. I had an uncle once, aged seventy-six, who, under the influence of old crusted port, would climb trees.

'Look here,' I said civilly but with what you might call a certain urgency, 'I know it's trespassing on your time, but could you tell me what all this is about?'

'You don't know?'

'No, I'm hanged if I do.'

'And you can't guess?'

'No, I'm dashed if I can.'

'Then I had best tell you from the beginning. Perhaps you recall my visiting you last night?'

I said I hadn't forgotten.

'I thought my daughter was in your cottage. I searched it. I did not find her.'

I twiddled a hand magnanimously.

'We all make mistakes.'

He nodded.

'Yes. So I went away. And do you know what happened after I

327

left you, Mr Wooster? I was coming out of the garden gate when your local police sergeant stopped me. He seemed suspicious.'

I waved my cigar sympathetically.

'Something will have to be done about Voules,' I said. 'The man is a pest. I hope you were pretty terse with him.'

'Not at all. I supposed he was only doing his duty. I told him who I was and where I lived. On learning that I came from this yacht, he asked me to accompany him to the police station.'

I was amazed.

'What bally cheek! You mean he pinched you?'

'No, he was not arresting me. He wished me to identify someone who was in custody.'

'Bally cheek, all the same. What on earth did he bother you with that sort of job for? Besides, how on earth could you identify anyone? I mean, a stranger in these parts, and all that sort of thing.'

'In this instance it was simple. The prisoner happened to be my daughter, Pauline.'

'What!'

'Yes, Mr Wooster. It seems that this man Voules was in his back garden late last night – it adjoins yours, if you recollect – and he saw a figure climbing out of one of the lower windows of your house. He ran down the garden and caught this individual. It was my daughter Pauline. She was wearing a swimming suit and an overcoat belonging to you. So, you see, you were right when you told me she had probably gone for a swim.'

He knocked the ash carefully off his cigar. I didn't need to do it to mine.

'She must have been with you a few moments before I arrived. Now, perhaps, Mr Wooster, you can understand what I meant when I said that, when I was a younger man, I would have broken your neck.'

I hadn't anything much to say. One hasn't sometimes.

'Nowadays, I'm more sensible,' he proceeded. 'I take the easier way. I say to myself that Mr Wooster is not the son-in-law I would have chosen personally, but if my hand has been forced that is all there is to it. Anyway, you're not the gibbering idiot I thought you at one time, I'm glad to say. I have heard since that those stories which caused me to break off Pauline's engagement to you in New York were untrue. So we can consider everything just as it was three months ago. We will look upon that letter of Pauline's as unwritten.'

You can't reel when you're sitting on a bed. Otherwise, I would have done so, and right heartily. I was feeling as if a hidden hand had socked me in the solar plexus.

'Do you mean—?'

He let me have an eye squarely in the pupil. A beastly sort of eye, cold and yet hot, if you follow me. If this was the Boss's Eye you read so much about in the advertisements in American magazines, I was dashed if I could see why any ambitious young shipping clerk should be so bally anxious to catch it. It went clean through me, and I lost the thread of my remarks.

'I am assuming that you wish to marry my daughter?'

Well, of course . . . I mean, dash it . . . I mean, there isn't much you can say to an observation like that. I just weighed in with a mild 'Oh, ah!'

'I am not quite sure if I understand the precise significance of the expression "Oh, ah!"' he said, and, by Jove, I wonder if you notice a rather rummy thing. I mean to say, this man had had the advantage of Jeeves's society for only about twenty-four hours, and here he was – except that Jeeves would have said "wholly" instead of "quite" and stuck in a "Sir" or two – talking just like him. I mean, it just shows. I remember putting young Catsmeat Potter-Pirbright up at the flat for a week once, and the very second day he said something to me about gauging somebody's latent potentialities. And Catsmeat a fellow who had always thought you were kidding him when you assured him that there were words in the language that had more than one syllable. As I say, it simply goes to show. . . .

However, where was I?

'I am not quite sure if I understand the precise significance of the expression "Oh, ah!"' said this Stoker, 'but I will take it to mean that you do. I won't pretend that I'm delighted, but one can't have everything. What are your views upon engagements, Mr Wooster?'

'Engagements?'

'Should they be short or long?'

'Well . . .'

'I prefer them short. I feel that we had best put this wedding through as quickly as possible. I shall have to find out how soon

329

that is on this side. I believe you cannot simply go to the nearest minister, as in my country. There are formalities. While these are being attended to, you will, of course, be my guest. I'm afraid I can't offer you the freedom of the boat, because you are a pretty slippery young gentleman and might suddenly remember a date elsewhere – some unfortunate appointment which would necessitate your leaving. But I shall do my best to make you comfortable in this room for the next few days. There are books on that shelf – I assume you can read? – and cigarettes on the table. I will send my man along in a few minutes with some pyjamas and so on. And now I will wish you good night, Mr Wooster. I must be getting back to the concert. I can't stay away from my son's birthday-party, can I, even for the pleasure of talking to you?'

He slipped through the door and oozed out, and I was alone.

Now, it so happened that twice in my career I had had the experience of sitting in a cell and listening to keys turning in locks. The first time was the one to which Chuffy had alluded, when I had been compelled to assure the magistrate that I was one of the West Dulwich Plimsolls. The other – and both, oddly enough, had occurred on Boat Race night – was when I had gone into partnership with my old friend, Oliver Sipperley, to pick up a policeman's helmet as a souvenir, only to discover that there was a policeman inside it. On both these occasions I had ended up behind the bars, and you might suppose that an old lag like myself would have been getting used to it by now.

But this present binge was something quite different. Before, I had been faced merely with the prospect of a moderate fine. Now, a life sentence stared me in the eyeball.

A casual observer, noting Pauline's pre-eminent pulchritude and bearing in mind the fact that she was heiress to a sum amounting to more than fifty million fish, might have considered that in writhing, as I did, in agony of spirit at the prospect of having to marry her, I was making a lot of fuss about nothing. Such an observer, no doubt, would have wished that he had half my complaint. But the fact remains that I did writhe, and writhe pretty considerably.

Apart from the fact that I didn't want to marry Pauline Stoker, there was the dashed serious snag that I knew jolly well that she didn't want to marry me. She might have ticked him off with great

330

breath and freedom at their recent parting, but I was certain that deep down in her the old love for Chuffy still persisted and only needed a bit of corkscrew work to get it to the surface again. And Chuffy, for all that he had hurled himself downstairs and stalked out into the night, still loved her. So that what it amounted to, when you came to tot up the pros and cons, was that by marrying this girl I should not only be landing myself in the soup but breaking both her heart and that of the old school friend. And if that doesn't justify a fellow in writhing, I should very much like to know what does.

Only one gleam of light appeared in the darkness – viz. that old Stoker had said that he was sending his man along with the necessaries for the night. It might be that Jeeves would find the way.

Though how even Jeeves could get me out of the current jam was more than I could envisage. It was with the feeling that no bookie would hesitate to lay a hundred to one against that I finished my cigar and threw myself on the bed.

I was still picking at the coverlet when the door opened and a respectful cough informed me that he was in my midst. His arms were full of clothing of various species. He laid these on a chair and regarded me with what I might describe as commiseration.

'Mr Stoker instructed me to bring your pyjamas, sir.'

I emitted a hollow g.

'It is not pyjamas I need, Jeeves, but the wings of a dove. Are you abreast of the latest development?'

'Yes, sir.'

'Who told you?'

'My informant was Miss Stoker, sir.'

'You've been having a talk with her?'

'Yes, sir. She related to me an outline of the plans which Mr Stoker had made.'

The first spot of hope I had had since the start of this ghastly affair now shot through my bosom.

'By Jove, Jeeves, an idea occurs to me. Things aren't quite as bad as I thought they were.'

'No, sir?'

'No. Can't you see? It's all very well for old Stoker to talk – er—'

'Glibly, sir?'

331

'Airily.'

'Airily or glibly, sir, whichever you prefer.'

'It's all very well for old Stoker to talk with airy glibness about marrying us off, but he can't do it, Jeeves. Miss Stoker will simply put her ears back and refuse to co-operate. You can lead a horse to the altar, Jeeves, but you can't make it drink.'

'In my recent conversation with the young lady, sir, I did not receive the impression that she was antagonistic to the arrangements.'

'What!'

'No, sir. She seemed, if I may say so, resigned and defiant.'

'She couldn't be both.'

'Yes, sir. Miss Stoker's attitude was partly one of listlessness, as if she felt that nothing mattered now, but I gathered that she was also influenced by the thought that in contracting a matrimonial alliance with you, she would be making – shall I say, a defiant gesture at his lordship.'

'A defiant gesture?'

'Yes, sir.'

'Scoring off him, you mean?'

'Precisely, sir.'

'What a damn silly idea. The girl must be cuckoo.'

'Feminine psychology is admittedly odd, sir. The poet Pope . . .'

'Never mind about the poet Pope, Jeeves.'

'No, sir.'

'There are times when one wants to hear all about the poet Pope and times when one doesn't.'

'Very true, sir.'

'The point is, I seem to be up against it. If that's the way she feels, nothing can save me. I am a pipped man.'

'Yes, sir. Unless—'

'Unless?'

'Well, I was wondering, sir, if on the whole it would not be best if you were to obviate all unpleasantness and embarrassment by removing yourself from the yacht.'

'What!'

'Yacht, sir.'

'I know you said "Yacht". And I said "What!" Jeeves,' I went on, and there was a quiver in the voice, 'it is not like you to come in here at a crisis like this with straws in your hair and talk absolute drip. How the devil can I leave the yacht?'

'The matter could be readily arranged, if you are agreeable, sir. It would, of course, involve certain inconveniences . . .'

'Jeeves,' I said, 'short of squeezing through the port-hole, which can't be done, I am ready to undergo any little passing inconvenience if it will get me off this bally floating dungeon and restore me to terra firma.' I paused and regarded him anxiously. 'This is not mere gibbering, is it? You really have a scheme?'

'Yes, sir. The reason I hesitated to advance it was that I feared you might not approve of the idea of covering your face with boot polish.'

'What!'

'Time being of the essence, sir, I think it would not be advisable to employ burnt cork.'

I turned my face to the wall. It was the end.

'Leave me, Jeeves,' I said. 'You've been having a couple.'

And I'm not sure that what cut me like a knife, more even than any agony at my fearful predicament, was not the realization that my original suspicions had been correct and that, after all these years, that superb brain had at last come unstuck. For, though I had tactfully affected to set all this talk of burnt cork and boot polish down to mere squiffiness, in my heart I was convinced that the fellow had gone off his onion.

He coughed.

'If you will permit me to explain, sir. The entertainers are just concluding their performance. In a short time they will be leaving the boat.'

I sat up. Hope dawned once more, and remorse gnawed me like a bullpup worrying a rubber bone at the thought that I should have so misjudged this man. I saw what that giant brain was driving at.

'You mean—?'

'I have a small tin of boot polish here, sir. I brought it with me in anticipation of this move. It would be a simple task to apply it to your face and hands in such a manner as to create the illusion, should you encounter Mr Stoker, that you were a member of this troupe of negroid entertainers.'

'Jeeves!'

'The suggestion I would make, sir, is that, if you are amenable to what I propose, we should wait until these black-faced persons have left for the shore. I could then inform the captain that one of them, a personal friend of mine, had lingered behind to talk with me and so had missed the motor launch. I have little doubt that he would accord me permission to row you ashore in one of the smaller boats.'

I stared at the man. Years of intimate acquaintance, the memory of swift ones he had pulled in the past, the knowledge that he lived largely on fish, thus causing his brain to be about as full of phosphorus as the human brain can jolly well stick, had not prepared me for this supreme effort.

'Jeeves,' I said, 'as I have so often had occasion to say before, you stand alone.'

'Thank you, sir.'

'Others abide our question. Thou art free.'

'I endeavour to give satisfaction, sir.'

'You think it would work?'

'Yes, sir.'

'The scheme carries your personal guarantee?'

'Yes, sir.'

'And you say you have the stuff handy?'

'Yes, sir.'

I flung myself into a chair and turned the features ceilingwards.

'Then start smearing, Jeeves,' I said, 'and continue to smear till your trained senses tell you that you have smeared enough.'

# =13=
# A VALET EXCEEDS HIS DUTIES

I MUST say, as a general rule, I always bar stories where the chap who's telling them skips lightly from point to point and leaves you to work it out for yourself as best you can just what has happened in the interim. I mean to say, the sort of story where Chapter Ten ends with the hero trapped in the underground den and Chapter Eleven starts with him being the life and soul of a gay party at the Spanish Embassy. And, strictly speaking, I suppose, I ought at this juncture to describe step by step the various moves which led me to safety and freedom, if you see what I mean.

But when a tactician like Jeeves is in charge of the arrangements, it all seems so unnecessary. Simply a waste of time. If Jeeves sets out to shift a fellow from Spot A to Spot B, from a state-room on a yacht, for instance, to the shore in front of his cottage, he just does it. No hitches. No difficulties. No fuss. No excitement. Absolutely nothing to report. I mean, one just reaches for the nearest tin of boot polish, blacks one's face, strolls across the deck, saunters down the gangway, waves a genial farewell to such members of the crew as may be leaning over the side, spitting into the water, steps into a boat, and in about ten minutes there one is, sniffing the cool night air on the mainland. A smooth bit of work.

I mentioned this to Jeeves as we tied up at the landing stage, and he said it was extremely kind of me to say so.

'Not at all, Jeeves,' I said. 'I repeat. An exceedingly smooth bit of work, and a credit to you.'

'Thank you, sir.'

'Thank *you*, Jeeves.' And now what?'

We had left the landing stage and were standing on the road that ran past my garden gate. All was still. The stars twinkled above. We were alone with Nature. There was not even a sign of Police-Sergeant Voules or Constable Dobson. Chuffnell Regis slept, as you might say. And yet, looking at my watch, I found that the hour was only a few minutes after nine. It gave me quite a start, I recall. What with stress of emotion, so to speak, and the spirit having been on the rack, as it were, I had got the impression that the night was particularly well advanced, and wouldn't have been surprised to find it one in the morning.

'And now what, Jeeves?' I said.

I noted a soft smile playing over the finely-chiselled face and resented same. I was grateful to the man, of course, for having saved me from the fate that is worse than death, but one has to check this sort of thing. I gave him one of my looks.

'Something is tickling you, Jeeves?' I said, coldly.

'I beg your pardon, sir. I had not intended to betray amusement, but I could not help being a little entertained by your appearance. It is somewhat odd, sir.'

'Most people would look somewhat odd with boot polish all over them, Jeeves.'

'Yes, sir.'

'Greta Garbo, to name but one.'

'Yes, sir.'

'Or Dean Inge.'

'Very true, sir.'

'Then spare me these personal comments, Jeeves, and reply to my question.'

'I fear I have forgotten what it was that you asked me, sir.'

'My question was – and is – "Now what?"'

'You desire a suggestion respecting your next move, sir?'

'I do.'

'I would advise repairing to your cottage, sir, and cleansing your face and hands.'

'So far, sound. It is just what I was thinking of doing.'

'After which, if I might hazard the advice, sir, I think it would be well if you were to catch the next train to London.'

'Again, sound.'

'Once there, sir, I would advocate a visit to some Continental resort, such as Paris or Berlin or even perhaps, as far afield as Italy.'

'Or Sunny Spain?'

'Yes, sir. Possibly Spain.'

'Or even Egypt?'

'You would find Egypt somewhat warm at this season of the year, sir.'

'Not half so warm as England, if Pop Stoker re-establishes connection.'

'Very true, sir.'

'There's a lad, Jeeves! There's a tough citizen! There's a fellow who chews broken glass and drives nails into the back of his neck instead of using a collar stud!'

'Mr Stoker's personality is decidedly forceful, sir.'

'Bless my soul, Jeeves, I can remember the time when I thought Sir Roderick Glossop a man-eater. And even my Aunt Agatha. They pale in comparison, Jeeves. Positively pale. Which brings us to a consideration of your position. Do you intend to go back to the yacht and continue mingling with that gruesome bird?'

'No, sir. I fancy Mr Stoker would not receive me cordially. It will be readily apparent to a gentleman of his intelligence, when he discovers your flight, that I must have been instrumental in assisting you to leave the boat. I shall return to his lordship's employment, sir.'

'He'll be very glad to get you back.'

'It is very kind of you to say so, sir.'

'Not at all Jeeves. Anybody would be.'

'Thank you, sir.'

'Then you'll push on to the Hall?'

'Yes, sir.'

'A very hearty good night, then. I will drop you a line to let you know where I am and how I have made out.'

'Thank you, sir.'

'Thank *you*, Jeeves. There will be a slight testimonial of my appreciation wedged into the envelope.'

'Extremely generous of you, sir.'

'Generous, Jeeves? Do you realize that if it hadn't been for you I should now be behind locked doors on that bloodsome yacht? But you know how I feel.'

'Yes, sir.'

'By the way, *is* there a train to London tonight?'

'Yes, sir. The 10.21. You should be able to catch it comfortably, sir. I fear it is not an express.'

I waved a hand.

'As long as it moves, Jeeves, as long as the wheels revolve and it trickles from point to point, it will do me nicely. Good night, then.'

'Good night, sir.'

It was with uplifted heart that I entered the cottage. Nor was my satisfaction lessened by the discovery that Brinkley had not yet returned. As an employer, I might look a bit askance at the idea of the blighter being given the evening off and taking a night and a day, but in the capacity of a private citizen with boot polish on his face, I was all for it. On such occasions, solitude is, as Jeeves would have said, of the essence.

I went up to the bedroom with all possible speed, and poured water from the jug into the basin, bath-rooms not being provided in Chuffy's little homes. This done, I dipped the face and instituted a hearty soaping. Then, having rinsed thoroughly, I moved to the mirror, and picture my chagrin and dismay when I discovered that I was still as black as ever. You might say I had hardly so much as scratched the surface.

These are the moments that make a fellow think a bit, and it wasn't long before I saw where the snag was. I remembered hearing or reading somewhere that in crises like this you have to have butter. I was just about to go downstairs and get some, when suddenly I heard a noise.

Now, a fellow in my position – virtually the hunted stag, I mean to say – has got to take considerable thought as to what his next move shall be when he hears a noise on the premises. Quite possibly, I felt, this might be J. Washburn Stoker baying on the trail, for if he had happened to drop into the state-room and observe that it was empty, the first thing he would do would be to come dashing to my cottage. So there was nothing of the lion leaping from its den about the way I now left the bedroom, but rather a bit more than a suggestion of a fairly diffident snail poking its head out of its shell during a thunderstorm. For the nonce, I merely stood in the doorway and listened.

There was plenty to listen to. Whoever was making the row was down in the sitting-room, and he seemed to me to be throwing the furniture about. And I think it was the reflection that a keen, practical man like Pop Stoker, if on my track, would hardly waste time doing this sort of thing, that braced me at length to the point of tiptoeing to the banisters and peeping over.

What I describe as the sitting-room, I must tell you, was really more in the nature of a sort of lounge-hall. It was rather liberally furnished for such a smallish place, and contained a table, a grandfather clock, a sofa, two chairs, and from one to three cases with stuffed birds in them. From where I stood, looking over the banisters, I had a complete view of the entire lay-out. It was fairly dim down there, but I could see pretty well, because there was an oil lamp burning on the mantelpiece. By its light I was able to observe that the sofa had been upset, the two chairs thrown through the window, and the stuffed-bird cases smashed; and at the moment of going to press, a shadowy form was in the far corner, wrestling with the grandfather clock.

It was difficult to say with any certainty which of the pair was getting the better of it. If in sporting vein, I think I should have been inclined to put my money on the clock. But I was not in sporting vein. A sudden twist of the combatants had revealed to me the face of the shadowy f., and with a considerable rush of emotion I perceived that it was Brinkley. Like a sheep wandering back to the fold, this blighted Bolshevik had rolled home, twenty-four hours late, plainly stewed to the gills.

All the householder awoke in me. I forgot that it was injudicious of me to allow myself to be seen. All I could think of was that this bally Five-Year-Planner was smashing up the Wooster home.

'Brinkley!' I bellowed.

I imagine he thought at first that it was the voice of the clock, for he flung himself upon it with renewed energy. Then, suddenly, his eye fell on me, and he broke away and stood stairing. The clock, after rocking to and fro for a moment, settled into the perpendicular with a jerk and, having struck thirteen, relapsed into silence.

'Brinkley!' I repeated and was about to add "Dash it!" when a sort of gleam came into his eyes, the gleam of the man who understands all. For an instant he stood there, goggling. Then he uttered a cry.

'Lor lumme! The Devil!'

And, snatching up a carving knife which he appeared to have placed on the mantelpiece with a sort of idea that you never knew when these things may not come in useful, he came bounding up the stairs.

Well, it was a close thing. If I ever have grandchildren – which, at the moment, seems a longish shot – and they come clustering round my knee of an evening for a story, the one I shall tell them is about my getting back into the bedroom just one split second ahead of that carving knife. And if as a result they have convulsions during the night and wake up screaming, they will have got some rough idea of their aged relative's emotions at this juncture. To say that Bertram, even when he had slammed the door, locked it, shoved a chair against it, and a bed against the chair, felt wholly at his ease would be a wilful overstatement. I cannot put my mental attitude more clearly than by saying that, if J. Washburn Stoker had happened to drop in at that moment, I would have welcomed him like a brother.

Brinkley was at the keyhole, begging me to come out and let him ascertain the colour of my insides; and, by Jove, what seemed to me to add the final touch to the whole unpleasantness was that he spoke in the same respectful voice he always used. Kept calling me "Sir", too, which struck me as dashed silly. I mean, if you're asking a fellow to come out of a room so that you can dismember him with a carving knife, it's absurd to tack a "Sir" on to every sentence. The two things don't go together.

At this point it seemed to me that my first move ought to be to clear up the obvious misunderstanding that existed in his mind.

I put the lips to the woodwork.

'It's all right, Brinkley.'

'It will be if you come out, sir,' he said civilly.

'I mean, I'm not the Devil.'

'Oh, yes, you are, sir.'

'I'm not, I tell you.'

'Oh, yes, sir.'

'I'm Mr Wooster.'

He uttered a piercing cry.

'He's got Mr Wooster in there!'

You don't get the old-fashioned soliloquy much nowadays, so I took it that he was addressing some third party. And, sure enough, there was a sort of rumbling puffing and a tonsil-ridden voice spoke.

'What's all this?'

It was my sleepless neighbour, Police-Sergeant Voules.

My first emotion on realizing that the Law was in our midst was one of pretty sizeable relief. There were lots of things about this vigilant man I didn't like – his habit of poking his nose into people's garages and potting sheds, for one – but, whatever you might feel about some of his habits, there was no denying that he was a useful chap to have around in a situation like this. Tackling a loony valet is not everyone's job. You need a certain personality and presence. These this outsize guardian of the peace had got in full measure. And I was just about to urge him on with encouraging noises through the door, when something seemed to whisper to me that it would be more prudent to refrain.

You see, the whole thing about these vigilant police-sergeants is that they detain and question. Finding Bertram Wooster in the equivocal position of going about the place with his face blacked up, Sergeant Voules would not just pass the thing off with a shrug of the shoulders and a light good night. He would, as I say, detain and question. Recalling our encounters of the previous night, he would view with concern. He would insist on my accompanying him to the police station while he sent for Chuffy to come and advise what to do for the best. Doctors would be summoned, ice packs applied. With the result that I would most certainly be confined to the neighbourhood quite long enough for old Stoker to discover that my room was empty and my bed had not been slept in and to come rushing ashore to scoop me up and carry me back to the yacht again.

On second thoughts, therefore, I said nothing. Merely breathed softly through the nose.

Outside the door, snappy dialogue was in progress; and I give you my honest word that, if I hadn't had authoritative information to the contrary, I should have said that this extraordinary bird, Brinkley, was as sober as a teetotal Girl Guide. All that one of the biggests toots in history had done to him was to put a sort of precise edge on his speech and cause him to articulate with a crystal clearness which was more like a silver bell than anything.

'The Devil is in there, murdering Mr Wooster, sir,' he was saying. And, except in radio announcers, I've never heard anything more beautifully modulated.

You would call that a fairly sensational announcement, I suppose; but it didn't seem to register immediately with Sergeant Voules. The sergeant was one of those men who like to take things in their proper order and tidy up as they go along; and for the moment, it seemed, he was interested exclusively in the carving knife.

'What are you doing with that knife?' he inquired.

Nothing could have been more civil and deferential than Brinkley's response.

'I caught it up to attack the Devil, sir.'

'What devil?' asked Sergeant Voules, taking the next point in rotation.

'A black devil, sir.'

'Black?'

'Yes, sir. He is in this room, murdering Mr Wooster.'

Now that he had at last got round to it, Sergeant Voules seemed interested.

'In this room?'

'Yes, sir.'

'Murdering Mr Wooster?'

'Yes, sir.'

'We can't have that sort of thing,' said Sergeant Voules, rather austerely. And I heard him click his tongue.

There was an authoritative rap on the door.

'Oy!'

I preserved a prudent silence.

'Excuse me, sir,' I heard Brinkley say, and from the sound of feet on the stairs I took it that he was leaving our little symposium. Possibly to have another go at the clock.

Knuckles smote the woodwork again.

'In there. Oy!'

I made no remark.

'Are you in there, Mr Wooster?'

I was beginning to feel that this conversation was a bit one-sided, but I didn't see what could be done about it. I moved to the window and looked out, more with the idea of just doing something to pass the time than anything else, and it was now — and only now, if you'll believe me — that the idea came to me that it might be possible to edge away from this distasteful scene. It wasn't so much of a drop to the ground, and with a good deal of relief I started to tie knots in a sheet with a view to the get-away.

It was at this moment that I heard Sergeant Voules suddenly give tongue.

'Oy!'

And from down below Brinkley's voice.

'Sir?'

'Look out what you're doing with that lamp.'

'Yes, sir.'

'You'll upset it.'

'Yes, sir.'

'Oy!'

'Sir?'

'You'll set the house on fire!'

'Yes, sir.'

And then there came a far-off crash of glass, and the Sergeant went bounding down the stairs. This was followed by a sound which gave me the impression that Brinkley, feeling that he had done his bit, had galloped to the front door and slammed it after him. And after that another slam, as if the Sergeant, too, had made a break for the open. And then, filtering through the keyhole, came a little puff of smoke.

I don't suppose there is anything that makes much better burning than one of these old country cottages. You just put a match to them – or upset a lamp in the hall, as the case may be – and up they go. It couldn't have been more than half a minute before a merry crackling came to my ears and a bit of the floor over in the corner suddenly burst into a cheerful flame.

It was enough for Bertram. A moment before, I had been messing about with knotted sheets with a view to what you might call the departure *de luxe* and generally loafing about and taking my time over the thing. I now quickened up quite a good deal. It was borne in upon me that anything in the nature of leisurely comfort was off. In the next thirty seconds cats on hot bricks could have picked up hints from me.

I remember reading in a paper once one of those Interesting Problem things about Suppose You were in a Burning House, what would you save? If I recollect rightly, a baby entered into it. Also a priceless picture and, if I am not mistaken, a bedridden aunt. I know there was a wide choice, and you were supposed to knit the brow and think the thing out from every angle.

On the present occasion I did not hesitate. I looked round immediately for my banjolele. Conceive my dismay when I remembered that I had left it in the sitting-room.

Well, I wasn't going down to that sitting-room even for the faithful old musical instrument. Already it was beginning to be a very moot point whether I wouldn't get cooked to a crisp, because that genial glow over in the corner had now spread not a little. With a regretful sigh I hopped hurriedly to the window, and the next moment I was dropping like the gentle dew upon the place beneath.

Or is it rain? I always forget.

Jeeves would know.

I made a smooth landing and shot silently through the hedge at the junction between my back garden and Sergeant Voules's little bit, and continued to leg it till I was in a sort of wood – I suppose about half a mile from the pulsing centre of affairs. The sky was all lit up, and in the distance I could hear the sound of the local fire brigade going about its duties.

I sat down on a stump, and took time off to pass the situation under review.

Wasn't it Robinson Crusoe or someone who, when things were working out a bit messily for him, used to draw up a sort of Credit and Debit account, in order to see exactly where he stood and ascertain whether he was behind or ahead of the game at that particular moment? I know it was someone, and I had always thought it rather a sound idea.

This was what I did now. In my head of course, and keeping a wary eye out for possible pursuers.

The thing came out about as follows:

| *Credit* | *Debit* |
|---|---|
| Well, here I am, what? | Yes, but your bally house has burned down. |
| Not mine, Chuffy's. | Yes, I know, but all your things are in it. |
| Nothing of value. | How about the banjolele? |
| Oh, my gosh! That's true. | I thought that would make you think a bit. |
| You needn't rub it in. | I'm not rubbing it in. I am merely saying that your banjolele has been reduced to a heap of ashes. |

Well, I'd have looked a damn sight sillier if it had been me.

A footling bit of reasoning.

Well, anyway, I've got away from old Stoker.

How do you know you have?

He hasn't caught me yet.

No, but he may.

I've still time to get that 10.21 train.

My poor ass, you can't go getting on trains with your face all black.

Butter will remove the blacking.

Yes, but you have no butter.

I can buy some.

How? Got any money on you?

Well, no.

Ah!

Why shouldn't I get someone to give me butter?

Who?

Why, Jeeves, of course. All I have to do is to go to the Hall and put the whole case before Jeeves and tell him to rally round, and there I'll be, as right as rain, with nothing more to worry about. Jeeves will know where to lay his hand on seas of butter. You see! It's perfectly simple if you think it out and don't lose your head.

And, by Jove, there didn't seem a single Debit to shove against that. I examined the position thoroughly, trying to find one, but at the end of five minutes I saw that I had got the Debit account stymied. I had baffled it. It hadn't a thing to say.

Of course, I mused, I ought to have thought of this solution right from the start. Dashed obvious, the whole thing, when you came to think of it. I mean, Jeeves would be back at the Hall by now. I had only to go and get in touch with him and he would bring out pounds of butter on a lordly dish. And not only that, but he would lend me enough of the needful to pay my fare to London and possibly even to purchase a packet of milk chocolate from the slot machine at the station. The thing was a walk-over.

I rose from my stump, braced to a degree, and started off. In the race for life, as you might term it, I had lost my bearings a bit, but I pretty soon hit the main road, and I don't suppose it was more than a quarter of an hour later that I was rapping at the back door of the Hall.

It was opened by a small female – a scullerymaid of sorts, I put her down as – who, on observing me, gaped for a moment with a sort of shocked horror, and then with a piercing squeal keeled over and started to roll about and drum her heels on the floor. And I'm not so dashed sure she wasn't frothing at the mouth.

# =14=

# THE BUTTER SITUATION

I MUST admit it was a fairly nasty shock. I had never realized before what an important part one's complexion plays in life. I mean to say, a Bertram Wooster with merely a pretty tan calling at the back door of Chuffnell Hall would have been received with respect and deference. Indeed, I shouldn't wonder if a girl of the social standing of a scullerymaid might not actually have curtsied. And I don't suppose matters would have been so substantially different if I had had an interesting pallor or pimples. But purely and simply because there happened to be a little boot polish on my face, here was this female tying herself in knots on the doormat and throwing fits up and down the passage.

Well, there was only one thing to do, of course. Already voices from along the corridor were making inquiries, and in another half-second I presumed that I might expect a regular susurration of domestics on the scene. I picked up the feet and pushed off. And, taking it that the neighbourhood of the back door was liable to be searched pretty soon, I hared round to the front and came to roost in a patch of bushes not far from the main entrance.

Here I paused. It seemed to me that before going any farther, I had better try to analyse the situation and find out what to do next.

In other circs. – if, let us say, I had been reclining in a deckchair with a cigarette, instead of squatting in a beastly jungle with beetles falling down my neck – I should probably have got a good deal of entertainment and uplift out of the scene and surroundings generally. I've always been rather a lad for the peace of the old-world English garden round about the time between the end of dinner and the mixing of the bedtime spot. From where I sat, I could see the great mass of Hall standing out against the sky, and very impressive it was, too. Birds were rustling in the trees, and I think there must have been a flower-bed fairly close by with stocks and tobacco plants in it, for the air was full of a pretty goodish sort of smell. Add the perfect stillness of a summer night, and there you are.

347

At the end of about ten minutes, however, the stillness of the summer night rather sprang a leak. From one of the rooms there proceeded a loud yelling. I recognized the voice of little Seabury, and remembered feeling thankful that he had his troubles, too. After a bit, he cheesed it – I assumed the friction had arisen from the fact that somebody wanted to put him to bed and he didn't want to go – and all was quiet again.

Directly after that there came a sound of footsteps. Somebody was walking up the drive to the front door.

My first idea was that it was Sergeant Voules. Chuffy, you see, is a local Justice of the Peace, and I imagined that one of the first things Voules would do after the affair at the cottage would be to call on the big chief and report. I wedged myself a bit tighter into the bushes.

No, it wasn't Sergeant Voules. I had just got him against a patch of sky and I could see he was taller and not nearly so round. He went up the steps and started knocking at the door.

And when I say knocking I mean knocking. I had thought Voules's performance at the cottage on the previous night a pretty good exhibition of wrist-work, but this chap put it all over him. In a different class, altogether. He was giving that knocker more exercise than I suppose it had ever had since the first Chuffnell, or whoever it was, had it screwed on.

In the intervals of slamming the knocker, he was also singing a hymn in a meditative sort of voice. It was, if I recollect rightly, 'Lead, Kindly Light', and it enabled me to place him. I had heard that reedy tenor before. One of the first things I had had to put my foot down about, on arriving at the cottage, was Brinkley's habit of singing hymns in the kitchen while I was trying to play foxtrots on the banjolele in the sitting-room. There could not be two voices like that in Chuffnell Regis. This nocturnal visitor was none other than my plastered personal attendant, and what he wanted at the Hall was more than I could understand.

Lights flashed up in the house, and the front door was wrenched open. A voice spoke. It was a pretty peevish voice, and it was Chuffy's. As a rule, of course, the Squire of Chuffnell Regis shoves the task of answering the door off on to the domestic staff, but I suppose he felt that a ghastly din like this constituted a special case. Anyway, here he was, and he didn't seem too pleased.

'What on earth are you making that foul noise for?'

'Good evening, sir.'

'What do you mean, good evening? What . . .'

I think he would have gone to some length, for he was evidently much stirred, but at this point Brinkley interrupted.

'Is the Devil in?'

It was a simple question, capable of being answered with a Yes or No, but it seemed to take Chuffy aback somewhat.

'Is – who?'

'The Devil, sir.'

I must say I had never looked on old Chuffy as a fellow of very swift intelligence, he having always run rather to thews and sinews than the grey cells, but I'm bound to say that at this juncture he exhibited a keen intuition which did him credit.

'You're tight.'

'Yes, sir.'

Chuffy seemed to explode like a paper bag. I could follow his mental processes, if you know what I mean, pretty clearly. Ever since that unfortunate episode at the cottage, when the girl he loved had handed him the mitten and gone out of his life, I imagine he had been seething and brooding and sizzling and what not like a soul in torment, yearning for some outlet for his repressed emotions, and here he had found one. Ever since that regrettable scene he had been wishing that he could work off the stored-up venom on somebody, and, by Jove, Heaven had sent this knocker-slamming inebriate.

To run Brinkley down the steps and up the drive, kicking him about every other yard, was with the fifth Baron Chuffnell the work of a moment. They passed my little clump of bushes at about forty m.p.h., and rolled away into the distance. And after a while I heard footsteps and the sound of someone whistling as if a bit of a load had been removed from his soul, and Chuffy came legging it back.'

Just about opposite my lair he paused to light a cigarette, and it seemed to me that the moment had come to get in touch.

Mark you, I wasn't any too keen on chatting with old Chuffy, for his manner at our last parting had been far from bonhomous, and had my outlook been a shade rosier I would most certainly have given him a miss. But he was by way of being my last hope. What with platoons of scullerymaids having hysterics every time I went near the back door, it seemed impossible to connect with

Jeeves tonight. It was just as impossible to go the round of the neighbourhood, calling on perfect strangers and asking for butter. I mean, you know yourself how you feel when a fellow you've never met drops in at your house with his face all black and tries to touch you for a bit of butter. You just aren't in sympathy.

No, everything pointed to Chuffy as the logical saviour of the situation. He was a man who had butter at his command, and it might be that, now that he had worked off some of the hard feelings on Brinkley, he would be in a frame of mind to oblige an old school friend with a quarter of a pound or so. So I crawled softly out of the undergrowth and came up in his immediate rear.

'Chuffy!' I said.

I can see now it would have been better to have given him a bit more warning of my presence. Nobody likes to have unexpected voices speaking suddenly down the back of their neck, and in calmer mood I should have recognized this. I don't say it was exactly a repetition of the scullerymaid episode, but for a moment it looked like coming very near it. The poor old lad distinctly leaped. The cigarette flew out of his hand, his teeth came together with a snap, and he shook visibly. The whole effect being much as if I had spiked him in the trousering with a gimlet or bodkin. I have seen salmon behave in a rather similar way during the spawning season.

I did my best to lull the storm with soothing words.

'It's only me, Chuffy.'

'Who?'

'Bertie.'

'Bertie?'

'That's right.'

'Oh!'

I didn't much like the sound of that "Oh!" It hadn't a welcoming ring. One learns to sense when one is popular and when one is not. It was pretty plain to me at this point that I was not, and I thought it might be wise if, before proceeding to the main topic, I were to start off with a stately compliment.

'You put it across that fellow properly, Chuffy,' I said. 'I liked your work. It was particularly agreeable to me to see him so adequately handled, because I had been wishing I had the nerve to kick him myself.'

'Who was he?'

'My man, Brinkley.'

'What was he doing here?'

'I fancy he was looking for me.'

'Why wasn't he at the cottage, then?'

I had been hoping for a good opportunity of breaking the news. 'I'm afraid you're a cottage short, Chuffy,' I said. 'I regret to report that Brinkley has just burned it down.'

'What!'

'Insured, I trust?'

'He burned the cottage? How? Why?'

'Just a whim. I suppose it seemed a good idea to him at the moment.'

Chuffy took it rather hard. I could see that he was brooding, and I would have liked to allow him to brood all he wanted. But if I was going to catch that 10.21 it was necessary to push along. Time was of the essence.

'Well,' I said, 'I hate to bother you, old man . . .'

'Why on earth should he burn a cottage?'

'One cannot attempt to fathom the psychology of blokes like Brinkley. They move in a mysterious way their wonders to perform. Suffice it that he did.'

'Are you sure it wasn't you?'

'My dear chap!'

'It sounds the sort of silly, fat-headed thing you would do,' said Chuffy, and I was distressed to note in his voice much evidence of the old rancour. 'What do you want here, anyway? Who asked you to come? If you think, after what has happened, that you can stroll in and out . . .'

'I know, I know. I understand. Painful misunderstanding. Coolness. A disposition to disapprove of Bertram. But . . .'

'And where did you spring from just now! I never saw you.'

'I was sitting in a bush.'

'Sitting in a bush?'

The tone in which he said the words told me that, always too prone to misjudge an old friend, he had once more formed a wrong conclusion. I heard a match scratch on its box, and the next moment he was examining me by its light. The light went out, and I heard him breathing deeply in the darkness.

I could follow the workings of his mind. He was evidently struggling with his feelings. The disinclination to have anything

more to do with me after last night's painful rift was contending
with the reflection that the fact that we had been pals for years
carried with it a certain obligation. A chap, he was thinking, may
have ceased to be on cordial terms with an old schoolmate, but he
can hardly let him go wandering about the countryside in the
condition he supposed I was in.

'You'd better come in and sleep it off,' he said in a weary sort of
way. 'Can you walk?'

'It's all right,' I hastened to assure him. 'It's not what you think.
Listen.'

And with convincing fluency I rattled off 'British Constitution',
'She sells sea-shells', and 'He stood at the entrance of Burgess's
fish-sauce shop, welcoming him in'.

The demonstration had its effect.

'Then you're not tight?'

'Not a bit.'

'But you sit in bushes.'

'Yes. But . . .'

'And your face is black.'

'I know. Hold the line, old man, and I will tell you all.'

I dare say you have had the experience of telling someone a
longish story and getting on to the fact, half-way through, that
you haven't got the sympathy of the audience. Most unpleasant
sensation. I had it now. It was not that he said anything. But a sort
of deleterious animal magnetism seemed to exude from him as I
passed from point to point. More and more, as I proceeded, did
the conviction steal over me that I was getting the silent raspberry.

However, I carried on stoutly and, having related the salient
facts, wound up with a pretty eloquent plea for the stearic matter.

'Butter, Chuffy, old man,' I said. 'Slabs of butter. If you have
butter, prepare to shed it now. I'll just saunter about out here,
shall I, while you pop to the kitchen and secure the stuff? And you
realize, don't you, that time is of the essence? I shall only just be
able to catch that train, as it is.'

He did not speak for a moment or two. When he did, there was
such a nasty tinkle in his voice that I confess the heart sank.

'Let me get all this straight,' he said. 'You want me to bring you
butter?'

'That's the idea.'

'So that you can clean your face and go off on this train to
London.'

'Yes.'

'Thus escaping from Mr Stoker.'

'That's right. Amazing the way you've followed it all,' I said in a congratulatory sort of voice, deeming it best to suck up a bit and apply the old salve. 'I don't suppose I know six fellows who would have grasped the plot with the same unerring accuracy. I've always thought highly of your intelligence, Chuffy, old man – very highly.'

But the heart was still sinking. And when I heard him snort emotionally in the darkness it touched a new low.

'I see,' he said. 'In other words, you wish me to help you back out of your honourable obligations, what?'

'What?'

'That's what I said – "What?" Good God!' cried Chuffy, and I dare say he quivered from head to foot, but I couldn't see properly, it being too dark. 'I didn't interrupt when you were telling me your degrading story, because I wanted to get it quite clear. Now, perhaps, you will let me say a word.'

He snorted a bit more.

'You want to catch trains to London, do you? I see. Well, I don't know what you think of yourself, Wooster, but, if you would come to know how your conduct strikes a perfectly unprejudiced outsider, I don't mind informing you that in my opinion you are behaving like a hound, a skunk, a worm, a tick, and a wart-hog. Good gosh! This beautiful girl loves you. Her father very decently consents to an early wedding. And instead of being delighted and pleased and tickled as – er – as anybody else would be, you are planning to edge away.'

'But, Chuffy . . .'

'I repeat, to edge away. You are brutally and callously scheming to oil out, leaving this lovely girl to break her heart – deserted, abandoned, flung aside like a . . . like a . . . I shall forget my own name next . . . like a soiled glove.'

'But, Chuffy . . .'

'Don't try to deny it.'

'But, dash it, it isn't as if she were in love with me.'

'Ha! Isn't she so infatuated with you that she swims ashore from yachts to get at you?'

'She loves you.'

'Ha!'

353

'She does, I tell you. It was you she swam ashore last night to see. And she only took on this binge of marrying me to score off you because you doubted her.'

'Ha!'

'So take the sensible viewpoint, old man, and bring me butter.'

'Ha!'

'I wish you wouldn't keep saying "Ha!" It doesn't advance the issue, and it sounds rotten. I must have butter, Chuffy. It is of the essence. If it be only a small pat, bring it out. Wooster speaking, old man – the chap you were at school with, the fellow you've known since he was so high.'

I paused. For a moment I had an idea that this had done the trick. I felt his hand fall on my shoulder with a distinct kneading movement. At that instant I would have put my shirt on it that he was softened.

And so he was, but not along the right lines.

'I will tell you exactly how I feel about all this, Bertie,' he said, and there was a sort of beastly gentleness in his manner. 'I won't pretend that I don't love this girl. Even after what has happened, I still love her. I shall always love her. I loved her from the first moment we met. It was at the Savoy Grill, I remember, and she was sitting on one of those chairs in that lobby place half-way through a medium dry Martini, because Sir Roderick and I were a bit late getting there and her father had thought they might as well be having a cocktail instead of just sitting. Our eyes met, and I knew that I had found the only girl in the world for me, not having the foggiest that she was really crazy about you.'

'She isn't!'

'I realize it now, and I know, of course, that I can never win her for myself. But I can do this, Bertie. Having this great love for her, I can see to it that she is not robbed of her happiness. If she is happy, that is all that matters. For some reason her heart is set on being your wife. Why, one cannot say, and we need not go into it. But for some unexplained reason she wants you, and she shall jolly well get you. Funny that you should have come to me, of all people, to help you shatter her girlish dreams and rob her of her sweet, childlike trust in the goodness of human nature! You think I will sit in with you on this foul project? My left foot I will! You get no butter from me, my lad. You will remain exactly as you are, and, after thinking it over, I have no doubt that you will find your better self pointing the way and that you will go back to the yacht, prepared to fulfil your obligations like an English gentleman.'

'But, Chuffy . . .'

'And, if you wish, I will be your best man. Agony, of course, but I'll do it if you want me to.'

I clutched at his arm.

'Butter, Chuffy!'

He shook his head.

'No butter, Wooster. You are better without it.'

And, flinging aside my hand like a soiled glove, he stalked past me into the night.

I don't know how long it was that I stood there, rooted to the s. It may have been a short time. It may have been quite a stretch. Despair was gripping me, and when that happens you don't keep looking at your watch.

Let us say, then, that at some point – five, ten, fifteen, or it may have been twenty minutes later – I became aware of somebody coughing softly at my side like a respectful sheep trying to attract the attention of its shepherd, and how can I describe with what thankfulness and astonishment I perceived Jeeves.

# =15=
# DEVELOPMENT OF THE BUTTER SITUATION

A BALLY miracle it seemed to me at the moment, but of course there was a simple explanation.

'I was hoping that you would not have left the grounds, sir,' he said. 'I have been searching for you for some little time. On learning that the scullerymaid had become a victim of hysterics as the result of opening the back door and observing a black man, I sprang to the conclusion that you must have been calling there, no doubt with a view to seeing me. Has something gone wrong, sir?'

I wiped the brow.

'Jeeves,' I said, 'I feel like a lost child that has found its mother.'

'Indeed, sir?'

'If you don't mind me calling you a mother?'

'Not at all, sir.'

'Thank you, Jeeves.'

'Then there is something wrong, sir?'

'Wrong! You said it. What are those sore things people find themselves in?'

'Straits, sir.'

'I am in the sorest straits, Jeeves. To start with, I found that soap and water won't get this stuff off.'

'No, sir. I should have informed you that butter is a *sine qua non*.'

'Well, I was on the point of getting butter when Brinkley – my man, you know – suddenly blew in and burned the house down.'

'Too bad, sir.'

'The expression "Too bad" scarcely overstates it, Jeeves. It landed me in the dickens of a hole. I came here. I tried to get in touch with you. But that scullerymaid gummed up that project.'

'A temperamental girl, sir. And by an unfortunate coincidence she and the cook, at the moment of your arrival, had just been occupying themselves with the Ouija board – with, I believe, some

356

interesting results. She appears to have regarded you as a materialized spirit.'

I quivered a bit.

'If cooks would stick to their roasts and hashes,' I said rather severely, 'and not waste their time in psychical research, life would be a very different thing.'

'Quite true, sir.'

'Well, then I ran into Chuffy. He stoutly declined to lend me butter.'

'Indeed, sir?'

'He was in a very unpleasant mood.'

'His lordship is undergoing a good deal of mental anguish at the moment, sir.'

'I could see that. He left me apparently to go for a country ramble. At this time of night!'

'Physical exercise is a recognized palliative when the heart is aching, sir.'

'Well, I mustn't think too harshly of Chuffy. I must always remember that he kicked Brinkley properly. It did me good to watch him. And now you've turned up, all is well. The happy ending, what?'

'Precisely, sir. I shall be delighted to procure you butter.'

'But can I still catch that 10.21?'

'I fear not, sir. But I have ascertained that there is another train as late as 11.50.'

'Then I'm on velvet.'

'Yes, sir.'

I breathed deeply. The relief was great.

'I shouldn't wonder if you couldn't even dig me up a packet of sandwiches for the journey, what?'

'Certainly, sir.'

'And a drop of something?'

'Undoubtedly, sir.'

'Then if you happened to have such a thing as a cigarette on your person at this moment, everything would be more or less perfect.'

'Turkish or Virginian, sir?'

'Both.'

There is nothing like a quiet cigarette for soothing the system. For some moments I puffed luxuriously, and my nerves, which had been sticking out of my body an inch long and curled at the ends, gradually slipped into place again. I felt restored and invigorated and in a mood for conversation.

'What was all that yelling about, Jeeves?'

'Sir?'

'Just before I met Chuffy, animal cries started to proceed from somewhere in the house. It sounded like Seabury.'

'It was Master Seabury, sir. He is a little fractious tonight.'

'What's biting him?'

'He is somewhat acutely disappointed, sir, at having missed the negro entertainment on the yacht.'

'Absolutely his own fault, the silly little geezer. If he wanted to go to Dwight's birthday-party, he shouldn't have started a scrap with him.'

'Just so, sir.'

'To attempt to touch your host for one and sixpence protection money on the eve of a birthday-party is the act of a fathead.'

'Very true, sir.'

'What did they do about it? He seems to have stopped yelling. Did they chloroform him?'

'No, sir. I understand that steps are being taken to provide something in the nature of an alternative entertainment for the little fellow.'

'How do you mean, Jeeves? Are they having the negroes up here?'

'No, sir. The expense rules that project out of the sphere of practical politics. But I understand that her ladyship has induced Sir Roderick Glossop to offer his services.'

I could not follow this.

'Old Glossop?'

'Yes, sir.'

'But what can he do?'

'It appears, sir, that he has a pleasing baritone voice and as a younger man – in the days when he was a medical student – was often accustomed to render songs at smoking concerts and similar entertainments.'

'Old Glossop!'

'Yes, sir. I overheard him telling her ladyship so.'

'Well, I would never have thought it.'

'I agree that one would scarcely suspect such a thing from his bearing nowadays, sir. *Tempora mutantur, nos et mutamur in illis.*'

'Then you mean that he is going to soothe young Seabury with song?'

'Yes, sir. Accompanied by her ladyship on the piano.'

I spotted the snag.

'It won't work, Jeeves. Reason it out for yourself.'

'Sir!'

'Well, here is a kid who has been looking forward to seeing a troupe of negro minstrels do their stuff. Is he likely to accept as an adequate substitute a white-faced loony-doctor accompanied by his mother on the piano?'

'Not white-faced, sir.'

'What!'

'No, sir. The question was debated, and it was her ladyship's view that something in the nature of a negroid performance was indispensable. The young gentleman, when in his present frame of mind, is always extremely exigent.'

I swallowed a puff of smoke the wrong way in my emotion.

'Old Glossop isn't blacking up?'

'Yes, sir.'

'Jeeves, pull yourself together. This can't be true. He is blacking his face?'

'Yes, sir.'

'It isn't possible.'

'Sir Roderick is very amenable at the moment, sir, you must remember, to any suggestion emanating from her ladyship.'

'You mean he's in love?'

'Yes, sir.'

'And Love conquers all?'

'Yes, sir.'

'But even so. . . . If you were in love, Jeeves, would you black up to entertain the son of the adored object?'

'No, sir. But we are not all constituted alike.'

'True.'

'Sir Roderick did endeavour to protest, but her ladyship overruled his objections. And, as a matter of fact, sir, I think that, on the whole, it is a good thing that she did. Sir Roderick's kindly act will serve to heal the breach between Master Seabury and himself. I happen to know that the young gentleman has been unsuccessful in his endeavour to extract protection money from Sir Roderick, and was resenting the fact keenly.'

'He tried to gouge the old boy?'

'Yes, sir. For ten shillings. I have the information from the young gentleman himself.'

'They all confide in you, Jeeves.'

'Yes, sir.'

'And old Glossop wouldn't kick in?'

'No, sir. Instead, he read the young gentleman something of a lecture. What the young gentleman described as "pi-jaws". And I happen to know that hard feelings existed as a consequence on the latter's side. So much so, indeed, that I received the impression that he had been planning something in the nature of a reprisal.'

'He wouldn't have the nerve to do the dirty on a future stepfather, would he?'

'Young gentlemen are headstrong, sir.'

'True. One recalls the case of my Aunt Agatha's son, young Thos., and the Cabinet Minister.'

'Yes, sir.'

'In a spirit of ill-will he marooned him on an island in the lake with a swan.'

'Yes, sir.'

'How is the swanning in these parts? I confess that I would like to see old Glossop shinning up something with a bilious bird after him.'

'I fancy that Master Seabury's thoughts turned more towards something on the order of a booby trap, sir.'

'They would. No imagination, that kid. No vision. I've often noticed it. His fancy is – what's the word?'

'Pedestrian, sir?'

'Exactly. With all the limitless opportunities of a large country house at his disposal, he is content to put soot and water on top of the door, a thing you could do in a suburban villa. I have never thought highly of Seabury, and this confirms my low opinion.'

'Not soot and water, sir. I think what the young gentleman had in mind was the old-fashioned butter-slide, sir. He was asking me yesterday where the butter was kept, and referred guardedly to a humorous film he had seen not long ago in Bristol, in which something of that nature occurred.'

I was disgusted. Goodness knows that any outrage perpetrated on the person of a bloke like Sir Roderick Glossop touches a ready chord in Bertram Wooster's bosom, but a butterslide . . . the lowest depths, as you might say. The merest A B C of the booby-trapping art. There isn't a fellow at the Drones who would sink to such a thing.

I started to utter a scornful laugh, then stopped. The word had reminded me that life was stern and earnest and that time was passing.

'Butter, Jeeves! Here we are, standing idly here, talking of butter, and all the time you ought to have been racing to the larder, getting me some.'

'I will go immediately, sir.'

'You know where to lay your hand on it all right?'

'Yes, sir.'

'And you're sure it will do the trick?'

'Quite sure, sir.'

'Then shift-ho, Jeeves. And don't loiter.'

I sat down on an upturned flower-pot, and resumed my vigil. My feelings were very different now from what they had been when first I had begun to roost on this desirable property. Then, I had been a penniless outcast, so to speak, with nothing much of a future before me. Now, I could see daylight. Presently Jeeves would return with the fixings. Shortly after that, I should be the old pink-cheeked clubman once more. And, in due season, I should be safely inside the 11.50 train, on my way to London and safety.

I was a good deal uplifted. I drank in the night air with a light heart. And it was while I was drinking it in that a sudden uproar proceeded from the house.

Seabury appeared to be contributing most of it. He was yelling his bally head off. From time to time, one caught the fainter, yet penetrating note of the Dowager Lady Chuffnell. She seemed to be reproaching or upbraiding someone. Blending with this, there could be discerned a deeper voice, the unmistakable baritone woofle of Sir Roderick Glossop. The whole appeared to be proceeding from the drawing-room, and, except for one time when I was sauntering in Hyde Park and suddenly found myself mixed up in a Community Singing, I've never heard anything like it.

It couldn't have been very long after this when the front door was suddenly flung open. Somebody emerged. The door slammed. And then the emerger started to stump rapidly down the drive in the direction of the gates.

There had been just a moment when the light from the hall shone upon this bloke. It had been long enough for me to identify him.

This sudden exiter, who was now padding away into the darkness with every outward sign of being fed to the eye-teeth, was none other than Sir Roderick Glossop. And his face, I noted, was as black as the ace of spades.

A few moments later, while I was still wondering what it was all about and generally turning the thing over in my mind, I observed Jeeves looming up on the right flank.

I was glad to see him. I desired enlightenment.

'What was all that, Jeeves?'

'The disturbance, sir?'

'It sounded as if little Seabury was being murdered. No such luck, I take it?'

'The young gentleman *was* the victim of a personal assault, sir. At the hands of Sir Roderick Glossop. I was not an actual eye-witness of the episode. I derive my information from Mary, the parlourmaid, who was present in person.'

'Present?'

'Peeping through the door, sir. Sir Roderick's appearance when she encountered him by chance on the stairs seems to have affected the girl powerfully, and she tells me that she had followed him about in a stealthy manner ever since, waiting to see what he would do next. I gather that his aspect fascinated her. She is inclined to be somewhat frivolous in her mental attitude, like so many of these young girls, sir.'

'And what occurred?'

'The affair may be said to have had its inception, sir, when Sir Roderick, passing through the hall, stepped upon the young gentleman's butter-slide.'

'Ah! So he put that project through, did he?'

'Yes, sir.'

'And Sir Roderick came a stinker?'

'He appears to have fallen with some heaviness, sir. The girl Mary spoke of it with a good deal of animation. She compared his descent to the delivery of a ton of coals. I confess the imagery somewhat surprised me, for she is not a highly imaginative girl.'

I smiled appreciatively. The evening, I felt, might have begun rockily, but it was certainly ending well.

'Incensed by this, Sir Roderick appears to have hastened to the drawing-room, where he immediately subjected Master Seabury to a severe castigation. Her ladyship vainly endeavoured to induce him to desist, but he was firm in his refusal. The upshot of the matter was a definite rift between her ladyship and Sir Roderick, the former stating that she never wished to see him again, the latter asseverating that, if he could once get safely out of this pestilential house, he would never darken its doors again.'

'A real mix-up.'

'Yes, sir.'

'And the engagement's off?'

'Yes, sir. The affection which her ladyship felt for Sir Roderick was instantaneously swept away on the tidal wave of injured mother love.'

'Rather well put, Jeeves.'

'Thank you, sir.'

'Then Sir Roderick has pushed off for ever?'

'Apparently, sir.'

'A lot of trouble Chuffnell Hall is seeing these days. Almost as if there was a curse on the place.'

'If one were superstitious, one might certainly suppose so, sir.'

'Well, if there wasn't a curse on it before, you can bet there are about fifty-seven now. I heard old Glossop applying them as he passed.'

'He was much moved, I take it, sir?'

'Very much moved, Jeeves.'

'So I should imagine, sir. Or he would scarcely have left the house in that condition.'

'How do you mean?'

'Well, sir, if you consider. It will scarcely be feasible for him to return to his hotel in the existing circumstances. His appearance would excite remark. Nor, after what has occurred, can he very well return to the the Hall.'

I saw what he was driving at.

'Good Lord, Jeeves! You open up a new line of thought. Let me just review this. He can't go to his hotel – no, I see that, and he can't crawl back to the Dowager Lady C. and ask for shelter – no, I see that too. It's a dead stymie. I can't imagine what on earth he'll do.'

'It is something of a problem, sir.'

I was silent for a moment. Pensive. And, oddly enough, for you would have thought my mood would have been one of sober joy, the heart was really rather bleeding a bit.

'Do you know, Jeeves, scurvily as that man has treated me in the past, I can't help feeling sorry for him. I do, absolutely. He's in such an awful jam. It was bad enough for me being a black-faced wanderer, but I hadn't the position to keep up that he has. I mean to say, the world, observing me in this condition, might quite easily just have shrugged its shoulders and murmured "Young Blood!" or words to that effect, what?'

'Yes, sir.'

'But not with a bloke of his standing.'

'Very true, sir.'

'Well, well, well! Dear, dear, dear! I suppose, if you come right down to it, this is the vengeance of Heaven.'

'Quite possibly, sir.'

It isn't often that I point the moral, but I couldn't help doing it now.'

'It just shows how we ought always to be kind, even to the humblest, Jeeves. For years this Glossop has trampled on my face with spiked shoes, and see where it has landed him. What would have happened if we had been on chummy terms at this juncture? He would have been on velvet. Observing him shooting past just now, I should have stopped him. I should have called out to him "Hi, Sir Roderick, half a second. Don't go roaming about the place in make-up. Stick around here for a while and pretty soon Jeeves will be arriving with the necessary butter, and all will be well." Shouldn't I have said that, Jeeves?'

'Something of that general trend, no doubt, sir.'

'And he would have been saved from this fearful situation, this sore strait, in which he now finds himself. I dare say that man won't be able to get butter till well on in the morning. Not even then, if he hasn't money on the person. And all because he wouldn't treat me decently in the past. Makes you think a bit, that, Jeeves, what?'

'Yes, sir.'

'But it's no use talking about it, of course. What's done is done.'

'Very true, sir. The moving finger writes and, having writ,

moves on, nor all your piety and wit can lure it back to cancel half a line, nor all your tears wash out a word of it.'

'Quite. And now, Jeeves, the butter. I must be getting about my business.'

He sighed in a respectful sort of way.

'I am extremely sorry to be obliged to inform you, sir, that, owing to Master Seabury having used it all for his slide, there is no butter in the house.'

# =16=
# TROUBLE AT THE DOWER HOUSE

I STOOD there with my hand out, frozen to the spot. The faculties seemed numbed. I remember once, when I was in New York, one of those sad-eyed Italian kids who whizz about Washington Square on roller skates suddenly projected himself with extraordinary violence at my waistcoat as I strolled to and from, taking the air. He reached journey's end right on the third button from the top, and I had much the same sensation now as I had had then. A sort of stricken feeling. Stunned. Breathless. As if somebody had walloped the old soul unexpectedly with a sandbag.

'What!'

'Yes, sir.'

'No butter?'

'No butter, sir.'

'But, Jeeves, this is frightful.'

'Most disturbing, sir.'

If Jeeves has a fault, it is that his demeanour on these occasions too frequently tends to be rather more calm and unemotional than one could wish. One lodges no protest, as a rule, because he generally has the situation well in hand and loses no time in coming before the Board with one of his ripe solutions. But I have often felt that I could do with a little more leaping about with rolling eyeballs on his part, and I felt it now. At a moment like the present, the adjective "disturbing" seemed to me to miss the facts by about ten parasangs.

'But what shall I do?'

'I fear that it will be necessary to postpone the cleansing of your face till a later date, sir. I shall be in a position to supply you with butter tomorrow.'

'But tonight?'

'Tonight, I am afraid, sir, you must be content to remain *in statu quo*.'

'Eh?'

'A Latin expression, sir.'

'You mean nothing can be done till tomorrow?'

'I fear not, sir. It is vexing.'

'You would go so far as to describe it as that?'

'Yes, sir. Most vexing.'

I breathed a bit tensely.

'Oh, well, just as you say, Jeeves.'

I pondered.

'And what do I do in the meantime?'

'As you have had a somewhat trying evening, I think it would be best, sir, if you were to get a good sleep.'

'On the lawn?'

'If I might make the suggestion, sir, I think you would be more comfortable in the Dower House. It is only a short distance across the park, and it is unoccupied.'

'It can't be. They wouldn't leave it empty.'

'One of the gardeners is acting as caretaker while her ladyship and master Seabury are visiting the Hall, but at this hour he is always down at the "Chuffnell Arms" in the village. It would be quite simple for you to effect an entrance and establish yourself in one of the upper rooms without his cognizance. And tomorrow morning I could join you there with the necessary materials.'

I confess it wasn't my idea of a frightfully large evening.

'You've nothing brighter to suggest?'

'No, sir.'

'You wouldn't consider letting me have your bed for the night?'

'No, sir.'

'Then I might as well be moving.'

'Yes, sir.'

'Good night, Jeeves,' I said moodily.

'Good night, sir.'

It didn't take me long to get to the Dower House, and the trip seemed shorter than it actually was, because my mind was occupied in transit with a sort of series of silent Hymns of Hate directed at the various blokes who had combined to land me in what Jeeves would have called this vexing situation – featuring little Seabury.

The more I thought of this stripling, the more the iron entered into my soul. And one result of my meditations regarding him was to engender – I think it's engender – an emotion towards Sir Roderick Glossop which came pretty near to being a spirit of kindliness.

You know how it is. You go along for years looking on a fellow as a blister and a menace to the public weal, and then one day you suddenly hear of some decent thing he's done and it makes you feel there must be good in the chap, after all. It was so in the matter of this Glossop. I had suffered much at his hands since first our paths had crossed. In the human Zoo which Fate has caused to centre about Bertram Wooster, he had always ranked high up among the more vicious specimens – many good judges, indeed, considering that he even competed for the blue ribbon with that great scourge of modern times, my Aunt Agatha. But now, reviewing his recent conduct, I must admit that I found myself definitely softening towards him.

Nobody, I reasoned, who could slosh young Seabury like that could be altogether bad. There must be fine metal somewhere among the dross. And I actually went so far as to say to myself with something of a rush of emotion that, if ever things so shaped themselves that I could go freely about my affairs again, I would look the man up and endeavour to fraternize with him. I had even reached the stage of toying with the idea of a nice little lunch, with him on one side of the table and me on the other, sucking down some good, dry vintage wine and chatting like old friends, when I found that I had arrived at the outskirts of the Dower House.

This bin or depository for the widows of deceased Lords Chuffnell was a medium-sized sort of shack standing in what the advertisements described as spacious and commodious grounds. You entered by a five-barred gate set in a box hedge and approached by a short gravel drive – unless you were planning to break in through a lower window, in which case you sneaked along a grass border, skipping silently from tree to tree.

This is what I did, though at a casual glance it didn't seem really necessary. The place looked deserted. Still, so far, of course, I had only seen the front of it: and if the gardener in charge had changed his policy of going down to the local pub for a refresher at this hour and was still on the premises, he would be round at the back. It was thither, therefore, that I now directed the footsteps, making them as snaky as possible.

I can't say I liked the prospect before me. Jeeves had spoken airily – or glibly – of busting in and making myself at home for the night; but my experience has been that whenever I try to do a bit of burgling something always goes wrong. I had not yet forgotten that time Bingo Little persuaded me to break into his house and pinch the dictaphone record of the mushy article his wife, neé Rosie M. Banks, the well-known female novelist, had written about him for my Aunt Dahlia's paper, *Milady's Boudoir*. Pekingese, parlourmaids, and policemen had entered into the affair, you may remember, causing me despondency and alarm: and I didn't want anything of that nature happening again.

So it was with a pretty goodish amount of caution that I now sidled round to the back: and when the first thing the eye fell on was the kitchen door standing ajar, I did not rush in with the vim I would have displayed a year or so earlier, before Life had made me the grim, suspicious man I am today: but stood there cocking a wary eye at it. It might be all right. On the other hand, it might not be all right. Time alone could tell.

The next moment, I was dashed glad I had held off, because I suddenly heard someone whistling in the house, and I saw what that meant. It meant that the gardener bloke, instead of going down to the "Chuffnell Arms" for a snifter, had decided to stay home and have a quiet evening among his books. So much for Jeeves's authoritative inside information.

I drew back into the shadows like a leopard, feeling pretty peeved. I felt that Jeeves had no right to say that fellows went down to the village for a spot at such and such a time when they didn't.

And then suddenly something happened that threw an entirely new light on the position of affairs, and I saw that I had misjudged the honest fellow. The whistling stopped, there was a single, brief hiccough, and then from inside came the sound of somebody singing 'Lead, Kindly Light'.

The occupant of the Dower House was no mere gardener. It was Moscow's Pride, the unspeakable Brinkley, who lurked therein.

The situation seemed to me to call for careful, unhurried thought.

The whole trouble with fellows like Brinkley is that in dealing with them you cannot go by the form book. They are such in-and-out performers. Tonight, for instance, within the space of little more than an hour, I had seen this man ravening to and fro with a carving knife and also tolerantly submitting to having himself kicked by Chuffy practically the whole length of the Chuffnell Hall drive. It all seemed to be a question of what mood he happened to be in at the time. If, therefore, I was compelled to ask myself, I were to walk boldly into the Dower House now, which manifestation of this many-sided man would greet me? Should I find a deferential lover of peace whom it would be both simple and agreeable to take by the slack of the trousers and bung out? Or should I have to spend the remainder of the night racing up and down the stairs with him a short head behind me?

And, arising out of this, what had become of that carving knife of his? As far as I could ascertain, he did not appear to have it on his person during the interview with Chuffy. But then, on the other hand, he might simply have left it somewhere and collected it again by now.

Reviewing the matter from every angle, I decided to remain where I was; and the next moment the trend of events showed that the decision had been a wise one. He had just got as far as that bit about 'The night is dark' and seemed to be going strong, though a little uncertain in the lower register, when he suddenly broke off. And the next thing I heard was a most frightful outbreak of shoutings and clumpings and bangings. What had set him off, I could not, of course, say; but the sounds left little room for doubt that for some reason or other the fellow had abruptly returned to what I might call the carving-knife phase.

One of the advantages of being in the country, if you belong, like Brinkley, to the more aggressive type of loony, is that you have great freedom of movement. The sort of row he was making now, if made in, let us say, Grosvenor Square or Cadogan Terrace, would infallibly have produced posses of policemen within the first two minutes. Windows would have been raised, whistles blown. But in the peaceful seclusion of the Dower House, Chuffnell Regis, he was granted the widest scope for self-expression. Except for the Hall, there wasn't another house within a mile: and even the Hall was too far away for the ghastly uproar he was making to be more than a faint murmur.

As to what he thought he was chasing, there again one could make no certain pronouncement. It might be that the gardener-caretaker had not gone to the village, after all, and was now wishing that he had. Or it might be, of course, that a fellow in Brinkley's sozzled condition did not require a definite object of the chase, but simply chased rainbows, so to speak, for the sake of the exercise.

I was inclining to this latter view, and wondering a little wistfully if there mightn't be a chance of him falling downstairs and breaking his neck, when I found that I had been wrong. For some minutes the noise had grown somewhat fainter, activities seeming to have shifted to some distant part of the house; but now it suddenly hotted up again. I heard feet clattering downstairs. Then there was a terrific crash. And immediately after that the back door was burst open, and out shot a human form. It whizzed rapidly in my direction, tripped over something, and came a purler almost at my feet. And I was about to commend my soul to God and jump on its gizzard, hoping for the best, when something in the tone of the comments it was making – a sort of educated profanity which seemed to give evidence of a better bringing-up than Brinkley could possibly have had – made me pause.

I bent down. My diagnosis had been correct. It was Sir Roderick Glossop.

I was just going to introduce myself and institute inquiries, when the back door swung open again and another figure appeared.

'And stay out!' it observed, with a good deal of bitterness.

The voice was Brinkley's. It was some small pleasure to me at a none too festive time to note that he was rubbing his left shin.

The door slammed, and I heard the bolts shot. The next moment, a tenor voice rendering 'Rock of Ages' showed that, as far as Brinkley was concerned, the episode was concluded.

Sir Roderick had scrambled to his feet, and was standing puffing a good bit, as if touched in the wind. I was not surprised for the going had been fast.

It struck me as a good moment to start the dialogue.

'What ho, what ho!' I said.

It seemed to be rather my fate on this particular night to stir up my fellow man, not to mention my fellow scullerymaid. But, judging by results, the magnetic force of my personality appeared to be a bit on the wane. I mean to say, while the scullerymaid had had hysterics and Chuffy had jumped a foot, this Glossop merely quivered like something in aspic when joggled on the dish. But this, of course, may have been because that was all he was physically able to do. These breathers with Brinkley take it out of a man.

'It's all right,' I continued, anxious to set him at his ease and remove the impression that what was murmuring in his ear was some fearful creature of the night. 'Only B. Wooster—'

'Mr Wooster!'

'Absolutely.'

'Good God!' he said, becoming a little more tranquil, though still far from the life and soul of the party. 'Woof!'

And there the matter rested, while he took in a supply of life-giving air. I remained silent. We Woosters do not intrude at such a time.

Presently the puffing died away to a soft whiffle. He took about another minute and a half off. And, when he spoke, there was something so subdued, so what you might call quavering, about his voice that I came within a toucher of placing a kindly arm around his shoulder and telling him to cheer up.

'No doubt you are wondering, Mr Wooster, what is the explanation of all this?'

I still wasn't quite equal to the kindly arm, but I did bestow a sort of encouraging pat.

'Not a bit,' I said. 'Not a bit. I know all. I am abreast of the whole situation. I heard what had happened at the Hall, and directly I saw you shoot out of that door I knew what must have occurred here. You were planning to spend the night in the Dower House, weren't you?'

'I was. If you have really been apprised of what took place at Chuffnell Hall, Mr Wooster, you are aware that I am in the unfortunate position of . . .'

'. . being blacked out. I know. So am I.'

'You!'

'Yes. It's a long story, and I couldn't tell you, anyway, because it's by way of being secret history, but you can take it from me that we are both in the same fix.'

'But this is astonishing!'

'You can't go back to your hotel, and I can't get up to London till we have taken the make-up off.'

'Good God!'

'It seems to bring us very close together, what?'

He breathed deeply.

'Mr Wooster, we have had our differences in the past. The fault may have been mine. I cannot say. But in this crisis we must forget them and – er—'

'Stick together?'

'Precisely.'

'We will,' I said cordially. 'Speaking for myself, I decided to let the dead past bury its dead when I heard that you had been giving little Seabury one or two on the spot indicated.'

I heard him snort.

'You are aware what that abominable boy did to me, Mr Wooster?'

'Rather. And what you did to him. I am thoroughly posted up to the time you left the Hall. What happened after that?'

'Almost immediately after I had done so, the realization of my terrible position came upon me.'

'Nasty jar, I imagine?'

'The shock was of the severest. I was at a complete loss. The only course it seemed possible to pursue was to seek refuge somewhere for the night. And, knowing the Dower House to be unoccupied, I repaired thither.' He shuddered. 'Mr Wooster, that house is – I speak in all seriousness – an Inferno.'

He puffed awhile.

'I am not alluding to the presence on the premises of what appeared to me to be a dangerous lunatic. I mean that the whole place is congested with living organisms. Mice, Mr Wooster! And small dogs. And I think I saw a monkey.'

'Eh?'

'I remember now that Lady Chuffnell informed me that her son had started to maintain an establishment of these creatures, but at the moment it had slipped my mind, and the experience came upon me without warning or preparation.'

'Of course, yes. Seabury breeds things. I remember him telling me. And you were snootered by the menagerie?'

He stirred in the darkness. I fancy he was mopping the b.

'Shall I tell you of my experiences beneath that roof, Mr Wooster?'

'Do,' I said cordially. 'We have the night before us.'

He handkerchiefed the brow once more.

'It was a nightmare. I had scarcely entered the place when a voice addressed me from a dark corner of the kitchen, which was the room in which I first found myself. 'I see you, you old muddler,' was the phrase it employed.'

'Dashed familiar.'

'I need scarcely tell you what consternation it occasioned me. I bit my tongue severely. Then, divining that the speaker was merely a parrot, I hastened from the room. I had scarcely reached the stairs when I observed a hideous form. A little, short, broad, bow-legged individual with long arms and a dark wizened face. He was wearing clothes of some description and he walked rapidly, lurching from side to side and gibbering. In my present cool frame of mind I realize that it must have been a monkey, but at the time . . .'

'What a home!' I said sympathetically. 'Add little Seabury, and what a home! How about the mice?'

'They came later. Allow me, if you will, to adhere to the chronological sequence of my misadventures, or I shall be unable to relate the story coherently. The room in which I next found myself appeared to be completely filled with small dogs. They pounced upon me, snuffling and biting at me. I escaped and entered another room. Here at last, I was saying to myself, even in this sinister and ill-omened house there must be peace. Mr Wooster, I had hardly framed the thought when something ran up my right trouser leg. I sprang to one side, and in so doing upset what appeared to be a box or cage of some kind. I found myself in a sea of mice. I detest the creatures. I endeavoured to brush them off. They clung the more. I fled from the room, and I had scarcely reached the stairs when this lunatic appeared and pursued me. He pursued me up and down stairs, Mr Wooster!'

I nodded understandingly.

'We all go through it,' I said. 'I had the same experience.'

'You?'

'Rather. He nearly got me with a carving knife.'

'As far as I could discern, the weapon he carried was more of the order of a chopper.'

'He varies,' I explained. 'Now the carving knife, anon the chopper. Versatile chap. It's the artistic temperament, I suppose.'

'You speak as if you knew this man.'

'I do more than know him. I employ him. He's my valet.'

'Your valet?'

'Fellow named Brinkley. He won't be my valet long, mind you. If he ever simmers down enough for me to get near him and give him the sack. Ironical, that, when you come to think of it,' I said, for I was in philosophic mood. 'I mean, do you realize that I'm giving this chap a salary all this time? In other words, he's actually being paid to chivvy me about with carving knives. If that's not Life,' I said thoughtfully, 'what is?'

It seemed to take the old boy a moment or two to drink this in.

'Your valet? Then what is he doing in the Dower House?'

'Oh, he's a mobile sort of fellow, you know. Now here, now there. He flits. He was at the Hall not long ago.'

'I never heard of such a thing.'

'New to me, too, I must confess. Well, you're certainly having a lively night. This'll last you, what? I mean, you won't need any more excitement for months and months and months.'

'Mr Wooster, my earnest hope is that the entire remainder of my existence will be one round of unruffled monotony. Tonight I have seemed to sense the underlying horror of life. You do not suppose that there could possibly be mice on my person still?'

'You must have shaken them off, I should say. You were pretty active, you know. I could only hear you, of course, but you seemed to be leaping from crag to crag, as it were.'

'Certainly I spared no effort to elude this man Brinkley. It was merely that I fancied I felt something nibbling at my left shoulder-blade.'

'You've had quite a night, haven't you?'

'A truly terrible night. I shall not readily recover a normal tranquillity of mind. My pulse is still high, and I do not like the way my heart is beating. However, by a merciful good fortune, all has ended well. You will be able to give me the shelter I so sorely need in your cottage. And there with the assistance of a little soap and water I shall be able to wash off this distasteful blacking.'

I saw that this was where I had to start breaking things gently to him.

'You can't get that stuff off with soap and water. I've tried. You have to have butter.'

'The point strikes me as immaterial. You can provide butter, no doubt?'

'Sorry. No butter.'

There must be butter in your cottage.'

'There isn't. And why? Because there isn't a cottage.'

'I cannot understand you.'

'It's burned down.'

'What?'

'Yes. Brinkley did it.'

'Good God!'

'A nuisance in many ways, I must confess.'

He was silent for a space. Turning the thing over in his mind. Looking at it from this angle and that.

'Your cottage is really burned down?'

'Heap of ashes.'

'Then what is to be done?'

It seemed time to point out the silver lining.

'Be of good cheer,' I said. 'We may not be so well off for cottages, but the butter situation, I am happy to say, is reasonably bright. We can't get any tonight, but it cometh in the morning, so to speak. Jeeves is going to bring me some as soon as the dairyman delivers.'

'But I cannot remain in this condition till morning.'

'Only course to pursue, I'm afraid.'

He brooded. Hard to see in the darkness, but discontentedly, I thought, as if his haughty spirit fretted somewhat. He must have been doing some good, solid thinking, too, because suddenly he came to life with an idea.

'This cottage of yours – had it a garage?'

'Oh, yes.'

'Was that burned down also?'

'No, I fancy it escaped the holocaust. It was well away from the scene of conflagration.'

'Is there petrol in it?'

'Oh, yes. Lots of petrol.'

'Why, then all is well, Mr Wooster. I am convinced that petrol will prove a cleansing agent equally as efficacious as butter.'

'But, dash it, you can't go to my garage.'

'Why not, pray?'

'Well, yes, you could, if you liked, I suppose. Not me, though. For reasons which I am not prepared to divulge, I propose to spend the rest of the night in the summer-house on the main lawn of the Hall.'

'You will not accompany me?'

'Sorry. No.'

'Then good night, Mr Wooster. I will not keep you any longer from your rest. I am greatly obliged to you for the assistance you have accorded me in a trying situation. We must see more of one another. Let us lunch together one of these days. How do I obtain access to this garage of yours?'

'You'll have to bust a window.'

'I will do so.'

He pushed off, full of buck and determination, and I, with a dubious shake of the old onion, trickled along towards the summer-house.

# =17=
## BREAKFAST-TIME AT THE HALL

I DON'T know if you have ever spent the night in a summer-house. If not, avoid making the experiment. It's not a thing I would advise any friend of mine to do. On the subject of sleeping in summer-houses I will speak out fearlessly. As far as I have been able to ascertain, such a binge doesn't present a single attractive feature. Apart from the inevitable discomfort in the fleshy parts, there's the cold, and apart from the cold there's the mental anguish. All the ghost stories you've ever read go flitting through the mind, particularly any you know where fellows are found next morning absolutely dead, without a mark on them but with such a look of horror and fear in their eyes that the search party draw in their breath a bit and gaze at each other as much as to say "What ho!" Things creak. You fancy you hear stealthy footsteps. You receive the impression that a goodish quota of skinny hands are reaching out for you in the darkness. And, as I say, the cold extremely severe and much discomfort in the fleshy parts. The whole constituting a pretty sticky experience and one to be avoided by the knowledgeable.

And what made the thing so dashed poignant in my case was the thought that if I had only had the nerve to accompany intrepid old Glossop to the garage there would have been no need for me to stay marooned in this smelly structure, listening to the wind howling through the chinks in the woodwork. Once at the garage, I mean to say, I could not only have scoured the face but could have hopped into the old two-seater, which was champing at its bit there, and tooled off to London by road, singing a gipsy song, as it were.

And I simply couldn't muster up the nerve to take a pop at it. The garage, I reflected, was right in the danger zone, well inside the Voules and Dobson belt, and I absolutely could not face the possibility of running into Police-Sergeant Voules and being detained and questioned. Those meetings with him the night before had shattered my *moral*, causing me to look upon this hell-hound of the Law as a sleepless prowler who rambled incessantly and was bound to appear out of a trap just at the moment when you could best have done without him.

So I stayed where I was. I hitched myself into position forty-six in the hope that it would be easier on the f.p's than the last forty-five, and had another shot at the dreamless.

The thing that always beats me is how on these occasions one ever gets to sleep at all. Personally, I abandoned all idea of it at an early stage, and no one, accordingly, could have been more surprised than myself when, just as I was endeavouring to give the miss to a leopard which was biting me rather shrewdly in the seat of the trousers, I suddenly awoke to discover that it had been but a dream, that in reality no leopards were to be noticed among those present, that the sun was up and another day had begun, and that on the greensward without the early bird was already break-fasting and making the dickens of a noise about it, too.

I went to the door and looked out. I could hardly believe that it was really morning. But it was, and a dashed good morning, at that. The air was cool and fresh, there were long shadows across the lawn, and everything combined to give the soul such a kick that many fellows in my position would have taken off their socks and done rhythmic dances in the dew. I did not actually do that, but I certainly felt uplifted to no little extent, and you might say that I was simply so much pure spirit, without any material side to me whatsoever, when suddenly it was as if the old tum had come out of a trance with a jerk, and the next moment I was feeling that nothing mattered in this world or the next except about a quart of coffee and all the eggs and b. you could cram on to a dish.

It's a rummy thing about breakfast. When you've only to press a bell to have the domestic staff racing in with everything on the menu from oatmeal to jams, marmalades, and potted meats, you find that all you can look at is a glass of soda water and a rusk. When you can't get it, you feel like a python when the Zoo officials have just started to bang the luncheon gong. Speaking for myself, I have, as a rule, to be more or less lured to the feast. I mean to say, I don't as a general thing become what you might call breakfast-conscious till I've had my morning tea and rather thought things over a bit. And I can give no better indication of the extraordinary change which had come over my viewpoint now than by mentioning that there was a young fowl of sorts not far away engaged in getting outside a large, pink worm, and I could willingly have joined it at the board. In fact, I would have taken pot luck at this juncture with a buzzard.

My watch had stopped, so I couldn't tell what time it was: and another thing I didn't know was when Jeeves was planning to go to the Dower House to keep our tryst. The thought that he might even now be on his way there and that, if he didn't find me, he would give the thing up as a bad job and retire to some impregnable fastness in the back parts of the Hall gave me a very nasty turn. I left the summer-house and, taking to the bushes, began to work my way through them, treading like a Red Indian on the trail and keeping well under cover throughout.

And I was just navigating round the side of the house and making ready for the dash into the open, when through the french window of the morning-room I saw a spectacle which affected me profoundly. In fact, you'd be about right if you said that it seemed to speak to my very depths.

Inside the room, a parlourmaid was placing a large tray on a table.

The sunlight, streaming in, lit up this parlourmaid's hair: and, noting its auburn hue, I deduced that she must be Mary, the betrothed of Constable Dobson: and at any other time the fact would have been of interest. But I was in no mood now to subject the girl to a critical scrutiny with a view to ascertaining whether the constable had picked a winner or not. My whole attention was earmarked for that tray.

It was a well-laden tray. There was a coffee-pot on it, also toast in considerable quantity, and furthermore a covered dish. It was this last that touched the spot. Under that cover there might be eggs, there might be bacon, there might be sausages, there might be kidneys, or there might be kippers. I could not tell. But whatever there was it was all right with Bertram.

For I had laid my plans and formed my schemes. The girl was on her way out by this time, and I estimated that I had possibly fifty seconds for the stern task before me. Allow twenty for nipping in, three for snaffling the works, and another twenty-five for getting back into the bushes again, and one had all the makings of a successful enterprise.

The moment the door closed I was speeding on my way. I recked little whether anybody saw me, and I should imagine that, had there been eyewitnesses, all they would have seen would have been a sort of blur. I did the first leg of the journey well inside the estimated time, and I had just laid hand on the tray and was about to lift and remove, when there came from outside the door the sound of footsteps.

It was a moment for swift thought, and such moments find Bertram Wooster at his best.

This morning-room, I should mention, was not the small morning-room where Dwight and little Seabury had had their epoch-making turn-up. In fact, I am rather misleading my public in alluding to it as a morning-room at all. It was really a study or office, being the place where Chuffy did his estate business, totted up his bills, brooded over the growing cost of agricultural apparatus, and gave the tenants the bird when they called to ask him to knock a bit off their rent. And as you can't get very far with that sort of thing unless you have a pretty good-sized desk, Chuffy had most fortunately had one put in. It stood across one whole corner of the room, and it seemed to beckon to me.

Two and a half seconds later, I was behind it, crouching on the carpet and trying to breathe solely through the pores.

The next moment, the door opened, and somebody came in. Feet crossed the floor, right up to the desk, and I heard the click as the hidden hand removed the telephone receiver.

'Chuffnell Regis, two-niyun-four,' said a voice, and conceive the sudden rush of relief when I recognized it as one that I had many a time shaken hands with in the past – the voice, in short, of a friend in need.

'Oh, Jeeves,' I said, popping up like a jack-in-the-box.

You can't rattle Jeeves. Where scullery maids had had hysterics and members of the Peerage had leaped and quivered, he simply regarded me with respectful serenity and, after a civil good morning, went on with the job in hand. He is a fellow who likes to do things in their proper order.

'Chuffnell Regis two-niyun-four? The Seaview Hotel? Could you inform me if Sir Roderick Glossop is in his room? . . . Not yet returned? . . . Thank you.'

He hung up the receiver, and was now at liberty to give the late young master a spot of attention.

'Good morning, sir,' he said again. 'I was not expecting to see you here.'

'I know, but . . .'

'I had supposed that the arrangement was that we should meet at the Dower House.'

I shuddered a bit.

'Jeeves,' I said, 'one brief word about the Dower House, and then I should like the subject shelved indefinitely. I know you meant well. I know that when you sent me there your motives were pure to the last drop. But the fact remains that you were dispatching me to a nasty salient. Do you know who was lurking in that House of Fear? Brinkley. Complete with chopper.'

'I am very sorry to hear that, sir. Then I assume that you did not sleep there last night?'

'No, Jeeves, I did not. I slept – if you can call it sleeping – in a summer-house. And I was just creeping round through the bushes to try to find you, when I saw that parlourmaid setting out food on the table in here.'

'His lordship's breakfast, sir.'

'Where is he?'

'He should be down shortly, sir. It is a most fortunate chance that her ladyship should have instructed me to ring up the Seaview Hotel. Otherwise we might have experienced some difficulty in establishing connection.'

'Yes. What was all that, by the way? That Seaview Hotel stuff.'

'Her ladyship is somewhat exercised in her mind about Sir Roderick, sir. I fancy that on reflection she has reached the conclusion that she did not treat him well last night.'

'Mother Love not so hot this morning?'

'No, sir.'

'And it's a case of "Return and all will be forgiven"?'

'Precisely, sir. But unfortunately, Sir Roderick appears to be missing, and we can secure no information as to what has become of him.'

I was in a position, of course, to explain and clarify, and I did so without delay.

'He's all right. After an invigorating session with Brinkley, he went to my garage to get petrol. Was he correct in supposing that that would clean him as well as butter?'

'Yes, sir.'

'Then I should think he was on his way to London by now, if not actually in the Metropolis.'

'I will notify her ladyship at once, sir. I imagine that the information will serve sensibly to lessen her anxiety.'

'You really think she loves him still and wishes to extend the *amende honorable*?'

'Or olive branch? Yes, sir. So, at least, I divined from her demeanour. I was left with the impression that all the old love and esteem were in operation once more.'

'And I'm very glad to hear it,' I said cordially. 'For I must tell you, Jeeves, that since we last got together I have completely changed my mind about the above Glossop. I see now that there is much good in him. In the silent watches of the night we formed what you wouldn't be far out in describing as a beautiful friendship. We discovered each other's hidden merits, and he left showering invitations to lunch.'

'Indeed, sir?'

'Absolutely. From now on, there will always be a knife and fork for Bertram at the Glossop lair, and the same for Roddy *chez* Bertram.'

'Very gratifying, sir.'

'Most. So if you're chatting with Lady Chuffnell in the near future, you can tell her that the match now has my full approval and sanction. But all this, Jeeves,' I proceeded, striking the practical note, 'is beside the point. The main issue is that I am sorely in need of nourishment, and I want that tray. So hand it across and look slippy.'

'You are proposing to eat his lordship's breakfast, sir?'

'Jeeves,' I said emotionally, and was about to go on to add that, if he had any doubts as to what I was proposing to do to that breakfast, he could remove them by standing to one side and watching me get into action, when once more I heard footsteps in the passage outside.

Instead of speaking along these lines, accordingly, I blenched, as near as a fellow can blench when his face is all covered with boot polish, and broke off with a brief heart-cry. Once more I perceived that it had become imperative that I vanish from the scene.

These footsteps, I must mention, were of the solid, sturdy, shoe-number-eleven type. It was natural, therefore, that I should assume that it was Chuffy who now stood without. And to encounter Chuffy, I need scarcely say, would have been foreign to my policy. I have already indicated with, I think, sufficient clearness, that he was not in sympathy with my aims and objects. That interview we had had on the previous night had shown me that he was to be reckoned as essentially one of the opposition – a hostile element and a menace. Let him discover me here, and the first thing I knew he would be locking me up somewhere in a spirit of chivalrous zeal and sending messengers to old Stoker to drop round and collect.

Long, therefore, before the handle had turned I was down in the depths like a diving duck.

The door opened. A female voice spoke. No doubt that of the future Mrs Constable Dobson.

'Mr Stoker,' it announced.

Large, flat feet clumped into the room.

# =18=
# BLACK WORK IN A STUDY

I WEDGED myself a little tighter in behind the old zareba. Not so good, not so good, a voice seemed to be whispering in my ear. Of all the unpleasant contingencies which could have arisen, this seemed to me about the scaliest. Whatever might have been said against Chuffnell Hall – and recent events had tended considerably to lessen its charm in my eyes – I had supposed that you could put forward at least one thing in its favour, viz. that there was no possible chance of encountering J. Washburn Stoker on the premises. And, in spite of having my time fairly fully occupied with feeling like a jelly, I was still able to experience quite a spot of honest indignation at what I considered a dashed unjustifiable intrusion on his part.

I mean to say, if a man has thrown his weight about in a stately home of England, ticking off the residents and asserting positively that he jolly well isn't going to darken its doors again, he has no right to come strolling in barely two days later as if the place were an hotel with "Welcome" on the mat. I felt pretty strongly about the whole thing.

I was also wondering how Jeeves would handle this situation. By this time a shrewd bloke like this Stoker was bound to have guessed that his were the brains behind my escape, and it seemed not unlikely that he would make some tentative move towards scattering these brains on the hearthrug. His voice, when he spoke, undoubtedly indicated that some such idea was floating in his mind. It was harsh and roopy, and though all that he actually said by way of a start was "Ah!" a determined man can get a lot of meaing into an "Ah!"

'Good morning, sir,' said Jeeves.

This business of lying curled up behind desks cuts both ways. It has its advantages and its drawbacks. Purely from the standpoint of the slinking fugitive, of course, fine. Indeed, could scarcely be bettered. But against this must be set the fact that it undoubtedly hampers a chap in his capacity of audience. The effect now was much the same as if I had been listening-in to a dramatic sketch on the wireless. I got the voices, but I missed the play of expression. And I'd have given a lot to be able to see it. Not Jeeves's, of course, because Jeeves never has any. But Stoker's, it seemed to me, would have been well worth more than a casual glance.

'So you're here, are you?'

'Yes, sir.'

The next item was an extremely nasty laugh from the visitor. One of those hard, short, sharp ones.

'I came here because I wanted information about where Mr Wooster has got to. I thought that Lord Chuffnell might possibly have seen him. I never reckoned I should run into you. Say, listen,' said the Stoker disease, suddenly hotting up, 'do you know what I've a mind to do to you?'

'No, sir.'

'Break your damned neck.'

'Indeed, sir?'

'Yes.'

I heard Jeeves cough.

'A little extreme, sir, surely? I can appreciate that the fact that I decided – somewhat abruptly, I admit – to leave your employment and return to that of his lordship should occasion displeasure on your part, but . . .'

'You know what I'm talking about. Or are you going to deny that it was you who smuggled that guy Wooster off my yacht?'

'No, sir. I admit that I was instrumental in restoring his liberty to Mr Wooster. In the course of a conversation which I had with him, Mr Wooster informed me that he was being detained on the vessel *ultra vires*, and, acting in your best interests, I released him. At that time, you will recall, sir, I was in your employment, and I felt it my duty to save you from what might have been an extremely serious contretemps.'

I couldn't see, of course, but I received the impression from a certain amount of gurgling and snorting which he put in during these remarks that old Stoker would have been glad to have the floor a bit earlier. I could have told him it wasn't any good. You can't switch Jeeves off when he has something to say which he feels will be of interest. The only thing is to stand by and wait till he runs down.

But though he had now done so, it wasn't right away that the party of the second part stated anything in the nature of a counter-speech. I imagine that the substance of Jeeves's little talk had given him food for thought.

In this conjecture, it appeared that I was correct. Old Stoker breathed a bit tensely for a while, then he spoke in almost an awed voice. It's often that way when you get up against Jeeves. He has a way of suggesting new viewpoints.

'Are you crazy or am I?'

'Sir?'

'Save *me*, did you say, from—?'

'A contretemps? Yes, sir. I cannot make the assertion authoritatively, for I am not certain to what extent the fact that Mr Wooster came on board the yacht of his own volition would weigh with a jury . . .'

'Jury?'

'. . . but his detention on the vessel despite his expressed desire to leave would, I am inclined to imagine, constitute an act of kidnapping, the penalties for which, as you are no doubt aware, sir, are very severe.'

'But, say, listen . . . !'

'England is an extremely law-abiding country, sir, and offences which might pass unnoticed in your own land are prosecuted here with the greatest rigour. My knowledge of legal *minutiæ* is, I regret to say, slight, so I cannot asseverate with perfect confidence that this detention of Mr Wooster would have ranked as an act in contravention of the criminal code, and, as such, liable to punishment with penal servitude, but undoubtedly, had I not intervened, the young gentleman would have been in a position to bring a civil action and mulct you in very substantial damages. So, acting, as I say, in your best interests, sir, I released Mr Wooster.'

There was a silence.

'Thanks,' said old Stoker mildly.

'Not at all, sir.'

'Thank you very much.'

'I did what I considered the only thing that could avert a most disagreeable contingency, sir.'

'Darned good of you.'

I must say I can't see why Jeeves shouldn't go down in legend and song. Daniel did, on the strength of putting in half an hour or so in the lions' den and leaving the dumb chums in a condition of suavity and *camaraderie*; and if what Jeeves had just done wasn't entitled to rank well above a feat like that, I'm no judge of form. In less than five minutes he had reduced this ravening Stoker from a sort of human wildcat to a positive domestic pet. If I hadn't been there and heard it, I wouldn't have believed it was possible.

'I've got to think about this,' said old Stoker, milder than ever.

'Yes, sir.'

'I hadn't looked at it that way before. Yes, sir, I've got to think about this. I believe I'll go for a walk and mull it over in my mind. Lord Chuffnell hasn't seen Mr Wooster, has he?'

'Not since last night, sir.'

'Oh, he saw him last night, did he? Which way was he headed?'

'I rather fancy it was Mr Wooster's intention to pass the night in the Dower House and return to London today.'

'The Dower House? That's that place across the park?'

'Yes, sir.'

'I might look in there. It seems to me the first thing I've got to do is have a talk with Mr Wooster.'

'Yes, sir.'

I heard him go out through the french window, but it wasn't till another moment or two had passed that I felt justified in coming to the surface. It being reasonable to suppose by then that the coast was clear, I poked the head up over the desk.

'Jeeves,' I said, and if there were tears in the eyes, what of it? We Woosters are not afraid to confess honest emotion, 'there is none like you, none.'

'It is extremely kind of you to say so, sir.'

'It was all I could do to keep from leaping out and shaking your hand.'

'It would scarcely have been judicious, in the circumstances, sir.'

'That's what I thought. Your father wasn't a snake-charmer, was he, Jeeves?'

'No, sir.'

'It just crossed my mind. What do you think will happen when old Stoker gets to the Dower House?'

'We can only conjecture, sir.'

'My fear is that Brinkley may have slept it off by now.'

'There is that possibility, sir.'

'Still, it was a kindly thought, sending the fellow there, and we must hope for the best. After all, Brinkley still has that chopper. I say, do you think Chuffy is really coming down?'

'At any moment, I fancy, sir.'

'Then you wouldn't advise my eating his breakfast?'

'No, sir.'

'But I'm starving, Jeeves.'

'I am extremely sorry, sir. The position at the moment is a little difficult. Later on, no doubt, I may be able to alleviate your distress.'

'Have you had breakfast, Jeeves?'

'Yes, sir.'

'What did you have?'

'The juice of an orange, sir, followed by Cute Crispies — an American cereal — scrambled eggs with a slice of bacon, and toast and marmalade.'

'Oh, gosh! The whole washed down, no doubt, with a cup of strengthening coffee?'

'Yes, sir.'

'Oh, my God! You really don't think I could just sneak a single sausage?'

'I would scarcely advocate it, sir. And it is a small point, but his lordship is having kippers.'

'Kippers!'

'And this, I fancy, will be his lordship coming now, sir.'

So down once more into the lower levels for Bertram. And I had hardly fitted myself into the groove when the door opened.

A voicy spoke.

'Why, hallo, Jeeves.'

'Good morning, miss.'

It was Pauline Stoker.

I must say I was a bit peeved. Chuffnell Hall, whatever its other defects, should, as I have pointed out, have been entirely free from Stokers. And here they were, absolutely over-running the place like mice. I was quite prepared to find something breathing in my ear and look round and see little Dwight. I mean to say, I was feeling — bitterly, I admit — that if this was going to be Old Home Week of Stokers, one might as well make the thing complete.

Pauline had begun to sniff vigorously.

'What's that I smell, Jeeves?'

'Kippered herrings, miss.'

'Whose?'

'His lordship's, miss.'

'Oh. I haven't had breakfast yet, Jeeves.'

'No, miss?'

'No. Father yanked me out of bed and had me half-way here before I was properly awake. He's all worked up, Jeeves.'

'Yes, miss. I have just been having a conversation with Mr Stoker. He did appear somewhat overwrought.'

'All the way here he was talking about what he was going to do if he ever found you again. And now you tell me he did find you. What happened? Didn't he eat you?'

'No, miss.'

'Probably on a diet. Well, where has he got to? They told me he was in here.'

'Mr Stoker left a moment ago with the intention of visiting the Dower House, miss. I think he hoped to find Mr Wooster there.'

'Somebody ought to warn that poor sap.'

'You need experience no anxiety for Mr Wooster, miss. He is not at the Dower House.'

'Where is he?'

'Elsewhere, miss.'

'Not that I care where he is. Do you remember my telling you last night, Jeeves, that I was thinking of becoming Mrs Bertram W.?'

'Yes, miss.'

'Well, I'm not. So you needn't save up for that fish slice, after all. I've changed my mind.'

'I am glad to hear that, miss.'

So was I. Her words were music to my ears.

'Glad, are you?'

'Yes, miss. I doubt whether the union would have been a successful one. Mr Wooster is an agreeable young gentleman, but I would describe him as essentially one of Nature's bachelors.'

'Besides being mentally negligible?'

'Mr Wooster is capable of acting very shrewdly on occasion, miss.'

'So am I. And that is why I say that, no matter if father does tear the roof off, I am not going to marry that poor, persecuted lamb. Why should I? I've nothing against him.'

There was a pause.

'I've just been talking to Lady Chuffnell, Jeeves.'

'Yes, miss.'

'Apparently she has had a little domestic trouble, too.'

'Yes, miss. There was an unfortunate rift between her ladyship and Sir Roderick Glossop last night. Now, I am glad to say, her ladyship appears to have thought matters over and decided that she made a mistake in severing relations with the gentleman.'

'One does think things over, doesn't one?'

'Almost invariably, miss.'

'And a fat lot of use that is, if the severed relation doesn't think them over too. Have you seen Lord Chuffnell this morning, Jeeves?'

'Yes, miss.'

'How was he looking?'

'Somewhat worried, it seemed to me, miss.'

'He was?'

'Yes, miss.'

'H'm. Well, I won't keep you from your professional duties, Jeeves: smack into them right away, as far as I'm concerned.'

'Thank you, miss. Good morning.'

For some moments after the door closed I remained motionless. I was passing the position of affairs under thoughtful review. To a certain extent you might say that relief was tingling through the veins like some rare wine, causing satisfaction and mental uplift. In the plainest possible language, weighing her words and speaking without dubiety or equivocation, this girl Pauline had stated that not even the strongest measures on the part of her father would induce her to shove on the old bridal veil and step up the aisle at my side. So far, so good.

But has she thoroughly estimated that father's powers of persuasion? That was what I asked myself. Had she ever seen him when he was really going good? Was she aware of what a Force he could be when in mid-season form? In a word, did she realize what she was up against, and know that to attempt to thwart J. Washburn Stoker, when in spate, was like entering a jungle and taking on the first couple of wildcats you encountered?

It was this thought which prevented my rapture from being complete. It seemed to me that, in opposing her will to that of a bally retired pirate like this male parent of hers, the frail girl was going out of her class and that her resistance to his matrimonial plans would be useless.

And I was musing thus when I suddenly heard the sloosh of coffee in a cup, and a moment later there came what Drexdale Yeats would have called a metallic clang, and with profound emotion I divined that Pauline, unable to resist the sight of that tray any longer, had poured herself out a steaming beaker and was getting at the kippers. For there was no longer any possible room for doubt as to the correctness of Jeeves's information. It was the scent of kippered herrings that was now wafted to me like a benediction, and I clenched my fists till the knuckles stood out white beneath the strain. I could mark every mouthful and each in turn went through me like a knife.

It's odd, the effect hunger has on one. You can't tell what you will do under the stress of it. Let the most level-headed bird get really peckish, and he will throw prudence to the winds. I did so at this point. Obviously the sound scheme was for me to remain under cover and wait till all these Stokers and what not blew over, and that was the policy which, in a calmer frame of mind, I would have pursued. But the smell of those kippers and the knowledge that with every moment that passed they were melting away like snow upon the mountain tops and that pretty soon all the toast would be gone as well, was too powerful for me. I came up from behind that desk like a minnow on a hook.

'Hi!' I said, speaking with a strong note of pleading in my voice.

It's rummy how experience never teaches us. I had seen the reaction of the scullerymaid to my sudden appearance. I had noted its effect on old Chuffy. And I had watched Sir Roderick Glossop at the moment of impact. Yet here I was, bobbing up in just the same sudden fashion as before.

And exactly the same thing happened again. If anything, rather more so. At the moment, Pauline Stoker was busy with a mouthful of kipper, and this for the nonce cramped her freedom of expression, so that all that occurred for about a second and a quarter was that a pair of horrified eyes stared into mine. Then the barrier of kipper gave way, and one of the most devastating yowls of terror I've ever heard in my puff ripped through the air.

It coincided with the opening of the door and the appearance on the threshold of the fifth Baron Chuffnell. And the next moment he had dashed at her and gathered her in his arms, and she had dashed at him and been gathered.

They couldn't have done it more neatly if they had been rehearsing for weeks.

# =19=
# PREPARATIONS FOR HANDLING FATHER

I ALWAYS maintain that it is by a chap's behaviour on this sort of occasion that you can really weigh him in the balance and judge if he's got the right chivalrous delicacy in him or not. It is the acid test. Come to me and say to me "Wooster, you know me pretty well. Tell me something. To settle a bet, would you consider that I was a *preux chevalier*, as the expression is?" and I reply "My dear Bates, or Cutherbertson, or whatever the name may be, I shall be able to answer that question better if you will indicate what you would do if you happened to be in a room where two loving hearts, after a painful misunderstanding, were in the process of getting together again on a basis of chumminess and mutual esteem. Would you duck down behind the desk? Or would you stand there and drink the performance in with bulging eyes?"

My own views are rigid. When a lovers' rconciliation is in progress, I do not remain goggling. As far as the conditions will permit, I withdraw and leave them to it.

But though, with the desk between us, I could not see these two, I could hear them, and most unpleasant it was. I have known Chuffy, as I say, practically from childhood, and in the course of the years I have seen him in a variety of differing circumstances and in many moods. And I never would have believed him capable of the revolting slush which now proceeded from his lips at the rate of about two hundred and fifty words to the minute. When I tell you that the observation "There, there, little girl!" was the only one I can bring myself to quote, you will be able to gather something of the ordeal to which I was subjected. And, to make matters worse, on an empty stomach, mind you.

Pauline, meanwhile, was contributing little or nothing to the dialogue. Until this moment I had considered that, in the matter of emotional reaction to my appearance, the scullerymaid had set a mark at which others who met me suddenly might shoot in vain.

But Pauline eclipsed her completely. She remained in Chuffy's arms gurgling like a leaky radiator, and it was only quite some little time later that she began to regain anything of a grip on her faculties. The girl seemed goofy.

I suppose the fact of the matter was that at the moment when I manifested myself she was undergoing considerable mental strain, and that my appearance served, as it were, to put the tin hat on it. At any rate, she continued to give this radiator impersonation of hers so long that in the end it seemed to strike Chuffy that it was about time he switched off the murmured endearments and got down to first causes.

'But, darling,' I heard him say. 'What was it, angel? What scared you, sweetheart? Tell me, precious. Did you see something, pet?'

It seemed to me that the moment had come to join the meeting. I rose above the top of the desk, and Pauline shied like a frightened horse. It annoyed me, I confess. Bertram Wooster is not accustomed to causing convulsions in the gentler sex. As a matter of fact, usually when girls see me, they incline rather to the amused smile, or, on occasion, to the weary sigh and the despairing "Oh, are *you* here again, Bertie?" But better even that than this stark horror.

'Hallo, Chuffy,' I said. 'Nice day.'

You might have thought that relief would have been the emotion uppermost in Pauline Stoker's bosom on discovering that the cause of her panic was merely an old friend. But no. She absolutely glared at me.

'You poor goof,' she cried, 'what's the big idea, playing hide-and-go-seek like that and scaring people stiff? And I don't know if you know it, but you've got a smut on your face.'

Nor was Chuffy behindhand in the recriminations.

'Bertie!' he said, in a sort of moaning way. 'My God! I might have guessed it would be you. You really are without exception the most completely drivelling lunatic that was ever at large.'

I felt it was time to check this sort of thing pretty sharply.

'I regret,' I said, with a cold hauteur, 'that I startled this young fathead, but my motives in concealing myself behind that desk were based on prudence and sound reasoning. And, talking of lunatics, Chuffnell, don't forget that I was compelled to overhear what you have been saying for the last five minutes.'

I was pleased to see the blush of shame mantle his cheek. He shuffled uncomfortably.

'You oughtn't to have listened.'

'You don't imagine that I wanted to listen, do you?'

Something of defiance or bravado came into his manner.

'And why the devil shouldn't I talk like that? I love her, blast you, and I don't care who knows it.'

'Oh quite,' I said, with a scarcely veiled contempt.

'She's the most marvellous thing on earth.'

'No, you are, darling,' said Pauline.

'No, you are, angel,' said Chuffy.

'No, you are, sweetness.'

'No, you are, precious.'

'Please,' I said. 'Please!'

Chuffy gave me a nasty look.

'You were saying, Wooster?'

'Oh nothing.'

'I thought you made a remark.'

'Oh, no.'

'Good. You'd better not.'

The first nausea had worn off somewhat by this time, and it was a kindlier Bertram Wooster who now displayed himself. I am a broad-minded man, and I reflected charitably that it was wrong to be hard on a fellow in Chuffy's situation. After all, in the special circumstances he could scarcely be expected to preserve the decencies. I struck a conciliatory note.

'Chuffy, old man,' I said, 'we must not allow ourselves to brawl. This is a moment for the genial eye and the affable smile. No one could be more delighted than myself that you and this old friend of mine have buried the dead past and started all square again together. I may look on myself as an old friend, may I not?'

She beamed in a cordial manner.

'Well, I should hope so, you poor ditherer. Why, I knew you before I ever met Marmaduke.'

I turned to Chuffy.

'This Marmaduke business. I want to take that up with you some time. Fancy you keeping that dark all these years.'

'There's nothing wrong in being christened Marmaduke, is there?' said Chuffy, a little heatedly.

'Nothing wrong, no. But we shall all have a good laugh about it at the Drones.'

'Bertie,' said Chuffy tensely, 'if you breathe a word of it to those blighters at the Drones, I'll track you to the ends of the earth and strangle you with my bare hands.'

'Well, well, we must see, we must see. But, as I was saying, I am delighted that this reconciliation has taken place. Being, as I am, one of Pauline's closest friends. We had some pretty good times together in the old days, didn't we?'

'You bet.'

'That day at Piping Rock.'

'Ah.'

'And do you remember the night the car broke down and we were stranded for hours somewhere in the wilds of Westchester County in the rain?'

'I should say so.'

'Your feet got wet, and I very wisely took your stockings off.'

'Here!' said Chuffy.

'Oh, it's all right, old man. I conducted myself throughout with the nicest propriety. All I am trying to establish is that I am an old friend of Pauline's and am consequently entitled to rejoice at the present situation. There are few more charming girls than this P. Stoker, and you are lucky to have won her, old man, in spite of the fact that she is handicapped by possessing a father who bears a striking resemblance to something out of the Book of Revelations.'

'Father's a good enough egg if you rub him the right way.'

'You hear that, Chuffy? In rubbing this bally old thug, be sure to do it the right way.'

'He is not a bally old thug.'

'Pardon me. I appeal to Chuffy.'

Chuffy scratched his chin. Somewhat embarrassed.

'I must say, angel, he does strike me at times as a bit above the odds.'

'Exactly,' I said. 'And never forget that he is resolved that Pauline shall marry me.'

'What!'

'Didn't you know that? Oh, yes.'

Pauline was wearing a sort of Joan of Arc look.

'I'm darned if I'll marry you, Bertie.'

'The right spirit.' I said approvingly. 'But can you preserve that intrepid attitude when you see Pop breathing flame through his nostrils and chewing broken bottles in the foreground? Will you not, if I may coin a phrase, be afraid of the big bad wolf?'

She wavered a bit.

'We're going to have a tough time with him, of course. I can see that. He's pretty sore with you, angel, you know.'

Chuffy puffed out his chest.

'I'll attend to him!'

'No,' I said firmly, '*I* will attend to him. Leave the whole conduct of the affair to me.'

Pauline laughed. I didn't like it. It seemed to me to have a derogatory ring.

'You! Why, you poor lamb, you would run a mile if Father so much as said, "Boo!" to you.'

I raised the eyebrows.

'I anticipate no such contingency. Why should he say "Boo!" to me? I mean, a damn silly thing for anybody to say to anyone. And even if he did make that idiotic observation, the effects would not be such as you have outlined. That I was once a little on the nervous side in your parent's presence, I admit. But no longer. Not any more. The scales have fallen from my eyes. Recently I have seen him in the space of something under three minutes reduced by Jeeves from a howling blizzard to a gentle breeze, and his spell is broken. When he comes, you may leave him to me with every confidence. I shall not be rough with him, but I shall be very firm.'

Chuffy looked a bit thoughtful.

'Is he coming?'

Outside in the garden, footsteps had become audible. Also heavy breathing. I jerked a thumb at the window.

'This, if I mistake not, Watson,' I said, 'is our client now.'

# JEEVES HAS NEWS

A ND SO it was. A substantial form appeared against the summer sky. It entered. It took a seat. And, having taken a seat, it hauled out a handkerchief and started to mop the brow. A bit preoccupied, I divined, and my trained sense enabled me to recognize the symptoms. They were those of a man who had just been hobnobbing with Brinkley.

That this diagnosis was correct was proved a moment later when lowering the handkerchief for a space, he disclosed what had all the makings of a very sweetish black eye.

Pauline, sighting this, uttered a daughterly yip.

'What on earth has been happening, father?'

Old Stoker breathed heavily.

'I couldn't get at the fellow,' he said, with a sort of wild regret in his voice.

'What fellow?'

'I don't know who he was. Some lunatic in that Dower House. He stood there at the window, throwing potatoes at me. I had hardly knocked at the door, when he was there at the window, throwing potatoes. Wouldn't come out like a man and let me get at him. Just stood at the window, throwing potatoes.'

I confess that, as I had heard these words, a sort of reluctant admiration for this bloke Brinkley stole over me. We could never be friends, of course, but one had to admit that he was a man who could do the right and public-spirited thing when the occasion called. I took it that old Stoker's banging on the knocker had roused him from a morning-after reverie to the discovery that he had a pretty nasty headache, and that he had instantly started to take steps through the proper channels. All most satisfactory.

'You can consider yourself dashed lucky,' I said, pointing out the bright side, 'that the fellow elected to deal with you at long range. For close-quarters work he usually employs a carving knife or a chopper, and a good deal of clever footwork is called for.'

He had been so wrapped up in his own concerns till now that I don't think he had got on to the fact that Bertram was with him once more. At any rate, he stared quite a bit.

'Ah, Stoker,' I said airily, to help him out.

He continued to goggle.

'Are you Wooster?' he asked, in what seemed to me a rather awed way.

'Still Wooster, Stoker, old man,' I said cheerily. 'First, last and all the time Bertram Wooster.'

He was looking from Chuffy to Pauline and back again almost pleadingly, as if seeking comfort and support.

'What the devil has he done to his face?'

'Sunburn,' I said. 'Well, Stoker,' I proceeded, anxious to get the main business of the day settled, 'it's most convenient that you should have dropped in like this. I've been looking for you . . . well, that's putting it a bit loosely, perhaps, but, anyway, I'm glad to see you now, because I've been wanting to tell you that the idea of yours about your daughter and me getting married is off. Forget it, Stoker. Abandon it. Wash it right out. Nothing to it, at all.'

It would be difficult to overpraise the magnificent courage and firmness with which I spoke. In fact, for a moment I rather wondered if I mightn't have overdone it a little, because I caught Pauline's eye and there was such a look of worshipping reverence in it that it seemed quite on the cards that, overcome by my glamour at this juncture, she might decide that I was her hero, after all, and switch back again from Chuffy to me. This thought caused me to go on a bit quickly to the next item on the agenda.

'She's going to marry Chuffy – Lord Chuffnell – him,' I said, indicating C. with a wave of the hand.

'What!'

'Yes. All set.'

Old Stoker gave a powerful snort. He was deeply moved.

'Is this true?'

'Yes, father.'

'Oh! You intend to marry a man who calls your father a pop-eyed old swindler, do you?'

I was intrigued.

'Did you call him a pop-eyed old swindler, Chuffy?'

Chuffy hitched up a lower jaw which had sagged a bit.

'Certainly not,' he said weakly.

'You did', said Stoker. 'When I told you I was not going to buy this house of yours.'

'Oh, well,' said Chuffy. 'You know how it is.'

Pauline intervened. She seemed to be feeling that the point was being wandered from. Women like to stick to the practical issue.

'Anyway, I'm going to marry him, father.'

'You are not.'

'I am too. I love him.'

'And only yesterday you were in love with this damned sooty-faced imbecile here.'

I drew myself up. We Woosters can make allowances for a father's chagrin, but there is a sharply defined limit.

'Stoker,' I said, 'you forget yourself strangely. I must ask you to preserve the decencies of debate. And it isn't soot – it's boot polish.'

'I wasn't,' cried Pauline.

'You said you were.'

'Well, I wasn't.'

Old Stoker got off another of his snorts.

'The fact of the matter is, you don't know your own mind, and I'm going to make it up for you.'

'I'm not going to marry Bertie, whatever you say.'

'Well, you're certainly not going to marry a fortune-hunting English lord.'

Chuffy took this fairly big.

'What do you mean, a fortune-hunting English lord?'

'I mean what I say. You haven't a cent, and you're trying to marry a girl in Pauline's position. Why, darn it, you're just like that fellow in that musical comedy I saw once . . . what was the name . . . Lord Wotwotleigh.'

An animal cry escaped Chuffy's ashen lips.

'Wotwotleigh!'

'The living spit of him. Same sort of face, same expression, same way of talking. I've been wondering all along who it was you reminded me of, and now I know. Lord Wotwotleigh.'

Pauline charged in again.

'You're talking perfect nonsense, father. The whole trouble all along was that Marmaduke was so scrupulous and chivalrous that he wouldn't ask me to marry him till he felt he had enough money. I couldn't think what was the matter with him. And then you promised to buy Chuffnell Hall, and five minutes later he came bounding up to me and started proposing. If you didn't mean to buy the Hall you ought not to have said you would. And I don't see why you won't, either.'

'I was planning to buy it because Glossop asked me to,' said old Stoker. 'The way I feel towards that guy now, I wouldn't buy a peanut stand to please him.'

I felt impelled to put in a word.

'Not a bad sort, old Glossop. I like him.'

'You can have him.'

'What first endeared him to me was the way he set about little Seabury last night. It seemed to me to argue the right outlook.'

Stoker was staring with his left eye. The other had now closed like some tired flower at nightfall. I couldn't help feeling that Brinkley must have been a jolly good shot to have plugged him so squarely. It's not the easiest thing in the world to hit a fellow in the eye with a potato at a longish range. I know, because I've tried it. The very nature of the potato, it being a rummy shape and covered with knobs, renders accurate aiming a trick business.

'What's that you're saying? Glossop soaked that boy?'

'With a will, they tell me.'

'Well, I'm darned!'

I don't know if you've ever seen one of those films where the tough guy hears the old song his mother used to teach him at her knee and you get a close-up of his face working and before you know where you are he's a melted man and off doing lots of good to all and sundry. A bit sudden I've always looked on it as, but you can take it from me that these lightning softenings do occur. Because now before our very eyes old Stoker was undergoing one of them.

One moment he had been absolutely the man of chilled steel. The next, he was practically human. He stared at me, speechless. Then he licked his lips.

'You really tell me old Glossop did that?'

'I was not present in person, but I have it straight from Jeeves, who got it from Mary, the parlourmaid, who was an eye-witness throughout. He put it across little Seabury properly – at a venture, I should say with the back of a hairbrush.'

'Well, I'm darned!'

Pauline was doing a big of eye-sparkling. You could see that

401

hope had dawned once more. I'm not sure she didn't clap her hands in girlish glee.

'You see, father. You got him all wrong. He's really a splendid man. You'll have to go to him and tell him you're sorry you were so snooty and that you're going to buy the house for him, after all.'

Well, I could have told the poor cloth-head that she was doing the wrong thing, butting in like this. Girls have no idea of handling any situation that calls for nice tact. I mean to say, Jeeves will tell you that on these occasions the whole thing is to study the psychology of the individual, and an owl could have seen what old Stoker's psychology was like. A male owl, that is. He was one of those fellows who get their backs up the minute they think their nearest and dearest are trying to shove them into anything; a chap who, as the Bible puts it, if you say Go, he cometh, and if you say Come, he goeth; a fellow, in a word, who, if he came to a door with "Push" on it, would always pull.

And I was right. Left to himself, this Stoker in about another half-minute would have been dancing round the room, strewing roses out of his hat. He was within a short jump of becoming a thing compact entirely of sweetness and light. Now he suddenly stiffened, and a mulish look came into his eye. You could see his haughty spirit resented being rushed.

'I won't do anything of the sort!'

'Oh, father!'

'Telling me what I'm to do and what I'm not to do.'

'I didn't mean it like that.'

'Never mind how you meant it.'

Affairs had taken an unpleasant turn. Old Stoker was gruffling to himself like a not too sunny bulldog. Pauline was looking as if she had recently taken a short-arm punch in the solar plexus. Chuffy had the air of a man who has not yet recovered from being compared to Lord Wotwotleigh. And, as for me, while I could see that it was a moment that called for the intervention of a silver-tongued orator, I felt it wasn't much use having a pop at being a silver-tongued orator if one hadn't anything to say, and I hadn't.

So all that occurred was a good deal of silence, and this silence was still in progress and getting momentarily stickier, when there was a knock at the door and in floated Jeeves.

'Excuse me, sir' he said, shimmering towards old Stoker and

presenting an envelope on a salver. 'A seaman from your yacht has just brought this cablegram, which arrived shortly after your departure this morning. The captain of the vessel, fancying that it might be of an urgent nature, instructed him to convey it to this house. I took it from him at the back door and hastened hither with it in order to deliver it to you personally.'

The way he put it made the whole thing seem like one of those great epics you read about. You followed the procedure step by step, and the interest and drama worked up to the big moment. Old Stoker, however, instead of being thrilled, seemed somewhat on the impatient side.

'What you mean is, there's a cable for me.'

'Yes, sir.'

'Then why not say so, damn it, instead of making a song about it. Do you think you're singing in opera, or something? Gimme.'

Jeeves handed over the missive with a dignified reserve, and drifted out with salver. Stoker started to rip open the envelope.

'I shall certainly not say anything of the kind to Glossop,' he said, resuming the discussion. 'If he cares to come to me and apologize, I may possibly . . .'

His voice died away with a sort of sound not unlike the last utterance of one of those toy ducks you inflate and then let the air out of. His jaw had dropped, and he was staring at the cable as if he had suddenly discovered he was fondling a tarantula. The next moment there proceeded from his lips an observation which even in these lax modern days I should certainly not have considered suitable for mixed company.

Pauline hopped towards him. Solicitous. When pain and anguish racks the brow stuff.

'What's the matter, father?'

Old Stoker was making gulping noises.

'It's happened!'

'What has happened?'

'What? What?' I saw Chuffy start. 'What? What? I'll tell you what. They're contesting old George's will!'

'You don't mean that!'

'I do mean that. Read it for yourself.'

Pauline studied the document. She looked up, rattled.

'But if this goes through, bang goes our fifty million.'

'Of course it does.'

'We shan't have a cent, hardly.'

Chuffy came to life with a jerk.

'Say that again! Do you mean you've lost all your money?'

'It looks like it.'

'Fine!' said Chuffy. 'Great. Ripping. Wonderful. Topping. Splendid!'

Pauline gave a sort of jump.

'Why, so it is, isn't it?'

'Of course it is. I'm broke. You're broke. Let's rush off and get married.'

'Of course.'

'This makes everything all right. Nobody can say I'm like Wotwotleigh now.'

'They certainly can't.'

'Wotwotleigh, on hearing the news, would have edged out.'

'I should say so. You wouldn't have been able to see him for dust.'

'It's marvellous!'

'It's magnificent'

'In my life, I've never heard of such a bit of luck as this.'

'Nor have I.'

'Coming just at the right time.'

'Exactly at the right time.'

'It's topping!'

'It's simply great!'

Their fresh young enthusiasm seemed to affect old Stoker like a boil on the cheek-bone.

'Stop talking that infernal rot and listen to me. Haven't you any sense at all? What do you mean, you've lost your money? Do you think I'm going to lie down and let this go through without making any come-back? They haven't a dog's chance. Old George was as sane as I am, and I've got Sir Roderick Glossop, the greatest alienist in England, to prove it.'

'But you haven't.'

'I've only to put Glossop on the witness stand, and their case collapses like a bubble.'

'But Sir Roderick won't testify for you now you've quarrelled with him.'

Old Stoker sizzled a bit. Or fumed, if you care to put it that way.

'Who says I've quarrelled with him? Show me the half-wit who

dares to assert that I'm not on the most cordial terms with Sir
Roderick Glossop. Just because we had a trifling, temporary
difference such as happens to the closest of friends, does that
mean that we're not like brothers?'

'But suppose he won't apologize to you?'

'There has never been any question of his apologizing to me. I
shall naturally apologize to him. I suppose I'm man enough to admit
it frankly when I realize that I have been in the wrong and have
wounded my best friend's feelings, aren't I? Of course I shall
apologize to him, and he will accept my apology in the spirit in
which it is given. There is nothing small about Sir Roderick Glossop.
I'll have him over in New York, testifying his head off, inside of two
weeks. What's the name of that place he's staying at? Seaview Hotel,
isn't it? I'll get him on the wire at once and arrange a meeting.'

I had to put in a word here.

'He's not at the hotel. I know, because Jeeves was trying to get
him just now and drew a blank.'

'Then where is he?'

'I couldn't say.'

'He must be somewhere.'

'Ah!' I said, following the reasoning and finding it sound. 'So he
is, no doubt. But where? Quite possibly he's in London by now.'

'Why London?'

'Why not?'

'Was he planning to go to london?'

'He may have been.'

'What's his address in London?'

'I don't know.'

'Don't any of you know?'

'I don't,' said Pauline.

'I don't,' said Chuffy.

'A lot of use you are to a man,' said old Stoker severely. 'Get
out! We're busy.'

The remark was addressed to Jeeves, who had come floating in
again. It's one of this man's most remarkable properties, that now
you see him and now you don't. Or, rather, now you don't see him
and now you do. You're talking of this and that and you suddenly
sense a presence, so to speak, and there he is.

'I beg your pardon, sir,' said Jeeves. 'I was desirous of speaking
to his lordship for a moment.'

Chuffy waved a hand. Distrait.

'Later on, Jeeves.'

'Very good, m'lord.'

'We're a little busy just now.'

'Just so, m'lord.'

'Well, it's not going to be so hard to locate a man of Sir Roderick's eminence,' said old Stoker, resuming. 'His address would be in *Who's Who*. Have you got a *Who's Who*?'

'No,' said Chuffy.

Old Stoker flung the hands skyward.

'Good God!'

Jeeves coughed.

'If you will pardon me for intruding the observation, sir, I think I can tell you where Sir Roderick is. If I am right in supposing that it is Sir Roderick Glossop that you are anxious to find?'

'Of course it is. How many Sir Rodericks do you think I know? Where is he, then?'

'In the garden, sir.'

'This garden, do you mean?'

'Yes, sir.'

'Then go and ask him to come here at once. Say that Mr Stoker wishes to see him immediately on a matter of the utmost importance. No, stop. Don't you go. I'll go myself. Whereabouts in the garden did you see him?'

'I did not see him, sir. I was merely informed that he was there.'

Old Stoker clicked the tongue a bit.

'Well, damn it, whereabouts in the garden did whoever merely informed you that he was in the garden merely inform you that he was?'

'In the potting-shed, sir.'

'The potting-shed?'

'Yes, sir.'

'What's he doing in the potting-shed?'

'Sitting, sir, I imagine. As I say, I do not speak from first-hand observation. My informant is Constable Dobson.'

'Eh? What? Constable Dobson? Who's he?'

'The police officer who arrested Sir Roderick last night, sir.' He bowed slightly from the hips and left the room.

# =21=
# JEEVES FINDS THE WAY

'JEEVES!' bellowed Chuffy.

'Jeeves!' screamed Pauline.

'Jeeves!' I shouted.

'Hey!' yelled old Stoker.

The door had closed, and I'll swear it hadn't opened again. Nevertheless, there was the man in our midst once more, an expression of courteous inquiry on his face.

'Jeeves!' cried Chuffy.

'M'lord?'

'Jeeves!' shrieked Pauline.

'Miss?'

'Jeeves!' I vociferated.

'Sir?'

'Hey, you!' boomed old Stoker.

Whether Jeeves liked being called "Hey, you!" I could not say. His well-moulded face betrayed no resentment.

'Sir?' he said.

'What do you mean by going off like that?'

'I was under the impression that his lordship, occupied with more vital matters, was not at leisure to attend to the communication I desired to make, sir. I planned to return later, sir.'

'Well, stay put for a second, won't you?'

'Certainly, sir. Had I been aware that you were desirous of speaking to me, sir, I would not have withdrawn from the room. It was merely the apprehension lest I might be intruding at a moment when my presence was not desired . . .'

'All right, all right, all right!' I noted, not for the first time, that there was something about Jeeves's conversational methods that seemed to jar upon old Stoker. 'Never mind all that.'

'Your presence is of the essence, Jeeves,' I said.

'Thank you, sir,'

Chuffy took the floor, Stoker being occupied for the nonce with making a noise like a wounded buffalo.

'Jeeves.'

'M'lord?'

'Did you say that Sir Roderick Glossop had been arrested?'

'Yes, m'lord. It was on that point that I wished to speak to your lordship. I came to inform you that Sir Roderick had been apprehended by Constable Dobson last night and placed in the potting-shed in the Hall grounds, the constable remaining on guard at the door. The larger potting-shed, m'lord, not the smaller one. The potting-shed to which I allude is the potting-shed on the right as you enter the kitchen garden. It has a red-tiled roof, in contradistinction to the smaller potting-shed, the roof of which is constructed of . . .'

I had never been, as you might say, frightfully fond of J. Washburn Stoker, but it seemed only neighbourly at this moment to try to save him from apoplexy.

'Jeeves,' I said.

'Sir?'

'Never mind which potting-shed.'

'No, sir.'

'Not of the essence.'

'I quite understand, sir.'

'Then carry on, Jeeves.'

He cast a glance of respectful commiseration at old Stoker, who seemed to be having a good deal of trouble with his bronchial tubes.

'It appears, m'lord, that Constable Dobson arrested Sir Roderick at an advanced hour last night. He was then in something of a quandary as to what means to take for his disposal. You must understand, m'lord, that in the conflagration which destroyed Mr Wooster's cottage that of Sergeant Voules, which is contiguous, was also burned down. And as this cottage of Sergeant Voules's is also the local police station, Constable Dobson was not unnaturally somewhat at a loss to know where to place his prisoner – the more so as Sergeant Voules was not there to advise him, he, in fighting the flames, having sustained an unfortunate injury to his head and having been removed to the house of his aunt. I refer to his Aunt Maud, who resides in Chuffnell Regis, not . . .'

I did the square thing again.

'Never mind which aunt, Jeeves.'

'No, sir.'

'Scarcely germane.'

'Quite so, sir.'

'Then carry on, Jeeves.'

'Very good, sir. So in the end, acting upon his own initiative, the constable arrived at the conclusion that as secure a place as any would be the potting-shed, the larger potting-shed . . .'

'We understand, Jeeves. The one with the tiled roof.'

'Precisely, sir. He, therefore, placed Sir Roderick in the larger potting-shed, and remained on guard there throughout the remainder of the night. Some little time ago, the gardener came on duty and the constable, summoning one of them – a young fellow named . . .'

'All right, Jeeves.'

'Very good, sir. Summoning this young fellow, he dispatched him to the temporary residence of Sergeant Voules in the hope that the latter would now be sufficiently restored to be able to interest himself in the matter. Such, it appears, was the case. A night's sleep, acting in conjunction with a naturally robust constitution, had enabled Sergeant Voules to rise at his usual hour and partake of a hearty breakfast.'

'Breakfast!' I couldn't help murmuring in spite of my iron self-control. The word had touched an exposed nerve in Bertram.

'On receiving the communication, Sergeant Voules hastened to the Hall to interview his lordship.'

'Why his lordship?'

'His lordship is a Justice of the Peace, sir.'

'Of course, yes.'

'And, as such, has the power to commit the prisoner to incarceration in a more recognized prison. He is waiting in the library now, m'lord, till your lordship is at leisure to see him.'

If the word "breakfast" was, as it were, the key word that had the power to set Bertram Wooster a-quiver, it appeared that "prison" was the one that tickled old Stoker up properly. He uttered a hideous cry.

'But how can he be in prison? What's he got to do with prisons? Why does this fool of a cop think he ought to be in prison?'

'The charge, I understand, sir, is one of burglary.'

'Burglary!'

'Yes, sir.'

Old Stoker looked so piteously at me – why me, I don't know, but he did – that I nearly patted him on the head. In fact, I might quite easily have done so, had not my hand been stayed by a sudden noise in my rear like that made by a frightened hen or a rising pheasant. The Dowager Lady Chuffnell had come charging into the room.

'Marmaduke!' she cried, and I can give no better indication of her emotion than by saying that as she spoke her eyes rested on my face and it made no impression on her whatsoever. For all the notice she took of it, I might have been the Great White Chief. 'Marmaduke, I have the most terrible news. Roderick . . .'

'All right,' said Chuffy, a little petulantly, I thought. 'We've had it too. Jeeves is just telling us.'

'But what are we to do?'

'I don't know.'

'And it is all my fault, all my fault.'

'Oh, don't say that, Aunt Myrtle,' said Chuffy, rattled but still *preux*. 'You couldn't have helped it.'

'I could. I could. I shall never forgive myself. If it had not been for me, he would never have gone out of the house with that black stuff on his face.'

I was really sorry for poor old Stoker. One thing after another, I mean to say. His eyes came out of his head like a snail's.

'Black stuff?' he gurgled faintly.

'He had covered his face with burnt cork to amuse Seabury.'

Old Stoker tottered to a chair and sank into it. He seemed to be thinking that this was one of those stories you could listen to better sitting down.

'You can only remove the horrible stuff with butter . . .'

'And petrol, so the cognoscenti tell me,' I couldn't help putting in. I like to keep these things straight. 'You support me, Jeeves? Petrol does the trick?'

'Yes, sir.'

'Well, petrol, then. Petrol or butter. At any rate, it was to get something that would take the stuff off that he must have broken into this house. And now . . . !'

She cheesed it in mid-sentence, deeply moved. Not, however, any more deeply than old Stoker, who seemed to be more or less passing through the furnace.

'This is the finish,' he said, in a sort of pale voice. 'This is where I drop fifty million dollars and try to like it. A lot of use any testimony in a lunacy case is going to be from a fellow who gets himself pinched while wandering around the country in a black face. Why, there isn't a judge in America who wouldn't rule out anything he said on the ground that he was crazy himself.'

Lady Chuffnell quivered.

'But he did it to please my son.'

'Anybody who would do anything to please a young hound like that,' said old Stoker, 'must have been crazy.'

He emitted a mirthless laugh.

'Well, the joke's on me, all right. Yes, the joke's certainly on me. I stake everything on the evidence of this man Glossop. I rely on him to save my fifty million by testifying that old George wasn't loco. And two minutes after I've put him on the stand, the other side'll come right back at me by showing that my expert is a loony himself, loonier than ever old George could have been if he'd tried for a thousand years. It's funny when you come to think of it. Ironical. Reminds one of that thing about Lo somebody's name led all the rest.'

Jeeves coughed. He had that informative gleam of his in his eyes.

'Abou ben Adhem, sir.'

'Have I *what*?' said old Stoker, puzzled.

'The poem to which you allude relates to a certain Abou ben Adhem, who, according to the story, awoke one night from a deep dream of peace to find an angel . . .'

'Get out!' said old Stoker, very quietly.

'Sir?'

'Get out of this room before I murder you.'

'Yes, sir.'

'And take your angels with you.'

'Very good, sir.'

The door closed. Old Stoker puffed out his breath in a stricken sort of way.

'Angels!' he said. 'At a time like this!'

I felt it only fair to stick up for Jeeves.

'He was perfectly right,' I said. 'I used to know the thing by heart at school. This cove found an angel sitting by his bed, writing in a book, don't you know, and the upshot of the whole affair was . . . Oh, all right, if you don't want to hear.'

I withdrew to a corner of the room and picked up a photograph album. A Wooster does not thrust his conversation upon the unwilling.

For some time after this there was a good deal of what you might call mixed chatter, in which – through dudgeon – I took no part. Everybody talked at once, and nobody said anything that you could have described as being in the least constructive. Except old Stoker, who proved that I had been right in thinking that he must at one time have been a pirate of the Spanish or some other Main by coming boldly out with a suggestion for a rescue party.

'What's the matter,' he wanted to know, 'with going and breaking the door down and getting him out and smuggling him away and hiding him somewhere and letting these darned cops run circles round themselves, trying to find him?'

Chuffy demurred.

'We couldn't.'

'Why not?'

'You heard Jeeves say Dobson was on guard.'

'Bat him over the head with a shovel.'

Chuffy didn't seem to like this idea much. I suppose, if you're a J.P., you have to be careful what you do. Bat policemen over the head with shovels, and the County looks askance.

'Well, darn it, then, bribe him.'

'You can't bribe an English policeman.'

'You mean that?'

'Not a chance.'

'My God, what a country!' said old Stoker, with a sort of whistling groan, and you could see that he would never be able to feel quite the same towards England again.

My dudgeon melted. We Woosters are human, and the spectacle of so much anguish in a moderately-sized room was too much for me. I crossed to the fire-place and pressed the bell. With the result that just as old Stoker was beginning to say what he thought about the English policeman, the door opened and there was Jeeves.

Old Stoker eyed him balefully.

'You back?'

'Yes, sir.'

'Well?'

'Sir?'

412

'What do you want?'

'The bell rang, sir.'

Chuffy did another spot of hand-waving.

'No, no, Jeeves. Nobody rang.'

I stepped forward.

'I rang, Chuffy.'

'What for?'

'For Jeeves.'

'We don't want Jeeves.'

'Chuffy, old man,' I said, and those present were, no doubt, thrilled by the quiet gravity of my tone, 'if there could ever be a time when you wanted Jeeves more than you do now, I . . .' I lost the thread of my remarks, and had to start again. 'Chuffy,' I said, 'What I'm driving at is that there is only one man who can get you out of this mess. He stands before you. I mean Jeeves,' I said, to make the thing clearer. 'You know as well as I do that on these occasions Jeeves always finds the way.'

Chuffy was plainly impressed. I could see that memory had begun to stir, and that he was recalling some of the man's triumphs.

'By Jove, yes. That's right. He does, doesn't he?'

'He does, indeed.'

I shot a quelling glance at old Stoker, who had started to say something about angels, and turned to the man.

'Jeeves,' I said, 'we require your co-operation and advice.'

'Very good, sir.'

'To begin with, let me give you a brief synopsis . . . do I mean synopsis?'

'Yes, sir. Synopsis is perfectly correct.'

'. . . a brief synopsis, then, of the position of affairs. I have no doubt that you recall the late Mr George Stoker. That cable you brought just now was to say that his will, under the terms of which Mr Stoker here has benefited so considerably, is being contested on the ground that the testator was as goofy as a coot.'

'Yes, sir.'

'In rebuttal of this, Mr Stoker had intended to bung Sir Roderick Glossop into the witness box to testify as an expert that old George was Grade A. in the sanity line. Not a gibber in him, if you see what I mean. And in ordinary circs this move could not have failed. It would have brought home the bacon infallibly.'

'Yes, sir.'

'But, and this is the nub of the thing, Jeeves – Sir Roderick is now in the potting-shed – the larger potting-shed – with his face covered with burnt cork and a sharp sentence for burglary staring him in the eyeball. You see how this weakens him as a force?'

'Yes, sir.'

'In this world, Jeeves, you can do one of two things. You can set yourself up as a final authority on whether your fellow-man is sane or not, or you can go blacking your face and getting put in potting-sheds. You cannot do both. So what is to be done, Jeeves?'

'I would suggest removing Sir Roderick from the shed, sir.'

I turned to the meeting.

'There! Didn't I tell you Jeeves would find the way?'

One dissentient voice. Old Stoker's. He seemed bent on heckling.

'Remove him from the shed, yes?' he said, and in an exceedingly nasty voice. 'How? With a team of angels?'

He started his buffalo imitations again, and I had to shush him pretty firmly.

'*Can* you remove Sir R. from the s., Jeeves?'

'Yes, sir.'

'You are convinced of this?'

'Yes, sir.'

'You have already formulated a plan or scheme?'

'Yes, sir.'

'I take it all back,' said old Stoker reverently. 'Forget I said it. Get me out of this jam and you can come and wake me up in the night and talk about angels, if you want.'

'Thank you, sir. By removing Sir Roderick before he is actually brought into the presence of his lordship, sir,' proceeded Jeeves, 'we shall, I think, obviate all unpleasantness. His identity is not yet known to either Constable Dobson or Sergeant Voules. The constable had never seen him before their meeting last night, and assumes that he is a member of the troupe of negroid minstrels who performed on Mr Stoker's yacht. Sergeant Voules is under the same impression. We have, therefore, only to release Sir Roderick before the matter is gone further into, and all will be well.'

I followed him.

'I follow you, Jeeves,' I said.

'If you will allow me, sir, I will now sketch out the method which I would advocate for accomplishing this end.'

'Yes,' said old Stoker. 'What is this method? Spill it.'

I held up a hand. A thought had struck me.'

'Wait, Jeeves,' I said. 'Just one moment.'

I fixed old Stoker with a compelling eye.

'Before we go any further, there are two things to be settled. Do you give your solemn word to purchase Chuffnell Hall from old Chuffy here at a price to be agreed upon between the two contracting parties?'

'Yes, yes, yes. Let's get on.'

'And you consent to the union of your daughter Pauline with old Chuffy, and none of that rot about her marrying me?'

'Sure, sure!'

'Jeeves,' I said, 'you may speak.'

I stepped back, and gave him the floor – noting, as I did so, that his eye was a-gleam with the light of pure intelligence. His head, as usual, bulged out at the back.

'Having given this matter a good deal of consideration, sir, I have come to the conclusion that the chief difficulty that confronts us in our attempt upon our objective lies in the presence before the entrance of the potting-shed of Constable Dobson.'

'Very true, Jeeves.'

'He represents the *crux*, if I may say so.'

'Certainly you may say so, Jeeves. Another way of putting it would be "the snag".'

'Precisely, sir. Our first move, accordingly, must be to eliminate Constable Dobson.'

'That's what I said,' put in old Stoker rather querulously. 'And you wouldn't listen to me.'

I squelched him.

'You wanted to hit him over the head with a spade or something. All wrong. What is needed here is . . . what's the word, Jeeves?'

'*Finesse*, sir.'

'Exactly. Carry on, Jeeves.'

'This, in my opinion, may be readily accomplished by sending word to him that the parlourmaid, Mary, wishes to see him in the raspberry bushes.'

I was stunned by the man's sagacity, but not so stunned as to be unable to turn to the others and add an explanatory footnote.

'This Mary, this parlourmaid,' I said, 'is betrothed to the blighter Dobson, and while I have only seen her in the distance, I can testify that she is exactly the sort of girl any red-blooded constable would come leaping into the raspberry bushes to meet. Full of sex-appeal, eh, Jeeves?'

'An exceedingly attractive young woman, sir. And I think that we might make matters even more certain by including in the message a word to the effect that she had a cup of coffee and a ham sandwich for him. The constable, I find, has not yet breakfasted.'

I winced.

'Skim lightly over this bit, Jeeves. I am not made of marble.'

'I beg your pardon, sir. I was forgetting.'

'Quite all right, Jeeves. You will have to square Mary, of course?'

'No, sir. I have been canvassing her views, and I find that she is extremely eager to convey refreshment to the officer. I would suggest giving her a message – ostensibly from the latter – to the effect that he is waiting at the spot indicated.'

I had to interrupt.

'A snag, Jeeves. A *crux*, in fact. If he wanted food, why wouldn't he come straight to the house?'

'He would be apprehensive of being observed by Sergeant Voules, sir. He is under strict orders from his superior to remain at his post.'

'Then would he leave it?' asked Chuffy.

'My dear old man,' I said. 'He has not yet breakfasted. And this girl will be dripping with coffee and ham sandwiches. Don't hold up the run of the dialogue with foolish questions. Yes, Jeeves?'

'In his absence, sir, it would be a simple task to remove Sir Roderick and lead him to some place of concealment. His lordship's bedroom suggests itself.'

'And Dobson wouldn't have the nerve to confess that he had abandoned the post of duty. That's what you're driving at?'

'Precisely, sir, his lips would be sealed.'

Old Stoker shoved himself forward again.

'No, good,' he said. 'Wouldn't work. I'm not saying we couldn't get Glossop away, but the cops would see that there had been funny business. Their man would have gone, and they'd figure it out that somebody had got him away. They would put two and two together and get wise to us having done it. Last night, for example, on my yacht . . .'

416

He stopped, not wishing, I suppose, to disinter the dead past, but I saw what he meant. When I had got away from the yacht, it hadn't taken him long to see that Jeeves must have been at the bottom of it.

'It's a point, Jeeves,' I was bound to say. 'The constabulary might not be able to do anything definite, but they would talk about it, and before we knew where we were, the story would be out that Sir Roderick had been roaming around with his face blacked up. The local paper would get hold of it. One of those gossip-writers you find at the Drones, always waiting with their ears flapping for good stuff about the eminent, would hear of it, and then we should be just as badly off as if the old boy went and picked oakum at Dartmoor or somewhere for years.'

'No, sir. The officers would find a prisoner in the shed. I would advocate substituting you for Sir Roderick.'

I stared at the man.

'Me?'

'It is vital, if I may be allowed to point it out, sir, that a black-faced prisoner be found in the shed when the moment arrives for the accused to be conducted before his lordship.'

'But I don't look like old Glossop. We're built on different lines. Me – slender and willowy; him ... well, I don't wish to say anything derogatory concerning one who is bound to the aunt of an old friend by ties warmer than those of ... well, what I'm driving at is that you couldn't by any stretch of the imag. call him slender and willowy.'

'You are forgetting, sir, that only Constable Dobson has actually seen the prisoner; and his lips, as I say, will be sealed.'

It was true. I had forgotten that.

'Yes, but, Jeeves, dash it, anxious as I am to bring aid and comfort to this stricken home, I'm not so bally keen on doing five years in the jug for burglary.'

'There is no danger of that, sir. The building into which Sir Roderick was breaking at the moment of his arrest was your own garage.'

'But, Jeeves. Reflect. Consider. Review the position. Am I supposed to have allowed myself to be pinched for breaking into my own garage and shut up in a shed all night without saying a word? It isn't ... what is it ... it isn't plausible.'

'It is only necessary to induce Sergeant Voules to believe it, sir.

What the constable may think is immaterial, owing to the fact that his lips are sealed.'

'But Voules wouldn't believe it for a minute.'

'Oh, yes, sir. I fancy that he is under the impression that it is a frequent practice of yours to sleep in sheds.'

Chuffy uttered a glad cry.

'Of course. He'll just take it for granted that you've been mopping it up again.'

I was frigid.

'Oh?' I said, and you couldn't have described my voice as anything but caustic. 'So I am to go down in the history of Chuffnell Regis as one of our leading dipsomaniacs?'

'He may just think him potty,' suggested Pauline.

'That's right,' said Chuffy. He turned to me pleadingly. 'Bertie,' he said, 'you aren't going to tell me at this time of day that you have any objection to being considered . . .'

'. . . Mentally negligible,' said Pauline.

'Exactly,' said Chuffy. 'Of course you'll do it. What, Bertie Wooster? Sacrifice himself to a little temporary inconvenience to save his friends? Why, he jumps at that sort of job.'

'Springs at it,' said Pauline.

'Leaps at it,' said Chuffy.

'I've always thought he was a fine young fellow,' said old Stoker 'I remember thinking so the first time I met him.'

'So did I,' said Lady Chuffnell. 'So different from so many of these modern young men.'

'I liked his face.'

'I have always liked his face.'

My head was swimming a bit. It isn't often I get as good a Press as this, and the old salve was beginning to unman me. I tried feebly to stem the tide.

'Yes, but listen . . .'

'I was at school with Bertie Wooster,' said Chuffy. 'I like to think of it. At private school and also at Eton and after that at Oxford. He was loved by everybody.'

'Because of his wonderful, unselfish nature?' asked Pauline.

'You've absolutely hit it. Because of his wonderful, unselfish nature. Because when it was a question of helping a pal he would go through fire and water to do so. I wish I had a quid for every time I've seen him take the blame for somebody else's dirty work on his own broad shoulders.'

'How splendid!' said Pauline.

'Just what I'd have expected of him,' said old Stoker.

'Just,' said Lady Chuffnell. 'The child is the father of the man.'

'You would see him face a furious headmaster with a sort of dauntless look in those big blue eyes of his . . .'

I held up a hand.

'Enough, Chuffy,' I said. 'Sufficient. I will go through this ghastly ordeal. But one word. When I come out, do I get breakfast?'

'You get the best breakfast Chuffnell Hall can provide.'

I eyed him searchingly.

'Kippers?'

'Schools of kippers.'

'Toast?'

'Mounds of toast.'

'And coffee?'

'Pots.'

I inclined the head.

'Well, mind I do,' I said. 'Come, Jeeves, I am ready to accompany you.'

'Very good, sir. If I might be permitted to make an observation—?'

'Yes, Jeeves?'

'It is a far, far better thing that you do than you have ever done, sir.'

'Thank you, Jeeves.'

As I said before, there is nobody who puts these things more neatly than he does.

# =22=
# JEEVES APPLIES FOR A SITUATION

THE sunlight poured into the small morning-room of Chuffnell Hall. It played upon me, sitting at a convenient table; on Jeeves, hovering in the background; on the skeletons of four kippered herrings; on a coffee-pot; and on an empty toast-rack. I poured myself out the final drops of coffee and sipped thoughtfully. Recent events had set their seal upon me, and it was a graver, more mature Bertram Wooster who now eyed the toast-rack and, finding nothing there, transferred his gaze to the man in attendance.

'Who's the cook at the Hall now, Jeeves?'

'A woman of the name of Perkins, sir.'

'She dishes up a nifty breakfast. Convey my compliments to her.'

'Very good, sir.'

I touched the cup to my lips.

'All this is rather like the gentle sunshine after the storm, Jeeves.'

'Extremely like, sir.'

'And it was quite a storm, what?'

'Very trying at times, sir.'

'Trying is the *mot juste*, Jeeves. I was thinking of my own trial at that very moment. I flatter myself that I am a strong man, Jeeves. I am not easily moved by life's untoward happenings. But I'm bound to confess that it was an unpleasant experience coming up before Chuffy. I was nervous and embarrassed. A good deal of the awful majesty of the Law about old Chuffy. I didn't know he wore horn-rimmed spectacles.'

'When acting as Justice of the Peace, invariably, I understand, sir. I gather that his lordship finds that they lend him confidence in his magisterial duties.'

'Well, I think someone ought to have warned me. I got a nasty shock. They change his whole expression. Make him look just like my Aunt Agatha. It was only by reminding myself that he and I once stood in the same dock together at Bow Street, charged with raising Cain on Boat Race night, that I was enabled to maintain my *sang-froid*. However, the unpleasantness was short-lived. I must admit he rushed things through nice and quickly. He soon settled Dobson's hash, what?'

'Yes, sir.'

'A rather severe reprimand, I thought?'

'Well phrased, sir.'

'And Bertram dismissed without a stain on his character.'

'Yes, sir.'

'But with Police Sergeant Voules firmly convinced that he is either an inveterate souse or a congenital loony. Possibly both. However,' I proceeded, turning from the dark side, 'it is no use worrying about that.'

'Very true, sir.'

'The main point is that once again you have shown that there is no crisis which you are unable to handle. A very smooth effort, Jeeves. Exceedingly smooth.'

'I could have effected nothing without your co-operation, sir.'

'Tush, Jeeves! I was a mere pawn in the game.'

'Oh, no, sir.'

'Yes, Jeeves. I know my place. But there's just one thing. Don't think for a moment that I want to detract from the merit of your performance, but you did have a bit of luck, what?'

'Sir?'

'Well, that cable happening to come along in what you might call the very nick of time. A fortunate coincidence.'

'No, sir. I had anticipated its arrival.'

'What!'

'In the cable which I dispatched to my friend Benstead in New York the day before yesterday, I urged him to lose no time in retransmitting the message which formed the body of my communication.'

'You don't mean to say—'

'Immediately after the rift had occurred between Mr Stoker and Sir Roderick Glossop, involving, as it did, the former's decision not to purchase Chuffnell Hall and the consequent unpleasantness to his lordship and Miss Stoker, the dispatching of the cable to Benstead suggested itself to me as a possible solution. I surmised that the news that the late Mr Stoker's will was being contested would lead to a reconciliation between Mr Stoker and Sir Roderick.'

'And there's nobody contesting the will really?'

'No, sir.'

'But what about when old Stoker finds out?'

'I feel convinced that his natural relief will overcome any possible resentment at the artifice. And he has already signed the necessary documents relating to the sale of Chuffnell Hall.'

'So that even if he's as sick as mud he can't do a thing?'

'Exactly, sir.'

I fell into a moody silence. Apart from astounding me, this revelation had had the effect of engendering a poignant anguish. I mean to say, the thought that I had let this man get away from me, that he was now in Chuffy's employment, and that there was a fat chance of Chuffy ever being chump enough to put him into circulation again . . . well, dash it, you can't say it wasn't enough to shove the iron into the soul.

It was with something of the spirit of the old aristocrat mounting the tumbril that I forced myself to wear the mask.

'Cigarette, Jeeves?'

He produced the box, and I puffed in silence.

'Might I ask, sir, what you intend to do now?'

I came out of the reverie.

'Eh?'

'Now that your cottage is burned down, sir. Is it your purpose to take another in this neighbourhood?'

I shook the head.

'No, Jeeves, I shall return to the metrop.'

'To your former apartment, sir?'

'Yes.'

'But . . .'

I anticipated the question.

'I know what you are going to say, Jeeves. You are thinking of Mr Manglehoffer, of the Honourable Mrs Tinkler-Moulke and Lieutenant-Colonel J. J. Bustard. But circumstances have altered since I was compelled to take the firm stand I did in regard to their attitude towards the old banjolele. From now on, there will be no friction. My banjolele perished in the flames last night, Jeeves. I shall not buy another.'

'No, sir?'

'No, Jeeves. The zest has gone. I should not be able to twang a string without thinking of Brinkley. And the one thing I do not wish to do till further notice is think of that man of wrath.'

'You are not intending to retain him in your employment, then, sir?'

'Retain him in my employment? After what has occurred? After finishing first by the shortest of heads in the race with him and his carving knife? I do not so intend, Jeeves. Stalin, yes. Al Capone, certainly. But not Brinkley.'

He coughed.

'Then, as there is a vacancy in your establishment, sir, I wonder if you would consider it a liberty if I were to offer my services?'

I upset the coffee-pot.

'You said – what, Jeeves?'

'I ventured to express the hope, sir, that you might be agreeable to considering my application for the post. I should endeavour to give satisfaction, as I trust I have done in the past.'

'But . . .'

'I would not wish, in any case, to continue in the employment of his lordship, sir, now that he is about to be married. I yield to no one in my admiration for the many qualities of Miss Stoker, but it has never been my policy to serve in the household of a married gentleman.'

'Why not?'

'It is merely a personal feeling, sir.'

'I see what you mean. The psychology of the individual?'

'Precisely, sir.'

'And you really want to come back with me?'

'I should esteem it a great privilege, sir, if you would allow me to do so, sir, unless you are thinking of making other plans.'

It is not easy to find words in these supreme moments, if you know what I mean. What I mean is, you get a moment like this – supreme, as you might say – with the clouds all cleared away and the good old sun buzzing along on all six cylinders – and you feel . . . well, I mean, dash it!

'Thank you, Jeeves,' I said.

'Not at all, sir.'

P. G. Wodehouse

# SHORT STORIES

# =1=
# THE RUMMY AFFAIR OF OLD BIFFY

'Jeeves,' I said, emerging from the old tub, 'rally round.'

'Yes, sir.'

I beamed on the man with no little geniality. I was putting in a week or two in Paris at the moment, and there's something about Paris that always makes me feel fairly full of *espièglerie* and *joie de vivre*.

'Lay out our gent's medium-smart raiment, suitable for Bohemian revels,' I said. 'I am lunching with an artist bloke on the other side of the river.'

'Very good, sir.'

'And if anybody calls for me, Jeeves, say that I shall be back towards the quiet evenfall.'

'Yes, sir. Mr Biffen rang up on the telephone while you were in your bath.'

'Mr Biffen? Good heavens!'

Amazing how one's always running across fellows in foreign cities – coves, I mean, whom you haven't seen for ages and would have betted weren't anywhere in the neighbourhood. Paris was the last place where I should have expected to find old Biffy popping up. There was a time when he and I had been lads about town together, lunching and dining together practically every day; but some eighteen months back his old godmother had died and left him that place in Herefordshire, and he had retired there to wear gaiters and prod cows in the ribs and generally be the country gentleman and landed proprietor. Since then I had hardly seen him.

'Old Biffy in Paris? What's he doing here?'

'He did not confide in me, sir,' said Jeeves – a trifle frostily, I thought. It sounded somehow as if he didn't like Biffy. And yet they had always been matey enough in the old days.

'Where's he staying?'

'At the Hotel Avenida, Rue du Colisée, sir. He informed me that he was about to take a walk and would call this afternoon.'

'Well, if he comes when I'm out, tell him to wait. And now, Jeeves, *mes gants, mon chapeau, et le whangee de monsieur.* I must be popping.'

It was such a corking day and I had so much time in hand that near the Sorbonne I stopped my cab, deciding to walk the rest of the way. And I had hardly gone three steps and a half when there on the pavement before me stood old Biffy in person. If I had completed the last step I should have rammed him.

'Biffy!' I cried. 'Well, well, well!'

He peered at me in a blinking kind of way, rather like one of his Herefordshire cows prodded unexpectedly while lunching.

'Bertie!' he gurgled, in a devout sort of tone. 'Thank God!' He clutched my arm. 'Don't leave me, Bertie. I'm lost.'

'What do you mean, lost?'

'I came out for a walk and suddenly discovered after a mile or two that I didn't know where on earth I was. I've been wandering round in circles for hours.'

'Why didn't you ask the way?'

'I can't speak a word of French.'

'Well, why didn't you call a taxi?'

'I suddenly discovered I'd left all my money at my hotel.'

'You could have taken a cab and paid it when you got to the hotel.'

'Yes, but I suddenly discovered, dash it, that I'd forgotten its name.'

And there in a nutshell you have Charles Edward Biffen. As vague and woollen-headed a blighter as ever bit a sandwich. Goodness knows – and my Aunt Agatha will bear me out in this – I'm no mastermind myself; but compared with Biffy I'm one of the great thinkers of all time.

'I'd give a shilling,' said Biffy wistfully, 'to know the name of that hotel.'

'You can owe it me. Hotel Avenida, Rue du Colisée.'

'Bertie! This is uncanny. How the deuce did you know?'

'That was the address you left with Jeeves this morning.'

'So it was. I had forgotten.'

'Well, come along and have a drink, and then I'll put you in a cab and send you home. I'm engaged for lunch, but I've plenty of time.'

We drifted to one of the eleven cafés which jostled each other along the street and I ordered restoratives.

'What on earth are you doing in Paris?' I asked.

'Bertie, old man,' said Biffy solemnly, 'I came here to try and forget.'

'Well, you've certainly succeeded.'

'You don't understand. The fact is, Bertie, old lad, my heart is broken. I'll tell you the whole story.'

'No, I say!' I protested. But he was off.

'Last year,' said Biffy, 'I buzzed over to Canada to do a bit of salmon fishing.'

I ordered another. If this was going to be a fish-story, I needed stimulants.

'On the liner going to New York I met a girl.' Biffy made a sort of curious gulping noise not unlike a bulldog trying to swallow half a cutlet in a hurry so as to be ready for the other half. 'Bertie, old man, I can't describe her. I simply can't describe her.'

This was all to the good.

'She was wonderful! We used to walk on the boat-deck after dinner. She was on the stage. At least, sort of.'

'How do you mean, sort of?'

'Well, she had posed for artists and been a mannequin in a big dressmaker's and all that sort of thing, don't you know. Anyway, she had saved up a few pounds and was on her way to see if she could get a job in New York. She told me all about herself. Her father ran a milk-walk in Clapham. Or it may have been Cricklewood. At least, it was either a milk-walk or a boot-shop.'

'Easily confused.'

'What I'm trying to make you understand,' said Biffy, 'is that she came of good, sturdy, respectable middle-class stock. Nothing flashy about her. The sort of wife any man might have been proud of.'

'Well, whose wife was she?'

'Nobody's. That's the whole point of the story. I wanted her to be mine, and I lost her.'

'Had a quarrel, you mean?'

'No, I don't mean we had a quarrel. I mean I literally lost her. The last I ever saw of her was in the Customs sheds at New York. We were behind a pile of trunks, and I had just asked her to be my wife, and she had just said she would and everything was perfectly splendid, when a most offensive blighter in a peaked cap came up to talk about some cigarettes which he had found at the bottom of my trunk and which I had forgotten to declare. It was getting pretty late by then, for we hadn't docked till about ten-thirty, so I told Mabel to go on to her hotel and I would come round next day and take her to lunch. And since then I haven't set eyes on her.'

'You mean she wasn't at the hotel?'

'Probably she was. But – '

'You don't mean you never turned up?'

'Bertie, old man,' said Biffy, in an overwrought kind of way, 'for Heaven's sake don't keep trying to tell me what I mean and what I don't mean! Let me tell this my own way, or I shall get all mixed up and have to go back to the beginning.'

'Tell it your own way,' I said hastily.

'Well, then, to put it in a word, Bertie, I forgot the name of the hotel. By the time I'd done half an hour's heavy explaining about those cigarettes my mind was a blank. I had an idea I had written the name down somewhere, but I couldn't have done, for it wasn't on any of the papers in my pocket. No, it was no good. She was gone.'

'Why didn't you make inquiries?'

'Well, the fact is, Bertie, I had forgotten her name.'

'Oh, no, dash it!' I said. This seemed a bit too thick even for Biffy. 'How could you forget her name? Besides, you told it me a moment ago. Muriel or something.'

'Mabel,' corrected Biffy coldly. 'It was her surname I'd forgotten. So I gave it up and went to Canada.'

'But half a second,' I said. 'You must have told her your name. I mean, if you couldn't trace her, she could trace you.'

'Exactly. That's what makes it all seem so infernally hopeless. She knows my name and where I live and everything, but I haven't heard a word from her. I suppose, when I didn't turn up at the hotel, she took it that that was my way of hinting delicately that I had changed my mind and wanted to call the thing off.'

'I suppose so,' I said. There didn't seem anything else to suppose. 'Well, the only thing to do is to whizz around and try to heal the wound, what? How about dinner tonight, winding up at the Abbaye or one of those places?'

Biffy shook his head.

'It wouldn't be any good. I've tried it. Besides, I'm leaving on the four o'clock train. I have a dinner engagement tomorrow with a man who's nibbling at that house of mine in Hereford-shire.'

'Oh, are you trying to sell that place? I thought you liked it.'

'I did. But the idea of going on living in that great, lonely barn of a house after what has happened appals me, Bertie. So when Sir Roderick Glossop came along – '

'Sir Roderick Glossop! You don't mean the loony-doctor?'

'The great nerve specialist, yes. Why, do you know him?'

It was a warm day, but I shivered.

'I was engaged to his daughter for a week or two,' I said, in a hushed voice. The memory of that narrow squeak always made me feel faint.

'Has he a daughter?' said Biffy absently.

'He has. Let me tell you all about – '

'Not just now, old man,' said Biffy, getting up. 'I ought to be going back to my hotel to see about my packing.'

Which, after I had listened to his story, struck me as pretty low-down. However, the longer you live, the more you realize that the good old sporting spirit of give-and-take has practically died out in our midst. So I boosted him into a cab and went off to lunch.


It can't have been more than ten days after this that I received a nasty shock while getting outside my morning tea and toast. The English papers had arrived, and Jeeves was just drifting out of the room after depositing *The Times* by my bedside, when, as I idly turned the pages in search of the sporting section, a paragraph leaped out and hit me squarely in the eyeball.

As follows:–

# FORTHCOMING MARRIAGES

## Mr C. E. Biffen and Miss Glossop

*The engagement is announced between Charles Edward, only son of the late Mr E. C. Biffen, and Mrs Biffen, of 11, Penslow Square, Mayfair, and Honoria Jane Louise, only daughter of Sir Roderick and Lady Glossop, of 6b, Harley Street, W.*

'Great Scott!' I exclaimed.

'Sir?' said Jeeves, turning at the door.

'Jeeves, you remember Miss Glossop?'

'Very vividly, sir.'

'She's engaged to Mr Biffen!'

'Indeed, sir?' said Jeeves. And, with not another word, he slid out. The blighter's calm amazed and shocked me. It seemed to indicate that there must be a horrible streak of callousness in him. I mean to say, it wasn't as if he didn't know Honoria Glossop.

I read the paragraph again. A peculiar feeling it gave me. I don't know if you have ever experienced the sensation of seeing the announcement of the engagement of a pal of yours to a girl whom you were only saved from marrying yourself by the skin of your teeth. It induces a sort of – well, it's difficult to describe it exactly; but I should imagine a fellow would feel much the same if he happened to be strolling through the jungle with a boyhood chum and met a tigress or a jaguar, or whatnot, and managed to shin up a tree and looked down and saw the friend of his youth vanishing into the undergrowth in the animal's slavering jaws. A sort of profound, prayerful relief, if you know what I mean, blended at the same time with a pang of pity. What I'm driving at is that, thankful as I was that I hadn't had to marry Honoria myself, I was sorry to see a real good chap like old Biffy copping it. I sucked down a spot of tea and began to brood over the business.

Of course, there are probably fellows in the world – tough, hardy blokes with strong chins and glittering eyes – who could get engaged to this Glossop menace and like it; but I knew perfectly well that Biffy was not one of them. Honoria, you see, is one of those robust, dynamic girls with the muscles of a

432

welterweight and a laugh like a squadron of cavalry charging over a tin bridge. A beastly thing to have to face over the breakfast table. Brainy, moreover. The sort of girl who reduces you to pulp with sixteen sets of tennis and a few rounds of golf and then comes down to dinner as fresh as a daisy, expecting you to take an intelligent interest in Freud. If I had been engaged to her another week, her old father would have had one more patient on his books; and Biffy is much the same quiet sort of peaceful, inoffensive bird as me. I was shocked, I tell you, shocked.

And, as I was saying, the thing that shocked me most was Jeeves's frightful lack of proper emotion. The man happening to float in at this juncture, I gave him one more chance to show some human sympathy.

'You got the name correctly, didn't you, Jeeves?' I said. 'Mr Biffen is going to marry Honoria Glossop, the daughter of the old boy with the egg-like head and the eyebrows.'

'Yes, sir. Which suit would you wish me to lay out this morning?'

And this, mark you, from the man who, when I was engaged to the Glossop, strained every fibre in his brain to extricate me. It beat me. I couldn't understand it.

'The blue with the red twill,' I said coldly. My manner was marked, and I meant him to see that he had disappointed me sorely.

About a week later I went back to London, and scarcely had I got settled in the old flat when Biffy blew in. One glance was enough to tell me that the poisoned wound had begun to fester. The man did not look bright. No, there was no getting away from it, not bright. He had that kind of stunned, glassy expression which I used to see on my own face in the shaving-mirror during my brief engagement to the Glossop pestilence. However, if you don't want to be of the What is Wrong With This Picture brigade, you must observe the conventions, so I shook his hand as warmly as I could.

'Well, well, old man,' I said. 'Congratulations.'

'Thanks,' said Biffy wanly, and there was rather a weighty silence.

'Bertie,' said Biffy, after the silence had lasted about three minutes.

'Hallo?'

'Is it really true – ?'

'What?'

'Oh, nothing,' said Biffy, and conversation languished again. After about a minute and a half he came to the surface once more.

'Bertie.'

'Still here, old thing. What is it?'

'I say, Bertie, is it really true that you were once engaged to Honoria?'

'It is.'

Biffy coughed.

'How did you get out – I mean, what was the nature of the tragedy that prevented the marriage?'

'Jeeves worked it. He thought out the entire scheme.'

'I think, before I go,' said Biffy thoughtfully, 'I'll just step into the kitchen and have a word with Jeeves.'

I felt that the situation called for complete candour.

'Biffy, old egg,' I said, 'as man to man, do you want to oil out of this thing?'

'Bertie, old cork,' said Biffy earnestly, 'as one friend to another, I do.'

'Then why the dickens did you ever get into it?'

'I don't know. Why did you?'

'I – well, it sort of happened.'

'And it sort of happened with me. You know how it is when your heart's broken. A kind of lethargy comes over you. You get absent-minded and cease to exercise proper precautions, and the first thing you know you're for it. I don't know how it happened, old man, but there it is. And what I want you to tell me is, what's the procedure?'

'You mean, how does a fellow edge out?'

'Exactly. I don't want to hurt anybody's feelings, Bertie, but I can't go through with this thing. The shot is not on the board. For about a day and a half I thought it might be all right, but now – You remember that laugh of hers?'

'I do.'

'Well, there's that, and then all this business of never letting a fellow alone – improving his mind and so forth – '

'I know. I know.'

'Very well, then. What do you recommend? What did you mean when you said that Jeeves worked a scheme?'

'Well, you see, old Sir Roderick, who's a loony-doctor and nothing but a loony-doctor, however much you may call him a nerve specialist, discovered that there was a modicum of insanity in my family. Nothing serious. Just one of my uncles. Used to keep rabbits in his bedroom. And the old boy came to lunch here to give me the once-over, and Jeeves arranged matters so that he went away firmly convinced that I was off my onion.'

'I see,' said Biffy thoughtfully. 'The trouble is there isn't any insanity in my family.'

'None?'

It seemed to me almost incredible that a fellow could be such a perfect chump as dear old Biffy without a bit of assistance.

'Not a loony on the list,' he said gloomily. 'It's just like my luck. The old boy's coming to lunch with me tomorrow, no doubt to test me as he did you. And I never felt saner in my life.'

I thought for a moment. The idea of meeting Sir Roderick again gave me a cold shivery feeling; but when there is a chance of helping a pal we Woosters have no thought of self.

'Look here, Biffy,' I said, 'I'll tell you what. I'll roll up for that lunch. It may easily happen that when he finds you are a pal of mine he will forbid the banns right away and no more questions asked.'

'Something in that,' said Biffy, brightening. 'Awfully sporting of you, Bertie.'

'Oh, not at all,' I said. 'And meanwhile I'll consult Jeeves. Put the whole thing up to him and ask his advice. He's never failed me yet.'

Biffy pushed off, a good deal braced, and I went into the kitchen.

'Jeeves,' I said, 'I want your help once more. I've just been having a painful interview with Mr Biffen.'

'Indeed, sir?'

'It's like this,' I said, and told him the whole thing.

It was rummy, but I could feel him freezing from the start. As a rule, when I call Jeeves into conference on one of these little problems, he's all sympathy and bright ideas; but not to-day.

'I fear, sir,' he said, when I had finished, 'it is hardly my place to intervene in a private matter affecting – '

'Oh, come!'

'No, sir. It would be taking a liberty.'

'Jeeves,' I said, tackling the blighter squarely, 'what have you got against old Biffy?'

'I, sir?'

'Yes, you.'

'I assure you, sir!'

'Oh, well if you don't want to chip in and save a fellow-creature, I suppose I can't make you. But let me tell you this. I am now going back to the sitting-room, and I am going to put in some very tense thinking. You'll look pretty silly when I come and tell you that I've got Mr Biffen out of the soup without your assistance. Extremely silly you'll look.'

'Yes, sir. Shall I bring you a whisky-and-soda, sir?'

'No. Coffee! Strong and black. And if anybody wants to see me, tell 'em that I'm busy and can't be disturbed.'

An hour later I rang the bell.

'Jeeves,' I said with hauteur.

'Yes, sir?'

'Kindly ring Mr Biffen up on the phone and say that Mr Wooster presents his compliments and that he has got it.'


I was feeling more than a little pleased with myself next morning as I strolled round to Biffy's. As a rule the bright ideas you get overnight have a trick of not seeming quite so frightfully fruity when you examine them by the light of day; but this one looked as good at breakfast as it had done before dinner. I examined it narrowly from every angle, and I didn't see how it could fail.

A few days before, my Aunt Emily's son Harold had celebrated his sixth birthday; and, being up against the necessity of weighing in with a present of some kind, I had happened to see in a shop in the Strand a rather sprightly little gadget, well calculated in my opinion to amuse the child and endear him to one and all. It was a bunch of flowers in a sort of holder ending in an ingenious bulb attachment which, when pressed, shot about a pint and a half of pure spring water into the face of anyone who was ass enough to sniff at it. It seemed to me just the thing to please the growing mind of a kid of six, and I had rolled round with it.

But when I got to the house I found Harold sitting in the midst of a mass of gifts so luxurious and costly that I simply hadn't the crust to contribute a thing that had set me back a mere elevenpence-ha'penny; so with rare presence of mind – for we Woosters can think quick on occasion – I wrenched my Uncle James's card off a toy aeroplane, substituted my own, and trousered the squirt, which I took away with me. It had been lying around in my flat ever since, and it seemed to me that the time had come to send it into action.

'Well?' said Biffy anxiously, as I curveted into his sitting-room.

The poor old bird was looking pretty green about the gills. I recognized the symptoms. I had felt much the same myself when waiting for Sir Roderick to turn up and lunch with me. How the deuce people who have anything wrong with their nerves can bring themselves to chat with that man, I can't imagine; and yet he has the largest practice in London. Scarcely a day passes without his having to sit on somebody's head and ring for the attendant to bring the strait-waistcoat: and his outlook on life has become so jaundiced through constant association with coves who are picking straws out of their hair that I was convinced that Biffy had merely got to press the bulb and nature would do the rest.

So I patted him on the shoulder and said: 'It's all right, old man!'

'What does Jeeves suggest?' asked Biffy eagerly.

'Jeeves doesn't suggest anything.'

'But you said it was all right.'

'Jeeves isn't the only thinker in the Wooster home, my lad. I have taken over your little problem, and I can tell you at once that I have the situation well in hand.'

'You?' said Biffy.

His tone was far from flattering. It suggested a lack of faith in my abilities, and my view was that an ounce of demonstration would be worth a ton of explanation. I shoved the bouquet at him.

'Are you fond of flowers, Biffy?' I said.

'Eh?'

'Smell these.'

Biffy extended the old beak in a careworn sort of way, and I pressed the bulb as per printed instructions on the label.

I do like getting my money's-worth. Elevenpence ha'penny the thing had cost me, and it would have been cheap at double. The advertisement on the outside of the box had said that its effects were 'indescribably ludicrous,' and I can testify that it was no overstatement. Poor old Biffy leaped three feet in the air and smashed a small table.

'There!' I said.

The old egg was a trifle incoherent at first, but he found words fairly soon and began to express himself with a good deal of warmth.

'Calm yourself, laddie,' I said, as he paused for breath. 'It was no mere jest to pass an idle hour. It was a demonstration. Take this, Biffy, with an old friend's blessing, refill the bulb, shove it into Sir Roderick's face, press firmly, and leave the rest to him. I'll guarantee that in something under three seconds the idea will have dawned on him that you are not required in his family.'

Biffy stared at me.

'Are you suggesting that I squirt Sir Roderick?'

'Absolutely. Squirt him good. Squirt as you have never squirted before.'

'But – '

He was still yammering at me in a feverish sort of way when there was a ring at the front-door bell.

'Good Lord!' cried Biffy, quivering like a jelly. 'There he is. Talk to him while I go and change my shirt.'

I had just time to refill the bulb and shove it beside Biffy's plate, when the door opened and Sir Roderick came in. I was picking up the fallen table at the moment, and he started talking brightly to my back.

'Good afternoon. I trust I am not – Mr Wooster!'

I'm bound to say I was not feeling entirely at my ease. There is something about the man that is calculated to strike terror into the stoutest heart. If ever there was a bloke at the very mention of whose name it would be excusable for people to tremble like aspens, that bloke is Sir Roderick Glossop. He has an enormous bald head, all the hair which ought to be on it seeming to have run into his eyebrows, and his eyes go through you like a couple of Death Rays.

'How are you, how are you, how are you?' I said, overcoming a slight desire to leap backwards out of the window. 'Long time since we met, what?'

'Nevertheless, I remember you most distinctly, Mr Wooster.'

'That's fine,' I said. 'Old Biffy asked me to come and join you in mangling a bit of lunch.'

He waggled the eyebrows at me.

'Are you a friend of Charles Biffen?'

'Oh, rather. Been friends for years and years.'

He drew in his breath sharply, and I could see that Biffy's stock had dropped several points. His eye fell on the floor, which was strewn with things that had tumbled off the upset table.

'Have you had an accident?' he said.

'Nothing serious,' I explained. 'Old Biffy had some sort of fit or seizure just now and knocked over the table.'

'A fit!'

'Or seizure.'

'Is he subject to fits?'

I was about to answer, when Biffy hurried in. He had forgotten to brush his hair, which gave him a wild look, and I saw the old boy direct a keen glance at him. It seemed to me that what you might call the preliminary spadework had been most satisfactorily attended to and that the success of the good old bulb could be in no doubt whatever.

Biffy's man came in with the nose-bags and we sat down to lunch.

It looked at first as though the meal was going to be one of those complete frosts which occur from time to time in the career of a constant luncher-out. Biffy, a very C-3 host, contributed nothing to the feast of reason and flow of soul beyond an occasional hiccup, and every time I started to pull a nifty, Sir Roderick swung round on me with such a piercing stare that it stopped me in my tracks. Fortunately, however, the second course consisted of a chicken fricassee of such outstanding excellence that the old boy, after wolfing a plateful, handed up his dinner-pail for a second instalment and became almost genial.

'I am here this afternoon, Charles,' he said, with what practically amounted to bonhomie, 'on what I might describe as a mission. Yes, a mission. This is most excellent chicken.'

'Glad you like it,' mumbled old Biffy.

'Singularly toothsome,' said Sir Roderick, pronging another half ounce. 'Yes, as I was saying, a mission. You young fellows nowadays are, I know, content to live in the centre of the most wonderful metropolis the world has seen, blind and indifferent to its many marvels. I should be prepared – were I a betting man, which I am not – to wager a considerable sum that you have never in your life visited even so historic a spot as Westminster Abbey. Am I right?'

Biffy gurgled something about always having meant to.

'Nor the Tower of London?'

No, nor the Tower of London.

'And there exists at this very moment, not twenty minutes by cab from Hyde Park Corner, the most supremely absorbing and educational collection of objects, both animate and inanimate, gathered from the four corners of the Empire, that has ever been assembled in England's history. I allude to the British Empire Exhibition now situated at Wembley.'

'A fellow told me one about Wembley yesterday,' I said, to help on the cheery flow of conversation. 'Stop me if you've heard it before. Chap goes up to deaf chap outside the exhibition and says, "Is this Wembley?" "Hey?" says deaf chap. "Is this Wembley?" says chap. "Hey?" says deaf chap. "Is this Wembley?" says chap. "No, Thursday," says deaf chap. Ha, ha, I mean, what?'

The merry laughter froze on my lips. Sir Roderick sort of just waggled an eyebrow in my direction and I saw that it was back to the basket for Bertram. I never met a man who had such a knack of making a fellow feel like a waste-product.

'Have you yet paid a visit to Wembley, Charles?' he asked. 'No? Precisely as I suspected. Well, that is the mission on which I am here this afternoon. Honoria wishes me to take you to Wembley. She says it will broaden your mind, in which view I am at one with her. We will start immediately after luncheon.'

Biffy cast an imploring look at me.

'You'll come too, Bertie?'

There was such agony in his eyes that I only hesitated for a second. A pal is a pal. Besides, I felt that, if only the bulb fulfilled the high expectations I had formed of it, the merry expedition would be cancelled in no uncertain manner.

'Oh, rather,' I said.

'We must not trespass on Mr Wooster's good nature,' said Sir Roderick, looking pretty puff-faced.

'Oh, that's all right,' I said. 'I've been meaning to go to the good old exhibish for a long time. I'll slip home and change my clothes and pick you up here in my car.'

There was a silence. Biffy seemed too relieved at the thought of not having to spend the afternoon alone with Sir Roderick to be capable of speech, and Sir Roderick was registering silent disapproval. And then he caught sight of the bouquet by Biffy's plate.

'Ah, flowers,' he said. 'Sweet peas, if I am not in error. A charming plant, pleasing alike to the eye and the nose.'

I caught Biffy's eye across the table. It was bulging, and a strange light shone in it.

'Are you fond of flowers, Sir Roderick?' he croaked.

'Extremely.'

'Smell these.'

Sir Roderick dipped his head and sniffed. Biffy's fingers closed slowly over the bulb. I shut my eyes and clutched the table.

'Very pleasant,' I heard Sir Roderick say. 'Very pleasant indeed.'

I opened my eyes, and there was Biffy leaning back in his chair with a ghastly look, and the bouquet on the cloth beside him. I realized what had happened. In that supreme crisis of his life, with his whole happiness depending on a mere pressure of the fingers, Biffy, the poor spineless fish, had lost his nerve. My closely-reasoned scheme had gone phut.

Jeeves was fooling about with the geraniums in the sitting-room window-box when I got home.

'They make a very nice display, sir,' he said, cocking a paternal eye at the things.

'Don't talk to me about flowers,' I said. 'Jeeves, I know now how a general feels when he plans out some great scientific movement and his troops let him down at the eleventh hour.'

'Indeed, sir?'

'Yes,' I said, and told him what had happened.

He listened thoughtfully.

'A somewhat vacillating and changeable young gentleman, Mr Biffen,' was his comment when I had finished. 'Would you be requiring me for the remainder of the afternoon, sir?'

'No. I'm going to Wembley. I just came back to change and get the car. Produce some fairly durable garments which can stand getting squashed by the many-headed, Jeeves, and then phone to the garage.'

'Very good, sir. The grey cheviot lounge will, I fancy, be suitable. Would it be too much if I asked you to give me a seat in the car, sir? I had thought of going to Wembley myself this afternoon.'

'Eh? Oh, all right.'

'Thank you very much, sir.'

I got dressed, and we drove round to Biffy's flat. Biffy and Sir Roderick got in at the back and Jeeves climbed into the front seat next to me. Biffy looked so ill-attuned to an afternoon's pleasure that my heart bled for the blighter and I made one last attempt to appeal to Jeeves's better feelings.

'I must say, Jeeves,' I said, 'I'm dashed disappointed in you.'

'I am sorry to hear that, sir.'

'Well, I am. Dashed disappointed. I do think you might rally round. Did you see Mr Biffen's face?'

'Yes, sir.'

'Well, then.'

'If you will pardon my saying so, sir, Mr Biffen has surely only himself to thank if he has entered upon matrimonial obligations which do not please him.'

'You're talking absolute rot, Jeeves. You know as well as I do that Honoria Glossop is an Act of God. You might just as well blame a fellow for getting run over by a truck.'

'Yes, sir.'

'Absolutely yes. Besides, the poor ass wasn't in a condition to resist. He told me all about it. He had lost the only girl he had ever loved, and you know what a man's like when that happens to him.'

'How was that, sir?'

'Apparently he fell in love with some girl on the boat going over to New York, and they parted at the Customs sheds, arranging to meet next day at her hotel. Well, you know what

Biffy's like. He forgets his own name half the time. He never made a note of the address, and it passed clean out of his mind. He went about in a sort of trance, and suddenly woke up to find that he was engaged to Honoria Glossop.'

'I did not know of this, sir.'

'I don't suppose anybody knows of it except me. He told me when I was in Paris.'

'I should have supposed it would have been feasible to make inquiries, sir.'

'That's what I said. But he had forgotten her name.'

'That sounds remarkable, sir.'

'I said that, too. But it's a fact. All he remembered was that her Christian name was Mabel. Well, you can't go scouring New York for a girl named Mabel, what?'

'I appreciate the difficulty, sir.'

'Well, there it is, then.'

'I see, sir.'

We had got into a mob of vehicles outside the Exhibition by this time, and, some tricky driving being indicated, I had to suspend the conversation. We parked ourselves eventually and went in. Jeeves drifted away, and Sir Roderick took charge of the expedition. He headed for the Palace of Industry, with Biffy and myself trailing behind.

Well, you know, I have never been much of a lad for exhibitions. The citizenry in the mass always rather puts me off, and after I have been shuffling along with the multitude for a quarter of an hour or so I feel as if I were walking on hot bricks. About this particular binge, too, there seemed to me a lack of what you might call human interest. I mean to say, millions of people, no doubt, are so constituted that they scream with joy and excitement at the spectacle of a stuffed porcupine-fish or a glass jar of seeds from Western Australia – but not Bertram. No; if you will take the word of one who would not deceive you, not Bertram. By the time we had tottered out of the Gold Coast village and were working towards the Palace of Machinery, everything pointed to my shortly executing a quiet sneak in the direction of that rather jolly Planters' Bar in the West Indian section. Sir Roderick had whizzed us past this at a high rate of speed, it touching no chord in him; but I had been able to observe that there was a sprightly sportsman behind the counter mixing things out of bottles and stirring them up with a stick in long glasses that seemed to have ice in them, and the urge came upon me to see more of this man. I was about to drop away from the main body and become a straggler, when something pawed at my coat-sleeve. It was Biffy, and he had the air of one who has had about sufficient.

There are certain moments in life when words are not needed. I looked at Biffy, Biffy looked at me. A perfect understanding linked our two souls.

'?'

'!'

Three minutes later we had joined the Planters.

I have never been in the West Indies, but I am in a position to state that in certain of the fundamentals of life they are streets ahead of our European civilisation. The man behind the counter, as kindly a bloke as I ever wish to meet, seemed to guess our requirements the moment we hove in view. Scarcely had our elbows touched the wood before he was leaping to and fro, bringing down a new bottle with each leap. A planter, apparently, does not consider he has had a drink unless it contains at least seven ingredients, and I'm not saying, mind you, that he isn't right. The man behind the bar told us the things were called Green Swizzles; and, if ever I marry and have a son, Green Swizzle Wooster is the name that will go down on the register, in memory of the day his father's life was saved at Wembley.

After the third, Biffy breathed a contented sigh.

'Where do you think Sir Roderick is?' he said.

'Biffy, old thing,' I replied frankly, 'I'm not worrying.'

'Bertie, old bird,' said Biffy, 'nor am I.'

He sighed again, and broke a long silence by asking the man for a straw.

'Bertie,' he said, 'I've just remembered something rather rummy. You know Jeeves?'

I said I knew Jeeves.

'Well, a rather rummy incident occurred as we were going into this place. Old Jeeves sidled up to me and said something rather rummy. You'll never guess what it was.'

'No. I don't believe I ever shall.'

'Jeeves said,' proceeded Biffy earnestly, 'and I am quoting his very words – Jeeves said, "Mr Biffen" – addressing me, you understand – '

'I understand.'

' "Mr Biffen," he said, "I strongly advise you to visit the – " '

'The what?' I asked as he paused.

'Bertie, old man,' said Biffy, deeply concerned, 'I've absolutely forgotten!'

I stared at the man.

'What I can't understand,' I said, 'is how you manage to run that Herefordshire place of yours for a day. How on earth do you remember to milk the cows and give the pigs their dinner?'

'Oh, that's all right. There are diverse blokes about the places – hirelings and menials, you know – who look after all that.'

'Ah!' I said. 'Well, that being so, let us have one more Green Swizzle, and then hey for the Amusement Park.'

When I indulged in those few rather bitter words about exhibitions, it must be distinctly understood that I was not alluding to what you might call the more earthy portion of these curious places. I yield to no man in my approval of those institutions where on payment of a shilling you are permitted to slide down a slippery runway sitting on a mat. I love the Jiggle-Joggle, and I am prepared to take on all and sundry at Skee Ball for money, stamps, or Brazil nuts.

But, joyous reveller as I am on these occasions, I was simply not in it with old Biffy. Whether it was the Green Swizzles or merely the relief of being parted from Sir Roderick, I don't know, but Biffy flung himself into the pastimes of the proletariat with a zest that was almost frightening. I could hardly drag him away from the Whip, and as for the Switchback, he looked like spending the rest of his life on it. I managed to remove him at last, and he was wandering through the crowd at my side with gleaming eyes, hesitating between having his fortune told and taking a whirl at the Wheel of Joy, when he suddenly grabbed my arm and uttered a sharp animal cry.

'Bertie!'

'Now what?'

He was pointing at a large sign over a building.

'Look! Palace of Beauty!'

I tried to choke him off. I was getting a bit weary by this time. Not so young as I was.

'You don't want to go in there,' I said. 'A fellow at the club was telling me about that. It's only a lot of girls. You don't want to see a lot of girls.'

'I do want to see a lot of girls,' said Biffy firmly. 'Dozens of girls, and the more unlike Honoria they are, the better. Besides, I've suddenly remembered that that's the place Jeeves told me to be sure and visit. It all comes back to me. "Mr Biffin," he said, "I strongly advise you to visit the Palace of Beauty." Now, what the man was driving at or what his motive was, I don't know; but I ask you, Bertie, is it wise, is it safe, is it judicious ever to ignore Jeeves's lightest word? We enter by the door on the left.'

I don't know if you know this Palace of Beauty place? It's a sort of aquarium full of the delicately-nurtured instead of fishes. You go in, and there is a kind of cage with a female goggling out at you through a sheet of plate glass. She's dressed in some weird kind of costume, and over the cage is written 'Helen of Troy.' You pass on to the next, and there's another one doing jiu-jitsu with a snake. Sub title, Cleopatra. You get the idea – Famous Women Through the Ages and all that. I can't say it fascinated me to any great extent. I maintain that lovely woman loses a lot of her charm if you have to stare at her in a tank. Moreover, it gave me a rummy sort of feeling of having wandered into the wrong bedroom at a country house, and I was flying past at a fair rate of speed, anxious to get it over, when Biffy suddenly went off his rocker.

At least, it looked like that. He let out a piercing yell, grabbed my arm with a sudden clutch that felt like the bite of a crocodile, and stood there gibbering.

'Wuk!' ejaculated Biffy, or words to that general import.

A large and interested crowd had gathered round. I think they thought the girls were going to be fed or something. But Biffy paid no attention to them. He was pointing in a loony manner at one of the cages. I forget which it was, but the female inside wore a ruff, so it may have been Queen Elizabeth or Boadicea or someone of that period. She was rather a nice-looking girl, and she was staring at Biffy in much the same pop-eyed way as he was staring at her.

'Mabel!' yelled Biffy, going off in my ear like a bomb.

I can't say I was feeling my chirpiest. Drama is all very well, but I hate getting mixed up in it in a public spot; and I had not realized before how dashed public this spot was. The crowd seemed to have doubled itself in the last five seconds, and, while most of them had their eye on Biffy, quite a goodish few were looking at me as if they thought I was an important principal in the scene and might be expected at any moment to give of my best in the way of wholesome entertainment for the masses.

Biffy was jumping about like a lamb in the springtime – and, what is more, a feeble-minded lamb.

'Bertie! It's her! It's she!' He looked about him wildly. 'Where the deuce is the stage door?' he cried. 'Where's the manager? I want to see the house-manager immediately.'

And then he suddenly bounded forward and began hammering on the glass with his stick.

'I say, old lad!' I began, but he shook me off.

These fellows who live in the country are apt to go in for fairly sizable clubs instead of the light canes which your well-dressed man about town considers suitable for metropolitan use; and down in Herefordshire, apparently, something in the nature of a knob-kerrie is *de rigueur*. Biffy's first slosh smashed the glass all to a hash. Three more cleared the way for him to go into the cage without cutting himself. And, before the crowd had time to realize what a wonderful bob's-worth it was getting in exchange for its entrance-fee, he was inside, engaging the girl in earnest conversation. And at the same moment two large policemen rolled up.

You can't make policemen take the romantic view. Not a tear did these two blighters stop to brush away. They were inside the cage and out of it and marching Biffy through the crowd before you had time to blink. I hurried after them, to do what I could in the way of soothing Biffy's last moments, and the poor old lad turned a glowing face in my direction.

'Chiswick, 60873,' he bellowed in a voice charged with emotion. 'Write it down, Bertie, or I shall forget it. Chiswick, 60873. Her telephone number.'

And then he disappeared, accompanied by about eleven thousand sightseers, and a voice spoke at my elbow.

'Mr Wooster! What – what – what is the meaning of this?'

Sir Roderick, with bigger eyebrows than ever, was standing at my side.

'It's all right,' I said. 'Poor old Biffy's only gone off his crumpet.'

He tottered.

'What?'

'Had a sort of fit or seizure, you know.'

'Another!' Sir Roderick drew a deep breath. 'And this is the man I was about to allow my daughter to marry!' I heard him mutter.

I tapped him in a kindly spirit on the shoulder. It took some doing, mark you, but I did it.

'If I were you,' I said, 'I should call that off. Scratch the fixture. Wash it out absolutely, is my advice.'

He gave me a nasty look.

'I do not require your advice, Mr Wooster! I had already arrived independently at the decision of which you speak. Mr Wooster, you are a friend of this man – a fact which should in itself have been sufficient warning to me. You will – unlike myself – be seeing him again. Kindly inform him, when you do see him, that he may consider his engagement at an end.'

'Right-ho,' I said, and hurried off after the crowd. It seemed to me that a little bailing-out might be in order.


It was about an hour later that I shoved my way out to where I had parked the car. Jeeves was sitting in the front seat, brooding over the cosmos. He rose courteously as I approached.

'You are leaving, sir?'

'I am.'

'And Sir Roderick, sir?'

'Not coming. I am revealing no secrets, Jeeves, when I inform you that he and I have parted brass-rags. Not on speaking terms now.'

'Indeed, sir? And Mr Biffen? Will you wait for him?'

'No. He's in prison.'

'Really, sir?'

'Yes. I tried to bail him out, but they decided on second thoughts to coop him up for the night.'

'What was his offence, sir?'

'You remember that girl of his I was telling you about? He

found her in a tank at the Palace of Beauty and went after her by the quickest route, which was *via* a plate-glass window. He was then scooped up and borne off in irons by the constabulary.'
I gazed sideways at him. It is difficult to bring off a penetrating glance out of the corner of your eye, but I managed it. 'Jeeves,' I said, 'there is more in this than the casual observer would suppose. You told Mr Biffen to go to the Palace of Beauty. Did you know the girl would be there?'

'Yes, sir.'

This was most remarkable, and rummy to a degree.

'Dash it, do you know everything?'

'Oh, no, sir,' said Jeeves with an indulgent smile. Humouring the young master.

'Well, how did you know that?'

'I happen to be acquainted with the future Mrs Biffen, sir.'

'I see. Then you knew all about that business in New York?'

'Yes, sir. And it was for that reason that I was not altogether favourably disposed towards Mr Biffen when you were first kind enough to suggest that I might be able to offer some slight assistance. I mistakenly supposed that he had been trifling with the girl's affections, sir. But when you told me the true facts of the case I appreciated the injustice I had done to Mr Biffen and endeavoured to make amends.'

'Well, he certainly owes you a lot. He's crazy about her.'

'That is very gratifying, sir.'

'And she ought to be pretty grateful to you, too. Old Biffy's got fifteen thousand a year, not to mention more cows, pigs, hens, and ducks than he knows what to do with. A dashed useful bird to have in any family.'

'Yes, sir.'

'Tell me, Jeeves,' I said, 'how did you happen to know the girl in the first place?'

Jeeves looked dreamily out into the traffic.

'She is my niece, sir. If I might make the suggestion, sir, I should not jerk the steering-wheel with quite such suddenness. We very nearly collided with that omnibus.'

# =2=
# THE ORDEAL OF YOUNG TUPPY

'What-ho, Jeeves!' I said, entering the room where he waded knee-deep in suitcases and shirts and winter suitings, like a sea-beast among rocks. 'Packing?'

'Yes, sir,' replied the honest fellow, for there are no secrets between us.

'Pack on!' I said approvingly. 'Pack, Jeeves, pack with care. Pack in the presence of the passenjare.' And I rather fancy I added the words "Tra-la!" for I was in merry mood.

Every year, starting about the middle of November, there is a good deal of anxiety and apprehension among owners of the better-class of country-house throughout England as to who will get Bertram Wooster's patronage for Christmas holidays. It may be one or it may be another. As my Aunt Dahlia says, you never know where the blow will fall.

This year, however, I had decided early. It couldn't have been later than Nov. 10 when a sigh of relief went up from a dozen stately homes as it became known that the short straw had been drawn by Sir Reginald Witherspoon, Bart., of Bleaching Court, Upper Bleaching, Hants.

In coming to the decision to give this Witherspoon my custom, I had been actuated by several reasons, not counting the fact that, having married Aunt Dahlia's husband's younger sister Katherine, he is by way of being a sort of uncle of mine. In the first place, the Bart. does one extraordinarily well, both browsing and sluicing being above criticism. Then, again, his stables always contain something worth riding, which is a consideration. And, thirdly, there is no danger of getting lugged into a party of amateur Waits and having to tramp the countryside in the rain, singing, 'When Shepherds Watched Their Flocks By Night.' Or for the matter of that, 'Noel! Noel!'

All these things counted with me, but what really drew me

to Bleaching Court like a magnet was the knowledge that young Tuppy Glossop would be among those present.

I feel sure I have told you before about this black-hearted bird, but I will give you the strength of it once again, just to keep the records straight. He was the fellow, if you remember, who, ignoring a lifelong friendship in the course of which he had frequently eaten my bread and salt, betted me one night at the Drones that I wouldn't swing myself across the swimming-bath by the ropes and rings and then, with almost inconceivable treachery, went and looped back the last ring, causing me to drop into the fluid and ruin one of the nattiest suits of dress-clothes in London.

To execute a fitting vengeance on this bloke had been the ruling passion of my life ever since.

'You are bearing in mind, Jeeves,' I said, 'the fact that Mr Glossop will be at Bleaching?'

'Yes, sir.'

'And, consequently, are not forgetting to put in the Giant Squirt?'

'No, sir.'

'Nor the Luminous Rabbit?'

'No, sir.'

'Good! I am rather pinning my faith on the Luminous Rabbit, Jeeves. I hear excellent reports of it on all sides. You wind it up and put it in somebody's room in the night watches, and it shines in the dark and jumps about, making odd, squeaking noises the while. The whole performance being, I should imagine, well calculated to scare young Tuppy into a decline.'

'Very possibly, sir.'

'Should that fail, there is always the Giant Squirt. We must leave no stone unturned to put it across the man somehow,' I said. 'The Wooster honour is at stake.'

I would have spoken further on this subject, but just then the front-door bell buzzed.

'I'll answer it,' I said. 'I expect it's Aunt Dahlia. She 'phoned that she would be calling this morning.'

It was not Aunt Dahlia. It was a telegraph-boy with telegram. I opened it, read it, and carried it back to the bedroom, the brow a bit knitted.

'Jeeves,' I said. 'A rummy communication has arrived. From Mr Glossop.'

'Indeed, sir?'

'I will read it to you. Handed in at Upper Bleaching. Message runs as follows:

*"When you come tomorrow, bring my football boots. Also, if humanly possible, Irish water-spaniel. Urgent. Regards. Tuppy."*

'What do you make of that, Jeeves?'

'As I interpret the document, sir, Mr Glossop wishes you, when you come tomorrow, to bring his football boots. Also, if humanly possible, an Irish water-spaniel. He hints that the matter is urgent, and sends his regards.'

'Yes, that's how I read it, too. But why football boots?'

'Perhaps Mr Glossop wishes to play football, sir.'

I considered this.

'Yes,' I said. 'That may be the solution. But why would a man, staying peacefully at a country-house, suddenly develop a craving to play football?'

'I could not say, sir.'

'And why an Irish water-spaniel?'

'There again I fear I can hazard no conjecture, sir.'

'What *is* an Irish water-spaniel?'

'A water-spaniel of a variety bred in Ireland, sir.'

'You think so?'

'Yes, sir.'

'Well, perhaps you're right. But why should I sweat about the place collecting dogs – of whatever nationality – for young Tuppy? Does he think I'm Santa Claus? Is he under the impression that my feelings towards him, after that Drones Club incident, are those of kindly benevolence? Irish water-spaniels, indeed! Tchah!'

'Sir?'

'Tchah, Jeeves.'

'Very good, sir.'

The front-door bell buzzed again.

'A busy morning, Jeeves.'

'Yes, sir.'

'All right. I'll go.'

This time it was Aunt Dahlia. She charged in with the air of a woman with something on her mind – giving tongue, in fact, while actually on the very doormat.

'Bertie,' she boomed, in that ringing voice of hers which cracks window-panes and upsets vases, 'I've come about that young hound, Glossop.'

'It's quite all right, Aunt Dahlia,' I replied soothingly. 'I have the situation well in hand. The Giant Squirt and the Luminous Rabbit are even now being packed.'

'I don't know what you're talking about, and I don't for a moment suppose you do, either,' said the relative somewhat brusquely, 'but, if you'll kindly stop gibbering, I'll tell you what I mean. I have had a most disturbing letter from Katherine. About this reptile. Of course, I haven't breathed a word to Angela. She'd hit the ceiling.'

This Angela is Aunt Dahlia's daughter. She and young Tuppy are generally supposed to be more or less engaged, though nothing definitely "Morning Posted" yet.

'Why?' I said.

'Why what?'

'Why would Angela hit the ceiling?'

'Well, wouldn't you, if you were practically engaged to a fiend in human shape and somebody told you he had gone off to the country and was flirting with a dog-girl?'

'With a what was that, once again?'

'A dog-girl. One of these dashed open-air flappers in thick boots and tailor-made tweeds who infest the rural districts and go about the place followed by packs of assorted dogs. I used to be one of them myself in my younger days, so I know how dangerous they are. Her name is Dalgleish. Old Colonel Dalgleish's daughter. They live near Bleaching.'

I saw a gleam of daylight.

'Then that must be what his telegram was about. He's just wired, asking me to bring down an Irish water-spaniel. A Christmas present for this girl, no doubt.'

'Probably. Katherine tells me he seems to be infatuated with her. She says he follows her about like one of her dogs, looking like a tame cat and bleating like a sheep.'

'Quite the private zoo, what?'

'Bertie,' said Aunt Dahlia – and I could see her generous

nature was stirred to its depths – 'one more crack like that out of you, and I shall forget that I am an aunt and hand you one.'

I became soothing. I gave her the old oil.

'I shouldn't worry,' I said. 'There's probably nothing in it. Whole thing no doubt much exaggerated.'

'You think so, eh? Well, you know what he's like. You remember the trouble we had when he ran after that singing-woman.'

I recollected the case. You will find it elsewhere in the archives. Cora Bellinger was the female's name. She was studying for Opera, and young Tuppy thought highly of her. Fortunately, however, she punched him in the eye during Beefy Bingham's clean, bright entertainment in Bermondsey East, and love died.

'Besides,' said Aunt Dahlia, 'There's something I haven't told you. Just before he went to Bleaching, he and Angela quarrelled.'

'They did?'

'Yes. I got it out of Angela this morning. She was crying her eyes out, poor angel. It was something about her last hat. As far as I could gather, he told her it made her look like a Pekingese, and she told him she never wanted to see him again in this world or the next. And he said "Right ho!" and breezed off. I can see what has happened. This dog-girl has caught him on the rebound and, unless something is done quick, anything may happen. So place the facts before Jeeves, and tell him to take action the moment you get down there.'

I am always a little piqued, if you know what I mean, at this assumption on the relative's part that Jeeves is so dashed essential on these occasions. My manner, therefore, as I replied, was a bit on the crisp side.

'Jeeves's services will not be required,' I said. 'I can handle this business. The programme which I have laid out will be quite sufficient to take young Tuppy's mind off love-making. It is my intention to insert the Luminous Rabbit in his room at the first opportunity that presents itself. The Luminous Rabbit shines in the dark and jumps about, making odd, squeaking noises. It will sound to young Tuppy like the Voice of Conscience, and I anticipate that a single treatment will make him retire into a nursing-home for a couple of weeks or so. At the

454

end of which period he will have forgotten all about the bally girl.'

'Bertie,' said Aunt Dahlia, with a sort of frozen calm, 'You are the Abysmal Chump. Listen to me. It's simply because I am fond of you and have influence with the Lunacy Commissioners that you weren't put in a padded cell years ago. Bungle this business, and I withdraw my protection. Can't you understand that this thing is far too serious for any fooling about? Angela's whole happiness is at stake. Do as I tell you, and put it up to Jeeves.'

'Just as you say, Aunt Dahlia,' I said stiffly.

'All right, then. Do it now.'

I went back to the bedroom.

'Jeeves,' I said, and I did not trouble to conceal my chagrin, 'you need not pack the Luminous Rabbit.'

'Very good, sir.'

'Nor the Giant Squirt.'

'Very good, sir.'

'They have been subjected to destructive criticism, and the zest has gone. Oh, and, Jeeves.'

'Sir?'

'Mrs Travers wishes you, on arriving at Bleaching Court, to disentangle Mr Glossop from a dog-girl.'

'Very good, sir. I will attend to the matter and will do my best to give satisfaction.'

That Aunt Dahlia had not exaggerated the perilous nature of the situation was made clear to me on the following afternoon. Jeeves and I drove down to Bleaching in the two-seater, and we were tooling along about half-way between the village and the Court when suddenly there appeared ahead of us a sea of dogs and in the middle of it young Tuppy frisking round one of those largish, corn-fed girls. He was bending towards her in a devout sort of way, and even at a considerable distance I could see that his ears were pink. His attitude, in short, was unmistakably that of a man endeavouring to push a good thing along; and when I came closer and noted that the girl wore tailor-made tweeds and thick boots, I had no further doubts.

'You observe, Jeeves?' I said in a low, significant voice.

'Yes, sir.'

'The girl, what?'

'Yes, sir.'

I tooted amiably on the horn and yodelled a bit. They turned – Tuppy, I fancied, not any too pleased.

'Oh, hullo, Bertie,' he said.

'Hullo,' I said.

'My friend, Bertie Wooster,' said Tuppy to the girl, in what seemed to me rather an apologetic manner. You know – as if he would have preferred to hush me up.

'Hullo,' said the girl.

'Hullo,' I said.

'Hullo, Jeeves,' said Tuppy.

'Good afternoon, sir,' said Jeeves.

There was a somewhat constrained silence.

'Well, good-bye, Bertie,' said young Tuppy. 'You'll be wanting to push along, I expect.'

We Woosters can take a hint as well as the next man.

'See you later,' I said.

'Oh, rather,' said Tuppy.

I set the machinery in motion again, and we rolled off.

'Sinister, Jeeves,' I said. 'You noticed that the subject was looking like a stuffed frog?'

'Yes, sir.'

'And gave no indication of wanting us to stop and join the party?'

'No, sir.'

'I think Aunt Dahlia's fears are justified. The thing seems serious.'

'Yes, sir.'

'Well, strain the brain, Jeeves.'

'Very good, sir.'

It wasn't till I was dressing for dinner that night that I saw young Tuppy again. He trickled in just as I was arranging the tie.

'Hullo!' I said.

'Hullo!' said Tuppy.

'Who was the girl?' I asked, in that casual, snaky way of mine – off-hand, I mean.

'A Miss Dalgleish,' said Tuppy, and I noticed that he blushed a spot.

456

'Staying here?'

'No. She lives in that house just before you come to the gates of this place. Did you bring my football boots?'

'Yes. Jeeves has got them somewhere.'

'And the water-spaniel?'

'Sorry. No water-spaniel.'

'Dashed nuisance. She's set her heart on an Irish water-spaniel.'

'Well, what do you care?'

'I wanted to give her one.'

'Why?'

Tuppy became a trifle haughty. Frigid. The rebuking eye.

'Colonel and Mrs Dalgleish,' he said, 'have been extremely kind to me since I got here. They have entertained me. I naturally wish to make some return for their hospitality. I don't want them to look upon me as one of those ill-mannered modern young men you read about in the papers who grab everything they can lay their hooks on and never buy back. If people ask you to lunch and tea and whatnot, they appreciate it if you make them some little present in return.'

'Well, give them your football boots. In passing, why did you want the bally things?'

'I'm playing in a match next Thursday.'

'Down here?'

'Yes. Upper Bleaching versus Hockley-cum-Meston. Apparently it's the big game of the year.'

'How did you get roped in?'

'I happened to mention in the course of conversation the other day that, when in London, I generally turn out on Saturdays for the Old Austinians, and Miss Dalgleish seemed rather keen that I should help the village.'

'Which village?'

'Upper Bleaching, of course.'

'Ah, then you're going to play for Hockley?'

'You needn't be funny, Bertie. You may not know it, but I'm pretty hot stuff on the football field. Oh, Jeeves.'

'Sir?' said Jeeves, entering right centre.

'Mr Wooster tells me you have my football boots.'

'Yes, sir. I have placed them in your room.'

'Thanks. Jeeves, do you want to make a bit of money?'

'Yes, sir.'

'Then put a trifle on Upper Bleaching for the annual encounter with Hockley-cum-Meston next Thursday,' said Tuppy, exiting with swelling bosom.

'Mr Glossop is going to play on Thursday,' I explained as the door closed.

'So I was informed in the Servants' Hall, sir.'

'Oh? And what's the general feeling there about it?'

'The impression I gathered, sir, was that the Servants' Hall considers Mr Glossop ill-advised.'

'Why's that?'

'I am informed by Mr Mulready, Sir Reginald's butler, sir, that this contest differs in some respects from the ordinary football game. Owing to the fact that there has existed for many years considerable animus between the two villages, the struggle is conducted, it appears, on somewhat looser and more primitive lines than is usually the case when two teams meet in friendly rivalry. The primary object of the players, I am given to understand, is not so much to score points as to inflict violence.'

'Good Lord, Jeeves!'

'Such appears to be the case, sir. The game is one that would have a great interest for the antiquarian. It was played first in the reign of King Henry the Eighth, when it lasted from noon till sundown over an area covering several square miles. Seven deaths resulted on that occasion.'

'Seven!'

'Not inclusive of two of the spectators, sir. In recent years, however, the casualties appear to have been confined to broken limbs and other minor injuries. The opinion of the Servants' Hall is that it would be more judicious on Mr Glossop's part, were he to refrain from mixing himself up in the affair.'

I was more or less aghast. I mean to say, while I had made it my mission in life to get back at young Tuppy for that business at the Drones, there still remained certain faint vestiges, if vestiges is the word I want, of the old friendship and esteem. Besides, there are limits to one's thirst for vengeance. Deep as my resentment was for the ghastly outrage he had perpetrated on me, I had no wish to see him toddle unsuspiciously into the arena and get all chewed up by wild villagers. A Tuppy scared stiff by a Luminous Rabbit – yes. Excellent business. The happy ending, in fact. But a Tuppy carried off on a stretcher in half a dozen pieces – no. Quite a different matter. All wrong. Not to be considered for a moment.

Obviously, then, a kindly word of warning while there was yet time, was indicated. I buzzed off to his room forthwith, and found him toying dreamily with the football boots.

I put him in possession of the facts.

'What you had better do – and the Servants' Hall thinks the same,' I said, 'is fake a sprained ankle on the eve of the match.'

He looked at me in an odd sort of way.

'You suggest that, when Miss Dalgleish is trusting me, relying on me, looking forward with eager, girlish enthusiasm to seeing me help her village on to victory, I should let her down with a thud?'

I was pleased with his ready intelligence.

'That's the idea,' I said.

'Faugh!' said Tuppy – the only time I've ever heard the word.

'How do you mean, "Faugh"?' I asked.

'Bertie,' said Tuppy, 'what you tell me merely makes me all the keener for the fray. A warm game is what I want. I welcome this sporting spirit on the part of the opposition. I shall enjoy a spot of roughness. It will enable me to go all out and give of my best. Do you realize,' said young Tuppy, vermilion to the gills, 'that She will be looking on? And do you know how that will make me feel? It will make me feel like some knight of old jousting under the eyes of his lady. Do you suppose that Sir Lancelot or Sir Galahad, when there was a tourney scheduled for the following Thursday, went and pretended they had sprained their ankles just because the thing was likely to be a bit rough?'

'Don't forget that in the reign of King Henry the Eighth – '

'Never mind about the reign of King Henry the Eighth. All I care about is that it's Upper Bleaching's turn this year to play in colours, so I shall be able to wear my Old Austinian shirt. Light blue, Bertie, with broad orange stripes. I shall look like something, I tell you.'

'But what?'

'Bertie,' said Tuppy, now becoming purely ga-ga, 'I may as well tell you that I'm in love at last. This is the real thing. I have found my mate. All my life I have dreamed of meeting some sweet, open-air girl with all the glory of the English countryside in her eyes, and I have found her. How different she is, Bertie, from these hot-house, artificial London girls! Would they stand in the mud on a winter afternoon, watching a football match? Would they know what to give an Alsatian for fits? Would they tramp ten miles a day across the fields and come back as fresh as paint? No!'

'Well, why should they?'

'Bertie, I'm staking everything on this game on Thursday. At the moment, I have an idea that she looks on me as something of a weakling, simply because I got a blister on my foot the other afternoon and had to take the bus back from Hockley. But when she sees me going through the rustic opposition like a devouring flame, will that make her think a bit? Will that make her open her eyes? What?'

'What?'

'I said "What"?'

'So did I.'

'I meant, Won't it?'

'Oh, rather.'

Here the dinner-gong sounded, not before I was ready for it.

Judicious enquiries during the next couple of days convinced me that the Servants' Hall at Bleaching Court, in advancing the suggestion that young Tuppy, born and bred in the gentler atmosphere of the metropolis, would do well to keep out of local disputes and avoid the football-field on which these were to be settled, had not spoken idly. It had weighed its words and said the sensible thing. Feeling between the two villages undoubtedly ran high, as they say.

You know how it is in these remote rural districts. Life tends at times to get a bit slow. There's nothing much to do in the long winter evenings but listen to the radio and brood on what a tick your neighbour is. You find yourself remembering how Farmer Giles did you down over the sale of your pig, and Farmer Giles finds himself remembering that it was your son, Ernest, who bunged the half-brick at his horse on the second Sunday before Septuagesima. And so on and so forth. How this particular feud had started, I don't know, but the season of peace and goodwill found it in full blast. The only topic of conversation in

Upper Bleaching was Thursday's game, and the citizenry seemed to be looking forward to it in a spirit that can only be described as ghoulish. And it was the same in Hockley-cum-Meston.

I paid a visit to Hockley-cum-Meston on the Wednesday, being rather anxious to take a look at the inhabitants and see how formidable they were. I was shocked to observe that practically every second male might have been the Village Blacksmith's big brother. The muscles of their brawny arms were obviously strong as iron bands, and the way the company at the Green Pig, where I looked in incognito for a spot of beer, talked about the forthcoming sporting contest was enough to chill the blood of anyone who had a pal who proposed to fling himself into the fray. It sounded rather like Attila and a few of his Huns sketching out their next campaign.

I went back to Jeeves with my mind made up.

'Jeeves,' I said, 'you, who had the job of drying and pressing those dress-clothes of mine, are aware that I have suffered much at young Tuppy Glossop's hands. By rights, I suppose, I ought to be welcoming the fact that the Wrath of Heaven is now hovering over him in this fearful manner. But the view I take of it is that Heaven looks like overdoing it. Heaven's idea of a fitting retribution is not mine. In my most unrestrained moments I never wanted the poor blighter assassinated. And the idea in Hockley-cum-Meston seems to be that a good opportunity has arisen of making it a bumper Christmas for the local undertaker. There was a fellow with red hair at the Green Pig this afternoon who might have been the undertaker's partner, the way he talked. We must act, and speedily, Jeeves. We must put a bit of a jerk in it and save young Tuppy in spite of himself.'

'What course would you advocate, sir?'

'I'll tell you. He refuses to do the sensible thing and slide out, because the girl will be watching the game and he imagines, poor lizard, that he is going to shine and impress her. So we must employ guile. You must go up to London today, Jeeves, and tomorrow morning you will send a telegram, signed "Angela," which will run as follows. Jot it down. Ready?'

'Yes, sir.'

' "So sorry – " . . .' I pondered. 'What would a girl say, Jeeves, who, having had a row with the bird she was practically engaged

461

to because he told her she looked like a Pekingese in her new hat, wanted to extend the olive-branch?'

' "So sorry I was cross", sir, would, I fancy, be the expression.'

'Strong enough, do you think?'

'Possibly the addition of the word "darling" would give the necessary verisimilitude, sir.'

'Right. Resume the jotting. "So sorry I was cross, darling . . ." No, wait, Jeeves. Scratch that out. I see where we have gone off the rails. I see where we are missing a chance to make this the real tabasco. Sign the telegram not "Angela" but "Travers".'

'Very good, sir.'

'Or, rather, "Dahlia Travers". And this is the body of the communication. "Please return at once." '

' "Immediately" would be more economical, sir. Only one word. And it has a strong ring.'

'True. Jot on, then. "Please return immediately. Angela in a hell of a state." '

'I would suggest "Seriously ill", sir.'

'All right. "Seriously ill". "Angela seriously ill. Keeps calling for you and says you were quite right about hat." '

'If I might suggest, sir —?'

'Well, go ahead.'

'I fancy the following would meet the case. "Please return immediately. Angela seriously ill. High fever and delirium. Keeps calling your name piteously and saying something about a hat and that you were quite right. Please catch earliest possible train. Dahlia Travers." '

'That sounds all right.'

'Yes, sir.'

'You like that "piteously"? You don't think "incessantly"?'

'No, sir. "Piteously" is the *mot juste*.'

'All right. You know. Well, send it off in time to get here at two-thirty.'

'Yes, sir.'

'Two-thirty, Jeeves. You see the devilish cunning?'

'No, sir.'

'I will tell you. If the telegram arrived earlier, he would get it before the game. By two-thirty, however, he will have started for the ground. I shall hand it to him the moment there is a lull in the battle. By that time he will have begun to get some idea of what a football match between Upper Bleaching and Hockley-cum-Meston is like, and the thing ought to work like magic. I can't imagine anyone who has been sporting awhile with those thugs I saw yesterday not welcoming any excuse to call it a day. You follow me?'

'Yes, sir.'

'Very good, Jeeves.'

'Very good, sir.'

You can always rely on Jeeves. Two-thirty I had said, and two-thirty it was. The telegram arrived almost on the minute. I was going to my room to change into something warmer at the moment and I took it up with me. Then into the heavy tweeds and off in the car to the field of play. I got there just as the two teams were lining up, and half a minute later the whistle blew and the war was on.

What with one thing and another – having been at a school where they didn't play it and so forth – Rugby football is a game I can't claim absolutely to understand in all its niceties, if you know what I mean. I can follow the broad, general principles, of course. I mean to say, I know that the main scheme is to work the ball down the field somehow and deposit it over the line at the other end, and that, in order to squelch this programme, each side is allowed to put in a certain amount of assault and battery and do things to its fellow-man which, if done elsewhere, would result in fourteen days without the option, coupled with some strong remarks from the Bench. But there I stop. What you might call the science of the thing is to Bertram Wooster a sealed book. However, I am informed by experts that on this occasion there was not enough science for anyone to notice.

There had been a great deal of rain in the last few days, and the going appeared to be a bit sticky. In fact, I have seen swamps that were drier than this particular bit of ground. The red-haired bloke whom I had encountered in the pub paddled up and kicked off amidst cheers from the populace, and the ball went straight to where Tuppy was standing, a pretty colour-scheme in light blue and orange. Tuppy caught it neatly, and hoofed it back, and it was at this point that I understood that an Upper

Bleaching versus Hockley-cum-Meston game had certain features not usually seen on the football-field.

For Tuppy, having done his bit, was just standing there, looking modest, when there was a thunder of large feet and the red-haired bird, galloping up, seized him by the neck, hurled him to earth, and fell on him. I had a glimpse of Tuppy's face, as it registered horror, dismay, and a general suggestion of stunned dissatisfaction with the scheme of things, and then he disappeared. By the time he had come to the surface, a sort of mob-warfare was going on at the other side of the field. Two assortments of sons of the soil had got their heads down and were shoving earnestly against each other, with the ball somewhere in the middle.

Tuppy wiped a fair portion of Hampshire out of his eye, peered round him in a dazed kind of way, saw the mass-meeting and ran towards it, arriving just in time for a couple of heavyweights to gather him in and give him the mud-treatment again. This placed him in an admirable position for a third heavyweight to kick him in the ribs with a boot like a violin-case. The red-haired man then fell on him. It was all good, brisk play, and looked fine from my side of the ropes.

I saw now where Tuppy had made his mistake. He was too dressy. On occasions such as this it is safest not to be conspicuous, and that blue and orange shirt rather caught the eye. A sober beige, blending with the colour of the ground, was what his best friends would have recommended. And, in addition to the fact that his costume attracted attention, I rather think that the men of Hockley-cum-Meston resented his being on the field at all. They felt that, as a non-local, he had butted in on a private fight and had no business there.

At any rate, it certainly appeared to me that they were giving him preferential treatment. After each of those shoving-bees to which I have alluded, when the edifice caved in and tons of humanity wallowed in a tangled mess in the juice, the last soul to be excavated always seemed to be Tuppy. And on the rare occasions when he actually managed to stand upright for a moment, somebody – generally the red-haired man – invariably sprang to the congenial task of spilling him again.

In fact, it was beginning to look as though that telegram would come too late to save a human life, when an interruption occurred. Play had worked round close to where I was standing, and there had been the customary collapse of all concerned, with Tuppy at the bottom of the basket, as usual; but this time, when they got up and started to count the survivors, a sizeable cove in what had once been a white shirt remained on the ground. And a hearty cheer went up from a hundred patriotic throats as the news spread that Upper Bleaching had drawn first blood.

The victim was carried off by a couple of his old chums, and the rest of the players sat down and pulled their stockings up and thought of life for a bit. The moment had come, it seemed to me, to remove Tuppy from the *abattoir*, and I hopped over the ropes and toddled to where he sat scraping mud from his wishbone. His air was that of a man who has been passed through a wringer, and his eyes, what you could see of them, had a strange, smouldering gleam. He was so crusted with alluvial deposits that one realised how little a mere bath would ever be able to effect. To fit him to take his place once more in polite society, he would certainly have to be sent to the cleaner's. Indeed, it was a moot point whether it wouldn't be simpler just to throw him away.

'Tuppy, old man,' I said.

'Eh?' said Tuppy.

'A telegram for you.'

'Eh?'

'I've got a wire here that came after you left the house.'

'Eh?' said Tuppy.

I stirred him up a trifle with the ferrule of my stick, and he seemed to come to life.

'Be careful what you're doing, you silly ass,' he said, in part. 'I'm one solid bruise. What are you gibbering about?'

'A telegram has come for you. I think it may be important.'

He snorted in a bitter sort of way.

'Do you suppose I've time to read telegrams now?'

'But this one may be frightfully urgent,' I said. 'Here it is.'

But, if you understand me, it wasn't. How I had happened to do it, I don't know, but apparently, in changing the upholstery, I had left it in my other coat.

'Oh, my gosh,' I said. 'I've left it behind.'

'It doesn't matter.'

'But it does. It's probably something you ought to read at once. Immediately, if you know what I mean. If I were you, I'd just say a few words of farewell to the murder-squad and come back to the house right away.'

He raised his eyebrows. At least, I think he must have done, because the mud on his forehead stirred a little, as if something was going on underneath it.

'Do you imagine,' he said, 'that I would slink away under her very eyes? Good God! Besides,' he went on, in a quiet, meditative voice, 'there is no power on earth that could get me off this field until I've thoroughly disembowelled that red-haired bounder. Have you noticed how he keeps tackling me when I haven't got the ball?'

'Isn't that right?'

'Of course it's not right. Never mind! A bitter retribution awaits that bird. I've had enough of it. From now on I assert my personality.'

'I'm a bit foggy as to the rules of this pastime.' I said. 'Are you allowed to bite him.'

'I'll try, and see what happens,' said Tuppy, struck with the idea and brightening a little.

At this point, the pall-bearers returned, and fighting became general again all along the Front.

There's nothing like a bit of rest and what you might call folding of the hands for freshening up the shop-soiled athlete. The dirty work, resumed after this brief breather, started off with an added vim which it did one good to see. And the life and soul of the party was young Tuppy.

You know, only meeting a fellow at lunch or at the races or loafing round country-houses and so forth, you don't get on to his hidden depths, if you know what I mean. Until this moment, if asked, I would have said that Tuppy Glossop was, on the whole, essentially a pacific sort of bloke, with little or nothing of the tiger of the jungle in him. Yet here he was, running to and fro with fire streaming from his nostrils, a positive danger to traffic.

Yes, absolutely. Encouraged by the fact that the referee was either filled with the spirit of Live and Let Live or else had got his whistle choked up with mud, the result being that he appeared to regard the game with a sort of calm detachment, Tuppy was putting in some very impressive work. Even to me, knowing nothing of the finesse of the thing, it was plain that if Hockley-cum-Meston wanted the happy ending they must eliminate young Tuppy at the earliest possible moment. And I will say for them that they did their best, the red-haired man being particularly assiduous. But Tuppy was made of durable material. Every time the opposition talent ground him into the mire and sat on his head, he rose on stepping-stones of his dead self, if you follow me. And in the end it was the red-haired bloke who did the dust-biting.

I couldn't tell you exactly how it happened, for by this time the shades of night were drawing in a bit and there was a dollop of mist rising, but one moment the fellow was hareing along, apparently without a care in the world, and then suddenly Tuppy had appeared from nowhere and was sailing through the air at his neck. They connected with a crash and a slither, and a little later the red-haired bird was hopping off, supported by a brace of friends, something having gone wrong with his left ankle.

After that, there was nothing to it. Upper Bleaching, thoroughly bucked, became busier than ever. There was a lot of earnest work in a sort of inland sea down at the Hockley end of the field, and then a kind of tidal wave poured over the line, and when the bodies had been removed and the tumult and the shouting had died, there was young Tuppy lying on the ball. And that, with the exception of a few spots of mayhem in the last five minutes, concluded the proceedings.

I drove back to the Court in rather what you might term a pensive frame of mind. Things having happened as they had happened, there seemed to me a goodish bit of hard thinking to be done. There was a servitor of sorts in the hall, when I arrived, and I asked him to send up a whisky-and-soda, strongish, to my room. The old brain, I felt, needed stimulating. And about ten minutes later there was a knock at the door, and in came Jeeves, bearing tray and materials.

'Hullo, Jeeves,' I said, surprised. 'Are you back?'

'Yes, sir.'

'When did you get here?'

'Some little while ago, sir. Was it an enjoyable game, sir?'

'In a sense, Jeeves,' I said, 'yes. Replete with human interest and all that, if you know what I mean. But I fear that, owing to a touch of carelessness on my part, the worst has happened. I left the telegram in my other coat, so young Tuppy remained in action throughout.'

'Was he injured, sir?'

'Worse than that, Jeeves. He was the star of the game. Toasts, I should imagine, are now being drunk to him at every pub in the village. So spectacularly did he play – in fact, so heartily did he joust – that I can't see the girl not being all over him. Unless I am greatly mistaken, the moment they meet, she will exclaim "My hero!" and fall into his bally arms.'

'Indeed, sir?'

I didn't like the man's manner. Too calm. Unimpressed. A little leaping about with fallen jaw was what I had expected my words to produce, and I was on the point of saying as much when the door opened again and Tuppy limped in.

He was wearing an ulster over his football things, and I wondered why he had come to pay a social call on me instead of proceeding straight to the bathroom. He eyed my glass in a wolfish sort of way.

'Whisky?' he said, in a hushed voice.

'And soda.'

'Bring me one, Jeeves,' said young Tuppy. 'A large one.'

'Very good, sir.'

Tuppy wandered to the window and looked out into the gathering darkness, and for the first time I perceived that he had got a grouch of some description. You can generally tell by a fellow's back. Humped. Bent. Bowed down with weight of woe, if you follow me.

'What's the matter?' I asked.

Tuppy emitted a mirthless.

'Oh, nothing much,' he said. 'My faith in woman is dead, that's all.'

'It is?'

'You jolly well bet it is. Women are a wash-out. I see no future for the sex, Bertie. Blisters, all of them.'

'Er – even the Dogsbody girl?'

'Her name,' said Tuppy, a little stiffly, 'is Dalgleish, if it happens to interest you. And, if you want to know something else, she's the worst of the lot.'

'My dear chap!'

Tuppy turned. Beneath the mud, I could see that his face was drawn and, to put it in a nutshell, wan.

'Do you know what happened, Bertie?'

'What?'

'She wasn't there.'

'Where?'

'At the match, you silly ass.'

'Not at the match?'

'No.'

'You mean, not among the throng of eager spectators?'

'Of course I mean not among the spectators. Did you think I expected her to be playing?'

'But I thought the whole scheme of the thing – '

'So did I. My gosh!' said Tuppy, laughing another of those hollow ones. 'I sweat myself to the bone for her sake. I allow a mob of homicidal maniacs to kick me in the ribs and stroll about on my face. And then, when I have braved a fate worse than death, so to speak, all to please her, I find that she didn't bother to come and watch the game. She got a 'phone-call from London from somebody who said he had located an Irish water-spaniel, and up she popped in her car, leaving me flat. I met her just now outside her house, and she told me. And all she could think of was that she was as sore as a sunburnt neck because she had had her trip for nothing. Apparently it wasn't an Irish water-spaniel at all. Just an ordinary English water-spaniel. And to think I fancied I loved a girl like that. A nice life-partner she would make! "When pain and anguish wring the brow, a ministering angel thou" – I don't think! Why, if a man married a girl like that and happened to get stricken by some dangerous illness, would she smooth his pillow and press cooling drinks on him? Not a chance! She'd be off somewhere trying to buy Siberian eel-hounds. I'm through with women.'

I saw that the moment had come to put in a word for the old firm.

'My cousin Angela's not a bad sort, Tuppy,' I said, in a grave elder-brotherly kind of way. 'Not altogether a bad egg, Angela, if you look at her squarely. I had always been hoping that she and you . . . and I know my Aunt Dahlia felt the same.'

Tuppy's bitter sneer cracked the topsoil.

'Angela!' he woofed. 'Don't talk to me about Angela. Angela's a rag and a bone and a hank of hair and an A1 scourge, if you want to know. She gave me the push. Yes, she did. Simply because I had the manly courage to speak out candidly on the subject of that ghastly lid she was chump enough to buy. It made her look like a Peke, and I told her it made her look like a Peke. And instead of admiring me for my fearless honesty she bunged me out on my ear. Faugh!'

'She did?' I said.

'She jolly well did,' said young Tuppy. 'At four-sixteen p.m. on Tuesday the seventeenth.'

'By the way, old man,' I said, 'I've found that telegram.'

'What telegram?'

'The one I told you about.'

'Oh, that one?'

'Yes, that's the one.'

'Well, let's have a look at the beastly thing.'

I handed it over, watching him narrowly. And suddenly, as he read, I saw him wobble. Stirred to the core. Obviously.

'Anything important?' I said.

'Bertie,' said young Tuppy, in a voice that quivered with strong emotion, 'my recent remarks *re* your cousin Angela. Wash them out. Cancel them. Look on them as not spoken. I tell you, Bertie, Angela's all right. An angel in human shape, and that's official. Bertie, I've got to get up to London. She's ill.'

'Ill?'

'High fever and delirium. This wire's from your aunt. She wants me to come up to London at once. Can I borrow your car?'

'Of course.'

'Thanks,' said Tuppy, and dashed out.

He had only been gone about a second when Jeeves came in with the restorative.

'Mr Glossop's gone, Jeeves.'

'Indeed, sir?'

'To London.'

'Yes, sir?'

'In my car. To see my cousin Angela. The sun is once more shining, Jeeves.'

'Extremely gratifying, sir.'

I gave him the eye.

'Was it you, Jeeves, who 'phoned to Miss What's-her-bally-name about the alleged water-spaniel?'

'Yes, sir.'

'I thought as much.'

'Yes, sir?'

'Yes, Jeeves, the moment Mr Glossop told me that a Mysterious Voice had 'phoned on the subject of Irish water-spaniels, I thought as much. I recognised your touch. I read your motives like an open book. You knew she would come buzzing up.'

'Yes, sir.'

'And you knew how Tuppy would react. If there's one thing that gives a jousting knight the pip, it is to have his audience walk out on him.'

'Yes, sir.'

'But, Jeeves.'

'Sir?'

'There's just one point. What will Mr Glossop say when he finds my cousin Angela full of beans and not delirious?'

'The point had not escaped me, sir. I took the liberty of ringing Mrs Travers up on the telephone and explaining the circumstances. All will be in readiness for Mr Glossop's arrival.'

'Jeeves,' I said, 'you think of everything.'

'Thank you, sir. In Mr Glossop's absence, would you care to drink this whisky-and-soda?'

I shook the head.

'No, Jeeves, there is only one man who must do that. It is you. If ever anyone earned a refreshing snort, you are he. Pour it out, Jeeves, and shove it down.'

'Thank you very much, sir.'

'Cheerio, Jeeves!'

'Cheerio, sir, if I may use the expression.'

# =3=
# BERTIE CHANGES HIS MIND

It has happened so frequently in the past few years that young fellows starting in my profession have come to me for a word of advice, that I have found it convenient now to condense my system into a brief formula. 'Resource and Tact' – that is my motto. Tact, of course, has always been with me a *sine qua non*; while as for resource, I think I may say that I have usually contrived to show a certain modicum of what I might call *finesse* in handling those little *contretemps* which inevitably arise from time to time in the daily life of a gentleman's personal gentleman. I am reminded, by way of an instance, of the Episode of the School for Young Ladies near Brighton – an affair which, I think, may be said to have commenced one evening at the moment when I brought Mr Wooster his whisky and siphon and he addressed me with such remarkable petulance.

Not a little moody Mr Wooster had been for some days – far from his usual bright self. This I had attributed to the natural reaction from a slight attack of influenza from which he had been suffering; and, of course, took no notice, merely performing my duties as usual, until on the evening of which I speak he exhibited this remarkable petulance when I brought him his whisky and siphon.

'Oh, dash it, Jeeves!' he said, manifestly overwrought. 'I wish at least you'd put it on another table for a change.'

'Sir?' I said.

'Every night, dash it all,' proceeded Mr Wooster morosely, 'you come in at exactly the same old time with the same old tray and put it on the same old table. I'm fed up, I tell you. It's the bally monotony of it that makes it all seen so frightfully bally.'

I confess that his words filled me with a certain apprehension. I had l.eard gentlemen in whose employment I have been speak in very much the same way before, and it had almost invariably meant that they were contemplating matrimony. It disturbed me, therefore, I am free to admit, when Mr Wooster addressed me in this fashion. I had no desire to sever a connection so pleasant in every respect as his and mine had been, and my experience is that when the wife comes in at the front door the valet of bachelor days goes out at the back.

'It's not your fault, of course,' went on Mr Wooster, regaining a certain degree of composure. 'I'm not blaming you. But, by Jove, I mean, you must acknowledge – I mean to say, I've been thinking pretty deeply these last few days, Jeeves, and I've come to the conclusion mine is an empty life. I'm lonely, Jeeves.'

'You have a great many friends, sir.'

'What's the good of friends?'

'Emerson,' I reminded him, 'says a friend may well be reckoned the masterpiece of Nature, sir.'

'Well, you can tell Emerson from me next time you see him that he's an ass.'

'Very good, sir.'

'What I want – Jeeves, have you seen that play called I-forget-its-dashed-name?'

'No, sir.'

'It's on at the What-d'you-call-it. I went last night. The hero's a chap who's buzzing along, you know, quite merry and bright, and suddenly a kid turns up and says she's his daughter. Left over from act one, you know – absolutely the first he'd heard of it. Well, of course, there's a bit of a fuss and they say to him, "What-ho?" and he says, "Well, what about it?" and they say, "Well, *what* about it?" and he says, "Oh, all right, then, if that's the way you feel!" and he takes the kid and goes off with her out into the world together, you know. Well, what I'm driving at, Jeeves, is that I envied that chappie. Most awfully jolly little girl, you know, clinging to him trustingly and whatnot. Something to look after, if you know what I mean. Jeeves, I wish I had a daughter. I wonder what the procedure is?'

'Marriage is, I believe, considered the preliminary step, sir.'

'No, I mean about adopting a kid. You can adopt kids, you know, Jeeves. But what I want to know is how you start about it.'

'The process, I should imagine, would be highly complicated and laborious, sir. It would cut into your spare time.'

'Well, I'll tell you what I could do, then. My sister will be back from India next week with her three little girls. I'll give up this flat and take a house and have them all to live with me. By Jove, Jeeves, I think that's rather a scheme, what? Prattle of childish voices, eh? Little feet pattering hither and thither, yes?'

I concealed my perturbation, but the effort to preserve my *sang-froid* tested my powers to the utmost. The course of action outlined by Mr Wooster meant the finish of our cosy bachelor establishment if it came into being as a practical proposition; and no doubt some men in my place would at this juncture have voiced their disapproval. I avoided this blunder.

'If you will pardon my saying so, sir,' I suggested, 'I think you are not quite yourself after your influenza. If I might express the opinion, what you require is a few days by the sea. Brighton is very handy, sir.'

'Are you suggesting that I'm talking through my hat?'

'By no means, sir. I merely advocate a short stay at Brighton as a physical recuperative.'

Mr Wooster considered.

'Well, I'm not sure you're not right,' he said at length. 'I *am* feeling more or less of an onion. You might shove a few things in a suitcase and drive me down in the car tomorrow.'

'Very good, sir.'

'And when we get back I'll be in the pink and ready to tackle this pattering-feet wheeze.'

'Exactly, sir.'

Well, it was a respite, and I welcomed it. But I began to see that a crisis had arisen which would require adroit handling. Rarely had I observed Mr Wooster more set on a thing. Indeed, I could recall no such exhibition of determination on his part since the time when he had insisted, against my frank disapproval, on wearing purple socks. However, I had coped successfully with that outbreak, and I was by no means unsanguine that I should eventually be able to bring the present affair to a happy issue. Employers are like horses. They require managing. Some gentlemen's personal gentlemen have the knack of managing them, some have not. I, I am happy to say, have no cause for complaint.

For myself, I found our stay at Brighton highly enjoyable, and should have been willing to extend it; but Mr Wooster, still restless, wearied of the place by the end of two days, and on the third afternoon he instructed me to pack up and bring the car round to the hotel. We started back along the London road at about five of a fine summer's day, and had travelled perhaps two miles when I perceived in the road before us a young lady, gesticulating with no little animation. I applied the brake and brought the vehicle to a standstill.

'What,' inquired Mr Wooster, waking from a reverie, 'is the big thought at the back of this, Jeeves?'

'I observed a young lady endeavouring to attract our attention with signals a little way down the road, sir,' I explained. 'She is now making her way towards us.'

Mr Wooster peered.

'I see her. I expect she wants a lift, Jeeves.'

'That was the interpretation which I placed upon her actions, sir.'

'A jolly-looking kid,' said Mr Wooster. 'I wonder what she's doing, biffing about the high road.'

'She has the air to me, sir, of one who has been absenting herself without leave from her school, sir.'

'Hallo-allo-allo!' said Mr Wooster, as the child reached us. 'Do you want a lift?'

'Oh, I say, can you?' said the child, with marked pleasure.

'Where do you want to go?'

'There's a turning to the left about a mile farther on. If you'll put me down there, I'll walk the rest of the way. I say, thanks awfully. I've got a nail in my shoe.'

She climbed in at the back. A red-haired young person with a snub nose and an extremely large grin. Her age, I should imagine, would be about twelve. She let down one of the spare seats, and knelt on it to facilitate conversation.

'I'm going to get into a frightful row,' she began. 'Miss Tomlinson will be perfectly furious.'

'No, really?' said Mr Wooster.

'It's a half-holiday, you know, and I sneaked away to Brighton, because I wanted to go on the pier and put pennies in the slot-machines. I thought I could get back in time so that nobody would notice I'd gone, but I got this nail in my shoe, and now

475

there'll be a fearful row. Oh well,' she said, with a philosophy which, I confess, I admired, 'it can't be helped. What's your car? A Sunbeam, isn't it? We've got a Wolseley at home.'

Mr Wooster was visibly perturbed. As I have indicated, he was at this time in a highly malleable frame of mind, tender-hearted to a degree where the young of the female sex was concerned. Her sad case touched him deeply.

'Oh, I say, this is rather rotten,' he observed. 'Isn't there anything to be done? I say, Jeeves, don't you think something could be done?'

'It was not my place to make the suggestion, sir,' I replied, 'but, as you yourself have brought the matter up, I fancy the trouble is susceptible of adjustment. I think it would be a legitimate subterfuge were you to inform the young lady's schoolmistress that you are an old friend of the young lady's father. In this case you could inform Miss Tomlinson that you had been passing the school and had seen the young lady at the gate and taken her for a drive. Miss Tomlinson's chagrin would no doubt in these circumstances be sensibly diminished if not altogether dispersed.'

'Well, you *are* a sportsman!' observed the young person, with considerable enthusiasm. And she proceeded to kiss me – in connection with which I have only to say that I was sorry she had just been devouring some sticky species of sweetmeat.

'Jeeves, you've hit it!' said Mr Wooster. 'A sound, even fruity, scheme. I say, I suppose I'd better know your name and all that, if I'm a friend of your father's.'

'My name's Peggy Mainwaring, thanks awfully,' said the young person. 'And my father's Professor Mainwaring. He's written a lot of books. You'll be expected to know that.'

'Author of the well-known series of philosophical treaties, sir,' I ventured to interject. 'They have a great vogue, though, if the young lady will pardon my saying so, many of the Professor's opinions strike me personally as somewhat empirical. Shall I drive on to the school, sir?'

'Yes, carry on. I say, Jeeves, it's a rummy thing. Do you know, I've never been inside a girls' school in my life.'

'Indeed, sir?'

'Ought to be a dashed interesting experience, Jeeves, what?'

'I fancy that you may find it so, sir,' I said.

We drove on a matter of half a mile down a lane, and, directed by the young person, I turned in at the gates of a house of imposing dimensions, bringing the car to a halt at the front door. Mr Wooster and the child entered, and presently a parlourmaid came out.

'You're to take the car round to the stables, please,' she said.

'Ah!' I said. 'Then everything is satisfactory, eh? Where has Mr Wooster gone?'

'Miss Peggy has taken him off to meet her friends. And cook says she hopes you'll step round to the kitchen later and have a cup of tea.'

'Inform her that I shall be delighted. Before I take the car to the stables, would it be possible for me to have a word with Miss Tomlinson?'

A moment later I was following her into the drawing-room.


Handsome but strong-minded – that was how I summed up Miss Tomlinson at first glance. In some ways she recalled to my mind Mr Wooster's Aunt Agatha. She had the same penetrating gaze and that indefinable air of being reluctant to stand any nonsense.

'I fear I am possibly taking a liberty, madam,' I began, 'but I am hoping that you will allow me to say a word with respect to my employer. I fancy I am correct in supposing that Mr Wooster did not tell you a great deal about himself?'

'He told me nothing about himself, except that he was a friend of Professor Mainwaring.'

'He did not inform you, then, that he was *the* Mr Wooster?'

'*The* Mr Wooster?'

'Bertram Wooster, madam.'

I will say for Mr Wooster that, mentally negligible though he no doubt is, he has a name that suggests almost infinite possibilities. He sounds, if I may elucidate my meaning, like Someone – especially if you have just been informed that he is an intimate friend of so eminent a man as Professor Mainwaring. You might not, no doubt, be able to say off-hand whether he was Bertram Wooster the novelist, or Bertram Wooster the founder of a new school of thought; but you would have an uneasy feeling that you were exposing your ignorance if you did not give the impression of familiarity with the name. Miss Tomlinson, as I had rather foreseen, nodded brightly.

'Oh, *Bertram* Wooster!' she said.

'He is an extremely retiring gentleman, madam, and would be the last to suggest it himself, but, knowing him as I do, I am sure that he would take it as a graceful compliment if you were to ask him to address the young ladies. He is an excellent extempore speaker.'

'A very good idea,' said Miss Tomlinson decidedly, 'I am very much obliged to you for suggesting it. I will certainly ask him to talk to the girls.'

'And should he make a pretence – through modesty – of not wishing – '

'I shall insist.'

'Thank you, madam. I am obliged. You will not mention my share in the matter? Mr Wooster might think that I had exceeded my duties.'

I drove round to the stables and halted the car in the yard. As I got out, I looked at it somewhat intently. It was a good car, and appeared to be in excellent condition, but somehow I seemed to feel that something was going to go wrong with it – something serious – something that would not be able to be put right again for at least a couple of hours.

One gets these presentiments.

It may have been some half-hour later that Mr Wooster came into the stable-yard as I was leaning against the car enjoying a quiet cigarette.

'No, don't chuck it away, Jeeves,' he said, as I withdrew the cigarette from my mouth. 'As a matter of fact, I've come to touch you for a smoke. Got one to spare?'

'Only gaspers, I fear, sir.'

'They'll do,' responded Mr Wooster, with no little eagerness, I observed that his manner was a trifle fatigued and his eye somewhat wild. 'It's a rummy thing, Jeeves, I seem to have lost my cigarette-case. Can't find it anywhere.'

'I am sorry to hear that, sir. It is not in the car.'

'No? Must have dropped it somewhere, then.' He drew at his gasper with relish. 'Jolly creatures, small girls, Jeeves,' he remarked, after a pause.

'Extremely so, sir.'

'Of course, I can imagine some fellows finding them, a bit exhausting in – er – '

'*En masse*, sir?'

'That's the word. A bit exhausting *en masse*.'

'I must confess, sir, that that is how they used to strike me. In my younger days, at the outset of my career, sir, I was at one time page-boy in a school for young ladies.'

'No, really? I never knew that before. I say, Jeeves – er – did the – er – dear little souls *giggle* much in your day?'

'Practically without cessation, sir.'

'Makes a fellow feel a bit of an ass, what? I shouldn't wonder if they usedn't to stare at you from time to time, too, eh?'

'At the school where I was employed, sir, the young ladies had a regular game which they were accustomed to play when a male visitor arrived. They would stare fixedly at him and giggle, and there was a small prize for the one who made him blush first.'

'Oh, no, I say, Jeeves, not really?'

'Yes, sir. They derived great enjoyment from the pastime.'

'I'd no idea small girls were such demons.'

'More deadly than the male, sir.'

Mr Wooster passed a handkerchief over his brow.

'Well, we're going to have tea in a few minutes, Jeeves. I expect I shall feel better after tea.'

'We will hope so, sir.'

But I was by no means sanguine.

I had an agreeable tea in the kitchen. The buttered toast was good and the maids nice girls, though with little conversation. The parlourmaid, who joined us towards the end of the meal, after performing her duties in the school dining-room, reported that Mr Wooster was sticking it pluckily, but seemed feverish. I went back to the stable-yard, and I was just giving the car another look over when the young Mainwaring child appeared.

'Oh, I say,' she said, 'will you give this to Mr Wooster when you see him?' She held out Mr Wooster's cigarette-case. 'He must have dropped it somewhere. I say,' she proceeded, 'it's an awful lark. He's going to give a lecture to the school.'

'Indeed, miss?'

'We love it when there are lectures. We sit and stare at the poor dears, and try to make them dry up. There was a man last term who got hiccoughs. Do you think Mr Wooster will get hiccoughs?'

'We can but hope for the best, miss.'

'It would be such a lark, wouldn't it?'

'Highly enjoyable, miss.'

'Well, I must be getting back. I want to get a front seat.'

And she scampered off. An engaging child. Full of spirits.

She had hardly gone when there was an agitated noise, and round the corner came Mr Wooster. Perturbed. Deeply so.

'Jeeves!'

'Sir?'

'Start the car!'

'Sir?'

'I'm off!'

'Sir?'

Mr Wooster danced a few steps.

'Don't stand there saying "sir?" I tell you I'm off. Bally off! There's not a moment to waste. The situation's desperate. Dash it, Jeeves, do you know what's happened? The Tomlinson female has just sprung it on me that I'm expected to make a speech to the girls! Got to stand up there in front of the whole dashed collection and talk! I can just see myself! Get that car going, Jeeves, dash it all. A little speed, a little speed!'

'Impossible, I fear, sir. The car is out of order.'

Mr Wooster gaped at me. Very glassily he gaped.

'Out of order!'

'Yes, sir. Something is wrong. Trivial, perhaps, but possibly a matter of some little time to repair.' Mr Wooster being one of those easygoing young gentlemen who will drive a car but never take the trouble to study its mechanism, I felt justified in becoming technical. 'I think it is the differential gear, sir. Either that or the exhaust.'

I am fond of Mr Wooster, and I admit I came very near to melting as I looked at his face. He was staring at me in a sort of dumb despair that would have touched anybody.

'Then I'm sunk! Or' – a slight gleam of hope flickered across his drawn features – 'do you think I could sneak out and leg it across country, Jeeves?'

'Too late, I fear, sir.' I indicated with a slight gesture the approaching figure of Miss Tomlinson, who was advancing with a serene determination in his immediate rear.

'Ah, there you are, Mr Wooster.'

He smiled a sickly smile.

'Yes – er – here I am!'

'We are all waiting for you in the large school-room.'

'But, I say, look here,' said Mr Wooster, 'I – I don't know a bit what to talk about.'

'Why, anything, Mr Wooster. Anything that comes into your head. Be bright,' said Miss Tomlinson. 'Bright and amusing.'

'Oh, bright and amusing?'

'Possibly tell them a few entertaining stories. But, at the same time, do not neglect the graver note. Remember that my girls are on the threshold of life, and will be eager to hear something brave and helpful and stimulating – something which they can remember in after years. But, of course, you know the sort of thing, Mr Wooster. Come. The young people are waiting.'

I have spoken earlier of resource and the part it plays in the life of a gentleman's personal gentleman. It is a quality peculiarly necessary if one is to share in scenes not primarily designed for one's co-operation. So much that is interesting in life goes on apart behind closed doors that your gentleman's gentleman, if he is not to remain hopelessly behind the march of events, should exercise his wits in order to enable himself to be – if not a spectator – at least an auditor when there is anything of interest toward. I deprecate as vulgar and undignified the practice of listening at keyholes, but without lowering myself to that, I have generally contrived to find a way.

In the present case it was simple. The large schoolroom was situated on the ground floor, with commodious French windows, which, as the weather was clement, remained open throughout the proceedings. By stationing myself behind a pillar on the porch or verandah which adjoined the room, I was enabled to see and hear all. It was an experience which I should be sorry to have missed. Mr Wooster, I may say at once, indubitably excelled himself.

Mr Wooster is a young gentleman with practically every desirable quality except one. I do not mean brains, for in an employer brains are not desirable. The quality to which I allude is hard to define, but perhaps I might call it the gift of dealing with the Unusual Situation. In the presence of the Unusual, Mr Wooster is too prone to smile weakly and allow his eyes to protrude. He lacks Presence. I have often wished that I had the power to bestow upon him some of the *savoir-faire* of a former employer of mine, Mr Montague-Todd, the well-known financier, now in the second year of his sentence. I have known men call upon Mr Todd with the express intention of horsewhipping him and go away half an hour later laughing heartily and smoking one of his cigars. To Mr Todd it would have been child's play to speak a few impromptu words to a schoolroom full of young ladies; in fact, before he had finished, he would probably have induced them to invest all their pocket-money in one of his numerous companies; but to Mr Wooster it was plainly an ordeal of the worst description. He gave one look at the young ladies, who were all staring at him in an extremely unwinking manner, then blinked and started to pick feebly at his coat-sleeve. His aspect reminded me of that of a bashful young man who, persuaded against his better judgment to go on the platform and assist a conjurer in his entertainment, suddenly discovers that rabbits and hard-boiled eggs are being taken out of the top of his head.

The proceedings opened with a short but graceful speech of introduction from Miss Tomlinson.

'Girls,' said Miss Tomlinson, 'some of you have already met Mr Wooster – Mr *Bertram* Wooster, and you all, I hope, know him by reputation.' Here, I regret to say, Mr Wooster gave a hideous, gurgling laugh and, catching Miss Tomlinson's eye. turned a bright scarlet. Miss Tomlinson resumed: 'He has very kindly consented to say a few words to you before he leaves, and I am sure that you will all give him your very earnest attention. Now, please.'

She gave a spacious gesture with her right hand as she said the last two words, and Mr Wooster, apparently under the impression that they were addressed to him, cleared his throat and began to speak. But it appeared that her remark was directed to the young ladies, and was in the nature of a cue or signal, for she had no sooner spoken them than the whole school rose to its feet in a body and burst into a species of chant, of which I am glad to say I can remember the words, though the tune eludes me. The words ran as follows:–

> 'Many greetings to you!
> Many greetings to you!
> Many greetings, dear stranger,
> Many greetings,
> Many greetings,
> Many greetings to you!
> Many greetings to you!
> To you!'

Considerable latitude of choice was given to the singers in the matter of key, and there was little of what I might call co-operative effort. Each child went on till she had reached the end, then stopped and waited for the stragglers to come up. It was an unusual performance, and I, personally, found it extremely exhilarating. It seemed to smite Mr Wooster, however, like a blow. He recoiled a couple of steps and flung up an arm defensively. Then the uproar died away, and an air of expectancy fell upon the room. Miss Tomlinson directed a brightly authoritative gaze upon Mr Wooster, and he blinked, gulped once or twice, and tottered forward.

'Well, you know – ' he said.

Then it seemed to strike him that this opening lacked the proper formal dignity.

'Ladies – '

A silvery peal of laughter from the front row stopped him again.

'Girls!' said Miss Tomlinson. She spoke in a low, soft voice, but the effect was immediate. Perfect stillness instantly descended upon all present. I am bound to say that, brief as my acquaintance with Miss Tomlinson had been, I could recall few women I had admired more. She had grip.

I fancy that Miss Tomlinson had gauged Mr Wooster's oratorical capabilities pretty correctly by this time, and had come to the conclusion that little in the way of a stirring address was to be expected from him.

'Perhaps,' she said, 'as it is getting late, and he has not very much time to spare, Mr Wooster will just give you some little word of advice which may be helpful to you in after-life, and then we will sing the school song and disperse to our evening lessons.'

She looked at Mr Wooster. He passed a finger round the inside of his collar.

'Advice? After-life? What? Well, I don't know – '

'Just some brief word of counsel, Mr Wooster,' said Miss Tomlinson firmly.

'Oh, well – Well, yes – Well – ' It was painful to see Mr Wooster's brain endeavouring to work. 'Well, I'll tell you something that's often done *me* a bit of good, and it's a thing not many people know. My old Uncle Henry gave me the tip when I first came to London. "Never forget, my boy," he said, "that, if you stand outside Romano's in the Strand, you can see the clock on the wall of the Law Courts down in Fleet Street. Most people who don't know don't believe it's possible, because there are a couple of churches in the middle of the road, and you would think they would be in the way. But you can, and it's worth knowing. You can win a lot of money betting on it with fellows who haven't found it out." And, by Jove, he was perfectly right, and it's a thing to remember. Many a quid have I – '

Miss Tomlinson gave a hard, dry cough, and he stopped in the middle of a sentence.

'Perhaps it will be better, Mr Wooster,' she said, in a cold, even voice, 'if you were to tell my girls some little story. What you say is, no doubt, extremely interesting, but perhaps a little – '

'Oh, ah, yes,' said Mr Wooster. 'Story? Story?' He appeared completely distraught, poor young gentleman. 'I wonder if you've heard the one about the stockbroker and the chorus-girl?'

'We will now sing the school song,' said Miss Tomlinson, rising like an iceberg.

I decided not to remain for the singing of the school song. It seemed probable to me that Mr Wooster would shortly be requiring the car, so I made my way back to the stable-yard, to be in readiness.

I had not long to wait. In a very few moments he appeared, tottering. Mr Wooster's is not one of those inscrutable faces which it is impossible to read. On the contrary, it is a limpid pool in which is mirrored each passing emotion. I could read it now like a book, and his first words were very much on the lines I had anticipated.

'Jeeves,' he said hoarsely, 'is that damned car mended yet?'

'Just this moment, sir. I have been working on it assiduously.'

'Then, for heaven's sake, let's go!'

'But I understood that you were to address the young ladies, sir.'

'Oh, I've done that!' responded Mr Wooster, blinking twice with extraordinary rapidity. 'Yes, I've done that.'

'It was a success, I hope, sir?'

'Oh yes. Oh, yes. Most extraordinarily successful. Went like a breeze. But – er – I think I may as well be going. No use outstaying one's welcome, what?'

'Assuredly not, sir.'

I had climbed into my seat and was about to start the engine, when voices made themselves heard; and at the first sound of them Mr Wooster sprang with almost incredible nimbleness into the tonneau, and when I glanced round he was on the floor covering himself with a rug. The last I saw of him was a pleading eye.

'Have you seen Mr Wooster, my man?'

Miss Tomlinson had entered the stable-yard, accompanied by a lady of, I should say, judging from her accent, French origin.

'No, madam.'

The French lady uttered some exclamation in her native tongue.

'Is anything wrong, madam?' I inquired.

Miss Tomlinson in normal mood was, I should be disposed to imagine, a lady who would not readily confide her troubles to the ear of a gentleman's gentleman, however sympathetic his aspect. That she did so now was sufficient indication of the depth to which she was stirred.

'Yes, there is! Mademoiselle has just found several of the girls smoking cigarettes in the shrubbery. When questioned, they stated that Mr Wooster had given them the horrid things.' She turned. 'He must be in the garden somewhere, or in the house. I think the man is out of his senses. Come, mademoiselle!'

It must have been about a minute later that Mr Wooster poked his head out of the rug like a tortoise.

'Jeeves!'

'Sir?'

'Get a move on! Start her up! Get going and *keep* going!'

I applied my foot to the self-starter.

'It would perhaps be safest to drive carefully until we are out of the school grounds, sir,' I said. 'I might run over one of the young ladies, sir.'

'Well, what's the objection to that?' demanded Mr Wooster with extraordinary bitterness.

'Or even Miss Tomlinson, sir.'

'Don't!' said Mr Wooster wistfully. 'You make my mouth water!'

'Jeeves,' said Mr Wooster, when I brought him his whisky and siphon one night about a week later, 'this is dashed jolly.'

'Sir?'

'Jolly. Cosy and pleasant, you know. I mean, looking at the clock and wondering if you're going to be late with the good old drinks, and then you coming in with the tray always exactly on time, never a minute late, and shoving it down on the table and biffing off, and the next night coming in and shoving it down and biffing off, and the next night – I mean, gives you a sort of safe, restful feeling. Soothing! That's the word. Soothing!'

'Yes, sir. Oh, by the way, sir – '

'Well?'

'Have you succeeded in finding a suitable house yet, sir?'

'House? What do you mean, house?'

'I understood, sir, that it was your intention to give up the flat and take a house of sufficient size to enable you to have your sister, Mrs Scholfield, and her three young ladies to live with you.'

Mr Wooster shuddered strongly.

'That's off, Jeeves,' he said.

'Very good, sir,' I replied.

# =4=
# JEEVES EXERTS THE OLD CEREBELLUM

'Morning, Jeeves,' I said.

'Good morning, sir,' said Jeeves.

He put the good old cup of tea softly on the table by my bed, and I took a refreshing sip. Just right, as usual. Not too hot, not too sweet, not too weak, not too strong, not too much milk, and not a drop spilled in the saucer. A most amazing cove, Jeeves. So dashed competent in every respect. I've said it before, and I'll say it again. I mean to say, take just one small instance. Every other valet I've ever had used to barge into my room in the morning while I was still asleep, causing much misery; but Jeeves seems to know when I'm awake by a sort of telepathy. He always floats in with the cup exactly two minutes after I come to life. Makes a deuce of a lot of difference to a fellow's day.

'How's the weather, Jeeves?'

'Exceptionally clement, sir.'

'Anything in the papers?'

'Some slight friction threatening in the Balkans, sir. Otherwise, nothing.'

'I say, Jeeves, a man I met at the club last night told me to put my shirt on Privateer for the two o'clock race this afternoon. How about it?'

'I should not advocate it, sir. The stable is not sanguine.'

That was enough for me. Jeeves knows. How, I couldn't say, but he knows. There was a time when I would laugh lightly, and go ahead, and lose my little all against his advice, but not now.

'Talking of shirts,' I said, 'have those mauve ones I ordered arrived yet?'

'Yes, sir. I sent them back.'

'Sent them back?'

487

'Yes, sir. They would not have become you.'

Well, I must say I'd thought fairly highly of those shirtings, but I bowed to superior knowledge. Weak? I don't know. Most fellows, no doubt, are all for having their valets confine their activities to creasing trousers and whatnot without trying to run the home; but it's different with Jeeves. Right from the first day he came to me, I have looked on him as a sort of guide, philosopher and friend.

'Mr Little rang up on the telephone a few moments ago, sir. I informed him that you were not yet awake.'

'Did he leave a message?'

'No, sir. He mentioned that he had a matter of importance to discuss with you, but confided no details.'

'Oh, well, I expect I shall be seeing him at the club.'

'No doubt, sir.'

I wasn't what you might call in a fever of impatience. Bingo Little is a chap I was at school with, and we see a lot of each other still. He's the nephew of old Mortimer Little, who retired from business recently with a goodish pile. (You've probably heard of Little's Liniment – It Limbers Up the Legs.) Bingo biffs about London on a pretty comfortable allowance given him by his uncle, and leads on the whole a fairly unclouded life. It wasn't likely that anything which he described as a matter of importance would turn out to be really so frightfully important. I took it that he had discovered some new brand of cigarette which he wanted me to try, or something like that, and didn't spoil my breakfast by worrying.

After breakfast I lit a cigarette and went to the open window to inspect the day. It certainly was one of the best and brightest.

'Jeeves,' I said.

'Sir?' said Jeeves. He had been clearing away the breakfast things, but at the sound of the young master's voice cheesed it courteously.

'You were absolutely right about the weather. It is a juicy morning.'

'Decidedly, sir.'

'Spring and all that.'

'Yes, sir.'

'In the spring, Jeeves, a livelier iris gleams upon the burnished dove.'

488

'So I have been informed, sir.'

'Right ho! Then bring me my whangee, my yellowest gloves, and the old green Homburg. I'm going into the Park to do pastoral dances.'

I don't know if you know that sort of feeling you get on these days round about the end of April and the beginning of May, when the sky's a light blue, with cotton-wool clouds, and there's a bit of a breeze blowing from the west? Kind of uplifted feeling. Romantic, if you know what I mean. I'm not much of a ladies' man, but on this particular morning it seemed to me that what I really wanted was some charming girl to buzz up and ask me to save her from assassins or something. So that it was a bit of an anti-climax when I merely ran into young Bingo Little, looking perfectly foul in a crimson satin tie decorated with horseshoes.

'Hallo, Bertie,' said Bingo.

'My God, man!' I gawped. 'The cravat! The gent's neckwear! Why? For what reason?'

'Oh, the tie?' He blushed. 'I – er – I was given it.'

He seemed embarrassed, so I dropped the subject. We toddled along a bit, and sat down on a couple of chairs by the Serpentine.

'Jeeves tells me you want to talk to me about something,' I said.

'Eh?' said Bingo, with a start. 'Oh yes, yes. Yes.'

I waited for him to unleash the topic of the day, but he didn't seem to want to get along. Conversation languished. He stared straight ahead of him in a glassy sort of manner.

'I say, Bertie,' he said, after a pause of about an hour and a quarter.

'Hallo!'

'Do you like the name Mabel?'

'No.'

'No?'

'No.'

'You don't think there's a kind of music in the word, like the wind rustling gently through the tree-tops?'

'No.'

He seemed disappointed for a moment; then cheered up.

'Of course, you wouldn't. You always were a fat-headed worm without any soul, weren't you?'

'Just as you say. Who is she? Tell me all.'

For I realized now that poor old Bingo was going through it once again. Ever since I have known him – and we were at school together – he has been perpetually falling in love with someone, generally in the spring, which seems to act on him like magic. At school he had the finest collection of actresses' photographs of anyone of his time; and at Oxford his romantic nature was a byword.

'You'd better come along and meet her at lunch,' he said, looking at his watch.

'A ripe suggestion,' I said. 'Where are you meeting her? At the Ritz?'

'Near the Ritz.'

He was geographically accurate. About fifty yards east of the Ritz there is one of those blighted tea-and-bun shops you see dotted about all over London, and into this, if you'll believe me, young Bingo dived like a homing rabbit; and before I had time to say a word we were wedged in at a table, on the brink of a silent pool of coffee left there by an early luncher.

I'm bound to say I couldn't quite follow the development of the scenario. Bingo, while not absolutely rolling in the stuff, has always had a fair amount of the ready. Apart from what he got from his uncle, I knew that he had finished up the jumping season well on the right side of the ledger. Why, then, was he lunching the girl at this God-forsaken eatery? It couldn't be because he was hard up.

Just then the waitress arrived. Rather a pretty girl.

'Aren't we going to wait –?' I started to say to Bingo, thinking it somewhat thick that, in addition to asking a girl to lunch with him in a place like this, he should fling himself on the foodstuffs before she turned up, when I caught sight of his face, and stopped.

The man was goggling. His entire map was suffused with a rich blush. He looked like the Soul's Awakening done in pink.

'Hullo, Mabel!' he said, with a sort of gulp.

'Hallo!' said the girl.

'Mabel,' said Bingo, 'this is Bertie Wooster, a pal of mine.'

'Pleased to meet you,' she said. 'Nice morning.'

'Fine,' I said.

'You see I'm wearing the tie,' said Bingo.

'It suits you beautiful,' said the girl.

Personally, if anyone had told me that a tie like that suited me, I should have risen and struck them on the mazzard, regardless of their age and sex; but poor old Bingo simply got all flustered with gratification, and smirked in the most gruesome manner.

'Well, what's it going to be today?' asked the girl, introducing the business touch into the conversation.

Bingo studied the menu devoutly.

'I'll have a cup of cocoa, cold veal and ham pie, slice of fruit cake, and a macaroon. Same for you, Bertie?'

I gazed at the man, revolted. That he could have been a pal of mine all these years and think me capable of insulting the old tum with this sort of stuff cut me to the quick.

'Or how about a bit of hot steak-pudding, with a sparkling limado to wash it down?' said Bingo.

You know, the way love can change a fellow is really frightful to contemplate. This chappie before me, who spoke in that absolutely careless way of macaroons and limado, was the man I had seen in happier days telling the head-waiter at Claridge's exactly how he wanted the chef to prepare the *sole frite au gourmet aux champignons*, and saying he would jolly well sling it back if it wasn't just right. Ghastly! Ghastly!

A roll and butter and a small coffee seemed the only things on the list that hadn't been specially prepared by the nastier-minded members of the Borgia family for people they had a particular grudge against, so I chose them, and Mabel hopped it.

'Well?' said Bingo rapturously.

I took it that he wanted my opinion of the female poisoner who had just left us.

'Very nice,' I said.

He seemed dissatisfied.

'You don't think she's the most wonderful girl you ever saw?' he said wistfully.

'Oh, absolutely!' I said, to appease the blighter. 'Where did you meet her?'

'At a subscription dance at Camberwell.'

'What on earth were you doing at a subscription dance at Camberwell?'

'Your man Jeeves asked me if I would buy a couple of tickets. It was in aid of some charity or other.'

'Jeeves? I didn't know he went in for that sort of thing.'

'Well, I suppose he has to relax a bit every now and then. Anyway, he was there, swinging a dashed efficient shoe. I hadn't meant to go at first, but I turned up for a lark. Oh, Bertie, think what I might have missed!'

'What might you have missed?' I asked, the old lemon being slightly clouded.

'Mabel, you chump. If I hadn't gone I shouldn't have met Mabel.'

'Oh, ah!'

At this point Bingo fell into a species of trance, and only came out of it to wrap himself round the pie and the macaroon.

'Bertie,' he said. 'I want your advice.'

'Carry on.'

'At least, not your advice, because that wouldn't be much good to anybody. I mean, you're a pretty consummate old ass, aren't you? Not that I want to hurt your feelings, of course.'

'No, no, I see that.'

'What I wish you would do is to put the whole thing to that fellow Jeeves of yours, and see what he suggests. You've often told me that he has helped other pals of yours out of messes. From what you tell me, he's by way of being the brains of the family.'

'He's never let me down yet.'

'Then put my case to him.'

'What case?'

'My problem.'

'What problem?'

'Why, you poor old fish, my uncle, of course. What do you think my uncle's going to say to all this? If I sprang it on him cold, he'd tie himself in knots on the hearthrug.'

'One of these emotional johnnies, eh?'

'Somehow or other his mind has got to be prepared to receive the news. But how?'

'Ah!'

'That's a lot of help, that "Ah"! You see, I'm pretty well dependent on the old boy. If he cut off my allowance, I should be very much in the soup. So you put the whole binge to Jeeves and see if he can't scare up a happy ending somehow. Tell him my future is in his hands, and that, if the wedding bells ring out, he can rely on me, even unto half my kingdom. Well, call it ten quid. Jeeves would exert himself with ten quid on the horizon, what?'

'Undoubtedly,' I said.

I wasn't in the least surprised at Bingo wanting to lug Jeeves into his private affairs like this. It was the first thing I would have thought of doing myself if I had been in any hole of any description. As I have frequently had occasion to observe, he is a bird of the ripest intellect, full of bright ideas. If anybody could fix things for poor old Bingo, he could.

I stated the case to him that night after dinner.

'Jeeves.'

'Sir?'

'Are you busy just now?'

'No, sir.'

'I mean, not doing anything in particular?'

'No, sir. It is my practice at this hour to read some improving book; but, if you desire my services, this can easily be postponed, or, indeed, abandoned altogether.'

'Well, I want your advice. It's about Mr Little.'

'Young Mr Little, sir, or the elder Mr Little, his uncle, who lives in Pounceby Gardens?'

Jeeves seemed to know everything. Most amazing thing. I'd been pally with Bingo practically all my life, and yet I didn't remember having heard that his uncle lived anywhere in particular.

'How did you know he lived in Pounceby Gardens?' I said.

'I am on terms of some intimacy with the elder Mr Little's cook, sir. In fact, there is an understanding.'

I'm bound to say that this gave me a bit of a start. Somehow I'd never thought of Jeeves going in for that sort of thing.

'Do you mean you're engaged?'

'It may be said to amount to that, sir.'

'Well, well!'

'She is a remarkably excellent cook, sir,' said Jeeves, as though he felt called on to give some explanation. 'What was it you wished to ask me about Mr Little?'

I sprang the details on him.

'And that's how the matter stands, Jeeves,' I said. 'I think we ought to rally round a trifle and help poor old Bingo put the thing through. Tell me about old Mr Little. What sort of a chap is he?'

'A somewhat curious character, sir. Since retiring from business he has become a great recluse, and now devotes himself almost entirely to the pleasures of the table.'

'Greedy hog, you mean?'

'I would not, perhaps, take the liberty of describing him in precisely those terms, sir. He is what is usually called a gourmet. Very particular about what he eats, and for that reason sets a high value of Miss Watson's services.'

'The cook?'

'Yes, sir.'

'Well, it looks to me as though our best plan would be to shoot young Bingo in on him after dinner one night. Melting mood, I mean to say, and all that.'

'The difficulty is, sir, that at the moment Mr Little is on a diet, owing to an attack of gout.'

'Things begin to look wobbly.'

'No, sir, I fancy that the elder Mr Little's misfortune may be turned to the younger Mr Little's advantage. I was speaking only the other day to Mr Little's valet, and he was telling me that it has become his principal duty to read to Mr Little in the evenings. If I were in your place, sir, I should send young Mr Little to read to his uncle.'

'Nephew's devotion, you mean? Old man touched by kindly action, what?'

'Partly that, sir. But I would rely more on young Mr Little's choice of literature.'

'That's no good. Jolly old Bingo has a kind face, but when it comes to literature he stops at the *Sporting Times*.'

'That difficulty may be overcome. I would be happy to select books for Mr Little to read. Perhaps I might explain my idea a little further.'

'I can't say I quite grasp it yet.'

'The method which I advocate is what, I believe, the advertisers call Direct Suggestion, sir, consisting as it does of driving an idea home by constant repetition. You may have had experience of the system?'

'You mean they keep on telling you that some soap or other is the best and after a bit you come under the influence and charge around the corner and buy a cake?'

'Exactly, sir. The same method was the basis of all the most valuable propaganda during the recent war. I see no reason why it should not be adopted to bring about the desired result with regard to the subject's views on class distinctions. If young Mr Little were to read day after day to his uncle a series of narratives in which marriage with young persons of an inferior social status was held up as both feasible and admirable, I fancy it would prepare the elder Mr Little's mind for the reception of the information that his nephew wishes to marry a waitress in a tea-shop.'

'*Are* there any books of that sort nowadays? The only ones I ever see mentioned in the papers are about married couples who find life grey, and can't stick each other at any price.'

'Yes, sir, there are a great many, neglected by the reviewers but widely read. You have never encountered "All for Love", by Rosie M. Banks?'

'No.'

'Nor "A Red, Red Summer Rose", by the same author?'

'No.'

'I have an aunt, sir, who owns an almost complete set of Rosie M. Banks'. I could easily borrow as many volumes as young Mr Little might require. They make very light, attractive reading.'

'Well, it's worth trying.'

'I should certainly recommend the scheme, sir.'

'All right, then. Toddle round to your aunt's tomorrow and grab a couple of the fruitiest. We can but have a dash at it.'

'Precisely, sir.'

# =5=
# NO WEDDING BELLS FOR BINGO

Bingo reported three days later that Rosie M. Banks was the goods and beyond a question the stuff to give the troops. Old Little had jibbed somewhat at first at the proposed change of literary diet, he not being much of a lad for fiction and having stuck hitherto exclusively to the heavier monthly reviews; but Bingo had got chapter one of "All for Love" past his guard before he knew what was happening, and after that there was nothing to it. Since then they had finished "A Red, Red Summer Rose", "Madcap Myrtle" and "Only a Factory Girl", and were halfway through "The Courtship of Lord Strathmorlick".

Bingo told me all this in a husky voice over an egg beaten up in sherry. The only blot on the thing from his point of view was that it wasn't doing a bit of good to the old vocal cords, which were beginning to show signs of cracking under the strain. He had been looking his symptoms up in a medical dictionary, and he thought he had got 'clergyman's throat'. But against this you had to set the fact that he was making an undoubted hit in the right quarter, and also that after the evening's reading he always stayed on to dinner; and, from what he told me, the dinners turned out by old Little's cook had to be tasted to be believed. There were tears in the old blighter's eyes as he got on the subject of the clear soup. I suppose to a fellow who for weeks had been tackling macaroons and limado it must have been like Heaven.

Old Little wasn't able to give any practical assistance at these banquets, but Bingo said that he came to the table and had his whack of arrowroot, and sniffed the dishes, and told stories of *entrées* he had had in the past, and sketched out scenarios of what he was going to do to the bill of fare in the future, when the doctor put him in shape; so I suppose he enjoyed himself, too, in a way. Anyhow, things seemed to be buzzing along quite satisfactorily, and Bingo said he had got an idea which, he thought, was going to clinch the thing. He wouldn't tell me what it was, but he said it was a pippin.

'We make progress, Jeeves,' I said.

'That is very satisfactory, sir.'

'Mr Little tells me that when he came to the big scene in "Only a Factory Girl", his uncle gulped like a stricken bull-pup.'

'Indeed, sir?'

'Where Lord Claude takes the girl in his arms, you know, and says – '

'I am familiar with the passage, sir. It is distinctly moving. It was a great favourite of my aunt's.'

'I think we're on the right track.'

'It would seem so, sir.'

'In fact, this looks like being another of your successes. I've always said, and I always shall say, that for sheer brains, Jeeves, you stand alone. All the other great thinkers of the age are simply in the crowd, watching you go by.'

'Thank you very much, sir. I endeavour to give satisfaction.'

About a week after this, Bingo blew in with the news that his uncle's gout had ceased to trouble him, and that on the morrow he would be back at the old stand working away with knife and fork as before.

'And, by the way,' said Bingo, 'he wants you to lunch with him tomorrow.'

'Me? Why me? He doesn't know I exist.'

'Oh, yes, he does. I've told him about you.'

'What have you told him?'

'Oh, various things. Anyhow, he wants to meet you. And take my tip, laddie – you go! I should think lunch tomorrow would be something special.'

I don't know why it was, but even then it struck me that there was something dashed odd – almost sinister, if you know what I mean – about young Bingo's manner. The old egg had the air of one who has something up his sleeve.

'There is more in this than meets the eye,' I said. 'Why should your uncle ask a fellow to lunch whom he's never seen?'

'My dear old fathead, haven't I just said that I've been telling him all about you – that you're my best pal – at school together, and all that sort of thing?'

'But even then – and another thing, why are you so dashed keen on my going?'

Bingo hesitated for a moment.

'Well, I told you I'd got an idea. This is it. I want you to spring the news on him. I haven't the nerve myself.'

'What! I'm hanged if I do!'

'And you call yourself a pal of mine!'

'Yes, I know; but there are limits.'

'Bertie,' said Bingo reproachfully, 'I saved your life once.'

'When?'

'Didn't I? It must have been some other fellow, then. Well, anyway, we were boys together and all that. You can't let me down.'

'Oh, all right,' I said. 'But, when you say you haven't nerve enough for any dashed thing in the world, you misjudge yourself. A fellow who – '

'Cheerio!' said young Bingo. 'One-thirty tomorrow. Don't be late.'

I'm bound to say that the more I contemplated the binge, the less I liked it. It was all very well for Bingo to say that I was slated for a magnificent lunch; but what good is the best possible lunch to a fellow if he is slung out into the street on his ear during the soup course? However, the word of a Wooster is his bond and all that sort of rot, so at one-thirty next day I tottered up the steps of No. 16 Pounceby Gardens, and punched the bell. And half a minute later I was up in the drawing-room, shaking hands with the fattest man I have ever seen in my life.

The motto of the Little family was evidently "variety". Young Bingo is long and thin and hasn't had a superfluous ounce on him since we first met; but the uncle restored the average and a bit over. The hand which grasped mine wrapped it round and enfolded it till I began to wonder if I'd ever get it out without excavating machinery.

'Mr Wooster, I am gratified – I am proud – I am honoured.'

It seemed to me that young Bingo must have boosted me to some purpose.

'Oh, ah!' I said.

He stepped back a bit, still hanging to the good right hand.

'You are very young to have accomplished so much!'

I couldn't follow the train of thought. The family, especially my Aunt Agatha, who has savaged me incessantly from childhood up, have always rather made a point of the fact that mine is a wasted life, and that, since I won the prize at my first school for the best collection of wild flowers made during the summer holidays, I haven't done a dam' thing to land me on the nation's scroll of fame. I was wondering if he couldn't have got me mixed up with someone else, when the telephone-bell rang outside in the hall, and the maid came in to say that I was wanted. I buzzed down, and found it was young Bingo.

'Hallo!' said young Bingo. 'So you've got there? Good man! I knew I could rely on you. I say, old crumpet, did my uncle seem pleased to see you?'

'Absolutely all over me. I can't make it out.'

'Oh, that's all right. I just rang up to explain. The fact is, old man, I know you won't mind, but I told him that you were the author of those books I've been reading to him.'

'What!'

'Yes, I said that "Rosie M. Banks" was your pen-name, and you didn't want it generally known, because you were a modest, retiring sort of chap. He'll listen to you now. Absolutely hang on your words. A brightish idea, what? I doubt if Jeeves in person would have thought up a better one than that. Well, pitch it strong, old lad, and keep steadily before you the fact that I must have my allowance raised. I can't possibly marry on what I've got now. If this film is to end with the slow, fade-out on the embrace, at least double is indicated. Well, that's that. Cheerio!'

And he rang off. At that moment the gong sounded, and the genial host came tumbling downstairs like the delivery of a ton of coals.

I always look back to that lunch with a sort of aching regret. It was the lunch of a lifetime, and I wasn't in a fit state to appreciate it. Subconsciously, if you know what I mean, I could see it was pretty special, but I had got the wind up to such a frightful extent over the ghastly situation in which young Bingo had landed me that its deeper meaning never really penetrated.

Most of the time I might have been eating sawdust for all the good it did me.

Old Little struck the literary note right from the start.

'My nephew has probably told you that I have been making a close study of your books of late?' he began.

'Yes. He did mention it. How – er – how did you like the bally things?'

He gazed reverently at me.

'Mr Wooster, I am not ashamed to say that the tears came into my eyes as I listened to them. It amazes me that a man as young as you can have been able to plumb human nature so surely to its depths; to play with so unerring a hand on the quivering heartstrings of your reader; to write novels so true, so human, so moving, so vital!'

'Oh, it's just a knack,' I said.

The good old persp. was bedewing my forehead by this time in a pretty lavish manner. I don't know when I've been so rattled.

'Do you find the room a trifle warm?'

'Oh, no, no, rather not. Just right.'

'Then it's the pepper. If my cook has a fault – which I am not prepared to admit – it is that she is inclined to stress the pepper a trifle in her made dishes. By the way, do you like her cooking?'

I was so relieved that we had got off the subject of my literary output that I shouted approval in a ringing baritone.

'I am delighted to hear it, Mr Wooster. I may be prejudiced, but to my mind that woman is a genius.'

'Absolutely!' I said.

'She has been with me seven years, and in all that time I have not known her guilty of a single lapse from the highest standard. Except once, in the winter of 1917, when a purist might have condemned a certain mayonnaise of hers as lacking in cream-iness. But one must make allowances. There had been several air-raids about that time, and no doubt the poor woman was shaken. But nothing is perfect in this world, Mr Wooster, and I have had my cross to bear. For seven years I have lived in constant apprehension lest some evilly-disposed person might lure her from my employment. To my certain knowledge she has received offers, lucrative offers, to accept service elsewhere.

You may judge of my dismay, Mr Wooster, when only this morning the bolt fell. She gave notice!'

'Good Lord!'

'Your consternation does credit, if I may say so, to the heart of the author of "A Red, Red Summer Rose". But I am thankful to say the worst has not happened. The matter has been adjusted. Jane is not leaving me.'

'Good egg!'

'Good egg, indeed – though the expression is not familiar to me. I do not remember having come across it in your books. And, speaking of your books, may I say that what has impressed me about them even more than the moving poignancy of the actual narrative, is your philosophy of life. If there were more men like you, Mr Wooster, London would be a better place.'

This was dead opposite to my Aunt Agatha's philosophy of life, she having always rather given me to understand that it is the presence in it of chappies like me that makes London more or less of a plague spot; but I let it go.

'Let me tell you, Mr Wooster, that I appreciate your splendid defiance of the outworn fetishes of a purblind social system. I appreciate it! *You* are big enough to see that rank is but the guinea stamp and that, in the magnificent words of Lord Bletchmore in "Only a Factory Girl", "Be her origin ne'er so humble, a good woman is the equal of the finest lady on earth!" '

'I say! Do you think that?'

'I do, Mr Wooster. I am ashamed to say that there was a time when I was like other men, a slave to the idiotic convention which we call Class Distinction. But, since I read your books – '

I might have known it. Jeeves had done it again.

'You think it's all right for a chappie in what you might call a certain social position to marry a girl of what you might describe as the lower classes?'

'Most assuredly I do, Mr Wooster.'

I took a deep breath, and slipped him the good news.

'Young Bingo – your nephew, you know – wants to marry a waitress,' I said.

'I honour him for it,' said old Little.

'You don't object?'

'On the contrary.'

I took another deep breath and shifted to the sordid side of the business.

'I hope you won't think I'm butting in, don't you know,' I said, 'but – er – well, how about it?'

'I fear I do not quite follow you.'

'Well, I mean to say, his allowance and all that. The money you're good enough to give him. He was rather hoping that you might see your way to jerking up the total a bit.'

Old Little shook his head regretfully.

'I fear that can hardly be managed. You see, a man in my position is compelled to save every penny. I will gladly continue my nephew's existing allowance, but beyond that I cannot go. It would not be fair to my wife.'

'What! But you're not married?'

'Not yet. But I propose to enter upon that holy state almost immediately. The lady who for years has cooked so well for me honoured me by accepting my hand this very morning.' A cold gleam of triumph came into his eyes. 'Now let 'em try to get her away from me!' he muttered, defiantly.


'Young Mr Little has been trying frequently during the afternoon to reach you on the telephone, sir,' said Jeeves that night, when I got home.

'I'll bet he has,' I said. I had sent poor old Bingo an outline of the situation by messenger-boy shortly after lunch.

'He seemed a trifle agitated.'

'I don't wonder, Jeeves,' I said, 'so brace up and bite the bullet. I'm afraid I've bad news for you.

'That scheme of yours – reading those books to old Mr Little and all that – has blown out a fuse.'

'They did not soften him?'

'They did. That's the whole bally trouble. Jeeves, I'm sorry to say that *fiancée* of yours – Miss Watson, you know – the cook, you know – well, the long and the short of it is that she's chosen riches instead of honest worth, if you know what I mean.'

'Sir?'

'She's handed you the mitten and gone and got engaged to old Mr Little!'

'Indeed, sir?'

'You don't seem much upset.'

'The fact is, sir, I had anticipated some such outcome.'

I stared at him. 'Then what on earth did you suggest the scheme for?'

'To tell you the truth, sir, I was not wholly averse from a severance of my relations with Miss Watson. In fact, I greatly desired it. I respect Miss Watson exceedingly, but I have seen for a long time that we were not suited. Now, the *other* young person with whom I have an understanding – '

'Great Scott, Jeeves! There isn't another?'

'Yes, sir.'

'How long has this been going on?'

'For some weeks, sir. I was greatly attracted by her when I first met her at a subscription dance at Camberwell.'

'My sainted aunt! Not – '

Jeeves inclined his head gravely.

'Yes, sir. By an odd coincidence it is the same young person that young Mr Little – I have placed the cigarettes on the small table. Good night, sir.'

# =6=
# AUNT AGATHA SPEAKS HER
# MIND

I suppose in the case of a chappie of really fine fibre and all that sort of thing, a certain amount of gloom and anguish would have followed this dishing of young Bingo's matrimonial plans. I mean, if mine had been a noble nature, I would have been all broken up. But, what with one thing and another, I can't let it weigh on me very heavily. The fact that less than a week after he had had the bad news I came on young Bingo dancing like an untamed gazelle at Ciro's helped me to bear up.

A resilient bird, Bingo. He may be down, but he is never out. While these little love-affairs of his are actually on, nobody could be more earnest and blighted; but once the fuse has blown out and the girl has handed him his hat and begged him as a favour never to let her see him again, up he bobs as merry and bright as ever. If I've seen it happen once, I've seen it happen a dozen times.

So I didn't worry about Bingo. Or about anything else, as a matter of fact. What with one thing and another, I can't remember ever having been chirpier than at about this period in my career. Everything seemed to be going right. On three separate occasions horses on which I'd invested a sizeable amount won by lengths instead of sitting down to rest in the middle of the race, as horses usually do when I've got money on them.

Added to this, the weather continued topping to a degree; my new socks were admitted on all sides to be just the kind that mother makes; and to round it all off, my Aunt Agatha had gone to France and wouldn't be on hand to snooter me for a least another six weeks. And, if you knew my Aunt Agatha, you'd agree that that alone was happiness enough for anyone.

It suddenly struck me so forcibly, one morning while I was having my bath, that I hadn't a worry on earth that I began to sing like a bally nightingale as I sploshed the sponge about. It seemed to me that everything was absolutely for the best in the best of all possible worlds.

But have you ever noticed a rummy thing about life? I mean the way something always comes along to give it you in the neck at the very moment when you're feeling most braced about things in general. No sooner had I dried the old limbs and shoved on the suiting and toddled into the sitting-room than the blow fell. There was a letter from Aunt Agatha on the mantelpiece.

'Oh gosh!' I said when I'd read it.

'Sir?' said Jeeves. He was fooling about in the background on some job or other.

'It's from my Aunt Agatha, Jeeves. Mrs Gregson, you know.'

'Yes, sir?'

'Ah, you wouldn't speak in that light, careless tone if you knew what was in it,' I said with a hollow, mirthless laugh. 'The curse has come upon us, Jeeves. She wants me to go and join her at – what's the name of the dashed place? – at Roville-sur-mer. Oh, hang it all!'

'I had better be packing, sir?'

'I suppose so.'

To people who don't know my Aunt Agatha I find it extra-ordinarily difficult to explain why it is that she has always put the wind up me to such a frightful extent. I mean, I'm not dependent on her financially or anything like that. It's simply personality, I've come to the conclusion. You see, all through my childhood and when I was a kid at school she was always able to turn me inside out with a single glance, and I haven't come out from under the 'fluence yet. We run to height a bit in our family, and there's about five-foot-nine of Aunt Agatha, topped off with a beaky nose, an eagle eye, and a lot of grey hair, and the general effect is pretty formidable. Anyway, it never even occurred to me for a moment to give her the miss-in-baulk on this occasion. If she said I must go to Roville, it was all over except buying the tickets.

'What's the idea, Jeeves? I wonder why she wants me.'

'I could not say, sir.'

Well, it was no good talking about it. The only gleam of consolation, the only bit of blue among the clouds, was the fact that at Roville I should at last be able to wear the rather fruity

505

cummerbund I had bought six months ago and had never had the nerve to put on. One of those silk contrivances, you know, which you tie round your waist instead of a waistcoat, something on the order of a sash only more substantial. I had never been able to muster up the courage to put it on so far, for I knew that there would be trouble with Jeeves when I did, it being a pretty brightish scarlet. Still, at a place like Roville, presumably dripping with the gaiety and *joie de vivre* of France, it seemed to me that something might be done.

Roville, which I reached early in the morning after a beastly chopping crossing and a jerky night in the train, is a fairly nifty spot where a chappie without encumbrances in the shape of aunts might spend a somewhat genial week or so. It is like all these French places, mainly sand and hotels and casinos. The hotel which had had the bad luck to draw Aunt Agatha's custom was the Splendide, and by the time I got there there wasn't a member of the staff who didn't seem to be feeling it deeply. I sympathized with them. I've had experience of Aunt Agatha at hotels before. Of course, the real rough work was all over when I arrived, but I could tell by the way everyone grovelled before her that she had started by having her first room changed because it hadn't a southern exposure and her next because it had a creaking wardrobe and that she had said her say on the subject of the cooking, the waiting, the chambermaiding and everything else, with perfect freedom and candour. She had got the whole gang nicely under control by now. The manager, a whiskered cove who looked like a bandit, simply tied himself into knots whenever she looked at him.

All this triumph had produced a sort of grim geniality in her, and she was almost motherly when we met.

'I am so glad you were able to come, Bertie,' she said. 'The air will do you so much good. Far better for you than spending your time in stuffy London night clubs.'

'Oh, ah,' I said.

'You will meet some pleasant people, too. I want to introduce you to a Miss Hemmingway and her brother, who have become great friends of mine. I am sure you will like Miss Hemmingway. A nice, quiet girl, so different from so many of the bold girls one meets in London nowadays. Her brother is curate at Chipley-in-the-Glen in Dorsetshire. He tells me they are connected with the Kent Hemmingways. A very good family. She is a charming girl.'

I had a grim foreboding of an awful doom. All this boosting was so unlike Aunt Agatha, who normally is one of the most celebrated right-and-left-hand knockers in London society. I felt a clammy suspicion. And, by Jove, I was right.

'Aline Hemmingway,' said Aunt Agatha, 'is just the girl I should like to see you marry, Bertie. You ought to be thinking of getting married. Marriage might make something of you. And I could not wish you a better wife than dear Aline. She would be such a good influence in your life.'

'Here, I say!' I chipped in at this juncture, chilled to the marrow.

'Bertie!' said Aunt Agatha, dropping the motherly manner for a bit and giving me the cold eye.

'Yes, but I say . . .'

'It is young men like you, Bertie, who make the person with the future of the race at heart despair. Cursed with too much money, you fritter away in idle selfishness a life which might have been made useful, helpful and profitable. You do nothing but waste your time on frivolous pleasures. You are simply an anti-social animal, a drone. Bertie, it is imperative that you marry.'

'But, dash it all . . .'

'Yes! You should be breeding children to . . .'

'No, really, I say, please!' I said, blushing richly. Aunt Agatha belongs to two or three of these women's clubs, and she keeps forgetting she isn't in the smoking-room.

'Bertie,' she resumed, and would no doubt have hauled up her slacks at some length, had we not been interrupted. 'Ah, here they are!' she said. 'Aline, dear!'

And I perceived a girl and a chappie bearing down on me, smiling in a pleased sort of manner.

'I want you to meet my nephew, Bertie Wooster,' said Aunt Agatha. 'He has just arrived. Such a surprise! I had no notion that he intended coming to Roville.'

I gave the couple the wary up-and-down, feeling rather like a cat in the middle of a lot of hounds. Sort of trapped feeling, you know what I mean. An inner voice was whispering that Bertram was up against it.

The brother was a small round cove with a face rather like a sheep. He wore pince-nez, his expression was benevolent, and he had on one of those collars which button at the back.

'Welcome to Roville, Mr Wooster,' he said.

'Oh, Sidney!' said the girl. 'Doesn't Mr Wooster remind you of Canon Blenkinsop, who came to Chipley to preach last Easter?'

'My dear! The resemblance is most striking!'

They peered at me for a while as if I were something in a glass case, and I goggled back and had a good look at the girl. There's no doubt about it, she was different from what Aunt Agatha had called the bold girls one meets in London nowadays. No bobbed hair and gaspers about *her*! I don't know when I've met anybody who looked so – respectable is the only word. She had a kind of plain dress, and her hair was plain, and her face was sort of mild and saint-like. I don't pretend to be a Sherlock Holmes or anything of that order, but the moment I looked at her I said to myself, 'The girl plays the organ in a village church!'

Well, we gazed at one another for a bit, and there was a certain amount of chit-chat, and then I tore myself away. But before I went I had been booked up to take brother and girl for a nice drive that afternoon. And the thought of it depressed me to such an extent that I felt there was only one thing to be done. I went straight back to my room, dug out the cummerbund, and draped it round the old tum. I turned round and Jeeves shied like a startled mustang.

'I beg your pardon, sir,' he said in a sort of hushed voice. 'You are surely not proposing to appear in public in that thing?'

'The cummerbund?' I said in a careless, debonair way, passing it off. 'Oh, rather!'

'I should not advise it, sir, really I shouldn't.'

'Why not?'

'The effect, sir, is loud in the extreme.'

I tackled the blighter squarely. I mean to say, nobody knows better than I do that Jeeves is a mastermind and all that, but, dash it, a fellow must call his soul his own. You can't be a serf to your valet. Besides, I was feeling pretty low and the cummerbund was the only thing which could cheer me up.

'You know, the trouble with you, Jeeves,' I said, 'is that you're too – what's the word I want? – too bally insular. You can't realize that you aren't in Piccadilly all the time. In a place like this a bit of colour and a touch of the poetic is expected of you. Why, I've just seen a fellow downstairs in a morning suit of yellow velvet.'

'Nevertheless, sir – '

'Jeeves,' I said firmly, 'my mind is made up. I am feeling a little low-spirited and need cheering. Besides, what's wrong with it? The cummerbund seems to me to be called for. I consider that it has rather a Spanish effect. A touch of the hidalgo. Sort of Vicente y Blasco What's-his-name stuff. The jolly old hidalgo off to the bull fight.'

'Very good, sir,' said Jeeves coldly.

Dashed upsetting, this sort of thing. If there's one thing that gives me the pip, it's unpleasantness in the home; and I could see that relations were going to be fairly strained for a while. And, coming on top of Aunt Agatha's bombshell about the Hemmingway girl, I don't mind confessing it made me feel more or less as though nobody loved me.

The drive that afternoon was about as mouldy as I had expected. The curate chappie prattled on of this and that; the girl admired the view; and I got a headache early in the proceedings which started at the soles of my feet and got worse all the way up. I tottered back to my room to dress for dinner, feeling like a toad under the harrow. If it hadn't been for that cummerbund business earlier in the day I could have sobbed on Jeeves's neck and poured out all my troubles to him. Even as it was, I couldn't keep the thing entirely to myself.

'I say, Jeeves,' I said.

'Sir?'

'Mix me a stiffish brandy and soda.'

'Yes, sir.'

'Stiffish, Jeeves. Not too much soda, but splash the brandy about a bit.'

'Very good, sir.'

After imbibing, I felt a shade better.

'Jeeves,' I said.

'Sir?'

'I rather fancy I'm in the soup, Jeeves.'

'Indeed, sir?'

I eyed the man narrowly. Dashed aloof his manner was. Still brooding over the cummerbund.

'Yes. Right up to the hocks,' I said, suppressing the pride of the Woosters and trying to induce him to be a bit matier. 'Have you seen a girl popping about here with a parson brother?'

'Miss Hemmingway, sir? Yes, sir.'

'Aunt Agatha wants me to marry her.'

'Indeed, sir?'

'Well, what about it?'

'Sir?'

'I mean, have you anything to suggest?'

'No, sir.'

The blighter's manner was so cold and unchummy that I bit the bullet and had a dash at being airy.

'Oh, well, tra-la-la!' I said.

'Precisely, sir,' said Jeeves.

And that was, so to speak, that.

# PEARLS MEAN TEARS

I remember – it must have been when I was at school because I don't go in for that sort of thing very largely nowadays – reading a poem or something about something or other in which there was a line which went, if I've got it rightly, "Shades of the prison house begin to close upon the growing boy". Well, what I'm driving at is that during the next two weeks that's exactly how it was with me. I mean to say, I could hear the wedding bells chiming faintly in the distance and getting louder and louder every day, and how the deuce to slide out of it was more than I could think. Jeeves, no doubt, could have dug up a dozen brainy schemes in a couple of minutes, but he was still aloof and chilly and I couldn't bring myself to ask him point-blank. I mean, he could see easily enough that the young master was in a bad way and, if that wasn't enough to make him overlook the fact that I was still gleaming brightly about the waistband, well, what it amounted to was that the old feudal spirit was dead in this blighter's bosom and there was nothing to be done about it.

It really was rummy the way the Hemmingway family had taken to me. I wouldn't have said offhand that there was anything particularly fascinating about me – in fact, most people look on me as rather an ass; but there was no getting away from the fact that I went like a breeze with this girl and her brother. They didn't seem happy if they were away from me. I couldn't move a step, dash it, without one of them popping out from somewhere and freezing on. In fact, I'd got into the habit now of retiring to my room when I wanted to take it easy for a bit. I had managed to get a rather decent suite on the third floor, looking down on to the promenade.

I had gone to earth in my suite one evening and for the first time that day was feeling that life wasn't so bad after all. Right through the day from lunchtime I'd had the Hemmingway girl on my hands, Aunt Agatha having shooed us off together immediately after the midday meal. The result was, as I looked down on the lighted promenade and saw all the people popping happily about on their way to dinner and the Casino and what-not, a kind of wistful feeling came over me. I couldn't help thinking how dashed happy I could have contrived to be in this place if only Aunt Agatha and the other blisters had been elsewhere.

I heaved a sigh, and at that moment there was a knock at the door.

'Someone at the door, Jeeves,' I said.

'Yes, sir.'

He opened the door, and in popped Aline Hemmingway and her brother. The last persons I had expected. I really had thought that I could be alone for a minute in my own room.

'Oh, hallo!' I said.

'Oh, Mr Wooster!' said the girl in a gasping sort of way. 'I don't know how to begin.'

Then I noticed that she appeared considerably rattled, and as for the brother, he looked like a sheep with a secret sorrow.

This made me sit up and notice. I had supposed that this was just a social call, but apparently something had happened to give them a jolt. Though I couldn't see why they should come to me about it.

'Is anything up?' I said.

'Poor Sidney – it was my fault – I ought never to have let him go there alone,' said the girl. Dashed agitated.

At this point the brother, who after shedding a floppy overcoat and parking his hat on a chair had been standing by wrapped in the silence, gave a little cough, like a sheep caught in the mist on a mountain top.

'The fact is, Mr Wooster,' he said, 'a sad, a most deplorable thing has occurred. This afternoon, while you were so kindly escorting my sist-ah, I found the time hung a little heavy upon my hands and I was tempted to – ah – gamble at the Casino.'

I looked at the man in a kindlier spirit than I had been able to up to date. This evidence that he had sporting blood in his veins made him seem more human, I'm bound to say. If only

I'd known earlier that he went in for that sort of thing, I felt that we might have had a better time together.

'Oh!' I said. 'Did you click?'

He sighed heavily.

'If you mean was I successful, I must answer in the negative. I rashly persisted in the view that the colour red, having appeared no fewer than seven times in succession, must inevitably at no distant date give place to black. I was in error. I lost my little all, Mr Wooster.'

'Tough luck,' I said.

'I left the Casino,' proceeded the chappie, 'and returned to the hotel. There I encountered one of my parishioners, a Colonel Musgrave, who chanced to be holiday-making over here. I – er – induced him to cash me a cheque for one hundred pounds on my little account in my London bank.'

'Well, that was all to the good, what?' I said, hoping to induce the poor fish to look on the bright side. 'I mean, bit of luck finding someone to slip it into first crack out of the box.'

'On the contrary, Mr Wooster, it did but make matters worse. I burn with shame as I make the confession, but I immediately went back to the Casino and lost the entire sum – this time under the mistaken supposition that the colour black was, as I believe the expression is, due for a run.'

'I say!' I said. 'You *are* having a night out!'

'And,' concluded the chappie, 'the most lamentable feature of the whole affair is that I have no funds in the bank to meet the cheque when presented.'

I'm free to confess that, though I realized by this time that all this was leading up to a touch and that my ear was shortly going to be bitten in no uncertain manner, my heart warmed to the poor prune. Indeed, I gazed at him with no little interest and admiration. Never before had I encountered a curate so genuinely all to the mustard. Little as he might look like one of the lads of the village, he certainly appeared to be the real tabasco, and I wished he had shown me this side of his character before.

'Colonel Musgrave,' he went on, gulping somewhat, 'is not a man who would be likely to overlook the matter. He is a hard man. He will expose me to my vic-ah. My vic-ah is a hard man.

In short, Mr Wooster, if Colonel Musgrave presents that cheque I shall be ruined. And he leaves for England tonight.'

The girl, who had been standing by biting her handkerchief and gurgling at intervals while the brother got the above off his chest, now started in once more.

'Mr Wooster,' she cried, 'won't you, won't you help us? Oh, do say you will! We must have the money to get back the cheque from Colonel Musgrave before nine o'clock – he leaves on the nine-twenty. I was at my wits' end what to do when I remembered how kind you had always been. Mr Wooster, will you lend Sidney the money and take these as security?' And before I knew what she was doing she had dived into her bag, produced a case, and opened it. 'My pearls,' she said. 'I don't know what they are worth – they were a present from my poor father – '

'Now, alas, no more – ' chipped in the brother.

'But I know they must be worth ever so much more than the amount we want.'

Dashed embarrassing. Made me feel like a pawnbroker. More than a touch of popping the watch about the whole business.

'No, I say, really,' I protested. 'There's no need of any security, you know, or any rot of that kind. Only too glad to let you have the money. I've got it on me, as a matter of fact. Rather luckily drew some this morning.'

And I fished it out and pushed it across. The brother shook his head.

'Mr Wooster,' he said, 'we appreciate your generosity, your beautiful, heartening confidence in us, but we cannot permit this.'

'What Sidney means,' said the girl, 'is that you really don't know anything about us when you come to think of it. You mustn't risk lending all this money without any security at all to two people who, after all, are almost strangers. If I hadn't thought that you would be quite businesslike about this I would never have dared to come to you.'

'The idea of – er – pledging the pearls at the local Mont de Pieté was, you will readily understand, repugnant to us,' said the brother.

'If you will just give me a receipt, as a matter of form – '

'Oh, right-o!'

I wrote out the receipt and handed it over, feeling more or less of an ass.

'Here you are,' I said.

The girl took the piece of paper, shoved it in her bag, grabbed the money and slipped it to her brother Sidney, and then, before I knew what was happening, she had darted at me, kissed me, and legged it from the room.

I'm bound to say the thing rattled me. So dashed sudden and unexpected. I mean, a girl like that. Always been quiet and demure and whatnot – by no means the sort of female you'd have expected to go about the place kissing fellows. Through a sort of mist I could see that Jeeves had appeared from the background and was helping the brother on with his coat; and I remember wondering idly how the dickens a man could bring himself to wear a coat like that, it being more like a sack than anything else. Then the brother came up to me and grasped my hand.

'I cannot thank you sufficiently, Mr Wooster!'

'Oh, not at all.'

'You have saved my good name. Good name in man or woman, my dear lord,' he said, massaging the fin with some fervour, 'is the immediate jewel of their souls. Who steals my purse steals trash. 'Twas mine, 'tis his, and has been slave to thousands. But he that filches my good name robs me of that which enriches not him and makes me poor indeed. I thank you from the bottom of my heart. Good night, Mr Wooster.'

'Good night, old thing,' I said.

I blinked at Jeeves as the door shut. 'Rather a sad affair, Jeeves,' I said.

'Yes, sir.'

'Lucky I happened to have all that money handy.'

'Well – er – yes, sir.'

'You speak as though you didn't think much of it.'

'It is not my place to criticize your actions, sir, but I will venture to say that I think you behaved a little rashly.'

'What, lending that money?'

'Yes, sir. These fashionable French watering places are notoriously infested by dishonest characters.'

This was a bit too thick.

'Now look here, Jeeves,' I said. 'I can stand a lot but when it comes to your casting asp-whatever-the-word-is on a bird in Holy Orders – '

'Perhaps I am over-suspicious, sir. But I have seen a great deal of these resorts. When I was in the employment of Lord Frederick Ranelagh, shortly before I entered your service, his lordship was very neatly swindled by a criminal known, I believe, by the soubriquet of Soapy Sid, who scraped acquaintance with us in Monte Carlo with the assistance of a female accomplice. I have never forgotten the circumstances.'

'I don't want to butt in on your reminiscences, Jeeves,' I said, coldly, 'but you're talking through your hat. How can there have been anything fishy about this business? They've left me the pearls, haven't they? Very well, then, think before you speak. You had better be tooling down to the desk now and having these things shoved in the hotel safe.' I picked up the case and opened it. 'Oh, Great Scott!'

The bally thing was empty!

'Oh, my Lord!' I said, staring. 'Don't tell me there's been dirty work at the crossroads after all!'

'Precisely, sir. It was in exactly the same manner that Lord Frederick was swindled on the occasion to which I have alluded. While his female accomplice was gratefully embracing his lordship, Soapy Sid substituted a duplicate case for the one containing the pearls and went off with the jewels, the money and the receipt. On the strength of the receipt he subsequently demanded from his lordship the return of the pearls, and his lordship, not being able to produce them, was obliged to pay a heavy sum in compensation. It is a simple but effective ruse.'

I felt as if the bottom had dropped out of things with a jerk.

'Soapy Sid? Sid! *Sidney*! Brother Sidney! Why, by Jove, Jeeves, do you think that parson was Soapy Sid?'

'Yes, sir.'

'But it seems extraordinary. Why, his collar buttoned at the back – I mean, he would have deceived a bishop. Do you really think he was Soapy Sid?'

'Yes, sir. I recognized him directly he came into the room.'

I stared at the blighter.

'You recognized him?'

'Yes, sir.'

'Then, dash it all,' I said, deeply moved. 'I think you might have told me.'

'I thought it would save disturbance and unpleasantness if I merely extracted the case from the man's pocket as I assisted him with his coat, sir. Here it is.'

He laid another case on the table beside the dud one, and, by Jove, you couldn't tell them apart. I opened it, and there were the good old pearls, as merry and bright as dammit, smiling up at me. I gazed feebly at the man. I was feeling a bit overwrought.

'Jeeves,' I said. 'You're an absolute genius!'

'Yes, sir.'

Relief was surging over me in great chunks by now. Thanks to Jeeves I was not going to be called on to cough up several thousand quid.

'It looks to me as though you have saved the old home. I mean, even a chappie endowed with the immortal rind of dear old Sid is hardly likely to have the nerve to come back and retrieve these little chaps.'

'I should imagine not, sir.'

'Well, then – Oh, I say, you don't think they are just paste or anything like that?'

'No, sir. These are genuine pearls and extremely valuable.'

'Well, then, dash it, I'm on velvet. Absolutely reclining on the good old plush! I may be down a hundred quid but I'm up a jolly good string of pearls. Am I right or wrong?'

'Hardly that, sir. I think that you will have to restore the pearls.'

'What! To Sid? Not while I have my physique!'

'No, sir. To their rightful owner.'

'But who is their rightful owner?'

'Mrs Gregson, sir.'

'What! How do you know?'

'It was all over the hotel an hour ago that Mrs Gregson's pearls had been abstracted. I was speaking to Mrs Gregson's maid shortly before you came in and she informed me that the manager of the hotel is now in Mrs Gregson's suite.'

'And having a devil of a time, what?'

'So I should be disposed to imagine, sir.'

The situation was beginning to unfold before me.

'I'll go and give them back to her, eh? It'll put me one up, what?'

'Precisely, sir. And, if I may make the suggestion, I think it might be judicious to stress the fact that they were stolen by – '

'Great Scott! By the dashed girl she was hounding me on to marry, by Jove!'

'Exactly, sir.'

'Jeeves,' I said, 'this is going to be the biggest score off my jolly old relative that has ever occurred in the world's history.'

'It is not unlikely, sir.'

'Keep her quiet for a bit, what? Make her stop snootering me for a while?'

'It should have that effect, sir.'

'Golly!' I said, bounding for the door.

Long before I reached Aunt Agatha's lair I could tell that the hunt was up. Diverse chappies in hotel uniform and not a few chambermaids of sorts were hanging about in the corridor, and through the panels I could hear a mixed assortment of voices, with Aunt Agatha's topping the lot. I knocked but no one took any notice, so I trickled in. Among those present I noticed a chambermaid in hysterics, Aunt Agatha with her hair bristling and the whiskered cove who looked like a bandit, the hotel manager fellow.

'Oh, hallo!' I said. 'Hallo-allo-allo!'

Aunt Agatha shooshed me away. No welcoming smile for Bertram.

'Don't bother me now, Bertie,' she snapped, looking at me as if I were more or less the last straw.

'Something up?'

'Yes, yes, yes! I've lost my pearls.'

'Pearls? Pearls? Pearls?' I said. 'No, really? Dashed annoying. Where did you see them last?'

'What does it matter where I saw them last? They have been stolen.'

Here Wilfred and Whisker King, who seemed to have been taking a rest between rounds, stepped into the ring again and began to talk rapidly in French. Cut to the quick he seemed. The chambermaid whooped in the corner.

'Sure you've looked everywhere?' I said.

'Of course I've looked everywhere.'

'Well, you know, I've often lost a collar stud and – '

'Do try not to be so maddening, Bertie! I have enough to bear without your imbecilities. Oh, be quiet! Be quiet!' she shouted in the sort of voice used by sergeant-majors and those who call the cattle home across the Sands of Dee. And such was the magnetism of her forceful personality that Wilfred subsisted as if he had run into a wall. The chambermaid continued to go strong.

'I say,' I said, 'I think there's something the matter with this girl. Isn't she crying or something? You may not have spotted it, but I'm rather quick at noticing things.'

'She stole my pearls! I am convinced of it.'

This started the whisker specialist off again, and in about a couple of minutes Aunt Agatha had reached the frozen grande-dame stage and was putting the last of the bandits through it in the voice she usually reserves for snubbing waiters in restaurants.

'I tell you, my good man, for the hundredth time – '

'I say,' I said, 'don't want to interrupt you and all that sort of thing, but these aren't the little chaps by any chance, are they?'

I pulled the pearls out of my pocket and held them up.

'These look like pearls, what?'

I don't know when I've had a more juicy moment. It was one of those occasions about which I shall prattle to my grand-children – if I ever have any, which at the moment of going to press seems more or less a hundred-to-one shot. Aunt Agatha simply deflated before my eyes. It reminded me of when I once saw some chappies letting the gas out of a balloon.

'Where – where – where – ' she gurgled.

'I got them from your friend, Miss Hemmingway.'

Even now she didn't get it.

'From Miss Hemmingway. Miss *Hemmingway*! But – but how did they come into her possession?'

'How?' I said. 'Because she jolly well stole them. Pinched them! Swiped them! Because that's how she makes her living, dash it – palling up to unsuspicious people in hotels and sneaking their jewellery. I don't know what her alias is, but her bally brother, the chap whose collar buttons at the back, is known in criminal circles as Soapy Sid.'

She blinked.

'Miss Hemmingway a thief! I – I – ' She stopped and looked feebly at me. 'But how did you manage to recover the pearls, Bertie dear?'

'Never mind,' I said crisply. 'I have my methods.' I dug out my entire stock of manly courage, breathed a short prayer and let her have it right in the thorax.

'I must say, Aunt Agatha, dash it all,' I said severely, 'I think you have been infernally careless. There's a printed notice in every bedroom in this place saying that there's a safe in the manager's office, where jewellery and valuables ought to be placed, and you absolutely disregarded it. And what's the result? The first thief who came along simply walked into your room and pinched your pearls. And instead of admitting that it was all your fault, you started biting this poor man here in the gizzard. You have been very, very unjust to this poor man.'

'Yes, yes,' moaned the poor man.

'And this unfortunate girl, what about her? Where does she get off? You've accused her of stealing the things on absolutely no evidence. I think she would be jolly well advised to bring an action for – for whatever it is and soak you for substantial damages.'

'*Mais oui, mais oui, c'est trop fort!*' shouted the Bandit Chief, backing me up like a good 'un. And the chambermaid looked up inquiringly, as if the sun was breaking through the clouds.

'I shall recompense her,' said Aunt Agatha feebly.

'If you take my tip you jolly well will, and that eftsoons or right speedily. She's got a cast-iron case, and if I were her I wouldn't take a penny under twenty quid. But what gives me the pip most is the way you've unjustly abused this poor man here and tried to give his hotel a bad name – '

'Yes, by damn! It's too bad!' cried the whiskered marvel. 'You careless old woman! You give my hotel bad names, would you or wasn't it? Tomorrow you leave my hotel, by great Scotland!'

And more to the same effect, all good, ripe stuff. And presently having said his say he withdrew, taking the chambermaid with him, the latter with a crisp tenner clutched in a vice-like grip. I suppose she and the bandit split it outside. A French hotel manager wouldn't be likely to let real money wander away from him without counting himself in on the division.

I turned to Aunt Agatha, whose demeanour was now rather like that of one who, picking daisies on the railway, has just caught the down express in the small of the back.

'I don't want to rub it in, Aunt Agatha,' I said coldly, 'but I should just like to point out before I go that the girl who stole your pearls is the girl you've been hounding me on to marry ever since I got here. Good heavens! Do you realize that if you had brought the thing off I should probably have had children who would have sneaked my watch while I was dandling them on my knee? I'm not a complaining sort of chap as a rule, but I must say that another time I do think you might be more careful how you go about egging me on to marry females.'

I gave her one look, turned on my heel and left the room.

'Ten o'clock, a clear night, and all's well, Jeeves,' I said, breezing back into the good old suite.

'I am gratified to hear it, sir.'

'If twenty quid would be any use to you, Jeeves – '

'I am much obliged, sir.'

There was a pause. And then – well, it was a wrench, but I did it. I unstripped the cummerbund and handed it over.

'Do you wish me to press this, sir?'

I gave the thing one last, longing look. It had been very dear to me.

'No,' I said, 'take it away; give it to the deserving poor – I shall never wear it again.'

'Thank you very much, sir,' said Jeeves.

# =8=
# JEEVES AND THE KID
# CLEMENTINA

It has been well said of Bertram Wooster by those who know him best that, whatever other sporting functions he may see fit to oil out of, you will always find him battling to his sixteen handicap at the annual Golf tournament of the Drones Club. Nevertheless, when I heard that this year they were holding it at Bingley-on-Sea, I confess I hesitated. As I stood gazing out of the window of my suite at the Splendide on the morning of the opening day, I was not exactly a-twitter, if you understand me, but I couldn't help feeling I might have been rather rash.

'Jeeves,' I said, 'Now that we have actually arrived, I find myself wondering if it was quite prudent to come here.'

'It is a pleasant spot, sir.'

'Where every prospect pleases,' I agreed. 'But though the spicy breezes blow fair o'er Bingley-on-Sea, we must never forget that this is where my Aunt Agatha's old friend, Miss Mapleton, runs a girls' school. If the relative knew I was here, she would expect me to call on Miss Mapleton.'

'Very true, sir.'

I shivered somewhat.

'I met her once, Jeeves. 'Twas on a summer's evening in my tent, the day I overcame the Nervii. Or, rather, at lunch at Aunt Agatha's a year ago come Lammas Eve. It is not an experience I would willingly undergo again.'

'Indeed, sir?'

'Besides, you remember what happened last time I got into a girls' school?'

'Yes, sir.'

'Secrecy and silence, then. My visit here must be strictly incog. If Aunt Agatha happens to ask you where I spent this week, say I went to Harrogate for the cure.'

'Very good, sir. Pardon me, sir, are you proposing to appear in those garments in public?'

Up to this point our conversation had been friendly and cordial, but I now perceived that the jarring note had been struck. I had been wondering when my new plus-fours would come under discussion, and I was prepared to battle for them like a tigress for her young.

'Certainly, Jeeves,' I said. 'Why? Don't you like them?'

'No, sir.'

'You think them on the bright side?'

'Yes, sir.'

'A little vivid, they strike you as?'

'Yes, sir.'

'Well, I think highly of them, Jeeves,' I said firmly.

There already being a certain amount of chilliness in the air, it seemed to me a suitable moment for springing another item of information which I had been keeping from him for some time.

'Er – Jeeves,' I said.

'Sir?'

'I ran into Miss Wickham the other day. After chatting of this and that, she invited me to join a party she is getting up to go to the Antibes this summer.'

'Indeed, sir?'

He now looked definitely squiggle-eyed. Jeeves, as I think I have mentioned before, does not approve of Bobbie Wickham.

There was what you might call a tense silence. I braced myself for an exhibition of the good old Wooster determination. I mean to say, one has got to take a firm stand from time to time. The trouble with Jeeves is that he tends occasionally to get above himself. Just because he has surged round and – I admit it freely – done the young master a bit of good in one or two crises, he has a nasty way of conveying the impression that he looks on Bertram Wooster as a sort of idiot child who, but for him, would conk in the first chukka. I resent this.

'I have accepted, Jeeves,' I said in a quiet, level voice, lighting a cigarette with a careless flick of the wrist.

'Indeed, sir?'

'You will like Antibes.'

'Yes, sir?'

'So shall I.'

'Yes, sir?'

'That's settled, then.'

'Yes, sir.'

I was pleased. The firm stand, I saw, had done its work. It was plain that the man was crushed beneath the iron heel – cowed, if you know what I mean.

'Right-ho, then, Jeeves.'

'Very good, sir.'

I had not expected to return from the arena until well on in the evening, but circumstances so arranged themselves that it was barely three o'clock when I found myself back again. I was wandering moodily to and fro on the pier, when I observed Jeeves shimmering towards me.

'Good afternoon, sir,' he said. 'I had not supposed that you would be returning quite so soon, or I would have remained at the hotel.'

'I had not supposed that I would be returning quite so soon myself, Jeeves,' I said, sighing somewhat. 'I was outed in the first round, I regret to say.'

'Indeed, sir? I am sorry to hear that.'

'And, to increase the mortification of defeat, Jeeves, by a blighter who had not spared himself at the luncheon table and was quite noticeably sozzled. I couldn't seem to do anything right.'

'Possibly you omitted to keep your eye on the ball with sufficient assiduity, sir?'

'Something of that nature, no doubt. Anyway, here I am, a game and popular loser and . . .' I paused, and scanned the horizon with some interest. 'Great Scott, Jeeves! Look at that girl just coming on to the pier. I never saw anybody so extraordinarily like Miss Wickham. How do you account for these resemblances?'

'In the present instance, sir, I attribute the similarity to the fact that the young lady *is* Miss Wickham.'

'Eh?'

'Yes, sir. If you notice, she is waving to you now.'

'But what on earth is she doing down here?'

'I am unable to say, sir.'

His voice was chilly and seemed to suggest that whatever had brought Bobbie Wickham to Bingley-on-Sea, it could not, in his opinion, be anything good. He dropped back into the offing, registering alarm and despondency, and I removed the old Homburg and waggled it genially.

'What-ho!' I said.

Bobbie came to anchor alongside.

'Hullo, Bertie,' she said. 'I didn't know you were here.'

'I am,' I assured her.

'In mourning?' she asked, eyeing the trouserings.

'Rather natty, aren't they?' I said, following her gaze. 'Jeeves doesn't like them, but then he's notoriously hidebound in the matter of leg-wear. What are you doing in Bingley?'

'My cousin Clementina is at school here. It's her birthday and I thought I would come down and see her. I'm just off there now. Are you staying here tonight?'

'Yes. At the Splendide.'

'You can give me dinner there if you like.'

Jeeves was behind me, and I couldn't see him, but at these words I felt his eye slap warningly against the back of my neck. I knew what it was that he was trying to broadcast – viz. that it would be tempting Providence to mix with Bobbie Wickham even to the extent of giving her a bite to eat. Dashed absurd, was my verdict. Get entangled with young Bobbie in the intricate life of a country-house, where almost anything can happen, and I'm not saying. But how any doom or disaster could lurk behind the simple pronging of a spot of dinner together, I failed to see. I ignored the man.

'Of course. Certainly. Rather. Absolutely,' I said.

'That'll be fine. I've got to get back to London tonight for revelry of sorts at the Berkeley, but it doesn't matter if I'm a bit late. We'll turn up at about seven-thirty, and you can take us to the movies afterwards.'

'We? Us?'

'Clementina and me.'

'You don't mean you intend to bring your ghastly cousin?'

'Of course I do. Don't you want the child to have a little pleasure on her birthday? And she isn't ghastly. She's a dear. She won't be any trouble. All you'll have to do is take her back to the school afterwards. You can manage that without straining a sinew can't you?'

I eyed her keenly.

'What does it involve?'

'How do you mean, what does it involve?'

'The last time I was lured into a girls' school, a headmistress with an eye like a gimlet insisted on my addressing the chaingang on Ideals and the Life To Come. This will not happen tonight?'

'Of course not. You just go to the front door, ring the bell, and bung her in.'

I mused.

'That would appear to be well within our scope. Eh, Jeeves?'

'I should be disposed to imagine so, sir.'

The man's tone was cold and soupy: and, scanning his face, I observed on it an 'If-you-would-only-be-guided-by-me' expression which annoyed me intensely. There are moments when Jeeves looks just like an aunt.

'Right,' I said, ignoring him once more – and rather pointedly, at that. 'Then I'll expect you at seven-thirty. Don't be late. And see,' I added, just to show the girl that beneath the smiling exterior I was a man of iron, 'that the kid has her hands washed and does not sniff.'

I had not, I confess, looked forward with any great keenness to hobnobbing with Bobbie Wickham's cousin Clementina, but I'm bound to admit that she might have been considerably worse. Small girls as a rule, I have noticed, are inclined, when confronted with me, to giggle a good deal. They snigger and they stare. I look up and find their eyes glued on me in an incredulous manner, as if they were reluctant to believe that I was really true. I suspect them of being in the process of memorizing any little peculiarities of deportment that I may possess, in order to reproduce them later for the entertainment of their fellowinmates.

With the kid Clementina there was nothing of this description. She was a quiet, saintlike child of about thirteen – in fact, seeing that this was her birthday, exactly thirteen – and her gaze revealed only silent admiration. Her hands were spotless; she had not a cold in the head; and at dinner, during which her behaviour was unexceptionable, she proved a sympathetic listener, hanging on my lips, so to speak, when with the aid of a fork and two peas I explained to her how my opponent that afternoon had stymied me on the tenth.

She was equally above criticism at the movies, and at the conclusion of the proceedings thanked me for the treat with visible emotion. I was pleased with the child, and said as much to Bobbie while assisting her into her two-seater.

'Yes, I told you she was a dear,' said Bobbie, treading on the self-starter in preparation for the dash to London. 'I always insist that they misjudge her at that school. They're always misjudging people. They misjudged me when I was there.'

'Misjudged her? How?'

'Oh, in various ways. But, then, what can you expect of a dump like St Monica's?'

I started.

'St Monica's?'

'That's the name of the place.'

'You don't mean the kid is at Miss Mapleton's school?'

'Why shouldn't she be?'

'But Miss Mapleton is my Aunt Agatha's oldest friend.'

'I know. It was your Aunt Agatha who got mother to send me there when I was a kid.'

'I say,' I said earnestly, 'when you were there this afternoon you didn't mention having met me down here?'

'No.'

'That's all right.' I was relieved. 'You see, if Miss Mapleton knew I was in Bingley, she would expect me to call. I shall be leaving tomorrow morning, so all will be well. But, dash it,' I said, spotting the snag, 'how about tonight?'

'What about tonight?'

'Well, shan't I have to see her? I can't just ring the front-door bell, sling the kid in, and leg it. I should never hear the last of it from Aunt Agatha.'

Bobbie looked at me in an odd, meditative sort of way.

'As a matter of fact, Bertie,' she said, 'I had been meaning to touch on that point. I think, if I were you, I wouldn't ring the front-door bell.'

'Eh? Why not?'

'Well, it's like this, you see. Clementina is supposed to be in bed. They sent her there just as I was leaving this afternoon. Think of it! On her birthday – right plumb spang in the middle of her birthday – and all for putting sherbet in the ink to make it fizz!'

I reeled.

'You aren't telling me that this foul kid came out without leave?'

'Yes, I am. That's exactly it. She got up and sneaked out when nobody was looking. She had set her heart on getting a square meal. I suppose I really ought to have told you right at the start, but I didn't want to spoil your evening.'

As a general rule, in my dealings with the delicately-nurtured, I am the soul of knightly chivalry – suave, genial and polished. But I can on occasion say the bitter, cutting thing, and I said it now.

'Oh?' I said.

'But it's all right.'

'Yes,' I said, speaking, if I recollect, between my clenched teeth, 'nothing could be sweeter, could it? The situation is one which it would be impossible to view with concern, what? I shall turn up with the kid, get looked at through steel-rimmed spectacles by the Mapleton, and after an agreeable five minutes shall back out, leaving the Mapleton to go to her escritoire and write a full account of the proceedings to my Aunt Agatha. And, contemplating what will happen after that, the imagination totters. I confidently expect my Aunt Agatha to beat all previous records.'

The girl clicked her tongue chidingly.

'Don't make such heavy weather, Bertie. You must learn not to fuss so.'

'I must, must I?'

'Everything's going to be all right. I'm not saying it won't be necessary to exercise a little strategy in getting Clem into the house, but it will be perfectly simple, if you'll only listen carefully to what I'm going to tell you. First, you will need a good long piece of string.'

'String?'

'String. Surely even you know what string is?'

I stiffened rather haughtily.

'Certainly,' I replied. 'You mean string.'

'That's right. String. You take this with you – '

'And soften the Mapleton's heart by doing tricks with it, I suppose?'

Bitter, I know. But I was deeply stirred.

'You take this string with you,' proceeded Bobbie patiently, 'and when you get into the garden you go through it till you come to a conservatory near the house. Inside it you will find a lot of flower-pots. How are you on recognizing a flower-pot when you see one, Bertie?'

'I am thoroughly familiar with flower-pots. If, as I suppose, you mean those sort of pot things they put flowers in.'

'That's exactly what I do mean. All right, then. Grab an armful of these flower-pots and go round the conservatory till you come to a tree. Climb this, tie a string to one of the pots, balance it on a handy branch which you will find overhangs the conservatory, and then, having stationed Clem near the front door, retire into the middle distance and jerk the string. The flower-pot will fall and smash the glass, someone in the house will hear the noise and come out to investigate, and while the door is open and nobody near, Clem will sneak in and go up to bed.'

'But suppose no one comes out?'

'Then you repeat the process with another pot.'

It seemed sound enough.

'You're sure it will work?'

'It's never failed yet. That's the way I always used to get in after lock-up when I was at St Monica's. Now, you're sure you've got it clear, Bertie? Let's have a quick run-through to make certain, and then I really must be off. String.'

'String.'

'Conservatory.'

'Or greenhouse.'

'Flower-pot.'

'Flower-pot.'

'Tree. Climb. Branch. Climb down. Jerk. Smash. And then off to beddy-bye. Got it?'

'I've got it. But,' I said sternly, 'let me tell you just one thing – '

'I haven't time. I must rush. Write to me about it, using one side of the paper only. Good-bye.'

She rolled off, and after following her with burning eyes for a moment I returned to Jeeves, who was in the background showing the kid Clementina how to make a rabbit with a pocket handkerchief. I drew him aside. I was feeling a little better now, for I perceived that an admirable opportunity had presented itself for putting the man in his place and correcting his view that he is the only member of our establishment with brains and resource.

'Jeeves,' I said, 'You will doubtless be surprised to learn that something in the nature of a hitch has occurred.'

'Not at all, sir.'

'No?'

'No, sir. In matters where Miss Wickham is involved, I am, if I may take the liberty of saying so, always on the alert for hitches. If you recollect sir, I have frequently observed that Miss Wickham, while a charming young lady, is apt – '

'Yes, yes, Jeeves. I know.'

'What would the precise nature of the trouble be this time, sir?'

I explained the circs.

'The kid is A.W.O.L. They sent her to bed for putting sherbet in the ink, and in bed they imagine her to have spent the evening. Instead of which, she was out with me, wolfing the eight-course table-d'hôte dinner at seven and six, and then going on to the Marine Plaza to enjoy an entertainment on the silver screen. It is our task to get her back into the house without anyone knowing. I may mention, Jeeves, that the school in which this young excrescence is serving her sentence is the one run by my Aunt Agatha's old friend, Miss Mapleton.'

'Indeed, sir?'

'A problem, Jeeves, what?'

'Yes, sir.'

'In fact, one might say a pretty problem?'

'Undoubtedly, sir. If I might suggest – '

I was expecting this. I raised a hand.

'I do not require any suggestions, Jeeves. I can handle this matter myself.'

'I was merely about to propose – '

I raised the hand again.

'Peace, Jeeves. I have the situation well under control. I have had one of my ideas. It may interest you to hear how my brain worked. It occurred to me, thinking the thing over, that a house like St Monica's would be likely to have near it a conservatory containing flower-pots. Then, like a flash, the whole thing came to me. I propose to procure some string, to tie it to a flower-pot, to balance the pot on a branch – there will, no doubt, be a tree near the conservatory with a branch overhanging it – and to retire to a distance, holding the string. You will station yourself with the kid near the front door, taking care to keep carefully concealed. I shall then jerk the string, the pot will smash the glass, the noise will bring someone out, and while the front door is open you will shoot the kid in and leave the rest to her personal judgment. Your share in the proceedings, you will notice, is simplicity itself – mere routine-work – and should not tax you unduly. How about it?'

'Well, sir – '

'Jeeves, I have had occasion before to comment on this habit of yours of saying "Well, sir" whenever I suggest anything in the nature of a ruse or piece of strategy. I dislike it more every time you do it. But I shall be glad to hear what possible criticism you can find to make.'

'I was merely about to express the opinion, sir, that the plan seems a trifle elaborate.'

'In a place as tight as this you have got to be elaborate.'

'Not necessarily, sir. The alternative scheme which I was about to propose – '

I shushed the man.

'There will be no need for alternative schemes, Jeeves. We will carry on along the lines I have indicated. I will give you ten minutes' start. That will enable you to take up your position near the front door and self to collect the string. At the conclusion of that period I will come along and do all the difficult part. So no more discussion. Snap into it, Jeeves.'

'Very good, sir.'


I felt pretty bucked as I tooled up the hill to St Monica's and equally bucked as I pushed open the front gate and stepped into the dark garden. But, just as I started to cross the lawn, there suddenly came upon me a rummy sensation as if all my bones had been removed and spaghetti substituted, and I paused.

I don't know if you have ever had the experience of starting off on a binge filled with a sort of glow of exhilaration, if that's the word I want, and then, without a moment's warning, having it disappear as if somebody had pressed a switch. That is what happened to me at this juncture, and a most unpleasant feeling it was – rather like when you take one of those express elevators in New York at the top of the building and discover, on reaching the twenty-seventh floor, that you have carelessly left all your insides up on the thirty-second, and too late now to stop and fetch them back.

The truth came to me like a bit of ice down the neck. I perceived that I had been a dashed sight too impulsive. Purely in order to score off Jeeves, I had gone and let myself in for what promised to be the mouldiest ordeal of a lifetime. And the nearer I got to the house, the more I wished that I had been a bit less haughty with the man when he had tried to outline that alternative scheme of his. An alternative scheme was just what I felt I could have done with, and the more alternative it was the better I would have liked it.

At this point I found myself at the conservatory door, and a few moments later I was inside, scooping up the pots.

Then ho, for the tree, bearing 'mid snow and ice the banner with the strange device "Excelsior!"

I will say for that tree that it might have been placed there for the purpose. My views on the broad, general principle of leaping from branch to branch in a garden belonging to Aunt Agatha's closest friend remained unaltered; but I had to admit that, if it was to be done, this was undoubtedly the tree to do it on. It was a cedar of sorts; and almost before I knew where I was, I was sitting on top of the world with the conservatory roof gleaming below me. I balanced the flower-pot on my knee and began to tie the string round it.

And, as I tied, my thoughts turned in a moody sort of way to the subject of Woman.

I was suffering from a considerable strain of the old nerves at the moment, of course, and, looking back, it may be that I was too harsh; but the way I felt in that dark, roosting hour was that you can say what you like, but the more a thoughtful man has to do with women, the more extraordinary it seems to him that such a sex should be allowed to clutter up the earth.

Women, the way I looked at it, simply wouldn't do. Take the females who were mixed up in this present business. Aunt Agatha, to start with, better known as the Pest of Pont Street, the human snapping-turtle. Aunt Agatha's closest friend, Miss Mapleton, of whom I can only say that on the single occasion on which I had met her she had struck me as just the sort of person who would be Aunt Agatha's closest friend. Bobbie Wickham, a girl who went about the place letting the pure in heart in for the sort of thing I was doing now. And Bobbie Wickham's cousin Clementina, who, instead of sticking sedulously to her studies and learning to be a good wife and mother, spent the springtime of her life filling ink-pots with sherbet –

What a crew! What a crew!

I mean to say, what a *crew!*

I had just worked myself up into rather an impressive state of moral indignation, and was preparing to go even further, when a sudden bright light shone upon me from below and a voice spoke.

'Ho!' it said.

It was a policeman. Apart from the fact of his having a lantern, I knew it was a policeman because he had said 'Ho!' I don't know if you recollect my telling you of the time I broke into Bingo Little's house to pinch the dictaphone record of the mushy article his wife had written about him and sailed out of the study window right into the arms of the Force? On that occasion the guardian of the Law had said 'Ho!' and kept on saying it, so evidently policemen are taught this as part of their training. And after all, it's not a bad way of opening conversation in the sort of circs. in which they generally have to chat with people.

'You come on down out of that,' he said.

I came down. I had just got the flower-pot balanced on its branch, and I left it there, feeling rather as if I had touched off the time-fuse of a bomb. Much seemed to me to depend on its stability and poise, as it were. If it continued to balance, an easy nonchalance might still get me out of this delicate position. If it fell, I saw things being a bit hard to explain. In fact, even as it was, I couldn't see my way to any explanation which would be really convincing.

However, I had a stab at it.

'Ah, officer,' I said.

It sounded weak. I said it again, this time with the emphasis on the 'Ah!' It sounded weaker than ever. I saw that Bertram would have to do better than this.

'It's all right, officer,' I said.

'All right, is it?'

'Oh, yes. Oh, yes.'

'What you doing up there?'

'Me, officer?'

'Yes, you.'

'Nothing, sergeant.'

'Ho!'

We eased into the silence, but it wasn't one of those restful silences that occur in talks between old friends. Embarrassing. Awkward.

'You'd better come along with me,' said the gendarme.

The last time I had heard those words from a similar source had been in Leicester Square one Boat Race night when, on my advice, my old pal Oliver Randolph Sipperley had endeavoured to steal a policeman's helmet at a moment when the policeman was inside it. On that occasion they had been addressed to young Sippy, and they hadn't sounded any too good, even so. Addressed to me, they more or less froze the marrow.

'No, I say, dash it!' I said.

And it was at this crisis, when Bertram had frankly shot his bolt and could only have been described as nonplussed, that a soft step sounded beside us and a soft voice broke the silence.

'Have you got them, officer? No, I see. It is Mr Wooster.'

The policeman switched the lantern round.

'Who are you?'

'I am Mr Wooster's personal gentleman's gentleman.'

'Whose?'

'Mr Wooster's.'

'Is this man's name Wooster?'

'This gentleman's name is Mr Wooster. I am in his employment as gentleman's personal gentleman.'

I think the cop was awed by the man's majesty of demeanour, but he came back strongly.

'Ho!' he said. 'Not in Miss Mapleton's employment?'

'Miss Mapleton does not employ a gentleman's personal gentleman.'

'Then what are you doing in her garden?'

'I was in conference with Miss Mapleton inside the house, and she desired me to step out and ascertain whether Mr Wooster had been successful in apprehending the intruders.'

'What intruders?'

'The suspicious characters whom Mr Wooster and I had observed passing through the garden as we entered it.'

'And what were you doing entering it?'

'Mr Wooster had come to pay a call on Miss Mapleton, who is a close friend of his family. We noticed suspicious characters crossing the lawn. On perceiving these suspicious characters, Mr Wooster dispatched me to warn and reassure Miss Mapleton, he himself remaining to investigate.'

'I found him up a tree.'

'If Mr Wooster was up a tree, I have no doubt he was actuated by excellent motives and had only Miss Mapleton's best interests at heart.'

The policeman brooded.

'Ho!' he said. 'Well, if you want to know, I don't believe a word of it. We had a telephone call at the station saying there was somebody in Miss Mapleton's garden, and I found this fellow up a tree. It's my belief you're both in this, and I'm going to take you in to the lady for identification.'

Jeeves inclined his head gracefully.

'I shall be delighted to accompany you, officer, if such is your wish. And I feel sure that in this connection I may speak for Mr Wooster also. He too, I am confident, will interpose no obstacle in the way of your plans. If you consider that circumstances have placed Mr Wooster in a position that may be termed equivocal, or even compromising, it will naturally be his wish to exculpate himself at the earliest possible – '

'Here!' said the policeman, slightly rattled.

'Officer?'

'Less of it.'

'Just as you say, officer.'

'Switch it off and come along.'

'Very good, officer.'

I must say that I have enjoyed functions more than that walk

535

to the front door. It seemed to me that the doom had come upon me, so to speak, and I thought it hard that a gallant effort like Jeeves's, well reasoned and nicely planned, should have failed to click. Even to me his story had rung almost true in spots, and it was a great blow that the man behind the lantern had not sucked it in without question. There's no doubt about it, being a policeman warps a man's mind and ruins that sunny faith in his fellow human beings which is the foundation of a lovable character. There seems no way of avoiding this.

I could see no gleam of light in the situation. True, the Mapleton would identify me as the nephew of her old friend, thus putting the stopper on the stroll to the police station and the night in the prison cell, but, when you came right down to it, a fat lot of use that was. The kid Clementina was presumably still out in the night somewhere, and she would be lugged in and the full facts revealed, and then the burning glance, the few cold words and the long letter to Aunt Agatha. I wasn't sure that a good straight term of penal servitude wouldn't have been a happier ending.

So, what with one consideration and another, the heart, as I toddled in through the front door, was more or less bowed down with weight of woe. We went along the passage and into the study, and there, standing behind a desk with the steel-rimmed spectacles glittering as nastily as on the day when I had seen them across Aunt Agatha's luncheon-table, was the boss in person. I gave her one swift look, then shut my eyes.

'Ah!' said Miss Mapleton.

Now, uttered in a certain way – dragged out, if you know what I mean, and starting high up and going down into the lower register – the word "Ah!" can be as sinister and devastating as the word "Ho!" In fact, it is a very moot question which is the scalier. But what stunned me was that this wasn't the way she had said it. It had been, or my ears deceived me, a genial "Ah!". A matey "Ah!" The "Ah!" of one old buddy to another. And this startled me so much that, forgetting the dictates of prudence, I actually ventured to look at her again. And a stifled exclamation burst from Bertram's lips.

The breath-taking exhibit before me was in person a bit on the short side. I mean to say, she didn't tower above one, or anything like that. But, to compensate for this lack of inches, she possessed to a remarkable degree that sort of quiet air of being unwilling to stand any rannygazoo which females who run schools always have. I had noticed the same thing when *in statu pupillari*, in my old head master, one glance from whose eye had invariably been sufficient to make me confess all. Sergeant-majors are like that, too. Also traffic-cops and some post office girls. It's something in the way they purse up their lips and look through you.

In short, through years of disciplining the young – ticking off Isabel and speaking with quiet severity to Gertrude and that sort of thing – Miss Mapleton had acquired in the process of time rather the air of a female lion-tamer; and it was this air which had caused me after the first swift look to shut my eyes and utter a short prayer. But now, though she still resembled a lion-tamer, her bearing had most surprisingly become that of a chummy lion-tamer – a tamer who, after tucking the lions in for the night, relaxes in the society of the boys.

'So you did not find them, Mr Wooster?' she said. 'I am sorry. But I am none the less grateful for the trouble you have taken, nor lacking in appreciation of your courage. I consider that you have behaved splendidly.'

I felt the mouth opening feebly and the vocal chords twitching but I couldn't manage to say anything. I was simply unable to follow her train of thought. I was astonished. Amazed. In fact, dumbfounded about sums it up.

The hell-hound of the Law gave a sort of yelp, rather like a wolf that sees its Russian peasant getting away.

'You identify this man, ma'am?'

'Identify him? In what way identify him?'

Jeeves joined the symposium.

'I fancy the officer is under the impression, madam, that Mr Wooster was in your garden for some unlawful purpose. I informed him that Mr Wooster was the nephew of your friend, Mrs Spenser Gregson, but he refused to credit me.'

There was a pause. Miss Mapleton eyed the constable for an instant as if she had caught him sucking acid-drops during the Scripture lesson.

'Do you mean to tell me, officer,' she said, in a voice that hit him just under the third button of the tunic and went straight through to the spinal column, 'that you have had the imbecility to bungle this whole affair by mistaking Mr Wooster for a burglar?'

'He was up a tree, ma'am.'

'And why should he not be up a tree? No doubt you had climbed the tree in order to watch the better, Mr Wooster?'

I could answer that. The first shock over, the old sang-froid was beginning to return.

'Yes. Rather. That's it. Of course. Certainly. Absolutely,' I said. 'Watch the better. That's it in a nutshell.'

'I took the liberty of suggesting that to the officer, madam, but he declined to accept the theory as tenable.'

'The officer is a fool,' said Miss Mapleton. It seemed a close thing for a moment whether or not she would rap him on the knuckles with a ruler. 'By this time, no doubt, owing to his idiocy, the miscreants have made good their escape. And it is for this,' said Miss Mapleton, 'that we pay rates and taxes!'

'Awful!' I said.

'Iniquitous.'

'A bally shame.'

'A crying scandal,' said Miss Mapleton.

'A grim show,' I agreed.

In fact, we were just becoming more like a couple of love-birds than anything, when through the open window there suddenly breezed a noise.

I'm never at my best at describing things. At school, when we used to do essays and English composition, my report generally read 'Has little or no ability, but does his best,' or words to that effect. True, in the course of years I have picked up a vocabulary of sorts from Jeeves, but even so I'm not nearly hot enough to draw a word-picture that would do justice to that extraordinarily hefty crash. Try to imagine the Albert Hall falling on the Crystal Palace, and you will have got the rough idea.

All four of us, even Jeeves, sprang several inches from the floor. The policeman uttered a startled 'Ho!'

Miss Mapleton was her calm masterful self again in a second.

'One of the men appears to have fallen through the conservatory roof,' she said. 'Perhaps you will endeavour at the eleventh hour to justify your existence, officer, by proceeding there and making investigations.'

'Yes, ma'am.'

'And try not to bungle matters this time.'

'No, ma'am.'

'Please hurry, then. Do you intend to stand there gaping all night?'

'Yes, ma'am. No, ma'am. Yes, ma'am.'

It was pretty to hear him.

'It is an odd coincidence, Mr Wooster,' said Miss Mapleton, becoming instantly matey once more as the outcast removed himself. 'I had just finished writing a letter to your aunt when you arrived. I shall certainly reopen it to tell her how gallantly you have behaved tonight. I have not in the past entertained a very high opinion of the modern young man, but you have caused me to alter it. To track these men unarmed through a dark garden argues courage of a high order. And it was most courteous of you to think of calling upon me. I appreciate it. Are you making a long stay in Bingley?'

This was another one I could answer.

'No,' I said. 'Afraid not. Must be in London tomorrow.'

'Perhaps you could lunch before your departure?'

'Afraid not. Thanks most awfully. Very important engagement that I can't get out of. Eh, Jeeves?'

'Yes, sir.'

'Have to catch the ten-thirty train, what?'

'Without fail, sir.'

'I am sorry,' said Miss Mapleton. 'I had hoped that you would be able to say a few words to my girls. Some other time perhaps?'

'Absolutely.'

'You must let me know when you are coming to Bingley again.'

'When I come to Bingley again,' I said, 'I will certainly let you know.'

'If I remember your plans correctly, sir, you are not likely to be in Bingley for some little time, sir.'

'Not for some considerable time, Jeeves,' I said.

The front door closed. I passed a hand across the brow.

'Tell me all, Jeeves,' I said.

'Sir?'

'I say, tell me all. I am fogged.'

'It is quite simple, sir. I ventured to take the liberty, on my own responsibility, of putting into operation the alternative scheme which, if you remember, I wished to outline to you.'

'What was it?'

'It occurred to me, sir, that it would be most judicious for me to call at the back door and desire an interview with Miss Mapleton. This, I fancied, would enable me, while the maid had gone to convey my request to Miss Mapleton, to introduce the young lady into the house unobserved.'

'And did you?'

'Yes, sir. She proceeded up the back stairs and is now safely in bed.'

I frowned. The thought of the kid Clementina jarred upon me.

'She is, is she?' I said. 'A murrain on her, Jeeves, and may she be stood in the corner next Sunday for not knowing her Collect. And then you saw Miss Mapleton?'

'Yes, sir.'

'And told her that I was out in the garden, chivvying burglars with my bare hands?'

'Yes, sir.'

'And had been on my way to call upon her?'

'Yes, sir.'

'And now she's busy adding a postscript to her letter to Aunt Agatha, speaking of me in terms of unstinted praise.'

'Yes, sir.'

I drew in a deep breath. It was too dark for me to see the superhuman intelligence which must have been sloshing about all over the surface of the man's features. I tried to, but couldn't make it.

'Jeeves,' I said, 'I should have been guided by you from the first.'

'It might have spared you some temporary unpleasantness, sir.'

'Unpleasantness is right. When that lantern shone up at me in the silent night, Jeeves, just as I had finished poising the pot, I thought I had unshipped a rib. Jeeves!'

'Sir?'

'That Antibes expedition is off.'

'I am glad to hear it, sir.'

'If young Bobbie Wickham can get me into a mess like this in a quiet spot like Bingley-on-Sea, what might she not be able to accomplish at a really lively resort like Antibes?'

'Precisely, sir. Miss Wickham, as I have sometimes said, though a charming – '

'Yes, yes, Jeeves. There is no necessity to stress the point. The Wooster eyes are definitely opened.'

I hesitated.

'Jeeves.'

'Sir?'

'Those plus-fours.'

'Yes, sir?'

'You may give them to the poor.'

'Thank you very much, sir.'

I sighed.

'It is my heart's blood, Jeeves.'

'I appreciate the sacrifice, sir. But, once the first pang of separation is over, you will feel much easier without them.'

'You think so?'

'I am convinced of it, sir.'

'So be it, then, Jeeves,' I said, 'so be it.'